Wil knew not to touch

He had been warned a hundred times, but, oh, the temptation to be first was irresistible. The book was perfection itself; he could have contemplated it for hours. He bent over it, pressing his lips to the cover. The iron was only blood-warm, yet his tears fizzed and steamed as they fell on the rough metal. He wanted to bawl. Wanted to slip the book inside his shirt, hug it to his skin and never let it go.

He shook off the fantasy. He was lowly Wil the Sump and he only had a minute. His trembling hand took hold of the cover. It was heavy, and as he heaved it open it shed scabrous grey flakes onto the white table.

The writing on the iron pages was the same sluggishly oozing crimson as on the cover, but his straining eye could not bring it into focus. Was it protected, like the other Solaces, against unauthorized use? *On Metallix* had to be heated to the right temperature before it could be read, while each completed chapter of *On Catalyz* required the light of a different chymical flame.

A mud-brain like himself would never decipher the protection. Frustrated, Wil flapped the front cover and a jagged edge tore his forefinger.

"Ow!" He shook his hand.

Half a dozen spots of blood spattered across the first page, where they set like flakes of rust. Then, as he stared, the glyphs snapped into words he could read. Such perfect calligraphy! It was the greatest book of all. Wil read the first page and his eyes did not hurt at all. He turned the page, flicked blood onto the book and read on.

"I can see." His voice soared out of his small, skinny body, to freedom. "I can see."

VENGEANCE

THE TAINTED REALM TRILOGY
BOOK ONE

IAN IRVINE

orbit

www.orbitbooks.net

Orbit
Hachette Book Group
237 Park Avenue, New York, NY 10017
www.HachetteBookGroup.com

First U.S. Edition: April 2012
Originally published in paperback by Hachette Livre Australia, 2011

Orbit is an imprint of Hachette Book Group, Inc. The Orbit name and logo are trademarks of Little, Brown Book Group Limited.

The Hachette Speakers Bureau provides a wide range of authors for speaking events. To find out more, go to www.hachettespeakersbureau.com or call (866) 376-6591.

The publisher is not responsible for websites (or their content) that are not owned by the publisher.

The characters and events in this book are fictitious. Any similarity to real persons, living or dead, is coincidental and not intended by the author.

Library of Congress Control Number: 2011945648
ISBN: 978-0-316-07284-7

10 9 8 7 6 5 4 3 2 1

RRD-C

Printed in the United States of America

To Laurie,
for webmastering way above and beyond the call

CONTENTS

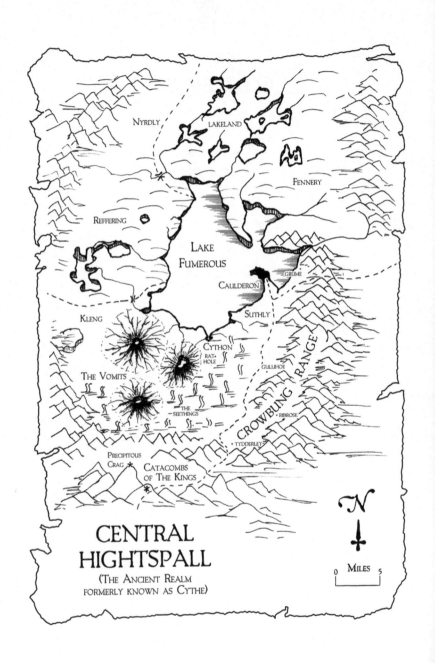

CENTRAL
HIGHTSPALL
(The Ancient Realm
formerly known as Cythe)

PART ONE

ESCAPE

CHAPTER 1

"Matriarch Ady, can I check the Solaces for you?" said Wil, staring at the locked basalt door behind her. "Can I, please?"

Ady frowned at the quivering, cross-eyed youth, then laid her scribing tool beside the partly engraved sheet of spelter and flexed her aching fingers. "The Solaces are for the matriarchs' eyes only. Go and polish the clangours."

Wil, who was neither handsome nor clever, knew that Ady only kept him around because he worked hard. And because, years ago, he had revealed a gift for *shillilar*, morrow-sight. Having been robbed of their past, the matriarchs used even their weakest tools to protect Cython's future.

Though Wil was so lowly that he might never earn a tattoo, he desperately wanted to be special, to matter. But he had another reason for wanting to look at the Solaces, one he dared not mention to anyone. A later *shillilar* had told him that there was something wrong, something the matriarchs weren't telling them. Perhaps— heretical thought—something they didn't know.

"You can see your face in the clangours," he said, inflating his hollow chest. "I've also fed the fireflies and cleaned out the effluxor sump. Please can I check the Solaces?"

Ady studied her swollen knuckles, but did not reply.

"Why are the secret books called Solaces, anyway?" said Wil.

"Because they comfort us in our bitter exile."

"I heard they order the matriarchs about like naughty children."

Ady slapped him, though not as hard as he deserved. "How dare you question the Solaces, idiot youth?"

Being used to blows, Wil merely rubbed his pockmarked cheek. "If you'd just let me peek . . ."

"We only check for new pages once a month."

"But it's been a month, look, *look*." A shiny globule of quick-silver, freshly fallen from the coiled condenser of the wall clock, was rolling down its inclined planes towards today's brazen bucket. "Today's the ninth. You always check the Solaces on the ninth."

"I dare say I'll get around to it."

"How can you bear to wait?" he said, jumping up and down.

"At my age, the only thing that excites me is soaking my aching feet. Besides, it's three years since the last new page appeared."

"The next page could come today. It might be there already."

Though Wil's eyes made reading a struggle, he loved books with a passion that shook his bones. The mere shapes of the letters sent him into ecstasies, but, ah! What stories the letters made. He had no words to express how he felt about the stories.

Wil did not own any book, not even the meanest little volume, and he longed to, desperately. Books were truth. Their stories were the world. And the Solaces were perfect books—the very soul of Cython, the matriarchs said. He ached to read one so badly that his whole body trembled and the breath clotted in his throat.

"I don't think any more pages are coming, lad." Ady pressed her fingertips against the blue triangle tattooed on her brow. "I doubt the thirteenth book will ever be finished."

"Then it can't hurt if I look, can it?" he cried, sensing victory.

"I—I suppose not."

Ady rose painfully, selected three chymical phials from a rack and shook them. In the first, watery fluid took on a subtle jade glow. The contents of the second thickened and bubbled like black porridge and the third crystallised to a network of needles that radiated pinpricks of sulphur-yellow light.

A spiral on the basalt door was dotted with phial-sized holes. Ady inserted the light keys into the day's pattern and waited for it to recognise the colours. The lock sighed; the door opened into the Chamber of the Solaces.

"Touch nothing," she said to the gaping youth, and returned to her engraving.

Unlike every other part of Cython, this chamber was uncarved, unpainted stone. It was a small, cubic room, unfurnished save for a white quartzite table with a closed book on its far end and, on the wall to Wil's right, a four-shelf bookcase etched out of solid rock. The third and fourth shelves were empty.

Tears formed as he gazed upon the mysterious books he had only ever glimpsed through the doorway. After much practice he could now read a page or two of a storybook before the pain in his eyes became blinding, but only the secret books could take him where he wanted to go—to a world and a life not walled-in in every direction.

"Who is the Scribe, Ady?"

Wil worshipped the unknown Scribe for the elegance of his calligraphy and his mastery of book making, but most of all for the stories he had given Cython. They were the purest truth of all.

He often asked that question but Ady never answered. Maybe she didn't know, and it worried him, because Wil feared the Scribe was in danger. If I could save him, he thought, I'd be the greatest hero of all.

He smiled at that. Wil knew he was utterly insignificant.

The top shelf contained five ancient Solaces, all with worn brown covers, and each bore the main title, *The Songs of Survival*. These books, vital though they had once been, were of least interest to Wil, since the last had been completed one thousand, three hundred and seventy-seven years ago. Their stories had ended long before. It was the future that called to him, the unfinished stories.

On the second shelf stood the thick volumes entitled *The Lore of Prosperity*. There were nine of these and the last five formed a set called Industry. *On Delven* had covers of pale mica with topazes embedded down the spine, *On Metallix* was written in white-hot letters on sheets of beaten silver. Wil could not tell what *On Smything*, *On Spagyric* or *On Catalyz* were made from, for his eyes were aching now, his sight blurring.

He covered his eyes for a moment. Nine books. Why were there *nine* books on the second shelf? The ninth, unfinished book, *On Catalyz*, should lie on the table, open at the last new page.

His heart bruised itself on his breastbone as he counted them again. Five books, plus nine. Could *On Catalyz* be finished? If it was, this was amazing news, and he would be the one to tell it. He would be really special then. Yes, the last book on the shelf definitely said, *On Catalyz*.

Then what was the book on the table?

A *new* book?

The first new book in three hundred and twelve years?

Magery was anathema to his people and Wil had never asked how the pages came to write themselves, nor how each new book could appear in a locked room in Cython, deep underground. Since magery had been forbidden to all save their long-lost kings, the self-writing pages were proof of instruction from a higher power. The Solaces were Cython's comfort in their agonising exile, the only evidence that they still mattered.

We are not alone.

The cover of the new book was the dark, scaly grey of freshly cast iron. It was a thin volume, no more than thirty sheet-iron pages. He could not read the crimson, deeply etched title from this angle, though it was too long to be *The Lore of Prosperity*.

Wil choked and had to bend double, panting. Not just a new book, but the first of the *third shelf*, and no one else in Cython had seen it. His eyes were flooding, his heart pounding, his mouth full of saliva.

He swallowed painfully. Even from here, the book had a peculiar smell, oily-sweet then bitter underneath, yet strangely appealing. He took a deep sniff. The inside of his nose burnt, his head spun and he felt an instant's bliss, then tendrils webbed across his inner eye. He shook his head, they disappeared and he sniffed again, wanting that bliss to take him away from his life of drudgery. But he wanted the iron book more. What story did it tell? Could it be the Scribe's own?

He turned to call Ady, then hesitated. She would shoo him off and the three matriarchs would closet themselves with the new book for weeks. Afterwards they would meet with the leaders of the four levels of Cython, the master chymister, the heads of the other guilds and the overseer of the Pale slaves. Then the new book would be locked away and Wil would go back to scraping muck out of the effluxors for the rest of his life.

But his second *shillilar* had said the Scribe was in danger; Wil had to read his story. He glanced through the doorway. Ady's old head was bent over her engraving but she would soon remember and order him back to work.

Shaking all over, Wil took a step towards the marble table, and the ache in his eyes came howling back. He closed his worst eye, the left, and when the throbbing eased he took another step. For the only time in his life, he did feel special. He slid a foot forwards, then another. Each movement sent a spear through his temples but he would have endured a lifetime of pain for one page of the story.

Finally he was standing over the book. From straight on, the etched writing was thickly crimson and ebbed in and out of focus. He sounded out the letters of the title.

The Consolation of Vengeance.

"Vengeance?" Wil breathed. But whose? The Scribe's?

Even a nobody like himself could tell that this book was going to turn their world upside-down. The other Solaces set out stories about living underground: growing crops and farming fish, healing, teaching, mining, smything, chymie, arts and crafts, order and disorder, defence. They described an existence that allowed no dissent and had scarcely changed in centuries.

But their enemy did not live underground—they occupied the Cythonians' ancestral land of Cythe, which they called Hightspall. To exact vengeance, Cython's armies would have to venture up to the surface, and even an awkward, cross-eyed youth could dream of marching with them.

Wil knew not to touch the Solaces. He had been warned a hundred times, but, oh, the temptation to be first was irresistible. The book was perfection itself; he could have contemplated it for hours. He bent over it, pressing his lips to the cover. The iron was only blood-warm, yet his tears fizzed and steamed as they fell on the rough metal. He wanted to bawl. Wanted to slip the book inside his shirt, hug it to his skin and never let it go.

He shook off the fantasy. He was lowly Wil the Sump and he only had a minute. His trembling hand took hold of the cover. It was heavy, and as he heaved it open it shed scabrous grey flakes onto the white table.

The writing on the iron pages was the same sluggishly oozing crimson as on the cover, but his straining eye could not bring it into focus. Was it protected, like the other Solaces, against unauthorised use? *On Metallix* had to be heated to the right temperature before it could be read, while each completed chapter of *On Catalyz* required the light of a different chymical flame.

A mud-brain like himself would never decipher the protection. Frustrated, Wil flapped the front cover and a jagged edge tore his forefinger.

"Ow!" He shook his hand.

Half a dozen spots of blood spattered across the first page, where they set like flakes of rust. Then, as he stared, the glyphs snapped into words he could read. Such perfect calligraphy! It was the greatest book of all. Wil read the first page and his eyes did not hurt at all. He turned the page, flicked blood onto the book and read on.

"I can see." His voice soared out of his small, skinny body, to freedom. "I can see."

Ady let out a hoarse cry. "Wil, get out of there."

He heard her shuffling across to the basalt door but Wil did not move. Though the crimson letters brightened until they hurt his eyes, he had to keep reading. "Ady, it's a *new book*."

"What does it say?" she panted from the doorway.

"We're leaving Cython." He put his nose on the page, inhaling the tantalising odour he could not get enough of. It was ecstasy. He turned the page. The rest of the book was blank, yet that did not matter—in his inner eye the future was unrolling all by itself. "It's a new story," Wil whispered. "The story of tomorrow."

"Are you in *shillilar*?" Her voice was desperate with longing. "Where are the Solaces taking us? Are we finally going home?"

"We're going—" In an instant the world turned crimson. "It's *the one*!" Wil gasped, horror overwhelming him. "*Stop her.*"

Ady stumbled across and took him by the arm. "What are you seeing? Is it about me?"

Wil let out a cracked laugh. "She's changing the story—bringing the Scribe to the brink—"

"Who are you seeing?" cried Ady. "Speak, lad!"

How could *the one* change the story written by the Scribe Wil worshipped? Surely she couldn't, unless ... unless the Scribe was *fallible*. No! That could not be. But if *the one* was going to challenge him, she must have free will. It was a shocking, heretical thought.

Could *the one* be as worthy as the Scribe? Ah, what a story their contest would make. And the story was everything—he had to see how it ended.

Ady struck him so hard that his head went sideways. "Answer me!"

"It's . . . it's *the one*."

"Don't talk nonsense, boy. What one?"

"A Pale slave, but—"

"A *slave* is changing our future?" Ady choked. "Who?"

"A girl." Wil tore his gaze away from the book for a second and gasped, "She's still a child."

"What's her name?"

"I . . . don't know."

Wild-eyed and frantic, Ady shook him. "When does this happen?"

"Not for years and years."

"When, boy? How long have we got to find her?"

Wil turned back to the last written page, tore open his finger on the rough edge and dribbled blood across the page. The story was terrible but he had to know who won. "Until . . . until she comes of age—"

"What are we to do?" said Ady, and he heard her hobbling around the table. "We don't know how to contact the Scribe. We must obey *The Consolation of Vengeance*."

The letters brightened until his eyes began to sting, to steam. Wil began to scream, but even as his vision blurred and his eyes bubbled and boiled into jelly that oozed out of his sockets, he could not tear his gaze away. He had longed to be special, and now he was.

She tottered back to him, wiped his face, and he heard her weeping. "Why didn't you listen to me?"

He took another sniff and the pain was gone. "Stupid old woman," sneered Wil. "Wil can see so much more clearly now. *Wil free!*"

"Wil, what does she look like?"

"She Pale. She *the one*."

"Tell me!" she cried, shaking him. "How am I to find this slave child among eighty-five thousand Pale—*and see her dead*."

CHAPTER 2

Whenever Mama wasn't watching, the huge man that Tali called *Tinyhead* poked his white tongue out at her. Black spots on it were like crawling blowflies and Tali had to turn away before she sicked up her breakfast.

She did not like Tinyhead, but he was helping them to escape. In a thousand years, no Pale had ever escaped from Cython, and Mama had tears in her eyes whenever she talked about going home. Not wanting to upset her again, Tali clutched Mama's hand and kept her worries to herself.

The further Tinyhead led them, the more alarming the tunnel art became, as if warning: try to escape and you'll die. For an hour of their journey the walls they passed were carved into the skeletons of burnt trees surrounded by ash like black snow. Then they walked along a dried-up river with water buffalo trapped in grey mud. Finally, as the passage became an endless desert where spiny lizards picked salt crystals off sharp rocks, Tinyhead heaved open a stone door and stood to one side so they could go through.

They had crossed into another world, one that was cold and dank and slimy underfoot, a vast oval cellar where mist hung in the stagnant air. It looked like the inside of a mouldy old skull and the stink of poisoned, decaying rats made Tali gag.

"Here you are." Tinyhead flopped out his tongue. "All your troubles are over, *Pale*."

Mama whirled, reaching up to him, but he slammed the door in her face. She let out a whimper.

"You're hurting my hand, Mama," said Tali.

Her mama crouched in front of Tali, holding her so tightly that she could hardly breathe. Mama's blue eyes were wet, and Tali hated to see her so sad.

"We're betrayed, little one. We're never going home."

"Why not?" said Tali, looking around in confusion. Why had Tinyhead shut them in? Why hadn't she told Mama her worries? Was this her fault?

A familiar face carved into the stone high on the wall made her shiver. It was Lyf, the enemy's last and wickedest king, who had died long ago. She had often seen the tattooed Cythonians kneeling before his image.

To her left, a series of dusty stone bins ran along the wall, partly concealed by tiers of barrels. On the right, hundreds of wooden crates were stacked nearly to the ceiling. In the centre, twenty yards away, stood a stained black bench. The floor was damp and littered with pieces of fallen stone.

Something rustled, far across the cellar. Mama looked around frantically. "Over here," she said, hauling Tali to the crates. "Squeeze into the middle where you can't be seen."

Tali clung to her. "I don't like this place, Mama."

"Me either. And yet, I feel close to our ancestors here. In, hurry."

Tali was a good little girl, so she bit her lip and edged into one of the gaps between the rotting crates. The floor was so slimy that her bare feet kept slipping.

"Don't cry. I know how brave you are." Her mama kissed her brow. "Tali," she choked, "if I don't come back, Little Nan will give you your papa's letter when you come of age."

"Mama?" Why would she say such a thing? Of course she would come back.

"Shh!" Mama took Tali's hands in her own and drew a ragged breath. "Our family has a terrible enemy—"

The dead rat smell thickened and grew fouler. "Who, Mama?"

"I don't know. He's never seen, never heard, but he flutters in my nightmares like a foul wrythen—"

"You're scaring me, Mama!"

"When you're older, you've got to find your *gift* and master it. It's the only way to beat him."

Tali shivered. In Cython, magery was forbidden. Magery meant death. Children were beaten just for whispering the word.

At a hollow click from the far side of the cellar, Mama jumped.

"But Mama," said Tali, lowering her voice, "if our masters catch any slave using . . . *magery*, they kill them."

"Even innocent little children," said Mama, hugging her desperately. "You must be very careful."

Tali's voice rose. "Then how am I supposed to find my magery?"

Mama clapped a hand over Tali's mouth. "I don't know, child. Don't tell anyone about your gift. Trust no one."

Tali pulled away. "Is Tinyhead the enemy?" She took hold of a splintered length of wood, wanting to jam it through his disgusting tongue.

"Shh! You know what happens when you get angry."

"I'm already angry, and I'm going—"

"Forget him. He's nothing."

"When I find my gift, his head will be nothing. I'll blast it right off."

"Tali, never say such things! You must lower your eyes and say, 'Yes, Master.'"

"*I won't!*" Tali said furiously. "I hate our masters and one day I'm going to escape."

"Yes, one day," said Mama, dully. "But for now, promise you'll be a good little slave."

"I can't."

Mama stroked Tali's golden hair. "You may *think* whatever fierce thoughts you like, little one, for one day you will be the noble Lady Tali vi Torgrist, but in Cython you must always act the obedient slave."

It frightened Tali to hear her mama say such things. "All right," she muttered. She had a bad temper, and knew it, but for Mama's sake she would try. "I promise."

Her mother looked doubtful. "I'll put a little glamour on you. It'll hide you, as long as they don't look directly at you. Hold still."

She put her hands on Tali's cheeks, whispered a word Tali could not make out, then drew her hands down Tali's sides, all the way to her feet. Tali's skin tingled and when she looked down, her body had blurred into the shadows. Magery! She ached for it. Feared it, too.

Something made an ugly scraping sound, closer this time, and her scalp felt as though grubs were creeping across it.

"Stay here," Mama said softly. "Don't look."

"Mama, what was that noise?"

"I don't know." Mama's teeth chattered. "But whatever happens, even if your gift comes, *don't use it here*."

Mama darted away, her pale blonde hair flying. Her bare feet skidded on the flagstones as she passed an ugly tapestry of three jackals fighting over the guts of a nobleman, recovered, then zig-zagged between the barrels and the stone bins. She was a beautiful little bird, leading a snake away from her nest.

But as she passed between a pair of stone raptors with flesh-tearing beaks, two masked figures came after her. Tali clutched at a crate, her fingers sinking into the powdery wood.

"Mama, look out!" she whispered, for the masks had fanged teeth and awful, angry eyes. "Don't let them catch you."

Then Mama slipped and twisted her ankle, and the moment they caught her Tali knew they were going to do something terrible.

"No!" she whimpered. "Mama, get away!"

The big man caught Mama's arms and held her while his accomplice, a bony woman, punched her in the mouth.

"Treacherous Pale scum!" the woman hissed.

Mama sagged, staring at them like a mouse trapped by two cats, and Tali's front teeth began to throb. Stop it, stop it! Mama, use your gift on them.

They dragged her to the black bench and heaved her onto it. The woman forced an oily green lump into Mama's mouth, then passed a stubby crystal back and forth over her head until the end glowed blue, scattering brilliant rays across the cellar. Mama moaned and her toes curled.

As the blue crystal glowed more brightly, pain stabbed around the whorled scar on Tali's left shoulder, her slave mark, and cold spread through her like venom. She shuddered and remembered to cover her eyes.

Born to slavery in underground Cython, she had learned life's lesson in her stone cradle—*obey, or suffer*. But the people who held her mama weren't tattooed like Cythonians, and they were too big to be Pale slaves. Who were they?

Something made an ugly grinding sound. Mama shrieked.

"Careful," the man cried. "He won't pay if—"

"It's stuck," said the woman, and the grinding grew louder.

What were they doing to Mama?

"It's got to be taken while she's alive," said the man.

"Do you think I don't know that?"

Tali peeped between her fingers and nearly screamed. Mama's arms and legs were thrashing, green foam was oozing from her nose and a strand of hair dripped blood. *Mama!* Tali could not breathe; for a moment she could hardly see.

"I can't hold her." The man's voice was hoarse, his eyes darting.

"Nor me if you don't!"

The woman was pressing a metal rod against the top of Mama's head, twisting and shoving as if trying to force it in. Through the mouth of the mask her grey teeth were bared. She was grunting and her hands were red.

Why were they talking like that? Why were they hurting Mama? Tali's breath came in painful gasps and her stomach was full of fishhooks. She had to help Mama. But Mama had told her not to move. Only magery could save Mama now, but she had told Tali not to use it here. Yet if she didn't, Mama was going to die. But Tali had promised . . .

No! She had to break that promise, and if she got into trouble she would take her punishment. Tali had used magery once before, when she was little. She had been really angry about something and her gift had burst forth out of nowhere. She tried to summon it now but it shrank from her mother's warnings, *Always hide your gift! Never use it or they'll find out and kill you.*

She tried and tried, but it would not come. Tali was desperate now. She had to save Mama. The glamour would hide her, wouldn't it? She crept out, picked up a piece of stone, took aim at the woman's head and hurled it with all the fury her small body could muster. And missed her.

"Ow!" cried the man, clapping a hand to the back of his head. "What was that?"

Tali eased backwards to the crates, praying the glamour would hold. She felt with her foot for a bigger stone.

The woman gave a last twist of her length of metal, withdrew it and flicked a white disc, trailing a clump of bloody hair, to the floor. Was that a piece of Mama's *head*? Tali was reaching for a fist-sized chunk of rock when the woman opened a pair of golden tongs behind Mama's head, pushed in and yanked. Tali heard an awful, squelchy *pop*. Mama's arms and legs jerked, then hung limp.

"You've ended her," the man said hoarsely, shying away.

"Who cares about a filthy Pale?" said the woman, holding up the steaming tongs. "I got it in time."

Tali's head spun and her eyes flooded. But for the crates she would have fallen down. Though she was only eight, she had seen all too many dead slaves. Why was this happening? Was it her fault? She should have run and led them away; she should have done something, *anything*. Had the evil woman killed Mama? No, she couldn't be dead.

"*Mama, Mama!*" she whimpered, hurting all over.

The man gasped, "Did you hear a cry?"

You stupid fool, thought Tali. Now they'll kill you too.

"Are you useless?" sneered the woman.

The man drew a long knife and waved it at her.

She laughed in his face. "Find the brat and finish it."

CHAPTER 3

The man took a lantern in his free hand and crept towards the stacked crates.

The woman put on a long glove that shone like woven green-metal—Tali sensed the whisper of magery coming from it—and removed something round from the tongs. It looked like a black marble. She stripped off the glove so it turned inside out, trapping the black object inside.

Now—horrible, horrible!—she opened a vein in Mama's neck and filled the glove with dribbling blood, then tied a knot in the long wrist and thrust the glove down her front. Tali made out a crimson glow there, shining through the glove, but it went out. She checked on the man, who was at the other end of the stacks, slowly moving her way.

On the far wall of the cellar, the carved face of Lyf shifted. Yellow moved in its stone eyes and a foggy hand reached towards the woman, stretching and stretching as if to pluck out the glove. It was more magery, but whose?

There came a purple flash from behind a pile of barrels, a *zzzt* like a spell going off and the hand recoiled, then faded out. The woman froze, staring at the stone face, then laughed and picked up the gory tongs.

"Oh!" she whispered. "Oh, yes!" and licked them clean.

Tali saw her muddy eyes roll up until the whites were showing through the holes in the mask. Tali wanted to punch her nose flat. After checking that the man wasn't looking, the woman filled a square, green-metal tin with Mama's blood, twisted on a brass cap and licked her bony fingers.

Tali's eyes burnt and her nose was running. She wiped it on the back of her hand, fighting the urge to scream. If she made a sound, the man would cut her open like Mama. But she was much more scared of the evil woman with the crab-leg fingers and those awful eyes. She pressed a finger to the slave mark on her left shoulder, for luck. Touching it always made her feel better.

The man was tall, with a round, jiggling belly like a pudding basin. He was outside her hiding place now and she caught a glimpse of the gleaming knife blade, as long as her arm. Tali recoiled and felt a shocking pain as a nail in one of the crates pierced her hip to the bone. Tears stung her eyes yet she dared not move. If she made a sound he would stab that knife right through her.

The man was panting and the spirits on his breath made her head spin. His hand shook as he raised the lantern, then lowered it. Silence fell, apart from a sickening *drip-drip* from the black bench.

After Papa's terrible death, Mama had taught Tali how to hide.

"A slave must be invisible," she had said. "Never be noticed and you'll be safe."

No slave was ever safe, but Tali was the best of the slave kids at hiding. She traced the loops and whorls of her slave mark with a fingertip, trying to find comfort there, but nothing could comfort her now. Mama couldn't be dead. It wasn't possible, yet she was gone.

He waited, as if he *knew* she was there. What if he pulled the crates away? She had to do something. She felt among the broken wood on the floor for the sharpest length, a piece as long as her forearm. If he came at her, she would shove it into his fat belly and run.

Her arm was trembling so much she could hardly hold the weapon. Then, to her shame, Tali realised that wee was running down her legs. She clamped her thighs together and, to distract herself, began to count her heartbeats, which were so loud that surely he could hear them. After another twenty beats, the man grunted and moved on. She kept still.

He sprang back, hacking at the crates with his knife and roaring, "Haaaaaa! Got you."

Tali's heart leapt up her throat and the nail ground into her hipbone. She was almost screaming from the pain but she did not move. She was going to win this contest, for Mama.

With savage hacks of the knife, the man began to tear down the crates to her left, *smash*, *crash*. He was going to find her. How could she stop him? She eased off the nail, took hold of the lowest crate and heaved. It did not budge; the weight of all the crates above it was too great.

More crates crashed down. It would not be long now. She could not go further backwards; the gap was too narrow. And she dared not wait. Once he saw her, he would jam the knife through her guts.

Tali crouched, took hold of the lowest crate and heaved, using her legs this time. Even little girl slaves were strong, and she forced upwards, slowly straightening her legs, until her back ached and her knees trembled. But she wasn't going to give in, ever.

The moving crates scraped and squealed. He swung around, trying to work out where the sound had come from. She gave an almighty heave, the ten-high stack swayed, then with a roar the lot fell down on him.

Tali scurried sideways into a new gap and hid in the darkness. The man groaned. The woman appeared, taking her time, and heaved the crates aside. The man's face was covered in blood. Ha! thought Tali. *Take that!* But it could never make up for what they had done to Mama.

"What happened?" he moaned.

"Stop whining," said the woman disgustedly. "You pulled them down on yourself. Did you find anything?"

Fifty heartbeats passed, then the man lurched away. "Must have been rats. Come on. I need another drink."

"I'll pour it down your throat until you choke."

Tali pressed a fingertip against the nail wound, trying to heal it the way Nurse Bet had taught her, but the hole went too deep. The beads of blood on her fingers were as bright as jewels, as bright as Mama's blood. *Mama!* Her eyes flooded.

The woman pulled on a dangling rope and, with a screech, an iron staircase corkscrewed down. Tali felt sure the point at the bottom was going to twist right through Mama, but it brushed by her tiny waist before grounding on the black bench. The man shot up the steps, a rat running away from a ferret. The staircase was a coiled spring quivering under his weight.

But then—*then* the woman picked up the tin of blood, climbed onto the bench and stepped onto Mama's chest as though she was rubbish. One of Mama's ribs snapped like the wishbone of a poulter and a scorching fury surged through Tali, an urge to smash the woman down. She fought it; Mama had told her to not make a sound.

The woman rocked back and forth as she scanned the cellar, *crack-crack*, standing on Tali's beautiful mama as if she were a piece of firewood, then followed the man.

Once they were gone, Tali darted across and touched the crimson beads on her fingers to her mama's head, as if her own blood could heal her. There was blood everywhere, but none left in Mama. Taking hold of her hand, Tali squeezed it tightly, trying to will Mama back to life, but the spirit had left her forever.

She had taught Tali not to fight back, to always bow her head and say, "Yes, Master," and it had killed her. Tali wasn't going to make that mistake. Mama said it was wrong to hate people, but Tali's rage had red-hot teeth and talons as sharp as spikes. How dare they treat her beautiful mama that way?

"When I'm grown up I'll find them out," she whispered, hand upon her mother's heart. "Once I get my gift I'll hunt them down and make them pay."

Someone took a heavy breath, close by. The murderers! Coming back to kill her! Tali scuttled into the shadows between two of the stone bins, grabbed a grey stick protruding from its broken top and prepared to defend herself.

But it was a handsome, black-haired boy, a few years older than herself, who stumbled out from behind a heap of empty barrels. He wasn't a slave, though, nor a tattooed Cythonian. He must have been rich, for he wore a plum-coloured velvet coat with gold buttons, an emerald kilt and shoes with shiny buckles. His face was white, his eyes a rich, purply brown, his yellow vest was covered in vomit and his teeth were chattering.

That wasn't the only odd thing about him. The faintest misty aura, pale pink as the gills of a mushroom, clung to his head and hands. The aura of magery—though not his. Tali could tell that he had no more gift than a log.

The boy reached out towards Mama then drew back sharply, staring at his hands. Tali's hair stood up. His hands were covered in blood, *yet he hadn't touched Mama.*

He doubled over, sicked onto his shoes and let out the moan of an animal in pain. Tali must have made a sound for his head shot around and he stared at her, then bolted up the stairs, yanking on the rope as he went. The iron staircase howled as it rose with him out of sight.

Tali could hold back no longer. "I'm going to get you!" she screeched, brandishing the stick. A trapdoor clanged shut and the greenish light began to fade.

What if Tinyhead was waiting outside? Tali shivered. What if he came after her? No, he had betrayed Mama and he had to pay. Rage swelled until her heart felt as if it was going to explode, then she pointed the stick at the stone door, willing Tinyhead's head to burst like a melon. With a sudden gush, the pressure was gone and her rage as well.

She was holding the stick so tightly that her knuckles hurt, and for the first time Tali saw it clearly. It wasn't a stick, it was a human thigh bone. There was nothing horrible about it, though. Oddly, it felt like a friend.

Tali put it back where she had found it. Now so exhausted that she could barely stand up, she stumbled to the door, trying not to think about the man with the knife or the woman and her golden tongs, trying to wipe out the memories forever. When she slipped into the painted tunnel that led back to Cython, there was no sign of Tinyhead.

Learn to lower your eyes and say, "Yes, Master".

"All right!" Tali said savagely. "But once I come of age, once I find my gift, *look out!*"

How could she find her gift when she couldn't trust anyone? How could she beat her enemy when no one knew who he was? Blinded by scalding tears, she crept home to Cython, and slavery.

At least she would be safe there.

CHAPTER 4

It takes an unnatural cold to touch a wrythen: cold bitter as bile and empty as a dead man's eyes. Cold so bleak that he felt his frostbitten *plasm* congealing and it took precious strength to maintain his uncanny, neither-live-nor-dead state. Strength he could not afford to waste.

Not when vengeance was so achingly near.

The wrythen suppressed his rage at the loss of a third nuclix. He had a plan to get all three back and avenge himself on the thief. It would not take long—not as he counted time.

He cleaned the hollow needle of a graver and filled it with

diluted *alkoyl*, the last of his hoarded store. The wrythen had to be exquisitely careful using it, for alkoyl was inimical both to his plasm and to most things he had created here in his five-fold caverns. The graver was made of purest platina, yet alkoyl would eat through it before he finished the iron book. No other substance could contain it at all.

He had to complete the book, if the alkoyl lasted, and transmit the completed pages to the Chamber of the Solaces as soon as he could find the strength for such challenging magery. *The Consolation of Vengeance* had to be finished soon. His people must be ready when the call came.

As the wrythen set his graver to the page, he was summoned. He did not have to go; nothing and no one had any hold on him. But in life he had been a decent and an honourable man, so he rose to the top of his home cavern.

Spaced around his lovingly imagined ancestor gallery, looking out from spectre sculptures as perfect as mind and memory could create, a hundred and seven pairs of regal eyes measured him. Their collective reign had lasted three thousand, six hundred and forty-two years; their wisdom could not be measured by any set of numbers. He had shaped them from his own plasm, had long relied on them for company, advice and support, had argued every point of his plan innumerable times, yet still they spoke to him, even the angry, red-throated shade of Bloody Herrie, in a single voice.

Don't do this!

It's the only way to save our people, the wrythen said, though what he meant was, *It's my sole reason for being*. Without the urge to vengeance he would have faded to a miserable ghost a thousand years ago.

We have *no people—with your blasphemous Solaces you've constructed these Cythonians just as you made us. And these caverns. And the vile* shifters *down below*.

What are you talking about? said the wrythen. *Our blood runs in Cython's veins.*

But nothing else. They've lost our language, been robbed of our history—

I won't discuss it, he said coldly. *It was our only hope.*

This must stop now, said Queen Hilga, whose luminous eyes protruded past her eyelashes. *Errek, tell him.*

The faded wisp of Errek First-King, so old that he found all human follies amusing, was not smiling now. *The price is too high.*

They destroyed our cities, our libraries and our art, said the wrythen, *and profaned all we held sacred.*

A monstrous crime, said Hilga, *but all things have their hour and their ending.*

Posterity is rife with oblivion, said Errek wryly. *Let it go.*

I CAN'T!

The wrythen returned to the iron book but was too agitated to finish the page. What if they were right? Since he could not speak to the matriarchs and they had no way to contact him, there was no way to judge their preparedness.

Like a trapped moth, he flitted around his home cavern, which he called a flaskoid. It resembled an upside-down alchymister's flask, save that the long neck looped down and up again, passing through its own wall and up through the bulb, its inside becoming its outside then its inside again. Though he had etched it in four dimensions out of solid rock, the shape even confused him at times.

Settling to the base of the loop, he drifted along the shelves of his memory library to the lovingly recollected epics that sustained him in the darkest times. Today they offered no comfort. All he saw were flames leaping high as the treetops as the treasures of ten millennia had been burned, along with the curators who had tended them. The epics of Cythe existed only through him now and, once he was gone, all would be lost.

But before that—vengeance.

Weeks had gone by and the wrythen still had to write the ending of the iron book. He drifted alongside the towering condenser of his platina still, tapping each of its thousand coils, but it yielded not a drop. The apparatus could only extract a few drops of alkoyl from the breath of the Abysm in a year, and even that was a sacrilege. The ending of the book would take twenty drops of the magical fluid, at least.

Frustrated, he ploughed up through solid rock to the top of the cloud-piercing crag. In warmer years the passage had been effortless but today every atom dragged through him like an anchor caught in weed. As a bodiless wrythen he was tied to his caverns. Bound forever, unless . . .

He could not afford to dream. His head slid through black ice into moving air, then stopped. Even here, a mile above the home cavern, it was warmer than down below.

Warm enough to feel the tension in sinews long gone to dust, in fingernails splintered from the stone with which his enemies had walled him in to die, in shinbone stumps where his feet had been hacked off with that accursed blade—Oh, yes! Vengeance, once he completed the *Consolation*. If his people followed the plan . . .

Swallowing the self-doubt, he looked around. From here he could see the whole of the great island he still called Cythe, which the enemy had renamed Hightspall, and south across the berg-crusted strait to ice-capped, uninhabitable Suden, two hundred miles away. To the north, he was pleased to see that the Brown Vomit was erupting again. One or other of the three Vomits had been erupting for the past hundred and seventy years, their ash sifting down on the bountiful lands of central Hightspall like grey flour, crushing the enemy's houses, burying their stock and choking the rivers with sludge.

Had it gone too far? What if the eruptions never stopped? What if they got worse? The cauldron at the heart of the world was unstable, he knew. But *how* unstable?

A king's highest duty was to protect his realm and it was torment to see his country so ravaged, but there was no other way to bring Hightspall to its knees. Volcanoes had made his country, then blown it to pieces and created it anew. Cythe was resilient; it was forever, and so were his people. When the enemy was no more, his people could come home.

But what would they return to? The wrythen wanted to weep for the ancient cities torn down, the temple gardens sown with salt, and for that desperate time when his noble people had been reduced to a handful of nomadic *origines* and a few thousand contemptible *degradoes*.

Save for the wrythen's intervention they would have vanished from the world, for the invading Hightspallers had set out to erase ten thousand years of history and they had been ruthlessly thorough. Only the king had stood in their way then, only the wrythen now. But he dared not weep—tears etched *quessence* out of him and he remained desperately weak.

The ash might not be enough, nor the poxes and pestilences that followed it. Nor even the vicious *shifters* he'd created with the blasphemous art of *germine*. Before ordering his remade people from their underground hiding place he must be sure.

The ice.

Further south, the globe-circling pall of ash and fume blanketed the sky all the way to the southern pole. The once mighty mountains of Suden were no more than pimples standing above mile-thick ice sheets and the ice crept further north each year. It would soon batter down the walls of accursed Hightspall, then freeze it solid like blood congealing in blocked veins.

It was time.

Back in his home cavern, the wrythen avoided the accusing eyes in his ancestor gallery and drifted down the curve to the cleft where the flaskoid passed back through itself in the fourth dimension.

He had to fold himself over seventeen times before he could fit through the infinitesimal cleft. New dimensions exploded out around him, then he was floating in the white shaft of the Abysm beside a disc of grass-green viridium, on which sat his prize, his joy and his terror. It was both the source and the limit of his magery. It represented all that had been lost, yet the means by which it might be regained. Though it sustained him, it must finally be the mode of his beautiful annihilation.

It was no bigger than a marble yet it represented the world; and it had taken him sixteen hundred years to create. It was so black that, even in the brightest light, it looked like a hole in the air, an emptiness nothing could fill, a cold that no fire could warm.

It was a nuclix. An ebony pearl.

Binding it to himself with magery so that the intangible could retain the tangible, he floated, holding his sensitive shin stumps well away from the wall of the shaft, and cupped the nuclix in his hands, waiting for the *call*.

Shortly it came, faint as the mewling of a newborn kitten.

He waited.

Nuclixes longed for the completion of unity, and after several minutes the second whispered its answer, followed by the third's shout and finally the dry chuckle of the fourth, the nuclix he'd been reaching for in the cellar when that thickening spell had blocked him.

Rage washed through the wrythen, that a third-rate magian had robbed him of treasures belonging to him alone. Until the Hightspallers invaded, magery had been a sacred and healing force belonging solely to the king. The enemy had perverted it, as they had corrupted beautiful Cythe, and he felt a special hatred for their magians.

He crushed the emotion—the three stolen nuclixes were still where the thief had hidden them. They would be his in time. He waited, as he had done so many times, for the fifth and last *call*.

The nuclix that had not yet answered.

The master.

A lesser shade might have twisted its plasm into knots. But if the king had not learned patience while starving to death walled up in a tomb, his wrythen had done so in the centuries of crushing defeat that had followed.

Once the master nuclix answered, the thief magian, Deroe, would try to take it. He must be killed. The wrythen could not take the nuclix himself, nor have the host brought here, because nuclixes were wildly unstable after extraction. It had to be taken by one of the enemy, but he would never use the man or the woman from the cellar, sickening predators that they were.

What about the boy?

He had been traumatised by the killing and, clearly, felt tainted by the blood on his own hands. Now the wrythen realised that the boy had been bathed by the aura of a heatstone since infancy. A *heatstone*—if only they knew!

For hundreds of years the wrythen had railed against Cython's vile heatstone trade with the enemy, but at this irony he allowed himself a small smile. Hightspall believed it was robbing a crushed enemy. In reality, it had carried the infected seed into its palace garden. Yes, with the heatstone the boy could be moulded, all unwitting, and once the fifth nuclix answered he would cut it out.

Months passed as the wrythen tweaked the heatstone from afar, setting it up to shape and influence the boy, and it was not easy. Though the wrythen knew where the boy lived, he could not travel there, and could only reach him when he was in dreaming sleep. Nonetheless, over the slow march of the years, the wrythen could command the lad as effectively as if he had possessed him.

Weeks went by.

Months.

Years, and still the wrythen lacked the strength to transmit the next set of pages to the Chamber of the Solaces. Ten years passed before a loud, angry *call* shivered the silence. The master nuclix was fully formed and it yearned for union with the lesser four.

It was time.

The wrythen knew nothing about the host's identity. All he could read was a roaring rage, so youthful and furious that it made him smile, for the Pale were cowed creatures whose anger threatened no one but themselves. And because all those with the gift had been culled, they were the only safe hosts.

Taking up a pale-blue ovoid like the egg of a small bird, he touched it to his forehead. Far away and deep underground, his sole servant stirred.

Master?

The host is a slave girl who has just come of age. Bring her to the cellar, unharmed, two nights from now.

How will I find her without a name, Master? There are many, many Pale.

Enquire of the overseers. The woken nuclix will trouble her and she lacks self-control. She will draw attention to herself. But tell no one.

No one, Master?

The host is a threat to Cython. No one must ever know about her.

Not even the matriarchs?

Especially not the matriarchs. You must protect the host from all dangers, and sacrifice yourself before you allow anyone to know what she carries.

Willingly, Master.

The wrythen drew *quessence* from the small store left to him and traced a link for twenty-six miles: out of the Crowbung Range, north-east around the treble cones of The Vomits, above the scalded lands and boiling mud pools of the Seethings then across the edge of bottomless Lake Fumerous which filled the chasm where the fourth Vomit had once stood two miles high, to the capital city of enemy Hightspall, Caulderon.

To a dirty, crumbling chateau overlooking the lake. To an upper room where the withered magian, Deroe, sat at a table before a selection of arcane instruments. His left hand was raised, ready to snatch the appropriate weapon at the first hint of intrusion.

The wrythen's consciousness edged along the link. Carefully now. The terrified magian had wards everywhere, in layers over-lapping layers, but there was a way through. The wrythen bypassed the wards, wrapped himself octopus-like around Deroe's mind before he had time to use his carefully prepared defences, and took possession again.

It sickened him to occupy such a foul instrument, but if he was to recover the stolen nuclixes there was no choice. Being physically bound to the caverns, the wrythen could only travel to two places: the mind of the magian he had first possessed a century before, when the blasphemer had broken into the Catacombs of the Kings, greedy for plunder; and the cellar that had once been the wrythen's own temple, where for aeons the kings had worked their magery to heal the land of Cythe.

You heard the call, the wrythen said into Deroe's mind. *You know the last of the five is ready. The host will be brought to the cellar two nights from now, but this time, I will take delivery.*

"Damn you," whined Deroe.

He was fighting the possession, growing stronger all the time, but the wrythen did not fight back. Nor did he look for the nuclixes Deroe had stolen in the hope of driving his possessor out. The master nuclix was Deroe's bait, the cellar a fatal trap. When Deroe came, he would bring the three with him.

And he would die.

It was time to mobilise the rich boy, now grown to a man. Time to send him the final nightmare, a horror like no other, and embed within it a command that must be obeyed.

Soon the wrythen would be strong enough to begin transmitting the completed sections of the iron book. Once that was done, with freshly distilled alkoyl he would begin on the last, terrible page. Then, when he had all five nuclixes . . .

Ruin upon his enemies.

Vengeance for his dispossessed people.

Annihilation and rebirth for his beloved country.

CHAPTER 5

He's coming for me. There's no way out. He's going to take me to the cellar and they're going to hack my head open like Mama's and *there's no way out*. He's coming for me.

Round and round it cycled, as it had ever since Tali had read her father's horrifying letter this morning. To survive, she had to escape, though in a thousand years no Pale slave ever had. There was only one way to gain your freedom here—the way Tali's mother had been given hers.

"Your eyes are really red," said Mia, arms folded over her pregnant belly. "Something the matter?"

They were in the sweltering toadstool grottoes where they worked twelve hours a day, every day of the month, every month of the year. At times the drifting spore clouds were thick enough to clog the eyes.

"Stupid spores," Tali lied. "They gunk everything up."

"You look terrible. Have a break; I'll do this row for you."

"Thanks, Mia."

Tali had woken in the middle of the night feeling as if a stone heart was grinding against her skull with every beat. And with each beat, brilliant reds and yellows swirled madly in her inner eye, like beams trying to find the way out of a sealed lighthouse until, with a spike of pain, they burst forth and she collapsed into sleep.

When the work gong had dragged her into wakefulness this morning, the inside of her skull felt bruised. She desperately needed to think, to plan, but now the colours were back, spinning like clay on a potter's wheel, and fits of irrational anger kept flaring. She had to restrain herself from smashing the toadstool trays against the bench.

He's coming for me and there's no way out. They're going to cut a hole in my head, just like Mama. No way out, *no way out!*

Tali pressed her cheek against the wet wall and after a minute the colours faded, the headache died to a dull throb. Take deep breaths and stay calm. Don't do anything silly. You've got time. He might not come for months, even years. Mama had been twenty-six, after all.

Her racing heartbeat steadied and Tali wiped her face. "I'm all right now."

"Be careful. The Cythonians are really agitated today."

"Why?"

"I don't know. Keep your head down and don't attract attention."

Tali managed a smile. "When did *I* ever do that?"

"I'm always getting you out of trouble." Shaking her head fondly, Mia turned away to her work.

The grottoes were a series of broad, low-ceilinged tunnels linked by arched doorways. Cages filled with fat-bellied fireflies provided a bluish light that barely illuminated the walls, which were sculpted to resemble a forest by moonlight—a humid glen whose every surface was covered in fungi, like the grottoes themselves. The air was so heavy with their mixed earthy, fishy, foetid and garlicky odours that it made Tali heave.

The floor shook, grinding the stone trays against the benches. It had been shaking all day. What was the enemy up to in the secret lower levels? Was that why they were so touchy?

"Tali, *try* to look like you're working."

"Sorry."

Today's job, one of the worst of her slave duties, was de-grubbing the harvest. Tiered stone benches running the length of each grotto were stacked with trays of edible toadstools and mushrooms, dozens of kinds, plus leathery cloud ear fungi and giant red puffballs as big as Tali's head. The puffballs had to be cut and bagged carefully lest they gush clouds of stinging flame-spores everywhere. In the darkest corners, tiny toadstools sprouted in clusters like luminous white velvet, though Tali wasn't fool enough to stroke them. They were delicious when properly cooked, but deadly to touch in their natural state.

Reaching between the brown toadstools in front of her, she found a red-and-yellow girr-grub by feel and crushed it, wincing as the sharp bristles pricked her fingers. After dropping the muck into her compost bucket she rinsed her hands under a wall spring. Last year she had sucked a sore finger covered in girr slime and spent the next three days throwing up the lining of her stomach.

Mia was humming as she worked. At least she could still dream. Tali's vow to hunt down her mother's killers had never faltered, but in ten years she had learned nothing more about them and this morning's revelation had extinguished all hope. This morning, her eighteenth birthday and coming-of-age day, Little Nan had given Tali the letter her father had written her mother only days before his own tragic death. The letter that made it clear Tali would be next to die.

Her hand clenched on the stone tray. "It's not right!" she hissed.

"What?" said Mia.

"Our servitude! Living in terror every day of our lives. Sleeping on stone beds. Being flogged for a scowl or a sideways look. Torn apart from our loved ones—"

"Don't say such things," Mia whispered. "What if the guards hear?"

Tali's voice rose. "Worked to death in the heatstone mines, killed for no reason at all." The blood was pounding in her head. "We've got to throw off our chains and cast the enemy down."

"Shh!" Mia slapped her hand over Tali's mouth. "They'll condemn you to the acidulators."

Tali yanked the hand away. "If they try," she said recklessly, "I'll smash—"

Mia shook her head and backed away, her eyes wide and frightened.

A ululating whistle sounded behind Tali and she sprang aside, too late. The chymical chuck-lash wrapped around her left shoulder and went off, *crack-crack-crack*.

She staggered several steps, clutching her blistered, bloody shoulder, and through a drift of brown smoke saw Orlyk, the bandy-legged guard, scowling at her. A fringe of chuck-lashes swung from Orlyk's belt like red bootlaces and she was raising another, ready to throw. Most of the guards were decent enough, but Orlyk was an embittered brute and she had been in a foul temper all day. And if she'd actually heard what Tali had said—

"Lazy, Pale swine," Orlyk grunted, her blue-tattooed throat rising and falling like a calling toad. "Come the day when Khirrikai leads us to take back our land and we don't need your kind any more. Oh, soon come the day!"

Tali's head gave another throb. She fantasised about tearing the chuck-lashes from Orlyk's belt, driving her to the nearest effluxor with them and dumping her head-first into the filth.

"Tali!" Mia hissed.

Lower your eyes and say, "Yes, Master".

Tali shivered at the hatred in Orlyk's bulging eyes, then managed to regain control and forced out the sickening words, "Thank you for correcting me, Master."

She bowed lower than necessary. One day, Orlyk, one day! Tali knew how to defend herself, for she had practised the bare-handed art with Nurse Bet every week since her mother's murder, but raising a hand against a guard was fatal.

Orlyk snapped the tip of a chuck-lash at Tali's left ear, *crack-crack*, grunted, "Work, slave," and headed after another victim.

The pain was like a chisel hammered through Tali's ear. She lost sight for a few seconds, the colours in her head swirled and danced, then her returning sight revealed Orlyk's broad back as she approached the archway. Scalding blood was dripping from Tali's ear onto her bare shoulder, and blood-drenched memory roused such fury that she snatched up a chunk of rock.

"Tali, no!" Mia hissed.

As the guard passed the puffball trays, Tali hurled her rock twenty yards and struck a giant puffball at its base. It disgorged an orange torrent of flame-spores, but then the shockwave set off a hundred other puffballs and she watched in horror as the guard disappeared behind churning spore clouds. When they settled, Orlyk was convulsing on the floor, choking, her face and throat swelling monstrously.

"Are you insane?" hissed Mia. "If she dies . . . "

"I didn't mean that to happen," Tali whispered.

"You never do."

"Sorry, Mia. I'm really sorry."

Mia ran down the far side of the bench, picked the rock out of the puffball tray and tossed it out of sight. Reaching up to the clangours beside the archway, she struck the square healer's bell with the ring-rod. The bell's chime was picked up by trumpet-mouthed bell-pipes running across the ceiling, and shortly Tali made out an echo from outside. Mia came back, glaring at her.

"I'm not taking it any longer," Tali said defensively. "If I have to die, I'm not going quietly."

"Leave me out of it," Mia snapped.

Shortly a lean, austere Cythonian, the red, linked-oval cheek tattoos of a healer standing out on his grey skin, ran in. "What happened?"

"Puffballs went off spontaneously," Mia lied.

He inspected the tray of burst puffballs and the thick layer of orange spores surrounding Orlyk, then stared at Tali. She kept working, watching him from the corner of an eye. Her cheeks grew hot.

"I tried really hard," Tali said under her breath once he had turned to Orlyk. "But when she hit me with the second chucklash—"

"I told you not to draw attention to yourself."

"Mama died because I didn't act quickly enough, and I'm never—"

"Shh!" said Mia.

Several slaves appeared on the other side of the archway, pretending to work while looking in sideways.

"You!" called the healer to the nearest slave, a thin girl with stringy yellow hair and eyes that must have seen a nightmare. "Run to the spagyrium. Get a sachet of blast-balm and a large head bag, quick!" He handed her a rectangular healer's token made from shiny tin.

"B-blast-balm and head bag, Master," she said, head dutifully lowered.

"*Large* head bag."

"Master!" She ran out, sweaty feet slap-slapping on the stone floor.

The healer dragged Orlyk away from the spore-covered area, dampened a cloth and began to clean the spores out of her eyes, mouth, ears and nose. Orlyk's face was scarlet, the swollen skin shiny and balloon-taut. Clotted sounds emerged from her throat as her lungs struggled to draw air.

"Pray she's all right," Mia said from the corner of her mouth. "If she dies—"

Tali could not meet her eyes. Why had she been so stupid?

The slave reappeared, panting, and handed the healer a clear bag made from the intestines of an elephant eel. The healer pulled it over Orlyk's head, inflated it with a small bellows, pulled the string on a pillow-like sachet of blast-balm, inserted it inside the bag and held the bag closed around Orlyk's tattooed neck while he counted to five.

A loud, wet *flupp* sounded, like gas bubbles bursting at the top of the squattery pits. Mustard-yellow vapour swirled inside the head bag then it shrank tightly against Orlyk's head. After a minute the healer peeled the bag off, thumped Orlyk in the chest and she took a gurgling breath. Red blisters protruded through the coating of yellow balm but the swelling was already going down.

As the healer and the slave girl carried Orlyk out to the Healery, her black eyes fixed on Tali and, with a convulsive snap of the wrist, Orlyk hurled another chuck-lash. Tali ducked, it soared over her head and struck Mia on her swollen belly, *crack-crack-crack*.

Stifling a cry, Mia pressed both hands to her wildly quivering belly.

Tali ran to her. "Are you all right?"

Mia nodded and took her hands away to reveal a red and white welt as long as a finger. "Only the tip caught me. Lucky."

"Lucky," said Tali, guilt churning in her. "Let me heal—"

"Someone's coming." Mia began to squash girr-grubs as though it was her sole delight.

Tali did the same. A replacement guard came in, stared at her for several minutes then went into the next grotto. Through the archway, a toothless slave was scattering compost onto trays of mauve, curly-tipped Sprite Caps. One cap could cure the worst toothache within minutes; three caps would cure life almost as quickly. It was not unknown for desperate slaves to take that way out.

"We got away with it."

Mia touched the welt on her belly and winced. She was paler than usual, and in evident pain. Her belly was churning, the muscles clenching and unclenching.

Any other slave would have sworn at Tali, or slapped her. Tali wished Mia would do the same. Anything would be better than this sickening shame. But Mia was too nice, too gentle. She reminded Tali of her mother.

"I'm really sorry, Mia. I just snapped."

"What is it with you? You've been acting strangely all day."

"You know what happened to Mama?"

"You've told me at least fifty times," said Mia. "You never stop talking about it."

Tali hadn't realised. "Well, according to Father's letter, Mama's mother, grandmother and great-grandmother were also killed the same way, and now I've come of age I'm marked to be next. Every time someone looks at me, every time I see a stranger pass by, I think they're the one. I can't take it any more. I've got to—"

"Shh!" Mia jerked her head towards the archway.

Tali glanced at the old slave. "Suba's no harm. She's simple."

"I think she's a *kwissler*." An informer.

Tali moved out of Suba's sight and pressed her hand against the welt on Mia's belly, beginning the charm Nurse Bet had taught her when she was little. Most Cythonians turned a blind eye to healing charms, since they weren't real magery, though a vengeful guard might still chuck-lash you for using one.

Healing charms were all Tali could do. She had practised her mother's gentle magery every night since her death, but it never worked. Tali's own gift had only come a handful of times, always when she was furious, though it was neither gentle nor controllable. It exploded out of her, wreaking unintended ruin, then vanished for years. Was that because she was so afraid of it?

To save herself and beat the enemy her mama had spoken of, the one that had fluttered in her nightmares like a wrythen, Tali had to find her buried magery and learn to control it. She had to find it fast, but who could she ask?

Trust no one.

CHAPTER 6

Tali pressed her back against the oozing wall. She always felt vulnerable with an open space behind her. Could Mia know magery? Tali had seen no evidence of any, though those few who had the gift hid it.

"We've got to escape," said Tali.

Another spasm shook Mia's small frame and she bit back a cry. "Leave me out of it. I'll soon have a baby to look after."

"All right, *I've* got to escape, and there's only one way. Mia, I don't suppose—"

"I hope you're not asking what I think you're asking." There was no warmth in Mia's voice now.

"Mia, please."

Mia checked over her shoulder. "I could be flogged for saying the word. And anyone who does say it is watched thereafter."

Sweat trickled down Tali's bare chest to soak her threadbare loin-cloth. "If I don't get away, I'm going to be killed."

Mia avoided her eyes. Maybe she did know magery.

"Mia, I'm desperate."

"I don't have the . . . the gift," she muttered. "And I don't know anyone who does."

Tali felt sure she was lying. "If you were my friend, you'd help me."

"If you were *my* friend, you wouldn't ask," said Mia, deeply hurt. "Haven't you done enough to me today?"

"Sorry." Tali put her arms around Mia. "I am a terrible friend, I know."

"You're a wonderful friend," said Mia, pulling free. "You just— you push too hard."

She staggered, catching at the bench as a spasm twisted her soft face. Everything about her was soft and sweet. Save for the matter of her belly she would have been the perfect slave.

"It's not your time yet, is it?" said Tali, holding her up.

The spasm passed and Mia resumed her work. "It's not due for two months."

"How did you get pregnant, anyway?"

She smiled. "The usual way."

But Pale boys were taken away at the age of ten to slave in Cython's mines, comminuteries, segregators, calciners and foundries, where most were worked to death before the age of thirty. The adult women only saw their partners on monthly mating nights, though, Tali had been told, some men were so weak that they weren't up to it. Besides, she had never seen Mia with a man. There weren't enough to go around.

Tali's stomach rumbled. Food production in the grotto farms, eeleries and poultyards was higher than ever, yet rations had been reduced again last week. Did slaves no longer matter? *Why not?*

They continued down the outside, steadily filling their buckets with girr-grubs. Mia kept well ahead, avoiding her, and Tali did not raise the topic again. She worked absently, making plan after plan, but all foundered on the same obstacle. No slave had ever escaped Cython, so how could she hope to? Many times she had sought the tunnels Tinyhead had led them along that terrible day, but she had never found them.

As they reached the end of the grotto, Mia gasped and doubled over.

"What is it?" Tali cried, holding her up.

Pink fluid was flooding down her friend's legs and puddling on the stone floor. Her waters had broken.

"Tali," wailed Mia, "it's too early!"

It must be coming because of the chuck-lash. Curse Orlyk! But Tali knew it was her own stupid fault. Mia had warned her, and yet again she had allowed her anger to control her. What a lousy friend she was.

Tali helped Mia to the floor, lifted the loincloth and her hands clenched involuntarily.

"What's the matter?" Mia grabbed Tali's wrist.

Tali shivered. Let it be stillborn. If it's born dead, we can hide the body and she *might* get away with it.

"Tali?" whispered Mia. "My baby is all right, isn't it?"

What to say? Tali looked again, but there was no doubt at all.

"It's small," she said, standing up to check on the guard in the next grotto. For bearing a Cythonian's baby Mia would be scourged, and Tali too, for witnessing the crime. "It'll come quickly."

"Babies can live at seven months, can't they?" Mia's tone was pleading.

"I don't know."

"Is it good and pink?"

Of course it's not *pink*, Tali wanted to scream, but then the slate-grey baby slipped out. Surely it couldn't live at seven months. What was she supposed to do? Scourging meant a life of agony that no healing charm could repair. There had to be a solution. But what, what, *what*? She could not think. Her mind had gone numb. "It's a boy, but . . ."

"My beautiful boy!" sighed Mia.

"I don't think he's breathing."

"Doesn't have to 'til the cord is cut. Give him here."

Tali cut the cord with her harvesting knife and knotted the end, carefully, respectfully. She picked the tiny baby up, feeling his lungs struggling as she embraced him with her hands and gave him to

Mia. If he died, they might escape punishment—no, what sort of a monster was she, wishing that on a helpless infant?

He took a faint breath. "You've got to hide him, Mia. Hurry! I'll say you've gone to the squattery to pee."

"Don't be silly," Mia said dreamily. "I've just had a baby."

Tali wanted to slap her. "A Cythonian baby! And you know the penalty."

"They wouldn't hurt my baby." Mia cradled the infant in her arms.

It was like standing beneath a toppling wall. "Come on!" Tali tried to lift her. "If you're quick, you can still get away with it."

"Leave me alone," wailed Mia. "You're spoiling everything." She looked down and her face cracked. "Tali, he's not breathing. Do something."

The baby's lips were turning blue. Tali put her hands around his tiny body. Heal, *heal*! But saving a life was far beyond her skill. He gave a little shudder and lay still. Tears welled in Tali's eyes. The poor little thing hadn't had a chance.

As she stood there, not knowing what to do, a rumbling voice echoed through the archway from the next grotto. Her stomach gave a sickening lurch. What was Overseer Banj doing here today? Investigating what had happened to Orlyk, of course.

Guilt rose up in her throat like vomit. She crouched in front of Mia, pressing the baby into her arms. "It's Banj, checking up. Hide it, quick!"

"Banj won't hurt me," said Mia. "Not when I show him my beautiful baby."

"Your son is gone," Tali said gently.

"No, he's not!"

"Mia, he's dead. Please—"

Mia's face crumpled. "Why are you doing this to me?"

Banj was kindly, as slave masters went, but he could not overlook a grey baby. "He'll have both of us scourged."

"Run away, then," said Mia, kicking Tali in the knee. "It's your fault my little boy is dead."

That hurt all the more because it was true. It was her fault Banj was here, too, and if ever there was a time for risking her mother's subtle magery it was now. Tali closed her eyes, whispered the words and made the gestures exactly as she had been taught, then focused her will to cast a concealing glamour over the baby. Mist churned in her inner eye and her scar tingled, but when she opened her eyes the baby was still visible.

It was too late to try again. "Put it in my bucket," she whispered. "I'll cover it up and carry it out to the composter."

The compost buckets were often checked in case the slaves were stealing food, and if she were caught the consequences would be dire, but Tali had to make up for the disaster she had caused.

"Lost everything," choked Mia. "Want to die."

"You'll get over it. Soon—"

Mia slapped Tali across the face. "Don't want to *get over* my baby. Go away! I hate you!"

The overseer was approaching the archway and the best option for both of them was for Tali to disappear. If no other slave had seen the grey baby, Banj might not punish Mia too severely. Tali kissed her damp cheek then ducked below the benches as he came down the central path. It was the only thing to do, so why did she feel like a faithless friend?

She reached the archway, rinsed her bloody hands under a spring and slipped into the next grotto. Suba had gone and the half dozen slaves were moving away, heads down.

Tali scuttled to the exit and out into the broad passageway, which was sculpted and painted to resemble a resin-pine forest under snow. Water gurgled by in one of the siphons, its stone sides carved to resemble a rivulet with reed beds cut in relief. Where to go? Idle slaves attracted attention; she could not wait here.

She headed for the squattery, then stopped. Further on, the passage was blocked by a Cythonian teacher, a buxom brunette with single, bright blue spot-tattoos on each cheekbone, who was instructing a dozen chattering children in the art of wall sculpting.

"First we take a measure of *solu*," the teacher said, pouring a cupful of palest green liquid from an orange-ringed carboy into a bucket. "Be careful with it. The waste *alk*–" She broke off, colouring. "Forget I said that."

"Yes, teacher," chorused the children.

"*Solu* is a thrice-diluted waste from the segregators, made for us by the master chymister, but it can still burn." She held out her forearm, where a long red scar cut across her smooth grey skin.

The children stared at the scar, big-eyed. Tali did, too. She had often wondered what *solu* was made from, that even thrice-diluted waste could do such damage. She stopped to watch, for she had never seen stone carving done up close before.

Every wall in Cython was carved into dioramas of forest or meadow, glade or stream, mountain or pool or wild seashore. Inlaid pieces of glowstone fostered the illusion of distance, as if the cramped caverns extended out into their lost homeland, while water gurgling in the siphons, and air sighing through wind-pipes brought each scene back to human scale.

No people, buildings or roads featured in these dioramas, which depicted a natural paradise empty of humanity. Could they not bear to think of Hightspallers occupying the land that had once been theirs, or was there a darker reason?

"We paint the *solu* on a small patch of wall, thus." The teacher dipped a broad Pale-hair brush in the bucket and swept it back and forth across a square yard of stone until the surface began to swell. "We wait one minute." She consulted the greenstone *chrono* around her neck, tapping her right sandal as she waited for the toothed wheels to mesh. "Then," she took up a small mallet and a chisel with a curved edge, "we carve away the unwanted stone like curd."

Within another minute she had cut a hollow elbow-deep into the softened stone and, at its centre, shaped a noble tree with spreading branches. A lump on one branch became a predatory wildcat, its long tail hanging down. It was staring out of the forest and, as the teacher shaped its eyes with a stone pick, it seemed to wake and the children gave a massed sigh.

"That's boring," said a round-faced boy. "Can I carve a crocodile eating a slave-girl?"

The teacher smacked his face. "No, you impertinent lout."

"Why not?" said the boy.

"Only those scenes set down in the fourth book of the Solaces are permitted."

She turned back to the wall. "Now, children, we roughen the fur with four-times-diluted *etchu*." She painted liquid from a yellow-ringed carboy onto the cat, then washed it off at once. "And finally, to make smooth areas we use *sheenu*—"

"Why do we have to live in this horrible place?" said the troublesome boy.

"Because the enemy stole Cythe from us."

"Who were we before we came here?"

"We don't ask that question."

"We're not allowed to ask *any* questions," the boy muttered.

"You don't need to. The matriarchs follow the Solaces, and the Solaces know best."

"I don't think we ever lived in Cythe," said the boy. "I think the matriarchs made it all up."

The teacher's face went purple, then she pulled a black wafer from her bag and said furiously, "Take this to your father."

The boy's grey skin went as pale as Tali's. "Sorry, teacher."

The teacher thrust the black wafer in his face. "Go! You have no place here."

The boy took the wafer and stumbled away, wailing. No one else in the class said a word and, after a minute or two, the teacher resumed her carving, though now her hand was shaking. It was rare for the enemy to reveal any dissension.

Tali headed back past the air wafters, praying that Mia had hidden the baby and she was all right. Here the only sound was the whisper of the wafter blades and the soft panting of the slaves who drove them, walking their treadmills hour after hour, year after year, life after life.

The gentle air current cooled her sweat-drenched skin. One of the treadmill runners made a faint *squeal-squeak*. It needed greasing but the best grease in Cython came from the fat of dead slaves and there was never enough—"Slave!" roared Banj, from inside.

Tali jumped. Cythonians never called the Pale by their names but she knew he meant her. The treadmill walkers did not look up—if she was in trouble, they wanted to know nothing about it.

What was she to say? Tali was better than most slaves at putting on an act and telling convincing lies. A heap of spilled compost lay against the wall, so she dirtied her feet in it and headed into the grottoes, holding her belly.

Banj, a compact, handsome man built like a bag of boulders, held up the dead baby. "Slave, what do you know about this?"

His tattooed face softened as he looked at Tali and he tugged on his lower lip. Banj didn't like scourging slaves. Could they get away with it? Then she glanced at the baby and it took all her self-control to stifle a gasp, to compose her face.

"N-nothing, Overseer." Tali clutched her belly, grimaced and looked down at her muck-covered feet. "Got a flux of the bowels." She heaved, as if she were going to throw up. "Been at the squattery."

Her stomach muscles tightened. She really did feel ill. Mia must have been out of her mind with grief—in trying to save herself a scourging, she had earned the Living Blade for them both.

Mia had lied. She did have the *gift*, but far better she'd not used it at all than in such a feeble way. She had turned the baby's grey skin pink, like a Pale child, but the night-black eyes and the sturdy little Cythonian frame proved otherwise. The faint aura surrounding the baby was an amateur's mistake, proof that she'd done it with forbidden magery.

Mia caught Tali's eye and a stricken look crossed her face at being caught out in the lie. *Sorry*, she mouthed. With Banj watching, Tali wasn't game to reply.

He studied Tali's hot face and her dirty feet, staring into her eyes as if trying to read her thoughts. It was hard to breathe; the sodden air stuck in her throat like glue.

Finally Banj grunted. "You're lucky today is Lyf's Day, slave."

The most sacred day in the Cythonian calendar. Tali choked. They were safe! It was unbelievable, but it had happened. She bowed to the floor. "Thank you, Overseer. Thank—"

"You're on a warning. Offend again and it's the acidulatory for you."

Then Banj drew Mia to her feet and, still holding her hand, bowed until his broad forehead touched the backs of her fingers.

Shivers scalloped tracks all the way up Tali's spine, because only one circumstance ever led the Cythonians to bow to their slaves. She sought for her gift, sought it recklessly, suicidally, but it failed her again.

"Alas," said Banj, and Tali knew his regret was genuine, "not even today can I forgive a Pale cursed with the abomination of *magery*. That art is forbidden to all except our long-lost kings, and you know the penalty."

From the broad sheath on his back he drew a long hilt which terminated in a plate-sized annulus of transparent metal, wickedly bladed all around. It sang as it moved through the air and the colours of the spectrum flickered across it before settling to red.

Mia's eyes widened, as if she finally understood what was happening. Her lips moved, *Tali, help!*

There was nothing Tali could do. One second Mia was warm, alive and real. The next, after a precise and poetic sweep of the overseer's Living Blade, she became a human fountain, painting the low ceiling crimson.

And for an hour afterwards the drunken blade kept singing.

CHAPTER 7

The ice leviathan rolled over the shanty town beyond the eastern palace wall, pulverising it and squeezing its miserable occupants dry. Their blood foamed into the leviathan's transparent tanks, the flattened husks were ejected at the rear. The tanks were already half full and one pass through the hive that was Palace Ricinus would fill them completely.

This is your fault, but you can stop it.

Go away, Rix gasped, but the split-ice voice kept echoing inside his head.

Two nights from now, at midnight, you will go down.

I won't!

You will cut it out and bring it to me.

White worms were crawling all over Rix's face. *Go away!*

It belongs to me.

Please leave me alone.

This is the only way for you to atone.

But I've done nothing wrong.

The voice became low, cunning. *Remember the cellar, and the blood on your hands?*

No, no, no!

Obeying me is the only way you can gain peace.

I'm not doing it. Get out of my head.

If you refuse, this is what will happen ...

The leviathan crushed the outer walls of the palace, then the inner, before toppling a dozen towers and smashing the Great Hall, the wonder and the glory of Hightspall, to powder. Finally, as it loomed outside Rix's tower, destroying everything that House Ricinus had achieved over four generations, coming directly for him because of what he'd done and what he refused to do, he screamed.

"What's the matter with you *now?*"

He roused, thrashing. A lovely young woman was shaking him, her breasts quivering in the golden light of his bedchamber. She was enchanting, all bosom and bottom and a waist that could be circled with a headband, yet he could not remember her name.

"Blood," he whispered. "It squeezed the blood right out of them, into tanks."

She thrust Rix back onto the pillows. "You're sick! Sick as dog vomit."

She marched out the door, across the hall and into Tobry's bedchamber. There was a mutter of feminine complaint, then Rix heard Tobry's amused drawl.

"Sorry, Liana. There isn't room."

"I'm not staying with him!" cried Rix's lover. "He's off his head."

Tobry sighed theatrically, then said, "Oh, all right. Squeeze up, girls."

Laughter tinkled. Rix slumped against the headboard of his bed, shuddering.

"I'm slipping out for a minute," said Tobry. "Don't do anything I can't do better."

He came through, wrapping a robe around his lean, duel-scarred form. Tobry was only of middle height, wiry and not handsome, but there was a look in his grey eyes that every girl wanted more of and no mother could ever trust. He drew up a dainty chair and sat by Rix's bed.

"You're dripping sweat. Another bad dream?"

"Ugh!" Rix rubbed his eyes, trying to wipe the images away. It was both his strength and his weakness that he could imagine the violence as clearly as if it had been painted. Two words kept ringing through his head and he could not rid himself of them. *It's time. IT'S TIME.*

"Worse?"

"Much worse . . . *and more urgent*. I dreamed I was in my salon, in a trance . . . then moving pictures appeared on the heatstone . . . as if someone had sent them to me. Do you think that's possible?"

"Dreams come from inside, not out," said Tobry. "Wait here."

He went out, then returned with a thick, square bottle and a vase-shaped goblet into which he poured a half measure of grey fluid.

Rix's nostrils tingled. "What's that?"

"A traditional remedy—best to take it in a gulp."

Rix did so, and wished he hadn't. It seared up his nose, leaving him breathless and his eyes watering, then burnt all the way down. And it stank.

"What the hell's in it? Smells like stink-damp."

"Sulphur water plus various volatiles and mercapts." Tobry clapped Rix's cheeks, grinning. "Rosy! It's already doing you good."

The nightmare was fading, though not the fear behind it. "They're getting worse. I've got to get away, Tobe, I can't take any more."

"Any more what?"

Rix told him about the ice leviathan. He did not mention the crackly voice like breaking ice, for he never remembered what it had said after he woke, but thought of the night after tomorrow made him feel so rotten that he wanted to run and never come back. "My nightmares are full of blood and butchery, and the fall of our house."

"After what happened to my family, I wouldn't wish that on anyone," said Tobry.

"The other night I dreamed someone was rubbing blood *into* my wounds. That's got to be an omen, hasn't it?"

"Dreams don't mean anything. Have a drink and go to sleep." Yawning, Tobry looked towards his bedchamber.

Rix felt the tension ease, the horrors fade. Nothing shocked Tobry, nor could anything faze him and, though he took few things seriously, he was as solid as the foundations of Palace Ricinus.

"It seemed so real. Could Cython be building an ice leviathan to attack us?"

"They'd hardly use something that'd melt when the sun came out."

"And I keep having these feelings . . ."

"Of impending doom?" said Tobry helpfully.

"As if the world is about to collapse around me." Rix glanced around the magnificent bedchamber, the walls of which were lined with yellow painted silk. The steepled cedar ceiling was inlaid with ivory and ebony, and touched with gilt. "Me, of all people. I mean . . ."

"Unlike me," said Tobry with a wry grin, "you're tall, handsome and heir to the biggest fortune in Hightspall. You turn twenty in a few weeks, and then you can spend as if there's no—" He broke off. "Sorry."

"No tomorrow," Rix intoned darkly. "You might as well say it."

"Stop fretting over nothing. You may be a conservative, dim-witted, irresponsible layabout—" Tobry laughed. "In fact, you are."

"Thanks!"

"But again, unlike me, you've never done anything truly bad. *Or have you?*"

"Not that I know of," Rix muttered. So why did he feel so festering inside, as though Hightspall's troubles ran right down the aeons to him?

"Don't take everything so seriously," said Tobry. "What can *you* possibly have to worry about?"

"Apart from Father? And Mother's crazy plan?"

"I'm sure she's thought it through," Tobry said carefully. "Lady Ricinus—"

"Oh yes. Mother calculates everything to a nicety." Rix bit the tip of his tongue at the disloyalty. "Forget I said that. I know she has our best interests at heart."

"She thinks of nothing save how to raise House Ricinus higher," said Tobry ambiguously. "And with plague and grandgaw bringing down the ancient families wholesale, there's never been a finer time to better one's own."

"House Ricinus hasn't been touched by plague or pox in a hundred years," said Rix.

"Something else to be thankful for." Tobry went across to the heatstone and put his back to it. "Why don't you try a new painting? That's cheered you up before."

Rix was a gifted artist, the best of the new generation, the chancellor said, but now he felt goose pimples rising on his arms. "One or two of my paintings have been divinations. I'm afraid . . . "

"That what you paint might come true?"

"Or I might paint something I don't want to see." Rix's art was everything to him. It was truth in a land of lies, an island of beauty in a corrupt, ugly world, and the one thing that House Ricinus's wealth had not bought.

He picked up a glass sphere from the bedside table and rotated it in his hands. Inside, a master craftsman had built a perfect model of Palace Ricinus in silver and gold—all eighty-eight towers, every dome and turret and buttress, even the fountains, pools and gardens. The chief magian himself had enchanted the sphere so it would mimic the weather outside, but lately it had only shown one season—wind-blasted winter.

"Don't drop it, whatever you do," said Tobry.

Rix had never liked it, priceless and perfect though it was, for magery unnerved him. He considered hurling the miniature into the fireplace. "Why not?"

"Considering your nightmare, it would be a bad omen."

Rix set the model back where it had come from, moodily watching the driving snow plastering the walls of the tiny palace, then sprang out of bed. He swung on a red and gold kilt and went down the hall to his salon, a six-sided chamber with a tented ceiling, dimly lit by an enormous heatstone. He looked at it askance, afraid of what he would see, for there was a wrongness about it, something brooding and baleful. But the heatstone displayed only its normal enigmatic shimmer.

"I could understand it if *you* were having the nightmares," said Rix over his shoulder.

He turned on the stopcock and caught a whiff of stink-damp. Using a flint snapper on a long pole, he ignited the gaslights in a series of small explosions and the rotten-egg stench was replaced by the cleansing odour of burnt sulphur.

"Because I'm a gentleman fallen so low I have to live on my wits?"

"You're not a gentleman."

"No, I'm the Lord of Nothing," Tobry said drily, "family disgraced, ancestral manor burnt down, lands confiscated to pay our debts and not a penny to my name." He brushed away an imaginary tear. "Forced to rely on the charity of my friends, and sleep in their hard beds—"

"With soft women," retorted Rix, managing a smile. "*My* women."

"Someone has to keep the poor girls warm after they flee from your bed."

The smile vanished; Rix wasn't feeling that good humoured. "Make yourself useful and ring the bell. I'm starving."

Tobry did so and, despite the hour, a manservant appeared at the outer door within seconds. Night or day, when the family rang, the servants jumped, or else. At the end of each month Lady Ricinus rated all the palace servants, and those in the lowest tithe were flogged as a lesson to all.

"Food and drink, please, Choom," said Tobry. "Something *traditional*, I think."

"At once," said Choom, who was so old and thin that his joints creaked as he walked. He lowered his voice. "I heard a cry. Is the young master—"

"I'm afraid so."

Rix scowled and stalked into his dressing room. Shortly, Tobry joined him, wearing his own kilt, black shot with threads of scarlet and gold.

"May I?" Tobry said, indicating the racks of garments.

Despite their long friendship, he never presumed, and Rix appreciated that. He waved a hand. Tobry went down the other end of the rack, where Rix kept clothes in his indigent friend's size. Rix selected a cream shirt, plain save for puffed-out shoulders and a diagonal sash of white lace across the front.

He climbed the stairs to his white studio, which encircled the core of his personal tower like a doughnut, and leaned on a malachite windowsill, looking down across the lawn to the shores of Lake Fumerous, the sapphire glory of Hightspall. The nightmare had been so real that he half expected to see the leviathan approaching, but the palace gardens, lit by a thousand hazy gaslights, were empty save for a gang of navvies in a trench, packing another layer of asbestos around the main hot water tubule.

"Waste of time," said Tobry from behind. "The heat's gone and it's never coming back."

Caulderon had been built on a geyser field and for two thousand years a network of tubules had carried hot groundwater around the city, but a century ago it had started to cool. Now, no amount of lagging could retain what little heat was left.

" 'Course it will," said Rix, without looking around. "We just have to delve deeper."

"The last hot-rock bakery went out of business two weeks ago, and it was four hundred feet down. And all the public scalderies have closed."

"No wonder the common folk are on the nose."

"In my grandfather's day, even the poorest folk were well fed and clean."

"Why don't they use heatstones?"

"Your mother would love that."

"What are you talking about?"

"Nothing," Tobry said hastily. "You have to be wealthy to afford heatstones, Rix. Life in the shanty towns is grim, and getting grimmer. The steam mills and screw pumps have to be driven by firewood boilers and we've stripped every hill bare for ten miles—"

"Enough bad news," snapped Rix. "Did you bring anything to eat?"

He turned and Tobry was levitating a tray above his head.

Involuntarily, Rix clenched his fists. "Do you have to? You know I hate anything uncanny."

"It's hardly magery at all," Tobry said mildly. "You know what a dilettante I am. Never done a day's work in my life."

A waggle of his fingers and the black bottle poured a goblet of a brown, foul-smelling wine. The tray turned upside down and floated towards Rix, yet nothing spilled or fell. Despite Tobry's self-deprecation, his forehead had a faint sheen. He was showing off, just to be annoying.

Rix resisted the urge to swat the tray out of the air. Stay calm. It's just his way. He clung to the carved green windowsill until his heart steadied and the pounding in his ears stopped.

"Why do you hate magery?" said Tobry.

"Don't know. I always have, since I was a kid."

"Did someone use it on you once?"

"Don't be ridiculous. Mother protected me from everything." Rix took a goblet, sniffed and made a face. "Yuk! What's this?"

"Fishwine. It's *traditional*. I know how important that is to you."

Tobry was mocking him because House Ricinus was so recently risen. Rix sipped. The wine left a foul taste in his mouth, but he drank it anyway. He wasn't going to be beaten that easily.

"Did you bring anything to eat?"

Tobry handed him a flat oval of hard yellow clay, the size of a small platter. His eyes were gleaming; he seemed to be restraining himself.

"What is it?" Rix said suspiciously.

"Hundred-year cod."

"Never heard of it."

"It's a rare delicacy. Very traditional in the *oldest* families."

"Baked?" Rix sniffed the clay, which had no odour.

"No, just matured for a hundred years. Or more."

Rix cracked the clay, gingerly. The hundred-year cod was brown as peat, hard, and had no odour. "This isn't one of your jokes, is it?"

"Would I joke about Hightspall's noble traditions?"

"You make fun of everything else I hold dear."

Rix picked a small piece out with the corner of a knife, put it in his mouth then, gagging, ran to the window and spat it out. "That's the most disgusting thing I've ever tasted."

"Too traditional for you?" Tobry was smirking.

Rix scrubbed his mouth with a handkerchief. "I don't see you eating any."

"I only live for the present."

Rix stalked away and uncovered a ten-foot-long canvas on which a nobleman in blood-spattered coil-armour was severing the head of a monstrous wyverin. The lava-streaked volcanoes in the background were nearly complete, and the wyverin had been painted in intricate detail, even down to the reflections in each pearly scale, but the nobleman was little more than a sketch. Only the purple, bloated nose looked finished.

"Not your father's best feature," Tobry said quietly.

How long could Lord Ricinus keep it up, Rix wondered. Surely the drinking would kill him before much longer. What had driven him to such sodden excess, anyway?

"How can I do it to him?" he said aloud.

"I'm sure he'd want you to paint him the way he is."

"Father wouldn't give a damn. It's Mother who ordered the portrait, and if it's not finished in time she'll crucify me. But that's not what I meant."

Rix opened a pot of red ochre and dabbed some on his palette. He mixed colours, picked up a large brush then threw it down with another heavy sigh.

"You used to love painting," said Tobry, sitting down. He brought out a liqueur bottle from behind his back, filled his own goblet and leaned back.

"I still do." Rix selected a smaller brush. "When I'm working, all my troubles disappear, but this picture won't come right."

"Your heart's not in it," said Tobry. "You don't want to do it." He sipped the liqueur and his eyes rolled upwards in bliss.

Rix's knuckles whitened around the brush, which snapped. He tossed it aside, irritated by the pleasure his friend could take from the simplest things while he, Rix ... "Of course I want to do it," he said. "It's for Father's great day."

"When is his Honouring?" said Tobry.

Rix glanced at the cherry wood month-clock by the stairs. The knife-blade hands seemed to be spinning towards him. He blinked, focused and it was just a clock.

"Eleven days," he said ominously. At this rate he wouldn't have his father's face finished by then, and the whole portrait had to be completed by the Honouring. That it not be done was unthinkable, for he was a dutiful son, and yet . . .

"Would you like me to leave you alone?"

"You'd better get back to *my* women," Rix said curtly, collecting crimson paint on the tip of another brush.

Laughter echoed up the stairs. "They seem happier without me." Tobry rubbed his chin. "And considering how hard I tried to please them, I find that a tad ironic."

"You find everything ironic." Rix dabbed at the line of his father's twisted mouth, then scraped it off. "You don't take anything seriously."

"With the world about to end in ice or fire," Tobry said lightly, "why should I? Life is a joke at our expense. I sometimes wonder if the entire universe isn't a farce."

As Rix reached out to the canvas, he felt the palace closing around him like dungeon walls. He was exhausted, but if he went back to bed the nightmare would batter him again, and again. He could not stay here, must not be here the night after tomorrow—

"Are you all right?" said Tobry.

"What?" Rix felt dislocated, as though a segment had been snipped from his life.

"You've been as still as a gargoyle for a good five minutes."

Rix cast the brush down. "I can't do it . . . Come on."

"Where are we going?" Tobry rose lazily, goblet in hand.

"Anywhere but here." Rix thought for a moment. "Let's go hunting in the mountains." He held his breath, waiting for Tobry to tell him what a bad idea it was, hoping he would. "Don't try to talk me out of it," Rix said half-heartedly.

"I wasn't planning to. I love it when people run away from their responsibilities."

"I'm not running away—" Of course he was, and Lady Ricinus would be furious. Rix stopped, wryly imagining her listing *him* into the month's flogging tithe. He wouldn't put it past her.

"I'd encourage you to neglect *all* your duties," said Tobry, studying the canvas. "For instance, it can't possibly take eleven days to finish this. Leave it 'til the last night, then fling the paint on with a bucket. None of the philistines at the Honouring will know the difference."

Had Tobry been talking to anyone else, Rix would have laughed. "Oh, shut up and come on. Bring the liqueur." Was he turning into his drunken father already? "No, leave it."

"What say I bring it and you don't have any?" Tobry said cheekily.

"I suppose we might need it," Rix rationalised. "For the cold, I mean."

He had to get away from Lady Ricinus who controlled every minute of his life, from the terrorised servants and the beautiful palace which was as suffocating as a coffin. Tobry didn't know how lucky he was, having nothing.

Rix ran down the stairs to the dressing room, exchanged his kilt for mustard-yellow woollen trews, selected a pair of black knee-boots and heaved them on. He reached for his favourite weapon, a magnificent red broadsword he had been given on his seventeenth birthday, then hesitated.

"Is that a new one?" said Tobry, pointing to a battered scabbard at the back. A square hilt, tightly wound with worn black wire, protruded from it.

"Actually, it's a family heirloom, and ages-old. Mother told me to use it but I don't like it."

"Why not?"

"It's too light. I'm afraid it'll break," Rix lied.

Tobry carried the scabbard out into the salon, drew the sword, sliced the air across and down, then diced it. "It's beautifully balanced." He flicked the tip, *ting*. "Lovely metalwork. It's titane, almost unbreakable. And damnably hard to forge."

It had a bluish tint and the blade was slightly curved, like a sabre, though it had cutting edges on front and back. An inscription down the blade was so worn as to be illegible save for the first two words, *Heroes must*.

"*Heroes must?*" said Tobry, looking from the blade to Rix, then back to the blade. "What does that remind me of?"

Rix had no idea. "Mother said it's enchanted to protect its owner," he said reluctantly. His throat tightened. He thumped his chest a couple of times to clear his air passages.

Tobry ran a finger along the flat of the blade and pale yellow swirls appeared in the air around it. "No ordinary charm, though."

"What do you mean?"

"It's not meant to work against soldiers, *or* wild beasts."

"Really? What's the good of it, then?"

"It protects against magery."

Sweat formed in Rix's armpits. "Why would anyone attack me with magery?"

"I can't imagine," Tobry said drily. He handed it to Rix and went out.

The sword jerked like a dowsing rod and swung around until its quivering tip pointed towards the heatstone. For a few seconds Rix strained to hold it, then it stilled like any other lifeless blade.

Was the magery of a sword enchanted to protect its owner worse than the attack of some uncanny creature? Probably not. He slammed it into its scabbard and belted it on, shuddering. After considering his kilt, head to one side, he tossed it into his bag in case the weather turned warm.

Tobry reappeared with a small case containing balms and potions, bandages and needles.

"What's that for?" said Rix irritably.

"When some beast tears your legs off, I'll be able to sew the loose skin over your stumps," Tobry said casually.

Rix felt a phantom pain at mid-thigh level, but shook it off.

"Why go at this time of night?" asked Tobry.

"It'll be light when we get there."

"And by the time the servants wake Lady Ricinus, she won't be able to order you back."

Rix didn't bother to reply. Tobry knew him better than he knew himself.

"What are we hunting?" Tobry went on.

"I don't care, the more savage the better. I need to cleanse myself."

"Of what?"

"I can't tell! But there's something wrong inside me."

"Drinking and wenching aren't crimes. Even Lady Ricinus encourages you in that."

"I'd feel better if she disapproved. What kind of a mother urges her only son into debauchery?"

Tobry opened his mouth, but wisely closed it again.

"*Something* is badly wrong with the world," said Rix. "And I feel as though it's all down to me."

"Hightspall's troubles began over a century ago."

"I know. Yet I still feel it's my fault!"

Tobry frowned at that. "Well, I'm not sure that killing some unfortunate beast is the answer."

"Right now," Rix said bleakly, "it's the only answer I've got."

CHAPTER 8

Tali kept seeing that frozen moment—the singing blade, Mia's body on its feet and her eyes begging Tali to save her even as her head flew through the air. She could not take it in, tried to deny it, rationalised that Mia had chosen to use her feeble magery, but Tali knew she had caused the tragedy. After her mother's death she had vowed not to be a docile slave. Now Mia was dead because she had been so reckless. She would never get it right.

If only she hadn't lost her temper with Orlyk. If only she hadn't woken with the blinding headaches that had driven her into that uncontrollable rage. If only she hadn't ducked the last chuck-lash. But she had, and gentle Mia, whose quick thinking had saved her life, was dead in her place. Nothing would ever be the same again.

Why were the innocent Pale held as slaves, anyway? Why was the wonderful gift of magery such a crime? What gave their masters the right of life and death over Mia, or any of them?

No other Pale posed such questions; they accepted the slaves' lot. Tali's aged tutors, Nurse Bet, Waitie and Little Nan, had always shushed Tali when she spoke up, and the other slaves avoided her. Only Mia had stood by her.

The body had been taken away and the other Pale were back at work, as far from Tali's grotto as possible. She was tainted now and they wanted nothing to do with her. She looked down at the blood spotting her hands. Nothing could bring Mia back—the best Tali could do was offer her own life in recompense.

She laid her right hand over the blood on her left, took a breath, then said, "On this precious blood, I swear to make up for what's been done to the Pale. For you, Mia. And your poor little boy who never had a chance."

It was done. A binding blood oath. But first she had to escape and she did not know how. In Cython, only docile, obedient Pale survived. Those who displayed boldness or daring earned a one-way trip to the heatstone mines. Yet to find a way out she had to be bolder than any of them.

Work in the grottoes had finished early because of Lyf's Day, but it was too early for dinner and Tali wasn't ready to face the accusing stares of the other Pale. She wandered down the outside passage to the entrance of a partly excavated tunnel. A team of Cythonian miners had been working there for weeks, using the chymical technique of *splittery* to cut a defile down to the next level.

A slave gang was pushing a heavily laden rock cart up the slope, the women gasping and grunting with every heave. Sweat carved runnels down their dusty faces. I'm going to free you, too, Tali thought. Every one of you.

Down at the workface, a Cythonian miner was trowelling the rusty, chymical powder called *thermitto* into channels chiselled into the rock. He turned away and a red-faced firer wearing smoked-glass goggles packed a length of silvery ribbon into the *thermitto*, ignited it and stood well back. Tali, who had seen *splittery* done before, hastily averted her eyes.

The *thermitto* burnt with a roar and such blinding, blue-white ferocity that molten rock trickled from the ends of the channel. Shortly, the rock split with resounding cracks and a second gang heaved the debris out of the way. The miners began to set up the next shot. Tali continued.

But a hundred yards past the tunnel she stopped, for there was a ward post around the corner and if she approached without a pass the guards would sound the clangours.

Having nowhere to go, she crept into an empty breeze-room where a little waterwheel in a stone flume drove a set of ticking box-fans, pumping air down to the lower levels of Cython. She huddled in its darkest corner, holding her throbbing head, and forced the bloody images of Mia's death out of her mind. She had to focus. The Cythonians were watching her, her enemy might be after her already, and she had to find a way out where no one ever had.

How could she save herself when she did not know who was hunting her? *Ticker-tick-sniffle-tick.* The box-fans might have been counting down her remaining moments. Or mocking her increasing panic as she struggled to think of any plan to escape.

There were only two possibilities: to find an unknown way out of Cython, or develop a plan to get through one of the four exits. But after years of searching, she had already exhausted the first possibility. And though a master of disguise *might* make her way through one of the four guarded exits, Tali had no such skills. Her only hope was magery, the key to everything.

She wiped her sweaty face. Cython was always sweltering and seemed to grow hotter every year. There came a muffled *boom*, the floor shook and an acrid smell gushed up from the cracked flange around the air duct. Absently, Tali waved it away. Peculiar bangs, shakes and reeks were commonplace here, from the digester chambers, amalgamators, abluters, sublimaters and elixerators on the chymical level below.

"Alkoyl spill!" someone roared, distantly. "Get help!" and the healers' bell began to ring.

Tali did not move—the Pale were not permitted to enter the lower levels. From down the passage she made out the squeaking axles of the rock carts, the crack of stone cloven by *splittery* and, once, a low rumble that could have been part of the excavation falling in.

She looked around distractedly. The breeze-room diorama offered an enticing glimpse of freedom, a steep mountainside where grey rocks angled up from cropped grass scattered with clumps of yellow sun-daisies. She imagined the doorway as a portal through which she could walk to safety, though even if she'd had command of her gift such magery was as far off as the moon.

Sniffle-sniff.

Tali's mouth went dry—there was someone in the breeze-room with her. Someone who had been waiting for her, hunting her? She rose to a crouch and began to edge along the wall. How had her hunter known she would come in here, anyway?

No one could have known; Tali hadn't known herself until she had reached the doorway. She stood up, peered over the box-fans, and started. A pair of huge hazel eyes, the left one black and bruised, stared at her from a grubby, tear-smeared face.

"What's yer name?" said the girl, who looked about ten. A livid handprint stood out on her left cheek.

"Tali. Who are you?"

"I'm Rannilt."

"Who's been hitting you?"

Rannilt shrugged. "Why are you hidin'? Are they pickin' on you too?"

She had a pinched face, a sharp little chin and unusually dark hair for a Pale—almost black. Both knees were scabbed and yellowing bruises covered her thin arms and legs.

"Not exactly," said Tali, wishing the girl would go away. "Better get back to work or you'll be in trouble." She returned to her hiding place.

Rannilt scurried around the box-fans and settled beside her. "I'm always in trouble."

"Well, I'm sure your mother is looking for you."

"She's dead," said Rannilt with a tragic sniffle. She wiped her nose in a shiny streak up her forearm, looked up at Tali, fat tears welling in her eyes, then said hopefully, "You could be my new mother."

"Don't be silly," Tali said as kindly as she could. "Off you go now, I'm really busy."

"You're not doin' nothin'." Rannilt peered into Tali's eyes. "You look really sad."

Tali choked, and suddenly it flooded out of her. "My best friend got the Living Blade today, and it's all my fault." She sank her head in her hands and wept as she had not done since she was a little girl.

Impulsively, Rannilt threw her arms around Tali and hugged her. "There, there. It'll get better, you'll see."

Tali knew it wouldn't, but could hardly say so to an urchin so much worse off than she was. She wiped her eyes.

"Got some gummery." Rannilt unfolded a toadstool skin wrapper to reveal a grubby orange chunk the size of her fist.

Tali salivated. She hadn't had the sweet since childhood. "Where did you get that?"

"Nicked it from an enemy dinner trolley," Rannilt said proudly. "Here." She cracked the chunk in half and, after a moment's hesitation, offered Tali the larger piece.

"You could be flayed alive for that," Tali whispered. All slaves stole food, though only the most reckless took it from the enemy's table.

"Got quick fingers." Rannilt held up her free hand. Her fingers were crooked, as if the bones had been broken and had set badly.

Tali could not refuse the child's earnest generosity. "Thank you." She broke a corner off the chunk, which was oozing wasp-honey, and handed the rest back. "I'm not very hungry just now."

It was a lie. Slaves were always hungry.

She was licking her fingers when a line of male slaves staggered past bearing massive crates on their shoulders, escorted by burly Cythonians with grim expressions. The slaves were gaunt and hollow-eyed, and all wore baggy knee-pants, for the enemy considered exposure of the male thigh to be obscene.

"Shh!" said Tali, pulling Rannilt close.

She had never seen male slaves labouring here before. They were held prisoner near the mines and foundries where they worked, and only brought to the women's quarters for a few days a month, to breed more Pale.

"What are men doin' here in daytime?" said Rannilt.

"Shh!"

A balding Cythonian guard stopped at the doorway, peering in with eyes so black they looked like holes in his head. The hot blood drained from Tali's face and her breath thickened in her throat. He seemed agitated. Was he after her? If he came inside he must see them. She squeezed Rannilt's thin wrist, *keep still*.

Outside, an emaciated slave stumbled, dropped his crate and it smashed open, spilling dozens of fist-sized, bizarrely shaped metal objects across the passage. Objects with too many legs, and jaws like iron traps, that went clacking and skittering in all directions. With a *scutter-click-clack*, one shot a foot into the air and its toothed jaws tore into the slave's calf. He shrieked, knocked it off in a spray of blood and Tali recognised him.

She covered her mouth; she had almost cried out his name. It was Sidon, Nurse Bet's son. Tali had been friends with him when they were little. Sidon was only two years older than her but his eyes had the death longing in them and his curly red hair had been charred off.

The bald guard turned away, raising a chuck-lash and shouting hoarsely, "Get the *skritters*. Now!"

Tali breathed again. He was just another guard, nothing to do with her.

Sidon drew on an armoured gauntlet and hobbled after the bloody *skritter*. As he bent to grab it, pieces of crisped skin the size of a hand flaked off his back. He looked like a roasted poulter.

"Poor man," whispered Rannilt, wringing Tali's forearm between her hands. "What have they done to him?"

"That's what happens when you work in the heatstone mines."

What had Sidon done, to be sent to the mines so young? He would be dead in days and it would kill Bet, too.

Tali could not look at him without imagining her father dying the same way, slaving for the vile trade that had caused so many deaths. Her mother and father had loved each other desperately, their passion all the stronger because they saw so little of each other, and his death had shattered her.

Cursed heatstones! They were unnatural, and the Cythonians

were afraid to go near them, but they were not afraid to profit from the Pale's agony, the stinking hypocrites.

Newly cut heatstones were barged down the floatillery to the neutral Merchantery on the southern shore of the lake. There they were bought in private rooms by nationless Vicini traders, and immediately sold, in other private rooms, to Hightspall. Neither Cython nor Hightspall soiled their hands by trading directly with the enemy, and everyone profited. Everyone save the Pale, she thought bitterly, and who cared about them?

"They got all kinds of lotions at the healery—" said Rannilt.

"The mine is a punishment. Men are sent there to die. They don't get lotions."

With a strangled sniff, Rannilt closed her mouth, and kept it closed for a minute before the next question burst out of her.

"What were those horrible things?" she said, once the *skritters* had been collected and the slaves driven on. "Were they *alive*?"

"I don't know," said Tali, swallowing. She had never seen anything like them, but the one that had attacked Sidon had been scarily fast. Did the enemy plan to use them on the Pale? She imagined one creeping towards her while she was asleep and bit down a scream.

"Can I stay with you?" said Rannilt. "Please."

Tali was tempted, for the girl was generous, and in great need. It was hard to refuse her, but there were thousands of children like her in Cython. Besides, Tali was a danger to everyone around her.

"I'm sorry. Run back to work, Rannilt, before they notice you're missing."

The girl went, with many a big-eyed backward glance, and Tali returned to her previous thoughts. Her father, Genry, had also been looking for a way out, for himself, her mother, Iusia, and *my precious daughter*.

She wiped her eyes. He had loved her enough to die for her, yet all she remembered of him was a thin, sad-eyed man covered in bruises. If he had found a way out, Genry had not lived to tell Iusia about it. He had died in the heatstone mine on Tali's sixth birthday.

CHAPTER 9

Her mother's murderers had been Hightspallers, her own people, but neither the whining man nor the crab-fingered woman was her real enemy. Nor was the treacherous Cythonian, Tinyhead. Tali's real enemy was *never seen, never heard,* her mother had said, *but he flutters in my nightmares like a foul wrythen.*

A wrythen was a terrible spectre from the past, far stronger than a feeble ghost or spirit. Wrythens were said to be immortal and rumoured to have powers of magery that made them invincible. The mere thought of such an unknown, unknowable creature turned her bones to water. How could she hope to defeat one?

Had the wrythen ordered her four direct female ancestors murdered in the same way, over nearly a hundred years? Why would he want to kill insignificant Pale? What passion ran so deep that it treated innocent women as though they were worthless?

Ticker-tick-tick went the box-fans, tolling down Tali's remaining days.

An overseer ran past, yelling, "Miners, come quickly! A terrible accident down at the elixerator. Bring your tools."

The miners hurried by. Last year an explosion far below had riven the floor of the wax-nut grottoes from one side to the other and blistering green vapour had gushed up, shrivelling ten thousand wax-nut plants as though they had been scorched by fire. Dozens of Pale and five Cythonians had died, choking on bleeding lungs.

The grottoes had been cleared, the fissure blocked with stone wedges shaped by splittery, and life had resumed, but Tali had been bent by a new burden. What was the green mist for? Why had the enemy's brilliant chymisters created something whose only use was to kill swiftly and painfully?

Her eyes followed the air ducts down. No one knew what they did in the secret levels, though all manner of ores and minerals mined by the slaves were lowered down shafts to the floors below, along with thousands of odd-shaped pieces of metal cast in the foundries. What were they making down there, apart from those clever, deadly *skritters*?

No one understood the Cythonians, or had any idea what they really wanted, but one thing was clear. They were more clever than anyone imagined, they were working to a plan, and it was rapidly coming to a head.

The dinner gong sounded. Tali slipped out, then noticed a tumble of stone down near the workface, evidently fallen from the tunnel wall in the collapse she had heard earlier. Dim light touched one corner of the pile, which was curious, since the miners had taken their lanterns. After checking behind her, she walked down. The rock fall had opened a small, triangular hole into a narrow service passage, and if she could wriggle through, she might be able to bypass the guard post around the corner. Had the miners not been called away they would have blocked the hole.

Bypassing the guard post did not help. Tali had no way to get through any of the heavily guarded exits from Cython. She turned back.

The tunnel was empty save for a ragged fellow up ahead, kneeling in one of the effluxor sumps. He was so thin that Tali first took him for a slave, until he turned and she saw the empty, blackened sockets and the seeing eye tattooed in the middle of his forehead. It was Mad Wil, also called Wil the Sump because he spent all his days doing slaves' work, cleaning the sumps until they shone.

Slaves never spoke to their masters unless answering a question, but Wil the Sump was not even master of himself. Tali nodded to him as she approached on silent feet, before remembering that he could not see her. But as she passed, he shot upright in a surge of grey water. His eye sockets were fixed on her and his toothless mouth was gaping.

"You *the one*. You *the one*."

He scrambled out, reaching towards her with cracked hands that were too big for his puny body. Tali recoiled, for his nasal septum had been eaten away, leaving him with one cavernous, red-rimmed nostril.

"Not Wil's fault," he wailed. "Wil didn't put them to death. Wil had to protect the story." He choked. "Ady made him tell. Poor Wil couldn't help it."

He turned aside, surreptitiously drawing a small metal tube from inside his coat and uncapping it, and Tali caught a sickly sweet, oily odour. He pressed the tube to his ragged nostril and took a gasping breath. Blood trickled down his upper lip.

She hurried away, but as she reached the corner his voice soared—"They all died for you."

What was he talking about? Her mother and her ancestors? But Wil hadn't been there when her mother died, and he wasn't old enough to have seen any of the earlier deaths. He'd been mad since an accident that had taken his eyes a dozen years ago, and maybe he said that to everyone, but it was one disturbing incident too many.

The entrance of the subsistery was carved to resemble the mouth of a grinning eel, one of the main foods in Cython. Tali had thought of it as a rare Cythonian joke, though today it felt like a threat.

Inside, the subsistery was lit in ghostly yellow by dozens of suspended circular plates encrusted with luminous fungi. The wall dioramas were views of the Seethings above Cython—an eerily beautiful wasteland of scalded soil, sinkholes of bubbling mud and glass-clear pools surrounded by concentric bands of red, orange and yellow salts. The dioramas seemed intended to teach another lesson—trying to escape led only to death.

Curved stone tables in various sizes, shapes and colours were scattered around the chamber like an eel's inner organs, while the kitchen slaves doled out the rations from a heart-shaped counter in the middle. All this month it had been eel-head and mushroom stew with yellow pea bread, though not on Lyf's Day.

Tali caught the haunting aroma from the doorway and her mouth flooded. The slaves were only given meat on the Cythonians' most important day of the year, Lyf's Day. The anniversary of the day their last and greatest king, Lyf, had disappeared two thousand years before.

From her lessons with Waitie, Tali knew that Hightspall also celebrated Lyf's death, though for a different reason. Hightspall knew Lyf as a liar and oath-breaker who had signed a solemn charter with the Five Heroes, then repudiated it. His treachery had caused the

Two Hundred and Fifty Year War between Hightspall and Cythe, which had ended with the Cythians' ruinous defeat. Centuries later, the broken survivors had taken refuge in their deepest mines, named their underground realm Cython, and had never come out again.

Heads turned as she entered, then a tall slave stood up, Tali's enemy since they were little girls together, the beautiful Radl. Her black hair shone like anthracite, her eyes were the colour of unpeeled almonds and her skin had the glow of rubbed amber. Radl's man had been executed last year, baked to death between two heatstones, and since then she had become feral. No one knew who she would turn on next, but she kept the Pale in her section in line more ruthlessly than any overseer.

"Give it to her," said Radl, raising her arms.

The slaves rose, their glares fixed on Tali, blaming her for Mia's death. Tali faltered. There were no guards inside the subsistery and the women could beat her to paste if Radl so ordered it.

Radl let out a low hiss, then table by table the slaves took it up until the hall echoed, *sssssssssss*. As Tali tried to stare them down, her face grew so hot it must have been glowing.

Don't let them beat you. If you can't take this, how can you hope to survive and escape? She forced herself to take another step, then another. Radl raised her hands like a chorus mistress and the women pulled together on their benches, three hundred unifying against one. The hissing rose and fell, the pressure of all that hatred undermined Tali and her courage cracked.

As she turned to flee, fighting to maintain a wisp of dignity, she noticed a small blonde slave sitting by herself near the entrance to the kitchens, head bowed over her dinner. She was not hissing; indeed, she seemed oblivious to what was going on. The slave was Lifka, and in appearance she was almost Tali's double.

Lifka's silence gave Tali heart. She stared down the slaves, met Radl's eyes and raised her chin in defiance, then went to the serving bench for the feast.

Baking trays held a number of crispy-skinned poulters, each with their four fat drumsticks upright. Cythonian legend held that Lyf had created the four-legged fowl with the magery called *germine*, as a gift to his suffering people.

A serving slave put the smallest drumstick on a square slate, added some curly, baked roots, a wedge of transparent glass-eel cake and a minute bowl of prawn-head soup. After decanting a measure of the purple-black drink called *hulee* into a narrow vase until foam rose above the top, she handed the slate to Tali.

Eyeing the glorious drumstick she would not be able to stomach, she took a seat opposite Lifka. Tali met her eyes and said in her most friendly voice, "Hello, I'm Tali."

Lifka inspected Tali's plate, drool beading on her lower lip, but did not answer.

Tali fished a prawn scale off the top of her soup and sipped the gloriously fatty broth. Through the kitchen doorway she could see slaves cleaning the oval heatstone ovens and benches, and other slaves on their knees, scrubbing the floor. No dirt or grime was permitted in Cython.

The top of her skull throbbed and she looked away; the uncanny shimmer of heatstone always unnerved her. Tali plucked a couple of charred pinfeathers from the poulter leg and put them on the edge of her platter, already tasting the gamy orange flesh from childhood memory. She sniffed the *hulee*, which she had never had before, then gagged and shoved it aside.

"Yuk. It smells like the seepage from the compost pits."

"I'll have it," Lifka said eagerly.

Tali pushed it across the table top and Lifka drained it in a gulp, as if afraid another slave would take it off her. She shuddered, licked the clinging foam from the vase with a pointed tongue, then bit the curly end off a baked piece of horse-parsnip.

The hissing died away, the pressure eased and Tali realised she was ravenous. The gobbled length of baked yam was a nutty explosion in the mouth, the spicy dregs of the prawn-head soup made her tongue tingle. She nipped a corner off the glass-eel cake, which had a pleasant tang but was otherwise flavourless.

Tali gave Lifka a tentative smile.

The vacant eyes inspected her. "Ya look like me. Though yer not as pretty."

Tali had never met anyone like Lifka, who uttered whatever thoughts came into her empty head. She studied her, side-on.

With her shaggy gold-blonde hair, high brow and neat, oval face, Lifka looked remarkably like Tali. She *was* prettier, Tali conceded, apart from the drooping lower lip which accentuated the vacant look in her eyes. Lifka wasn't as curvy, but appeared stronger. Her thighs were more muscular, there were callused indentations on her shoulders and her face and hands were lightly tanned, which was odd, since no sunlight ever penetrated into Cython . . .

Tali was wondering about that, trying to understand it, when the ghost of a plan whispered into her mind. Could it be possible?

"Aren't ya scared?" said Lifka, chewing with her mouth open.

"Of *them*?" Tali put on her most disdainful voice.

"No, of him."

Her stomach turned a back flip. The biggest Cythonian she had ever seen stood in the eel-mouth entrance, staring at her. His biceps were the size of her thighs, yet he had a tiny head no larger than a two-year-old's. A peculiar, purplish head, bulging in all the wrong places.

Tali had blocked out most of what had happened in the cellar that day ten years before, but she could never forget Tinyhead. Could this Cythonian be the same man? The man who had promised to show Iusia the way out, then betrayed her?

She did not think so. His head had neither been misshapen nor purple.

Then he flopped out a disgusting white-coated tongue flecked with black spots like crawling blowflies.

Yes, it was.

CHAPTER 10

"Free, free, and not a care in the world," Rix exclaimed as the sun rose.

Tobry raised an ironic eyebrow. His horse, a neat chestnut with a white blaze on its forehead and a muzzle that always seemed to be smiling, rotated its hairy ears as if it could not believe what it was hearing.

"All right, one or two cares." Rix drew the frigid air into his lungs and sighed. "But I can breathe up here; I'm not choked, stifled, cramped." He wouldn't suffer the nightmares here, either. He never had them anywhere but at the palace.

"Cramped? Your chambers are the size of a small mansion. No, make that a large mansion."

"I was born to live under the stars," Rix said lyrically, sweeping his arms towards the heavens, "to tickle fish in icy streams with my bare hands, to—"

"To paint in your studio while a hundred servants wait on your smallest whim."

Rix scowled. "After the stinking portrait is completed I may never paint again."

Tobry and his horse both snorted. "It's the one thing in your life that has nothing to do with house and heritage. You can't give it up."

"Watch me!"

"If you had to choose whether to give up painting or your inheritance, I believe you'd renounce your inheritance."

"Have you been at the flask while I wasn't looking?"

After an exhilarating race along the moonlit highway in the night, they were now mile-high in the Crowbung Range, which squeezed around Lake Fumerous and the city of Caulderon like the coils of a constrictor. Spear-point peaks pricked the belly of the sky behind them. Ahead, a monstrous bluff of tortured rock blocked a third of the horizon. It was snowing gently and bracingly cold.

Away to the right, the Red Vomit rumbled, shaking snow from tree branches and blasting steam and ash higher than any storm cloud could reach.

"Cursed Vomits," said Rix.

A change in the wind had drifted volcanic ash over House Ricinus's south-western estates for the past month, ruining the autumn crops, collapsing roofs and costing the family's treasury a fortune it no longer had.

"Cythonian legend says Lake Fumerous filled the hole where a fourth Vomit blew itself to bits in ancient times," said Tobry.

"If this one goes up, Caulderon will cease to be," said Rix, his good mood fading, "and probably half of Hightspall."

"Look on the bright side. Cython won't want to fight us for it any more."

"I see menace and doom everywhere, and all you can do is make jokes?"

"If you *really* want to see my dark side, I'll indulge you this once."

While Tobry sometimes hinted about his family's troubles, he had never spoken about them openly. Maybe he needed to. "I'm listening," said Rix.

"Did I ever tell you what really brought down the House of Lagger, or the terrible part I played in it—when I was a boy of thirteen?" Red flecks danced in Tobry's eyes.

Rix could not bear to look into them. "Perhaps some other time," he said hastily, and twitched the reins. "C'm on, Leather."

The great horse, black as the inside of a chimney and ferociously loyal, trotted to a rock platform that looked over the mountain chain encircling the fertile lands of central Hightspall, and towards the broad South Plains and the sea beyond.

He wished he had kept straight on. The strait between Hightspall and the long southern island of Suden was choked by icebergs, and that had never happened before.

Tobry came up beside him. "Until two hundred years ago, House Lagger's richest estates were in Suden."

"And now?" said Rix.

"Buried under half a mile of ice. Everyone and everything lost."

The wire-handled sword rattled in its scabbard. As Rix steadied it, an image flashed into his mind—a statue of a screaming man, rudely carved from a single piece of black opal, his arms and legs spread as though he was falling. Rix jerked his hand away and the image disappeared. He touched the hilt with a fingertip, but this time saw nothing.

He swallowed, looked where Tobry was pointing and goose pimples ran up his arms. "No wonder I dream about ice leviathans."

The coastline of Suden was ice-locked as far as he could see, and to either side the cliffs of oceanic ice crept ever north, closing in on Hightspall from the south, west and east. The northern sea passages remained open, but for how long? Only the most reckless sea captains dared venture into the mazy pack ice these days, and few returned.

"What's to become of us, Tobe? Is Hightspall to die under endless ice?"

Tobry shrugged. "Or a fiery eruption."

"The chancellor has doubled the prize," said Rix. "To fifty thousand."

"What prize?" Tobry was studying the strait with Rix's telescope.

"For anyone who can turn the ice sheets back. Mother says the chief magian has thirty assistants working on ice-wasting spells."

Tobry swung the telescope towards the descending moon. "Gramarye can no more turn back the ice than stop the moon in its orbit." The dire thought seemed to cheer him up.

Rix took a swig of water but his throat felt just as arid afterwards. "Is this the end of the world, then?"

"The world endures. But Hightspall may not."

"You're not helping my mood," Rix muttered. "Let's go hunting."

After a few hundred yards, the path angled to the right around a finger-like rock. Slantwise to the left, in front of the monstrous bluff, lay the slot-like entrance of a narrow valley, still dark inside, whose bare walls rose steeply to east and west.

Further right, a red, triangular peak rose out of a stubble of pines like a pointed head. A round opening near its base resembled a yawning mouth. "Is that . . . ?"

"Catacombs of the Kings," said Tobry. "A sacred place in old Cythe. We're not going there."

"Afraid of ghosts?" Rix teased.

"Wouldn't you be?"

"We should have torn the Catacombs down, like their other foul places."

"Take a closer look."

Scanning along the base of the peak with his telescope, Rix made out a line of stone figures carved into the red stone on either side of the entrance. The effigies to the far left and right were no more than thirty feet tall, but they grew progressively taller until the pair framing the entrance—the first kings of Cythe—towered at least five hundred feet high.

"Every king and ruling queen of Cythe for ten thousand years is represented there," said Tobry. "Save the last."

"Weird heads!"

Tobry gave Rix a sardonic glance.

He refocused on the statue to the left of the entrance. The red stone was crumbling, and ferns and small bushes had taken root in crevices here and there, but—"The head's upside-down."

"After we won the war, Chancellor Nidry ordered the head of every king taken off and replaced upside-down."

"Why?"

"It's a worse insult than pissing on their graves. Do you wonder that the Cythonians hate us so much?"

"They started the war!"

"Did they?"

Rix mentally inverted the head—an artist's trick—and fitted it to the body. And stared. "But . . . it's magnificent." He did the same for the others. "They're masterpieces. The finest sculptures I've ever seen."

"Haven't you seen their art before?" said Tobry.

"Didn't know there was any left."

"There are a few pieces in private collections. It's all like this."

"I was taught it was sentimental rubbish."

"I gather their art meant as much to them as yours does to you."

Rix soaked up the figures, marvelling at the artistry of those aeons-dead sculptors. "But . . . "

"Yes?" said Tobry.

"If what we were taught about their art is wrong . . . or a lie . . . ?"

Tobry did not respond. Rix pulled his cloak around him, already regretting the mad impulse that had brought him here. Only ten days remained until the Honouring. If the portrait was not perfect by then it would be a public insult to his father and Lady Ricinus would be choleric. Rix would sooner have had his skin flayed off than suffer another minute of her scarifying tongue.

Lately she had been more unbearable than usual, but he was not game to ask what the matter was. *You're not of age*, she would say coldly. *How dare you question me?*

Sometimes it seemed as though his mother was afraid, though that was preposterous. He had never known Lady Ricinus to be scared of anyone.

"Nice day," Tobry said laconically.

"What are you so happy about?" Rix snapped.

"I'm free, healthy and there's that beautiful bottle in the sad-dlebags. What more could any man want?"

"The moment I get something *I* want, all the pleasure dies inside me. What's wrong with me, Tobe?"

Tobry opened his mouth, again closed it without speaking. He studied the rearing peaks to the right, the steep slope on their left. "Which way?"

The finger rock appeared to be beckoning. Rix drew his sword and his malaise vanished—he felt as though he owned the world. "*Heroes must fight!*"

Tobry stopped dead. "What?"

"The rest of the inscription just came to me."

"That would only run halfway down the blade," said Tobry in a curiously flat voice. "Hold it out."

Rix did so. Tobry ran his fingers along the inscription, sub-vocalising a revelation charm. Black letters appeared on the blade, then faded. He looked up sharply. "*Heroes must fight to preserve the race.*"

Rix shrugged. "So what?"

"It's a notorious quote from the Herovians' *Immortal Text*."

"They're just words, Tobe."

"Words that toppled a nation." Tobry reached out. "I need a closer look."

Rix jerked the weapon away, irritated without knowing why. "When we get home you can look all you want."

He rode to the rock, balanced the sword there and spun it. It stopped with its tip pointing to the entrance of the valley.

"Not that way," said Tobry.

"Why not?"

"Trust me, you don't want to go up to Precipitous Crag."

"Why not?" Rix repeated tersely. Suddenly it was exactly where he wanted to go.

"The woods are too thick. If we flush out something big and it gets between us and the entrance . . . Spin it again."

On the second spin, the sword pointed the same way.

"I've heard there's good hunting up at the Crag," said Rix.

Tobry twitched the reins; his horse danced backwards on the narrow path. "For us, or for them?"

"I need this, Tobe."

"Why, exactly?"

Rix swallowed. "Yesterday's nightmare wasn't like the others. It—it's as though something is taking control of me, and when I'm at the palace I can't fight it. I've got to fight, Tobe, or I'm dead."

"All right. Give it another twirl."

This time the blade kept spinning, and spinning, for at least two minutes. Rix gave Tobry a suspicious glance. "Are you using magery?"

"Who, me?" Tobry said in injured tones.

"Well, stop."

The blade stopped, pointing towards the slot-like entrance.

"You're right about that sword," said Tobry. "I don't like it either."

CHAPTER 11

As Rix took his sword back, the shadows dwindled and the nightmare faded. "Oddly, I feel better when it's in my hand."

He swept it through the air. He was not a reckless man—unlike Tobry when one of those dark moods overcame him—but now Rix longed for the cleansing of violent action.

"And that doesn't bother you?"

"Why should it?"

"Where did you say the sword came from?"

"No idea. It's been in the family for ages." Rix was irritated by Tobry's persistence. "Let's go hunting."

"Not up there."

"There are more predators around than last year, and they're hungrier."

"Stands to reason, with the winters getting harder every year. But I don't—"

"Winter is weeks away, yet they're already attacking our outlying steadings and killing our serfs. Our scouts say they come from the Crag."

"That's why House Ricinus has an army," said Tobry. "It's not your responsibility."

"Army isn't as big as you think."

"Then hire mercenaries."

Rix looked away. "It's not a good time."

"Why ever not? House Ricinus could buy the chancellor himself."

Rix started; Tobry was awkwardly close to the truth. "Our treasury is a trifle short."

"Oh, come now," said Tobry.

How could Rix tell him about the wealth his drunken father had squandered, or the fortunes outlaid by social-climbing Lady Ricinus in bribes and kickbacks to a purpose only she knew? Even Rix, inexperienced though he was, could have managed House Ricinus better.

"As the heir to House Ricinus," he said pompously, "it's my duty to protect my lands and my people." It was another excuse. To avoid going home he would even lie to his best friend.

Tobry shook his head in disbelief. "You're a throwback. The heir never risks his own life—especially when he has no brothers or sisters."

Rix had often wondered why his mother, who was obsessed with the family line, had only one child. Had she refused to do it a second time, or did the problem lie with his father? Was that why Lord Ricinus drank, or was the problem *because* of his drinking?

"Earlier, you said I was running away from my problems, and it's true."

"It's an endearing weakness," said Tobry. "I wasn't suggesting you become *responsible*." He spat on the rocks.

"I come of age in a few weeks. It's time I started acting like the next lord."

"Until you are of age, leave the worrying to your parents."

"They're not doing any worrying!" Rix cried. "They're making things worse."

"Besides, you need to marry and produce an heir."

Rix frowned, not sure what he was hinting at. "Coming from you, that's rich."

"How do you mean?"

"You're five years older. Where's your heir?"

"I've got nothing to pass on save a ruined name. I don't need an heir." He studied Rix sidelong, grinning. "Actually, a good woman could be the making of you. I might have a word to Lady Ricinus about my cousin, Callista. Lovely girl, after a while you hardly notice the crossed eyes—"

"You swine! Don't you dare."

His friend arched an eyebrow. "Touched upon a sore point, have I?"

"Mother has lined up half a dozen candidates already," snapped Rix. "All mindless, simpering and *controllable*."

"It's a mother's right to propose suitable wives," Tobry said sententiously. "And as a dutiful son . . ."

"I'm not marrying some idiot who'll run from my bed to my mother, taking her orders and reporting everything I do."

"You certainly wouldn't want Lady Ricinus to know about your bedtime activities."

"I thought we came up here to kill something!" Rix snarled. "If you don't shut up it might well be you."

He turned Leather towards the valley entrance, checked his spear was to hand, his bow and quiver, then shook the reins. Leather looked him in the eye as if to say, *Do you really expect me to go in there?*

"The nag has more sense than either of us," said Tobry wryly.

It was dark as twilight under the canopy of the blood-bark trees, which clung to their leaves even in winter. The trunks, clotted with oozing red sap like the bloody wounds in his nightmares, grew so close together that he could not make out the obsidian walls of the valley to either hand. He felt their stifling presence, though.

The forest was silent apart from the horses' breathing and the muffled thud of hoof beats. A narrow trail led up the valley beside a partly frozen rivulet and Rix made out the tracks of rabbits, a scrub turkey and two kinds of deer. Shortly he stopped in a glade, looking down at the remains of a hare—ears, tail, back feet and some intestines draped like a string of bubbles across the bloody snow.

"Whatever ate that," said Tobry, no longer smiling, "it left no tracks. Yet a falling feather would mark this snow." He patted his trembling horse on the back of the head. "Steady, Beetle."

Rix's gut tightened. "I've heard reports of jackal shifters up here."

Small creatures, no bigger than scrawny children when *shifted* to human form, but either as jackals or jackal-men they were deadly in a pack.

Tobry greyed beneath his tan. "I wish you'd mentioned that before."

"I only just thought of it. Where do they come from? The pits of Cython, I'll bet."

Tobry did not reply.

"And to think the Pale serve the enemy there," said Rix. "Stinking traitors."

"Perhaps they don't have a choice."

"Everyone has a choice."

"Including House Ricinus's serfs," Tobry said sardonically. "They can work like dogs for a basin of gruel, or they can starve."

"They work for us. In return, we protect them, and that's getting harder every year." Rix swallowed and looked around, hand on sword. "Tobe, do you think Hightspall is haunted?"

"Why do you ask?"

"The winters are worse every year, our crops fail one season out of four, and now the ice—"

"Even the gramarye our ancestors brought here isn't a shadow of what it was. Everything fails, everything decays, and soon the world will end." Tobry said it with ghoulish relish.

"That's not what I meant," Rix said hastily.

"Really? What did you mean?"

"Do you think our land is rising up against us?"

"I'm not sure Hightspall was ever ours."

"Now you're talking like the enemy," Rix snapped.

"They *were* here first. We stole their land and drove them underground."

Rix spat in the snow. "It was all the filthy savages deserved after they broke their sworn oath to the Five Heroes." He made the sacred helix over his head, heart and sword arm.

"I don't share your worship of our *noble* founders," said Tobry.

It was so close to sacrilege that Rix wanted to thump him. Sometimes a punch in the mouth was the only rebuttal for a man who did not believe in anything.

"And I wouldn't advise you to think of the Cythonians as savages," Tobry went on. "They're a clever, cultured people."

Rix snorted. "Where are their monuments, their palaces, their –?" Remembering the defaced statues, he broke off.

"In the first years of the war, Axil Grandys ordered them razed to ground level. According to the *Axilead*, as I'm sure you know . . . "

"Haven't read it," Rix scowled. "Who's got time to waste reading books?"

"Don't you want to know your enemy? It says that the sky turned red from their burning libraries. Red as the soil watered with their blood."

"They started it." Rix hastily changed the subject. "Anyway, something has to be done about the shifters."

"If you'd told me before I'd never have encouraged you." Tobry rose in his stirrups to check all around them. Sweat shone on his brow and his left knee had a tremor.

Though they had often hunted together, and frequently talked about the hunting and killing of shifters, Rix had never encountered one, and this was a side of Tobry that he had never seen before. Rix had never known Tobry to be afraid of anything. Surely he wasn't worried about the little beasts? "What's the matter?"

"You do know what happened to my grandpère? My mother's father?"

"Can't say that I do."

"It was hushed up on the orders of the chancellor himself. Would have been disastrous for morale."

After a pause, Rix said, "I'm going on. If it's too much for you, go home." It was a low thing to say, for no man was braver than Tobry, but a fire was burning in Rix's veins and he did not take it back.

Tobry forced a smile. "I'll not run out on you. Though," he persisted, "surely it's the job of your house magians to deal with shifters and other uncanny creatures?"

"What sort of lord orders hirelings out to do the dangerous work?"

Tobry's look said, *Every other lord but you.*

They rode up a steep track where little snow had settled and the ground to either side was ankle-deep in purple moss. The bloodbarks had given way to tall pines whose branches were crusted with cinnamon-scented resin. Between the hanging needles, the sky was as grey as the zinc roof sheeting on Rix's tower.

"There's enough snow in those clouds to bury this valley thigh-deep," said Tobry. "If we don't turn back soon, we won't be going home for a week."

Rix could imagine Lady Ricinus's fury when she'd heard that he had sneaked out of the palace in the middle of the night. She would curse him for giving his word about the portrait then breaking it, for letting down his father on his Honouring Day, for jeopardising her plans for House Ricinus ...

In a numbing flash of insight, he understood that his mother had never loved him. He was just the means to raise House Ricinus to the most exalted heights, and if she were thwarted she would turn on him, as he had often seen her savage his father.

"Are you all right?" said Tobry.

Rix realised that he had cried out. "It's nothing." But the

realisation that he was just a tool to Lady Ricinus was everything, *everything*.

Even so, until he came of age he owed his mother obedience, and Rix did not neglect his responsibilities. Well, apart from the portrait, he thought uncomfortably.

"We'll just go to the bluff, then turn back."

He did not want to go home today. Once he returned to the palace the nightmares would come again, and the voice he could never remember, ordering him to do something dreadful ...

The resin pines terminated in a crescent of open ground littered with fallen boulders. Beyond, a vine thicket was so closely intergrown that no one could have pushed through it, though paths made by small animals wove beneath the tangled vegetation.

"And there she is," said Tobry.

The wall of indurated rock that was Precipitous Crag reared another mile above them, black, cold and forbidding.

"There are caves here somewhere," said Rix. "But I'd want a hundred men at my back before going inside one. Keep an eye out for tracks."

The vine thicket ran parallel to the curving base of the crag. As they rode towards it, Rix's stomach clenched—the boulder-strewn crescent was perfect for predators waiting in ambush.

"What did happen to your grandfather, Tobe?"

The muscles knotted along his friend's jawline. "Bitten by a shifter. Stupidly, our house magians tried to save him."

"Why was that a mistake?"

Tobry swung down off Beetle and pointed at something with his spear. "Fresh tracks."

The backs of Rix's hands prickled; he could not escape the feeling that they had been lured into this confined space. "Made by what?"

Tobry crouched in the snow. "These paw prints are as big across as my hand."

As Rix was dismounting, Tobry dropped his spear, drew his sword and cried, "Stay there!"

"What's the matter?"

"No claw marks."

"Retractable claws? So it's not a wolf or any other kind of dog—"

Leather whinnied and went up on her back legs. Rix clung on with his knees, realising he should not have looked around, but *up*.

Tobry was sprinting for his horse when a red-and-black cat the size of a lion streaked down from an overhanging branch. Its whip-tail extended behind it straight as a broom handle, its claws were extended, its small ears flattened against its head.

"Go left!" Rix bellowed. If the cat struck, it would bite through Tobry's spine—or tear his throat out.

Tobry threw himself sideways and the cat missed, though two claws ripped through the back of his left shoulder. The sword flew from his hand and he landed hard, rolling over through the snow and leaving red smudges behind him.

"Caitsthe!" he gasped, eyes bulging from his sockets. "Rix, run! You can't save me."

The most dangerous shifter of all. And Tobry was terrified of shifters.

The caitsthe's leonine head swung towards Rix, as if it had recognised his name. To his knowledge, nobody had ever killed a caitsthe in single combat. He hurled his spear, but Leather dropped to four hooves and it missed by the length of the shifter's black whiskers.

Rix's free hand was already raising his massive, wyverin-rib bow. As he nocked an arrow to the string, the caitsthe sprang onto Tobry's back, crushing him into the snow, which spurted up all around him like a trodden-on puffball. The shifter opened its jaws wide enough to bite off Tobry's head, then turned to Rix as if taunting him.

Tobry twisted sideways and there was a paralysed terror in his eyes that Rix had never seen before. It was not the fear of being maimed or dying, but something deeper, more primal. Then, with an effort Rix could only admire, Tobry pulled himself out of the paralysis.

"Fly!" he gasped. "You can't kill it with a hundred arrows."

Injuring the caitsthe could only make things worse, but if Rix didn't fire his dearest friend was dead.

CHAPTER 12

Tali didn't have years left. She didn't even have days. Only hours, and not many of them.

"He wants to kill ya dead," said Lifka. There was no malice in her tone, nor even dislike. Only indifference.

Tinyhead blocked the entrance, there was no other way out and no Pale would defend her against a Cythonian. No matter what he did to her, they would see nothing, admit to nothing. The self-defence arts Nurse Bet had taught Tali could not save her, either; Tinyhead was big enough to snap her backbone over his knee.

Her headache was like a ball hammer whacking the same bruised spot inside the top of her skull. She couldn't think. She would be lucky to stand up.

"He's comin' in," said Lifka. "Hope he doesn't ruin our special dinner."

She did not say it maliciously—Lifka appeared to be quite unfeeling. Tali felt an urge to punch her in the throat.

Tinyhead was weaving between the tables, heading this way. He looked from Lifka to Tali, frowning, perhaps struggling to tell them apart, then focused on Tali. His bloodshot eyes bulged and fury rose from him like steam—he loathed her. She clenched her thighs under the table in a vain attempt to stop her knees from trembling. What had she ever done to him?

Close up, his little head was covered in grotesque bulges, as if it had been pumped up with blood to bursting point. His ears were quivering purple monstrosities, engorged like overfed leeches, his eyes so crimson they appeared to be bleeding. The nose, once small and neat, protruded from his face like a segment of red cauliflower, while ragged scars radiated out from his mouth.

"How did you find me?" Tali whispered.

"Asked the overseers."

Not only had this morning's fit of rage led to Mia's death, it had betrayed Tali to an enemy who otherwise might not have found her for months.

"Why do you hate my family?" She had to know.

Tinyhead's hand rose to his left ear, touched it with a fingertip, and he winced. "*Hate?*" he said in bemusement. He was staring at her mouth, avoiding her eyes.

"Me, then? Why do you hate me?"

"Did this to me." Tinyhead indicated his ruined face.

"I've never touched you. The last time I saw you I was only eight."

He stooped and, before she realised what was happening, caught her ankles and tipped her onto her back on her bench. *What was he doing?* Cythonians never touched Pale if they could help it. Tali tried to pull free but he raised her legs until only her head and shoulders were touching the bench, holding her slight weight easily.

Dimly, Tali realised that every slave in the subsistery was on her feet. Drool threaded Lifka's lower lip and the excited gleam in her eyes was mirrored in all their eyes—another slave's suffering was the best entertainment available in Cython.

He extruded his white tongue, which was so enormous she could not imagine how it fitted inside his mouth, and licked the sole of her left foot, heel to toes.

Ugggh! Tali heaved, tasted baked yam in the back of her throat, then the fury fountained up and she thrust her hands out at Tinyhead. And, *yes*, this time her gift was rising with it. It was coming. It was nearly here, and she was going to make him pay for betraying her mother.

Tinyhead's face swelled, wrinkles popping, ears expanding like little pink balloons. His cheeks went scarlet and his red eyes rolled up. "Master?" he gasped.

Someone dropped a stone platter, which shattered, bringing her to her senses, and the gift drained away. Blood was dripping from Tinyhead's nose and Tali, trembling, knew how close she'd come. If he reported the attack she would be sent to the acidulatory, where the corrosive fumes of vitriol, aqua fortis and spirits of salts, made there for unknown chymical purposes, etched even stone away. There she would die within weeks, blind, toothless and blistered inside and out, of blood-lung.

She began to shudder uncontrollably. Fool! Remember your quest. He's not your real enemy. He's *nothing*.

"You—*abomination*!" he said thickly, as though it hurt to speak.

He licked the sole of her other foot, then dropped her legs as though she was poisonous. The soles of her feet were slimy-sticky, the skin crawling as if something was burrowing under it.

"Late tonight, when no one is watching," he said so softly that not even Lifka would have heard. "Wherever you run, wherever you hide, I'll find you." Tinyhead walked out.

The slaves sat down, scowling and muttering. Tali's head was pounding and the hall seemed to be rocking like the deck of a ship. She groped for the edge of the bench and clung to it, scrubbing the soles of her feet against the stone floor until they stung, but she could not get rid of the slimy feeling.

Late tonight, when no one is watching. Only hours to save herself, and nearly finding her gift meant nothing—next time she looked, it would not be there. She needed help, but who to ask, when having the gift was a death sentence. No Pale would dare admit to it.

Lifka wiped her lower lip, irritably. She had hoped to see Tali's blood. "Work in the grottoes, don't ya?"

Tali pressed her hands against her hot cheeks. Acid seared the back of her throat and the pit of her stomach was throbbing. It was a struggle to think, but if she was to turn the glimmer of hope she'd had earlier into a plan, she had to know more about Lifka. "Yes. What about you?"

"Carry sunstones up for rechargin'," said Lifka.

Only the most biddable and trustworthy slaves were allowed to do that vital job. Tali studied her double more closely. The heavy work explained Lifka's muscular thighs and flat feet, while the calluses on her shoulders would be from the sunstone harness.

Most of the light in Cython came from caged fireflies or pottery plates encrusted with luminous fungus, or from glowstones from the mine. But in the underground vegetable farms, and everywhere else that bright light was required, only sunstones would do.

They were cut from the halo of morphosed rock surrounding the heatstone mine, but their light only lasted for a week or two, after which they had to be lugged up the shaft to the one place in Hightspall where Cythonians were permitted to go, a little green valley in the middle of the Seethings. Once the stones had been recharged in sunlight they were carried down again.

"It must be hard work." Tali's faint hope retreated. She did not think she could even lift a sunstone.

"Like doin' it," said Lifka. "Workin' is better than thinkin'." She frowned at Tali, as if suspecting her of cogitation, then said, "Grow Purple Pixies in yer grotto?"

Tali shook her head. The little toadstools caused terrible visions, and sometimes madness. "We weed them out and chuck them in the composter."

Lifka's blue eyes revolved in a dizzying spiral. She glanced around, then licked her drooping lower lip. "Love 'em. Can you get me some?"

"Stealing from the grottoes earns us a chuck-lashing. Besides, they're locked at night."

"Take some from the composter."

"I'm already on a warning," said Tali.

Lifka leaned across the table. "I've seen Hightspall," she said slyly. "It's forbidden to talk about it, but for three Purple Pixies I'll tell ya what it's like."

Tali's heart gave a little jump. Apart from the trusted few who carried up the sunstones, in a thousand years no slave had felt wind or rain, had walked barefoot on grass or smelled a flower, had heard the call of a bird or the buzz of a bee. No other slaves had seen the sun in fifty generations; thus they were called the Pale.

"Aren't Purple Pixies dangerous?"

"Yeah," leered Lifka. "After one taste, I'll tell ya anythin'. But they numb the pain; numb it good."

Tali gnawed a fibrous curl of horse-parsnip. Taking a few Purple Pixies from the grotto's composter wasn't that risky, and it would be worth it to hear Lifka's story. That way out would be heavily guarded, protected in all kinds of ways, but still . . .

"Tell me about your work," she said in a low voice, "then I'll get the Pixies."

After checking that no one could overhear, Lifka described the enveloping robes the carriers wore for protection against sunburn, the eel skin sunstone harness and pouch, the loading station, the shaft of a thousand steps to the surface, and the watchful guards below, above and outside in the bowl-shaped valley.

"Ever thought about escaping?" said Tali, trying to sound casual.

"A girl tried it once," said Lifka, staring vacantly at Tali's nose. "Was even prettier than me—'til they cut everythin' off." She rubbed her shapely nose and full lips, cupped her piquant breasts and shuddered. "They let her live, as an example. Ya'd hafta be desperate."

Was Tali desperate enough to risk a fate worse than being killed? She had no choice; Tinyhead was coming *tonight*. Then, as she listened to Lifka's flat, colourless voice, an escape plan sprang into Tali's mind. A reckless plan, and if it failed, the guards would *cut everything off* her, too.

It wasn't a nice plan. Tali's mother would have been appalled; she would have forbidden it. But gentle Iusia was dead, and Mia, and so many others, and Tali was going to survive, whatever it took.

The plan had many obstacles, and even if she could overcome them all, she would have to use a concealment or confusion spell to get past the watch post, and again at the top of the shaft. Her gift had been close a few minutes ago, but it had retreated again. Who could help her to find it?

Trust no one.

Nurse Bet had taught Tali healing charms, but did she know real, darker spell work? Waitie had tutored Tali in the history of Hightspall and the Two Hundred and Fifty Year War, though she blanched every time Tali had even hinted at magery. Then there was Little Nan, who had read Tali the classics, however Nan's mind was going and she was prone to blurting out confidences.

Bet was Tali's only hope, though she had been acting strangely lately, laughing hysterically one minute, weeping the next. She must have discovered how the heatstone mine was killing her only child, and without Sidon she would have nothing to live for. Did that mean Bet could be trusted? There was no choice.

"Guard my dinner," she said, trying not to think about the acidulatory. "I'll get you the Pixies."

Tali looked down at the glorious piece of baked poulter, a perfectly cooked, crisp-skinned thigh. She craved meat as only a forced vegetarian could but, since the day that masked woman had stood on her mother, snapping her ribs like wishbones, Tali had not been able to choke down a morsel of poulter.

She swallowed her saliva and rose. Besides, she thought as she went out to the composter, I won't be doing Lifka *much* harm, and she was happy to see Tinyhead attack me. And if I don't do it the killers are going to cut my head open.

Just like Mama, and Grandmama, and her mama and grandmama.

CHAPTER 13

Let it die.

Rix's heavy arrow struck the caitsthe between the eyes with such force that it was tumbled across the snow to the edge of the vine thicket. It sprawled there, the fletching sticking out of its forehead, the arrowhead and half the shaft protruding from the back of its skull, its whiptail raising snow flurries as it tied itself in knots. A single thread of blood, luminous in the dull light and thicker than human blood, oozed down the yellow fletching to bead at its lower end.

Please, *please* let it die. It was a prayer, not a hope.

The caitsthe's back arched, its rear legs kicked three times and the green-gold eyes blinked, then took on a vacant stare, though Rix wasn't fool enough to think he'd killed it.

As Tobry scrambled for his sword, the beast howled. Glands at groin, armpits and belly squirted stinking brown fluids that fogged the air around it and shrivelled moss on nearby pebbles. Then, half concealed by vapour, it began to *shift*, as Rix had known it would—

any attack endangering its life must force it to change. Now he had no choice but to fight, for unlike other shifters the caitsthe was a more ferocious predator in its human form.

"Can't stop it," Tobry panted. "Shapeshifters heal by partial shifting. Caitsthes—fastest of all. Only way to kill one—" He gasped a breath, "—tear out its twin livers—"

"And burn them on a fire fuelled with powdered lead—which we don't have. But it can still feel pain. It must still breathe."

Rix nocked a club-head arrow. It could not kill the caitsthe either, though hitting a vital area might stop the beast for a minute or two. Could he cut out its livers in that time? Impossible! Caitsthes were terrifyingly strong and, even if it could be knocked down, it might take six men to hold it while another hacked open its belly and heaved out armloads of steaming intestines to reach the livers beneath.

The howl rose to an elongated shriek as the red and black fur began to withdraw through the skin. The tufted whiptail unknotted, the limbs lengthened, then shifted to a more human form so quickly that they blurred. Rix's skin crawled. The shrieks were shredding his eardrums and a wisp of the brown vapour burned up his nose. He doubled over the saddle horn, gagging—the beast was ranker than a bull warthog.

"Got to try," he said, slipping from the saddle.

"*Stay back!*" roared Tobry.

The air thickened in Rix's throat until he could hardly draw breath. This was his fault. He had known that coming up here was worse than reckless, and Tobry had warned him, but Rix had come anyway.

"I forced it to shift, Tobe. It's up to me to stop it."

It would not revert to cat form until it had slaked its blood-hunger, which might take the young maidens and undernourished children of half a village. And caitsthes' victims did not die easily. The beasts liked to play with their food.

The skull lengthened, the small ears glided to the sides and the bent arrow fell away, its metal tip clacking on a pebble. The only sign of injury was a red spot on the creature's forehead and a stroke-like stiffness to the left side of its face, probably temporary.

The caitsthe stood up and Rix choked. He was well over six feet but in human form it was seven feet tall and all lean, corded muscle. Man-shaped but lightly furred, it retained the retractable claws, bone-shearing jaws and whiptail of its cat form. To his artist's eye it was beautiful—a statue in repose, a silky, sensuous machine when it moved. Beautiful but vicious.

It bounded backwards, faster than any human could have, snatched up his spear and hurled it underhand as Rix fired. His club-head arrow took it in the throat, the impact knocking it off its feet, and the spear went wide.

"Now!" he roared, dropping his bow to draw the wire-handled sword.

Was its enchantment strong enough to hold back such an uncanny foe? It had better be. The caitsthe was mewling as it gasped for breath, its windpipe mashed, but they only had moments before it *shifted* the tissues and began to recover.

Tobry attacked from the left, swinging at its head. Rix went for the belly, planning to open it from chest to groin in one furious hack and tear out its livers bare-handed. Surely that would weaken the creature enough that they could escape to burn the livers elsewhere.

Before he reached the caitsthe it came to its knees and back-handed Tobry out of the way, lifting his feet a yard off the ground and spraying spit from his mouth. Rix struck at it but it swayed backwards then sprang at him, slashing with its left hand, then the right.

Though the creature wasn't fully recovered, it was faster than he was. Its left-handed blow tore the sleeve from his coat and opened a gash along his left forearm. The right ripped through coat and shirt, baring him from chest to belly the way he had planned to attack it and carving long gashes with its two middle claws. Pain sang in their tracks; an inch deeper and it would have torn his guts out. A few inches lower and Lady Ricinus's plans for an heir would have been lost.

Rix slashed across the left side of its furred chest. The shallow cut sealed over without shedding blood. The damn sword was supposed to protect him but it lay in his hand like any ordinary weapon.

Well, Rix was a master with any blade. He thrust at the caitsthe's throat, only pinking the right shoulder when it wove aside.

Tearing off the rags of his coat, he hurled them at the creature, hoping to entangle it, but it ducked. He lunged, making another attempt to open its belly. It sidestepped and sprang high.

The caitsthe was going for his throat and Rix had no hope of getting his sword into position in time. He dropped into a crouch, then sprang upwards as it passed above him, trying to head-butt it in the groin.

Its overpowering reek made him gag. Its foot-long, leathery organ struck his right cheek like a belaying pin, then he felt its furry cods split between his skull and its pelvis. His neck bones creaked as he forced with all the strength in his legs, driving the lower half of the creature straight up.

The caitsthe screamed, cat-like and shrill, turned an involuntary somersault and landed on its back, kicking wildly and clutching its groin. It doubled up, licked itself and, with a strangled howl, hobbled into the vine thicket on all fours. Rix heard it crashing away towards the Crag.

He swayed and had to hang onto a tree. The strength had gone from his legs and the top of his head, where he'd butted the caitsthe, throbbed as if he'd walked into a Stinging Tree. A hand-sized bruise was rising there, the sickening reek of the creature was all through his hair and his cheekbone burned as if he'd been whipped. The gashes along his arm and chest were just deep scratches ... though there was always the risk of infection, blood poisoning, pox or plague.

"Why did it run?" he said, shaking his head. The attack had passed so quickly that he could not remember how it had gone. "I don't understand."

Tobry was staring at him, open-mouthed.

"What?" said Rix.

"You hurt it in a way it's never been hurt before."

"They can feel pain, then? I never thought shifters could."

"Oh, yes," said Tobry. "They feel it more keenly than we do."

How did he know that?

Tobry was holding his bloodstained shoulder with one hand, his battered ribs with the other, but he was grinning broadly. "That's something I've never seen before. You're a treat, you really are." The grin faded and he wavered towards Rix, wobbly legged. "I've doubted many things about you—most things, actually—but never your courage . . ."

"Thanks!"

"But taking on a caitsthe to save my worthless life—that I will *never* forget."

"Where did it get to?" said Rix. Each throb was a nail hammered through his skull. He swayed and hastily sat down. "Can you see it?"

"It's gone."

"Gone?"

"You've discovered a way to stop the beasts," said Tobry. "Perhaps the only way."

But for how long? And how vengeful would it be when it healed itself? "It's a wonder no one else has done it."

"Only you would have the balls, if you don't mind the expression, to head-butt a caitsthe there," said Tobry, checking over his shoulder.

"Feels like I've been whacked with an iron bar." Rix pressed his fingers to his cheek and winced. The welt was exquisitely painful.

"You took a direct hit from a whang the size of a burglar's cosh." Tobry chuckled. "You're going to become a legend. They'll have to amend the bar sinister on your family crest to a bent todger." He snorted.

Rix imagined what Lady Ricinus would say about that. She was entirely lacking in a sense of humour. "How's your shoulder?"

"Not as sore as my ribs."

"Are they broken?"

Tobry probed them gingerly. "Might be cracked, but nothing can be done if they are." He took the case of potions and bandages from his saddlebags, one-handed.

Rix cleaned Tobry's shoulder wound, smeared on a lime-scented unguent and bandaged up the shoulder. Tobry did the same for Rix's forearm and the chest and belly gashes.

"I'd better attend your cheek as well," said Tobry.

"It didn't break the skin."

"You don't know where the caitsthe's been, or what its—"

"Proclivities are?"

"Quite. You wouldn't want to end up with pox or grandgaw."

Rix wondered about a caitsthe's proclivities while Tobry tended the welt across his cheek. No, that was a detail he would prefer to remain ignorant of.

"Now what?" said Tobry, checking behind him again. And again.

Rix avoided his eyes. Tobry had not blamed him, but he should have. In bringing him up here, Rix had traded on their friendship, risked Tobry's life, forced him to face his greatest fear, and for what?

The urge to cleanse himself in a life-or-death struggle had vanished. Exhausted, cold and aching everywhere, Rix wanted no more than his large, empty bed . . . but that reminded him why he had left in the first place.

"Let's go home," said Tobry.

"How can I? An injured caitsthe will be twice as vicious when it recovers."

"Seneschal Parby can send fifty men to hunt it down."

Rix could not return to the nightmares, nor the voice ordering him to do terrible things. He worked his thigh muscles. His legs still felt shaky.

"It could kill a dozen people before our soldiers get here."

Tobry's eyes darted towards the thicket, swept the boulders, checked the trees. "There's no one else up here."

"In a few hours it could be down in the lowlands, hunting women and children." Rix eyed the low passage the beast had taken. "It'll be in there somewhere, licking its wounds—"

"Not an image I care to dwell on." Tobry managed a feeble grin.

He took only friends and pleasure seriously, but Rix felt the overwhelming burden of responsibility. "Sorry, Tobe. I don't have any choice, I've got to deal with it. What do you know about the beasts?"

"Not much. They're uncanny creatures—"

"You mean enchanted?" Rix's voice rose—a block of wood had more magery than he did. His hand slipped to the hilt of his sword, hovered, then gripped it tightly and he felt better. At least its power was on his side.

"I mean they're not native to Hightspall. No shifters are."

"But—I thought they'd always been here?"

"The chancellor would like us to think so."

"What's that supposed to mean?"

"He doesn't like people to think he's not in control."

Rix put that worry aside for later. "Then where did they come from?"

"I don't know. The first records of shifters—little jackal-men—only go back a hundred years—"

"I'm not interested in them," Rix snapped. "What about caitsthes?"

"They weren't on the uncanny creatures list when I learned it as a boy."

Rix rubbed his cold arms. "So they're new. How did they get here?"

"How would I know?"

"You read books. You know everything. Have a guess."

"A wildcat fell into a pit of power and was transformed into a caitsthe?"

"What's a pit of power?"

"Didn't those expensive tutors teach you *anything*?"

"Sometimes my mind wanders."

"Let me know when it comes back." Acid had crept into Tobry's voice; his injuries must be troubling him.

"Just tell me what you know about caitsthes, Tobe."

"Well, in man-form they're reasonably intelligent."

"How intelligent?"

"Smarter than the average young lord, not that that's saying much."

Rix's fingers curled around the hilt of his sword, sprang away, clung to it. "Then it knows we'll come after it . . ."

"Yes."

"And it'll be waiting in ambush."

"They're vengeful, too. It'll be planning to attack you where you hurt it."

Knowing how close he'd gone to losing his manhood, Rix swallowed painfully. What folly had brought him up here? Well, no choice now. Going down on hands and knees, he headed into the thicket.

"I'm going first," said Tobry, coming after him.

"Bugger off." Rix centred himself on the track to block the way.

The path was barely the width of his shoulders and the vines formed a woven wall so close above his head that a three-year-old child could not have stood upright. If it attacked him here, he would not be able to swing his sword. With its superior weight and strength, the caitsthe could pin him against the brambles and tear him apart. Or come at his defenceless rear . . .

Halfway in, he stopped to sniff the air. Dark blood spotted the ground here and there and the caitsthe's rank tang was everywhere. How badly injured was it? Had it healed itself already?

A second path crossed the first. Rix checked left and right but could not tell if the caitsthe had turned aside. Now it could come at him from three directions.

"See anything?" said Tobry.

"No." It came out as a croak.

He emerged from the vine thicket, which terminated at a steep talus slope running up against the Crag, itself a mass of knotted rock towering so high that he cricked his neck trying to see the top. The sky had gone the colour of lead and the wind shrilling around the ragged edges of the bluff made his head throb.

"Where's it gone?" said Tobry, standing up beside him.

"Don't know. Haven't seen blood in a while."

"We'll never track it across all this rubble—"

"Something the matter?" said Rix, when Tobry did not go on.

"For a second, I thought the cliff face wavered up there."

"It's solid rock," Rix said derisively.

"Is it?"

Rix swallowed.

"You didn't see *anything*?" said Tobry.

"Of course not."

Tobry muttered something that might have been, "Bonehead,"

and crept up the rubble for about eighty feet. He crouched there, looking down at the cliff. "There's a spot of blood, right against the face."

"So what?"

"The caitsthe is too big to squat there." Tobry swung an arm and it disappeared into rock to the elbow.

"Tobe?" said Rix, not liking this at all.

"There's a concealed cave. Come up."

"Concealed by what?" Rix's stomach spasmed; his bruised cheek pulsed.

"What do you think?"

"Entering a caitsthe's lair is a really bad idea."

Tobry was beyond making a joke about it, which confirmed Rix's dismal conclusion. But if the shifter wasn't destroyed, dozens of people would die before it slaked the blood-hunger etched into its psyche. Previously, he had given little thought to the thousands of serfs on his family estates, but once he was lord they would be his people and it was his duty to protect them.

Rix reached the top. "Incidentally," he said, referring to their earlier conversation, "why was trying to save your grandfather from a shifter bite a mistake?"

Tobry shook his head. "The bite of a shifter is the one thing I truly fear." He laughed mirthlessly. "Don't tell my enemies."

CHAPTER 14

Lifka's principal recreation was chewing her dinner and she spent several open-mouthed minutes churning each morsel to a slimy pulp. Eyes averted from the repulsive sight, Tali handed over three shrivelled Purple Pixies, keeping another two. She felt stronger now. She had a plan and she was going to escape.

Most of the slaves had left the subsistery, but she hurled her defiance at those who remained, and they looked away—no doubt they considered her doomed. Damn you! she thought. I'm going to escape. *I'm going home.*

While Lifka vacantly gnawed a bone, Tali surreptitiously poked a red and yellow girr-grub deep into the orange flesh of her poulter leg. At the thought of what the grub would do, her cheeks grew hot. Though surely one grub would not cause lasting harm.

Lifka pushed back her chair and Tali rose hastily, tucking a small piece of yam into the inside pocket of her loincloth for her pet mouse, Poon.

"Left yer poulter leg," said Lifka tonelessly.

Any other slave, including Tali, would have stolen it. "Not hungry," she lied, swallowing a mouthful of saliva. "You can have it."

"Goody." Lifka pulled off shreds of crisp skin as she headed towards her cell, slipped them into her mouth and yawned. "Think I like ya after all."

The grudging admission did not make Tali feel any better. And what if Lifka was blamed for the crimes Tali was planning to commit, or punished as her collaborator? Surely no Cythonian would imagine Lifka to be part of a conspiracy? But if Tali did escape they would have to blame someone.

Her cheeks burnt, but Iusia and Mia cried out for justice and Tali had no other hope of getting it. No slave would help her. Anyone who learned her plans would betray her, and Tinyhead was coming in a few hours. If Lifka had to suffer for a day or two, that was too bad.

"Goin' ta bed," said Lifka.

Tali walked with her past the ever-guarded gates of the Cythonians' living area, whose name translated as *Away from Home*, then around a bend and through the carved entry hall of the Pale's Empound, where the wall dioramas changed dramatically.

No gentle, domestic-scale scenery here. Rather, a series of savage landscapes—cataracts in roaring flood, catastrophic eruptions, a forest torn apart by a hurricane, monster waves eating away at empty shores—and everywhere among the devastation, hungry eyes smouldered, warning the Pale of the consequences of trying to escape. Tali could not look at them. Even if she did get away, how would she cross such alien places to civilisation?

The enemy was paranoid about insurrection and every adult slave had her own tiny stone cell, these being clustered in tiers around each assembly area like chunks of curved honeycomb around an oval plate.

"If you don't eat that drumstick," said Tali as they approached Lifka's cell, "someone will steal it."

"Mind yer business." Lifka went into her cell and closed the door.

Anyone else would have gobbled the poulter leg at once. It had not occurred to Tali that Lifka would keep it for later. Now what was she supposed to do? Tinyhead might have lied. He could be coming now. She turned and kept turning, afraid that he would appear behind her with his blowfly tongue hanging out.

No, taking Tali out of Cython and selling her to the enemy was an act of treachery punishable by execution. Tinyhead would abduct her when there were no guards around to ask uncomfortable questions. He would come late at night.

The logic was sound, but Tinyhead also hated her and nothing he'd said could be trusted. She paced around the assembly area, which was empty, listening each time she passed Lifka's door, but heard nothing to indicate that she had swallowed the girr-grub.

A shadow hobbled past the entry to the Empound, fifty or sixty yards away. Tali's heart stopped, thinking it was Tinyhead, but the figure was too small and skinny. In the dim light it could have been Mad Wil. What had he meant by "You *the one*"?

She told herself that he wasn't called Mad Wil for nothing. But he was also known for his morrow-sight, and he had seemed to recognise her. Tali checked again. The figure was too short for Wil. It must be a slave going to the squattery.

She squinted through the triangular peephole in Lifka's door. The slave girl was on her bunk, apparently asleep. Tali pushed on the door, then hesitated. To attack another Pale, to injure someone who had done her no harm, went against everything her mother had brought her up to believe in.

If you can't do it, you die.

She rolled three prickly girr-grubs in the palm of her hand.

Should she use them all, to make sure? No, it might be a fatal dose. Tali put two back and kept the smallest, a squirming, blind-eyed creature whose brilliant red and yellow zigzags shrieked danger.

As she put her hand to the painted door, another of her mother's sayings came to mind—*harm no innocent*. Lifka wasn't exactly innocent, and she certainly wasn't nice, but she hadn't harmed Tali either. Yet Tali had sworn justice on her mother's body, on Mia's blood. She had to keep those promises and there was no other way.

Heart pounding, throat choked down to a thread, she eased Lifka's door open and slipped into the gloomy cell. The walls were unpainted, the floor waxy smooth from a thousand years of pacing slaves, and the solitary decoration was Lifka's red-brown loincloth hanging from a peg jammed into a crack. She lay on the stone bed-shelf, eyes closed and slack mouth wide, asleep.

Her legs and arms were hard with muscle from years of lugging heavy sunstones, and Tali dared not risk a fight she was bound to lose. She had to do it while Lifka was asleep.

Squeezing the girr-grub until its green innards oozed out, Tali reached towards Lifka's mouth, then hesitated. Could a whole girr-grub seriously harm the girl, even kill her?

Lifka's eyes shot open and before Tali could move a hard fist slammed into her jaw, lifting her off her feet. She hit the floor, head ringing, then Lifka was on her, slapping her face and clawing at her eyes in a frenzy.

Tali tried to push her off but Lifka jerked her up by the shoulders and shook her violently. Her small teeth were bared and her eyes had the sick gleam Tali had seen when Tinyhead had come into the subsistery—Lifka wanted blood. She lifted Tali higher. What was she doing? She was planning to slam her head against the floor, smash it open like a melon, and Tali was not strong enough to stop her.

She thrust the squashed girr-grub deep into Lifka's open mouth and jammed the heel of her hand against it. In an instant the girl's hands fell away, she began to jerk and shudder, then went rigid.

Tali scrabbled backwards out of reach. Lifka's eyes were starting from their sockets, green-tinged mucus flooding from her nose and mouth. She heaved, made a gagging sound, her face went scarlet and her open hands trembled as if on springs.

Was she choking? Having a fit? Fatally poisoned? Tali was bending over the girl when she jack-knifed upright and a torrent of vomit roared over Tali's left shoulder, onto the wall. Yellow, fizzing streaks oozed down, the stone bubbling from Lifka's stomach acids. Flecks of vomit stung Tali's neck and ear as Lifka fell back.

The smell made her belly heave. She fought it down and turned Lifka onto her side so she would not choke. Blood-tinged mucus dribbled from her swollen mouth. Her lips and tongue were blistered, her fingers opened and closed. She moaned.

Tali wiped her face, tilted her head then gave her a drink from the clay jug beside the bed. The water came straight up.

"Sorry," Tali whispered. "I'm really, really sorry."

Tali was lifting her onto the bed-shelf, as gently as she could, when Lifka's fist struck her under the chin. The back of Tali's head hit the floor and the cell went out of focus.

She roused slowly, pain splitting her head in two, lying on the floor with no memory of what she was doing there. She had been doing something urgent. What? The memory would not come, though she knew that a long time had passed and she should not be here.

Tali rolled over and forced herself to her knees. The back of her head had a lump and her whole jaw ached . . .

Someone groaned nearby and she smelled vomit. The cell reeked of it—Lifka's cell. The memories flooded back. How long had she been unconscious? Tali scrambled up.

Lifka was breathing shallowly. Yellow blisters clustered around her mouth and vomit had dried on her left cheek. What if she was seriously ill? It was too late to back out now. Tali put her hands on the girl's belly, then on her raw mouth, and worked the best healing charm she knew.

There was nothing more she could do. Every passing minute increased the probability of Tinyhead coming. She had to go now.

Tali studied the girl's spasming figure. Was the deception possible? Tali's own lack of shoulder calluses was an obvious difference, one that only a deception or concealment spell could fix, and getting that spell was her next task.

She could emulate the protruding lip, the low, colourless voice, the slow movements. What else? Tali's green loincloth marked her as a slave from the grotto gardens, so she swapped it for the red-brown rag the sunstone carriers wore.

A series of little dot-like scars ran around Lifka's left ankle, though Tali could not imagine what had caused them. Lifka's feet were broader, lightly tanned, and her arches were flattened from carrying the heavy sunstones, but who looked at a slave's feet? As long as slaves were hard-working and obedient, they were invisible, weren't they?

No, best be sure. Once Tali reached the sunstone station she would use a glamour to disguise her feet—assuming someone could release her gift. And if not, she would die.

"Why?" groaned Lifka. A tsunami rolled up her belly and she fountained masticated vegetables onto her own face.

Tali wiped the muck out of the girl's eyes and rinsed her off. "Tinyhead will kill me if I don't escape."

"Tell guards—cut everythin' off," Lifka slurred. "Glad. Hate you!" She turned her face to the wall.

Tali squirmed. "I'm really sorry. I had no choice."

"Won't escape. Die, horribly, ha, ha—*blurrggghh*." Up it came again, streaked with green bile now.

Tali washed the vomit off with the last of the water. "I'm going to get away," she said firmly, though she was beginning to doubt that she'd get as far as the sunstone shaft. If such a simple plan could go so wrong so quickly, how could she pull off the difficult parts?

"Didn't tell ya everythin', did I?"

"What do you mean?"

"Not sayin'." Lifka bared slime-coated teeth, puked onto the wall beside her bed-shelf and lay still, breath rasping in her raw throat.

After tossing a ragweed blanket over the girl, Tali took back the poulter leg, then hurried down the painted tunnels to her own cell, ten minutes away, picking the girr-grub out of the poulter flesh as she walked. She felt self-conscious in the sunstone carrier's red-brown loincloth and, if she encountered anyone who knew Lifka, she was lost.

This time she saw no one. In her cell, Tali was washing her hands when she realised how easily she could have saved Mia. If she'd only thought to shove a mucky finger into Mia's mouth, girr-grub slime would have made her violently ill. Tali could have cleaned up the birth mess, hidden the dead baby until Banj had gone and the healers had taken Mia away, then buried it in the composter. By the time Mia recovered from the girr-grub she might have come to terms with her loss, and no one need ever have known about the grey baby.

Tali stared at the wall, rubbing her eyes with the backs of her hands. Why hadn't that occurred to her? No matter how hopeless things were, there was always a way out. She just had to find it.

Her pet mouse squeaked. Poon had grey fur, small feet and big ears, and Tali loved her. She poked the piece of yam into the ramshackle cage she had fashioned from poulter bones and gum. Poon took the yam in her front paws, ate it with delicate nibbles and looked up for more.

"Sorry," said Tali. "Had greater need of it." She swallowed. "Poon, I've got to set you free."

She unlatched the cage, stroked the mouse's ears and set her on the floor. "Go," she whispered. "Run and hide."

Poon stood up on her back legs, reaching for the swinging cage.

"I'm scared to leave my cage, too," said Tali.

CHAPTER 15

"I've got to fly, Poon. Tinyhead's after me." Tali, her eyes prickling, urged the mouse away with the back of her hand. "Off you go."

Poon ran inside and scrabbled against the side of her bed.

Tali sighed, gave her a shred of poulter leg, wrapped the rest in a length torn from her ragweed blanket and slipped it into her pocket. She gathered her only possessions: a swirling silver ornament on a chain—the seal of her ancient house—and her father's letter, which she fixed into the hem of her loincloth with a purloined brass pin. Finally, a pretty blue gown made of the finest silk cloth. Her ancestor Eulala vi Torgrist had worn it proudly as she left her home a thousand years ago, one of a hundred and forty-four noble children sent into exile.

They had been told that they were going on a grand adventure to serve their country, but had been given over to the Cythonians as hostages and never ransomed. Why not? If Hightspall was prepared to trade with the enemy, why couldn't they ransom their own children? Tali could only see it as a betrayal.

Eulala had been just twelve but the gown was a good fit on Tali and she would wear it when—if—she escaped. She could not go home wearing a loincloth.

The silver seal had burned the slave's mark into her left shoulder. She pocketed it and went out, carrying Poon. Now came her biggest challenge—finding someone to release her hidden gift.

"What if Bet won't tell me?" Talking to Poon created the illusion that Tali was not alone. "What do I do then?"

Poon's brown eyes peered at Tali from the cave of her coiled fingers. The mouse was trembling. You and me both, Tali thought. I've only a few hours to find a slave who knows magery, convince her to release my gift, assuming she can, and practise the glamour. Not long at all. And what if no one will help?

"Would I," she said to Poon, "if a madwoman burst into my cell in the middle of the night, demanding I tell her about forbidden magery?"

Poon's flanks heaved, then she ducked out of sight. You can't do it, the lifetime slave jeered. No slave has ever escaped.

But Tali had to succeed, whatever it took. She had sworn a blood oath.

She fingered the Purple Pixies in her pocket. *After one taste, I'll tell ya anythin'*, Lifka had said. If there was no other way to get Bet to talk, Tali would feed her a Pixie. It would be a wicked betrayal of the old lady, but without magery the quest would fail. Without magery she could never defeat her enemy. Without magery, Tinyhead would carry her to the cellar and the killers would cut her head open.

Once her gift had been released Tali would squeeze through the hole she had noticed this afternoon, run for the sunstone loading station and practise her glamour. When the carrier slaves came at dawn, she would use the glamour on herself and take her place in the line as Lifka.

It wasn't much of a plan, but at least she had one.

But what if Lifka recovered and gave the alarm? What if she died of girr-grub poisoning and someone found the body? No, Lifka was tough; she'd be all right. Wouldn't she?

The painted tunnels of the Pale's Empound were empty. The other slaves were asleep in their cells, since the going-to-work gongs sounded at dawn and any slave more than three minutes late went without breakfast. The luminous plates in the assembly areas had been turned to the wall to dim their glow; the slaves walking the air wafter treadmills had slowed to a lulling *thump-thump*. Their eyes were closed, their arms hung limp. Some, Tali knew, were able to doze as they walked.

It was not forbidden to be out of one's cell in the middle of the night, but it would attract the attention of any guard she encountered. Tali slipped into the shadows and was on her way to Nurse Bet's cell when heavy footsteps sounded behind her. Since slaves went barefoot, it had to be a Cythonian.

The huge shoulders and little head gave him away. Tinyhead was heading towards her cell. Another few minutes and he would have caught her there. What would he do when he discovered she was gone? Check the squattery, then search the cells of her associates, like Bet. Then he would come hunting.

She dared not go to Bet's cell now, but where else could she go? Tali ran the curving corridor on tiptoes, out of the Pale's Empound, past the subsistery, the composters and the toadstool grottoes, then darted down the tunnel where the miners had been working, praying that they had not come back and blocked the collapsed hole. If they had, it was over. No, it was still open, though the gap was tiny.

A clangour sounded down by the grottoes, a shrill, tearing sound that scraped her raw nerves. Dozens of other clangours answered it, then Cythonians were shouting, yelling and running. Had they discovered Lifka? Tali had to disappear.

She climbed the rubble pile, careful to make no noise. The hole was roughly triangular, though she wasn't sure her small shoulders would fit. Tali put her head through into an oval passage where widely spaced luminous plates provided meagre pools of light. She put Poon down on a rock, hunched her shoulders, wriggled through with only a few scratches, then stuck at the hips.

If anyone went past the tunnel, they would see her waving legs and she would die. Tali put her hands flat against the wall and heaved, but did not budge. Wriggling backwards a couple of inches, she pulled her loincloth down over her hips and shoved. A sharp projection scored down her left hip then she toppled head-first into the passage.

She landed on her hands, recovered and looked back. Tinyhead was far too big to follow, though it would only gain her a minute or two. There would be other ways in.

Tali collected a quivering Poon, packed broken stone into the hole so it could not be seen from the main passage and was con-gratulating herself on her little victory when she realised that she could not reach Bet's cell from here. Without Bet, Tali had no hope of magery, but she could not turn back.

She turned right, away from the guard post, passed a set of ticking box-fans driven by the flow of a siphon, walked a plank where a yellow pipe dribbled waste into a reeking effluxor sump and was trudging along when another clangour went off, above her head.

Tali was about to bolt when she realised that it wasn't an alarm but the more melodious healer's bell. Distantly, other bells repeated the signal and she heard a man's voice, shouting frantically, and run-ning feet, coming this way. And then the shredded scream of a woman in uttermost agony.

Tali's hair stood up. Over the years she had seen many slaves injured by rock falls, accidents and cruel Cythonian punishments, but she had never heard such an awful cry. She slipped Poon into her pocket and backed away. The passage was broad here and there was nowhere to hide, though behind the effluxor sump she noted a recess in the left-hand wall. She squeezed into it and crouched in the shadows.

A vibration in her pocket was Poon nibbling at the poulter leg, but Tali didn't begrudge her. The least she could do was to set her free with a full belly.

The screaming grew louder and shortly a group of hurrying figures appeared, all Cythonian: a tall man and a stocky one carrying someone on a stretcher, a bald man wearing a foreman's sash and a thin, elderly fellow in the red gown of a master chymister. He was dreadfully scarred about the face, hands and arms, and carried a platina bucket. A heavy, green, slightly luminous fluid, dripping from the stretcher, smoked where it touched the stone floor. A drop fell on a clump of straw, which caught fire and burnt with a bright red flame.

From the other direction, a white-haired female healer, bearing the annular cheek tattoos of a master, came hurtling past Tali's hiding place, robes flapping.

"What happened?" she panted. "Put her down."

The bearers set the stretcher down in the light of a glowing fungi plate, thirty yards from Tali. The injured woman shrieked and writhed.

"Hold her," yelled the healer, "or she'll tear that leg right off."

The bearers held the young woman down. The scarred chymister glanced at her leg and gagged. Tali rose to her feet, staring in awful fascination at the melon-sized hole in the woman's thigh and the sickening brown fumes rising from it. Poon came creeping out of the pocket and poked her head above the waistband of the loincloth. Tali stroked her silky fur.

"What took you so long?" said the healer.

The foreman stared at the floor before him, wringing his meaty hands. "Took the miners all afternoon to dig 'er out."

"I don't understand how this happened," the healer said furiously. "Alkoyl must be contained in capped platina ware at all times, yet it's dripped all over her leg. Don't you bother to follow the procedures?"

Tali had never heard the word *alkoyl* before, though everything done below was a secret.

"We follow 'em to the letter." The foreman looked as though he wanted to sink through the floor. "Had urgent orders from the matriarchs, yesterday morning. All us foremen did—abluters, crystallisers, sublimaters, the lot! And down on the smything level, too."

"Matriarchs' orders?" the healer said sharply. "What orders?"

"Get everything ready by month's end, and no excuses."

That's only eleven days away, thought Tali. What are they up to?

"Why wasn't I informed?" the healer said coldly.

"I don't know, Master Healer."

"Go on."

The foreman glanced at the woman on the stretcher and his face crumpled. "We were workin' double time. It had to be done *at any cost*."

"So you cut corners."

"Never! I check the alkoyl store every time we use it. You don't muck around with that stuff. Twice I checked, last night. The dribblers were in and all the caps were double-tight."

"So what happened?" said the healer, tapping one foot.

The white-faced foreman looked down at the victim. "She were up on the third elixerator, toppin' up the alkoyl level, but someone had taken the dribbler out. The whole flask poured in." He groaned. "Blew the elixerator to pieces, and a whole flask of precious alkoyl lost—"

"And a woman dying in agony," the healer said caustically.

"My little sister, Flix," said the foreman, burying his face in his hands and weeping so violently that his whole body heaved.

"How could this happen? You must have made a mistake."

The master chymister, shaking his head, drew the healer away from the others. "It's not the first time a flask has been interfered with," he said quietly, "or a dribbler removed. Someone's been stealing alkoyl for ages."

"But . . . that's preposterous," said the healer. "No Pale is allowed down—"

"It's not a Pale. It's one of us, and we can never catch him."

The healer goggled at him, then returned to the woman, who let out a chilling scream and fell silent. The healer, her face blanched, gingerly lifted away the severed, fuming leg and put it down against the wall. Poon squeaked and hid.

"I'm sorry, Hyme," the healer said to the foreman, "there's nothing anyone can do. Alkoyl is dissolving her flesh and bones, and it can't be neutralised." She turned to the thin man dressed in red. "Master Chymister, you'd better fetch your stilling apparatus. You'll want to recover as much as you can."

"Won't be enough," he croaked, as if his throat was as scarred as his face. "And we can't do without it. I'll have to send down the Hellish Conduit for more, if I can get anyone to go." He shuddered. "After last time—"

"If no one else can take that path, you must do your duty," the healer said coldly.

"I always do my duty. And look what it's done to me."

Once the chymister had headed back the way he had come, the healer gestured to the stretcher bearers. They picked up their burden and the grim cavalcade passed by Tali, out of sight. As it did, she smelled blood and seared flesh, and under that, very faint, an unnaturally sweet, oily odour with a hint of bitterness. A vaguely familiar odour. Where had she smelled it before?

She went towards the severed leg, which was still smoking against the wall. The green fluid had already eaten pits in the stone, each the depth of a knuckle, and the odour was strong enough to sting her nose from yards away.

Wil's nose was eaten away on the inside. Could he be the thief? He had been sniffing something from a platina tube, she recalled. Tali backed away. Whatever it was, and whatever urgent chymical purpose the enemy needed it for, she wanted to know no more about it.

The incident had cost her another twenty precious minutes. Tinyhead could not be far behind. Her options were closing off one by one and all she could do was run.

She lifted Poon out, kissed her head and set her down beside the effluxor. "Off you go, little Poon. You'll be a lot safer on your own."

Poon looked up at Tali reproachfully then, when she gently urged her away, took off towards the darkened hole in the wall. She was outside it when a ginger cat sprang from the rubble and pounced.

Poon squeaked once, then went limp. The cat carried her away, grinning.

As Tali fled, so shocked she was unable to weep, she could not but see the parallel with her own fragile existence.

CHAPTER 16

Tobry walked through solid rock and vanished.

"Tobe?" said Rix, unnerved.

"Maybe the caitsthe's hurt worse than we thought," Tobry said from inside.

"More likely it's putting on an act to lure us in."

It wasn't the caitsthe he was most afraid of, though. It was the illusion—or the wizardry behind it. Who had made it, and what was it protecting?

Tobry came out again. "And maybe it's circled back to kill the horses and strand us here." He chuckled. "We're a dismal pair, aren't we?"

Rix grimaced. At times his friend's relentless nihilism grew irksome, yet he could not have done without him. Damn it, he thought, I'm going through. Taking his sword in hand, he walked into the illusion.

It parted around the blade like a twinkling curtain and he found himself in a broad, lens-shaped cave that, oddly, was far colder than it had been outside. Even odder, he could see the vine thicket and the forest beyond—the illusion only worked one way. The floor had been swept so clean by the incessant wind that the single fist-sized stain was a bloody signpost pointing into the dark.

"It crouched there for a moment." Tobry's eyes were darting again.

To their left, water dripped from dagger-blade stalactites into a natural stone basin shaped like a kidney dish, encrusted with white and yellow concretions and full of clear water. Rix's throat was dry as paper. He dipped a hand into the basin, the world tilted and turned upside-down, and his sight vanished in a tangle of whirling colours.

"Rix? *Rix?*"

He groaned. Tobry was distorted and wild colours were streaming out of him.

"What the hell happened?" said Tobry.

"Don't know. Help me up."

"Stay down until you're better."

"'S nothing. Just felt dizzy for a bit."

Tobry gave a barking laugh. "You've been out for ten minutes."

"Can't have . . ." Rix tried to get up but his head was spinning and his hands did not know where the floor was. Again he felt as though part of his life had vanished.

Tobry heaved him to his feet. Rix clung to him, afraid of falling, shivering, shaking.

"Joints feel funny—not sure knees will hold me up." The colours were fading, Tobry and the cave becoming clearer, the vertigo easing. "It's getting better. Think I'm all right now."

Tobry peered into his eyes. "Ever had a turn like that before?"

"Never. I just put my hand in the basin." Rix let go and did not fall down, though he still felt wobbly.

Tobry studied Rix's hand, which was unmarked, then extended a fingertip towards the water. His hand jerked downwards as if it was being pulled into the basin, and it took all his strength to hold it back. One fingertip touched the water and his head wobbled in a circle. He stumbled to the entrance and scrubbed his finger with a clump of moss.

Rix wiped his own hands and the sensations passed, apart from a trembling weakness of the knees and a worrying liquidity in his bowels. Just what I don't need right now, he thought wryly.

"Bad water," said Tobry, making a couple of passes over it with his right hand and murmuring words that raised goose pimples on Rix's arms.

"Enchanted?"

"Not by any gramarye I understand. Lucky you didn't wash your face in it."

"Lucky I didn't drink it," said Rix. "I was going to." Death by magery—*his* personal nightmare. Well, one of those in the queue.

"I'll take some back, see if I can find out what it is." Tobry emptied out a glass potion phial and filled it with water from the basin, using a couple of twigs as tongs.

Rix could not see the back of the cave, though an air current suggested it ran for some distance. He swallowed painfully. "Let's get on."

"You're not up to it and neither am I."

"I told you—"

"I'm not going any further. This is a trap."

The place bothered Rix too, but he could not turn back. "How could it be? No one knew we were coming."

"That damned sword of yours did."

"Now you're being ridiculous."

"When you spun it that last time, I tried to turn it away," said Tobry. "I used my strongest magery on it but it kept spinning. It fought me, Rix. The sword was determined to bring us here."

"Whatever!" Rix swallowed his unease. "Look, you know what shifters are like—after they heal themselves they have to feed. I've got to finish it . . . but you don't have to come."

"I'm not."

Deep in the cave, something went *thunk*. The water in the basin rippled and a rush of frigid air stirred Tobry's hair.

"What was that?" Rix whispered.

"Falling rock," Tobry said, too quickly.

Rix took a few steps towards the back of the cave. It was hard to move; the heavy air clung to his legs like molasses.

"You'll need light," Tobry added, too casually. He was fighting his fear of shifters, and what if he cracked? Every man had his breaking point.

Including Rix. Had he taken a mouthful of the uncanny water he would now be dead or insane. Had the caitsthe made it? They were intelligent creatures, the product of uncanny forces, and maybe they could do magery, too.

And if he had been lured, or *led*, here, why?

Tobry went out, hacked an oozing branch off the nearest resin pine, came back and lit the resinous end with flint and tinder. Rix reached for it.

"I'll carry it," said Tobry curtly.

"You don't have to come."

"Shut up!"

Once the flame grew to a yellow sputter Rix raised the torch in his left hand, took his sword in his right and headed into the dark. Ahead, the shadows writhed like a shapeshifter's nightmare. The cave narrowed, then sloped down beyond sight, but at least it ran straight and smooth-walled, leaving nowhere for their quarry to lurk.

Unless it could shift into a less visible form . . .

Weather-worn images appeared on the walls, and as they descended the pictures became clearer and brighter, as if they had only recently been painted: peaceful scenes of forest and glade, seashore and mountain, fruits and flowers and beasts of the field.

"Cythonians must have lived here long ago," Tobry said.

With the sword in his hand, Rix saw their art for what it was. "Sentimental, *pretty* rubbish. Why don't they show the world as it really is?"

"Nasty, violent and brutal?"

"You can't hide from reality."

"I'm doing my best." Tobry stopped. "Shh!"

Ahead, the passage turned sharply to the left. Rix edged around the corner. Ten yards further on, the floor was covered in debris fallen from the roof—a tumbled pile of iron-stained stone large enough to provide cover for a prone caitsthe.

He sniffed the air. "If it's behind that, we'd smell it."

Tobry licked a finger, not the one he'd dipped into the basin, and held it up. "The air's moving down past us; it'd carry any scent away."

"And our smell to the shifter. Anyway, wherever it is, it'll nose out the torch from a hundred yards away."

"Hold it higher."

Rix went up on tiptoes and moved left and right. "Don't think it's hiding there."

"If the beast attacks, we go for its weak point—the nuts."

"*You* go for its nuts." Rix touched the welt across his cheek.

Here, the passage was wide enough for them to walk abreast. The space behind the rubble was empty, though twenty paces further along the cavern branched into five passages, their walls being oddly blurred. Rix poked the torch into each in turn. Further on, they all split into more passages.

"A maze." Rix stumbled. "Sorry, head's spinning again." He could barely focus.

Tobry steadied him. "It's enchanted to confuse anyone who gets this far."

"How come I feel it worse than you?" Rix said dully.

"Weaker mind," said Tobry with a thin smile.

"Which way?"

Tobry got out a hand-sized piece of silver-streaked wood, carved into interlocking swirls that did not seem physically possible.

"That thing makes me uneasy," said Rix.

"Not thing, *elbrot*."

"I know what they're called."

"It focuses my magery. And without magery, we may not get out of here."

Tobry swept the elbrot back and forth before the five passages, studied it, sniffed the air, grunted and waved it towards the second on the left. For a second or two, the elbrot shimmered with emerald cold-fire.

Rix's fingers clenched on the wound-wire hilt.

"Something the matter?" said Tobry.

"What did the glow mean?"

"A warning—don't take that passage."

"So that's the way we're going."

"Need you ask?"

CHAPTER 17

At each new junction, Tobry took the way his elbrot warned against.

After some minutes they emerged from the maze to see two passages ahead, the left-hand path slowly descending, the right tunnel

plunging down a steep set of stairs. Its walls and the steps themselves were glassy smooth, as if moulded from a molten state.

Tobry indicated the left passage but, as he headed down, Rix
could feel the trap closing. The caitsthe was probably lurking in the
maze, and now it could pen them in. He whirled, nearly skewering
Tobry with his sword tip.

"With friends like you," Tobry said laconically.

And I was worried about Tobry cracking up, Rix thought.

The air grew ever colder and thicker. Now it was like wading
through a pool of smashed ice. A drip froze on the tip of his nose.

"How can it be so cold this far underground?"

"You might ask, what's making it so cold?"

Emerald green light was pulsing through the fabric of Tobry's
coat. He must be fingering the elbrot in his pocket. "Or you might
just tell me," said Rix.

"We won this land two thousand years ago, yet we know nothing about it."

Shivers crept down Rix's half-exposed chest and he wished he'd
recovered his coat, torn though it was. "Are you saying this cold
isn't natural?"

"How can it be? It should get warmer as we go deeper."

The slope steepened. Ahead, seeps formed two lines of ice nip-
ples along the roof, like the belly of a sow.

"That stone looks none too solid," Tobry said from behind him.

Rix glanced up. Another shear zone, this one several yards wide,
angled across the passage, and so much rock had fallen from it that
a hollow ran up for several feet. He hunched his shoulders and
moved on. Something grated underfoot; a broken human thigh
bone.

"Split to get at the marrow," Rix muttered. He blew on his fingers but could not warm them.

"What's that?" Tobry whispered a few seconds later.

Rix stopped. "I didn't hear anything."

"A faint mewling noise."

The hairs rose on the back of Rix's neck. "Like kittens?"

"Very big kittens . . ."

"I didn't think caitsthes were able to breed."

"With the equipment our hairy friend has, I'm surprised it can think of anything else."

Even the torch was struggling now, as if the darkness was pressing in on it, the cold dousing its fire. Rix sniffed. "Smells like cat piss. And it seems to be opening out further down. Can you see anything?"

"Only in my inner eye."

"What's that supposed to mean?"

"Can't explain it. It's just what I'm seeing."

"And that is?"

Tobry stopped and closed his eyes. "Below us, the tunnel coils down deep—very deep, like a spiral ... no, two spirals, winding down together. Um ... there are cross-passages linking the spirals ... hollowed out into chambers ..." He caught at Rix's shoulder, his breath rasping in and out.

"What is it?" Rix said hoarsely.

Tobry's eyes flicked open, staring. "It's enormous."

"Who could have made such a place?"

"I don't think we should go any further."

"I know damn well we shouldn't, but we've come this far and I'm never coming back."

Rix held the sword out before him. It felt heavier; he needed two hands to hold it steady and the hilt was so cold that his skin was sticking to it.

"Rix, I *really* don't like this place."

"Stay here. I've got to know what's down there." He went forwards.

"We're trespassing, and when the owner catches us—"

"The spirals could have been empty for five thousand years."

Tobry caught Rix by the left shoulder and jerked him back. "Stay here."

Tobry pushed past, down into the darkness, his footsteps making odd, rustling echoes. Rix waited, fuming and afraid in equal measure. After some minutes, Tobry reappeared.

"I don't need to be protected, Tobe."

"Yes, you do."

"Well, what's down there?"

"Pens," said Tobry.

"For animals? What kind?"

"Couldn't see. But I'd guess shifters . . . "

"I'm getting a bad feeling—"

From below them came another heavy thud, as if a stone door had been slammed, followed by a rush of air so cold that it crackled. Rix's ears and the tip of his nose began to hurt; the next breath pricked his nostrils as if he'd breathed in a cloud of icy needles. He turned and thrust the torch forwards but the flames died until it gave out no more light than a match.

"Back," Tobry croaked.

They hurried back. The flames kept low. At the passage with the steep, glassy-smooth steps, Rix stopped. Tobry caught his shoulder, as if to stop him again, then let go.

"This time, *I'm* going down," said Rix. "Stay here."

He sheathed his blade and went on, feeling his way down the precipitous stair, which had neither railing nor landings. Tobry followed.

"Feels like ice," Rix whispered. "Like we're in a flow tube melted through a glacier. We're not though, are we?"

"No." Tobry was panting.

"Now would be a good time for your magery to work, Tobe."

"As I keep telling you, I don't know enough—*stop*!" Tobry's fingers clamped Rix's shoulder, hard enough to hurt.

Rix's hair stirred. "What's the matter?"

"You're about to walk off the end of the stair."

It ended in mid-air three steps below them. The feeble torchlight reflected back from odd, alien curves a long way down, though he could not see enough to discern the shape they formed.

"What's down there, Tobe?" he said softly. "*Tobe?*"

Tobry was waving the elbrot furiously but here it had no aura at all. "Weird," he muttered. "It's shaped like some gigantic alchymical vessel."

"A what?"

"An upside-down retort, and we're above the top of the bulb."

As Rix moved the torch, curved reflections shifted along arcs. "Can't make any sense of it."

"It's an impossibility," said Tobry in a low voice, "nothing can curve around and back through itself that way."

As they peered down, Rix thought he could see spectral figures watching with dead eyes. His own eyes were watering from the cold, tears freezing as they formed.

"Turn around," Tobry said in his ear. "We're going up. Don't make a sound. Don't even breathe."

For once, Rix was glad to do as he was told. His sword rattled in its sheath as if trying to get out. He clamped onto the hilt, sensed something moving below him and glanced over his shoulder.

From far below the spectral figures, a shadow was rising, so black that it stood out against the darkness.

"Caitsthe?" he whispered.

"Too big," Tobry said hoarsely.

Too big? What could be bigger?

"And it's shooting up towards us."

The steps below their feet undulated like water rippling in a basin. Rix's knees wobbled. The air felt as though it had been charged up by a thunderstorm, and his hair was crackling.

Tobry swallowed audibly. "We're getting out *now.*" He pulled on Rix's shoulder. "Pray to your Five Heroes."

It was not in Rix to retreat from a fight. "You don't believe in the Heroes."

"I'd pray to a pickled onion if it would get us home safely. *Come on.*"

"What is that thing?" Rix made out a pair of yellow pinpoints, racing upwards. Through the rents in his shirt, cold stabbed at his chest like icicle daggers.

"We shouldn't be here!" Tobry yanked Rix's arm. "Run, like you've never run before."

Rix ran, glancing over his shoulder but the black shadow reflected nothing. Their hunter might have been man-shaped or it might have been winged. It was too large to be the caitsthe in cat form or human but, whatever it was, it was fast. There was a faint luminance about its middle, a reddish, uncanny glow, and shimmers of light further out. He could smell the magery on it, magery that gave him the blind horrors.

They scrambled up the steep steps, through the pool of bitter cold, and were approaching the maze when Rix stumbled on a loose stone, twisted his right ankle and landed on his knees. Tobry, who was ahead, came running back and heaved him up. Wrenching the torch from Rix's hand, he whirled it around his head until it flared, then hurled it at the onrushing shape.

Momentarily the figure was outlined in tinges of red—swirling robes, staff like a shepherd's crook, a vaguely human shape that was glacier blue at the centre. It was like a wrythen from the nightmares Rix had been having lately, then the torch went out as if it had been swallowed whole.

"The land *is* haunted," Rix gasped. "How are we going to survive?"

"How are *we* going to survive?" Tobry retorted.

He waved the elbrot furiously and it lit, telling him which path to take through the maze. Rix was glad of the enchantment now, for he could never have found the way. But then, he would not have seen the concealed cave in the first place.

"It's gaining," said Rix. "Can you hold it off?"

Tobry laughed hollowly. "Not even if I were Hightspall's chief magian."

They were approaching the rubble pile below the cave entrance, Rix limping badly, when a blast woven from a thousand shrieking souls howled up at the fissured roof ahead of them. It touched it with a pearly flicker, drifted forwards, and stone spalled away everywhere it touched. Crevices opened, fractures ground over rock fractures.

"It's trying to bring the roof down," gasped Tobry.

Rock began to fall, making a deadly curtain across the passage.

"Don't stop!" Tobry dragged Rix on. "Dive through!"

"We'll never make it."

"Better we don't than be trapped here with *that*."

The wrythen hated them—Rix could see the rage shimmering all around the creature. It had never met them before, yet it loathed and despised them, wanted nothing but to crush them into oblivion. Why?

He ignored the pain and ran harder, preparing to leap the rubble pile and dive through the falling rocks. They might just make it.

Then something rose up from the other side of the rubble, its eyes reflecting the pearly light coming off the roof. Eyes that were higher than the top of Rix's head.

The caitsthe was blocking the way out.

CHAPTER 18

What was *alkoyl*, and why had the master chymister shuddered at the thought of going down the Hellish Conduit, whatever that was, to get more? What were the enemy readying in such haste? And why?

Without warning, fingers thin and cold as knotted wire closed around Tali's upper arms and she was jerked backwards into darkness. Tinyhead? No, her attacker was far too small. Biting her tongue to stifle a cry that was bound to bring guards running, Tali tried to pull free.

The fingers locked like manacles. "Stupid little scrag. Hold still." The woman's voice was a croaky rasp, like the call of some aged bird.

"Who are you?" Tali whispered, struggling fruitlessly. There was something unnatural about the wiry fingers, which were draining the strength from her. "Are—are you taking me to Tinyhead?"

A bony fist cracked Tali on her sore ear. A series of lurching heaves took her backwards into a tunnel as black as her own terror. She was jerked around, thrust through a doorway and a latch clacked. The room was airless, confining and dank. She felt sure she was going to die here.

She swayed, so disoriented that she could hardly tell which way was up. "What are you going to do to me?"

"Shut up."

Tali gained the impression that her captor had an ear to the door. After a minute or two a brown, streaky glimmer appeared from that direction, and grew.

It revealed a tiny, birdlike Pale, a woman so ancient she was bald save for a few strands of white silk dangling from either side of a mottled skull with a jagged scar across the top. Her face was sharp as an axe, the eyes round like a bird's eyes, the nose a parrot's beak. Her shrunken lips appeared to have been sucked inside a toothless mouth and her fingers might have been lengths of wire knotted at the knuckles. As well as a grey loincloth, she wore a blouse made from frayed ragweed.

But Pale did not mean friend. The other slaves would either ignore her or betray her for the enemy's favour. Tali assumed that this woman intended the latter.

The light, which sprang from her fingertip, was pure white where it shone on the wall, though transmitted through her broken nail it became a dingy brown.

The illuminated patch of wall was deeply sculpted to resemble a dripping forest in which every rock and fallen tree trunk was carpeted in bright green moss. Only the gritty stone beneath Tali's feet told her that she was in a subterranean slave camp, not a primeval woodland.

"Who—" said Tali.

"Shut it, you little turd!"

The eviscerated mouth had not moved. It sounded as though the words issued through the old woman's gaping nostrils. Her head was tilted sideways like a crow studying an undersized worm and wondering if it was worth the effort.

Tali dragged her eyes back to the light, which was too bright to come from a chip of glowstone. Its source could only be magery, and no slave revealed that gift to a stranger—unless the old woman planned to kill Tali after getting what she wanted.

Tali tensed. Could she knock her aside and get away? But if she did, the old woman might sound the clangours.

"Don't try it," the old woman said.

"Wasn't going to," Tali lied.

"My name is Mimoy," said the old woman, "and I'm dying."

She didn't look it. Though she was as aged and leathery as a mummy, her eyes were bright and her grip had been unbreakable. Perhaps that had been magery, too.

"You are Thalalie vi Torgrist, of the noble House vi Torgrist," said Mimoy.

"Yes," Tali said faintly.

"You're planning to break out of Cython," said Mimoy. "I require a service of you."

Tali's diaphragm spasmed, forcing the air from her lungs, and for several seconds she could not draw breath. How could Mimoy know her plans when she'd told nobody?

She focused on the second sentence. "A service" could only mean blackmail—do what I say or I'll betray you. Or was Mimoy a *kwissler*, here to lull Tali into admitting her plans? Planning to escape got you the Living Blade—after various tortures.

"Don't know what you're talking about," she said hoarsely. A bead of sweat ran down her forehead into her left eye. She blinked it away.

The knotted-wire knuckles struck Tali's ear where Orlyk had gashed her with the chuck-lash. Pain lanced through the lobe.

Mimoy dragged her forwards, pressing the forefinger nail of her unlit hand into Tali's breastbone. "I've been watching over you all my life. I know everything about you."

"I've never seen you before," Tali said weakly.

Mimoy's smile was as ragged as her nail. "Your mother tried to teach you your gift. She failed."

The sweat bursting from Tali's brow turned icy. Mimoy knew too much, and they were both going to die for it. "Wizardry is evil," Tali said, parrot fashion. "It's forbidden to all save the lost kings of Cython."

"Iusia vi Torgrist failed," said Mimoy, prodding Tali to emphasise each word, "because *your* gift is not the feeble heritage magery of House vi Torgrist."

"Don't say that word," Tali cried. How could the old woman talk so casually about the forbidden? "I have no gift."

Mimoy indented a series of crescents down Tali's breastbone. "When you were three, a slave boy was beaten in front of you and you were so furious that you made a geyser burst from the wall. It washed the guard a hundred yards down the tunnel and broke both his legs."

Shivers crept up Tali's bare arms. Could it be true? She vaguely remembered a flood, then her mother shrieking and carrying her away . . .

"You next used magery when you were eight—"

"No," Tali moaned, shaking her head furiously. "I know nothing about it."

"Three days after your mother's murder the man called Tinyhead, whose real name is Sconts, was discovered crawling along a distant tunnel, bleeding from the mouth, nose, eyes and ears. He claimed to have been attacked by a horde of slaves, yet there was not a mark on him."

"It wasn't me."

"You struck him down with a spell of your own devising. You nearly killed him."

"It's not true," Tali whispered.

She had suppressed most of the memories of the worst day of her life, though she could remember the rage. She had directed it at the big man who had betrayed her mother, willing his tiny head to explode. Had she really done that to Tinyhead, *through a stone door*? The grotesquely bulging skull and ruined face, still engorged with blood ten years later, was evidence that she had.

"Yet your gift mostly fails you. It let you down yesterday when you tried to save your only friend. That's why you forced a girr-grub down Lifka's throat and stole her uniform." Mimoy's white-filmed eyes were on the red-brown loincloth.

"How do you know all that?" Tali whispered. Ah, the small, hobbling shadow she had seen earlier. "You've been following me."

"Watched over you ever since your mother was killed," said Mimoy. "And over her mother before that. Failed and failed!"

"Why? Who are you?" Perhaps Mimoy didn't intend to betray her after all. Tali restrained the surging hope. First, she had to know the price.

"Your mother died because she was *weak*," Mimoy spat.

"How dare you?" Tali cried, restraining an urge to slap the old woman.

"Also your grandmother, and your great-grandmother and great-

great-grandmother. All murdered; all weak! Are you going to let
the enemy kill you too?"

"No!" Tali snapped. "I'm strong."

"The first time I saw your quality was when you attacked Lifka,"
said Mimoy. "The same ruthless quality that's made me the oldest
Pale in Cython. One hundred and nineteen yesterday."

"A hundred and nineteen?" Tali echoed. In Cython, anyone who
lived to fifty was regarded as old. "No one lives to that age."

"Not *naturally*," said Mimoy.

"What are you saying?"

Mimoy shrugged her skeletal shoulders. "You're going to do me
a service."

Could the old woman be genuine? Mimoy's eyes gave nothing
away, but any Pale to survive so long with the gift would be adept
at concealing her thoughts.

"My mother told me to trust no one."

"Sound advice to a gifted child," said Mimoy, "but it won't keep
you alive until breakfast. Do you remember what else she told
you?"

"*You must find your . . . your . . .*" It almost choked Tali to say the
forbidden word aloud. "*You must find your gift, and master it. It's the
only way to beat him.*"

The sucked-in mouth twitched. "You haven't found it, have
you?"

"I've tried," Tali said grudgingly, "but nothing ever happens."
Her fingers clutched at her frayed waistband. "I don't know what
I'm doing wrong."

"We have three kinds of gramarye," said Mimoy, and held up her
splintered fingernail. "House vi Torgrist—"

"How do you know?" Tali burst out. "Who –?"

The wiry fingers pinched Tali's lips together until her eyes
watered, and held her for a painful minute. "I talk, you listen, yes?"

Tali balled her fists, then unclenched them. Had Mimoy come to
help her? It must be so. "Yes!" Damn you.

"The *old magery* came from our ancestral homeland of Thanneron, now lost beneath the creeping ice, with the First Fleet that
brought the Herovians to Hightspall. But none of magery's three

forms worked as well in Hightspall. The land fights it and it grows ever weaker."

Mimoy turned her head to one side then the other, like a crow watching for a cat.

"Is that why—?"

Mimoy raised a hand and Tali broke off, touching her bruised lips. The vicious old woman was her only hope, but any help would be on Mimoy's terms.

"A few of the original houses, including vi Torgrist, possessed *heritage magery*—a subtle gift which can only be mastered by looking within oneself. Wizard training ruins it."

"So that's what I've been doing wrong—"

"Are you as stupid as you look?" hissed Mimoy.

Tali looked at her blankly.

"Is your gift *subtle*?"

Blowing up Tinyhead's head could hardly be described as subtle. The thought gave her strength.

"There's also traditional magery," Mimoy continued. "The study and practice of the lore under a master."

Clearly, Tali did not have that branch of magery, either.

"And finally, magery that comes from the use of enchanted objects. Spells any fool can set off."

Tali had never seen an enchanted object. If there were any in Cython, their owners kept them well hidden. And that meant –

"You may speak," said Mimoy.

"If there are three kinds of magery, and I have none of them . . . I don't understand."

Taking Tali's head between her wire claws, Mimoy pressed the blade-beak nose against Tali's nose and stared into her eyes.

Tali tried to glare back but the pressure of Mimoy's will was, like water squirting from a break in the Siphons, enough to wash her away. *Turn aside*, the eyes said. *Don't take me on, you little fool.*

I may be young but I'm not a fool. And I won't be beaten by you. Tali raised her chin and forced herself to meet Mimoy's old eyes, to hold her gaze.

After a few seconds, the old woman drew back. "Stronger than I thought," she said grudgingly. "But are you strong enough?"

"Yes, I am," said Tali, and the strength that Mimoy had drained away at the beginning came surging back. "I'm going to beat Tinyhead. I'm going to escape and punish the people who killed my mother—every one of them."

"Brave words," sneered Mimoy, "but how are you going to get away from the matriarchs?"

"What have they got to do with me?"

With a disgusted snort, Mimoy turned and headed for the door. "Useless after all."

Tali watched her go, not understanding. "Wait," she cried, realising that the old woman had given up on her. "Where are you going? Don't leave me—"

Mimoy turned and struck Tali across the face. "Never beg!"

She rubbed her stinging cheek. "I've never even seen the matriarchs. Why do they want me?"

"Wil the Sump told you." Mimoy dripped scorn. "Have you no brains at all?"

"He called me *the one*. What did he mean by that?"

"You don't *know*?"

"How could I know? I'm not psychic."

"It means," gritted Mimoy, "that after many years of searching, the matriarchs finally know the name of the girl they failed to kill as a child. The girl they have to see dead, immediately and secretly. You."

Tali choked. "They want me dead. Why?"

"Because of a *shillilar*. A foretelling."

"Then why didn't Tinyhead kill me in the subsistery?"

"He serves another master."

Tali was struggling to process this. "So I have *two* separate enemies. The matriarchs want to kill me here, and our family's enemy wants to hack my head open in the cellar."

"Your snail's intellect has finally grasped the danger." Mimoy looked down at her tiny, twisted feet. "I suppose you'll have to do." She turned away.

"Why do the matriarchs want to kill me?" said Tali, more confused than ever.

"To prevent the *shillilar* coming true, of course."

"What did it say?"

"How would I know? It's a secret." Mimoy hobbled towards the door.

"Wait. What about my gift? I've got to practise the spell."

"No, you haven't."

"I can't escape without it."

"Can't you?"

"What are you saying?" cried Tali, but Mimoy, who was wincing with every step, did not answer. "When will we next meet?"

"Before dawn," said Mimoy.

"Where are you taking me, anyway?"

"I'm not taking *you* anywhere. You're taking me."

"Where?"

Mimoy cracked her knuckles and the finger light vanished. In the sudden darkness Tali heard the latch being raised.

"Home to Hightspall, to die," came the old woman's voice, moving away, and the naked longing in her voice brought tears to Tali's eyes.

"But I can't find my magery—"

Mimoy was gone.

CHAPTER 19

Wherever you run, wherever you hide, I'll find you.

But how was Tinyhead following her down these tunnels floored with clean, hard stone? Magery was an insult to their lost kings and no Cythonian would think of doing it.

Turning aside, she fled down one random passage after another, running until her knees went wobbly, yet twenty minutes later he was behind her again. Without a weapon she could not hope to beat him, and their masters were careful to lock away anything that might be used as a weapon. That only left one thing.

Since Tali's gift was not any of the three old kinds of magery, there must be a new magery, but where did it come from and why had it come to her? Was that why her family were targeted by killers from Hightspall? It did not make sense. How could outsiders know about magery in some insignificant slave trapped in Cython, and why would they care?

After passing down a broad passage, she slipped into an unlit cross-tunnel and waited on hands and knees. And soon he came, down on all-fours, sniffing the floor like a dog. He moved into a patch of light and she caught a flicker of white. Not sniffing—he was *licking* the floor with that repulsive tongue. Tracking her by her taste! She could hear him breathing, and a thick slurping as he licked, swallowed, licked again.

The soles of Tali's feet crept. The horrible, disgusting brute.

After backing away down the tunnel, she slipped the front and back sections of her loincloth off its waist cord and bound them around her feet, hoping that Lifka's stronger odour would confuse him. Tali hurried away, feeling tainted.

She had to concentrate on her plan though, without magery, how could she hope to impersonate Lifka? When she failed, she would be mutilated and beheaded. But there was no other way—or was there? Tali began to think the unthinkable.

Tinyhead knew a secret way out of Cython, and if anyone could elude the matriarchs, he could. If she allowed him to catch her, he would take her to the cellar. But what if she couldn't find her gift on the way? No, the risk was too great. She had to keep going. If she failed, at least she would have done her best.

Then a shadow moved, a long way behind, and it was the wrong shape to be Tinyhead or Mimoy. It must be one of the matriarchs' agents. Tali turned left and ran down a random passage, trying to work out why they wanted her dead.

They all died for you, Wil had said. Who had died?

Because of the *shillilar* about *the one*, the matriarchs had tried to kill her many years ago, but they had failed. How had they tried, and why had they failed? Because they hadn't known her name? But now they did, and they planned to kill her immediately and secretly. Why? What had the *shillilar* said about her? It must be dramatic if they had been trying to identify her all this time. Who could she ask?

Wil had called her *the one*, and he had a seeing eye tattooed on his forehead—the mark of morrow-sight. It must have been Wil who'd had the *shillilar*, but he was the enemy and would never tell her.

Tali scented water, burst out into a broad cross-passage and skidded to a stop inches from the edge of the floatillery. She knew where she was now. The underground canal ran to the Merchantery on the southern shore of vast Lake Fumerous, though that exit was the most closely guarded of all.

The dim, bluish light of a roof-mounted glowstone revealed a line of barges tied up along the stone quay, low in the water, heavily laden. Tali's hackles rose, and faint scintillations from within confirmed her unease. The barges were stacked high with rectangular slabs of heatstone, each as large as the bed of a wagon, all no doubt intended for the wicked trade with Hightspall.

There was something wrong about the twinkling slabs, as though the rock protested at the uncanny force trapped inside it, but Tali also saw an opportunity to shake her pursuers. Cythonians were superstitious about heatstones and would not touch them.

She clambered over the side of the nearest barge onto the stacked heatstones, shuddering at the sickly feeling on the soles of her feet and the moving colours it set off in her head. Within a minute her feet were burning hot. She ran down and leapt into the next barge, then the ones after that until she reached the end of the line. From there she sprang for the far side of the floatillery. Her pursuers would have to divert to the nearest bridge, which might gain her a respite.

Tali knew roughly where she was, though she had no idea how to get to the sunstone area from here and time was running out. She had to get there first—it would take a long time to prepare herself.

In Cython, people often found their way by the smell of a passage, and Tali's nose was one of the keenest, though only after hours of searching and sniffing did she scent a tunnel heading in the right direction. She unbound her feet, put on the crumpled loincloth and, as she hurried on, tried to resolve the enigma of Mimoy. The old woman knew things about Tali that no one *could* know without magery. Clearly, she had been spying on her for years. Yet, since Mimoy had not made herself known before, she could hardly be on Tali's side.

Trust no one.

Only Mimoy could show Tali how to release her gift. She had to go along with the old woman's plan and be ready to break free if Mimoy betrayed her.

By the time Tali reached the maze behind the sunstone shaft, only half an hour before dawn, she was panicking. Time was running out and if Tinyhead or the matriarchs' killers had arrived before her she would be walking into a trap. Even if they were not, without magery escape seemed impossible.

She had planned to slip through into the loading station and practise putting on the leather harness, but the maze entrance was blocked by crisscrossing bars, and beyond them, guards were pacing. There was no sign of Mimoy.

It was almost time for the breakfast gong. If Mimoy didn't appear soon, it would be too late. When Tali and Lifka did not join the lines outside their cells to march to work, the guards would go looking for them. Tali's crime would be discovered and the hunt would be on.

Could she escape without magery? Fifty yards back she had passed a series of storerooms stacked with crates and boxes. She slipped inside the first storeroom and sat in the dark, wondering if she could impersonate Lifka without magery.

It could go wrong in so many ways: if the guards checked each slave before they donned the harness; if she could not get Lifka's speech or mannerisms right; if Lifka had already been found; if the sunstone proved too heavy; if what Lifka *hadn't* told Tali was vital . . .

Her burdens came down on her with the weight of a sunstone. If the guards caught her, they would cut everything off. If Tinyhead took her, her family's enemy would hack her head open while she was still alive. If the matriarchs found her, she would be killed without ever knowing why *the one* was such a threat.

There was a reason why no Pale had ever escaped—it was impossible. Thus far, all she had done was run and hide, but there was nowhere else she could run to.

Yet she had sworn a binding oath and, no matter what else happened, the oath remained: unbreakable, unyielding, stiffening her spine no matter the burden. She would go on, to the bitterest end, or die in the attempt. She would not break her oath.

The breakfast gong sounded and her empty stomach rattled. Tali consumed the mouse-gnawed poulter leg shred by shred and, to a half-starved slave, it was the most delicious thing she had ever eaten.

If Mimoy did not turn up, Tali was going to put on the performance of her life. She wasn't just going to look like Lifka, she would become her in every way. She was rehearsing how her double moved, the way she spoke, the drooping lower lip and the glazed look in the girl's eyes, when her thumbs pricked.

Scutter-clack.

There was something in the storeroom with her, high up. Something guarding the crates. One of the beasts rumoured to guard the secret levels of Cython? Tali rose to a crouch, arms up to protect her face. Could it see her? She strained for any sound that would tell her where it was, what it was. Was it on top of the crates to her left, or the ones on the right? She had to pass between them to reach the door, and it could go for her face or attack her throat.

She was creeping along, arms stretched out to either side so she did not blunder into the stacks, when a fingertip picked up the faintest vibration in the side of a crate. Was it inside?

Using the poulter bone, she felt for a gap between the boards of the crate and poked the bone in. It touched something hard, with a complicated, curved shape ... and serrations. *Scutter-clack-snap.* The bone was torn from her fingers and crunched to splinters.

Tali scrambled away, fingertips stinging. It sounded like the skritter that had made that bloody assault on Sidon's calf. Each crate must hold dozens of them, and there were dozens of crates. What were they for? Why were they stored here? What if they got out?

From the feebly lit passage, she watched the storeroom door until her heart stopped pounding. The skritters had to be for hunting and attacking, but the Pale did not need to be hunted . . .

An unpleasant suspicion arose. Why had their rations been cut when Cython was producing more food than ever? She peered into the next storeroom, which was full of boxes. More skritters?

A foreman's coat hung from a peg on the wall. She wrapped it around her hands and eased up the lid of the nearest box, sweating. It contained spearheads, hundreds of them. The next box was the same, and the one after.

In recent days, several guards had talked about getting rid of the Pale, as if Cython would soon have no need for them. And the foremen below had been ordered to get everything ready by the end of the month *at any cost*.

Cython was going to war, a war they must have been planning for a very long time, and they now held the advantage. Hightspall occupied the Cythonians' ancestral land of Cythe; their maps showed every inch of it and they could swarm out through secret tunnels anywhere, any time.

Hightspall, however, knew nothing about Cython, for no Hightspaller had ever been allowed inside the underground realm. Its few entrances were defended by a maze of traps, dead ends and killing rooms for any enemy who broke through.

Unless Hightspall was prepared for war in eleven days, it would not have a chance.

CHAPTER 20

Rix's lungs were burning, but he could never run fast enough to escape what was behind them. Or what lay ahead.

As the caitsthe went up on its toes, Tobry let out a shuddery moan and Rix knew their lives hung from a cobweb. If Tobry cracked they would both fall.

"Keep going," he panted. "Better a hundred shifters than that uncanny wrythen."

"Easy for you to say," Tobry said hoarsely. "You've got an enchanted sword."

"If we get through, I'll take the shifter."

"Damned if—"

Another bolt of tormented sound screamed overhead, struck the fissured roof further along and, *crack-crack*, began to pick the stone apart. Rix looked back and a scream bubbled up his throat—the wrythen was like something out of his night horrors.

The broken rock formed a rubble waterfall and diving through it was a lottery, their survival a matter of chance. But chance was better than the certainty if they were trapped with the thing behind them.

"Go!" Rix cried, and they dived together.

Rock was falling on the left and right sides of the gap, dust billowing out to obscure what little light there was. The roof gave an almighty groan and he knew that it was all coming down. His ankle shrieked as he soared over the rubble, small rocks whacked him on the back and buttocks, then the mountain fell in.

Broken stone was flying everywhere, bouncing off the walls, rap-rapping down his backbone, stinging his left ear. He hit the floor hard, skinning both elbows, rolled over and raised his sword in the one movement. Where was the caitsthe?

Until the dust settled, the creature would be impossible to see while it stood still, no more than a shadow when it moved. Though no doubt it could scent him. Rix suppressed a sneeze, put his back to the wall and probed with the blade. Despite the exertion, he was freezing—the depths of the tunnel seemed to be breathing up cold. Where was it? It could strike from anywhere and he would not see it until it was too late.

He could not see Tobry, either. "Tobe?" he whispered.

No reply. Rix swept the flat of his sword around like a paddle but it did not touch flesh. Tobry was either unconscious or dead. Rix was on his own with one enemy before him and another at his back, and if they attacked together he would die.

Why was the caitsthe here, anyway? What was it guarding? What didn't the wrythen want him to see?

He couldn't see it now, but he could *feel* it coming as an icy ache in places where he had never felt anything before—inside his arm and leg bones, in the marrow—and a creeping and crawling of the skin on the back of his thighs. Whatever it was, it was no honest, natural creature. Why didn't it attack? What was it waiting for? Was it driving them towards the caitsthe ... or was the caitsthe penning them in for the wrythen?

Their survival depended on the answer.

"Tobe?" he repeated.

Nothing.

Something grated on stone, low to his left. It might have been Tobry, twitching on the floor, but Rix did not think so. Tobry's presence wouldn't make the little hairs on the back of Rix's neck stand up.

He caught a faint exhalation, the snick of a set of massive jaws closing, a liquid sound in a long throat. What was the caitsthe up to? He turned slowly, the hilt slipping in his sweaty palm, his eyes struggling to penetrate the dust. Where was it? Those weren't the sounds made by a beast preparing to attack. Caitsthes took the easy prey first. It was going for Tobry and he didn't know where either of them were. And Tobry was unconscious, helpless. All it had to do was close its jaws around his throat ...

Rix had to make the beast go for him. Picking up a handful of small rocks, he flung them horizontally, one after another, turning as he did. The fourth rock made a faint thud, as if hitting flesh. The caitsthe drew a sharp breath and he knew where it was.

Then it went for him.

Rix fought best when he relied on instinct and he allowed it to take over, angling his sword to the right as if planning a swinging blow while surreptitiously freeing the knife on his left hip. It would not be easy to fight with such different-sized weapons at once, nor was it a defence he'd ever practised. And if his hunch proved wrong ...

His only warning was the hiss of exhaled breath, foul as a jackal that fed on carrion. Rix swung the sword, deliberately leaving his front and left side exposed. If his guess about either the caitsthe's position or mode of attack was wrong, it would gut him.

"Re-ven-ge," it said in a halting purr. As if, even in human form, its throat struggled to shape words.

Was it parroting something its master had taught it, or was a cunning mind at work inside the caitsthe? If it was truly intelligent his strategy would fail.

And where was the wrythen? Rix glanced over his shoulder. The cold was getting closer. Was its plan to attack from behind as the caitsthe came at him from the front? To his left the air flurried and faint, swirling red lines appeared there. Caitsthe magery? Rix was glad of his enchanted blade now.

He caught the blur of movement as it sprang and more swirls of red, but before he could strike the beast had him by the shoulders, digging its claws in and holding his sword arm so tightly that he could not use the weapon. It could have torn his throat out with a snap of those teeth. The fact that it did not suggested it had other plans, and the toothy smile confirmed it.

It'll be planning to attack you where you hurt it.

The urge to protect his groin was almost irresistible. It took all Rix's will to follow his instinct and wait for the one second when he would have a chance.

The caitsthe arched its back, opened its maw and began to lower its head. To divert his true intentions, he drove a knee up at its belly where the twin livers would be. The glancing blow had too little power to do serious damage, yet the caitsthe groaned and threw its head back.

No time to wonder why. He jerked his unnoticed knife out and up at the caitsthe's belly at the same instant as it went for him. The knife encountered unexpected resistance—the woven belts of belly muscle were taut as wire. Rix swayed backwards and its snapping teeth grazed his chin, its foul breath blasting up his nostrils. His right forearm hit the side of its head but his sword was now behind the caitsthe and at the wrong angle to strike.

There was only one chance and he used it, forcing the knife through its belly muscles to the hilt then dragging it sideways. The caitsthe's grip relaxed fractionally. He brought his knee up into its groin this time, putting all his weight behind it, and the shifter must not have been completely healed there, for it howled.

Rix slammed up again, gave the knife another twitch then put one foot against its crotch and shoved the creature backwards, tearing its claws from his shoulders.

The caitsthe slid off the knife and he lost sight of it as it hit the floor, though he could hear it panting and the oily squelch of intestines in its opened abdominal cavity. Any other creature would be dying from such an injury but the shifter seemed more troubled by the battering its groin had taken. He was safe for a minute or two until it healed itself—safe from it, at least—and had Rix been by himself he would have bolted.

Blood ran down his upper arms from his shoulders, each gouge throbbing as if a nail had been dragged through his flesh. He cleaned the caitsthe's blood off his knife, very carefully, then scanned the air for the wrythen, the floor for Tobry. There was no sign of either.

Rix sheathed the knife but kept the sword out and, using his free hand, groped along the piled rubble. "Tobe, where are you?"

He had always taken Tobry for granted, had not realised how much he mattered to him or relied on him. His mocking, believe-in-nothing friend could not be dead. "Tobe, speak to me. I need you."

He could not be far away. They had been side by side before they jumped, but if Tobry was under two feet of rubble there would be no helping him.

"Tobe, if you're conscious, I need light badly."

The irony did not escape Rix, but his phobia about the uncanny had to take a back seat now. He was moving along the face of the rock fall when he realised that he could no longer hear the squelch of intestines. He couldn't hear anything from the place where the caitsthe had fallen. Had it healed itself already?

A faint bluish glow lit the tunnel from behind. Tobry had come through; he was alive! But as Rix spun around, his smile died. The wrythen was hovering a yard above the ground on the other side of the rubble, blocking his retreat. Even if by some miracle he beat the caitsthe, he must next face an opponent he had no means of fighting.

Out of nowhere, the caitsthe launched itself head-first at his groin and there wasn't time to raise the sword. Rix jammed its tip against the floor and wriggled the blade from side to side, pathetically trying to protect himself with the narrow blade.

The caitsthe's jaws snapped, trying to close around him, but the blade cut across its mouth. It yelped, withdrew, then dived at him. Rix braced himself and jerked the edge of the blade into its path.

It twisted its head out of the way, losing only an ear, but momentum drove it hard onto the blade, which sliced a hand-span deep down the side of its neck and through its inner shoulder. The arm went limp but the caitsthe's other hand came curling around behind Rix to wrench his feet from under him.

He lost his grip on the sword, then landed so hard on the rubble that he went numb from the waist down. The caitsthe was snapping and snarling, blood pouring from the terrible wound in its shoulder. It attempted a lunge to finish him off but the sword blade was caught on bone and the lunge only drove it deeper. Nothing else could have saved him.

It lurched backwards, reaching across with its good arm to pull the sword free, then jerked away as though the hilt had burnt it. The enchantment was the only thing protecting Rix now.

Yellow-brown fluid squirted from glands behind the caitsthe's ears onto the wound; froth foamed up to cover it. The creature's eyes glazed and it made several uncoordinated snapping motions with its teeth.

Rix's numbness was fading but the smell of the glandular fluid made his nose drip and his stomach heave. As he tried to get up, the strength drained from him; the warmth fled from his body and was replaced with ice. His limbs might have been weighed down with rubble—he could barely move them. What was the caitsthe doing to him?

A convulsive blow sent the sword clattering across the rubble. Rix managed to rise to his hands and knees, though there were pins and needles in his feet and his shoulders had an unpleasant, jelly-like quality. The caitsthe was temporarily incapacitated as it shifted the tissues and bone to heal itself. Was it drawing on his strength for that purpose? Could it do such a thing?

It let out a groan; its free hand skimmed its stomach and it winced. Rix's knife gouge was no longer visible but its belly bulged like a melon above its livers and the sweat running down its front was steaming there. What if the twin livers were involved in shapeshifting or healing? Were they painful because they had been so overworked, forced to heal by shifting again and again?

He groped behind him for a chunk of rock, then flung it at the bulge. The caitsthe screamed and convulsed, flinging its arms up and out repeatedly like a grotesque mechanical toy.

The cold and the weakness eased suddenly. Rix staggered forwards, fumbling for his knife, knowing that this was his last chance to finish the beast but not sure his legs would hold him up. If he had guessed wrong about the caitsthe it would tear his head off.

He swayed on his feet, the icy numbness creeping up his bones again. Should he try to cut the twin livers out? Rix wasn't sure he was up to it. The caitsthe struck at him feebly. A feint intended to draw him in? He had to take the risk.

It struck again, at his head this time. Rix ducked but it was too much for his shaky knees, which collapsed under him. He landed on his kneecaps, scrabbled forwards and hacked upwards with the knife.

His aim was true and the caitsthe's severed gonads went flying across the tunnel. It screamed shrilly, clutched at its groin and every gland on its body squirted pungent fluids, fogging the air around it. It let out an echoing howl, the same cry it had made when it had first changed to man-form, and its dim outline began shifting again, turning back to the huge cat that was its natural form. Was shifting a quick way of healing itself?

Rix crawled across to his sword and, using it as a crutch, forced himself to his feet. He had never fought anything this tough before. He swayed back and forth, trying to will strength into his limbs for the next battle. His last. He could not take on a healed caitsthe and win, not now that he was being drained again. So cold; so very cold. He tried to lift the sword but his arm had the weight of an iron ingot. How was the caitsthe doing that?

Mother will be furious, he thought oddly. My death is going to ruin all her plans. It would also leave House Ricinus vulnerable and its people unprotected, and Rix regretted that far more. Why hadn't he given thought to his responsibilities before he came up here?

He realised that he had been standing still for minutes, watching the outline through the yellow fog. Now it dispersed, revealing the caitsthe still in man-form save for the tufted ears and furry tail—the shifting had not gone to completion. He could feel heat radiating off it. The shifter was as hot as he was cold, far hotter than any live creature should be. It seemed thinner and its formerly taut skin was baggy, as though it had burnt a lot of weight in a short time.

Its glands dribbled, though not enough to form the fog. Again it howled and tried to shift to cat-form but the howl died away in a frustrated yelp. After another series of dribbles it snapped weakly at its injured shoulder and in the direction of its groin. Steam hissed from its mouth, ending in a series of puffs like smoke rings. Its head lolled.

"Kirikay, Kirikay," it gasped, reaching out towards the wrythen. The caitsthe tried to stand up, made it halfway then crashed to the floor and did not move.

Rix suspected another trick, though this did not look like one. The creature's body seemed to shrink as it cooled, the skin sagging like a deflated balloon, and its limbs had the limpness of death. Could it be dead? If it was, how had he done it without cutting out its livers?

Rix felt the draining again, the creeping cold and heaviness of his arms and legs, but this time instinct prompted him to look over his shoulder. The hovering wrythen had no feet, its lower legs terminating in stumps of shattered bone. His gaze travelled upwards and he saw that its right arm was extended towards him. A pale blue thread of light connected them. The draining had not come from the caitsthe at all.

The wrythen was attacking him with the one thing he had no defence against—magery. It made a swirling motion with one hand, as if snapping a length of string, and the blue thread broke.

All light in the cavern was extinguished.

CHAPTER 21

The work gong sounded three times. The sunstone carriers, who started early to catch the dawn light, would be here any minute, while, back at the Empound, Tali's absence would soon be noted.

Lifka would be questioned and would reveal Tali's plan. The overseer's fastest runners would be sent racing to the loading station, and it would take them less than half an hour to get here. That was all the time she had to get away . . .

Her heart stuttered. Fool! Banj won't send runners, he'll sound the clangours, and the alarm will echo through the bell-pipes all the way to here. The guards on the other side of the grille will hear it a minute after Banj signals, and they'll seal the exit, unless . . .

She ran into the storeroom, carried out one of the heavy boxes of spearheads, then stacked another onto it, and another, until she could reach the hall ceiling. Tali wrenched one of the boards off the box, making rather a lot of noise. Had anyone heard? She checked the grille. The guards were out of sight.

Reaching up, she inserted the board between a join of the bell-pipe and the ceiling, and heaved. The pipe did not budge. She heaved again, with the same result. The work gangs must be close; she had to break the join *now*. Hanging onto the board, she sprang up, put her feet against the ceiling and forced with all the strength in her legs, and the pipe came apart at the soldered join.

The alarm might still carry. She jammed the foreman's coat into the end of the bell-pipe and pushed it in until it could not be seen. It would have to do.

Was that the tramp of guards? She heaved the boxes back, crouched in the dark storeroom and forced herself to concentrate. Everyone at the sunstone station had worked with Lifka for years and knew everything about her. One tiny mistake, one word or gesture out of character and Tali would be discovered. Only magery could guarantee the deception but she did not think Mimoy was coming.

Outside, an alarm clangour sounded, faint and muddy, from the blocked pipe. That would be Banj, signalling the maze guards to be on alert. She did not think they would hear it, but when they failed to acknowledge the alarm he would send his fastest runners.

Mimoy did not appear, Tali's frantic efforts to reach down to her gift failed as they always had and directly the slaves began to pass by. Her heartbeat was so fast that it was painful and she felt an overwhelming urge to throw up but she had to keep going. The fate of her country now depended on her escaping.

Sticking out her bottom lip, she imitated Lifka's listless, stoop-shouldered stance, mentally rehearsed her flat speech one more time and joined the end of the line.

The maze guards opened the grille; the slaves began to file through the passages of the maze. Tali surreptitiously weighed the defences as she went. The walls were slotted high up so hidden archers could fire down on the enemy. Stains etched into the stone below each slot suggested that the Cythonians also used chymical weapons.

She passed over a series of clanking grids, each covering a deep pit. The first pit had iron spikes embedded in the base. From an oily liquid in the second pit, breath-tearing fumes wisped up. If intruders passed the pits, stone doors ahead and behind could trap attackers in a series of killing rooms. She shivered and hurried through.

Her upper arms were encircled by lines of bruises where Mimoy's wire-like fingers had clamped around her, though bruises on a slave would not arouse suspicion. Ahead, two lines of Pale were donning brown robes under the eyes of a pair of guards. Tali pressed her fingers to her shoulder scar, for luck. I'm Lifka. Don't notice me; there's nothing to see.

Eyes lowered like a cowed slave, she took a set of thigh-length robes from a peg and pulled them over her head. They fastened around her neck but opened at the front so as not to hinder the climb. A guard scanned Tali's face, scowled at her grubby, crumpled loincloth, then waved her on. One obstacle down.

Half a dozen young slave girls appeared, each carrying two pails of water. The first two girls filled jugs for the guards. The next three carried the pails along the line of slaves so they could wash their faces, hands and feet. Tali was familiar with the morning ritual, for the enemy bathed twice a day and tolerated no filth on their slaves.

The last girl went to the head of the line with her buckets. Her eyes were shining; she was bursting with pride for the important job she had been entrusted with. Tali's mouth went dry, for the girl was Rannilt and if she called Tali by name, she was lost.

Tali dropped her lower jaw, pushed her lip out further and tried to look like a congenital idiot. Rannilt held up her buckets so two slaves at a time could scoop water with cupped hands and drink. The girls with the empty buckets waited to one side. Along the line Rannilt came, then, just ahead of Tali, a tall slave girl thrust her foot between Rannilt's ankles and she crashed to the floor, spilling her water.

"Stupid Rannilt can't do anything right," said the tall girl, and the other four sniggered. The guards took no notice.

"Sorry, sorry." Rannilt was rubbing a gashed knee and blushing. Tali had never seen anyone go so red. "Always doin' that. Really clumsy, I am."

Tali could hardly ignore the girl; that was bound to arouse suspicion. She helped Rannilt up. "Blood's runnin' down yer leg," she said, trying to imitate Lifka's stolid indifference and knowing her voice did not sound right.

"It's nothin'. I'm always fallin' over."

Or being pushed. Bullying was common among the slaves. The terrorised herd picked on the weakest.

Rannilt looked up at Tali, stared and her eyes widened. She smiled, she was going to say hello. Tali put on a ferocious scowl, gave a stiff jerk of the head and waved her away. Rannilt looked hurt, sniffled and wiped her nose on an arm covered in shiny streaks.

"More water," snapped the nearest guard.

Rannilt gathered her buckets and limped off. "Sorry, sorry," she said to every Pale she went by.

Tali let out her breath. The line of slaves moved around the corner, then stopped. Up ahead, the leading slave put her left foot on a square stone. A black-haired Pale locked a bracelet around her ankle while a guard looked on. The bracelet had an odd bulge at the front, the size of a child's fist. Tali began to sweat. Lifka hadn't mentioned this.

Didn't tell ya everythin', she had gloated. What was the bracelet for?

Panic swelled until it was choking Tali. This was her punishment for using Lifka so cruelly, for being such a hypocrite. She should have worked harder to find out everything Lifka knew. Instead of attacking the girl, she should have befriended her.

Too late now. If she left the line, the guards would know something was wrong. Besides, Banj's most fleet-footed guards would be racing this way. How long before they got here? Ten minutes? Fifteen at the most. She had to put on an act such as she had never done before.

As she lifted her small, pale foot onto the stone, ice formed along her backbone. *Who looked at a slave's feet?* The guard supervising the ankle bracelets, that's who.

Instinctively, Tali pressed her fingers to her slave's mark. Don't notice any difference, she prayed. I'm Lifka. *I am*. She licked dry lips, allowed her jaw to sag and put on a listless stare.

The black-haired slave's eyes were on Tali's ankle as her fingers locked the silver bracelet in place. It was heavy and uncomfortably warm, and the ominous bulge at the front was made from a reddish metal engraved with Cythonian glyphs which Tali could not read.

The guard came forwards, bearing a graduated brass squirter, and squeezed a single drop of an orange, chymical fluid into a small hole on the top of the bulge. The bulge gave forth a faint ticking sound and Tali felt it vibrating against her shinbone, reminding her uncomfortably of a skritter.

Then the slave frowned, looked up sharply, and she was the last Pale Tali wanted to see—the beautiful savage who had led the hissing in the subsistery, Tali's childhood enemy, Radl.

Don't betray me. Please, please don't betray me.

Radl smiled, displaying her pointed teeth.

Tali rubbed her scar. Time stopped, then jerked forward a second; another.

Radl said something to the guard, too softly for Tali to hear. Now the guard was studying Tali's ankle, frowning. *He knew!* It was all over.

She pressed harder on her scar. *You can't see anything different. I'm Lifka and I've got broad, tanned feet.*

The guard's black eyes crossed, then he waved her on, irritably. Tali met Radl's blue eyes. Her lips moved and Tali read, *Leaving you to your enemy, bitch.*

Tali forced herself to not react, but as she went on her legs felt de-boned. The twin lines moved towards the loading station, where a pair of burly Pale eunuchs, their smooth, indecent thighs well covered, lifted the rectangular, faintly shimmering sunstones from a stack and lowered one into the leather pouch on the back of each slave's harness. A Cythonian foreman studied the faces and checked each woman off on his list.

Sunstones were the size of tombstones and each slave shrank an inch or two under the enormous weight. Tali braced herself and moved forwards, trying to look as docile and vacant-eyed as Lifka. The bulge on the ankle bracelet seemed to be ticking more loudly than before and the vibration felt as though teeth were meshing inside it.

The foreman inspected Tali, checked her off but then, instead of waving her past, thrust back her hood and turned her head from side to side. Tali's mouth went dry. If he made her remove the harness, her lack of calluses would reveal the deception at once.

"Name?"

"Lifka, Master," she said in Lifka's colourless voice.

"What's the matter with you?"

Was the voice wrong? Her skin too pale? Not knowing what had alerted his suspicions, Tali had no idea how to remedy things. "Master?"

"Why are you sweating?"

"Gripe, Master." Tali touched her belly and winced. "Gut gripe."

Her belly looked like Lifka's, at least. She pushed it out and swayed forwards, praying he would not notice her pale feet.

CHAPTER 22

Tali felt like screaming hysterically, head-butting the guard in the belly then running wild and pushing over all the sunstones. The guard was staring at her as though he knew she was an impostor and was waiting for her to crack. She kept her eyes lowered like a docile slave, bit her tongue until it hurt, and waited. And waited. In her mind's eye she could see Banj's runners sprinting down the tunnels, surely only minutes away. He would also have informed the matriarchs that a slave was trying to escape, and that there had been no reply from the maze guards. They would know she was *the one* and their executioners would also be on the way.

After an agonising minute the guard grunted, flipped the hood over Tali's golden hair and gestured her to the loading station. The Pale eunuchs were built like wrestlers, yet they grunted as they lifted each sunstone from the stack and rotated it to the vertical. As the first eunuch raised Tali's stone, it slipped.

"Don't drop it!" cried the second eunuch, steadying the sunstone with both hands. He cast an anxious glance at the guards.

"Ready?" the first eunuch said to Tali. Sweat was running down his round face and dripping from his chin.

"Yes," she said in Lifka's empty voice, then realised that she had forgotten to push out her lower lip.

The first eunuch did not move. He was holding the weight of the stone, his gaze travelling up and down her small form as if he did not believe she could carry it. Now he was looking at her feet. His eyes flicked to the second eunuch, then he smiled, ever so faintly. He knew!

She met the eunuch's eyes, praying that he would not give her away, yet knowing that most slaves would. Betraying another slave meant favour with the guards, and extra rations. And for many, the pleasure of seeing a troublesome rebel brought down.

Please, she said through her eyes.

The eunuch's eyes misted, as if looking upon a daughter he would never have, and his lips moved. *Good luck.*

There was one good man left in Cython, at least, and it gave her heart. She tilted her head to him.

"Move it," the second eunuch said curtly.

As Tali braced herself for the weight, heat flickered around the loops and whorls of the scar on her shoulder and she felt a momentary dizziness. She put her hand across her shoulder and the dizziness passed, though the scar still felt hot.

Holding the sunstone vertically, the first eunuch slipped it into the long leather pouch at the back of her harness and stepped away. Tali's knees almost collapsed and a groan was squeezed out of her. It was impossible; her backbone was compressing, her arches flattening until her feet looked like twin tortoises. She could barely stand up under the weight. No way could she carry the sunstone a thousand steps to the surface.

The second eunuch was looking at her curiously so she lurched off, following the line of carriers. If she did not reach the top of the shaft before Banj's runners arrived, she was lost.

The sunstone should have been cool, its absorbed sunlight being reduced to the faintest shimmer, but Tali could feel its presence at her back as if an alien force was surging and ebbing in its core. How many thousands of Pale men and boys had died mining heatstone, and the concentric layers of sunstone and glowstone that surrounded the blistering heatstone mine?

An arched opening led into a ten-sided shaft running vertically to the surface. A stairway with shallow stone steps coiled around it and the leading carriers were already halfway up. The walls around the base of the shaft were blackened, as if a fire had once burnt there, and the edges of several steps looked glassy. The upper section of the shaft was dimly lit and she could not tell how high it was, but it had to be hundreds of feet to the top. To Hightspall, the beloved realm, the homeland the Pale had yearned for all the thousand years of their enslavement.

The leading slaves were striding up the steps as if it were a race. Tali pressed back against the wall, waiting her turn, and it felt as though the bones of her feet were cracking.

"What's wrong with you, Lifka?" a stocky slave girl said, elbowing Tali in the side.

"Gut gripe," Tali said faintly.

"If you can't take it, call sick. If you drop a sunstone . . . " The slave girl shivered.

The entire sunstone gang would be punished. It was the Cythonian way—the group suffered for the failings of the individual, therefore the group enforced the enemy's will as ruthlessly as any slave master.

"I'm all right," said Tali. "I can do it."

She stepped onto the lowest step, but as she stretched for the second the weight of the sunstone pulled her off balance. Her arms flailed and she was falling backwards with no hope of recovery, failing at the first hurdle.

As abruptly, she went flying forwards. The slave behind her had shoved hard on her sunstone.

"Thanks," she choked, stumbling but recovering.

"Keep right, sluggard."

She lurched to the wall side of the stair and the slave barged past, cursing her. The ankle bracelet vibrated, *scutter-click-click*, reminding her of the skritter that had embedded itself in the flesh of Sidon's calf. Tali took another step, careful to lean forwards, then another. Her breath was wheezing in and out, her knees wanted to collapse and her thigh muscles were ablaze.

By the time she made it to the first landing half the line of slaves had passed her. She stopped, gasping, but could not drag enough air into her lungs to satisfy her desperate needs. Her face was burning, sweat flooding down her chest. At her back, the core of the sunstone seemed to be throbbing in time with her racketing heart.

Scutter-click-click. The bracelet tightened around her ankle and she felt a series of little prickings there, like a warning of pain to come. That's where those little scars around Lifka's ankles came from.

From high above, great bolts were drawn back, clanking against their brackets. She heard the thud of heavy doors pushed wide and yellow light washed in. Tali caught her breath and her eyes misted—it was the first daylight she had ever seen.

She lurched up to the next landing and stopped again, her legs unable to drive her any further. Leaning back against the wall, she allowed it to take part of the weight and prayed she would be able to stand upright again.

By the time she made the third landing her heart was palpitating. At this rate she would not have to worry about being caught; she would die of apoplexy. Her muscles were melting, the shoulder straps felt as though they had torn her flesh down to the collarbones and her vision was going in and out of focus. Was this how her poor father had died, worked to death for seeking a way out?

Click-scutter-clack. The bracelet tightened again, its points pricking and biting all around her ankle. Horror froze her for a second, somehow worse because the bracelet was a relentless mechanical weapon driven by that drop of chymical fluid. It felt nothing, cared about nothing, and there was nothing she could do to get it off her ankle.

The pain cleared her head, though, temporarily pushing the burden of the sunstone into the background. The first slaves had reached the top. Even the stragglers were two flights above Tali and the Cythonians at the exit were eyeing her suspiciously. Yet even if she got there, and even if they let her outside, how could she hope to escape so many guards without a spell of concealment?

Tali had no energy to think. She had to get to the top before the teeth around her ankle tore through to the bone. *Never give up*, her mother had taught her. If you begin something, you must complete it. And so she would, her own small monument to Iusia.

Her agony could get no worse, or so she had thought, but each flight proved harder than the one before. As she reached the fourth landing, her body a mass of spasming pain, the first of the slaves were on their way down again. By the sixth landing, even the tail-enders were descending. Tali wanted to lie down and die. Only will drove her on.

At the exit, a hard-faced Cythonian who might have been

Orlyk's brother was uncoiling a yard-long, bright yellow chuck-lash, a punishment far worse than the little ones Orlyk used in the grottoes. Yellow chuck-lashes burst against the skin like miniature bombasts.

A second guard raised a piece of metal in the shape of a musician's triangle, then struck it with a rod. The triangle chimed, an answering *ting* came from Tali's bracelet and, with a *clacketty-scutter-clack*, it drove a series of needle-sharp teeth into the bone of her ankle.

The pain was a shriek from a torture chamber. She stumbled, nearly fell, and trying to stand upright again was like lifting a mountain. It felt as if the sunstone itself was resisting her. She could not pretend to be Lifka now—Tali could no longer remember the way her double spoke. Was it her lower lip that gaped, or the upper?

The last of the slaves reached the blackened floor of the shaft and went out through the archway for their next load. The teeth in her ankle withdrew, though only so they could bite deeper next time. At the top, three more guards came in from outside to join the watching pair. The guard with the triangle raised it and Tali braced herself for more pain.

She staggered across another landing and kept going; if she stopped for a second she would never start again. Fantasies ran through her mind—the slaves' bathing chamber and cool water flowing over her overheated body; pressing her face against the green, bubbly ice in the cool rooms. Her stomach was cramping, her knees vibrating like a fiddler's bow, her ankle throbbing with every shuddery vibration of the bracelet.

Then, as she glanced down, a tiny, skin-and-bone figure lurched through the archway. Mimoy had come. Tali's heart jumped and she felt a surge of hope, but it swiftly faded. The old woman looked exhausted. She was leaning on a knob-headed cane, swaying from side to side, and her twisted feet left bloody prints on the floor.

Tali's heart went out to the old woman, who must be in agony on those ruined feet. But what could Mimoy do? If she used magery under the eyes of the guards they would take her head at once.

"Move, slave!" shouted the guard with the yellow chuck-lash.

Tali tried to go on but her thigh muscles cramped. She should not have stopped.

"I—can't—"

The guard with the triangle began to come down, one step at a time, never taking his eyes off her, the rod held high above his head as if to strike a mighty blow. The teeth of the ankle bracelet pricked into her, quivering. Tali imagined the next snap shearing right through her ankle, the teeth meeting in the middle, but she had nothing left.

With the cane, Mimoy gave a feeble wave. Not even the most suspicious Cythonian would have taken it for magery, yet Tali felt the cramps ease, a little strength trickle into her legs, then the teeth in the ankle bracelet withdraw. She looked up and down, biting her lip. What did Mimoy want her to do? *You're taking me*, she had said, but Tali could not go down for her, nor could Mimoy follow. Only sunstone carriers were allowed up the shaft, so how did she plan to get out?

Mimoy met Tali's eyes and nodded, almost imperceptibly. Did that mean Tali was to continue up? She climbed the next flight, stronger now than she had been at the beginning, and the guard lowered his triangle.

A tiny bubble of optimism carried her on. She would climb to the exit, then haul her burden out to the racks where the stones were exposed to sunlight. And once there? Cold logic defeated every plan, every hope. Without magery, she could not escape the ever-watchful guards. Without magery, she would be driven down the shaft again, where Overseer Banj would be waiting with his blood-drinking blade.

But life was hope: once outside in Hightspall her gift might come. Or Mimoy might have a plan to help her find it. And Mimoy must know who had ordered her mother's death. It was enough to keep Tali going.

She was two flights from the top when a big man entered the base of the shaft. Her vision was blurred from exhaustion and at first she thought it was one of Banj's runners, though there was no tumult below, no shouts of, *Stop her*! He looked up, saw her desperate eyes on him and his ruined mouth cracked wide. Tinyhead licked the wall she had rested against, up and down, his bloodshot eyes rolling. Even from this distance the sound turned her stomach.

One word from him and the guards would stop her. The only way to escape him was to give herself up, though if she did the Cythonians would *cut everything off.*

It would be better to jump, yet jumping meant failure to punish her mother's killers and breaking the oath sworn on Mia's blood. Failure meant victory for her family's enemy; it meant no warning for Hightspall about the coming war; it meant the Pale being slaughtered as soon as war began. It meant more than her own life.

Since she was going to die, was there a way to make her death meaningful, as her parents' deaths had not been? Tali slumped against the wall, every breath hurting. Iusia's killers were beyond her reach but she might be able to punish her betrayer.

She was turning to the rail when Mimoy pointed her cane at Tinyhead and this time the pose was unmistakable—she was attacking him with magery. As she croaked the words of a spell, he struck her a ferocious backhander across the chest, sending her flying out through the archway. Mimoy's breaking ribs made the same sound as Iusia's had that day in the cellar, and a terrible, killing rage surged through Tali. Surely, now at the moment she was about to die, she could use that rage to find her gift?

Die, she raged, willing his head to burst, his heart to tear open, his eyes to explode from their sockets. Tinyhead stumbled, pressed a hand to the right side of his head, and shook it, then a round, blue stone hanging around his neck glowed and faded. He began to climb the stairs, wincing with each step but clearly unharmed. Tali's gift had not come. Her last hope had failed.

The killers would go unpunished, but at least she could have the satisfaction of revenge on Tinyhead before she was killed. What if she dragged him over the edge? No, he was far too strong.

Then she had it. "Tinyhead!" she yelled.

The ankle bracelet shuddered violently and Tali knew it was going to chew her foot off, but that did not matter now. She turned and staggered towards the stair rail. Only three steps but it felt like a mile.

High above, a guard bellowed, "Stop her!"

Over the pounding in her ears, Tali heard them scrambling down, and she could see other guards running up. She was dead but she was going to take Tinyhead with her.

As she reached for the rail, her knees went. She forced up on will alone, fell forwards and landed against the rail, gasping. Her heart felt as though it was bursting, and the rail was breast-high on her. Could she get the sunstone over it? She had to.

The guards were close. Do it! Taking a firm grip on the rail, Tali went up on tiptoes and bent over it. She was directly above Tinyhead, who had stopped nine flights below her, looking up. She drew her head down out of the way and aimed the sunstone.

"This is for you, Mama."

CHAPTER 23

Naked, pants-wetting terror overwhelmed Rix. Magery was the terror he could not overcome, the enemy he could never fight. And the wrythen wasn't just a creature of magery. It was supernatural, incomprehensible and, since it had no physical body, there was nothing he could do to harm it.

In utter darkness he clung to his sword, which for all he knew was the only real thing left in creation. It was like being in one of the recurring nightmares that woke him screaming and sweating, knowing that the world was ending and it was all his fault because of the terrible thing he'd done, and the service he kept refusing to do ...

Pull yourself together. Nightmares aren't real, and neither are the whispers in your head. That's why you can never remember them afterwards. Nor is this footless spirit real. It's just a wrythen, a semi-solid Cythonian shade, and shades can't touch you. You're not a coward—you've just beaten a caitsthe, for the Gods' sakes, and no one's ever done that before. A caitsthe!

It did not help, for this was no ordinary shade. It had brought down the roof with powerful magery the like of which Rix had never seen. Where did it get it from? How could a shade wield such power?

Even in total darkness Rix could sense the fury smoking out of it. Was that because he and Tobry were trespassers, or because they had found those shifter pens down below?

He rotated, boots grating on the gritty floor, and strained until his eyeballs ached. Nothing appeared. The wrythen hadn't just extinguished itself—it had withdrawn all light from the cavern as it had previously driven the torchlight back into Rix's burning brand. Presumably, so it could hunt him at its leisure.

It need not have bothered. He truly feared only three things: the bile-dripping tongue of Lady Ricinus, the end-of-the-world night-mares he could never escape when he was home, and uncanny, incomprehensible magery. The wrythen had magery at its com-mand that even Tobry had no understanding of, and Rix feared it the way a bullock feared the slaughterman's knife.

Devoid of hope, he waited for it to attack. Would he know when it did? In the dark it could come from any direction. It could blast him apart the way it had unpicked the stone in the fissure, or simply stand off and drain him as it had done before, until his mus-cles died and the creeping cold froze him from the inside out, as the southern ice cap was steadily surrounding Hightspall to crush it out of existence.

"Light," he said softly, hopelessly. "Please, let there be light."

And the faintest emerald glimmer appeared from the rubble. Rix's heart jumped. "Tobe? Is that you?"

There was no answer and the light faded again, but it had to be Tobry, for the wrythen's light was glacier-coloured. Tobry was alive, and it gave Rix new hope. He had to find a way out. He could not allow his friend to die here and be sucked dry by that fell creature.

Something scraped across the rocks, close by, like the side of a leather boot. "Tobe?"

Was the wrythen dragging him away? Rix sheathed his sword

and began to crawl across the piled rubble, feeling all around. Another scrape came, this time from his left. He lunged and caught the shank of a wiry, hairy leg. Tobry must be unconscious.

Rix tugged gently. A powerful return jerk nearly pulled the leg out of his hand. He took hold with both hands, prepared to give an almighty heave. No! If the wrythen had Tobry by the head, he might break his neck.

Tobry moaned. His boots thumped a tattoo on the rubble and his left hand blinked several times, as though the uncanny light was being forced back into him. How was the wrythen doing that? Rix squinted into the darkness, which was thickest directly above his friend's head. It seemed to be forming paired whirlpools over Tobry's eyes, spinning down as if the wrythen was pulling itself towards his skull.

Or reaching into it. What for? What was it doing to him?

Another blink from Tobry's hand revealed steam wisping up from his eyes. He convulsed, thudded back on the rubble, and Rix knew that if Tobry wasn't dead now, he soon would be—*or worse than dead.* He wrenched out his sword and thrust several feet above Tobry's head, praying that the ancient enchantments on the blade would turn the black whirlpools aside.

A shock almost tore the sword from his hand, then every muscle in Rix's arm began to spasm and the weapon flailed about wildly. The wrythen reappeared as a bare outline. Rix caught the hilt in his free hand, controlled it, and lunged at its middle.

But the blade dipped of its own accord and struck much lower. The wrythen lit up from the top of its head to the stumps of its shins and a thin scream issued from its gaping mouth, as if the blade had carved real flesh and smashed live bone. The sword's tip had passed through its leg at the point of one spectral stump and wisps of its ethereal substance were separating from the wound, dripping silently onto the rubble.

In the eerie light, Tobry's mouth was opening and closing, his eyes fluttering. An incoherent moan issued from low down in his throat, *n-n-n-n.* What had it done to him?

Rix drew back and was preparing to strike again when the wrythen withdrew half a yard. Its eyes were huge and staring, its plasm quivering. Could it be afraid of him? Then it spoke in a rusty creak, as though it had not used its true voice for centuries.

"That—sword. Where . . . ?"

It wasn't Rix the wrythen feared—it was the *sword*. But why? *Heroes must fight to preserve the race.* A notorious quote, Tobry had said. Rix wished he had paid attention to his history tutors, and that he had allowed Tobry to test the blade.

Or did the wrythen fear the enchantment against magery? Rix swiped at it.

The wrythen pointed a finger at his chest. "Heart—sunder!"

The pain in his heart was like the flesh being torn in two. A molten ache seared up into his head, accompanied by a sick dizziness that drained the strength from him, and his sword arm went so weak that the sword fell to the rubble. The pain in his heart grew; it was going to burst inside his chest; he was about to die.

A hard hand clenched around his calf, fell away, clenched again. "Heart-heal," croaked Tobry, "heart-heal, *heart-heal*!" and the bursting pain and icy sickness eased.

"Heart—sunder!" repeated the wrythen. This time the finger wavered.

Rix's heart gave another throb, though the edge of the pain was dull, bearable now. He picked up the sword, feeling so drained that he needed both hands to lift it, and shoved it at the wrythen's middle. Its plasm recoiled from the blade in all directions, leaving a hole where its belly had been.

"Upstart, who—are—you?" it said hoarsely.

He should have kept his mouth shut, used the advantage the sword had given him and hacked the spectre to pieces, but Rix had always been better at fighting than thinking and the insult rankled. He was proud of his House and his ancestors who, in little more than a hundred years, had built Ricinus from nothing to the greatest fortune in the land. Let no man call him upstart. Let no stinking wrythen think that House Ricinus was afraid to speak its name.

"I am Rix," he said. "Only child of the noble House Ricinus."

All motion ceased. The wisps, clumps of nebulosity and enigmatic darknesses of which the wrythen was made hung in the air in a watchful stillness. An alarming stillness. What was it doing? Why wasn't it speaking?

Rixium Ricinus!

The words weren't spoken this time, the voice was in his mind again. Why the switch?

"Do you know me?" said Rix.

Again that elongated pause. Rix gained the impression that the wrythen was wrestling with a dilemma.

I have not seen you since you were a boy.

The marrow-freezing cold crept upwards and he began to fear that giving the wrythen his name had been a fatal mistake, but he kept his voice steady. "I've never seen you before."

No, you haven't.

Yet the way the wrythen spoke was troublingly familiar.

"The—sword—is—yours?" it said aloud.

Rix's unease swelled. "Handed down since forgotten times. In ages past, this sword was the making of our House."

"Traitor's blade," cried the wrythen. "Liar's blade. *Oathbreaker's blade.*"

"It's a noble weapon," Rix cried. "I've—"

"You belong to me. Put down the sword and come."

"I ... don't ... belong ..." Rix said thickly.

He was bending to lay his sword on the floor when he realised what was happening. How could it have commanded him so easily? How could he have obeyed? He tried to say, "Be damned," but all that emerged was a grunt.

Rix gathered every ounce of will and managed to say, "No," though it did not convince him.

"Yesssss," said the wrythen.

Without appearing to move, it had halved the distance between them. Its right hand shot towards Rix's eyes, shimmying through the air the way it had gone for Tobry. It was trying to get inside Rix's head, and instinct rose up to defend what his will could not.

He reacted instantly, with the shattering violence and precision that made him such a ferocious warrior. Ducking the hand, he swung his sword out then brought it straight up so it passed up through the wrythen from crotch to chest.

This time he was too quick for it. The enchanted blade parted something too soft to be living flesh yet more solid than any shade, then began to shake so violently that Rix could barely hold it. Tobry jerked as if struck by lightning, let out a thin cry and steam gushed from his mouth, nose and eyes.

The wrythen's plasm closed around the blade but instantly recoiled, hissing like hot metal quenched in ice. Frost ran along the blade and Rix smiled grimly. The enchantment had done some good after all—no ordinary sword could have touched such a creature.

Both hands shot for Rix's eyes this time. He jerked the sword out, shook a crust of black ice off it, drew back and swung hard for the region of its heart. The blade went straight through the wrythen, bisecting it, and its halves fluttered in the air for several seconds before it reformed. He swung higher, carving through something more solid, *sssss*. A hot shock ran up his arm, his hand went numb and again the sword slipped from his fingers. This time Tobry was directly beneath it.

Rix barely caught the hilt in time, took it in both hands and slashed across the wrythen's neck, then back. The numbing shocks were not so bad now; he was able to hang onto the blade as the wrythen's fading segments hissed down the slope of the tunnel, stopped twenty yards away and slowly began to creep together. Had he hurt it? He thought so, for it seemed weaker and was taking much longer to reform than before. But had he done it any serious damage? Unlikely.

"House—Ricinus," it ground out, as though committing the name to memory.

As clearly as if rays of were-light had painted the scene on the wall of the cavern, Rix saw the ice leviathan of his nightmares rolling over the palace walls, crushing them to dust and his people to paste. The cold crept to his throat. What if it wasn't a nightmare, but a premonition, like past scenes he had painted from his imagination that had come true? Why, why had he come up here? The wrythen had nearly taken control of him, and it gave the impression that it already owned him.

Taking Tobry under the arms, Rix dragged him away, keeping

well clear of the fallen caitsthe, though he felt sure it was dead. Further down the tunnel, the segments of the wrythen merged, though it did not come after him. How long until it would? As he heaved Tobry onto his shoulder, his right ankle, which he had managed to ignore during the battle, flared with pain.

He staggered to the entrance, losing sight of the wrythen when he turned the corner, and carried Tobry out past the basin with its perilous water, through the illusion into a leaden gloom, and onto the rubble slope.

"How the hell are we going to get home?" he said quietly.

The wind had dropped and snow was falling so thickly that he could barely make out the vine thicket. Leather and Beetle would be in the boulder-strewn clearing on the other side, assuming they had not run off. Or been eaten.

"How are you feeling?" said Rix.

No reply. The top of Tobry's head was bloody, presumably from being struck by a rock, and yellow, oozing blisters were clustered around his eyes, nose and mouth where the wrythen had tried to enter. He had been out for a long time. Too long. After such a blow, sometimes people faded away and not even the healers knew why.

"You were right about the weather," he said, talking for the company. "You're always right and I should have listened."

He was dragging Tobry through the vine thicket when a jackal let out a barking howl. Tobry's unconscious body twitched, his eyes shot open, staring straight up, then his blistered eyelids shuddered shut.

Rix gripped his friend's shoulder. For the cry of a jackal shifter to break through Tobry's unconsciousness, his terror of them must be monumental. And I led you up here, he thought. I pressured you to stay even when the danger became obvious, and you put your fears to one side because you can never let a friend down.

"Sorry, Tobe. Some friend I am."

Every second's delay was a ticking heartbeat further from survival. Rix crawled along the low passage through the vine thicket, heaving Tobry behind him. If a single jackal shifter attacked in here, they would both die.

There was no sign of the horses when he reached the lower side of the vine thicket, and panic flared. Rix fought it down. One thing at a time. He propped Tobry against a tree and checked him all over. The skull beneath the bloody bruise felt sound, yet his eye sockets were almost black beneath the weeping blisters and his eyelids were hot. What had the wrythen been up to?

Tobry's pupils were dilated, though at least they were the same size. If it was only a mild concussion, he would recover with no more than a bad headache. But if the concussion was severe, he could die.

And if the wrythen had done something to him, something unnatural? Then the Gods help him, for Rix would not be able to.

CHAPTER 24

The wrythen tasted fear on the ice-laden air. He felt it quaking the bones of his native land, heard it in the cracked howling from the shifter pens in his doubly coiled germinerium.

His form shifted and churned. After that savage dissection yesterday, he could not settle into his true shape, and his phantom stumps ached worse than they had when his feet had been freshly severed.

But that was nothing to his terror of the accursed sword whose magery he could never forget. The very sword with which that Herovian brute had hacked off his feet all those centuries ago, when the wrythen had still been a man.

He had sworn revenge on the five who had been involved, and as a wrythen had taken it. The sword had been lost long ago; he had thought it destroyed. Now, at the moment he was poised to take back Cythe, it appeared again, wielded by a warrior like an enemy risen from the dead—Rixium, of the House of Ricinus. The very boy whose nightmares the wrythen had shaped via the heatstone all these years. A boy now grown to a formidable man, and where had he found that vile sword?

In desperation, the wrythen had attempted to command Rixium via the compulsion inside him, and it should have worked. Years of the whispering nightmares had almost broken him, yet with the sword in hand he had proven unexpectedly resistant. The sword had worked its cursed magery yet again, one that the wrythen could not defeat, for neither magery nor sword were native to Hightspall and he did not understand either.

Determination had always been the wrythen's great strength, but the old self-doubt was creeping back. Had he made a fatal blunder? He hovered, tugging restlessly on his fingers. There were many things he could do, though he could not choose between them. He no longer had confidence in his own judgement.

Seeking the only comfort available to him, he floated to the top of his cavern, then recoiled. All one hundred and seven figures in his ancestor gallery were roaring, *Desist!*

The king is supposed to heal *the land, not corrupt it*, spat scar-faced Ruris. He had been the greatest master of spagyre, the healing art, that had ever lived, yet Ruris had refused to use it to heal himself. *You have profaned what you should have held sacred.*

At thought of what he had done in his spagyrium, the wrythen flushed. His memory library offered no surcease, either. It only reminded him of all that had been lost. And as for his germinerium—one of the creations caged there gave even him the horrors.

It's the only way to ensure our people's survival, he said coldly. *The enemy bitterly resent the price they must pay for heatstones. They will soon decide to take them for themselves, using their profane magery.*

An army of a hundred thousand would founder on the defences of Cython, said the shade of Rovena the Wise. Her long white hair was in constant motion, like feathers drifting in a breeze.

Remember the tactics they used in the Secret War? What if they poison the streams that Cython's Siphons draw from? Or seed anthrax into the air breathers? Or empty wagon loads of brimstone into one of the tunnels and set fire to it? They could wipe our people out in a day. We have to strike first.

The wrythen had not drawn breath in two millennia, but suddenly he was choking on the horror of his people's annihilation. It could not be endured.

Every man has his allotted span, said Errek First-King. *Every people, too. If Cython's time is up, let it go.*

I can't let my people go, he cried. The thought was pure agony, the worst he had ever felt. *I won't!*

Better they vanish than you continue this monstrous sacrilege, thundered Ruris. *How dare you distil alkoyl from our holy Abysm! How dare you perform that profane nucleation spell in the place of sacred dissolution?*

The wrythen hurtled away until their ghostly recriminations could no longer be heard. There is a way. Focus!

But he was too agitated, too afraid that the Herovians were rising again. Only one remedy remained, one he doled out to himself grudgingly lest it lose its effect. A hundred and forty years had passed since he'd last resorted to it.

The wrythen slipped into the sacred Abysm, then down, down to the glittering speck that floated far below. The speck became a statue carved from black opal, the figure of a great warrior contorted in bone-snapping torment.

As the wrythen looked upon the remains of his ancient enemy, he felt the tension ease, the self-doubt fade. The warrior had been a tyrant everyone had thought invincible; he had torn Cython apart. Yet the wrythen had brought him down and frozen him in perpetual agony.

As the man, so too his people. Only vengeance could cleanse the tainted land.

Calmly now, he returned to his chamber. Time to get on with it. But first—Rix.

The nightmares embedded in Rix's heatstone had implanted the required orders, guilts and fears so he would obey when the call came, but the wrythen, unable to travel into Palace Ricinus, had no insights into either Rix's adult mind or his character.

He had seemed slow-witted yet, after the way he had dealt with the caitsthe, the wrythen could deny neither Rix's courage nor the power of his sword arm. Indeed, there was much to admire in him, and in olden times they might well have become friends. But Rix could become a great leader of men, a deadly and unpredictable opponent.

Had the wrythen created his own nemesis? Could he still use Rix, or must he destroy him? The wrythen's plan depended on surprise. Rix must not get back to Caulderon with his news and his deadly blade, nor the other, far more clever man, that wielder of foul magery whose mind and gift the wrythen had gone so close to taking.

Should he send shifters after Rix and cut him down? The man was exhausted, injured and burdened with the unconscious friend he had refused to abandon, which revealed a nobility the wrythen had not expected in the enemy.

Killing him was the easy solution, but without Rix the wrythen would be forced to rely on Deroe, who had betrayed him thrice already. And Deroe was growing stronger by the day.

No, Rix must be back at the palace when the host girl was brought to the cellar. Once there, the compulsion would drive him down to do the bloody business . . .

The wrythen faltered. The struggle had left him desperately short of *quessence* and he had no safe way of getting more. It was all he could do to hold his severed plasm together. He would never find the strength to get to the cellar and do what must be done.

Wait! If he plundered the gift of Rix's friend, Tobry, it would last him for weeks. And once he had the fifth nuclix he would cut Rix down, then topple him and the cursed sword down the Hellish Conduit to be consumed by the Engine far below.

Three packs of jackal shifters hunted out in the valley. And shifters, being his own creatures, could be commanded from a mile away. He sent a compulsion to the leader of the closest pack.

Bring the smaller man here. Let the big one go. No feeding.

The wrythen headed across to the linked spirals of his germinerium. The next task should have been a week and a half away, for he did not have quite enough alkoyl to complete *The Consolation of Vengeance*. Initiating the plan without completing the book was reckless, but Rix's escape had changed everything. And he dared not contact his faithful servant in Cython again. The matriarchs must never know about him.

After settling into the frigid depths, the wrythen stopped outside a cage whose bars were made of green olivine. Within was a shifting creature, part shadow, part flesh, the greatest horror he had ever shaped. Even from this distance he could feel the pressure of its infected psyche. The despair it radiated was eating at his own resolve.

It wasn't ready. Its mind was only half formed, making it dangerous even to a wrythen and difficult to control, but it was all he had. He opened the cage.

Hold out your hand, the wrythen said softly, and the facinore obeyed. He had not been sure it would. He focused on the creature's dark palm, then seared his message there.

Run to Cython, he said. *Seek out the matriarchs and show them your hand.*

The facinore loped off, its open right hand swinging. Even when it was fifty yards away the wrythen could read the blazing letters there.

MAKE WAR.

CHAPTER 25

The sunstone did not fall.

The weight was crushing Tali against the rail, preventing her from drawing breath. She shook herself frantically, trying to dislodge the stone. The guards were only one flight above her and could reach her in a leap. She had to get rid of it now.

She gave an almighty heave. The sunstone slid from its pouch, rasped across the back of her head and fell.

When the weight left her back an even heavier weight slipped from her heart. She watched it plummet towards Tinyhead and, momentarily, all her cares were gone. The enemy would kill her but at least she had ended her mother's betrayer.

Then the blue stone around Tinyhead's neck emitted an angry blink of light and he moved so fast she lost sight of him.

"Look out!" yelled the guard above. She heard him scrambling up again, desperate to get to the outside door.

"Get down!" shrieked another guard. "Cover yourselves."

Used to obeying instantly, Tali scrunched herself up against the wall of the landing and yanked the leather pouch over her as the sunstone hit the steps far below and smashed. There came an immense flash, so bright that she could see it through the leather, and white rays seared up the shaft. It was as bad as the time the pyrites calciner had exploded, punching a hole through a small floatillery and scalding twenty slaves to death with superheated steam, save that this cataclysm took place in silence empty as a vacuum.

Her head throbbed and a single, pure note sounded in her inner ear, like the highest note of a clarinet. She did not want it to stop, she yearned for it as much as any Pale had ever yearned for Hightspall, but it died away in a little upturn, like an unanswered question.

In the silence that followed, the bracelet burned around her ankle as if all those pointed spikes had turned red-hot, then tinkled and fell off. Her slave mark turned to ice embedded under the skin.

The shaft shook so violently that Tali's head cracked against the wall. Scalding reds and yellows whirled and tumbled, then pain screamed through her skull as it had the night before last, when she had come of age. Shattered rock hammered at the underside of the landing, glancing off the rails and skidding up along the walls. A whirlwind of dusty air carried the pungency of overheated stone and the stench of burning flesh. She scrunched against the wall, sure she was going to die. Gravel rained onto the leather pouch, pressing it against her, and it was burning hot.

Finally it ended and the eerie silence resumed. She heard no shouts, no cries of pain, no sound at all. She shoved the pouch off and the thick leather was deeply charred on the outside, though not as charred as she would have been without it. So that's why the slaves were so afraid of dropping a sunstone, why the edges of the steps had been glassy, why the stone at the bottom was soot-stained. A churning power lay at each sunstone's core and, when liberated, it was deadly.

As she stood up on shaky knees, a long object, black and smoking and trailing a burnt meat stench, fell past and smashed below her. She caught at the rail. Her head felt so peculiar, hot and bruised, that it was a struggle to focus, but she had to make sure of Tinyhead. She could not see him. Surely he must be dead.

It was her chance to escape, though she would have to be quick—the cataclysm would bring armed troops running from all directions, thinking Cython was under attack. If she could slip by the guards stationed outside, she might get away.

She hesitated. After the sunstone implosion, and Tinyhead's rib-shattering blow, could Mimoy still be alive? Tali could not see the base of the shaft for dust. There was no way to tell without going down, nor any time to do so. And the wicked old woman had planned to use Tali—only a fool would risk everything to check on her. In Cython it was every slave for herself.

But the Pale had been slaves for the past thousand years *because* the enemy had pitted them against each other, and they could only survive the coming war by working together. What's more, Mimoy had been struck down trying to help. Tali, imagining what it must have cost the old woman hobbling all this way on her ruined feet, could not abandon her.

Her head throbbed and a series of coloured patterns drifted through her inner eye, as if she were looking ever deeper into a maze of brightly coloured loops and whorls that were continuously expanding around her. Tali shook herself and the colours faded, though now she felt a tight fullness in her head, a build-up of pressure that longed for release. She squeezed her head between her palms and the pressure eased, though it did not entirely disappear.

Covering her nose, she felt her way down the gravel-littered steps. On nearing the bottom, she put her hand down on something that crunched and crumbled—her hand had broken through into a chest turned to charcoal. Tali gasped and sprang aside, shaking off sticky red char and shuddering violently. Tinyhead? No, the body wasn't big enough.

In her brief life she had seen more than enough dead people: many killed in ghastly work accidents; a few, like Mia, executed by the guards; suicides hanging in their cells or twisted in convulsions from eating Sprite Caps; an occasional woman killed in a fight over a man; her mother murdered in the cellar. But she never got used to it. Only minutes ago this object had been a living, breathing guard. Her enemy, and yet a man, and she had done this to him.

She had not intended to harm anyone save Tinyhead but, she rationalised, the Cythonians would kill her without a qualm. To survive, save her country and punish her mother's killers she must be prepared to kill them.

She did not have to like it, though.

Grains of bloody charcoal clung to her fingers. She wiped them on her robes, scrubbed her fingers with the coarse cloth, and continued down. There was no sign of Tinyhead and she dared to hope, if he had taken the full force of the sunstone implosion, that it had burned him to ash.

Tali put her head through the archway. The visibility was better beyond the shaft and she saw all six guards scattered around the loading station, unburnt but unconscious. There was no sign of the slaves, who must have stampeded back towards the Empound. Why hadn't they been knocked out? Why hadn't she? And how long before the guards came to?

"Mimoy?" she said urgently.

Tinyhead's blow had driven the old woman diagonally through the archway, which had sheltered her from the blast, though she lay like a heap of bones, twisted toes hooked, fingers locked around her cane. The only colour on her was the blood on her shrunken lips. She looked like a bald, dead crow, save for her eyes, which were open, glinting.

As Tali bent over the old woman, a ray of golden-yellow light lit the wall above her head, reflecting off something in the defence maze. Lantern light from Banj's runners? No, the light was the wrong colour, too warm.

"What—you do?" Mimoy cawed.

"Tried to kill Tinyhead with my sunstone ... but it imploded. They're coming. We've got to go."

The old woman's mouth stretched into a grin, or a grimace. "Take me home to die."

"All right." Tali took a deep breath. She almost did not speak, for it felt wrong to bargain at a time like this, but she had to know. "And in return, you'll tell me who killed my mother."

Tali could not tell whether the glister in the crow eyes was fury or glee. "Once you've dug my grave."

Tali did not know what to say to that. She nodded stiffly.

Though Mimoy weighed no more than an armload of sticks, it hurt to lift her. Tali was at the entrance to the shaft when another golden ray caressed her cheek and she heard a faint, wrenching groan. She turned back towards the maze.

"What are you doing?" grated Mimoy.

"Someone's hurt. It sounds like a child."

"Stupid girl! It's a trap. Take me up, I must die in Hightspall."

Doing otherwise was madness, but Tali could not turn away from a child in pain. Ignoring Mimoy's raucous protests, then a series of stinging blows from the cane, she limped through the maze. The light was reflecting from the polished clangours, the golden flashes growing brighter the further she went, and shortly Tali saw a slave girl lying on the floor at the far end of the maze, convulsing. It was Rannilt, the water carrier.

"What's the matter with her?" whispered Tali.

Rannilt's head snapped backwards, her back arched, she groaned, then light fountained from her eyes, mouth, ears, nostrils and fingertips. A clean, beautiful light, so soft and warm that as it fell on Tali's face it was like being stroked with golden feathers.

"Sunstone woke a gift she never knew she had." The old woman's voice was stronger now, and Mimoy dug her splintered nails into Tali's left ear. "Go! She's not worth a turd in a teacup."

Suppressing an urge to slap the vile old woman, Tali prised Mimoy's nails out, set her down and crouched beside the slave girl.

"Rannilt," she whispered, "you've got to stop the light."

The girl's eyes fluttered and the light brightened until it was dazzling. Tali checked up the dark tunnel, her stomach fluttering. The enemy must be close by now. They would see the light hundreds of yards away but Tali would not see them. What was she supposed to do? The fullness in her head was growing ever tighter. She could hardly think for it.

"Brat can't control it," said Mimoy. "Leave her."

"But when the enemy sees she's got the gift, they'll kill her."

"Are you weak, like your mother?"

"She *wasn't* weak," Tali hissed. "She was brave and kind."

"Aren't you bitter that she left you an orphan? That she failed to teach you magery? That she left you to the mercy of Tinyhead?"

"She loved me. She gave everything for me."

"She taught you nothing," Mimoy spat, "then abandoned you."

It was the wrong thing to say. Tali lifted the girl to a sitting position. "Well, I'm not abandoning Rannilt."

"They kill Pale every day, and we'll be next if you don't get moving. Carry me up!"

Rannilt's huge eyes fixed on Tali. The girl smiled and gave a little sigh and snuggled up to her, as if to say, I'm safe now.

When they had first met, Rannilt had said, with such childlike, wistful hope, *you could be my new mother*. Tali's eyes misted. She checked down the tunnel, her toes clenching. What was she supposed to do? She couldn't carry them both.

Mimoy whacked Tali around the ankles with her cane. "The little scutter's worthless. Take–me–up!"

Distantly, someone swore in the guttural Cythonian tongue. Tali jumped.

Mimoy gave her another whack. "They're coming."

Tali looked down at Rannilt's bruised legs, the knees covered in scabs, and her heart went out to the skinny little girl. Though taking her would surely lead to disaster, she could not leave her behind to be killed like a cockroach. But how could she abandon the old woman to a worse fate?

"Chuck her away," hissed Mimoy, delivering a hail of blows to Tali's backside and right hip, from the floor.

"If you're strong enough to beat me, you're strong enough to walk up by yourself," Tali snapped, for the blows were hard enough to bruise.

"I've got five broken ribs, you little bitch."

"They don't seem to be hindering you." The vicious old cow had probably healed them already. Tali picked Rannilt up. "Put your arms around my neck."

With another sigh, the girl cuddled against Tali. She was shorter than Mimoy, but heavier. Mimoy dealt Tali another ferocious blow to the buttocks then levered herself to her feet and her cane rap-tapped away.

A set of robes lay on the floor. Tali, remembering her mother's warnings about sunburn, wrapped them around the girl. Rannilt convulsed and more golden light burst from her, so brightly that it illuminated a group of creeping figures a hundred yards down the tunnel.

"Enemy," Rannilt moaned, clinging so tightly that her arm was cutting off Tali's air. "Coming to kill us."

"Foul, forbidden magery!" a guard bellowed. "Stop them."

Tali lurched through the maze, knowing she couldn't possibly beat the Cythonians up the shaft while carrying Rannilt. Why had she wasted so much time?

As she climbed the first step, she realised how weak she was—the strength Mimoy's earlier spell had given her was gone and she ached from the base of her skull to the soles of her feet. There was no sign of the guards who had been up above, and she dared to hope that they had also been knocked out. If they were waiting outside—no, one thing at a time. Just get to the top.

Mimoy was halfway up, her cane flashing. Despite her twisted feet and broken ribs she was moving faster than Tali.

"You all right, Rannilt?" Tali gasped. "Can't carry you much fur-ther."

The girl jerked. Again the golden light poured from her and she made a rasping noise in her throat. Tali forced against the bone-ache, crunched across a rubble-littered landing and up the next set of steps.

The pressure in her head was building; once more those coloured patterns whorled and looped their way across her inner eye, con-fusing her. Her foot missed the next step and she stumbled and nearly dropped the girl. The enemy was close behind. Their lantern beams were shining through the archway and Tali could hear them speaking in low voices.

Why hadn't they come through? They must be checking the guards at the loading station, trying to work out what had hap-pened here and wondering how someone could have knocked them all out without leaving a mark, probably fearing it had been done with magery. Their fear was her friend. How could she use it against them? She had to have her gift, and the wilder and more dangerous the better.

"Mimoy?" Tali called. "Wait, I need—"

"You chose that worthless brat over me," Mimoy spat. "Beg her for aid."

"I'm sorry. Please, help me with . . ." she was too indoctrinated to say it aloud. The best she could do was whisper, " . . . my *magery*."

"Don't need you any more." Mimoy tossed her head, her white hair floating up like strands of silk, and continued.

A handful of Cythonians edged through the archway into the shaft and stood there, gaping at the smashed steps, the rubble, the greasy charcoal that had once been a man. Tali had six flights to go and if she had to lug Rannilt all the way she would never make it.

Then they looked up and saw the golden light dribbling from Rannilt's dangling hand.

"Aieee!" a woman cried. It was Orlyk, her face still grey-pink and bloated from the puffball spores. From a belt pouch she withdrew a crimson, chymical death-lash. Yellow bands circled each end. It was a foot long and as thick through as her pudgy thumb. "Forbidden magery. The Pale filth spit in Khirrik-ai's face. Kill them—"

A man cut her off, pushed to the front and Tali recognised the compact, muscular figure of Overseer Banj. She was not surprised to see him. It was his responsibility to find any slave from the grottoes who ran.

At heart he was a kindly man, to those who obeyed the rules, and Tali had always felt that he liked her. But Banj was not a thinker and, as Mia's death had shown, he was quick to enforce Cython's rigid rules at need. He could show an escaping slave no mercy. And perhaps he was doing the matriarchs' work for them. Tali was going to die without ever knowing why she was *the one*.

"Slave," he said to Tali in the voice that every Pale was conditioned to obeying instantly. "Come down."

CHAPTER 26

"The devil you doin'?" Tobry slurred. "Put me down."

"You're not up to it," said Rix, heaving him higher on his shoulder. "You've been out for half an hour."

"Just restin'."

Rix lowered Tobry onto his feet. He fell down.

"Told you so."

"Noble of you to point it out." Tobry lay on his back in the snow and momentarily his pupils widened until his eyes went black. He shivered and looked away. "Thanks."

Rix's chill deepened. Whatever the wrythen had done to him, it was Rix's fault. He had pressured Tobry to come up here, ignored his arguments and overridden his fears. Some friend!

"What for?"

"Getting me out."

"Any time," said Rix absently, keeping watch up the slope.

It was mid-morning now but the gloom was thickening, the snow falling more heavily than ever, and miserably cold. Now the action was over, the chill was creeping into him. The fresh snow was untracked and there was no way of telling where the horses had gone, which could prove fatal.

A branch cracked somewhere behind him, then he heard a tearing rustle as though something big was forcing its way through the vine thicket. A jackal yelped, its hoarse call identifying it as a shifter. And jackals never hunted alone.

Tobry was the most strong-willed man Rix knew, so what was it about shifters that terrified him so? Rix heaved him over his shoulder, then put him down again. It was too late to run.

"That's twice you've saved my life today," said Tobry.

"Don't keep on about things. You're worse than my mother."

"How did you get past the caitsthe, anyway?"

"Later!" Rix snapped.

"What's the matter?"

"Jackal shifters, coming through the vine thicket." Even so, he had to ask the question. "What did the wrythen do to you? Your eyes were steaming."

Tobry shuddered and one foot kicked involuntarily. "Don't want to think about it. Where are the nags?"

"Ran off," said Rix. "Can't think why."

"Didn't they come when you called them?"

"Leather doesn't come when called."

Tobry put two fingers into his mouth and let out a whistle that shook snow off the twigs of the blood-barks. There came a frenzy of barking and yelping from upslope.

Rix helped Tobry to his feet. "Your face looks like a warthog's arse."

"It never was my fortune." Tobry swayed and had to grab Rix's arm. "Skull feels like it's packed with needlebush."

Something crashed through the trees, sending snowballs rolling down the slope towards them, growing as they came. Rix pulled Tobry behind a tree and watched them pass. Then a brindled, scarred cur loped out from the trees to their left. The jackal shifter was no bigger than a dog, though heavier in the shoulders, and its jaws were massive.

Tobry tried to make a joke, "Any last words?" but choked.

Rix shoved him back against the trunk, put Tobry's sword in his hand and drew his own. "Stay on your feet."

"Never would have thought of that."

Putting most of his weight on his good ankle, Rix stood in front of Tobry, sweeping the titane blade from side to side. The cur's eyes did not follow it, which was worrying.

"Whistle the nags again, Tobe."

As he did so, three more jackals appeared on the left, then another four to the right. They moved in slowly, black tongues lolling, yellow eyes focused on the same point—the tree trunk. No, *on Tobry*.

Rix's alarm swelled. Their first instinct should be self-preservation, so why weren't they watching his sword? He could only think of one reason: their instincts had been overridden by the shade that had sent them, and he wanted Tobry dead.

Rix took a half step backwards, trying to shield him.

"What the hell are you doing?" said Tobry. "Nearly jammed my blade through your kidneys."

"We're in trouble, Tobe."

"They only want me. Clear out—I'll be all right."

Rix ignored that. The jackals were showing no signs of shifting, which was bad—unlike caitsthes, they were more formidable in the animal form. Cowardly creatures that they were, they only shifted when their victims were helpless.

The brindled leader darted in, snapped at Rix's sword and retreated. The others on the left did the same, trying to draw him away from Tobry. He hacked at them but they were too fast; all he managed was a cut to the black nose of the third.

He saw it from the corner of an eye—the rest of the pack attacking from the right—and whirled, battle instinct guiding his hand. The blade made a muffled thump as it took the first cur's head off and cleaved through the snow into hard ground.

Rix wrenched it out and was going for the second jackal when another, unseen, snapped its jaws around his calf and held him. He froze. It hadn't broken the skin, but if it did, and shifter saliva got into the wound, it might *turn* him. Its blood definitely would.

The other jackals could have leapt on Rix and taken him down, but they were silently watching.

"What the blazes are they up to?" he said aloud.

Rix dared not move. He could kill the jackal with a blow, though before he did its jaws would have torn through his calf into the bone and, with such a crippling wound, the pack would soon finish him.

And where was the brindled leader?

There was a scuffle behind him and Tobry hit the ground, dropping his sword into the snow. The pack leader had leapt on him from around the trunk, pulling him off his feet and cracking his head against it.

As Rix swung around, the jaws tightened, the teeth passing

through his trews and pricking the skin. Why didn't the jackal bite? Why was it just holding him?

"Tobe?" he called, but Tobry was too dazed to answer.

Only one thing could be preventing them from indulging their natural viciousness. The beasts must be acting on the wrythen's orders and it wanted them alive. Rix could do nothing to save them. Only Tobry could, but how to get through to him?

"*TOBE!*"

Tobry grunted. Two more jackals sank their teeth into his collar and began to drag him up the slope, pulling his weight easily across the snow.

"You're letting me down, Tobe," said Rix. "You owe me." What a lie that was.

"Ugh?"

"I saved your miserable life. You could at least do the same for me."

"Can't," Tobry groaned.

"Useless bastard! Use your damned magery."

Tobry's limp fingers stiffened. He raised his head and managed to focus on Rix, then the jackal with its jaws around his calf. Pressing one hand against the elbrot in his pocket, Tobry pointed the other. With a muffled crack, snow blasted out of a trench stretching from his fingers to the jackal and every tooth in its head shattered. Its jaws snapped convulsively on Rix's calf, which was like being bitten with a mouthful of gravel, then it ran, howling.

Another jackal came at Rix, and another, but blood-fury was driving him now and he bisected both with the one stroke. He leapt at another, spearing it through the chest. Rix whirled and, refusing to admit any pain from his ankle, took a hopping bound towards Tobry, who was holding his head with both hands. Snatching up Tobry's fallen sword, Rix hurled it left-handed past his ear and through the skull of the brindled pack leader.

It fell dead, and immediately the pressure eased. The remaining two jackals retreated several feet, stinking saliva dripping from their black tongues, then ran. A horse whinnied, there was a gruesome thud, then the first jackal came flying through the air, a mangled mess.

Beetle, Tobry's black-faced nag, poked its head out from between the trees. Leather was behind it.

"I told *you* so," said Tobry feebly. "Put me in the saddle, there's a good fellow—"

Rix heaved Tobry onto his saddle and slapped Beetle on the left flank. "Go!"

Beetle bolted. Rix wrenched Tobry's sword from the jackal's skull, dragged himself into Leather's saddle and followed. A second pack of jackals came loping down, then stopped, their tongues lolling.

"What happened to that liqueur?" said Tobry later, as they passed the entrance to the Catacombs of the Kings and all the upside-down heads. Rix, who might have died and been reborn in the past hours, no longer thought the insult a good idea.

He took the flask from the saddlebags and passed it across. Tobry took a deep swig and offered it back.

Rix shook his head. "I've never felt less like a drink in my life."

"I've never wanted one more." Tobry took another healthy swig. "How's your head?"

"Better. Ankle?"

"No better."

After a while, Tobry said, "That didn't go so well."

"Tell me about it."

"Well," Tobry was trying to sound his normal self and almost pulling it off, "we've no idea what the wrythen is up to but we know it's bad, the snow is getting thicker by the second, you've got one day less to finish the portrait, Lady Ricinus will be apoplectic by now—"

"I meant, *don't* tell me about it," Rix snarled.

"And to cap it off," Tobry continued, "you came all this way to kill something big, and haven't."

He didn't know the caitsthe was dead and there wasn't time to explain. "I still might!" Rix brandished his sword.

Tobry chuckled and urged Beetle on.

Rix followed, trying to make sense of all that had happened. Something had changed the moment the wrythen had recognised his sword. Where had it come from? *Traitor's blade. Liar's blade.*

Oathbreaker's blade, he had said, and suddenly the attack had become personal, vengeful. He wanted revenge for an injury done in the past, by some previous owner of this sword.

And he had committed House Ricinus to memory.

CHAPTER 27

Tali was frozen to the step. Though she knew Banj was going to kill her, obedience was so ingrained that it was a struggle to ignore his direct order. But she had to fight it.

"I'm not letting Rannilt be killed by that vicious toad," she muttered, avoiding Banj's stare. No, she had to be stronger. She must openly defy him—for her own sake, nothing less would do. Raising her head, Tali steadied her shaking knees, looked Banj in the eye and said firmly, "I refuse. Damn the matriarchs, damn Cython and damn you. I'm *the one!*"

Banj's handsome features registered shock at the defiance, perhaps more so at the secret she should have known nothing about. Purple crept up his cheeks and he glanced over his shoulder. "Archers?"

"Not here yet." Orlyk waved the crimson and yellow death-lash. "But with this I can sever her backbone from twenty feet away."

"Are you her overseer?" Banj said stiffly.

Orlyk bent her head in angry submission.

Banj drew the Living Blade with which he had beheaded Mia. Red-tinged rainbows wavered around its transparent annulus and it began to keen gently as he lumbered up the steps. Tali retreated, knowing he would catch her before the top. Rannilt convulsed again and light blazed out of her in all directions. Tali could barely hold the jerking girl; it was all she could do to keep climbing.

"Not now, Rannilt, please." Tali hugged her tightly, hoping to overcome her inner torment, but Rannilt did not respond.

Tali looked up desperately. Despite Mimoy's earlier words, she was waiting at the doors, watching. The pressure in Tali's head was almost unbearable now, and every flash from Rannilt's fingers set off such a whirling of the coloured lights in her inner eye that she had to clutch at the rail to hold herself up.

"Stop, slave!" Banj, only two flights below her now, was taking three steps to her one.

"Mimoy!" Tali cried. "Help me."

Mimoy did not reply.

"Please don't kill Rannilt," Tali begged Banj. "She didn't ask for the gift. It just came to her."

Banj was inexorable. "Magery is forbidden, obscene, and an abomination."

"But she's an innocent little girl."

"Hightspall's magery was conceived in treachery and birthed in blood. No one bearing its taint is innocent."

"Kill her and it makes you a child-murderer."

Banj's eyes slid away from hers, but he said, "All those bearing the taint must be put down. It's our law and I swore to uphold it."

"It proves you're nothing but savages!" she shouted. "Your ancestors were too gutless to fight Hightspall so they enslaved its children."

Banj's dark eyes flashed. "Oh, we fought," he said softly. "For two hundred and fifty years our ancestors battled the barbarian invaders. If not for their sly, depraved magery, Cythe would still be ours."

He said it with such passion that Tali had no reply. Her knees were shaking; she could carry Rannilt no further. Prising the girl's arms from around her neck, Tali put her on the steps above the landing. Rannilt whimpered and reached out blindly, the warm yellow light flowing in waves from her fingertips.

Tali could only see Banj severing the little girl's head. She shook her. "Rannilt, wake up. You've got to run, *now*."

She did not wake, and Tali had no choice. She had to fight Banj bare-handed or they would both die. She stumbled to the front of the landing, facing him in the defensive posture Nurse Bet had taught her. Tali had practised the moves ten thousand times but had never fought a real opponent, much less an armed one. She would be lucky to get in one blow before he killed her, yet even one blow was more than her gentle mother had dared. Even one blow would be a blow for justice and an inspiration to all the Pale. The enemies were only human. They could be beaten. Though not here, not by her.

As she raised her hands, the pressure in her head grew until her skull bones creaked. The colours swirled furiously, she lost vision for a second and when it came back Banj was on the step below the landing, only six feet away, the annular blade pointing at her breast.

"Surrender, Tali," he said, using her name for the first time. He inclined his head to her, then reached out as if to take her hand.

Prickles ran down her front at his mark of respect—Banj was honouring the doomed one. He was no savage. He was a decent man, within his limits. She shook her head. "You'll have to kill me ... Banj."

No slave dared speak a Cythonian's name to his face, but Tali wasn't going to die a slave. She was any man's equal.

"I'm sorry," he said, another first in a day of firsts, and bowed as he had bowed to Mia before he decapitated her.

Tali had never heard a Cythonian say *sorry* to a slave before. Banj drew back the Living Blade in the precise, balletic movement prescribed for execution of slaves with the gift. Tali had to get in the first blow, or die. She sprang forwards, swinging at his neck with the rigid edge of her right hand. Such a blow might bring down a frail slave, though she had little hope of hurting Banj through those corded neck muscles.

Perhaps disconcerted that a little Pale was attacking him, he swayed backwards and her blow missed. The Living Blade began to keen, the blood waves racing across it.

Rannilt screamed and the golden light seared out from her. The colours in Tali's inner eye went wild, the pressure in her head made her skull creak and she felt a warm gush as if something had burst open. Then, as she frantically tried to beat Banj's out-arcing blade with a backhanded strike, needles of boiling whiteness burst from her fingertips.

Tali tried to pull away but her arm continued its inexorable sweep. With a hypersonic screech the whiteness swept across the

Living Blade, shattering the annulus of transparent metal and spraying splinters into Banj's face, throat and chest. Blood sprang from a dozen wounds, then to Tali's horror her white-light needles carved across his throat, peeling the skin back before tearing all the way through, cutting off his hoarse scream and sandblasting the wall with fragments of bone.

Banj's body toppled backwards, slid down a dozen steps and came to rest, his blood flooding down to pool on the landing below. His handsome head bounced down the stairs, following the curve of the ten-sided shaft, and thudded bloodily into Orlyk's thick shins.

Her toad mouth was sagging, her eyes black and white buttons in her grey face. Her arm twitched involuntarily and the death-lash went flying across the shaft, exploding so violently that it carved an s-shaped groove in the stone. She backed towards the doorway, along with the rest of the enemy, then bolted.

The white needles vanished. The colours in Tali's head were gone, the pressure too. Her knees gave, she fell against the wall and her head began to throb. Her fingertips were speckled with blood as if by a hundred pinpricks—the only sign of the magery that had torn out of her. But the rise of her gift gave her no joy. She felt sick at the thought of what it had done.

"How did that happen?" she said dazedly, turning away from the shambles and crouching before Rannilt to block her view. "What were those white needles?"

Had she seen? Tali hoped not. She shook the child, gently.

Rannilt sat up and her eyes sprang open. The golden light was gone. She looked her normal self again. "You're all bloody. Tali, you all right?"

Tali wiped her face on her sleeve. "What have I done?"

"Saw it in my mind's eye," Rannilt whispered. "You saved me. With *magery*."

She said it as though it was the most wonderful thing in the world. Had she no memory of her golden display? Had she not seen what Tali had done? Perhaps it was for the best.

"Run! Get reinforcements," Orlyk bellowed from below.

A grey face appeared in the doorway, looking up, then ducked out of sight. Tali clung to the rail. Her head had never hurt this badly before. She could barely see.

"Tali, come," whispered Rannilt.

"Can't—move." Tali felt faint, and cold, and so weak she could barely hold her head up.

Rannilt took her hand, hauled her to her feet and put a skinny arm around her waist. "I'm lookin' after you. I'll never leave you, *never*."

Tali submitted to her, confused and shivering and unable to speak. She kept seeing Banj's head flying off, then Mia's, then Banj's again. And blood. So much blood. When she'd used magery before, it had never been like that. It had never been *visible*; it had never killed before. Where had that tearing white hail come from?

Something had jumped from Rannilt to her. Had the golden force flowing from the girl kindled that deadly fire in Tali? The light-storm had burst out as if she were just a conduit for a greater force.

The top landing was covered in pulverised rock and there was no sign of the other guards, save for one whose remains were fused to the right-hand wall beside a hat rack, like a blackened *bas relief*. The rays from the sunstone implosion had turned him to char, though the stone around him and the hats on the rack were unmarked.

Rannilt put her skinny fingers over Tali's eyes, as if to protect her. They reached the exit, a square arch of stone whose pair of carved stone doors stood open.

"Careful." Tali clung to the door for a moment, for her legs felt as though the bones had been removed. "Guards out there."

Rannilt slipped out, but soon returned. "They're lyin' on the ground with their eyes closed."

Unconscious like the ones at the loading station, Tali prayed. Why had the blast knocked them down yet left her and the other Pale unharmed? It was an important question for later—if they escaped.

"It's beautiful outside, Tali," said Rannilt, eyes wide. "Oh, come see!"

Tali roused. All her life she had dreamed of Hightspall and now it was only a few steps away. She rubbed her eyes, longing for it, then the girl took her hand and led her out into a world she had never seen, into the glorious sunlight of an autumn morning, to her beloved country at last.

Though it was not long after sunrise, the daylight was so bright that her eyes flooded with tears. Tears for the homeland she had never seen, and the mother and father who had sacrificed their lives to try and find it. She wiped her face and was looking around when her head spun and she had to grab Rannilt's shoulder.

"What's the matter?" said the girl, gazing in open-mouthed wonder. "Tali, look at all the flowers. I can see a hundred kinds."

"It's—too big," said Tali. "I—I didn't realise it would go so far, in every direction."

In Cython, no chamber or passage extended more than a few hundred yards without a bend or barrier. All her life she had been used to tunnel vision, to having walls on either side and a roof close above her head. Now she was surrounded by a vast emptiness and the dome of the sky was rocking. It felt as though it was going to overturn on her head.

Her heart raced and she felt a peculiar tingling in her fingers. It was hard to breathe; she swayed on her feet; suddenly she felt cold, ill, dizzy.

Rannilt caught her by the arm. "You're shakin' all over. What's the matter?"

Tali's mouth was so dry she could barely speak. She turned her head and the sky seemed to detach from the earth. Instinctively she covered her face with her arms.

"Be all right in a minute," she croaked. "Hat, hat!"

But the tingling and dizziness were getting worse, and she had never felt this way before. What was wrong? She wanted to scream and run but could not move. A wave of dread passed over her; she needed to huddle in a hole, covering her head, blocking out the world she had so longed for and which now felt utterly alien.

Rannilt came back, wearing a bright orange, broad-brimmed hat and carrying another. She gave the hat to Tali, then gasped and backed away, a hand over her mouth.

A huge Cythonian rose from behind one of the defensive walls, and he was so covered in blood and burns and weeping blisters that for a second she did not recognise him. He had a remarkably small, bulging head, all blackened save for the streaming eyes, and his charred clothes were falling to pieces. A small, egg-shaped blue stone, the one that had lit up as she dropped the sunstone, hung around his neck. How had Tinyhead survived? Why wasn't he unconscious like all the other Cythonians?

"Tali, run!" yelled Rannilt.

But even when Tinyhead came stalking towards her, she could not move. The tingling ran up her arms, down her legs to her toes, and her heart was beating so wildly it must soon burst. The sky began to rock violently and she felt sure it was going to overturn. Was she dying? Going mad?

Tinyhead caught her arms, wound a leather belt three times around her wrists and jerked it tight.

"Oh, Master," he slurred through red-raw lips. "Master, I have her at last."

He looked around for Rannilt but the child had vanished.

"Mimoy, help," said Tali in a whispery croak.

"There is no help." Tinyhead heaved her out through the defensive walls surrounding the shaft.

The old woman lay sprawled over a low stone barricade, blood running from her mouth. More blood than Tali would have imagined Mimoy's tiny body could hold.

CHAPTER 28

Tobry's blistered eyes, now thickly coated in bile-green unguent, made him look like a corpse risen from the dead, yet he was unnaturally cheerful. He still wasn't meeting Rix's eyes, though. He seemed to be *acting* himself, trying to appear normal though clearly he was not.

Outside the valley an avalanche filled the central saddle of the pass to a depth of thirty feet, blocking the way they had come. Rix assessed the area, despair rising like a sickness in him.

"Doesn't look as though you'll be finishing the portrait any time soon," said Tobry.

"I gave my word it'd be done," Rix snapped, imagining the interview with Lady Ricinus, who could remove more skin with her acid tongue than the palace's Master of the Floggings with his metal-tipped flails. "Is there any other way back?"

Tobry rubbed the top of his head and winced. "Only one—north over Hasp Pass, then down a series of unmarked mountain tracks. After that we'll have to skirt around the eastern side of the Red and Grey Vomits, avoiding any fresh lava flows . . . and, er, head across the Seethings to the Caulderon Road."

Rix had never been into that treacherous wasteland of hot springs, boiling mud lakes, bottomless sinkholes and lifeless pools corrosive enough to etch the toenails off anyone foolish enough to wade into them. He had no wish to go there now.

"Didn't someone ride into a hidden pool in the Seethings and get boiled alive?"

"And then there was the fellow who took a dump in a geyser hole," said Tobry. "Did I tell you—?"

"Don't bother," said Rix.

"Blew him three hundred feet into the air and welded his arse to the back of his head. Gave a whole new meaning to the term—"

"I'm not in the mood, Tobe. Can we get home tomorrow?"

Tobry shook his head. "Dinner time the day after. Finding your way through the Seethings can be agonisingly slow."

"Gods! Mother is going to cut out my kidneys." Rix felt the area, which was painfully inflamed where the caitsthe's claws had scraped down his belly.

"Why go home?"

"Sorry?" said Rix.

Tobry grinned. "Defy Lady Ricinus. Neglect your responsibilities."

"What are you talking about?"

"Every misery in your life comes from the palace, but you come of age in a few weeks and there's enough coin in your saddlebags to last a year. Run away. Make your own way in the world."

"Mother would disinherit me."

"And release you from your greatest burden."

"I can't do it."

"Why not? You're strong, vigorous, clever ... " Tobry studied Rix, head to one side. "Perhaps *clever* is too strong a word—" He ducked as Rix hurled a coin pouch at him, and they both laughed.

Rix retrieved it, smiling for the first time since they had come up here. Of course Tobry was all right. He was recovering amazingly well, after all he had been through. But, tempting as the suggestion was, Rix could never do it. From the moment he had been able to walk, his destiny and duty had been to become the next Lord Ricinus. Given his father's focus on drinking himself to death as quickly as possible, Rix might have to assume that responsibility any day.

"My house needs me," he said quietly. "It's what I was born for."

"It's what people *told* you that you were born for. Your destiny lies in your own hands."

"I want to be Lord Ricinus. It's the very meaning of my existence."

"Our existence has no meaning. We just *are*, and then we die and there's an end to it."

"I hate it when you talk that way," Rix snapped.

"I'll lie if it'll make you feel better. Tra-la-laa, tra-la-loy," Tobry sang in a girly falsetto, "life's so wonderful I could skip for joy."

Rix ground his teeth. "I can't run away from my duty at a time like this."

"Duty will consume you and crap you out."

"I'm in charge of my life."

"You, and Lady Ricinus."

Rix scowled and rode ahead. They picked their way through fetlock-deep snow, heading towards Hasp Pass. To the north he could just make out the fuming top of the Red Vomit. On his right, the dark face of Precipitous Crag reared up behind a series of white-covered ridges. What else did those caverns hide?

The swirling wind that plastered snow on their faces carried a faint, cleansing scent from the resin pines, and it cleared his head. "What did you make of those pens?" he said shortly.

Tobry rubbed his face so furiously that several blisters burst. He jerked around in the saddle and once more his eyes dilated to vacancy.

Rix shivered. Not recovering so well after all. Or was there a darker reason? *"Tobe?"*

It was a long time before he answered. "They had the look of breeding pens."

Every claw wound throbbed at once. "For shifters?"

"That's my guess."

"Why would a wrythen want to breed shifters?"

"Because no living person could do so safely?"

"Are you saying it's working for the enemy?"

"I can't think of any other explanation."

"What are they up to? How does a wrythen manage it, anyhow?"

"I don't know."

"And that weird cavern below the stair. What was it for?"

"Trying not to think about it."

"Why?"

"It didn't look possible, yet it was there."

"It had an odd smell, did you notice?"

"Sickly sweet," said Tobry, "but masking something that left a bitter taste in the back of my mouth."

"Any idea what it was?"

"Never smelt it before."

Rix digested that as they rode. "The wrythen recognised my sword."

"What?" Tobry said sharply. "When?"

"After I killed the caitsthe."

Tobry reined in sharply. "You—*killed*—it? How?"

As Rix explained, Tobry's mouth turned down. "All while I lay unconscious?"

"Yes," said Rix. What was the matter now?

"And then you fought the wrythen?"

"That's right. Anyway—"

"Great!" Tobry said. "So when you most needed help—"

"He recognised my sword," Rix said hastily. *"Oathbreaker's blade,* he called it. What do you suppose that means?"

"It means things are a lot worse than my worst imaginings."

"I wish you'd explain something," said Rix when Tobry did not go on. "*Anything!*"

"The moment we get home, I'll have to go away for a bit. I need to talk to people."

"What about talking to me?"

"You've got the portrait to finish," said Tobry, deliberately misunderstanding him. "And Lady Ricinus to explain to."

"You sure know how to ruin my day."

"Thought I'd already done that." Tobry looked away.

Finally Rix realised what the matter was. Tobry felt that he had let Rix down. "It wasn't your fault a rock knocked you out."

"When you needed my magery, it wasn't there. That *was* my fault."

"If I'd listened to you, we wouldn't have gone within miles of that place."

"I could have stopped you, and I didn't," Tobry said bitterly.

Leaving him to his dark thoughts, Rix looked ahead. Hasp Pass was a vertical slot between white mountains, like a jawbone missing one front tooth, and the wind whistling through it was a wrythen wailing in a boneyard.

His thoughts returned to the sword. Why had it led him to the wrythen's caverns? Why had the sword attacked the wrythen of its own accord? "And what was that opalised figure all about?"

"Beg pardon?" said Tobry.

Rix hadn't realised he had spoken the last thought aloud. "Several times, when I've touched the hilt, I've seen a life-sized sculpture of a man carved from a single piece of black opal. A twisted figure; a man in agony."

"I don't know what that means."

After a minute or two, Rix said, "Why is that quote on my sword notorious?" He braced himself for another lecture about not paying attention to his tutors.

"The *Immortal Text* said that the Herovians were the chosen race and Hightspall was their promised land. That's why they left Thanneron and sailed here."

"I heard they were brawling barbarians, always drunk and fighting everyone."

"They were, but in their eyes the book justified their supremacist war against Cythe. And their right to this land."

A layer of ice formed on the back of Rix's neck.

"That's where the word *hero* comes from," Tobry added. "The Five Heroes who led the war were originally called the Five Herovians."

"What happened to them?"

"The *Immortal Text* disappeared in the Ten Day War. That—was—a—thousand—years—ago," said Tobry as if talking to a slow child.

Rix ground his teeth. "I know!"

Tobry chuckled. "After that, the Herovians faded from view, though there are still plenty of them in Hightspall. In fact, I wouldn't be surprised . . . " He stared at Rix for a moment.

"What?" said Rix.

"Nothing." Tobry rode ahead.

Rix called out, "Why is everyone against the Herovians anyway?"

"Arrogance and deceit," Tobry said over his shoulder.

Rix spurred up to him. "What's that supposed to mean?"

"When they landed here and discovered how numerous and strong the Cythians were, the Herovians pretended friendship, but sent a ship racing back to Thanneron, calling thousands of settlers here with the lie that the land was empty. As soon as the Second Fleet landed, they went to war against the Cythians. The people on the Second Fleet had come in peace but they had no choice other than to fight beside the Herovians. And we've never forgotten how they lied to us and manipulated us."

Rix rode on, thoughtfully. It did not answer the main question—how House Ricinus had ended up with the sword.

Directly, they emerged from the slot and headed down. It wasn't snowing here but a drifting mist obscured the way ahead and covered every surface in tiny droplets. The clammy cold made Rix's bones ache.

Out in the Seethings, they would be riding over the mines and tunnels of Cython. "Why does the chancellor let the filthy rock rats come up onto our land, anyway?" he said irritably. "If I were him, I'd tumble their shaft down on them."

"You do know where heatstones come from—like the gigantic one that warms your chambers?"

"I hate them. I don't understand why we trade with the enemy for the wretched things."

Tobry gave him a sideways glance. "Don't you?"

"The trade should be banned."

"Rix," said Tobry patiently, "House Ricinus holds a third of the heatstone monopoly. Your family has made a fortune from the trade."

"I don't believe it!" Rix cried.

"Where do you think your wealth comes from?"

Lady Ricinus was constantly harping on about preparing him for the time when he would be lord, yet kept every detail of House Ricinus's affairs from him. "Our estates, mines and manufactories, of course."

"With the ash falls, the creeping cold, the shifter raids and crop failures, your estates lose money one year in two. All the profit is in trade."

"We *lose* money?" Things must be even worse than Rix had thought.

"The estates lose money, but most of the losses are made up in trade ... and I've heard that House Ricinus has *other* sources of income."

The track sloped down steeply here, with a sheer drop only two feet to the left and an equally steep rise on the right. Rix held his breath as Leather picked his way around a fallen boulder shaped like his father's head, complete with the misshapen drunkard's nose and sagging jaw. A beret of snow crusted its flat top.

"Like what?" Rix didn't much like the way Tobry had said *other*. "What are you hinting at?"

"You'll have to ask your parents."

Rix imagined how that conversation would go. *Mother, would you care to tell me about the shady ways House Ricinus makes its money?* He would sooner be strapped to the toenail puller in the fourth basement.

"We survived without heatstones in the olden days. We can do without again."

"It was a lot warmer in the olden days."

"When I'm lord, we'll abandon the filthy trade. And . . . and I'll personally tumble the Rat Hole down on the enemy."

"If you mean the shaft where the Pale carry the sunstones up—"

"Filthy white slugs!" Rix snapped. "Mother is right about them. The Pale should be put down. When I think about them going over to the enemy, *willingly* living with them for the past thousand years—ugh! They sicken me."

"Everything is black and white to you, isn't it? There's no middle ground."

"Everything *is* black and white," said Rix. "The Cythonians have always been our enemies, and they always will be. Since the Pale choose to serve them, they should suffer the punishment due to traitors."

They rode out of the fog. Ahead, the rocky path wound down through forest hung with tendrils of mist.

"Be that as it may," said Tobry, "any attack on the Rat Hole would be a declaration of war."

"We *should* declare war on the mushroom eaters," said Rix. "Why pay their usurious prices for heatstones when we can take them for ourselves? We should wipe them out once and for all."

"We fought a two-hundred-and-fifty-year war against them, if you remember your history lessons, and they're still around."

"We drove them out of Hightspall. Sent the bastards creeping underground."

"But they got the better of us in the Ten Day War—and in the Secret War two hundred years ago."

"I've never heard of a Secret War."

Tobry smirked. "It was a secret. Hightspall tried to poison their water, among other dirty ways to wage war. But it failed."

"Next time it'll be different," said Rix, raising his sword as if commanding a company of Hightspall's finest. He cried, "To fight for my country—"

"Watch the cliff!"

Rix swerved Leather to the centre of the track then rose up in his stirrups, cutting and parrying at an imaginary foe. "When I come of age in two weeks, I'm going to raise an army."

Tobry's horse shied sideways. "And pay for it how?"

"Um . . . I'll train the best of our serfs."

Tobry rolled his eyes. "Armies are expensive, wars ruinously so. You'll need all the profits from your heatstone monopoly to pay for it."

"Er . . ."

"And once your war begins, there won't be any heatstone trade. Where will you get the money then?"

"If everyone was like you," Rix snapped, "we'd never go to war."

"Now you're talking like a *brawling barbarian*." Tobry sighed. "Rix, there are no good wars."

"Nonsense. Defending one's country is the highest calling of all. I don't understand you, Tobe."

Tobry rode on. "No, you never have."

"Sooner or later we'll have to fight them."

"I don't see why."

"If the land is rising up against us, I reckon they're behind it."

"Behind what, specifically?"

"The winters that get colder every year. The wet summers where our crops struggle to ripen—"

"We can hardly blame the enemy for the weather."

"We have weather wizards," said Rix. "Why can't they?"

"Cythonians hate and despise all forms of magery."

"So they say!" Rix sneered.

"No, it's a matter of faith to them. Besides, even our best weather magians can't do more than cause a cloudburst here, a local frost or gust of wind there. To change the very climate of Hightspall is beyond all their spells put together."

"What about all the new plagues and poxes, then? And the shifters—" Rix reined in again, trying to pull his jumble of worries together.

"What's the matter now?" said Tobry.

"The caitsthe. The packs of jackal shifters. The breeding pens in the wrythen's cavern. Tobe—they're getting ready for war."

Tobry stared at him. "For once, I believe you're right. And jackal shifters first appeared a hundred years ago, which means Cython has been planning war for a long time."

"I don't know what to make of the wrythen, though."

"The enemy is forbidden to do magery, so it's doing magery for them. And if they do attack, we'll lose."

Rix jerked on the reins, restraining an urge to knock Tobry off his horse. "That's traitor's talk."

"Is Hightspall ready to fight?"

"Our armies could march within a week ... or two. Well, a month, anyway."

"A *month*! Wars have been lost in days—ugh!" Tobry hunched over, pressing his palms against his blistered eyes.

"Are you all right?" Had the wrythen left something *inside him*?

"I've felt worse."

"I wish you'd heal your eyes. They look horrible."

"I thought you were against magery," said Tobry.

"I'll make an exception in this case."

Tobry put his hands over his eyes and subvocalised a healing charm.

Rix studied his eyes. "Didn't do any good."

"It takes time to work."

At this lower altitude, the track was fringed with aromatic shrubs. A fleeting ray of sunlight penetrated the clouds before they closed again and the chill wind picked up. The slopes to either side were clad in Haunted Rosewood forest, the small-leaved trees so dense that it was black inside. It had no better reputation than the valley they were running from.

It was late afternoon after a night without sleep, and Tobry was swaying in the saddle. They would have to camp soon, though Rix wanted nothing more than to get out of the mountains as quickly as possible. Even the deadly Seethings would be better than this. At least, camped by a geyser or boiling mud lake, it would be warm. He thought longingly of freshly poached trout.

"Our generals' tactics come from the first war," Tobry said, as though an hour's silence had not passed. "They're way out of date."

"What are you saying?"

"The next war won't be fought that way."

"If our tactics worked then," said Rix, "why wouldn't they work now?"

"The enemies have long memories. And they could strike any-where, through tunnels built in secret hundreds of years ago."

"We'll tunnel down to them."

"Whenever we've tried, they've collapsed our tunnels and killed our best miners."

"Then we'll attack their entrances."

"Every way into Cython is a maze. We'd need ten times their number to break in, and even then we'd lose most of our men."

"You're starting to piss me off, Tobe," Rix snarled.

He whirled and galloped down the path, hacking at the shrub-bery with his sword. Hightspall was going to win. They had to. He wiped his blade and, feeling a trifle foolish, rode back.

And had another flash of the ice leviathan grinding over the walls of his beautiful palace—surely a metaphor for what was coming. He could not shake off the dread that it was somehow his fault, that his house was going to fall because of something he had done, or had refused to do.

With the cold eye of reality, he assessed the defences of Palace Ricinus. Its grounds were vast, the surrounding walls so extensive that it would take an army to defend them. Yet the palace was a fortress compared to Caulderon, which had outgrown its city walls centuries ago and now lay open to attack on all sides.

Tobry was right. The defences of Hightspall were poorly main-tained, its armies ill-equipped, while not a single soldier had been blooded in war. It would take weeks to mobilise the armies and if the enemy attacked without warning ... Rix tried not to think about the worst. Defeat meant annihilation. Defeat could not be countenanced.

"We've got to find out what they're up to," he said.

"I can't go back to the caverns." Dread showed in Tobry's blis-tered eyes.

"The way through the Seethings takes us close to the Rat Hole, doesn't it? If the enemy are gathering to attack, we might see signs there."

"It's hours out of our way. We've got to warn the chancellor and hours could be vital."

"Not as vital as knowing what the enemy is up to."

"No, Rix. We could go all that way and see nothing, and our news is urgent."

Rix wasn't listening. The diversion would put off his interrogation by Lady Ricinus for another half a day, which could only be a good thing. "I need to do this. We'll take a look, then ride home as though our backsides are on fire."

"One misstep in the Seethings and they will be," muttered Tobry.

Rix heaved a great sigh. War would change everything, but as the son of a nobleman he had spent half his life perfecting the warrior's arts. Hightspall's armies might not be ready, but he was. He already had the chancellor's favour, and he would be most grateful for advance warning about war. If Rix could add useful intelligence about the enemy's movements at the Rat Hole, the chancellor might even give him command of a company.

And that would free him from Lady Ricinus's thrall. She would not dare to stand against the absolute ruler of Hightspall.

Yes, war was just what he needed.

CHAPTER 29

"Hat," gasped Tali.

Sweat was flooding down her chest and back. Tinyhead crammed the orange hat onto her head and dragged her away from the shaft. The hat came down to her eyebrows and, as the broad brim blocked out the sky, the tingling in her fingers eased and her thundering heart slowed. She tilted her head back, experimentally. The sky wobbled.

It must be a panic attack. Tali had seen other slaves have them, in dire situations, though it seemed unfair that she should be brought low by sight of the world she so yearned for. She looked down and the phobia eased.

This was her opportunity to uncover her mother's killers, and her family's enemy if Tinyhead knew it. She had to outwit him and that would not be easy. Having had no sleep last night, it was a struggle to think at all.

He hauled her through the maze of defensive walls into a bowl-shaped valley a few hundred yards across, and the world outside, the real world she had never seen before, overwhelmed her senses. A hundred unfamiliar scents flooded her nose. Her ears rang with trills and whistles, chirps and a dozen other bird calls. Soft grasses caressed her toes.

She looked up, too suddenly. Sky and ground seesawed, the tightness in her chest and the tingling in her fingers roared back, panic overwhelmed her and she froze. Tinyhead yanked on the strap, the hat slipped down over her eyes and she stumbled on.

Once she felt better Tali checked around her, careful to manage her field of view, and everywhere she looked was a wonder of wild-flowers, birds and trees. Brown rocks, humped like flocked sheep, outcropped around the valley's steep rim. To her left, a series of rusty iron racks held the sunstones the Pale had carried up earlier. Tinyhead stopped beside the racks, gnawing on a thumb. What was he worried about?

Again the images coruscated in her inner eye: white needles shearing Banj's head from his body, and blood everywhere, spraying on the wall and flooding down the steps. Blood on her too—the front of her robes was soaked with it.

She had slain a Cythonian who had always treated her well. Killed him savagely, whether she had meant to or not, and it did not help that Banj would have executed her. Tali could not get past the ruinous violence she had done to him. She shivered and closed her eyes but the images would not go away.

Tinyhead crushed her wrist bones. She winced but refused to cry out. Forget Banj—she had to focus. How could she get the killers' names out of Tinyhead?

A hollow thud echoed up the shaft. Sweeping Tali into his arms, he ran across closely cropped grass to a boulder cluster shaped like a handful of sticky peas and thrust her behind them. He crouched and peered around the left-hand side of the boulders, his jaw clenched.

"You're afraid of your own people," said Tali, to needle him.

"I love my people," he said with bitter scorn.

He touched his blistered mouth and his face spasmed. Tinyhead had been in pain when she'd seen him at dinner last night, pain her eight-year-old self had inflicted in that unconscious attack after her mother's murder. He must be in agony now, and if she kept at him she might create an opportunity to escape. Alternatively, he might knock her unconscious and carry her to her doom.

There was no sign of Rannilt, who had vanished the moment Tinyhead appeared, and Tali couldn't blame her. One slave had escaped, which made today a very good day, the best for the Pale in a thousand years. Run, little Rannilt, and don't stop until you get to Caulderon.

He began to whisper to himself, though Tali could not make out the words. His plans were in trouble. Five people had seen her cut down her overseer with forbidden magery, and for such a crime she must be executed in a way that set an example to every slave. If Tinyhead took her back into Cython, he would lose her.

But if he remained here, and the matriarchs discovered that he planned to sell *the one* to the enemy, he would be put to a traitor's death, the worst fate any Cythonian could suffer.

Tinyhead drew a rattling breath. Tali peered around the side of her boulder as five Cythonians, led by the red-faced figure of Orlyk, emerged through the stone doors. She climbed onto the highest wall and scanned the valley, then snapped an order. The other guards carried two of the unconscious ones through the doorway. Orlyk dragged Mimoy's body across the grass to the rim of the valley, dumped her over the edge and went down the shaft.

"You'll never sneak me inside," said Tali. "You're stuck."

Taking the blue ovoid from around his neck, Tinyhead rolled it back and forth in his hands. It might have been made from the mineral turquoise but, whatever it was, she felt sure it had saved him from the blast. A muscle began to twitch along the left side of his jaw. With a grimace, he thrust the ovoid into a pouch hanging from his sash, then stared at the doors to the shaft.

To claim his blood money Tinyhead would have to take Tali through Hightspall to the murder cellar, but any Cythonian caught in Hightspall would be killed on sight. What was he going to do?

He was watching her again, hatred rising from him like smoke. Tali surreptitiously tested the leather belt, which was tight enough to numb her fingers. The leather was unbreakable.

Tinyhead unwrapped a half loaf of yellow pea bread, cut a cylinder out of the top and filled it with the slimy red mushroom pickle known as *glorn*. Tali's mouth watered but he did not offer her any. He was about to take a bite when rock clicked on rock, along the ridge to their left. Setting down the bread, he drew a knife the length of her arm.

It had to be Rannilt, and if Tinyhead caught her she would die. He crept to the far end of the pile of boulders, his gaze sweeping the ridge. How could she stop him? Tali remembered her unused plan from last night.

After one taste, I'll tell ya anything, Lifka had said.

Tali fumbled one of the withered Purple Pixies out of her pocket, poked it under the surface of the *glorn* and resumed her position, surreptitiously wiping the pickle off her finger. She was not game to lick it.

Tinyhead took several steps towards the ridge crest.

Tali shouted, "Rannilt, run, hide!"

He stalked back, the knife jerking up and down with each stride. She shrank away, expecting him to strike her, but he merely picked up his breakfast.

"When we reach the cellar, she'll cut your head open like this loaf." Tinyhead opened his mouth to take a bite.

"Who's *she*?"

Tali's memories of the masked woman who had killed her mother were lost, save for her icy contempt. She had despised the Pale, viciously mocked the man who had been her accomplice and stood on Iusia's chest as though she was rubbish.

Tinyhead froze for a second, mouth open, and a muscle on his jaw twitched. He tried to smile but it failed. "A traitor to her own people," he gasped.

"Just like you, then."

She had gone too far. Tinyhead dragged her upright by her

bound hands and clubbed a fist. His misshapen face had gone purple; his whole body shook. With a visible effort he withheld the blow and shoved her backwards onto the grass.

"You think I've suffered all this for *gold*?" he spat. "For the enemy's filthy coin?"

She tried to calm her galloping heart. His outrage was genuine. She had been wrong about Tinyhead all along, and it changed everything. Clearly, she had mortally insulted him by comparing him to the woman who had killed her mother. But if he wasn't acting out of greed, or some deep-seated hatred of the Pale, what did move him?

"Why do you do it?" she said softly. She needed to know. She had to understand him.

For the first time, he met her eyes. "I love my country. I was chosen. I serve."

He took a huge bite from the loaf, through the cavity filled with *glorn*, then chewed twice and swallowed. Had he eaten the Purple Pixie? How long would it take to work? She found it hard to breathe. Would it work on a Cythonian?

"Who do you serve?" said Tali.

It was the vital question. If he wasn't betraying Pale for money, if he was following some Cythonian's secret orders, then whose? And why did that person require him to lead the women of Tali's family to a distant cellar, to be killed in a particular way by that evil, masked woman—a Hightspaller and an enemy? It made no sense. Why not kill them in Cython? Why involve the enemy at all?

Could the women of her family pose a threat to someone in Cython, a threat most safely eliminated by having them killed by the enemy? It seemed far fetched; much simpler to kill the mother and her little daughter, thus eliminating the threat forever. Why allow each daughter to grow up and have another daughter?

Tinyhead squatted and attacked the rest of the loaf. His bloodshot eyes were on her mouth again. He was definitely afraid of something about her. Her gift?

Tali attacked the problem from another direction. What if the women of her house were not a threat? What if there was something valuable in them—some promise that had to mature: their magery, perhaps? But if so, why didn't the Cythonians take it for themselves? Why hand it to an enemy? Unless, she thought with a sudden chill, there was something wrong with this unknown gift in her family . . .

Her stomach began to throb. What if there was something poisoned inside her? If she escaped and went home to Hightspall, might she carry that corruption to her own people? But she could not live her life on *what ifs*. She had to continue with her plan.

Tinyhead swayed and fell backwards, his eyes describing ovals in their sockets. He tried to sit up but fell down again—the Purple Pixie was starting to work. Tali had to get the truth out of him quickly. Once he began to hallucinate she would not be able to trust anything he said.

She checked on the shaft. Orlyk's reinforcements must arrive any minute, to begin the search for her. She had to be gone by then, because the well-fed, tireless Cythonians would soon run her down. They could not afford to let her warn Hightspall about the coming war.

But first Tali needed the name of the woman who had killed her mother, or the man who had aided her, though they weren't her ultimate quarry. Iusia had called House vi Torgrist's enemy *he*.

And Tinyhead had said, *I love my country. I was chosen. I serve.* Who did he serve, and why was it such a secret that he would risk his life rather than allow his fellow Cythonians to discover it? It had to be her *real* enemy.

Voices came from the top of the shaft. The Cythonians were back. Tinyhead began to grunt and gasp. His pupils were so dilated now that his eyes were watering.

Tali bent over him. "Who killed my mother?"

"Lay-lay-lay—" he gasped, white tongue lolling from his open mouth.

"Is that the woman's name? Layla, Ladis, Layyalie?"

"Lay—" Tinyhead's eyes rolled, then focused on somewhere behind her. "No!" he said, trying to scramble away on his back like a four-legged spider. "Get away."

There was nothing behind her—he was beginning to hallucinate.

She was almost out of time; forget the woman's name. Tali took him by the shoulders and whispered, "Who do you serve?"

"The dead—the dead—"

Tinyhead convulsed so violently that she was knocked aside, then stood up and began to reel about, waving his arms and bellowing incoherently. "M—M—Master—"

Someone shouted, "I heard something, over there," from the direction of the shaft. Orlyk.

Tali only had seconds to get the name. Still hidden behind the boulders, she said, "Who is your master?"

"Master . . ."

Tinyhead jerked like a loose-stringed marionette, then his left arm stilled and, moving at a calm purpose at odds with the rest of his uncontrollable body, he drew from his pouch the blue ovoid he'd been toying with earlier. It was glowing again.

"Master? Help me, Master."

His hand smashed the ovoid against the right side of his blistered forehead and blue light fled in all directions, leaving a small blue-green blob like thick jelly stuck to his brow. His dilated pupils contracted to pinpoints, swung onto Tali and focused like twin telescopes.

She gasped, for the air had gone so frigid that her lungs crackled with each breath. His eyes had turned an eerie yellow and someone was looking out of them, someone cold as death, patient as time, radiating rage and an implacable determination. The House vi Torgrist's enemy had found her.

"The name!" hissed Tali, praying that the Purple Pixie still had some influence over Tinyhead.

"Master—is . . . is—"

With a boiling hiss, the blob vanished. Smoke rose from a small circle burned deep into Tinyhead's forehead, then something white and gluey squirted from his left ear. He swayed in a circle but remained on his feet.

A piercing pain stabbed through Tali's own brow. Her head began to throb like a beating heart and suddenly she felt exposed, naked, vulnerable. Her enemy knew where she was, yet she knew nothing about him.

Behind her, the Cythonians were shouting down the shaft for reinforcements, yelling at Tinyhead, gasping, choking.

Whatever he knew about her enemy, it was lost.

And Tali had but seconds to get away.

CHAPTER 30

Something was very wrong. The scheme the wrythen had fed, nurtured, honed and tweaked for so many centuries, his plan that was in the last but one stage of completion, was sliding off track like a wagon on wet clay. And if the plan failed, all failed, for he had invested everything in it.

The last nuclix—the fifth—was the master, and once he held it his power would rise a thousandfold. He might even get his long-lost body back, might *live* again rather than merely existing. Everything rested on the master nuclix now. If he lost it, if even the least of Cython's enemies obtained it, the plan would fail so utterly that it would be better never to have begun it. His people would be driven from their underground refuge and expunged.

He had tried to anticipate every problem and find a solution. Deroe might attempt to break free and add the master nuclix to the others he had stolen, but the wrythen had a plan to stop him and get them back. The Hightspallers who had cut out the other nuclixes might try to take the fifth for themselves, and ruin it. Or sell it to one of their own. He had schemes for those eventualities too.

Of all possible failures, it had not occurred to the wrythen that his one faithful servant might be outwitted by the miserable slave girl who was the host. The Pale were half-starved, illiterate and con-temptible, a beaten race from which all those manifesting the gift for magery had been culled long ago.

The girl hosting the master nuclix should have been as cowed as the others—she should have gone blindly to her doom. Why, then, was the wrythen's blue signal ovoid shrieking out a warning of imminent betrayal?

He shot towards it and, as he touched the ovoid, *saw* his servant outside Cython's sunstone shaft, fifteen miles away. The man was raising his own ovoid to his forehead, crying, "Master? Help me, Master."

Then he smashed it there—

The shockwave of its destruction split the wrythen's ovoid and tore him to fluttering wisps. His disembodied consciousness did not try to pull himself together—there wasn't time.

It should not have been possible, but he forced himself along the link formed between the two ovoids, settled into his servant's addled mind then cut through the hallucinations to look out from his eyes.

And the wrythen's distant heart-plasm stopped.

The host girl was a slip of a thing, barely out of childhood. She should have had no gift, yet it burnt in her so brightly that he could see the flares wavering all around her. And she was clever, too. Without using her gift, she had beaten his servant. Unease fluttered within him—*who was she?*

"Tell me the name!" she hissed to his servant.

And his servant, all restraint destroyed by the hallucinogenic toadstool, tried to answer. "Master—is . . . is—"

The wrythen's name could not be revealed. Though it would throw his plan into utter disarray, he had no choice but to burn through his faithful servant's brain.

Ah, how it hurt, even worse than the cursed sword. It felt as though a hole had been burnt through the wrythen's own head from front to back. There were hot needles in his eyes and his vision went redly in and out of focus as though blood was running down his servant's eyeballs. The slave girl was staring at his servant in horror, her small hands beating the air.

With a supreme effort, the wrythen took command of his smouldering consciousness. Think! Several of his people had gathered by the shaft doors and would soon come after the girl. He could not allow them to catch her—if they killed her, the master nuclix would be ruined and his plans set back by decades. But if they discovered the nuclix and kept her alive until they cut it out and used it, his plan would fail utterly and, in the end, Cython would be destroyed.

His servant's vision was fading, the man's tongue flopping uncontrollably from his mouth. The wrythen had to act quickly. His people had to be kept back, no matter the price. He raised his servant's twitching right arm, reached towards the arched roof over the shaft and directed all the power that remained in him at the keystones.

Stone grated on stone. The bones of the earth groaned and there came a dull rumble as part of the shaft house collapsed, crushing the guards inside, his own people whom he had dedicated his life to protecting.

Look what I have become, he thought bitterly as his consciousness was hurled back to his home cavern. But the girl—what a magnificent creature she was. The fire in her almost equalled his own. A tragedy that one so gifted had to die.

He dragged himself up to the ancestor gallery to confess his folly. His long-dead nerves should not have been capable of feeling pain, yet pain throbbed through each phantom limb and digit.

I have made terrible blunders, he said to the massed faces, and the wrythen bent his head to them. *Yesterday I sent the facinore—*

You made a facinore? cried Rovena the Wise, her voice shivering. *What if it breaks free and turns on our people?*

It won't, the wrythen said uncomfortably.

You can never tell with them. Never!

You sent it where? said Bloody Herrie.

To the matriarchs, ordering them to make war on Hightspall. The first attack will come tonight and I have no means of calling them back.

Send the caitsthe.

It was a long time before the wrythen spoke. *Rixium killed it.*

You boasted that no man could kill a caitsthe.

I was wrong.

He also hurt you grievously. With that sword, he's a formidable foe.

He will die.

What else have you done? said Bloody Herrie, icily.

The host girl got out through the sunstone shaft, outwitted my servant and almost forced him to reveal my identity. I had to burn through his

*brain, and now she will escape into Hightspall, bearing the master nuclix
within her. If the enemy realises—*

They will cut the nuclix from her and use it to control the others,
including your own, said Ruris.

Their failing magery will be rejuvenated, said the wrythen. *It will
take on the power of the land itself and tip the balance against us. To the
ruin of all.*

The matriarchs' soldiers will find her, said Ruris.

They must not take her, cried the wrythen. *If our people find the
master nuclix, it will be worse than the enemy getting it.*

You said the Pale were sad, cowed creatures, said Bloody Herrie. *You
said all their magery was gone. How did this girl come to be so strong, so
bold?*

I don't know.

What will she do next?

I cannot say . . .

But you're afraid.

He did not reply. He wanted to plunge through the floor.

Order the matriarchs to take the girl, but leave her untouched for you,
said Rovena.

I have no way to contact them.

Then write another page to the Solaces and transmit it.

I have no alkoyl.

The ghostly ancestors consulted among themselves, then Bloody
Herrie said, *Can you take command of Rixium?*

Not until he's near the heatstone in his own chambers, said the wrythen.

*What about his spell-casting friend, Tobry? You went close to pos-
sessing him, did you not?*

I . . . might be able to reach him, though he will be difficult to control.

Do it. Have him find the girl and bring her here.

*The master nuclix may not be brought here in a host who has the gift
of magery.*

A tiny gift, surely. Untutored, unpractised—

Nuclixes call to each other, said the wrythen. *The master nuclix
might attempt to command the one I hold, and the girl's magery could be
so different to my own that I might not be able to stop it. There is only one*

safe way. The girl must be taken to the cellar—our healing temple of olden times—and the nuclix cut from her by a Hightspaller under my command. One who lacks even a whisper of magery.

It will not be easy to get her there through a land at war, said Ruris.

You must. If you fail, all fails, said Bloody Herrie.

CHAPTER 31

The sky was visible through Tinyhead's skull.

A hole the diameter of a thick wire had been burnt through his head from front to back, like a hole burnt through a plank with a red-hot poker. He swayed on his feet, his tongue flap-flopping like a spotted eel. A tendril of smoke drifted from the back of his head and white gloop continued oozing from his right ear, but the greater horror was that he was still alive.

Pain was shrieking through Tali's temples and her face felt as though it was aflame. Was her enemy trying to attack her the same way? And if he could reach her from his unknown hiding place, was there any point running?

She had to. His power over her was uncertain, but the Cythonians milling in the shaft entrance were an immediate threat. She had to run *now*. But Tali could not move; her strained thigh muscles had locked in cramp.

Healing charm, *healing charm*. She massaged the muscles, subvocalising the charm, and the cramp eased, though the healing was far more draining than usual and would not last. The white torrent that had killed Banj had drained her to the marrow, and the damage from carrying the sunstone went too deep.

Tinyhead's arm swung out, his fingers pointed towards the shaft house and one side collapsed on the guards inside. She looked sideways at his eyes. They were empty now, the yellow and the presence gone.

Pulling her orange hat well down, she took his knife and hobbled diagonally up the slope to a sheep-shaped outcrop near the rim of the valley. Crouched behind it, she sawed through the strap binding her wrists and tried to make sense of the images burned into her consciousness.

She'd learned a clue to the killers—*Lay*, part of a woman's name—and had been close to discovering her enemy's name as well, the man Tinyhead called *Master*. She would have succeeded had not Tinyhead, a Cythonian she had believed to be beneath contempt, called on his master to sacrifice him rather than be forced to reveal the name. And if so contemptible a man could reveal unexpected nobility, what did that say about—

"Get after the slave," Orlyk yelled.

Tali peeped through the longer grass beside her rock as Orlyk and four others rounded the cluster of boulders and stopped, staring at Tinyhead. He was still lurching aimlessly, white clots quivering on his shoulders.

Orlyk doubled over and threw up into the grass. Tali ducked down and worked the charm on her churning belly but the icy sickness did not abate. The Cythonians would also blame her for the attack on Tinyhead. It might make them more cautious but they could not allow her to get away. If they were unable to take her back, their archers would shoot her down.

Orlyk ran up to the steep rim of the basin, looking all around. Tali shrank into the grass. If Orlyk saw Rannilt she would kill her on sight.

Orlyk returned to the boulders and issued orders. Two guards took Tinyhead by the arms, walked him to the broken shaft doors and inside. Orlyk followed. The remaining two guards, who were armed with Living Blades, kept watch. Tali could hear the keening of the thirsty blades.

She wriggled up a shallow fold towards the rim of the bowl, which here rose steep and bare. After making sure the guards weren't looking her way, she wriggled across several yards of broken rock to the other side and looked out.

As the vastness of the Seethings opened out before her, both ground and sky began to seesaw. Chills ran down her arms and her heartbeat accelerated. She wrenched the hat brim down at front and sides, fighting the irrational dread. But she had to be able to see, had to know where to go.

The bowl was shaped like a crater at the top of a small, round peak, an oasis of green in the middle of a wasteland so barren that it might have been scorched with *thermitto*. Her mother had warned her of the dangers of the Seethings, and so had Waitie, who had also taught Tali geography. Her overwhelming urge was to scurry down the slope to cover, and hide, though first she must locate Caulderon. Once down into the flatlands of the Seethings it might be impossible to find.

The Seethings were mottled in reds, browns and yellows, littered with gigantic boulders and dotted with thousands of lakes, ponds and sinkholes, all steaming. Directly in front of her, not many miles away, a volcano reared up like a broken horn. Its slopes were brown and grey, as if everything that had once grown there had been swept away under landslides of ash, and grey clouds billowed from its top.

. There were three large volcanoes called The Vomits, though she was not sure which one this was. The Brown Vomit, perhaps. Another, reddish Vomit lay to its left, partly concealed behind it. She could not see the third.

Behind her, across more steaming wasteland and grass-covered plains beyond that, a range of snow-blanketed mountains curved around on her left, growing higher and steeper until it disappeared behind The Vomits. The Crowbung Range. To her right, a little further than the closest Vomit, she made out an enormous blue lake.

After consulting her mental map she concluded that she was looking at the southern end of Lake Fumerous, maybe three miles away. Caulderon would be to the right along the shore, three times that distance, though if she headed east across the Seethings she should reach the main south road within five or six miles, and once there she should be safe.

Tali sighted on various landmarks that she should be able to see from the Seethings, and was making her way down, taking advantage of the cover of a boulder here, a gully there, when someone rose up from behind the bush in front of her.

Tali jumped, then muffled her cry of surprise. "Rannilt—I thought you'd be miles away by now."

"Where would I go?" said Rannilt, taking her hand. "Who'd look after me?"

A vague unease stirred but Tali thrust it away. "Where's your hat?"

Rannilt looked around vaguely. "Left it over there."

"Get it, or the sun will cook you like poor Sidon in the heatstone mine."

Rannilt scurried away to retrieve her hat and pulled it down until it shaded her narrow shoulders.

A few hundred yards further on, the grassland merged into a band of woodland sweeping down a series of corrugated hills. They had to reach the trees before the enemy came over the rim. But even if they got as far as the Seethings they would be visible for miles on the flat surface. And they were bound to leave tracks . . .

One worry at a time. Tali was hobbling down the slope when Rannilt said, "What about old Mimoy?"

There was only one way to say it. "She's dead."

Rannilt took a shuddering breath and cried, "But I saw her move!"

Tali froze. The girl must have imagined it. After losing all that blood, after being thrown down the slope, Mimoy could not be alive. Her body had been dumped further around the curving rim of the basin and wasn't visible from here but, if they went back to check, any guard coming to the crest of the hill would see them at once.

"You're not goin' to leave her there, are you?" Rannilt said anxiously.

Tali swallowed, her dry throat rasping. Just when she'd thought she had a chance.

"Of course not." She took the girl's cold hand. "The things you say, child."

They spotted Mimoy's body twenty feet down from the rim, dumped like an unwanted bag of bones. Her cane lay a few yards further on. The slope where she lay was bare of any kind of cover.

"Rannilt, can you do a tricky job for me while I get Mimoy?"

She nodded vigorously.

"Can you creep to the top and check on the enemy without being seen? You'll have to be really careful."

Rannilt's eyes shone. "Anything for you, Tali."

She bent low and darted up the slope.

"Quietly!" hissed Tali.

Rannilt turned to wave, tripped and fell headlong, sending stones clattering down. Tali winced. Had the sound carried? She limped across to Mimoy and lifted her head. There was blood on the grass and on her torn ragweed blouse, and she was cold. Tali felt sure she was dead, until Mimoy's left eye fluttered.

A clicking sound issued from her wattled throat, a whispered, "Where?"

Mimoy's clouded eye focused on Tali, who saw a desperate longing there. She chewed on a knuckle. Mimoy was almost dead and every second they remained here increased the risk of discovery, but she could not ignore the entreaty in the old woman's eyes.

Tali smoothed Mimoy's wrinkled brow. "In Hightspall. Mimoy, you're the first Pale to escape Cython—*the very first.*"

She picked the old woman up, every strained muscle groaning. How could she still be alive? Only by the agency of her own gift.

"Hightspall," Mimoy sighed. "Home, at last." She looked up and her lipless mouth cracked into a grin. "Ha, ha! Beat you, Evvie. You said I'd never do it."

Tali wondered who Evvie was. Probably some childhood rival, dead for a hundred years.

Mimoy's bones settled, she gave a tiny groan and Tali thought she had died, but the old woman wheezed, "Lay me in the good earth, won't you, daughter?"

A fist squeezed the air from Tali's lungs. It was too much to ask. The time it would take to dig a grave and bury the selfish old woman would eat up their one chance of escape. She should offer Mimoy the comfort of a lie, then abandon her the moment she died. It was the sensible thing to do, the only way Tali could hope to escape, warn her people and complete her own quest. The dead had no needs, only the living.

But when Tali looked down at the ache in the old woman's eyes she could not say no to her.

"Yes, Mimoy. You're going to tell me the names of Mama's killers, and I'm going to lay you in the good earth of Hightspall. Where would you like to rest?"

"Tell you when we get there."

"Psst!" said Rannilt from above. "Someone's comin' out the shaft."

She ducked down. "Get my cane, brat," said Mimoy.

Rannilt handed it to Mimoy, who promptly whacked her with it.

Tali snatched the cane. "What did you do that for?"

"You chose her over me. Give it here."

"So you can whack her again?" Tali snapped the cane over her knee and threw the pieces away.

Pain speared through her head. She stumbled and fell to her knees.

"You'll come to regret that," Mimoy said maliciously. "Cane, now!"

CHAPTER 32

Rannilt fetched the pieces of cane. Mimoy snatched them, hugged them to her, and they hurried down the slope. Tali's back felt like a target all the way to the trees.

After taking shelter behind a comfortingly solid trunk, she looked back. The rim of the valley was clear—no, someone was climbing it. A head appeared, and broad shoulders. The guard scanned the slope, checked along the rim then shouted and raised his Living Blade. Red flowed around the annulus and it howled. He ran back the way he had come.

"What's with him?" said Rannilt, rubbing a trickle of blood from another skinned knee.

"He's noticed Mimoy is gone. Keep watch. They'll soon be after us."

As they were moving on, the ground quivered. A loud rumble

issued from behind them and a small cloud of dust drifted above the rim.

"What was that?" whispered Rannilt, pressing against Tali. "I'm scared."

It was an open secret that the enemy had invented many terrible weapons of war. Slaves in the know spoke of burrow-burrs, shriek-arrows, bombasts, fire-flitters and grenadoes. No one knew what they were, though some were rumoured to kill at great distances. Tali assumed the enemy was testing some weapon to attack the escaping slaves from afar, though there was no point telling Rannilt that.

"I don't know." She held Mimoy with one arm and put the other around the girl's skinny frame. "But I'll look after you."

"She's useless, and you're a fool," said Mimoy. "I'm the only one who can help you."

Tali ignored her. If the enemy found them, she would have to abandon the old woman and run with Rannilt. The living must take precedence over the dying.

She took a random route through the woodland, taking care to leave no tracks, then hobbled up a shallow stream, her burden growing heavier with every step and her resentment with it. How far did Mimoy expect to be carried? All the way to Caulderon? Selfish old witch!

At once she felt guilty for wanting to get rid of the old woman who, after all, had been struck down trying to help her. Besides, Tali had been brought up to respect her elders, but where did that duty begin and end? Surely not in sacrificing herself?

They climbed three low, knobbly hills, one after another, creeping over their crests where they might be seen against the sky. The Seethings lay beyond the last hill and as they climbed it the knot in Tali's gut tightened. She fixed the chosen landmarks in her mind and trudged on.

"I can see all the way back," said Rannilt, skipping beside Tali as though she had not a care in the world.

How resilient she was. How quickly she had forgotten her terror of half an hour ago. Tali felt the burden and the threat growing with each step.

Mimoy's eyes opened a crack and she scowled at Rannilt. "Get me a drink."

Rannilt skipped off towards a rivulet.

"Why are you so mean to her?" said Tali.

"She brings out your weaknesses and distracts you from your purpose."

"I don't see caring for an abused child as a weakness," Tali snapped.

"Survival is the only thing that matters."

"Not if I end up a sour old witch like you."

Mimoy slapped her across the face.

"Do that again and I'll abandon you right here," Tali said coldly.

"No, you won't. You're too soft, too *kind*." Mimoy spat the word at her.

Rannilt came back with a double handful of water. Mimoy lapped at it then shoved her away.

"Can you see the enemy?" said Tali.

"Can't see no one," said Rannilt.

"Why are they holding back?"

"Afraid," said Mimoy.

Tali hadn't thought of that, but they had seen her kill Banj with the torrent of white needles, and doubtless they blamed her for Tinyhead's gruesome fate too. She was no longer a despised slave; she was an enemy using forbidden magery that was an insult to the lost kings of Cython. An enemy who had to be crushed so bloodily that no Pale would ever contemplate using their gift again. She was also *the one*, and the matriarchs had her under a death warrant.

They continued over the hill and down. Tali's robes were sodden with sweat and she was so weary that she had to talk herself into each step. She no longer had the strength to look ahead, nor the courage to look behind.

"Why is it so hot?" said Rannilt, wiping her face.

Tali had been wondering that too, since it was late autumn. "I suppose it's because we're not used to the sun. The temperature is always the same in Cython."

Suddenly, a hundred feet from the base of the hill, Mimoy dug her nails into Tali's wrist. "Bury me here, before the Brown Vomit."

Tali set her down. They were in a little dip where mossy ground squelched underfoot. The bottomlands skirting the hill were scattered with scrubby bushes, though they soon died out in the barren, steaming Seethings. The great volcano looked twice as big here, and far more menacing. It was not just erupting steam and ash—great boulders were wheeling through the air and crashing down on the slopes, smashing the rubble to powder. And judging by the rock scattered about, they sometimes fell out in the Seethings . . .

She shook the fear off. "What about my mother's killers?" said Tali. Her hot feet sank into the cool, sodden ground.

"Here, you stupid little fool! Now!" hissed Mimoy, sounding stronger than before.

"But . . . you're not dead," cried Rannilt.

"Wretched child." Mimoy's trembling hand drew a small knife from beneath her loincloth. "Use it. Cut swift and deep."

"No!" cried Rannilt.

Mimoy's eyes met Tali's and Mimoy smiled grimly. Surely she didn't mean . . . ? Of course not; it was another test.

"Rannilt," said Tali, "it's all right. Go to the top of the hill and keep watch."

She settled Mimoy on the ground, then took the knife and made four deep cuts, carving a rectangle into the moss. After peeling it off, she hacked out sections of the peaty ground and stacked them to one side. Half an hour of heavy labour and she had excavated a wet grave an arm's length deep.

"It's done."

Mimoy did not open her eyes. "Put me in."

Again the unease. Surely Mimoy did not want to be buried alive? But her voice was strong; she knew what she was asking. Tali made a pillow with a clump of moss, then lowered Mimoy's withered body into the grave. She lifted her twisted, bloody feet in afterwards, neatly arranged her frail limbs and pulled together her bloodstained ragweed blouse. It must have been painful but Mimoy made no sound, poor old woman. Tali laid the broken cane beside her, close to her right hand, for it was Mimoy's only possession.

Tali rubbed her eyes. "Are you comfortable?" She touched the old woman's scarred skull. Had she also been attacked, but had survived?

"I'd prefer it was drier, and warmer." Mimoy's eyes opened and she looked up at Tali. "Are you stupid?"

"I—er . . . " Tali had no idea what she was talking about.

"I picked you because you showed the ruthlessness required for survival. If you blub into my grave, I'll pull you in with me."

"I'm not blubbing." Tali wiped her eyes.

"Why are you wasting time on a wicked old woman who only ever abused you?"

"You longed to go home to Hightspall, and I knew how you felt. It's what I've wanted all my life."

A hand rose from the grave and whacked Tali's shins with a length of the cane, hard enough to hurt. "Imbecile! What about your quest?"

"I'm lost." Remembering those pinpoint-pupilled eyes, Tali shuddered. "I saw the enemy not long ago, looking out from Tinyhead's eyes. Iusia said he can only be beaten with magery but I don't know where mine is. Help me, please."

"You broke my cane."

"I'm sorry, but—"

"I was going to give it to you, but now the magery is lost."

"Your gift was in the cane?" Tali whispered.

"I told you that you'd regret it."

"But—why didn't you say?"

"Why don't you ever think before you act?"

Yet again, Tali's temper had let her down, and this time it could be fatal. "I don't understand a thing about my magery. Where does it come from?"

"Don't know. It's unique."

"Then how am I to master it?" Tali cried.

Mimoy gave a pained shrug.

"But back in Cython you said you'd help me with my gift," said Tali.

"You broke my cane."

Tali tore at her hair. "Please help me."

"Had to come home to die," said Mimoy, her voice faint now. She was fading.

"Mimoy, I can't do this by myself."

Mimoy's blue-veined eyelids fluttered.

Tali took the wire-like fingers in her own. "Please tell me what to do."

Mimoy slumped, her head thudding into the wet peat. "Only—" she croaked.

Tali bent over her. "Yes?"

"Only one person ... can show you ... how ... to master ... your ... gift."

She was slipping from the world. *Please, give me some answers first.* "Who?"

"Your—your enemy."

"*My enemy?* Is this a cruel joke?"

"No—joke." Mimoy's voice was little more than a sigh.

"But who is my enemy?" Then, hastily, for if Mimoy did not say the name now it would be lost forever. "And who killed my mother?"

Mimoy's pupils contracted and expanded, as if she did not know which question to focus on. "Poison—"

"Just the names," Tali said softly. "My enemy, and my mother's killer. That's all I need from you, Mimoy. Then you can rest."

"Poison," Mimoy repeated. "The worst."

"What's that supposed to mean? She wasn't poisoned."

Mimoy reached up to Tali and her throat moved, but the effort was too much for her. Her eyes became fixed.

Tali was adjusting the torn blouse when it came apart at Mimoy's left shoulder, revealing her slave mark. A very familiar mark, the same as Tali's own—the mark of House vi Torgrist.

Mimoy must have been Mimula vi Torgrist, Tali's great-great-great-grandmother. Her only living relative was dead.

CHAPTER 33

"The Rat Hole," said Rix.

They had spent all the previous day following a series of unmarked tracks and dead ends until they finally found a way out of the mountains, then making their slow way around the flank of the Red Vomit and through the morass of the southern Seethings. Now they were on the rim of a small, bowl-shaped valley, looking towards the maze of fortifications around the roofed shaft. Rix lifted his kilt to scratch his gnat-bitten rump. The wind had turned north-westerly during the night and it was unseasonably warm here, a good six thousand feet lower than the wrythen's caverns.

He added, "I could take it with a hundred men."

"Since it's unguarded, you could take it with a one-legged rabbit," said Tobry. "And you'd die as soon as you reached the bottom of the shaft."

"The grass isn't worn," Rix mused. "There's no sign that any army has ever exercised here." He let out a heavy sigh. "And they'd have to—you can't practise battle manoeuvres in a tunnel. They're not planning war at all."

Tobry was staring at the shaft. "Unless it's a different kind of war . . . "

Rix checked the angle of the sun—midday. "Come on. I've got to get home." Lady Ricinus would be honing her flaying knives by now.

"Can I have the 'scope?"

Rix handed it across.

Tobry extended it to full length and focused on the maze. "I can see bodies."

"Bodies?" cried Rix.

"And part of the shaft roof has collapsed."

"Has Hightspall attacked? I'll be really pissed off if war has begun and I've missed it."

Tobry gave him a pitying glance. "Make up your mind, Rix."

"What?"

"There are no dead horses, no bodies outside the maze." They rode to the walls. "Everything's coated in dust. Whatever happened here, it came from within."

"So that's what the mushroom eaters look like," said Rix, dismounting to study an unconscious Cythonian, a muscular young man with blue wings tattooed on his temples. He had never seen the enemy up close before. "Ugly brutes, aren't they?"

Tobry rolled his eyes. "They're alive, but unconscious. And there's no sign of violence, plague or poison. That only leaves one thing."

"Magery." Rix shifted uneasily. "But you said they don't use it."

"They don't."

"So who did this?"

Tobry shrugged.

Grating sounds echoed up the shaft. Rix eased one of the broken doors open, started when he came face to face with the charcoaled corpse of a guard fused to the wall, then edged by and peered down into a rubble-choked hole.

"They're clearing the shaft," said Tobry, beside him.

Rix turned away. "Come on."

"Don't you want to know what happened here?"

"I don't imagine it's that important." Rix could think of nothing save the verbal crucifixion that awaited him at home.

They were riding down to the Seethings when Tobry, who was ahead, stopped so suddenly that Leather had to swerve aside.

"Hey?" said Rix.

Tobry had gone as still as a sphinx. As Rix rode up beside him, the wire-handled sword rattled furiously in its scabbard. He punched the hilt down with his fist.

"Tobe?"

His pupils were enormous, his eyes even blacker than before, though after a minute they shrank to normal. Tobry shook himself.

"Why is your mouth hanging open?" Rix said mildly. "You looked as though your brain was in another place."

"Just thinking." Tobry frowned, as if trying to remember something, then looked down and said sharply, "Hello, what's this?" He dismounted, studying the ground. "A faint track through the grass."

They followed it down into a dip where the ground was moist and soft, to a freshly cut grave neatly covered with stones. Two pairs of small footprints continued down.

"Kids!" Rix shook Leather's reins. "I have to get home." And face Lady Ricinus's fury.

*

"My enemy can only be beaten with magery," mused Tali. "But the one person who can show me how to use *my* magery is my enemy."

No matter how she turned Mimoy's words around, it was impossible. She tried to dismiss it as the raving of a dying woman, but could not. She felt sure it meant something.

They had been trudging across the Seethings for hours. The autumn sun was still surprisingly hot, baking her head and shoulders through the heavy robes, and her mouth was as dry as the scalded ground beneath her. They had found no drinkable water since leaving the hills.

"Rannilt, what do you know about your gift?"

Tali was trying to work out how it had sparked hers off. And how she might discover where it had retreated to, for she could find no trace of it.

"Until this mornin', never knew I had a gift. Where are we goin', Tali?"

"Caulderon, the greatest city in Hightspall. And when we get there, my family, House vi Torgrist, will help us. We'll sleep in real beds—"

"Not made of stone?"

"No, child. Our beds will be as soft as that fluffy little cloud up there." Without thinking, she looked up and the dome of the sky tilted. Tali jerked the hat down. Her phobia was worse out here; she was constantly fighting the urge to curl up into a ball inside her robes. She forced herself to continue. "We—we'll wear lovely gowns and eat our dinner off silver plates. You can have a whole poulter to yourself, if you want."

"I've never tasted poulter," Rannilt said wistfully. "The big girls steal all the good stuff."

She went skipping off to their left, following the tracks of some small creature that led across a smooth, grey expanse—alarmingly smooth.

"Stop!" Tali screamed.

Rannilt froze, left foot in the air. Tali tossed a stone onto the grey area, which rippled, emitted a burst of steam then smoothed out as the stone sank with a thick *gloop*. She felt a sharp pain in her middle.

"If you stepped on that, you'd be *cooked* like a poulter. Stay beside me."

"Yes, Tali," said the girl, still beaming. Having adopted Tali, nothing could faze Rannilt.

But she had no common sense and, though Tali liked Rannilt, she was needy. She was a burden Tali could have done without.

You took her on, now you're responsible for her. She looked ahead, trying to find the shortest path to the road, knowing the Cythonians would be much faster. They would have spied out the land years ago; they would know the quickest way through the Seethings, and how to get ahead to block her path.

Rannilt looked back anxiously. "Still not coming. Do you think they've given up?"

"Maybe they have," Tali said, knowing it was probably a lie.

The attempt to assuage Rannilt's fears only heightened Tali's. They would never give up. Why weren't they coming? Were they setting a trap?

It was impossible to go in a straight line here. The Seethings was a maze of mud pools, sinkholes, steaming bogs and chymical lakes surrounded by crystalline haloes of red, orange, yellow and green salts. Some pools were hot enough to boil eggs.

As she limped on, her thoughts returned to that image of her enemy, glaring out through Tinyhead's eyes. Tinyhead had called him master and had broken that blue object against his own forehead to prevent himself revealing his master's name. He was selflessly doing his master's bidding, following some plan kept secret even from his own people.

It did not change Tali's view of her enemy—an evil master could surround himself with well-meaning servants. He had been killing the women of her line for a hundred years; he was powerful enough to destroy Tinyhead's mind from a great distance. And he had seen her. Was he watching her meandering passage across the Seethings, smiling as he moved the pieces to trap her? Was he after her because she was *the one*?

The thought made it hard to maintain hope. Some traps were perfect, some enemies all-powerful . . . and some people were born to be crushed, as the Pale had been beaten down these past thousand years. Even if she got away, even if she discovered her enemy's name and where he dwelt, what could she do? She was neither fit nor ready. She would never be ready.

She fought down the despair, the surety that her quest was impossible and that she was a tiny fly trapped in a gigantic web. Clearly, her enemy needed something from her, and she was determined to stop him getting it.

"Trees!" yelled Rannilt, half an hour later. "Tali, we're nearly through."

Some distance ahead, a flat-topped mound covered in tall palm trees and shrubbery made a green blister on the ravaged flatlands. "It's just an . . . " Tali had to dredge up the right word, ". . . an oasis. But at least there's shade, and maybe good water."

And, she hoped, relief from the endless open spaces that so panicked her.

They wove through tall, dense shrubbery, and the moment Tali lost sight of the horizon the pressure eased. High above, a canopy of palm fronds hid most of the sky, and it wasn't rocking. Her pulse slowed to normal; the dread faded. They pushed through the bushes to a deep, heart-shaped pool touched by slanting sunbeams and surrounded by tussocks of coarse grass.

"Will we get to Caulderon tonight?" said Rannilt.

The girl had no sense of distance, but then, how could she have? "Not at this rate." Tali scooped a handful of water, which tasted fresh. She drank, then worked the healing charm again. It helped, though only a little. "In the morning, if my legs hold out."

She wasn't looking forward to it. As soon as she went out into the open, the phobia would return. Tali felt a momentary pang; she had never felt this insecure in Cython.

What? her other self cried. You spent your whole life trying to escape, and now you want to go back?

"Are you all right?" said Rannilt.

Tali came back to reality. "I expected too much," she said absently. "I thought once we escaped, our troubles would be over."

"But we're *free*. What can go wrong now?"

Tali smiled at the girl's naïveté. She scratched her itching head and could hardly force her fingers through her hair. Sweat had caked it with dust from the sunstone implosion; she was covered in it and spotted with Banj's blood.

She looked longingly at the pool. Uncleanliness was not permitted in Cython, and being so dirty felt disgusting. Besides, she rationalised, no proud lady of House vi Torgrist could present herself to her people looking like a filthy tramp.

"Rannilt, can you do an important job for me?"

"Yes, Tali."

"Can you keep watch while I bathe? You'll have to be careful, though."

"Yes, Tali." Rannilt's eyes were glowing. All it took was a little kindness.

Tali washed her dusty gown in the pool and spread it over a rock to dry. It was beautiful and would make her feel like a lady of House vi Torgrist. Wearing it would also symbolise putting her slave past behind her. Then she scrubbed herself clean, combed her hair with her fingers, donned the gown, still damp, and felt sure she looked her best. She did feel like a lady, just a little.

Never again would she be a slave, or serve unwillingly. She pinned her father's letter into the hem and put the silver seal around her neck, taking comfort from its link to her ancestors all the way back to the Second Fleet. Now, what about dinner? In Cython they ate fish or eel twice a week, though they were farmed in stone tanks and only had to be scooped out with a net.

She was crouched by the water, wondering if there were fish in this pool, and if she could catch one with her hands, when Rannilt whispered, "Tali, Tali?"

"What's the matter?"

"Heard somethin' in the bushes."

The backs of Tali's hands prickled; why hadn't she been more careful? "What was it?" A pool of fresh water in the middle of the Seethings would attract all kinds of predators. She looked for a stick or a stone, but saw neither.

A long pause. "A man, a *really big* man. And he looks cross."

CHAPTER 34

"I think the kids from the Rat Hole are there," said Tobry.

"Where?"

Rix fanned himself with his hat. It was hot in the Seethings, for there was neither cloud nor breeze and the baked ground reflected the heat up at them. They were heading for an oasis whose dense halo of palms and green shrubs indicated that the waterhole was neither scalding, saline nor, hopefully, poisonous.

At the outer edge of the shrubbery they dismounted and crept on until they could see through a fringe of leaves to the pool.

Rix stopped abruptly, making a strangled noise in his throat.

"Well, *she's* not a kid," Tobry murmured.

Standing by the water twenty yards away, in a blue gown that clung to her small yet feminine form, a young woman was squeezing water from chin-length, golden-blonde hair. A skinny child, nine or ten years old with a pinched face and scabbed knees, was talking non-stop.

"Close your gob," said Tobry. "You're gawping like a yokel."

"I've never seen a woman with such luminous skin, such silky hair, such a soft mouth. Her eyes are the colour of sapphires—"

Tobry drew him backwards until they were out of earshot. "I concede she's an engaging little wench, but she's not for you."

"You stinking hypocrite," Rix hissed. "You've seduced whole villages of women."

"Only *small* villages," said Tobry wryly. "And I don't debauch innocents. Look at her; she could have been hatched last night."

"You're not stopping me, Tobe."

"What makes you think she'll say yes?"

Rix looked at his friend in astonishment. "No woman has ever said no."

Tobry opened his mouth to say something, but closed it again.

"What?" said Rix.

"Nothing."

"You're doing it again. If there's something I need to know, tell me."

"I'm not sure you need to know."

"Don't patronise me, Tobe."

"Haven't you wondered *why* no woman has ever said no?"

"No," said Rix smugly. "Why would they?"

"They say no to me all the time. But then, I don't have your looks, your title, your wealth—*or your mother.*"

Rix frowned. "What's Mother got to do with anything?"

"Can't you work it out?"

Rix strained until his eardrums bulged. "No, I can't."

"She makes sure all the young women you meet are *the right kind.* And clean, and willing."

The cold sweat was back. "What do you mean, *willing?*"

"Lady Ricinus makes it clear what will happen to any woman who refuses her precious son—"

"Are you saying they come to my bed because they're too scared to refuse?"

"I dare say they *like* you—you can be charming enough, when you make the effort. And no doubt Lady Ricinus encourages their forlorn hopes—"

"What hopes?"

"That you'll make them the next Lady Ricinus."

"But . . . surely they realise it's just a bit of fun?" said Rix.

"You're such a babe," said Tobry. "Do I have to spell it out?"

"I guess you do," Rix said sullenly. He peered through the vegetation but the young woman had moved out of sight.

"To most of those girls, snaring you is a way out of miserable poverty, for them and their families."

"That's . . . that's just like—" Rix could not say it. He'd never paid in his life.

Tobry's mouth opened; closed. Heavy sigh. "Family duty matters to you, doesn't it?"

"Of course. Family is everything."

"To them as well. For their entire extended families, you're the difference between the gutter and the palace. And be sure, their families pressure them."

"Are you serious?" The idea that those sweet girls had been forced into lying with him, that they had been pretending the whole time, desperately trying to please him for their families' sakes, was sickening.

"Lady Ricinus can destroy them with a snap of her fingers," said Tobry.

Black fury smoked inside Rix. "The horrible, scheming bitch! I'm going to have it out with her the minute we get back."

"It might be an idea to finish the portrait first."

The cursed portrait of his wretched father. "You're right, of course."

"What can I say?" grinned Tobry. "It's a gift."

"Damn Mother! Well, I've had it. I'm swearing off women."

Tobry stifled a roar of laughter. Rix did not smile.

"What?" said Tobry, alarmed. "Forever?"

Rix raised his right hand, "Upon my family's honour, until the war is over I take no wench to my bed. And after the war, no woman I haven't sought out by myself." It was the only way to be sure.

"You won't last a day."

"You want me to fail?" Rix cried.

Tobry fought to restrain himself. "Yes, I do."

"Anyway, I've got to be ready for battle. I'm going to train night and day."

"You might be killed in the war," Tobry said slyly. "And never make love again."

"At least I'll die knowing I'm not abusing girls too afraid to refuse me."

Tobry went forwards until he could see the young woman again. "She doesn't look as though she's afraid of anything."

Rix pushed past, deliberately jostling him. "From this moment she's under my protection, so keep your eyes off her."

"*My* eyes weren't on her."

"I mean it, Tobe."

Tobry sighed. "Have I ever mentioned that you overdo everything?"

*

Who were these men? What did they want? Were they safe? Tali might be innocent but she was not naïve. She knew what could happen.

Her bare feet felt cold. "Get down. Don't let him see you."

Rannilt scurried behind a broad clump of grass. "He already has."

Tali edged towards the rocks where she had left her robes, surreptitiously picked up Mimoy's small knife and slipped it through the back of her waist sash. "Is he a Cythonian?"

"Can't see any face tattoos," said Rannilt. "And he doesn't have grey skin."

He must be one of Tali's own people. What was he doing here? Or was it just a coincidence?

"Keep talking; don't look around."

"There's two of them. They know we're here."

Though they were well back in the bushes, Tali's eyes were used to the dim light of Cython and she had no trouble picking them out—definitely Hightspallers. She swallowed. Why were they watching her? Then she saw that they wore kilts that exposed their thighs. She looked away, her cheeks hot.

Rannilt's head was visible above the clump of grass, her mouth agape. "Ooh, they'll be in trouble!"

"We're home now," Tali said softly. "That's how noblemen and warriors dress in Hightspall. Men's thighs are only indecent in Cython." She peeped again and they were still shocking. "Creep away and hide. Don't come out until I call you."

"What if they take you away?" the girl whispered. "Who'll look after me?"

"Go!" Tali hissed, and turned to face them.

The man with the black hair was far bigger than any Pale man, the other fellow more normal-sized. Both wore swords and looked as though they knew how to use them. Both were richly dressed, and therefore noble or wealthy. Tali knew that not all Hightspallers could be trusted but they did not look like hard men. She swallowed and turned towards them. They were her people. Surely they would help her. But first she had to convince them that she was also noble . . .

"Hello?" she said, trying to smile.

They came through the bushes. What was she to say? How could she prove herself to them? Tali wasn't used to meeting new people. In Cython she had known most of the slaves she worked with all her life. What if these men wouldn't listen?

Her smile felt odd. The muscles had not been used in a long time. She needed their help but must also appear proud and confident, for she was a lady now and would never act like a cringing slave again. Did ladies go barefoot out of doors? She suppressed her anxiety—surely a lady was a lady no matter how she was dressed.

As the black-haired man stepped into the clearing, Tali moved back involuntarily. His face was flushed—he looked as though he had been arguing. And he was even bigger than Tinyhead; she had never seen any man like him. Most Pale men were small and thin, their skin mottled with bruises and scars. Many had teeth missing and feet misshapen from rock falls in the mines.

This fellow was handsome, appeared well fed and looked as though he owned the world, yet there was something soft, almost melting in his eyes. Some trouble that made him seem vulnerable, that made her warm to him, though . . . no, the thought was gone.

"I'm Rix, of House Ricinus," he said, holding his hands up to show that they were empty. "Don't be afraid."

Tali did not realise how engagingly the damp gown clung to her. Having lived her life among female slaves, where no one wore more than a loincloth and male visits to the mated women were doled out even more meagerly than dinner rations, she was ignorant of the effect her figure might have on the opposite sex. Nonetheless, she found him disturbing. His eyes kept drifting towards her, then flicking away as if he did not want to look at her.

"I'm not afraid. I'm home now."

Even the baked lands of the Seethings were part of Hightspall. It still did not seem possible that she could be here, and free. Had her legs not been so sore, she would have danced for joy.

"My friend is Tobry Lagger," said Rix, indicating the man behind him. "Who are you?"

"I am Thalalie of House vi Torgrist," said Tali, formally, for that was how she imagined a lady would speak. She bowed; she was determined to put the life of a slave behind her forever. She paused so Rix would have the opportunity to recognise her noble name, then added, to be friendly, "But you may call me Tali."

Now he would help her, and the Cythonians would hardly dare to take him on.

Tobry chuckled. Unlike Rix, he was not at all handsome, especially with those bruised and blistered eye sockets, though he had a pleasantly craggy face. His arms and legs were scratched, and through a tear in his shirt she saw that his left shoulder was bandaged. Both men looked as though they had been in a fight and she wondered about that.

Rix's brow wrinkled and he turned to Tobry, murmuring, *vi Torgrist?* Tobry said something that Tali did not catch and Rix turned back to her.

"Ta-lee." He might have been tasting her name with his tongue.

"I can see that you are gentlemen. Would you be so kind as to escort me to my family's manor?" Tali did not mention Rannilt; first, she had to be sure it was safe for her to come out.

Rix choked. "Gentlemen!"

Tobry laughed ironically. Rix glowered at him.

"I beg your pardon," said Tali. Had she unwittingly offended them? "Is something the matter?"

"My friend is noble," said Tobry, and the mischievous humour in his eyes made her smile. "Rix is heir to the vast wealth and endless estates of *House Ricinus*." He pronounced the name with weighty import. "One day he will be Lord Ricinus, one of the most powerful men in all Hightspall. Therefore he finds the term *gentleman* a trifle . . . er, vulgar."

Tali went through the list of ancient noble houses her mother had made her memorise as a child. "House Ricinus?" she said, frowning. "Is that a *new* House?"

Rix's jaw tightened and his eyes went flinty. "How can you not know of House Ricinus? For a hundred years—"

He broke off, breathing heavily, but regained control of himself and forced a smile. His gaze passed down her gown to her bare feet, up again, but flicked away once more. What was the matter with him?

"I have urgent business elsewhere and cannot escort you to your home," he said, "wherever that is. However I will provide you with silver enough to outfit yourself respectably."

He did not call her *lady*, nor even use her name. Clearly, she had angered him, though Tali had no idea how. However, his offer of coin to *outfit herself respectably* was an insult. House vi Torgrist did not ask for charity. She had to make it clear who she was without antagonising him further. She needed his help, for Rannilt's sake as well as her own.

"House vi Torgrist is not wealthy, nor powerful," she said with cool dignity, "yet our line extends unbroken back to the Second Fleet and the founders of Hightspall."

"Why only the Second Fleet?" Rix said mockingly. "Why not claim the First?"

"Only Herovians came on the First Fleet. Clearly, I am not descended from those big, black-haired, brawling buffoons." Her eyes raked his huge frame, his black hair, then, remembering her manners, she said coolly, "Thank you for your offer, but we do not accept pennies from strangers."

"Pennies!" cried Rix. "Are you suggesting that I'm cheap?"

Tali's self-restraint foundered. "How dare you insult me by offering charity, sir!" she snapped. "Has House Ricinus no nobility at all?"

His face flushed and he strode towards her.

"Rix!" Tobry called, warningly.

Rix stopped, his massive chest rising and falling. "I show you more respect than a scallyscragging impostor deserves," he cried, still keeping his eyes averted.

She did not know what the word *scallyscragging* meant, though it must have been an insult. "I am not an impostor," she said coldly, drawing herself up to her full, meagre height. "Every word I've said—"

"My lady Tali?" said Tobry.

Was he mocking her? No, all she saw in his eyes was a bitter-sweet amusement. "Yes?"

"I know every noble house in Hightspall. House vi Torgrist was wiped out in the Fester Plague seven centuries ago, along with one-third of the other First Families. So, who are you?"

Tobry's words were like a sunstone imploding inside her—burning heat followed by shards of ice, then a sickening dizziness. She sagged, clutching her stomach. Her house *wiped out*? It could not be.

She studied him from under her lashes. He had the air of a man stating facts that were well known to all, so it must be true. Yet again she had allowed her expectations to run away from reality. What was she to do now? Without the aid of her people, how could she hope to complete her quest? The cellar where Iusia had died might have been anywhere and she had no idea where to begin.

"I *am* Tali vi Torgrist," she said, raising her chin and looking him in the eye.

"It's a crime to pretend you're noble when you are not," said Rix, still smouldering. "You can be stoned for that."

Tali, proud lady that she was determined to be, could take no more. "I can recite the names of every one of my ancestors back to the Second Fleet. Can you do the same, sir?"

His fists knotted and red waves flooded his face. "I've had enough of this—"

Tali fought an urge to scream and bolt. He might be twice her size but he was not going to dominate her. She had to take control, and there was only one way to do that—with calm, clear logic.

After taking several breaths, she said gently, "I understand that you feel inferior because your House is newly risen, but there's no need to get angry. It's the way things are, and if you'll just—"

At Rix's bellow of rage, she yelped and took an involuntary leap backwards.

Tobry caught Rix by the arm and dragged him off for several yards. "Given your vow of a few minutes ago," Tobry said savagely, "I'd have thought you'd treat a girl down on her luck more honourably."

Rix might have been smacked in the mouth with an eel. He jerked free and turned away, clenching and unclenching his fists, then snapped, "Thank you for reminding me. Despite her insults, I will take her to her house. *If she has one.*"

Tobry said softly, "What about the portrait?"

"Damn it! And Mother, too. And damn you to hell, Tobry Lagger."

Stalking back towards Tali, he bowed and said stiffly, "Forgive me, Lady Tali. My manners do my house no credit. I will personally escort you wherever you wish to go."

She bowed back, her mind racing. If her house had fallen centuries ago, where could she go? She knew the names of the other noble houses but why would any of them help her? Tali looked up at Rix, gnawing her lip, his sheer physicality intimidating her. Despite his bad temper, she did not think he had any ill intentions towards her. Even so, there was something about him she could not read. And also, now that he was close, something vaguely familiar about the eyes . . .

Unconsciously, Tali ran her fingers through her hair. She had to have food and somewhere safe to stay; and clothing and boots. Without help, her quest would fail. Besides, with Rannilt to look after and the enemy hunting her, there was no choice but to go with them. But go where?

"Thank you," she said, bowing again.

His sword rattled in its sheath and shivers ran in waves along her arms. He struck the hilt an angry blow with his fist and the rattling stopped, though her unease did not go away. A darkness lay on him, or within him, something she had not sensed before.

"Does Torgrist Manor still stand?" said Tali.

"More or less," said Tobry. "It's a plague house. The whole of House vi Torgrist died there, and most of their servants. There are terrible stories—"

"What kind of stories?"

"The townsfolk wouldn't let them out the gates, nor let any food in. The survivors were starving and the Lady vi Torgrist tried to escape underground with her children to the palace down the hill . . ." Tobry went still for a moment. "Some say they were walled up in the tunnels, others that they were massacred there. No one ever got out and the plague house has lain empty ever since."

"Where is it?"

"Not far from Palace Ricinus, as it happens."

She raked her hair again. "I'll go to my house. I'm not afraid of some ancient plague."

Rix's eyes narrowed. He was staring at her shoulders, exposed where the loose sleeves had slipped down when she raised her arms.

"Your arms are black and blue," he said. "Have you been beaten?"

They were the bruises that Mimoy's wire-like fingers had made last night. Tali dropped her arms. "It's nothing."

Rix took her left arm, and she was almost overpowered by his physical presence. He was a handsome man ... and yet, there was something about him that made her uneasy, that she could not fathom.

A deep, inflamed gash ran the length of his left forearm, as if he had been clawed by some large beast. Without thinking, she reached inside herself for a healing charm. No, what was she thinking? *Always hide your gift.* Revealing it to a stranger could be fatal.

"Who did this to you?" said Rix.

"It doesn't matter." She jerked her arm free. "Let me go."

He held her, pushed the sleeve up, then drew a sharp breath.

He was staring at the scar on her left shoulder, at the complicated pattern that was both her slave mark and the symbol of her nobility—the unique and instantly recognisable seal of House vi Torgrist. Now he would believe her. Now he would know that she was as noble as anyone in Hightspall ...

"You came from the *Rat Hole*!" he cried.

Tali did not know what he was talking about.

He thrust her away so hard that she tripped and fell backwards onto a tussock. Rix's eyes were ablaze, his mouth curled down in disgust.

"You're no lady, you're a lying, stinking *Pale*!" he cried. "An enemy collaborator. How dare you try to inveigle me?"

He stalked away, but had only gone a few steps when he clutched at his stomach, doubled over and, with a moan like an animal in pain, vomited onto the ground.

He wiped his mouth on the back of his hand. "Run, little Tali," he said savagely. "Run back to the Rat Hole where you belong. If anyone catches you spying on the land your people betrayed, you're dead."

CHAPTER 35

Tali watched Rix's great horse career away, feeling worse than she had after the encounter with Tinyhead in the subsistery. As a slave, she was used to domination and humiliation, but Rix's reaction was an attack on her very identity.

Tobry was staring after him, shaking his head. He lifted her to her feet then stepped away, hands rigidly at his sides as if to prove that his intentions were honourable.

It was not enough. She should not have trusted Rix and she wasn't going to make that mistake twice. Why had Tobry stayed behind? *What did he want?* She wanted to be rid of him. But if he went, how would she escape the enemy who must be coming closer by the minute? How could she protect Rannilt when just the sight of the open sky drove her into a panic?

Why had Rix said those foul things about her? The Pale were more noble than he was. They had come from the highest families in the land, ancient, respected houses. The hostage children hadn't betrayed anyone—they were the ones who had been betrayed.

"May I see?" said Tobry.

She wanted to scream out her anguish. Not even in Cython had she been treated as foully as this. Mutely, she drew up her sleeve.

He studied the scar, frowning. "I've seen that before . . ."

"It's made by my family seal." Tali showed it to him. "I spring from Eulala vi Torgrist, one of the child hostages Hightspall gave Cython to end the Ten Day War."

"What child hostages?" said Tobry, clearly perplexed.

Her fury flared. "How can you not know? There were a hundred and forty-four of them, all children, all from noble families. All of us Pale come from them, *because they were never ransomed.*"

"We were taught that the Pale willingly went over to the enemy and serve them to this day," said Tobry. "I've never heard your tale before."

"It's not a *tale*," she snapped. Her voice rose. "For a thousand years we've been their *SLAVES!*"

Tobry raised his hands. "I believe you."

"It's Hightspall's greatest shame. And now you tell me we're blamed? Seen as *traitors*." She advanced on him, wanting to thump him.

"I never called you that," said Tobry.

"Your friend did. The sight of me made him vomit."

"I'm sorry." Tobry was clenching his fists by his sides again.

"Yesterday my dearest friend was beheaded because she used magery to save herself from a flogging." Tali looked sideways, wondering where Rannilt was hiding. "They would have killed Rannilt—" She broke off, cursing herself.

"Ah, yes," said Tobry. "Where is the child?"

"Promise you won't hurt her?" Tali said desperately.

"What do you take me for?"

"All my life I've dreamed about coming home, about being *welcomed* home." Tears were forming in her eyes and she dashed them away, furiously. She had to be strong. "I don't know my own country. I don't know my people." She glared at Tobry. "And I certainly don't know you."

"I'm a simple man. What you see is all there is to me."

"Ha!"

She studied the craggy face, the blistered eyes and the claw marks on his arms. Tali also sensed something buried deep in him, a hurt he had carefully concealed. "I suppose *you're* all right," she muttered.

He grinned. "Thank you for that ringing endorsement of my character. You were saying about the girl?"

The warmth of his smile made her feel better. Could she tell him? *Trust no one.* But she had no choice—without help, she and Rannilt would be killed within hours.

Besides, magery wasn't a crime in Hightspall; it was a valued gift. "Something set off a gift for magery Rannilt didn't know she had, and the enemy would have killed her for it. I had to bring her with me."

She told him, briefly, about their escape.

"They kill little children because they can do magery?" cried Tobry.

"Anyone who has the gift must die. That's the lot of the Pale in Cython." She glared at him as though he was responsible for all their suffering, daring him to deny it.

"I believe you," he repeated. "And I'll get to the truth, too." He turned away to the pool and washed his face, drank deeply and came back, rubbing a bristly jaw. "What are you going to do?"

"I don't know. I've nowhere to go." She thought for a while. "Eulala was the only child of House vi Torgrist, and I think I'm her only descendant among the Pale."

"Then you're the heir," said Tobry, and bowed. "Lady vi Torgrist."

"Lady vi Torgrist," Tali repeated. Her mother had said that she would be Lady Tali one day.

Barefoot Lady Tali, a despised Pale with not a brass *chalt* to her name. How was she to survive?

"Why did Rix throw up at the sight of me?" she said plaintively, feeling like a little slave girl again, in trouble for no fault of her own.

"House Ricinus is conservative and full of prejudices," said Tobry. "Rix isn't a bad man . . . not really. *Bastard!*" he said under his breath.

"I don't know what to do."

He untied a canvas pouch hanging on his left hip and reached inside. Tali caught a faint glimmer through the weave, as if a glowstone had been uncovered, and a single tendril of emerald light quivered across her inner eye.

He withdrew a little cloth bag and held it out. "Take this."

Both the glow and the light tendrils faded. "What is it?" she said warily.

"Silver, all I have. Not much." He smiled ruefully. "*I'm* not wealthy."

Pride told her to scornfully reject his charity. Reason said she would need it, since she had no house to help her. Tali bowed and took the bag. Her hand was still trembling; she could not stop it. "Thank you, Lord Tobry." He was a good man. He would help her.

"Just Tobry. My house has fallen; there's nothing noble about me."

He glanced along the path Rix's flight had flattened through the bushes. A brown horse waited near the edge of the oasis. Tobry whistled and the horse pulled its reins free, trotted to the pool and drank noisily.

"You're leaving us behind," Tali said dully.

Escaping from the enemy had been the easy part compared to relations with her own people. Why had she taken Rix on? If she had bowed and thanked him she would be halfway to safety by now. The enemy would never catch riders on horseback.

Tobry mounted, grimacing and rubbing his bandaged shoulder. "My horse is worn out. It can't carry me and both of you. I'll bring Rix back."

"But—the enemy—"

"I won't be long. But keep out of sight, just in case . . . " He rode off.

"Tobry!" she cried, remembering her urgent news. "Cython is going to war in eleven days—no, ten days now."

He whirled and came back. "How do you know?"

She told him about the stockpiled food, the preparations on the chymical level, the crates of weapons and the threats that they would soon put the Pale down. "What if my escape makes them bring forward their plans?"

"Why would it? You're just—" Tobry bit the rest off, then had the grace to look embarrassed.

"Just a slave," said Tali. "A worthless Pale. Don't worry, I'm used to it. They told us so every hour of every day."

"They won't be saying it now. They'll be working like a swarm of rats to discover how you escaped."

"What if they attack before Hightspall can get its army together?"

"They'll get a nasty surprise," said Tobry, though not convincingly.

Tali remembered what Tinyhead had said. "They've been

planning this war for a thousand years. Hightspall *is* ready for war, isn't it?"

"Of course . . . " He glanced at her, then away, biting his lip. "I'd better go."

Hightspall isn't prepared, she thought, but he dares not say so. He's afraid I might be a spy. Tali knew what happened to spies and informers at a time of war. They were killed, but only after everything they knew had been tortured out of them.

As he rode away, her head began to throb, in the particular way it had when her enemy's eyes had been looking out from Tinyhead's eyes. She went back to the pool. Did her enemy know she was here? Was he directing the Cythonians to the oasis? Were they close?

Half an hour passed, then an hour, but Tobry did not return. Had he lied? Or what if he and Rix had run into a band of the enemy?

"Rannilt?" Tali called. The girl was up the tree again, keeping watch. "Any sign of them?"

"No."

"What about the enemy?"

"Can't see no one."

Tali was running out of options. They could not hide here; a small band of Cythonians could search the oasis in half an hour. Yet if she went back into the Seethings they would see her from a mile off.

"Come down. You must be thirsty."

Rannilt came creeping down, washed her face in the pool and took Tali's hand. "Why did that wizard—?"

"What do you mean, *wizard*?" cried Tali.

"He had gramarye in his pocket," said Rannilt.

"Are you sure?"

"I saw it, clear as anything."

Relief flooded her. Tobry was clever. He must know far more about magery than any slave, and he was a kind man who did not despise the Pale. Could he teach her? Yes, she would appeal to him. It was absurd to think that the only person who could teach her magery was her enemy. How would Mimoy know, anyway?

"Tali?" said Rannilt.

"Shh, child, I'm trying to think." She had to go after Tobry and
Rix. "Come on." Tali crammed her hat well down and put the robes
on over her gown.

How had Rix known she was one of the Pale, anyway? If no Pale
had ever escaped from Cython before, how could any Hightspaller
know what they looked like, or that they bore a slave mark on their
left shoulders?

She was trying to understand his reaction to her when a long-lost
memory came flooding back, one she had suppressed after the terrible day in the cellar. By the time she found her way back to the
Pale's Empound, a day later, Tali had buried the memories so deep
that, even as an adult, she had not been able to find them.

A handsome, black-haired boy, his eyes tormented and his fine
clothes covered in vomit, reaching out to her mother's hair then
staring at the blood on his fingers. The look in Rix's dark eyes had
been vaguely familiar, but the way he had thrown up, like an
animal in pain, was unmistakable.

He was her first real clue to who had murdered her mother.

Rix was the boy from the cellar.

CHAPTER 36

An hour later, as darkness raced across Lake Fumerous towards
the west, the hatches were lifted on nine cunningly concealed
tunnels. Three lay close by the fishing towns on the southern shore
of the lake, three more were scattered along the triangle of fertile
farmland that made up Suthly County, on the eastern side of the
Caulderon Road, and one was insolently close to the main gates of
Caulderon.

Four thousand *cloaked* Cythonian warriors synchronised their
chronos then, armed with shriek-arrows, pox-pins, cling-metal and
other chymical horrors, made their silent way to the richest farming communities, the wealthiest towns and the most important

bridges. At the appointed minute of the appointed hour, they attacked.

Carefully placed bombasts, exploding in pyrotechnic crimson arcs, collapsed three bridges and the left-hand side of the city gate. Fire-flitters, hurled in hissing swarms from small, wheeled *pults*, turned fields, warehouses and granaries into chymical furnaces. Sunstone grenadoes, tossed into palaces and hovels alike, imploded with silent, brain-numbing violence that rendered most of the occupants catatonic. Shriek-arrows cut swathes through those nobles and commoners who managed to claw their way out into the dark. Finally an epidemic of tiny pox-pins, falling in a whispering rain from the black sky, delivered their hideous cargo into the unfortunate survivors.

After ten minutes, one-fifth of the harvest of the region was ablaze. Hundreds of people were dead, thousands lay unconscious and thousands more were yet to feel the indigo buboes forming inside them. Hightspall did not know what had happened; not a single Cythonian had been seen. They withdrew to their tunnels, erasing their tracks as they went, to sleep like just warriors and dream of vengeance.

The other two tunnels opened onto the Seethings, one to the north of the Rat Hole and one to the south. Twenty soldiers emerged from the northern tunnel, led by a big captain, once handsome, with a deep, powerful voice. The left side of his face was pocked with craters so deep that the tip of a little finger could be inserted in them, surrounded by starkly white scar tissue.

"Where is she, Wil?" he said to a skinny little man of indeterminate age with blackened, empty sockets and a seeing eye tattooed in the middle of his forehead.

Wil the Sump fingered the platina containers secreted in his pouch. Just the thought of their deadly contents sharpened his inner eye. He needed to sniff—he ached for the pretty pictures alkoyl made in his mind and the burning bliss that drove all his cares away.

He wiped his dripping nose. He had to find *the one*. No one else could do it. No one else could truly *see*. He turned away, took a surreptitious sniff and his eroded single nostril burned like chymical fire.

His heart pounded whenever he thought about the contest between the Scribe and *the one*. Who would prevail? The Scribe's story, what he had read of it in the iron book, was sliding off track. But so was *the one's* story Wil had seen in his *shillilar*, and he had to know how the story ended. Sometimes, under the influence of alkoyl, he imagined writing it himself.

Wil turned around once, twice, thrice, then pointed south-east.

"The one, *the one*."

"Take us to her."

"You won't hurt her, will you?" said Wil. "She could change our story all by herself. I told the matriarchs so."

"And so the matriarchs told me." The captain fingered his Living Blade and said, below Wil's hearing, "I guarantee that she will feel no pain."

The squad from the southern tunnel, the one closest to the Rat Hole, was captained by the squat, toad-faced woman called Orlyk. Behind her lurched a huge, empty-eyed man with a red, ruined face and a narrow hole burnt through his tiny head from front to back.

Orlyk jerked the barbed rope around his neck, dragged him all the way to the Rat Hole and knocked him down by the faint track that could still be seen through the grass.

"Find the Pale slave called Tali, you treacherous hog-rat. Find the vile spell-caster this night, or die a cursed, unshriven traitor."

Tears ballooned out Tinyhead's raw eyelids, but they were stuck together and would not open. He grunted, groaned, then flopped out a white and black tongue and began to lick Tali's scent from the grass.

PART TWO

PURSUIT

CHAPTER 37

The wrythen made another fluttering circuit of his alkoyl still, and another. Despite centuries of planning, every single thing had gone wrong.

Deroe was breaking the possession. If he discovered where the host was, he would gouge the master nuclix out of her in a place the wrythen could not reach, which was practically everywhere, and the battle would be lost.

Now the wrythen's own people were hunting the host, planning to kill her for escaping, and that would ruin the nuclix. But if they realised it was inside her, and took it, it would destroy them.

He had to get to her first, but how? His faithful servant was somewhere in the Seethings, still clinging to a shambling kind of life, though there was no way to reach him. However, Rix's friend Tobry must be exhausted, and sooner or later he would relax his guard. When he did, the wrythen would renew the link, possess Tobry and send him after the host.

But what if Tobry broke free?

Only one weapon remained, the facinore, though it sickened the wrythen to use it. It was a reminder of how far he had fallen, and he had a healthy fear of it, too. The facinore's strength was its changeability and it was evolving rapidly, becoming harder to command by the day, but there was no choice.

Activating the pathways imprinted in the creature when he had created it by the uncanny art of *germine*, the wrythen sent it the image of the host he had seen through his faithful servant's eyes, then imitated the strident, angry *call* of the master nuclix she bore.

She is in the Seethings. Locate her via this call *and bring her to the cellar, unharmed.*

In the labyrinth between the caverns and Cython, the facinore stopped suddenly, head cocked. It gave a savage nod, scraped a morsel of deliciously decayed flesh from between its teeth and swallowed it, then loped away.

CHAPTER 38

"Are you all right?" said Rannilt, creeping up beside Tali. She sat by the water, shivering. She could not stop remembering now.

The skull-shaped cellar that had stunk of poisoned rats. Her mama darting and weaving as she tried to lead the hunters away from her little daughter. The masked woman so cold and cruel. The tall, round-bellied man, afraid to stand up to her. The shiny knife, the nail sticking deep into Tali's hip, the woman standing on Mama's chest as though she were rubbish and her frail ribs snapping like wishbones.

Tali jumped up, caught sight of her reflection in the still pool, and cried, "Mama!"

"Tali?" said Rannilt anxiously.

Tali could not look away. There were no mirrors in the Empound and she had never seen her face clearly before, but it could have been Iusia looking up at her. She studied every detail, tears stinging in her eyes as she remembered all the good times. Despite their slavery, she had always felt safe before Iusia had been killed.

She dashed the tears away and rage surged so furiously that her jaw clicked. How dare they treat her mama that way? She had never done anything to hurt them. How they were going to pay.

But first she had to find the killers and Rix was the best lead she had. Why had he been in the cellar anyway? Tobry had said that Rix was not a bad man, but had he, even as a boy, been part of the crime? Tali could not believe that of any child ... yet she had a faded memory of blood on his hands.

"What's the matter?" said Rannilt.

Tali shuddered and pulled the coarse robes around her, struggling to think. Her plan had collapsed. She had assumed that, as the first Pale ever to escape from Cython, she would be welcomed home as a hero. In reality, the Pale were despised as traitors. And there was no House vi Torgrist to help her. She had no one in the world save this grubby little urchin staring at her so anxiously.

Tali forced a smile. "When I looked at my reflection in the water, for a minute I thought it was my mother. Don't fret, I'm all right now."

"She must have been very beautiful." Rannilt twined her arms around Tali, sighing and snuggling.

"Yes, she was," Tali said absently.

"Why was that big man so nasty? How could anyone not like you?"

Tali gave her a hug. Why did Rix hold the Pale in such contempt? Did he blame them for not escaping from their masters? It was like a sick joke, save that Rix believed every word he had said. The woman in the cellar had called Iusia *Pale scum*, and if everyone in Hightspall thought that way, Tali and Rannilt would be in more danger in their homeland than they had been in Cython. What could she do? How could she go on when everything she believed in was regarded as a lie?

Someone had been lied to, but she did not think it had been the Pale. They had definitely been taken to Cython a thousand years ago as child hostages, for she had often heard the Cythonians laugh about it. And she did not think the Pale had made up the story about being noble. Therefore, Hightspall's view of the Pale was wrong—wickedly so.

"Your slave's mark is better than mine," said Rannilt.

"Nonsense, child," said Tali.

It was true, though. Rannilt's mark was just a squiggle burnt into her shoulder, while Tali's was an elegant pattern of lines and swirls, identical to her family seal and as beautiful as it was old.

She ran a finger around it. To the Cythonians, the slave mark had been a sign of eternal bondage. To Rix it was the mark of treachery and collaboration—it raised feelings so powerful that he had thrown up at the sight of it. But to her it would always be the symbol of House vi Torgrist, one of the oldest of the noble houses, and of vi Torgrist's strength, longevity and steadfastness. It was also a symbol of hope—that she could succeed despite the opposition of both her enemies and her own people.

Tali pressed the seal against her arm, leaving a white impression there. It made her feel better so she made a series of marks down her arm. She was the last of her line and the heir to House vi Torgrist, therefore, her house *wasn't* extinct. It was up to her to raise it again. After she had gained justice for Mama, Grandmama, Great-Grandmama and Great-Great-Grandmama, that's what she was going to do.

Despite Rix's threat, and the foul things he had said about her, she had to find a way to get the truth out of him. And she had better hurry; night was bound to bring the enemy.

Her thoughts turned to Tobry, who had magery in his pocket and might be able to help her uncover her own. Tobry had been kind to her, and clearly he did not despise the Pale—another positive. Her world was beginning to tilt back.

Tali tried to rise but could not move. "Help me up, Rannilt. My muscles have locked."

As the girl heaved her to her feet, every bone and sinew protested. Tali hobbled around the pool like old Mimoy until her muscles came back to life.

"Where are we goin'?" said Rannilt.

"After Rix and Tobry."

"But he was so mean to you."

"Not as mean as the enemy will be."

"If he does it again, he'll be *really* sorry."

The girl's fierce loyalty warmed Tali more than she could have imagined. A third positive. "Yes, we'll fix him."

She drank from the pool, bathed her hot face and told herself that the open spaces could not harm her. It was a silly, irrational phobia and she was going to overcome it. She wove grass into a band and tied the hat brim down to her eyebrows. Her legs and back ached down to the bones, but pain was a slave's lot and she had learned to endure it.

"I'm a really hard worker," said Rannilt. She was plodding along, exhausted and trying to hide it. They had been following Rix's tracks for hours.

There was no sign of anyone in the scorched lands. It was late afternoon now, at most an hour of daylight left. Tali walked faster. The Seethings was no place to navigate after dark.

Her head was aching again. She kept seeing the swirling lights and coloured patterns, and twice more she heard that distant note in her inner ear, pealing like an unanswered question. She had first heard it as the sunstone imploded and had associated it with freedom and liberation. Now it sounded angry.

"I can wash clothes and carry water," said Rannilt. "And when I clean fish, I don't leave a speck of meat on the bones."

The girl had been nattering about her accomplishments for ages. "I'm sure you're really good."

"I know how to massage achin' muscles," Rannilt said shrilly. "I'm really quiet, too. You hardly know I'm there."

A pointed suggestion was on the tip of Tali's tongue when she realised what was behind it. She stopped abruptly.

"Is somethin' the matter?" Rannilt cried, and began to bite a bloody knuckle.

"Rannilt, I can't be your mother. But I'm not going to turn you away either."

"You're not?" cried the girl, throwing her arms around Tali and bursting into tears.

"Of course not. We're going to stay together. Don't worry, I'll look after you."

"And I'm goin' to look after you."

Rannilt looked up, eyes shining and nostrils running rivers. She burrowed her face into Tali's chest, inadvertently wiping her nose on the silk gown, then went skipping off.

Tali looked down at the claggy smears and sighed. How was she supposed to look after the child when she didn't know how to look after herself? She looked up and the sky overturned. She wrenched on the hat brim.

"I wish the sun would go down." Sunset had better take the phobia with it.

"I don't." Rannilt shuddered.

"Why not?"

"Things live in the dark. Things come out of the dark."

"Nonsense, child. That's just an irrational—" Tali broke off. They weren't so different—they just feared different things. "What sort of things?"

"I can feel somethin' bad. Really bad, waitin' for the dark."

It didn't help Tali's own frame of mind. "I'm sure we'll find Tobry and Rix before then."

Several weary minutes passed. "Why do you keep doin' that?" said Rannilt.

"What?"

"Tracin' your slave mark."

Tali had not realised that she was doing it. "When I've got a problem, sometimes it seems to help . . ." Should she tell Rannilt? It would be wrong to shield her. "I keep hearing an angry note in my head and I'm worried the enemy are using it to track me. I don't think they're far behind."

She glanced over her shoulder. If the Cythonians were closing in, they were concealed by the mirages that shimmered and danced in every direction.

"Why don't you block it?" said Rannilt. "That's how I hide from the mean girls."

"How?"

"I make their eyesight go foggy so they can't see me."

"And that works?"

"Sometimes. But it'd be different for you." Rannilt took Tali's arm, staring at the slave mark, then traced the central part with a dirty finger. "Why don't you close it?"

"Close what?" Tali said irritably, for her feet and back and head hurt and she was very afraid.

"This, in the centre." Rannilt was looking anxious again. "See this bit here, it's like an open shell, and if you close it the note can't get out. Then they won't be able to find you . . ." She bit her lip.

Tali realised that she was frowning. It sounded like nonsense. She inspected the central part of her slave mark and supposed that the pair of touching semicircles there did resemble a shell open at its hinge.

"How am I supposed to close it?" She felt obtuse.

"In yer mind. It helps if you close yer eyes."

Tali did so and tried to visualise her slave mark. Though she could have drawn it from memory, creating a visible image in her inner eye proved more difficult than she had imagined. Ah, there it was.

As she focused on the shell, she heard the angry note again. "Can you see anyone coming, Rannilt?"

"No. Take hold of the shell," Rannilt said, sounding deliberately calm. "Push it closed."

As Tali mentally grasped the two sides of the shell the angry note cut off, to be replaced by a higher one, faint and rarefied as though it came from far away. As though, she thought, her angry note was a call, and this note was an answer. She pushed on the two sides of the shell, forced them shut and the distant note was gone, and so were the swirling patterns and the coloured lights. Her head spun; she staggered and grabbed blindly at the girl.

"Tali?" Rannilt cried.

"Sorry. I've been wading through fog for days and suddenly I'm free. Thank you."

The relief was so great that Tali felt weak in the knees. She had not felt her normal self since the night she had come of age, when she had woken feeling as though a stone heart was grinding against her skull.

They trudged on and the sun went down. Tali looked up at the sky and it did not rock.

"It's waitin' in the dark," whispered Rannilt. "Waitin', waitin'."

Instinctively, Tali checked behind her. "Now you've got me worried."

The light faded and the temperature dropped sharply. She pulled her robes around her and was gazing at the dark sky and the jewel-like points of stars, the first she had ever seen, when Rannilt stopped, moaning deep in her throat. Tali caught her thin wrist, afraid the girl was lapsing back into the enraptured state where her magery had burst out in those golden rays.

But Rannilt's eyes were fixed on a hollow fifty yards ahead, from which at least a dozen of the enemy were rising, including a stumbling giant with a little head. Somehow, incredibly, despite the hole through his head, Tinyhead had led them to her.

"Run!" Tali said softly. "Run, Rannilt, and don't look back."

"I'm not leavin' you." Rannilt's teeth were chattering.

"Find Rix and Tobry. Get help, go!"

Rannilt bolted. Tali broke into the fastest hobble she could manage, but she had not gone ten yards when a whirling missile went *zivva-zivva-zivva* past her left ear, struck a small salt mound not far ahead and went off, flinging scorching white crystals everywhere.

Salt shards stung her cheeks. A spinning chunk the size of a fist struck her in the belly hard enough to double her over, then the dust was stinging her eyes and they were watering so badly that she could not see. Tali choked on air laden with salt dust, so much salt in her nose and mouth and throat that she began to retch and could not stop.

She was lurching around, knowing she was lost, when a chucklash wrapped around her bottom and went off in a series of cracks that drove her to her knees. The pain was excruciating. As she was clawing at the crusted ground, a heavy boot drove into her side, knocking her down.

"Got you," said Orlyk, tight with glee, and kept kicking.

CHAPTER 39

"You're a piece of work, you really are," said Tobry when he finally caught up to Rix, miles from the oasis.

Dark was settling shroud-like over the Seethings, though the way ahead was lit by wisps of marsh light and uncanny yellow glows from several of the lifeless pools.

Leather's flanks were crusted with dried foam. Rix had dismounted and was leading her along a burnt-black isthmus meandering between a series of steaming ponds. The ground here was so hard that the horses' hooves clicked with each step. The air had an alkaline tang and left a slippery, soapy taste in the mouth.

"I don't want to talk about it." The anger had passed and he felt a sick emptiness now. He had behaved shamefully, but . . . how dare a Pale speak to him that way?

"I do. Tali said—"

"I don't want to hear it." Rix glared at his friend. "You fancy her. That's why you're taking her side."

Tobry tried to smile but it wasn't convincing. "You know me— I never get attached. And Tali said something rather interesting—"

"Whatever she said, I don't believe it."

Tobry's jaw was clenched and so was his fist. "She said that the Pale spring from noble children, a hundred and forty-four of them, given by Hightspall as hostages to Cython a thousand years ago. *And never ransomed.*"

Rix kicked a stone into the pool to his right. It sank below the surface with a viscous *gloop*, as though it had plopped into a vat of glycerine. "You must like the wench. I've never seen you get so worked up about anything."

Tobry ground his teeth and continued. "She said the Pale are enslaved, and beaten for the smallest infringement. She said her best friend was beheaded yesterday because she used magery to save herself from a flogging."

"She's lying," Rix said half-heartedly, for he knew how hard it was to lie to Tobry. He could read people the way anyone else might read a map. Rix stared ahead, refusing to meet his friend's eyes.

"Tali said magery is forbidden in Cython."

"We know that."

"Will you listen!" roared Tobry. "They kill every slave who shows a gift for it—*even children*. They were going to kill that little urchin hiding behind the tussocks—"

Rix swung around. "WHAT?"

"You heard."

"They kill *children*, because they have the gift?"

"That's what she said."

Rix did not want to believe it, yet Tobry could sniff out a half-truth a mile away. "Can the Pale really spring from child hostages?"

"Never ransomed, Tali said. Hightspall's noblest children, abandoned to the enemy. She was furious about it."

"Why haven't we heard about it before? Everyone knows the Pale are traitors. All the history books say so."

"How would you know?" said Tobry. "You've never read a schoolbook in your life."

Rix scowled. "Who has time for that rubbish?"

"You saw the bruises on Tali, and the little girl was covered in them. Does that sound like they serve willingly?"

"All right, I believe you," Rix snarled. If Tali was telling the truth, it made his behaviour even more inexcusable. "How did they escape from Cython?"

"A question the chancellor will certainly be asking, once he hears." Tobry came up close. "Listen! Tali said they're going to war in ten days."

At last! Rix thought. "Then we'd better ride home like a hurricane." He took hold of the saddle horn.

"Not yet."

"Why not?" Rix snapped. If there was to be a war, his life would mean something at last.

"The Caulderon road can't be far ahead. We can send warnings with the first riders we meet—they'll be a lot faster than our worn-out horses. Then we're going back."

Rix prepared to swing into the saddle. "There isn't time."

Tobry's fingers dug into Rix's shoulder, holding him back. "You've acted dishonourably to a woman and abandoned a child in danger. You can't run away."

"I'm not running away," said Rix, all the more irritated with Tobry for pointing out the uncomfortable truth. Rix had offered Tali help, then insulted her and fled. His cheeks burnt. "All right! But if they're not at the oasis, I'm not searching the Seethings for them. My house is in danger. My country."

They had just reached the Caulderon road, a broad, well-built thoroughfare paved with slabs of white sandstone, when a crimson fireball erupted many miles to their right, bursting and billowing upwards in silence.

"What the hell was that?" said Rix. "Was it an eruption?" Though it wasn't in the right place. The Vomits were west of here, not east.

Small white flashes twinkled around the base of the fireball, and shortly flames lit up the rising cloud. Uncanny flames, not orange or red, but a lurid, unnatural crimson.

"I've never seen any fire like that before," Tobry said slowly.

The ground quivered and thunder rumbled, though not normal thunder. It had a brittle, crackling quality.

"New volcanoes sometimes appear from nowhere."

"It's not a volcano." Tobry consulted his map by a glimmer of mage light. "Close to Gullihoe, I'd say."

"Then what is it?" The answer was obvious but Rix did not want to jinx them by putting it into words. He looked up and down the road but saw no lights, no travellers. "We'd better find out."

As they rode across undulating country, the dry grass swishing around the horses' fetlocks, more fireballs appeared behind them. Two were towards the south coast of the lake on the far side of the Seethings, three others in the direction of Caulderon. Rix wheeled Leather about and drew his sword.

"It's war! Come on."

Tobry caught the reins. "They'll be long gone by the time we can reach Caulderon."

"What if they're not? What if they're in the city?" Was this what his nightmares meant? Were they blasting the palace walls right now, butchering his helpless people and murdering children they suspected of having the gift?

"Caulderon isn't *that* unprepared. We can't do anything for them, but we may be able to help Gullihoe."

Rix strained forwards. "I've got to fight."

"We could learn vital intelligence in Gullihoe." Rix did not reply. "Besides," Tobry added, "the enemy might still be there. You could put that sword to good use."

It was well after ten o'clock when they crested a gravel-topped hill and looked down on the smoke-wreathed ruins of the stone town. The central arch of the thousand-year-old bridge across the river had fallen. The granaries, warehouses and barges along the shore were ablaze, and hundreds of cottages, and the mayoral mansion lay in ruins.

"What can have done this?" said Rix. He sniffed the smoky air. "That's not blasting powder."

"Something far stronger," Tobry said quietly. "I don't like this, Rix."

They rode down, keeping to the shadows, though it soon became evident that the attackers had gone. Dead lay everywhere in the main street, women, children and men, yet few bore any sign of injury.

"What's going on?" said Rix, more unnerved than he would have been by a battlefield full of dead. "How can the enemy kill without leaving a trace?"

He crouched beside an elegantly dressed old woman who lay in the middle of the street as if she had fallen asleep. A red wig lay beside her; her own hair was white, wispy and scant. The only sign of trauma was a dribble of blood from her ears. The child beside her had a bloody nose and red eyes, but no bruises or evident wounds.

"I'm not seeing any enemy dead," said Tobry, who was walking down the middle of the street, sword in hand. "Nor any spears, arrows or other abandoned weapons. Nothing to indicate a fight."

Rix checked another group of bodies: a stout woman with grey hair, dressed like a nurse, and two little boys in nightgowns, all dead without a mark on them. Rix felt a sharp pain in the centre of his chest, as though they had been his own sons.

Tobry emerged from the doorway of a substantial home. "There's been no looting either."

"What kind of enemy doesn't loot afterwards?"

A long pause, then Tobry said, "One that values nothing of ours. Or expects to soon have it all."

"I don't like that kind of talk."

Someone groaned, not far away. He swung down and made his

way towards a half-naked figure convulsing in the shadow cast by a broken wall, a short, balding man with skinny little legs and a massive belly.

"Stop!" Tobry said urgently.

Rix froze, blade out, eyes searching the shadows. Tobry conjured a tiny light from his fingertips and came up beside him.

"What's the matter?" said Rix.

The light touched on the man's bare back and side, where the skin was embedded with dozens of small spines like red pins.

"Looks like he's backed into a needlebush," Rix added.

The man made a clotted sound in his throat. His watering eyes were blank—he did not appear to have seen them. Rix was bending over when Tobry drove a shoulder into him, knocking him out of the way.

"Don't touch anything!"

Rix took another look at the man, whose skin was red and raised around each of the spines. Purple nodules were swelling visibly as though a handful of bean seeds were embedded under the skin. He felt his hackles rising.

"Those aren't needlebush spines," said Tobry.

"What are they?"

The man kicked with a bare foot, rolled onto his back, screamed and wrenched himself onto his side again, thrashing and keening. His nails tore at one of the nodules, which burst, discharging red-black pus with a foul smell. Rix leapt backwards.

Tobry passed his elbrot over the man and subvocalised several words. A blurred shadow appeared around him, kicking and squirming, then came into focus. It lurched up from the ground, reeled about and staggered backwards down the street. His shirt rose from the ground, fitted itself to him. He began to scratch and claw at himself as the sky rained millions of tiny streaks. Rix made out a thin squeal, the lost echo of the man's first cry, perhaps, and the shadow faded into the night.

Tobry crouched and sniffed. "A new kind of pox, not one I've seen before, and it came from that rain of needles fired into Gullihoe by the enemy. Back away, Rix. You can't do anything for him."

Rix's stomach heaved at the sight and the smell. "There's no hope?"

"He's going to die most unpleasantly."

"I'll put him out of his misery, then."

"At the cost of your own life?"

"Tobe?" said Rix.

"The pestilence may be contagious."

"What pox is it?"

"How the hell would I know?"

"But . . . this is against all the rules of war. What scum would do this?"

"The Five Heroes did it to the enemy two thousand years ago. I dare say that's where they got the idea."

Rix felt blood bloom in his cheeks. "This isn't the time to undermine morale."

"It's in the *Axilead*. Axil Grandys boasted that he collected plague corpses and catapulted them over the enemy's walls."

Rix put his hands over his ears. "Don't tell me any more. Leave me some illusions."

As they moved on, the man began to thrash and squeal. Rix quickened his pace, but down the street they saw more infected people, many more.

"None of the dead are armed," said Rix. "They were taken by surprise. I can't believe that the enemy would attack without declaring war."

"Axil Grandys did."

"Damn you, Tobe!" Rix stalked away. "I've got to get home."

"The other blasts were much closer to home," said Tobry. "All Caulderon will know by now. Go if you must, but I'm staying. We can learn a lot about the enemy by the way they've attacked."

Tobry was right. If they could decipher the enemy's tactics it would be vital intelligence. "Why haven't they put in a garrison?" said Rix.

"Maybe they don't want to hold Gullihoe."

Tobry continued down the street, using magery to reconstruct the attack. Ahead, a stocky young man lay on his back, milky eyes staring upwards. His clothes were charred on the left-hand side and his face was as red as sunburn, though there was no mark of injury on him.

"Dead?" said Rix.

Tobry nodded.

There were more bodies, though far less than the number Rix would have expected for a town as big as Gullihoe. No one called out to them, though they heard groaning coming from beneath rubble they could not have shifted without ropes and winches. The rest of the survivors had fled.

Ahead, a young woman also lay dead with sunburnt face and milky eyes. Her body was twisted, as though she had been writhing before she died, her fingernails broken where she had clawed at the ground.

Rix straightened her out, pulled her gown down and closed her staring eyes. A slash-shaped burn mark across her belly was deeply charred as if a length of red-hot metal had struck her.

Rix shivered. "Magery?"

Tobry waved his elbrot above the mark. Rix saw a linear flash and a shadow figure clutching at her belly. He shook his head. "Not an iota." He stood upright, looking grey and weary and twice his age. "But there's something dark at work here."

"Tali had a welt on her shoulder," said Rix. "Nothing as bad as that, but the shape was the same."

Tobry sniffed the charred wound. "Smells like an alchymical device."

The hair rose on Rix's scalp. "What kind of war is this, where they can do such destruction and we don't know how?"

"Magery isn't telling me as much as I'd hoped. All the more reason to find Tali, who knows the enemy." He looked at Rix questioningly.

"I've seen enough," said Rix. "If we're going to find her, let's go."

They mounted and headed back, as fast as it was safe to ride in the dark.

"Who are the Cythonians, anyway?" said Tobry an hour later. They were riding down a country road and there was just enough light to see stubbled fields to either side. To their right, a series of small hills made dark mounds against the sky.

"We know who they are," Rix said irritably.

"We know who they *were* when they were called Cythians. We haven't seen them in fifteen hundred years."

"What rot! Our traders deal with them at the Merchantery. We buy the damned heatstones off them."

"*We* don't trade with them. Our traders deal with the Vicini out-landers, and they trade with Cython. I've never heard of anyone setting eyes on a Cythonian until we came on those unconscious ones at the Rat Hole."

"How did they come to go underground, anyway?"

Tobry gave him a sardonic glance. "Regretting the history books you didn't read?"

"I'm starting to see the use of them. But, Tobe, after they lost the war the Cythians were nothing but filthy *degradoes*, living in muck and killing each other. They were thought to have died out, then they reappeared as a force living underground where we couldn't touch them—as the Cythonians. What happened?"

"That's a good question."

"Do you have a good answer?"

"No one does . . . though I've heard that an early chancellor—just before they disappeared—tried to wipe them out in secret."

Worms wriggled up Rix's spine. "I haven't heard that."

"It's not in the history books, nor taught by the tutors. One night, according to the tale, bands of nameless mercenaries sur-rounded the *degradoes'* three camps, locked the gates and set the camps ablaze. Then archers shot everyone trying to escape."

"The writer must have meant their army camps." Rix could jus-tify the torching of an enemy army camp in wartime, though he would not have locked the gates.

"They had no army, Rix. The *degradoes* hadn't been allowed weapons since their defeat, two hundred years before. The camps were miserable shanty towns, even more squalid than the ones sur-rounding Caulderon, and they burnt like kindling."

Rix shifted uneasily in the saddle. "How do you know the chan-cellor was behind it?"

His artist's eye, sometimes a blessing but lately a curse, showed him every terrible detail clearly enough to paint it. He could hear the screams, see the flesh charring and smell the burnt bodies as though he was there.

"Some of the mercenaries were so sickened by their part in genocide that they revealed the name of their paymaster."

"If the enemy were wiped out, how did Cython come about?"

"No one knows. For two hundred years they were thought extinct, then suddenly it revealed itself—a new civilisation with defences we could never break—"

"Taunting us by their very presence," said Rix, half-heartedly, still seeing the burning camps.

"The *degradoes* were a ruined people, raddled by pox and drink and *sniffily*," said Tobry. "So how did a handful of them—for any who did escape could have been no more than a handful—set up such a powerful civilisation, so quickly?"

Rix said nothing.

"That may turn out to be the most vital question of all," said Tobry.

CHAPTER 40

"I killed Overseer Banj with magery and I can do you too," Tali blustered. If she did not resist they would crush her like a slave, yet she knew she would pay for her defiance.

The guards formed a line with her in the middle and Tinyhead ahead of her, and roped themselves together. Orlyk waddled down the line, inspected Tali's bonds then brought a meaty knee up into her belly.

Tali hit the baked earth, the stars going in and out of focus. A guard unshuttered his lantern and the bluish light of a glowstone shone into her eyes.

"We can drag you all the miles back to the shaft," said Orlyk, "grinding your face off against the ground. I'd enjoy that."

Tali's back felt as though she was still carrying the sunstone. She tried to get up but there was no strength in her legs. The guards heaved her upright and jerked on the rope. She stumbled on, the bindings already chafing her wrists and despair whispering in her ear. Rannilt would not find help. Lost in the Seethings on a dark night, the terrified child would be lucky to survive. *It's waitin' in the dark*, she had said. *Waitin', waitin'*.

Tali's last hope, in Tobry, was fading by the minute. Rix must have refused him. She could only rely on herself. Well, she had been in hopeless situations before and succeeded. She *would* find a way.

"I met two Hightspallers back at the oasis," said Tali, testing her bonds. They did not budge. "Powerful men riding fast horses. They'll come howling out of the darkness and cut you down."

"Hightspall despises the Pale. They won't come," sneered Orlyk.

Tali flexed her wrists until the skin tore, trying to stretch the bonds enough to slip a hand free. The rope did not give. "How do you know that?"

"We feed stories to the heatstone merchants."

"What stories?"

"About how lovingly the Pale serve us. Your people lap up every word."

"But Tobry liked me," said Tali plaintively, then cursed her lack of self-control.

Glee lit Orlyk's dark eyes. "Once they see that, they won't even remember your name."

In the distance a cloud, tinted with crimson fire, gushed up. Another appeared far to the left, in the direction of Caulderon, while a third mushroomed on the right. Tali bit down on a cry. The war had begun.

"We have tactics to defeat every weapon Hightspall possesses," said Orlyk. "Caulderon will fall within a week, and we'll show the survivors the same mercy they showed us in the first war."

The enemy must have advanced their plans because of Tali's escape, and the attack had come before Tobry could have sent warning. Could Caulderon fall that easily? She did not want to believe it . . . but the enemy had terrible new weapons.

Tali scanned the darkness and saw only ill omens: behind her, the eerie clouds rising ever higher; ahead, red flickering above the crater of the Brown Vomit. It was erupting again. From somewhere close by, steam whistled up through a crack. The Seethings was a boiling pressure-kettle and they were walking across the top.

The trudge resumed. The small hole through Tinyhead's skull had scabbed over. How could he still be alive? Yet alive he was, and in pain. She thought he was suffering more than she was.

"Mathter," he groaned. "Mathter, help me."

Tali felt an aching pressure in her skull, as if something was attempting to prise open the shell with which she had blocked the *call*. She tightened her mental grip and after a minute or two the pressure died away.

The trek continued, one stumbling, exhausting hour after another. Tinyhead made a gurgling sound in his throat and extended his arms towards the unseen mountains beyond the Vomits.

"Mathter," he wailed, "help me."

Orlyk came stalking back, swinging a chuck-lash in one meaty hand. "Enough!" She snapped it against his chest, hard enough to sting though not hard enough to set it off, and returned to the front.

Was Tinyhead in anguish because he had failed his master? She thought so. Could she make use of that devotion? Tali choked back hysterical laughter. He had betrayed her mother, and she loathed him more than anyone save her killers. Yet back at the Rat Hole he had revealed an unexpected nobility—he did nothing for his own gain, only for love of his master.

"Mathter? Help me do your will, Mathter."

Orlyk stalked down and struck him across the mouth with the chuck-lash, *crack-crack-crack*. Tinyhead lurched around, spitting out blood and broken teeth. A blistered welt ran from ear to ear and his gory mouth was stretched in agony. His eyes wept red tears but he made no sound.

How could he hold back such pain? Tali would have screamed loudly enough to bring up her oesophagus. Here is a man! she marvelled. How I've underestimated him. She would always hate Tinyhead for what he had done, yet she could also admire his unswerving dedication. And his master did not want her taken back to Cython and executed . . .

Using him was a faint hope, almost non-existent, but better than nothing.

"Tinyhead?" she said softly, praying that the crackling of salt crystals underfoot would mask her voice.

His nodular head creaked around as though his joints were choked with sand. His ruined mouth moved silently.

"There's only one way you can serve your master now," said Tali.

The inflamed eyes bulged. His throat quivered, his tongue squelched around in his wet mouth.

"Betrayer, away . . . " he said under his breath.

"You have to take me to the cellar."

The thought of returning to that place made her tremble, yet, whether the murder cellar was her doom, or a step on the road of her quest, she had to go there.

"Can't betray . . . own people," said Tinyhead.

She leaned forwards. If any of the guards realised what she was up to, Orlyk's next chuck-lash would take half her face off. "You betrayed them when you led my mother there."

"Different now. War!"

"If Orlyk takes me back I'll be killed . . . and the thing your master wants will be lost." It was a guess, but there was evidence for it. "Cleave to your people and you betray your master. You have to choose."

"Can't."

"You must."

"Can't do anything. *Blocked*."

"Who blocks you?" Tali repeated, more loudly than she had intended.

From five yards away, Orlyk hurled a chuck-lash across Tali's belly. She did not hear it explode, for the linear flare of pain, like a burning blade cutting her in half, overwhelmed all her senses. She doubled over, wanting to scream then wanting to vomit, jamming her knuckles into her mouth to prevent herself from doing either.

Not for anything would she give Orlyk the satisfaction: not even if it killed her.

Tali straightened, her midriff a shriek of pain, expecting to see a mortal gash across her belly and entrails spilling out, but there was only a red welt an inch across and a foot and a half long. Her robes were burnt through, though, and the beautiful gown was ruined. That hurt more than her own pain.

With a grunt of satisfaction, Orlyk urged the group to greater speed. Tali wiped her flooding eyes. Tinyhead was staring at her, and she thought she saw compassion in his eyes, though they were swiftly hooded. No, she must have imagined it.

A panacea occurred to her, though she could not waste it on herself. "I have something that can numb your pain," she murmured.

"Don't speak to me."

"It might *unblock* you so you can do what your master requires."

It was a guess, though who else could have blocked such a powerful man?

"What is it?" said Tinyhead.

"Purple Pixie." A last, shrivelled toadstool lay in the bottom of her pocket, so desiccated that the Cythonians had not noticed it when searching her. Could the hallucinations it brought release the block?

"I'll have it," said Tinyhead.

"Stop for a second."

He stopped, grimacing and rubbing his thigh, and the lead rope slackened enough for her to fish the Purple Pixie out and palm it. Orlyk brandished another chuck-lash at him. He faced her stolidly. She glanced at the rising columns of crimson-tinged smoke, and the angle of the stars, and her mouth turned down. She was afraid.

"The enemy will have a hundred patrols out by now," said Orlyk. "Faster!"

They continued, limping across rippled salt crusted so hard that every footstep jarred. To the left, mist rose from a suspiciously smooth expanse; on the right, a long, narrow pool was so clear that Tali could see the shining shapes of crystals on the bottom, reflecting the starlight. She judged that they would reach the edge of the Seethings in another hour, after which they had at least an hour's climb to reach the Rat Hole. Once there, she had no hope. It had to be now.

Tinyhead reached back with a hand that could have enveloped her skull and she pressed the Purple Pixie into it. As he raised the hand to his face, she saw that his coordination was improving. Another marvel—he was beginning to recover.

The toadstool would take a few minutes to take effect but, even if it unblocked him, what could he do against twenty? If he tried to escape, Orlyk would cut him down.

This part of the Seethings belied its name. The night was silent. No hoof beats, no Tobry. All she could hear was the crunch of boots on salt and a distant *gloop-gloop* of bubbling mud.

The big man lurched sideways, and in the same instant Tali heard that distant *call* in her head, her enemy, searching for her. Did he know Tinyhead was recovering? Her mental shell was gaping. She forced it to close, cutting the *call* off.

Tinyhead groaned, "Master?"

Something bright flashed in arcs through the lantern light, before him and behind, and Tali's lead rope slackened. He had cut it. Before she could run he elbowed her out of the line, wound one rope around each wrist and heaved with all his strength, ducking aside so the fore and after guards cannoned into each other. Glowstone lanterns tumbled through the air and went out, save for one whose slanting rays lit up a strip of the unnaturally smooth ground to the right.

"What happened?" yelled Orlyk. The heaped Cythonians were all shouting, yelling and trying to untangle themselves.

Tinyhead snapped the bows of the three archers over his knee, swept Tali up in one arm and ran over the piled guards. He stepped with a crunch onto Orlyk's broad nose, twisted, and bolted onto the smooth expanse.

"Go back!" Tali cried. "You'll fall through."

The surface rocked, quaking under his massive feet like an ice floe on a pond. But it was not ice; she could feel the heat radiating up from underneath. He was running across the baked crust on a pool of scalding mud, and if it broke, as it surely must under Tinyhead's weight, they would be cooked alive.

CHAPTER 41

"Ged avter dem!" howled Orlyk, blood belching from her mashed nose.

Lanterns were righted and their beams directed towards Tinyhead. Tali looked back as a lanky, big-footed fellow stepped onto the crusted mud. White circles ringed his eyes—he was sure he was going to die. But the crust did not crack. Feet that size would spread the load—a smaller load than Tinyhead plus Tali. He moved forwards, gingerly.

"All ob you!" screeched Orlyk. "Ib dey ged away, ve faze Libbing Blade."

The rest of the guards moved onto the crust, then Orlyk hurled a black and yellow length at Tinyhead. Tali, helpless in his grip as he fleeted across the quaking surface, watched the death-lash spinning towards them. It could take off a limb in one flaring excruciation.

"Left!" she yelled in Tinyhead's quivering ear.

He sprang two yards to the left, landing with a thump that shook the surface, and one foot broke through three inches of crust into steaming mud. He was heaving his foot out when the whirling death-lash struck the point he had sprang from and went off in yellow and black fire, blasting jagged chunks of crust and gouts of boiling mud everywhere.

Tali shrank into the shelter of Tinyhead's torso. He was struck on the face and arms by chunks of crust and clots of boiling mud, though he showed no pain. The toadstool must still be numbing him. From the point of the blast the crust fractured like ice, one crack snaking towards Tinyhead, a bigger, broader crack zipping the way they had come.

"Nod dogedder," yelled Orlyk, for the guards were moving in a mass. "Zpread out, zpread out!"

A line of cracks was sweeping towards Tinyhead, the crust breaking into angular pieces which would not have supported a child's weight. He leapt sideways onto solid crust, though as he landed it cracked again.

"Slide on it," said Tali in her Lady vi Torgrist voice. "Three inches of crust might take our weight if there's no impact."

Tinyhead knew when to obey. He slid his right foot forward one stride, took his weight on it with a creaking that cracked the crust around him but did not break through, then slid the other foot up and past it.

As the broad crack from the death-lash zigged and zagged in the direction of the guards, they scattered in all directions, two scrambling back towards the shore, the others sweeping out to Tinyhead's right and left, then ahead, moving as fast as they could to cut him off.

They were twenty yards ahead now and coming together to form a line. Tinyhead was hesitating when the woman on the left-hand end of the line screamed, dropped her lantern and flung out her arms. The crust was cracking around her, for she was big and solid, and her small feet concentrated the load.

Had she kept moving she might have made it, but she froze as the overloaded crust cracked on all sides, leaving her on a mud floe only a yard across. It tilted, she threw her weight the other way and the floe split, dumping her into the mire. Steam gushed out as she slid down to chest level, floating in hot quick-mud with the consistency of glue. She struggled furiously but there was no solid ground below her, and nothing to take a grip on.

"Help me," she said shrilly, but the other Cythonians dared not move her way.

Tinyhead slid a yard towards her, then another. Tali could hear each breath rasping into his lungs.

The woman threw out her hands towards him. "It's burning, it's burning!"

They were only yards away now. Her face was scarlet; she was in such agony that no human being could have passed her by ... yet if Tinyhead tried to save her, he would surely fall through.

Tali checked on the other guards. They were moving carefully around the cracked area, closing the gap.

"You can't save her," Tali said. It was cruel, but nothing could be done.

Taking a firm grip on her, Tinyhead slid forwards another yard and stretched out his free arm. The woman caught his fingers, clinging desperately, and he slowly drew back, straining to lift her from the sucking mud without cracking the surface beneath him. Her chest came free, her waist. The exposed skin was raw, blistered, weeping.

Then she stuck at the hips. She gasped, "Pull harder," and began to flail about.

"Don't move," said Tinyhead, swinging her arm gently to try and break the suction.

"It's burning. Get me out!" she howled.

Overcome by panic, she thrashed wildly, lost her grip and slid down into the hot mud again, and the crust cracked to pieces. Nothing could save her now.

Tali watched in helpless horror as Tinyhead carried her away, and she had to cover her ears to block out the screaming. The woman's thrashing widened the cracks and one zipped towards the line of guards, who backpedalled hastily.

A burly fellow wearing red tasselled boots made a desperate bid for the edge of the pond and almost made it, moving so fleetly that he was off each breaking chunk of crust before it could collapse under him. But, only a few yards from safety, he made the mistake of lunging, trying to reach the edge in a single leap.

It was too much for the fragile crust. His feet broke through, he made a desperate tumbling drive for the edge but fell short and went in head-first. There was no scream, for he had plunged down to the waist. One beating arm broke the surface, his legs kicked furiously for half a minute, then flopped, lifeless, as his overheated brain expired.

Tinyhead, still sliding forwards and barely outrunning the spreading cracks, looked over his shoulder. The trapped woman was still now, her face the colour of a boiled lobster. Three more guards had also gone in and their desperate efforts to escape only sank them deeper. The heat would kill them in minutes, and then they would slowly cook.

"Master," whispered Tinyhead, shaking his head from side to side as he slid on. What must it have cost him to put his master's needs ahead of the lives of his own people? "Master, I will never fail you . . . but the price . . . the price is very high."

Tali thought so too. Five more guards dead because she had dared to escape where no one else ever had. Where would it end? Her toes curled at the thought of such a death.

Orlyk, whose face and chest were drenched in blood, tossed another two death-lashes high and hard, trying to break through the crust and plunge Tinyhead in. One landed short, the other went over his head, but Tinyhead was adept at this game now. He found a smooth path to the left and soon they were out of range.

His foot struck a rough patch that was no longer crust, he stepped up onto indurated ground and all was solid underneath him. They were safe. By the time Orlyk's remaining troops reached this point, he would have disappeared into the maze of the Seethings.

Safe, ha! Tali thought with a bitter smile—if she could not free herself, she'd merely have swapped one unpleasant death for another. And even if she did escape, how far would she get with bound hands when Hightspall was at war and the enemy were swarming everywhere?

So the night proceeded, one step, then another and another. Tinyhead must have been exhausted but his grip on her never relaxed. Their passage through the Seethings was punctuated by his tormented cries to his master. She tried to ignore them. Could she extract the name his master had blocked last time?

"Who killed my mother?" she said quietly.

He did not reply. In the darkness to their left, a geyser spurted, the water having a violet luminescence. It went up so far into the frigid night that the spray falling on them was icy.

Tali worked her chafed wrists back and forth, attempting to free her hands, but the ropes had been tied too cunningly. "Who's your master, Tinyhead?"

He stopped. The ruined mouth stretched wide, though no one would have called it a smile, and he opened his free hand. On his palm lay the shrivelled Purple Pixie, complete but for the tip of its pointed hood.

"Only ate enough to unblock. Not enough to lose control." He tossed it away.

He was recovering rapidly, physically and mentally, and would soon be back to the strength he'd had when she first met him. If she was to escape, she had better try soon.

Tali gave an experimental wriggle. His arm clamped so tightly around her chest that she could not draw a full breath.

"Know what you're about," said Tinyhead. "On guard."

He began to trot, weaving between a myriad of pools and mires, quick-mud seethes and holes that, despite the phosphorescent water in them, appeared to have no bottom. Tali looked back and could no longer see the glowstone lanterns. It would take a miracle for Orlyk to catch them in this dark and deadly labyrinth.

Little consolation to her. She contemplated the possibility that Tinyhead would get her to the murder cellar after all. Caulderon could not be more than seven miles from here. Once out of the Seethings he could reach the city before dawn, even in the dark, and get inside, too. Tinyhead was a driven man. He would find a way.

An hour went by, and another, and Tali was counting down the miles. They must be close to the north-eastern edge of the Seethings. The ponds, mires and sunken lands were further apart now and she had not seen a geyser in ages. How far to Caulderon? Five miles? Four? She could see lights in the distance, probably the thickly clustered villages of Suthly County on the other side of the main road. Not long at all.

The land was lumpy here, covered in nodules and round mounds. She could hear bubbling to left and right, and a slow, oily gurgling issued up through crusted cracks. The air had the acrid smell of sulphur.

She rubbed the painful weal across her belly. Unarmed and exhausted as she was, what could she do to save herself? Tinyhead would avoid all forms of habitation, but in the densely populated land ahead a chance meeting was likely. She had to be ready to call for help.

He stopped abruptly. More lights appeared, brighter than before, revealing that the ground, the lumps and the nodules were solid yellow sulphur. But the lights were both ahead and to either side now. They weren't village lights, they were glowstone lanterns, though not Orlyk's.

"She *the one*," came a familiar voice from the darkness, an awed, enraptured voice. "Found her. She *the one*."

Wil the Sump was at the head of a second squad of Cythonians and he had led them straight to her.

CHAPTER 42

Tinyhead let out another of those shivery groans. "Master? I can't turn on my own people. Not again."

His master, if he had heard, gave no answer.

"Put the slave down, Sconts, and get out of the way," said a voice from the darkness. A deep voice, confident in its authority.

Tinyhead tightened his grip around Tali's chest. The white-coated tongue licked his ruined lips as he looked for a way of escape, but the lights blocked three sides now and distantly, on the fourth, Tali saw more glowstone lanterns. Orlyk was coming.

Tinyhead's eyes fixed on a gap in the lights ahead. His muscles tensed and his bulging head swung from side to side as he assessed his chances. Tali's right ear was squashed against his chest and she could hear the breath crackling in his lungs. Was he going to run?

"She has to die," said the deep voice, and an annular blade shone as it was raised above the speaker's head—a Living Blade. "Here and now."

"Wil saved her," moaned Wil. "She Wil's now."

"She may not die at your hands," said Tinyhead, and bolted towards the gap.

Down a gentle slope he pounded, through a patch of shadow and straight into a concealed pit of mud, the reason for the gap. But there was no crust here and he let out a gasp as his feet sank deep. For a second she thought he was going to be trapped the way

Orlyk's troops had been, but his feet found the base of the shallow pit, his thighs bunched and drove him through the hot, knee-deep mud.

Steam gushed up from each footfall and pungent gases stung Tali's nostrils, but Tinyhead was an automaton no wound or pain could stop. He reached solid ground, his mud-coated feet slipping and skidding as he climbed a gentle slope, and drove for the gap between the guards. He almost made it.

The man to the left hurled his sword, hilt forwards, its flat end striking Tinyhead above the ear. He let out an explosive grunt, dropped Tali and began to stagger around blindly. The blow had driven him back into the zombie state he'd been in after the hole had burnt through his head.

Tali landed on her shoulder, the impact numbing her whole arm, and was struggling to her feet when the guard dived on her, flattening her on the yellow ground. He put his knees in the middle of her back and held her down with all his weight. Two more guards stood to either side, their blades out-thrust, and the others ran in and held Tinyhead at bay. It was over.

He shook his head, then reeled off into the darkness, wailing, "Master, I failed you."

The man giving the orders said, "Take a firm grip on the slave. Should she escape again, our families will suffer the fate set down for her."

The guard took his weight off Tali, keeping hold of her arms. The captain was a strong, handsome fellow with a clear brown eye and a confident manner. Then he turned, and the other side of his face was a ruin of raised white scars and deep pock marks. The survivors of that explosion on the lower levels of Cython a few years ago had looked like this.

"Raise her and hold her," he said.

He examined Tali's face and slave mark, nodded and issued orders in a low voice. Ten guards formed a line to block Tinyhead in case he attacked from the darkness.

A thin, owl-eyed woman was studying the bobbing lanterns through a pair of night glasses. "Captain, it's Orlyk's squad. They'll want to take her back to Cython."

"Orlyk has allowed the Pale to escape *twice*," said the captain. "We have our orders and we're not giving her up."

"Said you wouldn't hurt her," cried Wil the Sump, waving his skinny arms.

"Nor will I," said the captain, rubbing his cheek with a callused thumb. "She won't even feel it as I take her head off."

This was it. She was going to die. Even if Rix and Tobry were to ride up with an army of a thousand, the captain would behead her before they could get close.

Tali shook off the despair. Never give up. Think, think!

Wil tried to pull the captain away from Tali. "But she *the one*."

"And *the one* has to die, Wil. The Living Blade gives a merciful death. It's more than she deserves, considering her crimes."

Could she work on Wil the way she had swayed Tinyhead? It was the faintest hope, because any of the guards would be his match in strength, and they were all around, all armed, all watchful.

Whatever Wil had seen in her, it mattered deeply to him. Could she manipulate him to create a chance of escape? How far would he go to protect her?

"You're right, Wil," said Tali. "I am *the one* and you've got to help me."

"See!" cried Wil, and stretched out his thin arms imploringly. His gruesomely enlarged nostril was dripping blood, his hands and wrists were so scarred and cracked that fluid was weeping through the skin, and there was an odd, oval bulge across his belly. "Mustn't touch her. You'll ruin the ending."

As he surged forwards, Tali caught the oily, oppressively sweet odour of alkoyl. Where did a nobody like Wil get such precious stuff? Could he be the thief that the master chymister had mentioned—the one whose clumsy theft had caused the explosion on the lower levels and burnt through that young woman's leg?

"Don't be silly, Wil." The captain held him off with one hand, gently and respectfully. Wil might be mad, but when he went into *shillilar* the matriarchs listened. "The matriarchs have decreed that *the one* has to die, to protect our future."

Tears began to drip from Wil's empty eye sockets. "Must not interfere with *shillilar*. She vital to Cython's story."

"The matriarchs look after the future, Wil. You clean out sumps."

"Tali *special*," wailed Wil.

"The matriarchs have given their orders," said the captain, "and they will be carried out."

Wil stiffened, then went rigid save for his fingers, which hooked into talons and raked at the air. "*Wil sees her*," he uttered in an ecstatic voice. "She whispers to Khirrik-ai. She—"

The captain jerked his head at the nearest guard, who took Wil around the chest with one brawny arm and stopped his mouth with the other hand.

The captain shook his head. "Sorry, Wil. The matriarchs said you might pretend to have a *shillilar*."

"Not pretend, not pretend."

"Take him away, Borst," the captain said to a stocky fellow with a shock of sulphur-yellow hair. "Treat him kindly; don't let him see."

Wil was led away, struggling feebly.

"Wil, help me," whispered Tali.

But they did not allow him to look back and, though she knew Tinyhead still lurked in the darkness beyond the lantern light, neither could he break through the captain's cordon. Tali had nothing left. She hoped she could face her end the way a lady of House vi Torgrist should, with dignity.

Two guards stood her on her feet, holding her so tightly that she could not move. Both men were leaning backwards, making room for the captain's swing. Tali pictured the Living Blade taking Mia's head off her slender neck. She had sworn a blood oath to Mia, and she had failed, failed at everything.

The captain studied Tali and his eyes softened. "So brave, so clever. What I have to do is indeed a waste."

"Then don't do it," Tali burst out. "Take me back. I promise—"

"My orders are to bring your head home to Cython, as proof that *the one* is dead and the *shillilar* has been averted."

As he raised his Living Blade, red highlights chased themselves around the annulus and the blade began to keen. He did not bow to her, though, nor reach out to take her hand. The captain was not planning to honour the doomed one—not after she had killed her overseer.

He drew the blade back. Then a girl screamed, "No!" and yellow rocks were falling all around them. One bounced off the left-hand guard's chin, rocking him backwards like a punch in the face, and another struck the captain in his right eye.

"Come on, Tali!" shrieked Rannilt from the darkness.

Before Tali could run, the second guard locked his arms around her and held her.

"Get after the child," said the captain, rubbing his streaming eye.

Two men advanced into the darkness.

"Run, Rannilt," yelled Tali.

"Hold her while I do the business," said the captain. The guards held Tali upright and again leaned away.

"Master, help me!" howled Tinyhead.

"Him too," snapped the captain. "Cut the traitor down."

More guards ran into the dark. The captain wiped his eye and hefted the Living Blade.

Wil let out a shriek and burst free of the man holding him. "She *the one*. Kill *the one* and Cython burns."

CHAPTER 43

Wil had alkoyl, Tali was sure of it. And alkoyl ignited combustible materials at a touch. But the Living Blade was swinging back. There wasn't time to think things through—only to pray that it would work.

"Wil!" she yelled. "Run your alkoyl across the ground."

"What's she talking about?" said the captain. "What's Wil got? Check him, Borst."

The yellow-haired guard made a lunge for Wil, who twisted the cap off a platina tube and scuttled away, dribbling green alkoyl across the sulphur ground from one mud pit to the other.

The ground seethed up knee-high in yellow foam, caught fire and the sulphur burnt with a towering red flame and dense clouds of white smoke. A breeze drifted it into the faces of the guards, who began to reel about, gasping and choking.

Tali brought her elbow up into the throat of the man holding her, doubling him over, then ducked under the Living Blade and drove her head into the captain's belly. He went over backwards, dropping the blade, which sang as it cut into the sulphurous ground.

She dived on it and tried to wrench it free, but the Living Blade sent such a shock through her fingers that she could not hold it.

Whoomph! Alkoyl must have eaten through the upper layer of sulphur and melted that which lay below, for a yellow geyser erupted upwards from the centre of the flame, a fountain of molten sulphur burning bright as the sun and blasting up for fifty feet. Fire crept in a blocking line from pond to pond and Tali saw her chance . . . though if it went wrong she would be cooked.

She hobbled towards the lowest part of the line of fire, praying that she could get there before it erupted. Then she ran, held her breath and dived through the belching smoke, and made it. Wisps of white smoke clung to her face and hair, stinging her eyes, nose and mouth, and when she took her first breath it carved a searing track down to her lungs. Coughing out stinging saliva, she darted away.

"After her," gasped the captain. "For your families' lives."

The guards hesitated on the other side of the line of fire, afraid to follow. A beaky-nosed fellow gathered his courage and ran, but as he soared above the fire it erupted in a molten sulphur geyser which lifted him high and tumbled him about, blazing like a moth in a flame. He was dead before he thudded to the ground and the other guards drew back. The fire was now yards high and extended from one mud pool to the next, blocking the track and cutting them off from Tali.

Wil was standing by himself, his arms stretched out towards her and his mouth working, though she could not make out what he was saying over the roaring of the fires. And Orlyk's squad was not far away.

As she turned to go, Wil came flying out of the flames, his mouth gaping and his remaining hair shrivelled, to land sprawling on the crusted ground. He had skinned both knees and blood was running down his shins, but he did not appear to have noticed.

He swivelled his head from side to side as if using some otherworldly sense, then his empty eye sockets fixed on her. The brilliant light threw his face into high contrast. His cheeks and chin were dotted with faded scars, his single nostril was bleeding again and clusters of brown nodules were growing in his eye sockets.

"Take Wil with you," he said, craning his head and upper body forwards, raptly. "Wil special."

"I don't think—"

"Wil saved you twice now."

"Twice?" said Tali. "What are you talking about?"

"All put to death in your place. You owe Wil."

His words chilled her. The first time she met him he had mentioned people being put to death, but what did *in her place* mean?

There was no time to ask, and the last thing she wanted was the company of a blind madman who had visions, yet without Wil's swift action the captain would be packing her head in a bag and taking it back to Cython. How could she refuse him?

"This way," she said, turning in the direction of Caulderon.

Wil reached out to her like a shy youth. She took his cracked hand, uncomfortably.

"Where you going?" he said in a childlike, breathy voice.

"I don't know," she lied.

"Wil the Sump, they call me. Not respectful, is it?"

"No," Tali said absently, checking for lanterns. The enemy could not track her without light, though to conceal themselves they would open their lantern shutters as seldom as possible. Unless she kept watch every minute, she could miss them.

"First to see the *new book*, Wil was," said Wil. "First to read it, too."

"What book was that?" said Tali. Books were rare in Cython— at least, in the Pale Empound—though it was said the enemy had huge libraries containing hundreds of volumes.

His face took on a closed expression. It was remarkably mobile, considering he had no eyes.

"Can't tell you about the Solaces. You Pale, you our enemy."

"What are the Solaces?" She had never heard the term before.

"Secret books. They tell the stories of our past and our future."

"Who wrote them?"

He did not reply.

"Why do you want to go with an enemy, Wil?"

He looked around as if afraid someone would overhear. "Touched the iron book, Wil did," said Wil in an awed whisper. "Saw you change the future."

"What iron book?" She reminded herself that he was mad, and that, no matter how clever he had been in leading the enemy to her, his words might not mean anything.

"Can't speak of it. Contest still going. Have to see the ending."

Tali shivered. "Did you see what was going to happen?"

He hugged himself around the chest. "Change the story, change the truth. Mustn't touch it."

"What story?"

"Saw it first." He let out a high-pitched laugh. "They can't take that away. Earned his tattoo, Wil did. Wil *is* special."

"I believe you," said Tali, pitying the unfortunate man for a life so lowly that even the slaves had mocked him as they trudged by.

"Not Wil's fault," said Wil, his face crumpling. "Wil didn't put them down."

The chill was back. "Who, Wil?"

"Matriarchs made Wil tell. Wil just protecting the ending. All those children, all those children."

The fine hairs stood up on Tali's arms. "Are you saying that children were killed *instead of me*?"

He crumpled to the ground, rolling over and over, his face covered by his forearms. "How was Wil to know? It wasn't in *shillilar*."

She could not stop here; the pursuit was too close. She lifted him and led him by the hand. "What have you done, Wil?"

"Couldn't let matriarchs find you." Wil moaned like an animal in a trap. "They kill you, it ruin the story. But ah, the children, the little children."

She checked around her, saw no lights, then shook him. "When was this? Tell me!"

He could barely get the words out. "Twelve years ago. Lied to matriarchs. Had to protect *the one*. They must not change her story."

"What did you tell the matriarchs?"

"That *the one* had black hair—olive skin—mother cleaned effluxors. Wil didn't know," he said shrilly.

The hair stirred on Tali's head as a childhood memory surfaced—screaming mothers, uproar among the effluxor slaves and a rebellion bloodily put down. Her own mother would never talk about it.

"The matriarchs took other children in my place. How many?"

"All the ones that fitted. Thirty-nine black-haired little girls. Put to death to prevent *shillilar*."

It was dreadful, but she had to know why it had happened. "What is the *shillilar*?"

"Not Wil's fault. Why they make Wil watch? Horrible, horrible."

"All those little girls killed instead of me," Tali whispered. "Why, Wil? What am I supposed to do?"

"Can't say."

"Why not?" she snapped, shaking him again.

"Change the contest. Ruin the ending," said Wil. "Anyway, can't remember."

Obviously a lie. Perhaps Wil did that filthy work cleaning sumps as a penance for what he had done, but it could never be enough. How could anyone atone for thirty-nine black-haired girls killed in the place of one who was blonde?

Yet despite his protests, Wil still feasted on his discovery of her. Tali did not like him at all.

It prompted her to question everything she had done, though. What was it about her that created havoc wherever she went? Why did those innocent children have to die, that she should live? She'd had nothing to do with it, yet she felt an obligation to make up for the waste of their young lives. And her mother's. And Mia's. It strengthened the blood oath. She had to find a way.

They might have travelled a mile since the escape, but there was still a long way to go and in the dark she could not be sure she was going in the right direction.

"Wil?" she said. "How do you find your way around?"

He shrugged. "Just *see*, better than Wil could with eyes."

"Which way is Caulderon?"

He pointed to the left of her heading.

"How far?"

He shrugged.

"What about my enemies? The captain, and Orlyk? And Tinyhead?"

"Can't *see* own people."

Damn! "Well, we'd better hurry if we're to get to Caulderon before the sun comes up."

"Not going to Caulderon," said Wil.

It solved her problem. "I am. You can go wherever you want."

She was turning away when he grabbed her with those hands that seemed too big for him.

"Saved your life." Wil held her arms behind her back in a grip she could not break. "You Wil's now."

He had only hauled her a hundred yards when there was a soggy thud behind her and his grip relaxed. Tali turned to run but Orlyk dealt her an even harder blow. By the time she swam back to consciousness she was bound so tightly that there was no hope of escape.

"I'm putting Mijl the pothecky in charge of you," said Orlyk, shining a glowstone lantern in Tali's eyes. "She's an expert in chymical pain: one whiff of her distillates sets the nerves ablaze, her congelas can etch the skin from living flesh, her refracts set living innards solid as stone. And unlike me," Orlyk bared her teeth in a sickening smile, "Mijl has good reason to hate Pale."

Mijl, a small, sinewy woman with nostrils like mine tunnels and stubby, spatulate fingers, touched Tali on the temple with a yard-long glass tube as thick as a magian's staff. Its rounded tip was thickly smeared with a brown substance.

Bright pain sparkled at the touch and slowly spread across Tali's temples like a flame consuming a sheet of paper. She tried to brush the gunk off her forehead but a similar pain seared through her hand, which stiffened until she could not bend her fingers.

"What was that for?" gasped Tali.

"Advance payment, slave," said the pothecky. "After interrogation in Cython, you will serve as a terrible warning to the other Pale. With congela, I will take the skin off and lay bare the living flesh. For every one of us who suffered in the shaft, and all those who died in the mud mire, and even for the traitor Sconts, you will feel every minute of their pain."

The pothecky paused.

"Then I will extract the cost of the destroyed sunstone from your living flesh with the distillate called *red noddy*. Then, for impersonating the slave, Lifka, I will bath you in a tincture reduced from a thousand girr-grubs. You will find it ... *exquisite*."

CHAPTER 44

"What if they've blasted the city gates?" said Rix. "They could be rampaging through Caulderon right now."

Fear tightened his throat. A contagious pox could cripple Caulderon in a few days, then the enemy could march into the undefended city. Could Hightspall, after standing unchallenged for seventeen hundred years, be toppled that easily?

"I don't think so," said Tobry. "These attacks are just a warning, intended to spread as much fear as possible."

"I should be there. Who else can protect my family? Not Father."

They had ridden along the edge of the Seethings for an hour, searching for any light or sound that might indicate Tali was nearby, but had seen nothing. Rix was so tired he could barely stay in the saddle and even Leather was reduced to a plod.

"Look on the bright side," said Tobry. "Now we're at war, they're bound to postpone your father's Honouring."

"They won't," Rix said dully.

"How do you know?"

"It's a secret."

"Oh, come on."

"All right." Rix took a sharp breath. "We need the Honouring, desperately."

"I don't see why. House Ricinus has everything."

"Including more enemies than the rest of the great families put together—people who envy our wealth and despise us for rising so high. They can't bear our successes, Tobe. There are moves afoot to have Father stripped of his title, lands, monopolies . . . "

"What for?"

"Behaviour unbecoming to the chief of a noble house."

"The chiefs of the noble houses *invented* bad behaviour," said Tobry. "It's their art form."

"But in his drunkenness Father has insulted all the senior Houses, as well as their wives and daughters, households, dogs and chickens. And Mother—well . . . " Rix could not say it aloud.

"Lady Ricinus is not universally loved," Tobry said helpfully.

"They bow and smile as they take her bribes and douceurs, then stab her from behind. House Ricinus is teetering under their malice."

"How's the Honouring going to help? What's your father done to deserve it?"

"He's personally paid for a new force of five thousand men, to be Hightspall's Third Army. Wages, uniforms, weapons, training and supplies for up to a hundred days in the field—the lot."

Tobry whistled. "That's a generous act, even for one of the richest families in Hightspall."

"It was Mother's idea, so generosity doesn't come into it—she would have weighed the costs and calculated the benefits to the last penny. Without it, House Ricinus might have been toppled. But after he's been publicly Honoured by the chancellor . . . and if Mother's other surprises come off—"

"There's more?" said Tobry.

"A couple of things she's been scheming and plotting and bribing for, for years."

"I'm intrigued. Tell on."

"Only Mother knows what they are. But if they come to pass—"

"House Ricinus will be untouchable."

"We'd better be—the Third Army has almost bankrupted us. That's why everything has to be perfect, including my portrait of Father."

"No offence to your artistic genius, but I don't understand why the damn portrait is so important."

"Mother has been boasting about how her brilliant son has captured the perfect likeness of her noble husband. She's built it up to be the greatest painting of the age, and if it's not finished it'll be a public humiliation. It'll be as though I've spat in my father's face."

"No matter how much we loathe each other behind closed doors," said Tobry, "in public the family must kiss each other's bottoms."

Rix looked out across the Seethings. Tali could be anywhere within that treacherous labyrinth, which stretched east all the way to Lake Fumerous and the Brown Vomit, and south for fifteen miles almost to the Crowbung Range.

"Even in daylight it could take a week to find her," he said. "In darkness, there's no hope. I've got to get home, while I still can. If they besiege the city ... "

"We might not be able to get in," said Tobry. "I know."

Rix turned down the Caulderon Road, heading for Palace Ricinus and his crucifixion at Lady Ricinus's hands. She might have already sent her seneschal out to drag him back. His cheeks flamed at the thought.

"It's for the best," said Tobry after they had gone a mile or two in silence. "Tali's nothing special."

Rix restrained the urge to punch his friend into next Tuesday.

"I've always felt chivalry to be overrated," Tobry went on. "I mean, why should a woman be treated different from a man just because she's small and curvy and vaguely decent on the eye?"

"If you don't shut it, Tobe, you'll be excreting teeth for a fortnight."

"Actually, I found Tali to be rather plain. I mean, her skin is fine enough, if you like it the colour of paper, but those horrible blue eyes and golden hair. Uggh!"

"You're a dead man, Tobe."

Tobry grinned. "We're doing the right thing, the sensible thing—"

"Since when did you ever do the sensible thing?" Rix snapped. "You don't believe in anything, you mock all that I hold dear and you think life is a joke at our expense."

"I've changed," Tobry said loftily. "I've achieved maturity and I'm closing in on wisdom."

"Well, change back. I only keep you on because you amuse me, and I've had precious few laughs out of you lately . . . "

Tobry had stopped. "What was that?" he said, standing up in the stirrups.

"Didn't hear anything," said Rix dully.

"Thought I saw a light."

"Probably another enemy attack."

"No, it was out in the Seethings."

"Bog gas catching fire, then."

"Bog gas burns blue. This light was pure gold."

"Lord Tobry, Lord Tobry?" a child's voice piped from the darkness.

"Who the hell is that?" said Rix.

"At a guess," said Tobry complacently, "the slave girl, Rannilt."

"You don't have to sound so pleased about it."

"You might turn Tali away, but you won't abandon a child to certain death."

"Why would you even think I would?" Rix snarled. "I may be a fool but I'm not a brute."

"Did I say you were?" Tobry said innocently. He raised his elbrot and conjured light. "Come forward, child. We won't harm you."

Rannilt edged across the gravel road towards Tobry, keeping as much distance between Rix and herself as possible. She was an unprepossessing little urchin, thin and bruised and grubby, her skin tinged pink from sunburn and a dozen shiny streaks up her right forearm where she had wiped her nose.

Yet despite the late hour she moved lightly, bouncing on the balls of her feet, and there was a light in her eye and a set to her small, pointed jaw that spoke of considerable determination. It made Rix uneasy. Kids her age should be safely in bed, not lost in the middle of a war, begging aid from strangers.

"Well, child," he said. "You called and we're here. What do you want?"

"It's Tali," said Rannilt, speaking to Tobry. "They got her."

Rix bit off the curse as it was bursting forth. He was not so far gone as to swear in front of a child.

"Who's got her?"

The girl moved closer to Tobry, as if for protection. Rix regretted his terseness, though not as much as he regretted the situation he was being manoeuvred towards.

"The enemy. They're takin' her back to Cython and ... and they're goin' to kill her horribly, for sure."

"How can you know that?" Rix said uncomfortably.

"It's what they do to slaves with magery," said Rannilt, limping into the middle of the road. "If Tali hadn't saved me, they would have cut my head off, hack! Just like that. Seen it done to other Pale," she added quietly. "The blood spurts up for six feet—"

Rix blanched. "A child should not be dwelling on such things."

"How can I ever forget?" She reached up with her grubby hands and snot-covered arm. "Tali is the kindest lady in the world and you've got to save her."

"Caulderon's under attack, look." He indicated the glowing skyline. "I have to save my own people, child. How can I do both at the same time?"

"You said you'd help her."

"How many of the enemy are there?" said Tobry.

"Four, I think," said Rannilt, though she did not meet his eyes.

"Are you sure that's all?"

"There's another squad somewhere, more than twelve of them."

"But not travelling with the first squad?"

"The second squad doesn't want to take Tali back. Just her ... her *head*."

Tobry exchanged glances with Rix, who scowled and looked away.

"Have you had anything to eat?" said Tobry.

"Got no food," said Rannilt.

He took bread, cheese and sausage from his saddlebags. "Why don't you sit on one of those rocks while Rix and I see what we can do."

They walked down the empty road, out of earshot. The crimson-tinged plumes were dying away now, the fuel they fed on almost consumed. Soon, no doubt, the road would be thick with desperate refugees.

"Two of us," said Rix. "At least sixteen of them. We're both worn out and so are our horses. It can't be done."

Tobry looked at him.

"What if the enemy has broken into Caulderon?" said Rix. "What if they're firing pox pins into the palace right now?

"We've still got to try."

"Tobe, listen." Rix took a deep breath.

"I know what you're going to say."

"Really?"

"You're going to say that you've neglected your responsibilities too long. That only you can pull the defences of Palace Ricinus together in time, but you've got to go now. That your highest duties are to your country and to your house, and it's not in you to shirk them at such a time—no matter how worthy the individual might be."

"Well put. Let's go."

"And I thoroughly agree," said Tobry. "Waste time trying to save Tali, and hundreds might die because you're not there to rally your troops."

"Exactly," said Rix.

"There is one thing, though," said Tobry.

"I knew it."

"No one's ever been inside Cython."

"So what?"

"When the chancellor plans to counterattack, Tali's knowledge of Cython's layout and defences will be priceless."

"You might have mentioned this when we could have done something about it."

"Probably would have, if you hadn't ridden off in such a tantrum."

Rix let it pass. Tobry was right, and the chancellor would be doubly pleased if they could pull it off. "That was twelve hours ago. They'll have her down the Rat Hole by now."

"Rannilt?" Tobry called. "How long ago was she taken?"

Rannilt got up and trudged towards them, almost out on her feet but refusing to give in. "Just on dark, the first time. Evil Orlyk got her, the nasty old toad."

"First time?" Tobry's face lit. "You mean Tali escaped?"

"'Course," said the girl with such glowing pride that Rix's steely heart was touched. "I was watchin' from the dark. Tali tricked Tinyhead into leadin' half the guards across the crust over a hot mud pond ... They broke through and fell in, and it cooked 'em like chickens in a pie. Cooked 'em good."

"That's a very bloodthirsty attitude for a child," said Rix sternly.

"They kill kids with the gift," said Rannilt.

"But they caught Tali again?" asked Tobry.

"The other squad did, a few hours ago. Mad Wil led them to her." Rannilt caught her breath.

"Who's Mad Wil?"

"No eyes. Sees the future. Pretends to be nice but he's a nasty little man. Pinches when no one's lookin'."

"And then?" said Tobry.

"Second squad was goin' to kill her right away. I shouted and threw rocks and ... and ... but they came after me and I had to run and hide ... They nearly got me ... " She shuddered. "The Living Blade was singin', dyin' to take her head ... " Rannilt faltered and tears appeared in her eyes. "Dyin' ... "

Rix realised that he was up on his toes, leaning forwards. "But it didn't. What happened this time?"

"Tali got to Wil."

"She's a clever woman," said Tobry, admiringly.

"Wil's funny about Tali," said Rannilt. "He led the enemy to her but when captain was goin' to kill her ... Wil set fire to the ground and—"

"You can't burn dirt, or salt," said Rix. "Tobe, I thought you said they don't use magery?"

"I didn't think they did. What did Wil do, child? This is important."

"Wasn't magery. In Cython, it's called chymie."

"What's the difference?" said Rix.

"It's a kind of alchymie, isn't it?" said Tobry.

"That's right," said Rannilt. "Wil had some thick green water in a metal tube. He tossed the water on the ground ... it was all yellow there—"

"Layers of sulphur fumed out of vents," said Tobry. "I know the place, it's only a couple of miles from here. Treacherous country in the night, though."

"—everywhere the green water landed, it burned so high and fierce that the enemy couldn't get past," Rannilt went on.

"The 'green water' must be an alchymical combustion agent," said Tobry. "Fascinating."

"Mad Wil ran off with Tali," said Rannilt. "But not long after that, Evil Orlyk whacked her on the head and took her away. Couldn't do nothin' so I ran for help."

"And there were four in her squad, you said?"

"Think so," said Rannilt.

"Four's a lot better odds than sixteen," Tobry said, giving Rix a significant stare. "How long ago?"

"Maybe two hours," said Rannilt.

"They've got a long start," said Rix. "Could be halfway to the Rat Hole by now. If we can cut them off, can you stop them with gramarye?"

"It'll take more than my conjuror's tricks," Tobry said with that hint of bitterness.

"Do we have a garrison near here?"

"Plegm is the closest, but they'll be out hunting enemy by now. Besides, if we rode after Tali with a squad of soldiers ... "

Rix ran through half a dozen plans, but they all ended the same way. "Orlyk would cut her throat. She's doomed if we attack, doomed if we don't."

Rannilt let out a little cry. "You've got to save her."

"I'm sorry," said Rix, and he was. Tali was brave and determined and wholly admirable, and even if the Pale *were* traitors, about which he now had serious doubts, he could not bear to think of her killed like a chicken for the pot. "I don't see what we can do."

He climbed into the saddle and closed his eyes, the better to think, but imagined Lady Ricinus's icy rage. *House Ricinus can't afford a hint of scandal until the Honouring is over. Association with a despised Pale could be ruinous. Forget the scrag and do your duty!*

Rix's fingers tightened on the reins. He was tempted to go after Tali out of sheer defiance. But how could he, with war raging and Caulderon under threat?

Do your duty! Rix tried to focus on the portrait of his father, but all he could see was the bloated drunkard's nose. He opened his eyes and Rannilt was staring up at him, reproachfully. He looked away.

"Tobry?" Rannilt was swaying, almost out on her feet but refusing to give in. "You've got to—"

"Hush, child," said Tobry. "It can't be done. Hop up here, in front of me."

"No!" She turned and walked into the Seethings.

"What the blazes is she up to?" said Rix.

"How would I know?" snarled Tobry. "Rannilt? Where are you going?"

Rannilt's face was wet and her nose was running. She wiped it on her crusted forearm. "Goin' to save Tali."

Tobry took hold of handfuls of his hair as though planning to tear it out. He glared at Rix, then dismounted and ran after her. Rix followed.

"Rannilt," said Tobry, "they'll kill you too. You can't—"

"Tali risked her life to save me," said the girl, over her shoulder. "*I* don't desert my friends."

The reproach stung. Rix wanted to scream, *I'm not like that. You don't understand. It's not that simple.*

"She's right," said Tobry, quietly.

For the first time Rix saw that his friend was in pain and doing his best to cover it up, but he had no idea what to say to him. "What are you talking about?"

"The bravest and cleverest girl we've ever set eyes on is in mortal trouble and we made a commitment to her."

"What would you do?" said Rix.

"I wouldn't be running home to paint my father's poxy portrait."

"Easy for you to say, since you've got no responsibilities."

"That's the wonderful thing about losing my house and all my family," said Tobry. "I'm free! Free as a bird."

"Sorry," said Rix. "Didn't mean it that way. All right—how would you rescue her?"

"Haven't got the faintest." Tobry took the reins. "Come up here, Rannilt. We'll do what we can."

Her eyes lit up like twin full moons. "You're goin' to save Tali?"

"We're going to try. But we might all be killed."

"Could have died four times since I met her," said Rannilt.

Tobry heaved her into the saddle. Rannilt looked around in amazement, and not a little terror, at being so high on such an unfamiliar beast, then threw her skinny arms around him and burrowed her snotty nose against his chest.

"We're goin' to save Tali," she murmured.

She closed her eyes, sighed, and within seconds she was asleep. Tobry enclosed her with one arm, looked up, and his eyes were suspiciously shiny. "What are you staring at?" he muttered to Rix.

"The way you've gone all protective," said Rix, "you'd think she was your own daughter."

After a long pause, Tobry said softly, "I wish she was."

"But you never get involved. You don't believe in anything."

"It's amazing how the end of the world gives you focus. I recommend you try it."

Rix nudged Leather forwards. "How do we find Tali?"

Tobry waved his elbrot and a handful of golden motes sparkled in the air. "Rannilt came this way."

"What are you doing?"

"Her gift is uncontrolled—it leaves traces that gramarye can read for a little while. If we backtrack her, we'll discover where Tali was taken."

"We know where she was taken—near where the ground is made of sulphur."

"So we do," said Tobry, consulting the map. "From there, they'd take this path back to the Rat Hole. Come on."

A weight had lifted from Rix's shoulders but, as they rode on, the familiar burden settled on him. He *was* neglecting his responsibilities, and if this went wrong, as it probably would, House Ricinus might well come tumbling down.

CHAPTER 45

"How are we going to do this?" said Rix. "I can't think of any plan save going at them full gallop, and we can't do that carrying a kid."

"With respect, Lord Rixium," said Tobry, "full gallop is the only plan you ever have. Subtle you are not."

"It's worked in the past."

"Not this time. Once they see us, they'll cut Tali's throat just like that." Tobry mimed it, his face a death mask. "Two seconds. Gone!"

Rannilt jerked in her sleep and let out a muffled cry.

"Sorry, little one, I'm a stupid old fool." He stroked her hair and she settled. "Rix, next time I open my big mouth, do me a favour and put your boot in it."

Rix studied the girl, sidelong. "She's a tough little thing."

"Tougher than I am. Suppose slaves have to be."

Tobry delved in his saddlebags for the map and conjured a small light above it. "There is one place we might ambush them."

Rix nudged his horse closer.

"The quickest way to the Rat Hole," said Tobry, "is via the track between this cluster of salt lakes." He traced it with a fingertip. "If we were to race out west, *this way*, then get to this point first, we might manage a surprise attack. They've been going all day and night—they'll be worn out and not as vigilant as they should be. Not expecting an ambush, hopefully."

"We've been going longer."

"We're used to long days of travel. They can't be."

Rix frowned at the map. "Looks risky. For Tali, I mean."

Tobry's eyes went black for a moment and his arm tightened around Rannilt. He was expecting the worst.

"If you can come up with a better idea, we'll try it," he said.

"What about Rannilt? If we're caught, they'll kill her."

Tobry tightened his grip around her tiny frame. Rannilt sighed and snuggled, without waking. "I—We'll have to leave her with the horses."

"What if we're killed?"

Tobry's eyes went that desolate black again.

There was just enough starlight to see. Soon they were winding between the bubbling lakes and steaming mud pools of the Inner Seethings, where the air was almost too foul to breathe and pungent vapours bit at their mucous membranes until their noses ran and their eyes wept.

Tobry was wrapped in his own thoughts. Rix studied him in the dim light, marvelling at the change in Tobry since they'd escaped the wrythen's caverns, and especially since they'd met Tali and the child. Barely a trace remained of the reckless Tobry he'd grown up with, the man who had thought about nothing save friendship and pleasure. He seemed older, sadder, yet deeper and more subtle. And he cared!

Rix knew he was changed, too. The encounter with the wrythen had shaken him; it knew who he was and he felt sure it planned to avenge itself on his house. Now every day brought a greater burden of responsibility; every day it became clearer how disastrously his parents were managing House Ricinus. Whether the war went well or badly, his house could well fall, as Tobry's own ancient house had been crushed in a few terrible years. Rix had to save it.

So why wasn't he racing home as fast as his weary horse could carry him? If he were killed trying to rescue Tali, who would rally the palace guard? Not his father, who could not stay sober to save his life, and certainly not Lady Ricinus. Rix could not name one servant who did not fear her monthly flogging tithe, and loathe her. When he became Lord Ricinus, he would turn the palace upside-down to scour away the taint of its previous lord and lady.

"Where did we go wrong, Tobe?"

"What kind of a question is that?"

"We were happy when I was little. Oh, Mother was always sharp-tongued, Father always drank more than he ought, but life was good. Then I got sick, and after I was well again everything had changed."

"Sometimes terrible choices have to be made—as in my house."

Rix said no more. Compared to the catastrophe that had crushed House Lagger, the problems between Lord and Lady Ricinus were insignificant.

As the first glow of dawn touched the eastern horizon, they were walking their horses across the broken country between the simmering salt lakes of the Inner Seethings. The earth here was baked like a burnt biscuit, and just as lifeless. Rix felt a sudden terror that the beautiful estates of House Ricinus would soon look this way. The enemy had terrible new weapons, ones Hightspall did not understand. How could they fight chymie when they did not know how it worked?

All the more reason to rescue Tali, who might know some of the enemy's secrets. Surely even his mother would see the sense in that. Ha!

"Where are we?" said Rannilt, yawning.

"Not far now," said Tobry. "Hungry?"

"Always hungry."

He handed her hard bread and even harder sausage. She gnawed at one, then the other in the dim light.

"You're goin' to save Tali," she said with childlike certainty.

"We'll try. Have you known her long?"

"Two days. I asked her to be my mother. She said I was being silly."

"What happened to your mother?"

"The enemy killed her when I was five, because she could do magery." Rannilt said it without a trace of self-pity.

"Is that where your gift comes from?"

"Suppose so. Never knew my father. He was minin' out a sunstone and his heart burst."

"What can you do with magery, apart from that golden light?"

Rannilt shrugged. "Scared to try. If you say *magery* in Cython they beat you. If they know you have it, they kill you."

"You're in Hightspall now and you can use magery all you want," said Rix, amazing himself. Until he had saved them both with the enchanted sword, he'd had a deep-seated fear of magery.

"Do you know anything about Tali's gift?" said Tobry.

"It's different. Strong. Buried deep and she can't find it." Rannilt frowned at Rix, who pretended he hadn't been listening. "Do you have a palace too, Lord Tobry?"

He let out a barking laugh. "No, child. I'm not rich like Rix."

"I could be a servant in your house. I'd love that . . . you don't beat your servants all the time, do you?"

"I have no servants. But when I did, I didn't beat them."

"I'd work all day, every day, and all I'd want is a little tiny room. Ever since Mama died I've dreamed about having a room to myself."

"Is that your only dream?"

"I dream about Mama and Papa, but they're gone. Until I met Tali, nobody cared about me. No one in the world."

Tobry hugged her and she closed her eyes. Rix looked away, swallowing.

After another mile, ahead of them the land rose several hundred feet to a doorknob-shaped hill whose flanks were covered in grey-leaved bushes, though the knob itself was bare rock the rich, reddish hue of iron ore.

"From the crest we should be able to see the other track," said Tobry.

"Let's pray they've taken it. If they took some other route, we'll never find them."

As they climbed the hill, concealed from the track by tall scrub, Rix felt his pulse rise and the backs of his hands prickle. If they'd guessed wrong, Tali would die in Cython and everything she knew about the enemy would be lost.

"Rannilt?" Tobry roused her with a touch on the shoulder.

She woke with a start, flinched as though expecting a blow, then a lovely smile transformed her thin features. "Lord Tobry." She turned towards Rix and the smile slipped a little, though it did not go out.

Rix felt an ache in his chest, that a child should be wary of him.

"We're going to try and rescue Tali now, and you've got to stay here."

Her eyes widened in alarm. "Don't leave me. I can help. I'm quick and quiet."

And brave, Rix thought, but clumsy. "No."

"But it's out there. Huntin'."

"What's out there?" Tobry said sharply.

"The thing in the dark. Shadow and shape, shiftin', always shiftin'." She shuddered. "Please don't leave me."

CHAPTER 46

"**D**oes she mean a shifter?" Rix mouthed.

"I hope not," Tobry mimed back. "Rannilt, it won't come in daylight, and we need someone really brave to watch the horses. It's a vital job. Can you do it?"

Rannilt studied the huge beasts, chewing on her bottom lip. She nodded jerkily. "What if—what if you don't come back?"

"Can you ride?" said Rix.

"Of course she can't ride," said Tobry. "There aren't any horses in Cython."

He scribbled on a scrap of paper, then laid a hand on his horse's muzzle, speaking in a low voice. The horse stamped its front feet, one after the other.

"My horse is called Beetle," he said as he shortened the stirrups. "If we're not back by nightfall, Beetle will take you to Caulderon, to a friend of ours, a kind old lady called Luzia. She'll look after you. Give her this note; don't lose it." He handed the scrap of paper to her. "You can ride there in a few hours." He gave Rix an anxious glance.

The chances of a despised Pale child making it, through war and the Seethings, was remote. Though not as remote as their attack succeeding.

"Beetle," said Rannilt. "That's a nice name."

"He's very gentle," said Tobry. Beetle folded his right ear over. "Look, he likes you. But don't try to ride Leather. She has a very bad temper."

"Like Rix," said Rannilt, then covered her mouth and turned scarlet.

Tobry snorted. By the words of a child I stand revealed, thought Rix.

Tobry put various items in a small pack and tossed it over a shoulder. They shook her grubby hand, then Rix followed Tobry around the curve to the other side of the knob. When he looked back, Rannilt was a tiny, fragile figure, staring after them.

"I hate this," said Tobry. "Leaving her all alone is wrong."

Rix clasped his shoulder. "We'll make it quick."

As the light grew they had a good view over the broken landscape to their left—a myriad of lifeless salt lakes and brilliantly blue, boiling pools, each surrounded by a concentric banding of red, orange and yellow crystals.

"Looks like the Gods vomited the place up," said Rix, who had not previously seen the Seethings from on high. "Why did the enemy delve Cython here? There are caves aplenty in the mountains."

"There's rich ore under the Seethings. They already had mines here when our First Fleets came."

"Plus the heatstones they sell us for such usurious prices."

"Oh, how House Ricinus would suffer," said Tobry, the sarcasm floating light as cobweb, "if it didn't hold a third of the heatstone monopoly."

"It's no good to us now we're at war."

"There's the path." Tobry pointed. "They'd better be on it."

A narrow isthmus meandered between two large, ragged lakes, a faint path running along it then skirting the shore of the larger lake not far below them. Half a mile on, the lake's outflow passed down a sinuous channel and over a series of cascades into a third, smaller lake, and that into another, and another. Finally, several miles away, the outlet river tumbled over a precipice into Lake Fumerous, which extended north for twenty miles.

"Unless I'm mistaken," Tobry went on, "the rock rats should appear from behind that little ridge and pass along the shore below us. And since they're not in sight and I had no sleep last night, I'm trying for a nap."

"How can you sleep?"

"How can I help Tali if I can't think straight?"

"I don't like it," said Rix. The steep slope was littered with broken red rock. "There's nowhere we can wait in ambush; no cover at all."

"We'll have to attack from here."

"We're two hundred yards away. It's impossible."

"I'm too tired to think. Ask me when I wake."

Tobry pillowed his cheek on his folded arms. Rix longed for a quick nap to freshen his own muddy head, but dared not close his eyes. He pressed himself into a fold in the rock and stared down at the track. How to pull off an ambush from so far away? With his mighty wyverin-rib bow, stronger than any bow made from wood, he could shoot an arrow right over the path into the lake, though not with any accuracy.

He strung the bow, nocked an arrow and drew the string back a few times, aiming at a spot where the track passed this side of a cluster of boulders near the water. He would be lucky to hit a man at such extreme range. Tobry might; he was a better shot, but he was not strong enough to fully draw Rix's bow.

Tobry grunted in his sleep and kicked both feet. His eyes began to flick back and forth beneath his closed lids in an unpleasantly familiar way, and he began to moan incoherently, *n-n-n-n, n-n-n-n.*

Rix's throat went dry. Everyone had nightmares, but why was this one so familiar, so hackle-rearing? He could not remember, could not penetrate the mental fog of exhaustion.

Then suddenly he knew. Tobry had looked like this when the wrythen had been trying to possess him in the caverns. Was it making another attempt? But the mountains were a day's ride from here; how could it reach Tobry from so far away? *And what if it succeeded?*

"Tobe?" Rix nudged him with the toe of a boot.

Like a cat, Tobry went from sleep to full wakefulness in a second, and sat up. "Are they coming?"

"Not yet. You were having a bad dream, making a racket."

"Was I? Don't remember a thing."

He did not look troubled, which was comforting. After Rix had one of his doom-laden nightmares he could feel the shudders running through him for hours afterwards. This was just a bad dream, nothing to worry about . . .

He rubbed his face with his hands. Nothing could have induced him to doze now. What if the wrythen's power strengthened further? What if it could reach Tobry when he was awake?

Cold sweat trickled down Rix's sides. If he could not rely on his best friend, if he had to watch his back whenever he was with Tobry, he was bound to fail.

"Tobe, do you reckon you could shoot a man on the path, from here?"

"Not with my bow."

"What about mine?"

"It takes a gorilla to pull your bow."

"Thanks." Rix pulled the arrow back a couple of times, straining until his biceps creaked and showing off a little. Right now, his physical strength was the one thing he could rely on. "What if I pull it and you aim?"

Tobry snorted. "That'd be like two men wheeling a wheelbarrow." He sighted along the arrow. "Maybe. Bugger of a shot, downhill."

"If we can kill their leader without warning, we'll have a minute to disable the others before they kill Tali."

Something flashed in Tobry's eyes. Pain? Regret? "It's possible. Just."

"It'd better be. Can you kill Orlyk from here if I draw my bow?"

"I don't know."

"Can you hit her?"

"I expect so."

"Not good enough." Rix released the tension on the string. "If you can't be sure of bringing her down, we might as well go home."

"I can hit her, just can't be sure of killing her. A flesh wound won't stop her from shouting an order to kill Tali. Wait a minute . . ." He felt in his pack.

"What are you thinking?"

"Still got that club-headed arrow?" said Tobry.

"Yes, but it doesn't have the range of the others."

"What if you took the head off and put this in its place?"

Tobry handed him the little conical phial of hallucinogenic water he'd collected from the entrance to the wrythen's caverns.

Rix weighed it in his hand. "Stopper's nicely pointed. But there's not much water in it . . . "

"There's more than you got on your hand the other day."

"True. And it disabled me instantly."

"So it should work . . . as long as I hit her."

"Make sure you do."

Tobry took off the club-head, bound the phial in its place and fixed it with arrowhead gum. His hand had a slight tremor; it took him three attempts to get it right. He checked the balance, adjusted the position of the phial, checked everything again and put the arrow in the sun so the gum would set.

Rix had to forcibly unclench his jaw. It was a lunatic plan that could get Tali killed. The minutes passed.

"You're worried about Rannilt, aren't you?"

Tobry did not answer.

"I hate waiting," said Rix. "What if you miss? What if one of the guards cuts Tali's throat before we can stop him?"

"It'll be a better fate than awaits her in Cython."

Rix had seen throats cut before. That was how thieves in Palace Ricinus were dealt with, and Lady Ricinus required the household to bear witness. His artist's eye could see bright pearls of blood all over Tali's luminously pale skin . . .

"You'd better not miss."

"Shut up, they're coming," said Tobry.

Orlyk, a heavyset, squat woman, was limping along the track towards the nearer end of the isthmus. Behind her came a small sinewy woman wearing a large pack, then a tall male guard, then Tali, her hands bound in front of her, followed by the big man Rannilt called Tinyhead, and another guard.

Tobry cursed. "There's five. Rannilt only said four."

"They're too close together," Rix said hoarsely, "and Tali's hands are tied. Even if you take the leader down, any of the others can kill her in seconds. I don't like the look of that small woman, either."

"What don't you like about her?"

"Just an instinct."

"She doesn't seem to be armed."

"Even more worrying. Get ready, but we don't shoot until they're well clear of those boulders or they'll run for cover."

Rix laid the phial arrow to hand, plus four ordinary arrows. In practice he could shoot ten arrows a minute, even with the heavy draw of this bow, but with the extreme range, and the awkwardness of him drawing and Tobry aiming, they would be lucky to get three arrows off in that time. And there were five targets.

After firing the arrows they had two hundred yards to run. On level ground he could do that in twenty-five seconds but it would take more than a minute down this rubbly slope. Tali could be dead by then. And what if the wrythen *had* got to Tobry, and was planning to take command of him at the critical moment? Rix shot a quick glance his way, afraid of what he might see in his friend's bruised eyes.

"Something the matter?" said Tobry.

"Nah!"

Then it got worse.

"More of them." Tobry was staring to the east. "Coming the other way. Hope Rannilt has sense enough to keep out of sight."

"It must be the second squad. The ones who were going to kill Tali straight away."

"They're between us and the horses," said Rix. "Even if we can rescue Tali, how do we get back to Rannilt?"

CHAPTER 47

Mere thought of the Oathbreaker's Blade froze the wrythen's plasm. The *Immortal Text* must be found and destroyed in case the Herovians were rising anew, though he did not know where to look for it.

He dismissed that worry for a more immediate one. He was floating in the white shaft of the Abysm. His nuclix, which was black as a hole in space, kept calling, calling, and the stolen three kept replying, but the master nuclix no longer answered and the wrythen was very afraid.

Had Deroe taken it already? He was growing stronger all the time, feeding on the raw power of the three stolen nuclixes and preparing to break free. The wrythen shivered; the cold radiating from his nuclix seemed to intensify.

And yet, he did not think Deroe had taken the master nuclix. Several times, after burning through his servant's brain, the wrythen had glimpsed enigmatic flashes of a band of his own people, and behind them the scenery of the Seethings, as though seeing it from another's eyes—the host's eyes. He had also seen a scrawny little slave girl and, once, his brain-burnt servant, arms out-thrust as though pleading to his master. Unfortunately, the wrythen had not been able to find them again. Had the host discovered how to block the *call*?

What else might she do? He could not guess—she was unpredictable. What if she discovered how to use her nuclix to bolster her own magery? That risked everything and could not be allowed.

It was remarkable that his faithful servant had survived at all, but a matter of wonder that he had recovered enough to try and follow the wrythen's orders. Could he succeed? The wrythen did not think so. The host girl was more than his match. And since he could not contact his servant, it left him no choice.

The facinore was evolving, which made it even more perilous to use, but it was all he had. He would direct it to the place from where the last *call* had come, and urge it to make haste. The host had to be taken now, or killed if she could not be taken alive. Her death would set his plans back by decades but it was better than the alternatives. If she got out of the Seethings he would lose her, either to his own people or the enemy.

Either alternative would be disastrous.

CHAPTER 48

"**R**eady?" said Tobry. "If we can hit Orlyk, and take the others down, we run and ... and try to get Tali away before the other squad arrives."

"What if we miss?" said Rix.

Tobry did not answer.

"We might take down three," Rix added, focusing his telescope on the sinewy woman behind Orlyk. Something about her still bothered him, and it wasn't just her thick glass tube, half the length of a magian's staff, that was suspiciously yellow at the tip, "Though that still leaves two. It only takes one to cut Tali's throat."

"You don't need to spell it out," Tobry said faintly.

He was unnaturally pale. "You like her," said Rix.

Tobry shrugged. "I like lots of people."

"No, you *really* like her." Tobry remained friends with all the women he had ever known, though Rix could not recall him *really* liking anyone before.

"Do your damned job and keep your thoughts to yourself!"

Rix managed a smile. They watched the line. Tali was a diminutive figure in the middle, with Tinyhead head and shoulders above her.

"What's the tube for?" said Rix.

"How would I know?" Tobry studied the line. "Bastard of a shot, side-on, but if we can get Orlyk to stop and turn this way—"

"Toss a stone across onto the rubble," said Rix. "She'll look up at the noise."

"If she knows we're here—"

"Rocks fall down hills all the time. Besides, it'll take her a few seconds to pick us out among the boulders. By then your arrow will spit her."

"It had better."

"Don't suppose you can help it on its way with magery?"

"My magery isn't that subtle."

"Let's hope your aim is."

Rix drew back the phial-headed arrow to the fullest extent of the string and sighted on Orlyk's middle, then moved his head so Tobry could correct the aim.

Tobry felt the curve of the bow, the tension of the string, then nudged the tail of the arrow slightly down, slightly across.

"Your hand's shaking," said Rix. Tobry was normally iron in a crisis.

As Tobry steadied his hand, a drop of sweat ran down his cheek.

What if the wrythen can get to him when he's awake? What if he possesses Tobry now and makes him aim for Tali instead of Orlyk? Rix could not tell from his angle.

Forcing himself to dismiss worries he could do nothing about, he visualised the arrow flying all the way to the target. Tali's life rested in the steadiness of his hands, possibly the survival of Hightspall as well, and Rix was rock-calm. He might not be the sharpest sword in the armoury but action was what he was made for.

Tobry nudged the arrow with a fingernail. "Perfect. Tossing the stone, *now.*"

It clacked twenty yards across the slope. Orlyk stopped and turned, looking up.

Rix fired, picked up the second arrow in one smooth movement and fixed on the sinewy woman. Tobry adjusted aim for the slightly heavier arrow. Rix fired, took the third arrow, fired again.

Orlyk was turning away when the phial smashed against her upper chest and the shaft of the arrow buried itself deep. She fell, alternately hurling her arms out and snapping them tight around her. The sinewy woman with the glass tube was snatching at something on her belt when the second arrow speared through her belly muscles from side to side. Her face twisted, but she hurled the object high and barbed sparks exploded upwards from it like a skyrocket—a call for help.

She was crumbling now, holding her belly, though she managed to skid an apple-sized object across the ground and thick, opaque smoke belched out. The third arrow skimmed Tinyhead's forehead and Rix cursed. It would have killed anyone with a normal-sized head.

The rear guard was turning to run for the boulders when the fourth arrow skewered him in the buttocks, doubling him over like a rooster with a single tail feather and driving him to all-fours.

"This isn't good," said Tobry, leaping up in a scatter of gravel.

Only three hits, none of the five killed, and the two on the ground could not be seen through the low-hanging smoke.

"Where's Tali?" Rix had lost sight of her. He ran.

The uninjured guard yanked the man with the tail arrow to his feet, shouting and waving a long knife. The injured man drew a curved knife and began to creep about, looking for Tali.

"Tinyhead's dragged her behind the boulders," choked Tobry, who was yards ahead. "Come *on*."

Rix's inner calm had vanished. Tinyhead could be knifing her right now. Compounding his problems, the troop at the other end of the isthmus was running. They had seen the signal. He lengthened his stride to pass Tobry and thundered down the rubble slope, bow in hand. Firing on the run from this distance would mean wasting his last arrow, but as soon as he was within range he would take Tinyhead down. Rix prayed that the man had not slain Tali already.

A gust cleared the smoke at the front of the line. Orlyk was still convulsing on the ground, almost tying her stocky body into knots. How long would she be disabled? It would depend how much hallucinogenic water had touched her, and she might recover suddenly. Rix prayed that the water had been carried deep into her bloodstream.

"Can you see Tali?" panted Tobry, now five yards behind.

Rix did not answer. He lacked the breath.

"Watch out for woman—glass tube," yelled Tobry. "Think she's a *pothecky*."

Chills spiralled down Rix's back. "A what?"

He could not make out Tobry's reply. Rix sprang over a corrugated outcrop of orange rock. While in the air he saw Tinyhead struggling with Tali near the boulders, then the flash of sunlight, as if off a knife.

Rix could not shoot—he was as likely to hit her. The sinewy pothecky was standing now, heaving out the arrow. She was one tough woman. Blood was pouring from both sides of her belly and the pain must be extreme, but she thumbed something into the end of the glass tube and swung it around towards Tali. Rix knew it was intended to kill. He aimed his last arrow and fired on the run, but could his arrow reach his target before the pothecky blew her deadly dart?

The arrow thumped into her upper arm. She swayed, almost dropped the tube but caught it again and began to raise it. Could nothing take her down? She lowered it, looking around in puzzlement, then slumped to the ground.

Tali was out of sight behind the boulders. Rix leapt another rock and saw Tinyhead stagger out from the other side of the boulders, blood running from his nose and right cheek. He reached out towards the distant mountains, as if in supplication, then swung back towards Tali's hiding place.

Rix could not stop him; he had no arrows left. He dropped the useless bow, wrenched out his sword and ran harder. Tali appeared from behind the boulders.

"Take the guards," Rix yelled back to Tobry. "I'll deal with Tinyhead."

But he had vanished in dense smoke, and so had Tali. Rix pounded down to the track, skidding on gravel, bounding over rocks, his blood roaring in his ears and his teeth bared. With his speed and bulk he must be a frightening sight. He hoped so.

The uninjured guard was almost as tall, though slightly built, and armed with a short spear with a jagged tip. He braced himself and thrust it out towards Rix. It would be difficult to avoid but Rix did not falter. He hurtled towards the fellow and, as he moved the tip of the spear to track Rix, Rix sprang and swung hard.

The spear point was only inches from his belly when his blade sheared through the shaft and sent the severed half spinning. Something thumped against his chest. Rix doubled up his legs and kicked out, taking the guard under the chin and driving his head back so hard that his neck snapped. He tumbled backwards and did not move again.

Rix landed awkwardly and felt a sharp pain in his chest. The spear point was embedded there, half an inch deep. He twisted it out and swept his gaze around the battlefield. Orlyk was still down. The pothecky was swaying on her knees, trying to pull out the arrow in her shoulder.

Tali was backing this way around the boulders, retreating from Tinyhead. The last guard crept towards her, the feathered arrow in his buttocks wagging like a puppy's tail. He raised his sword for a blow that would take Tali's head off, and she did not know he was there.

"Tali, behind you!"

Rix sent the half spear spinning at the man. The shaft cracked into the back of his head, though not hard enough to do any damage. Rix ran.

Tali turned late, saw the looming guard and let out a little cry. He took a swipe at her pale stomach, which showed though her torn garments. She gave a convulsive backwards heave and he missed by layers of skin. She threw something at his eyes, a handful of dust or grit, but the pitiful weapon had no effect.

The guard went for her again and Tali, trying to scramble away, stumbled. Rix could not reach her in time; he was still twenty yards away.

"Hoy, you!" he trumpeted, hoping to startle the man into turning, which would gain him a few seconds.

The guard was well trained. He half-turned, then swung back to kill Tali. Rix's remaining option was pure recklessness but he did not hesitate. Relying on the lightning judgement of hand and eye, he swung his sword sideways and let it fly, willing it to go true. He had never thrown a sword before, for that was suicide on the battlefield. And the guard was very close to her.

Thunk! The blade went through the man's backbone above the embedded arrow, and came out his chest. His legs collapsed and he fell at Tali's feet.

Tali was staring at the corpse when Orlyk sat upright, blood pouring from the chest wound. She was swaying, white-faced and clearly not fully recovered from the hallucinogenic water, but she raised a small brass triangle in one hand and a knife in the other.

Rix tried to change direction but skidded on the gravel,

aggravating the sore ankle he had twisted in the caverns. He snatched at the knife on his belt, knowing he could not draw and throw it in time.

Orlyk struck the triangle with her knife, *ting*, and Tali cried out as smoke wisped up from a bulbous ankle bracelet the enemy must have put on after they caught her. She bent, clawing at it in a panic, but could not get it off. Orlyk lurched towards her, blood running down her chest and her legs and arms moving in shuddering arcs, but every step was firmer than the one before. She was recovering far more quickly than Rix had.

The pothecky was still on her knees. She had broken off the arrow in her shoulder and now swung the glass tube in Tobry's direction. It had to be some deadly chymical weapon, one neither of them could combat, and for the first time in a fight Rix didn't know what to do—whether to try and save Tali, or his best friend.

He could not do both, and if he didn't act fast they were both going to die. He flung his knife at the pothecky but she calmly wove aside. The glass tube was aimed at Tobry again, the pothecky put her lips to the end, and *pfft*!

Tobry bellowed and fell, creating a miniature landslide. From the corner of an eye Rix saw him carried down with it. A deeper pain sheared through him and for a second he lost concentration. No—between Tobry and Tali there was no choice at all.

Rix was turning to run back when the glass tube fixed on his own chest. He felt no impact, though when he looked down a tiny, hollow-tipped dart was embedded beside his breastbone. In an instant his heart caught alight. He tried to knock the dart out but the blow squirted more of its chymical contents into him, belling out the skin all around.

His heartbeat accelerated to a gallop, spreading fiery pain in all directions. He could feel it rising up the arteries in his throat, burning like boiling acid, and when the blood reached his brain it was going to stew inside his skull.

He reached for the dart. At least, he tried to, but his arm did not move.

"Tobe?" he gasped, and was horrified to see steam gush from his own mouth. "Tobe?"

It felt as though he was boiling from the inside out. Rix managed to lurch around. Tobry lay on the rubble slope twenty yards away, unmoving. Dead?

As Rix soon would be. And, oddly, all he could think was how furious Lady Ricinus would be, and how badly he had let her down. He had failed his house, neglected to provide it with an heir, and when his father died House Ricinus would be no more.

He felt himself falling sideways and could do nothing about it. He hit the ground but felt no pain. His field of view tilted until the pothecky appeared to be standing out from the vertical face of a cliff. She advanced towards Rix, the broken arrow still quivering in her shoulder, thumbing another dart into the tube and aiming it at his right eye.

CHAPTER 49

Orlyk fell with an arrow in her chest, then Mijl was struck, and a third arrow whistled between Tali and Tinyhead. Before she could move, the tall guard spun her around and jerked her head back to expose her throat. Her hands were still bound and she could not help herself.

Whack! The guard's knife spun past her ear—Tinyhead had kicked it out of his hand. Another kick to the groin dropped the man. Tinyhead grabbed Tali, raced for the boulders, dropped her on her feet, one giant paw crushing her shoulder, and peered around the side.

Tali doubled over, shuddering. It had been so close. But she had to get free. She rasped at her bonds with the brass pin that had pinned her father's letter in place. She had been working on the ropes for an hour; and now the last strands tore through. She could not see the attackers through the claggy smoke. What if they thought she was Cythonian and shot her too?

A big man came charging towards her, running so fast down the rubbly slope that he was likely to break his neck. Tali caught her breath; it was Rix, carrying a bow, and behind him was Tobry, sword in hand. She had been wrong about them. They were risking their lives for her.

Mijl rose from the smoke, swinging the glass tube towards Tali. Mijl's middle and thighs were blood-drenched and a broken arrow protruded from her belly muscles, yet her hand was steady. Tinyhead had not noticed and his grip prevented Tali from ducking out of sight.

Mijl took aim. Tali was staring at the round opening in the end of the tube, unable to move, when the pothecky let out a pained grunt. Another arrow had gone through her upper arm, pinning it to the side of her chest. She tried to raise the tube, then it wavered and she fell down through the smoke.

Tinyhead caught Tali up but this time she was ready. She slashed him across the forehead with the brass pin, beads of blood bursting from the deep scratch, then back across the nose and cheek. He was so shocked that he dropped her. She bounced on her bruised bottom, scrambled up and, as he lunged, she thrust out the pin to hold him off.

Tinyhead flicked blood out of his eyes and reached for her. With Nurse Bet's lessons guiding her hand, Tali slashed and the pin tore through his fingertips. He took a backwards step, raising his arms skywards and silently beseeching his master. She pushed forwards. A chymical dart whirred past her cheek and struck him in the left shoulder. He plucked it out, stared at the fluid dripping from its hollow tip for several seconds, then crumbled.

Tali backed away, turned and cried out. Rix was flying through the air, straight towards one of the guard's spears—he was going to impale himself through the chest. But then, with a mid-air dexterity beyond her imagination, he hacked the spear shaft in two and killed the man with a kick to the jaw.

"Tali, behind you!"

The warning came almost too late. Only instinct got her out of the way and she felt the wind of the tall guard's sword blow, the tug as it sliced through her baggy robes. She scrambled away, snatching a handful of dirt and tossing it at his eyes. He kept coming, slashing across and back, aiming to kill.

With a sickening crunch, a sword came out through the left wall of his chest and he died on his feet. It had gone right through him. She was staring at the impaled corpse when Orlyk sat up, struck a triangle, *ting*, and the ankle bracelet went from cold to burning in a few seconds. Smoke rose from Tali's ankle as the skin blistered. The pain was hideous but there was no way to get the bracelet off—the squat Cythonian was advancing with her throat-cutting knife.

Tali tried to heave Rix's sword out of the man's back, but it was jammed through the ribs. She grabbed a stone and hurled it at Orlyk. It missed, and so did the next; throwing stones was not an art Tali had ever practised. Orlyk was almost on her when her third stone struck the arrow wound in the squat woman's upper chest. She dropped like a boulder, convulsing again, and the bracelet began to cool.

The smoke billowed high, drifted low. All was a chaos of screams and shouts, blows and counter-blows. Tali kept turning and turning, squinting through the eye-stinging smoke, never sure which direction the next attack was coming from but always knowing that the enemy was determined to cut her throat.

She could not have said whom she fought or what was the result, but suddenly everyone was down save the pothecky, who had dropped Rix and Tobry with chymical darts and was thumbing another into her tube. Tobry lay thirty yards away up the slope, unmoving. Steam gushed from Rix's mouth and he was making inarticulate grunts. His red face looked as though it was about to burst.

The pothecky turned on Tali, who took careful aim with a jagged chunk of red stone, and flung it. This time it went true, thudding into the pothecky's forehead. Her arms flailed, she fell to her knees on rock and Tali heard an unpleasant crack, as if a kneecap had broken.

She was drenched in sweat, staggering from exhaustion, and every movement aggravated her blistered ankle, but Tinyhead was lurking somewhere, and Mijl and Orlyk were still alive.

The sensible thing was to kill them while they were helpless but that was too cold-blooded for Tali. She limped to Rix and put a hand on his face. He was almost too hot to touch—he seemed to be burning from the inside. The lake was only ten yards away yet it might as well have been a mile—she could never drag his dead weight that far. She would have to try and heal him.

Even the most minor healing was draining, but it was going to take far more than that to save him and she had little strength left. Tali pressed hard on his cheeks with her healing hands, summoning every iota of her little gift to draw the heat out of him. Her hands went as hot as his face, yet he seemed to be getting worse.

He clawed weakly at his chest and she saw the dart embedded there, the bubble of fluid under the skin. Taking hold of the feathered tail, she eased the dart out, then opened his shirt. She shot a glance around her, saw no Tinyhead lurking, no Orlyk or Mijl. Tali pressed her fingers in under the bubble so as to drive out the remaining poison, then carefully wiped it off his skin, stroking outwards so none would be drawn into the puncture.

She laid hands on his chest again. He was even hotter now and his heart was going like a galloping horse; it was a wonder it had not burst. Tali murmured the strongest healing charms she knew, trying to draw the heat into her hot hands. They became scaldingly hot, red and painful, and after a minute she felt the heartbeat slow its frantic pace.

The smoke was settling, forming an opaque, knee-deep layer she could not see through. Mijl and Orlyk might be creeping up on her or they might be dead. She could not tell.

"Tobe?" Rix groaned, eyelids fluttering. "Tobe, that you? Thought you—dead." He tried to sit up.

She could not think about that. "It's me, Tali. Stay down."

"Help Tobe. He's . . . the better man."

Noble, perhaps, but stupid. "Shut up and let me do my job."

Tobry was on his hands and knees, attempting to crawl, though he only managed a yard before flopping like a dying man. *Was* he dying? Tali had seen so many dead—in her brief life she had lost everyone she cared about. It was a struggle to help Rix, whose heart raced every time she lifted her hands. How could Tobry survive the same poison without healing aid?

Ting! White smoke belched up from the bracelet again, burning her scorched ankle. She shook her foot, trying to ease the pain, and caught the stench of burning skin—Orlyk must have roused. Yes, she was lurching towards Tali, knife out, and the look on her face was murderous.

"I am so going to enjoy cutting your throat," said Orlyk.

Without thinking, Tali picked up the chymical dart she had taken from Rix's chest and tossed it into Orlyk's open mouth.

Her crimson-faced, steam-gushing death was not pretty, but it was mercifully brief.

"Better now," whispered Rix. "Help Tobe."

Dare she? If she left Rix now, both he and Tobry could die. Where was Tobry? He must have crawled off and there was no time to look for him. The chymical smoke was thinning, blowing away, and the pothecky was on her feet, blood running from cheek, shoulder, belly and knee. Mijl must have been in agony but she was determined to do her duty. She lurched around towards Tali, each step a struggle, and there was no one to stop her.

She raised the tube and, after three fumbling attempts, inserted a killing dart. Tali scrambled backwards, looking for a fallen weapon. There was nothing within reach.

"Aah!" gasped Rix. "Heart burning, burning."

He pressed his hands over his chest, tried to get up and succeeded in raising his head, but it fell back on the path, *thud.*

Tali found a pebble. It was too small to do any damage unless it struck Mijl in the eye. It would have to. She hurled it and missed by feet.

The pothecky raised her tube and tried to hold it steady but swayed and slammed down onto her cracked kneecap. She screamed and something fell onto the ground and smashed—a glass eye. Mijl turned her empty socket and good eye on Tali, then raised the tube again. It was wobbling a little, though at this range she could not miss.

Tali wondered if she could dive and outrun the dart. Surely not. Mijl's cheeks puffed out to blow, but as she did, and Tali ducked, a staggering, scarlet-faced Tobry came at Mijl from behind and with a ferocious slash lifted her domed head four feet off her hunched shoulders.

Rix was on his feet. "Burning, burning."

He swayed, jammed the point of his sword into the ground to hold himself up and almost took a big toe off. Tali pressed her hands against his chest, muttered her healing charm and forced until her fingers burned and her knees wobbled. Slowly the crimson receded from his face.

"Water," whispered Rix.

Tali and Tobry dragged him to the edge of the lake and rolled him in. Tali stepped into the water, quenching the ankle bracelet in a hissing cloud of steam, and it cracked and came to pieces. Her ankle was red-raw, blistered in a circle and, now that she had nothing to distract her, excruciatingly painful.

Tobry drank half a gallon, Rix even more, and after several minutes he sat up.

"Where—Orlyk?" he rasped. "Watch out for her."

"Dead," said Tali. "They're all dead, save for Tinyhead, and he's gone." But how far?

"Thank you." Rix tried to struggle upright.

"Lie down. You're not well."

"No time," said Rix. "The other squad's coming. Tali, Tali, got to say it."

"You don't have to say anything," she muttered.

"Yes, I do." He extended his hand. "Sorry about yesterday. I'm a fool. Everyone will tell you that."

"He's not lying," said Tobry, managing a grin. "You'll look hard to find a bigger idiot in all Hightspall. I'm thinking about writing a book about him."

"Don't go on, Tobe," said Rix.

"But his heart's in the right place."

"It is now," said Rix, pressing his free hand against his chest.

As Tali stared at him, the heat swept back into his face. Was he thinking that she was going to spurn his apology? "Yesterday you threw up at the sight of my slave mark."

He bent his head to her. "I was taught that the Pale willingly served the enemy. I'm not proud of myself."

"We're enslaved! We've always been enslaved."

"I understand that now."

She could see what an effort he was making. And, having saved each other's lives, there would forever be a bond between them. It was no small thing.

"I've made plenty of mistakes," said Tali, "and not all could be remedied with a handshake." His huge, tanned hand engulfed her small, pale one. "Shall we call truce?"

"Truce." He turned to Tobry. "I thought you were dead. How did you survive?"

"Don't know," said Tobry, in a voice as dry as a crackling blaze. "After the dart hit me, my heart was on fire. I was burning up; knew I was going to die. Nothing I could do. Tried to heal myself but didn't know how. Then I . . . I lost a minute or two. When I roused, the hot pain was being pushed back down . . . and out."

"Pushed back down?" said Rix incredulously.

"I can't explain it. Must have a strong constitution, I guess."

Tali looked from one to the other. Rix was studying Tobry side-on as if he did not believe what he was hearing. No, as if he thought his closest friend was lying.

CHAPTER 50

Tobry broke Mijl's tube underfoot, tossed the pieces into the lake and rummaged through her pouches and pack, taking out small items and stuffing them in his own pack.

"We don't have time for that," said Rix, looking up the path. He thought he could hear the enemy coming, though it might have been his own racketing heart. His face still felt scalding. "The second squad can't be more than five minutes away."

"If we can discover how their chymical weapons work it'll be a big help," said Tobry, unhitching a death lash from Orlyk's belt and jamming it into the pack.

"Careful," cried Tali. "That can take your whole arm off."

Tobry winced, then stripped the sandals off Mijl's small feet and tossed them to Tali. "Here. You can't run across the Seethings in bare feet."

She put them on.

"They'll see us as we climb the slope," said Rix, "and run us down long before we can reach the horses." He eyed Tobry surreptitiously, unnerved by his miraculous recovery from the dart. "We'll have to take to the lake." He took off his boots, tied them to his belt and waded in.

"I'm not going without Rannilt," said Tobry. He seemed to be in pain.

"You found her?" said Tali, standing on the edge. "Is she all right?"

Rix drew her into the water. She was shivering and resisted him. "She found us. Made us come after you, too."

"We can't leave her." Tali jerked on his arm.

"Can't take on a dozen of the enemy, either. Rannilt's well hidden; she's safer than we are. We'll come back for her."

He drew Tali out until the cool water was mid-chest on him, throat level on her, and it was glorious on his inflamed skin.

"What if we don't get back?" said Tali.

Rix explained about the note and the gramarye Tobry had put on Beetle. "Luzia is my old nurse in Cauldron. She'll look after Rannilt. It's the best we can do."

Tali bit her lip, then nodded.

"Can Cythonians swim?" said Rix.

Her eyes were darting, her breathing fast and shallow. "I don't know—but I can't."

She seemed close to panic, but she was such a little thing she could hardly cause him any trouble. "Stay with me and you'll be all right. Tobe, we'll swim across to the outlet and go down the cascades. Once we're far enough ahead, we'll double back to Rannilt and the horses."

"What if we can't get back?" Tali's voice cracked.

"We'll think of something else."

"Better dump the swords," said Tobry.

"I'm keeping mine. If they beat us to the cascades—"

"A sword will be no use at all. They'll pick us off with arrows from the bank."

"I'm not going unarmed. Tali, ditch those baggy robes."

Tali shrugged them off and Rix pushed them under. She was still wearing the silk gown from yesterday, though a tear across the waist revealed a livid welt on her pale skin. She pulled her orange hat down as far as it would go. She was trembling, her breathing fast and shallow. Shock, he thought. This could get tricky.

"Take hold of my belt, Tali. Don't let go."

She did so and he swam out using sidestroke. She was clinging so tightly that her knuckles were jammed into his belly. Every so often her eyes rolled back; she was fighting not to scream.

"What is a pothecky, anyway?" said Rix to Tobry.

Tobry's eyes never left Tali's face. "Cross between an alchymist and a healer, but uses chymical potions for war. How are you feeling?"

Rix put his head under for a few seconds. "Still hot. I don't ever want to go that close to death again. Ah, this water's good."

They were only a hundred yards out when the second squad came charging down the track and stopped at the bodies.

"No splashing." Rix put an arm around Tali and sank down in the water. "We can still get away with this."

They managed another twenty yards before they were spotted.

"Go!" Rix took off, Tali trailing behind like a wide-eyed corpse.

The enemy ran to the water's edge and several troops waded in to chest level, but headed back and the archers began to fire.

"Keep low," said Tobry. "A head shot is quite an ask from there."

"You could do it," said Rix, "so maybe they can." Tali's teeth chattered. "How are you doing?" He turned over and swam on his back to watch her.

Her eyes were enormous blue pools. She was clutching his belt desperately, yet kept letting go with one hand to pull her hat down. Rix could not identify with her fear of the water. He had learned to swim before he could walk.

"If you can do it, I can," she said, shuddering.

"The water isn't that cold."

"It is to me. In Cython, all the water is warm."

"And you're such a little thing."

"I'm strong," she said, with a determined tilt of the head. "In Cython, if you're weak, you die."

"How's your ankle?"

"It's excruciating. But in Cython we learn to endure pain."

"You don't give much away, do you?"

"Reveal your weaknesses and everyone takes advantage of them."

"I just saved your life," he said irritably, "and you saved mine. I don't expect to be your friend but I think I've earned a little trust."

"Father said never trust anyone who says, 'Trust me.' Father said you learn how to trust by seeing what people do, not by hearing what they say."

"I've just ridden six miles through the blasted Seethings, risked my life and nearly died, for you."

He could see the unspoken questions in her eyes—*Why did you risk your life? What do you want from me?*

An arrow plucked at the surface of the water a hand span from Tali's right shoulder. She rolled over and the hat came off. Letting out an incoherent cry, she grabbed it and jammed it on. Two more arrows splashed near Tobry.

"Hang on tight and hold your breath, Tali," said Rix. "Tobe, dive!"

Rix dived deep, pulling her under with him, and swam away from the shore for as long as his breath held, nearly two minutes.

He surfaced twenty yards ahead of Tobry. Tali bobbed up behind him, hatless, her gown up around her shoulders, coughing up water. She let go of his belt and covered her eyes with a forearm. Her other arm thrashed feebly. Arrows rained down.

"Tobe?" Rix turned towards him. "We've got to get further out."

"Where's Tali?" cried Tobry.

Rix churned the water to foam as he turned. Her hat was floating several yards away. "She was just here."

"She was in a bad way when you came up. Why didn't you hang onto her?" Tobry dived.

Rix did too, squinting through the murky water. He could only see down a yard or two. He swept his arms out to either side as he swam, cursing his stupidity.

As he surfaced, Tobry was also coming up. "You're a moron, Rix," he said furiously.

"I know." Rix scanned the water but there was nothing to see save arrow splashes. "She seemed to be doing fine . . ."

"You swam underwater for forty yards! I couldn't hold my breath that long."

Rix dived again. Fool! You could see how afraid she was. You've drowned her! He surfaced and dived again, swimming around in circles, feeling sicker and sicker. Finally he burst up. Tobry was treading water with his back to him.

"Tobe?"

"I've got her," said Tobry. "She's not in a very good state."

Rix swam across. Tobry had his arms around Tali from behind. He put his knotted fists in under her ribcage, thrust hard, and water and mucus dribbled down her chest. Tobry thrust again but nothing more came up.

"Let me . . ." began Rix.

"Piss off, Rix."

Tobry, the most even-tempered man Rix knew, was angrier than he had ever seen him. Treading water furiously, Tobry raised himself out to the waist and tipped Tali upside down, holding her back to his chest. He pushed under her ribcage again, water gushed from her mouth and nose and she took a shuddering breath.

He turned her the right way up and sank down, panting. "Better now?"

Tali clung to him like a raft in the middle of the ocean. "*Hat!*" she croaked.

Rix collected her floating hat and put it on her head. Her ragged breathing steadied.

"They're heading around both sides of the lake," he said, watching the men on the shore. "It's a long trek but they could still beat us to the outlet. I'd better take—"

"No!" Tali cried.

"I think it's best if I get her across, don't you?" said Tobry pointedly.

Rix did not need to be told twice. Cursing himself, the enemy and Tobry in turns, he swam for the outlet, churning through the water for ten minutes before discovering that he had left Tali and Tobry a hundred yards behind. If they got into trouble he would be too far away to help them. Grow up, you fool. It'll be a long time before *you're* ready to be Lord Ricinus.

He swam back slowly, conserving his strength. Tobry had tied a piece of cord around Tali's waist and the other end around his own, and was swimming steadily, stopping to check on her every minute.

Rix pushed himself higher in the water to watch the running enemy. Because of the meandering track they had to travel many times the distance, but they appeared to be halfway, perhaps more. They were winning the race.

"We've got to pick up the pace, Tobe, or they'll be waiting when we get to the outlet."

"Can't swim any faster," said Tobry. "That dart has left me weaker than I'd thought. Tali, go with Rix."

"No!" She clung to Tobry.

Her voice was still hoarse, as if it hurt to talk. Rix had heard that drowning was a painful way to die.

"If we can't beat them to the outlet, we all die," said Rix.

Again, that little tilt of her chin. She swallowed, then something shifted in her eyes. Was it the slave's habit of obedience, or the determination that had taken her where no other Pale had ever gone? Whatever it was, he had to admire it.

"Then of course I must go with ... *him*."

Tobry handed Rix the cord. He tied it to his waist and Tali gripped his belt. She looked like a convicted felon being led to the blood gallows above the gates of Palace Ricinus.

"I'm sorry," he said quietly. "Sometimes I forget that other people aren't like me."

She stared at him, unblinking. "*I* certainly wouldn't want to be like you."

"I'll be swimming as fast as I can," he said. "If you lose hold, shout. Ready?"

"I don't make the same mistake twice." Her teeth chattered; she clamped her jaw.

"Neither do I."

He swam slowly at first, accelerating once he was confident that she was secure, and revelling in his strength and endurance. But also, if he could admit it to himself, putting on a display, to both of them, that no one else could have equalled.

Tobry came up beside him, blowing hard, going all out. Rix, even wearing his sword and towing Tali, had a bit in reserve.

"We're gaining," Tobry said. "Another ten minutes should do it."

"We've got to beat them by more than a bowshot. A lot more."

Rix accelerated away. As he approached the outfall, and the racing enemy coming along either side of the lake resolved into separate figures, he knew that he and Tali would make it with minutes to spare. The seven Cythonians on the left were half a mile off, at least five minutes in this rough country, while the nine approaching from the right were a little further back.

But Tobry was a couple of minutes behind and flagging badly. Rix swam into the shallows and stood up, feeling mud beneath his feet. He felt no triumph now. The urge to trump his friend had vanished a quarter of a mile back.

"Hurry, Tobe," he said softly.

Tali waded ashore, holding her hat on. Her lips moved; her eyes yearned towards Tobry. *Come on.*

Rix emptied the water from his boots and sword sheath and scrambled up a rocky beach to the far bank of the outflow from the lake. It was about ten yards wide and three or four deep, a sinuous cataract that ran fast for a mile or two before emptying into the next, lower lake. He climbed a little mound and went up on tiptoes, trying to see what lay ahead.

There were three cascades, at least. Even had he been on his own they would have been perilous to negotiate, but the cataract was their only chance of escaping.

He walked downstream for a hundred yards, working out how best to tackle it. When he came back, Tobry was staggering from the water, breathing like a stranded dolphin.

"What's it like?" he gasped.

"Ugly," said Rix.

CHAPTER 51

"I'm never going in the water again," said Tali, trembling all over. She hugged the gown around her but the morning wind blew right through it.

If they escaped, found Rannilt and made it through the war zone to Caulderon, she might never see Rix and Tobry again. Or if Rix was killed . . . it felt callous, but she had to find out what he knew about her mother's murder.

"Ready?" said Rix.

Tobry bent double, slipped to his knees and stayed down. "Only if you can tow me too."

Tali ran across. "Lean on me."

He rose, holding onto her slender shoulders and breathing hard. Tobry was heavier than she had expected but she had borne greater burdens.

"Why do you keep staring at me, Rix?" said Tobry.

"Just concerned for you."

To Tali's mind, his reply was unconvincing. What was Rix worried about?

"Getting a bit old for this adventuring lark," said Tobry, letting go. "A maiden should be bathing my feet by a hearty fire while I sip—"

"They're nearly within bowshot," Rix said curtly, and moved to the edge of the channel. "Ready?"

"Give me one more minute."

The cataract looked far more dangerous than the placid lake. The water had burnt all the way down into her lungs and without Tobry she would have drowned. Tali never wanted to feel that helpless again.

"Ready, Tali?" said Rix.

She shook her head. "I can't go back in the water."

"Don't you trust me to get you through?"

She took a sharp breath. She had to raise it now, while he was off-guard, and hope he would be shocked enough to give something away.

She met his eyes. "The last person I trusted was my mother . . . "

"And?" said Rix, when she did not go on.

"She was murdered when I was eight."

"I'm sorry," he said politely.

Tali had expected him to start, or look away guiltily. Expected to see a reflection of that horror she had seen in his eyes ten years ago, or for Rix to conceal his feelings behind a liar's mask. She had not expected polite sympathy. But he *had* been that boy, she was positive of it. How could her mother's murder have meant nothing to him?

Rix was a man whose passions ran deep and she did not think he could be indifferent to such a childhood trauma, any more than she could. And how come he had not recognised her, when she looked so like her mother? Tali saw no recollection in his eyes, no guilt or shame or horror—nothing save mild curiosity.

"I look just like my mother did, I'm told," said Tali.

He frowned, doubtless wondering why she was babbling about such things, then turned to Tobry.

"We've got to go *now*, Tobe."

"I'm ready."

He did not look it. His face was blotchy and his left knee had a worrying tremor. Rix lifted Tali's hat off, the sky went up and down and panic exploded inside her. She snatched the hat and crammed it on, gasping.

"What's with the hat?" said Rix, frowning. "You're bound to lose it in the cataract."

Tali pressed a hand against her chest, unable to speak.

Tobry peered at her. "You're not used to being in the open, are you? Does it make you feel panicky?"

She jerked her head up and down. He drew a length of twine from a pocket.

"We don't have time," said Rix. "They're almost within bow-shot."

"If she has a panic attack in there, you both drown," said Tobry. He tied the hat on. "Go!"

Tali swallowed and took hold of Rix's belt. He put an arm around her waist.

"You don't need—" she said hastily, uncomfortable with the physical contact.

"If the current tears us apart, there's nothing I can do to save you. We'll go in together."

She had to trust him. Though how could she trust someone hiding such a terrible secret?

He stepped off, carrying her with him, and before they sank to the waist the current had whirled them away, far faster than Rix had swum across the lake. Tali stifled a shriek and locked her hands onto his belt. If they got into trouble, not even his great strength could fight the power of the water.

They shot downstream, the current thumping the sheathed sword against her legs and his tied boots against her shoulder. Rix was steering them with scoops of his free arm and powerful kicks. A cascade appeared ahead, the water straining between smooth, slime-covered boulders. They were heading straight for one. They were going to smash into it and be torn apart! Tali shrieked. Rix gave a mighty double-kick, they shot between it and the next boulder and she felt slime-covered rock gliding under her thigh.

Tobry had tied the hat on so tightly that the cord was cutting into her throat, making every breath a struggle. It reminded her of drowning. Her legs thrashed, instinctively.

"Don't do that," said Rix.

She fought to contain the panic. Ahead the water ran straight and fast for a couple of hundred yards before another cascade, a bigger one, though the rocks were further apart and Tali wasn't so worried this time.

She should have been—a dip in the water surface hid a little whirlpool. They shot into it and it hurled them out sideways, straight towards a ramp-shaped boulder, and Rix could do nothing to avoid it. He half-turned, sheltering Tali with his body, and struck it with his backside. A grunt of pain escaped him, then they were shooting up the slimy slope and hurtling into the air with his kilt up around his waist and Tali, clinging two-handed to his belt, trailing behind. Her cold hands were slipping. She was losing grip! A moan escaped her.

His arm clamped around her waist, crushing her against him, and she did not flinch from the contact this time. Did she trust him? In the water, she had to. Without him, she was dead.

There were rocks below them too, but they were moving so fast they passed over them and splashed into deep water. It hurled them away down the race, moving faster and faster. They curved around a bend and shot down another long straight towards a third cascade.

"You all right?" said Rix.

Tali nodded stiffly. How far had they gone? A couple of miles? They must be well ahead of the enemy by now, but her escape was a threat to Cython's security and they would never give up.

She relaxed enough to look upstream. Where was Tobry? He had been exhausted before entering the cataract. What if he'd hit the rocks and broken his legs, or had been knocked out?

"Tobry?" she yelled. Water surged into her mouth; she choked and coughed it out. "Rix?" Her voice went squeaky. "I can't see him."

If Rix was anxious, he did not show it. "He'll be all right. Old Tobe is indestructible."

"Aren't you worried?" Tobry felt like an old, reliable friend. He could not drown; he could not. And yet, anyone could go under in this cataract. "He could be dead."

"If I take my eyes off the river to look for him, we *will* be dead. Hang on."

"What?" said Tali, still scanning upstream.

"*Hang on!*"

She was turning when he crushed her so tightly against his iron-hard chest that it forced the breath out of her.

"Can't breathe," she gasped.

His grip relaxed a little, then they were on the brink—and it wasn't a cascade. It was a waterfall and they were going over the edge.

Though Tali wasn't a screamer, she let out a shriek of desperation, then threw her arms around Rix's solid body as they fell in a torrent of water. Down they plunged, she could not see where to. They were surrounded by whirling spray going in a hundred directions at once, hitting her face so hard that it stung—

He rolled over in the air so he would hit the water first and not crush her beneath him, and they struck. But it did not feel like water—it was foamy and offered no resistance, supported no weight. They plunged through it, down and down and down. Why hadn't she taken a deep breath before they hit? She had hardly any air.

This was worse than the other time. This time Tali knew what to fear—the desperate urge to breathe, while knowing that the only thing she could breathe was water. Water that would burn all the way down and fill her lungs with that terrible, aching cold.

Her lungs were beginning to heave; funny lights were dancing in her head. Tali kicked furiously, trying to get to the surface, but could not free herself of Rix's grip. What if he had drowned and was carrying her to the bottom? She could not tell which way was up.

She thumped him with a fist. His big hand went across her nose, mouth and two-thirds of her face, and then she could not have breathed if she had wanted to. She tore at his hands but he did not let go. She was suffocating; panic was overwhelming her; they were tossed upside-down and jerked in three different directions. Then, when she was blacking out, he drove them up to the surface and she felt blessed air on her face.

The hand pulled away. Tali sucked in air so full of spray that it was half water, breathed it out just for the joy of being able to, and took another gulp. The waterfall was pouring down on her head and she could not see a thing. It would have driven her under had Rix not been holding her.

Then they were moving, Rix dragging them out of the flow. The hammering on her head faded. She opened her eyes and they were in a broad, deep pool carved out by the waterfall. He kicked towards the edge, a sandy shore, and dropped her onto solid ground.

Tali concentrated on breathing, in, out, in, out. A minute passed before she realised that she was alone. Where had he gone? He was out in the middle of the pool, diving, disappearing. Tali climbed to her knees. Why wasn't he coming up?

Her breath caught in her throat. What if he had drowned? The Cythonians would be here before long and she could not bear to go through that again. Better to cast herself into the pool, holding a rock, and sink to the bottom.

Don't be stupid. You're not a helpless slave now. You're the last of the ancient line of House vi Torgrist. You have a duty to perform and you will do it, or die trying. *You will never give up.*

Rix bobbed to the surface, floating on his back, head towards her, arms and legs spread, prone upon the flood. Had he drowned? A few minutes ago he had exploded out of the water with her, a physical force that had overcome even the power of the river, but now he was limp as wet rags. One crooked arm held Tobry up in a headlock—or was it Tobry's body?—but Rix's eyes were closed.

Tali waded out as far as she could go, but from there the bottom sloped steeply and she felt sand slipping beneath her feet. She scrambled back, thrashing with her arms. How could she get them out?

A nest of tangled branches was wedged between the trees to her left, carried down by a flood. She heaved one out, snapped off the side branches to stubs and ran back. Wading in as far as she dared, Tali hooked a stub end into the belt of Rix's kilt, and pulled gently. The kilt pulled up then slipped free.

She reached further down, caught something and jerked.

"Aaarrgh!" Rix roared. He convulsed and his head went under.

She panicked. Get him out, quick, before he drowns. She heaved on the branch with all her strength.

He let out a bellow that echoed off the rock walls, even louder than the waterfall. "What the hell are you doing? Let go."

She kept dragging him backwards, and Tobry with him, still in the headlock, until Rix grounded on the shore. Tobry was not moving. She pulled Rix's hooked arm away from Tobry's neck, dug her toes into the sand and dragged him up the beach.

Rix groaned, rolled over, gasping and clutching at himself under the kilt, and only then did Tali realise where the branch had caught him.

Oh dear, she thought, flushing.

Tobry was barely breathing. She turned him onto his side and drove her knee into his diaphragm, imitating the way he had pressed the water out of her. None came out. She opened his shirt and put her ear to his chest, which was bruised and scratched where he must have hit the rocks, and red from healing cuts made days ago. She could not hear any gurgling, just his fluttering heartbeat.

She was about to drive her knee into his belly again when his eyes opened and he took a deeper, more reassuring breath. He was all right! She rolled him onto his back. His chest had a number of thin white scars across it, healed wounds, and some went perilously close to the heart.

"Is Rix—?" he whispered.

"He's alive, but—" She bit her lip.

"What's the matter?"

"I was hooking him out with a branch but . . . er, it caught on something under his kilt. I'm afraid I've hurt him."

"It caught on *something under his kilt?*"

"I'm afraid so. He seems quite upset about it."

Tobry made a muffled noise in his throat, looked at Rix, who was still writhing, and chuckled. "Serves the sod right."

"He's in pain," said Tali, shocked at his callousness.

"But hilarious pain," Tobry hooted.

"What if I've damaged him?" She knew men were sensitive down there.

His laughter echoed off the cliff face.

"He just saved your life," snapped Tali.

"And in ten years' time I'll still be getting free drinks to tell this story."

CHAPTER 52

"They're only minutes away," called Tali from her vantage point up a tall tree.

"Come down, Tali," said Rix.

"Can't go back in the water," said Tobry. "Another ride like that one will finish me."

"Besides," Rix added, "we'd end up in Lake Fumerous and the last waterfall has a thousand-foot drop. We'll swim the pool and head overland."

Rix towed Tali across but she saw no animal power in him now, just a bone-creaking weariness. Tobry was even slower. The hundred and fifty yards across the pool took him minutes and with every laboured stroke she was afraid he would fail and sink. She looked upstream, expecting to see grey heads beside the waterfall. Tobry reached the shore and Rix dragged him out.

"How do we get back to Rannilt?" said Rix. "You know this country better than I do."

"Map's lost." Tobry checked the angle of the sun and pointed to the right. "This way. I think."

Rix squeezed Tali's shoulder, the way an old friend might have done. "You did well."

"Thank you," said Tali, disconcerted by the change in him. But then, they had been through a year's worth of adventures today. "Are you sure Rannilt's all right?"

Rix and Tobry exchanged glances. For a few seconds, Tobry's eyes went black.

"We've led the enemy away from her ..." said Rix.

"What is it?" said Tali.

"Nothing to worry about," Rix said slowly. "But ... Rannilt kept talking about something that comes out of the dark. *Shadow and shape, shiftin', always shiftin'*, she said. But kids are afraid of the dark. It's probably nothing."

Frosty fingers scraped down Tali's back. "She told me about it, too."

"Do you think it's real?" Tobry's voice crackled like ice.

"Yes, I do."

"And it's hunting her?"

Tali's chest was tight. She pushed the words out. "*Me!* It's using her to get to me."

There was a long silence. "We'd better split up," said Rix. "Tobe, take Tali and head for Caulderon. I'll go after Rannilt."

"If you think I'm running away—" began Tali.

"I'm with Rix on this," said Tobry. "If you're right, it wants you to come after Rannilt. It's luring you in."

"Do you think I don't know that?" snapped Tali, for she was desperately afraid. "She saved my life and I'm going after her. I'm not debating the matter."

"This way," said Tobry, turning left.

Away from the incised channel of the river, the barren plain was unnaturally warm and dotted with sinkholes and fuming pits. The soil was a rusty orange, scattered with round black pebbles the size of marbles that rolled beneath them and hurt Tali's feet through Mijl's thin sandals. In the distance, the Brown Vomit fumed and roared. Red lava was trickling over the rim, though it quickly congealed.

"Eruption's getting worse," said Tobry laconically.

"Does lava ever flow this far?" said Tali.

"It's too sticky. The Vomits tend to blow up."

"H-how often?"

"Might not happen for a thousand years. But when it does, it'll empty the lake and wash Cauldron clean away."

Tali wished she had not asked. "How far is it to Rannilt?"

"Three miles in a direct line," said Tobry. "But it'll take hours on our winding route."

In hours the enemy could catch them. In hours the shifting thing could kill Rannilt and eat her.

"How did you escape Cython, where no other Pale ever has?" asked Rix, sometime later.

She explained about the sunstone knocking all the enemy out.

"Yet you escaped?"

"It didn't affect me—apart from a terrible headache." Or had it? The power that had killed Banj had appeared soon afterwards.

"I wonder why not?" mused Tobry.

She did not answer, for a chilling possibility had occurred to her. How come Rix, the one person she could identify from the murder scene, had appeared at the shaft within hours of her escape? It could be a coincidence, though it seemed a little too neat.

If he knew the killers, had he been blackmailed into protecting them? But in that case, why had he rescued her, and why was he doing his best to make up for his earlier insult? She couldn't make sense of it.

She had to confront him, tell him she knew he was the boy from the cellar, and demand answers ... though, after he had risked his life for her, to do so now felt more than a little ungrateful. It must be soon, though, and in the meantime she would try the subtle approach.

"Why was Tinyhead hunting you *before* you escaped?" said Tobry.

"He's *why* I escaped." She turned to Rix, watching his face. "He betrayed my mother to her killers and now he's after me."

"Then he's a traitor to his own country," said Rix.

"He serves a higher master." She told them how Tinyhead's master had burnt through his head to prevent him revealing the name. "For a few seconds, I could see his eyes looking out of Tinyhead's eyes, staring at me."

Rix jumped, and he and Tobry exchanged glances. "I don't like this at all," Tobry said in a low voice. "When we get home, Rix, we've got to talk."

"He wants me desperately and I've no idea why," said Tali, moving closer to Rix and watching his face. "Wants to kill me the way that woman killed my mother."

"What woman?" said Rix. His voice rose. "Were you there when she died?"

"I saw her killed," said Tali, staring at his eyes. She saw no flicker of guilt, shame or even recognition. "The killers were masked, but they were definitely from Hightspall."

"Hightspallers in Cython?" said Rix to Tobry.

"I don't know that we were in Cython. Tinyhead led us a long way underground."

"Doing secret deals with the enemy is treachery, even without conspiring to murder Pale. Treachery of the worst kind, a capital offence. What scum would sink so low?"

She wanted to scream, *then what were you doing there?*

"They're behind us," said Tobry. "Nine of them."

"Can we shake them off?" said Tali. Rannilt was lost in a

deadly land and Tali had to get to her before the *thing in the dark* did.

"Not a hope," said Tobry. A cluster of cone-shaped peaks broke the horizon a mile and a half away. "If we can reach those hills we might hold them off . . . for a while. Run!"

She set off, and every stride was like having the soles of her feet beaten. Rix passed her, jogging, his wet boots squeaking with every stride. Tobry laboured along beside her.

"Are you better?" she said.

"It's been a while since I've had a day like this."

"Did you get the scars on your chest in battle?"

Tobry shook his head. "There hasn't been war in many life-times . . . " He did not speak for a while. "I didn't get those scars respectably."

"I don't understand," said Tali.

"A woman's husband challenged me to a duel of honour. *His* honour, not mine, if you take my meaning."

More than a little shocked, she mulled it over as she ran. Such things were unheard of in Cython. When the men came back for their monthly visits, many were too exhausted to service their own wives. An especially vigorous man could be called upon to honour the wife of an incapable friend, but that was by mutual consent. Clearly, things were different in Hightspall.

She looked sideways at Tobry. He was half a head shorter than Rix, wiry rather than muscular and no one would have called him handsome, yet in Cython he would have been a rare prize. Moreover, she felt safe with him, as she had never felt safe since her mother was murdered.

"I think you *are* honourable," she said.

"How little you know me. My noble house has fallen, not unrelated to a terrible choice I had to make as a lad. Now I'm forced to rely on the kindness of my friends. I believe in nothing save the here and now, and I think the whole universe is a joke. So there."

"You're brave and kind," she panted. "You gave me the last coins you had. You risked your life for me."

"They're gaining fast," said Tobry.

They had crossed half the distance now. Even if they made it to the peaks, three could not fight nine when Rix was the only one armed.

The peaks were shaped like cones and only a few hundred feet high. Tali could see four of them and thought there might be others beyond.

"Those mountains are oddly neat," she said.

"Cinder cones," said Tobry. "Baby volcanoes."

"Do you think there could be caves there? Or anywhere we can hide?"

"No. They're just steep piles of broken rock, and dry as bones."

Rix reached the face of the nearest cinder cone, climbed twenty feet then turned to look out over the plain. Tali scrambled up to him, wincing. It was hard climbing, the surface being loose rock which slipped underfoot.

"How are you doing?" Rix said pointedly.

She wasn't giving anything away. "In Cython we learn—"

"To endure pain. I'm getting sick of hearing that."

"Sorry. My feet hurt like blazes. Everything hurts." It was a big admission, for her.

He put an arm around her. "We'll stand together and make them pay."

No, she thought, we won't.

CHAPTER 53

The enemy reached the base of the cinder cone, hundreds of feet below them. Rix drew his sword, Tobry a knife. Tali picked up a stone that fitted neatly in her hand, and waited.

"Come down," said the pock-faced captain.

"Go to hell," shouted Rix.

"Send down the slave and we'll allow you a merciful death."

"We know all about Cythonian honour," Rix sneered. "And Cythonian treachery. That's why the war started in the first place."

The captain clenched his grey fists. "The war started," he said, biting off each word and spitting it in their faces, "because your *Five Heroes* used vile sorcery to forge King Lyf's name on a charter—"

"They made a solemn agreement with your king which gave us half your country."

"Cythe belonged to the people. No king ever had the power to give it away."

"Well, that was two thousand years ago and what's done can't be undone," said Rix. "Go back to the Rat Hole where you belong."

"I'm not sure it's wise to insult them," Tobry murmured.

"I've had enough of their stinking lies."

"Take them!" ordered the Cythonian.

The enemy had just begun to climb the slope when Tali, who was higher than Rix and Tobry, noticed a cloud of dust back the way they had come. She climbed onto a honeycombed rock as tall as she was, then up onto a cart-sized boulder. Could they be that lucky?

"Tobry, riders!"

He scrambled up beside her and stared across the raddled plain. "Dozens of riders, coming this way. The Cythonians don't have horses, do they?"

"They could have stolen them."

"What do you think, Rix?" said Tobry.

Rix shaded his eyes with his hand. "They're flying our standard." He raised his voice. "You're too late, rock rats! Run back to the Rat Hole and some of you might survive."

"Don't taunt them, Rix," said Tobry.

The enemy turned to study the galloping horsemen. "Our blood will nourish the motherland stolen from us," said the captain. "But before it does, *cut them down*."

The Cythonians whirled and their archers raised their bows.

"Down!" cried Tobry, throwing himself behind the boulder.

Rix dropped flat. Tali could not get down quickly enough. A blinding pain speared through her right thigh and she was driven backwards off the boulder. Arrows were smashing against the rubble all around.

"Kill the Pale!" bellowed the captain.

Tobry pulled Tali into cover. The Cythonians were scrambling up the steep slope and the riders were still several minutes away. She touched the arrowhead, which was protruding from the back of her thigh, and a worse pain lanced through her.

"The riders won't get here in time," said Rix. "Tobe, put your shoulder behind this."

Through a haze of pain she saw them heaving on the smaller boulder. They rolled it out from behind the larger one and sent it crashing and bouncing down the slope, carrying smaller rocks with it and turning into a fan-shaped landslide. A man screamed. The sound of falling rocks grew to a roar, though it soon rattled away into silence. Dust drifted up the slope.

"Got two," Rix said with grim satisfaction. "And swept another four down to the bottom. Give us a hand, Tobe. Let's see if we can tidy up the rest of them."

More arrows fell as they pushed another boulder, and another. "The survivors are turning to face the riders," said Tobry. "They can't get to you now."

He crouched beside Tali. She opened her eyes but even the dull daylight made them ache.

Tobry pulled the hat brim down. "How are you feeling?"

She was hard pressed not to whimper. "Leg hurts."

"I'm not surprised." He raised his voice. "Rix? Get up here."

She heard him scrambling up the slope and smelled his sweat amidst the dust. Tobry stood up. He and Rix spoke in low voices, though not low enough.

"Better pray it's not poisoned," said Rix. "Or covered in plague pox. I wouldn't put that past the bastards."

"Let's just worry about the wound," said Tobry.

They bent over her thigh. Tali hurt too much to be embarrassed. Rix wiggled the arrow. She gasped, but bit her tongue.

"There's not a lot of blood," said Rix, "and it's only ebbing, so it hasn't hit an artery." He reached out, then jerked his hand back. His tanned face had gone pale.

"What's the matter?" said Tobry sharply.

"What's wrong with my blood?" said Tali.

"Take no notice," said Tobry. "Rix has nightmares about tanks of blood."

"Thanks for telling the world," Rix snapped. "Some poxes and pestilences are spread from bad blood, and it's getting worse all the time."

"There's nothing wrong with my blood," said Tali, insulted. "Besides, there aren't any diseases in Cython."

"What, none?" Tobry sat back on his heels.

"I've never known anyone to be ill. Save from overwork or food poisoning."

Tobry felt under her thigh. "The head's gone through, luckily. Hold her leg up. I'll cut it off."

"No!" cried Tali. "You're not—"

"He's cutting off the arrowhead, not your leg," said Rix gruffly.

She felt like a fool as he raised her leg. Tobry sawed at the tough shaft. It took ages and every movement sent shudders of pain through her.

"There," he said. "Pull it out."

Rix lowered her leg to the rubble. Tobry took her hands in his. "This is going to hurt."

"Just do it," she said. "In Cython we learn to endure—"

"We know!" Tobry and Rix said in a chorus.

As Rix pulled on the shaft, agony echoed along nerve endings down as far as her toes, as high as the middle of her back. She squeezed Tobry's hand so hard that he winced. Tali arched her back, clenched her toes, then the shaft came free and the pain died to a series of sharp throbs, each one matched to a heartbeat.

Rix pressed a big thumb against the wound. "Don't think it's done too much damage, though it'll scar."

Tali took his hand away, pressed her palm against the entry wound and murmured her healing charm. Warmth extended along the arrow line but the pain did not diminish. Her healing gift was drained, which was not surprising. She had used it more in the past few days than in her previous life. And even at full strength, treating such a deep wound would have taxed her.

"But I'll still be able to walk?"

"When it's healed. In a week or two."

She groaned and lay back. Rix rose. "I'm going to check on the enemy."

He crunched away. Tobry tore a strip off his shirt and bound it several times around her thigh. That hurt too. Tali closed her eyes and drifted.

In the distance she heard battle cries, the clash of steel weapons, the screams of men dying brutal deaths.

Tobry stroked her brow. "Don't look now."

"Why not?"

"The riders have surrounded the enemy. It's going to be rather unpleasant."

Tali drifted again, not knowing whether minutes were passing, or hours.

"Shit!" said Rix, from below.

"What's the matter?" said Tobry.

"That's Seneschal Parby. What the hell is he doing here?"

"Lady Ricinus must have sent him to find you and drag you back by the—"

"He's got a telescope. He's seen me. I'll have to go."

"Yes, Tali needs a good healer."

"We can't take her to the palace!" cried Rix. "You know what Lady Ricinus is like."

Tali's eyes shot open. What manner of a woman was his mother, to drive a brave man to such panic?

"Not going to any palace," she said limply. "Going after Rannilt."

"No, you're not," said Tobry. "Rix, if that wound gets infected, Tali will die."

"I know." Rix crunched back and forth across the slope, scattering rubble like confetti. "She needs the best healer there is. Where can we send her that's safe?"

"I thought the Cythonians were dead," said Tali, clutching at Tobry's wrist.

"They are. But you're not safe from our allies."

CHAPTER 54

Parby's commanding voice echoed up the slope. "Lord Rixium?"

"Go!" hissed Tobry. "They mustn't see her."

"Why not?" said Tali. "What's going on?"

Rix stood up. "Seneschal Parby! Thank you—"

"Lady Ricinus sends her compliments," boomed Parby, "and bids you to return home *immediately*."

Rix bowed from the waist. "And I come running, like a cringing lapdog," he said in an aside. "Tobe, think of something—"

Tali could scarcely credit the change in Rix. He looked like a naughty boy who had been caught out and was about to be punished.

"I'll fix it," sighed Tobry. "Get me a horse—"

"What about Rannilt?" said Tali.

He took her hand. "Do you think I'd forget her? Rix, tell Parby I've got urgent business elsewhere. We're going back."

"That's bloody dangerous—but of course . . . "

"I know," said Tobry.

Rix clasped his arm. "You can't go unarmed."

"I'll collect a blade from the dead. There are plenty to choose from."

"No." Impulsively, Rix unbuckled his sheath and held it out. "Take mine."

"You sure?"

"Its enchantment saved us the other day."

"Thanks," said Tobry, buckling it on. "It might help with Rannilt's *shadow and shape*, too."

"Lord Rixium?" the seneschal called, curtly.

"I'm coming!" Rix turned down the slope, turned back. "Where will you take her, Tobe?"

"To Abbess Hildy."

"Hildy doesn't love House Ricinus."

"She's not fond of me, either, but she's the best healer I know."

"I know how to soothe her ruffled feelings." Rix handed him a small leather bag.

Tobry pocketed it. "Tali, if I come up straight away, Parby will be suspicious. I'll ride a little way with Rix and double back."

Don't leave me. Please don't leave me here all alone.

She lay in the shadow of the boulder, listening as they scrambled down to the plain and rode away. Time drifted in a haze of pain, her helplessness magnifying every fear tenfold. What if he didn't come back? The bodies would attract predators from all directions and they would soon sniff her out. What if Tobry encountered more Cythonians? Or they came up to investigate?

A horse approached; footsteps crunched up the slope.

"Tobry?" she croaked.

"It's me, Tali. It's just me."

Then he was beside her, lifting her in his arms, and she clung to him like a lost lover, all reserve gone. She closed her eyes. She was safe; she could leave it to him now . . .

The next hour was torn into fragments: being lugged, Tobry slipping and sliding, down the slope; hanging head-down across a saddle, every bump and jounce sending pulses of agony through her thigh; Tobry helping her drink from his cupped hand, the water having a mouth-puckering bitterness that left a residue on her teeth; night falling and him riding on, now holding her against his chest; the elbrot flaring. He seemed to be finding his way with a magery that sensed the firmness of the ground ahead, or perhaps the heat of it. Then, finally, sleep. Blessed oblivion.

The *call*, more urgent and strident than ever, shocked her awake. She snapped the shell closed, trembling. It was still dark, the end-less hunt still went on and her hunter was closer than before. Much closer.

"Tobry," she whispered, "I'm afraid."

"It's all right," he said softly.

"He's out there, tracking me."

"There's no one behind us."

"You don't understand." She twisted around in the saddle.

"Mama said *he's never seen, never heard, but he flutters in my nightmares like a foul wrythen.*"

Tobry stiffened and reined in. "What did you say?"

"The people who killed my mother aren't my worst enemies, and neither is Tinyhead. My real enemy is his master—"

"You told me that before. Why did you call him a *wrythen?*"

"My mother said it, though I never thought she meant a *real* wrythen."

Tobry's eyes were darting. "Tell me about him."

"Since the night I came of age, I've been hearing an angry little note in my head. I think of it as the *call* because it feels like one, and I'm sure he's tracking me by it. Sometimes I hear a higher, distant note that feels like a reply." She explained about closing the *call* off with her mental shell.

Tobry said nothing, though she could tell that he was disturbed.

"Why does a wrythen bother you so much?" said Tali.

"We were nearly killed by one in the mountains a few days ago." He briefly related their encounter with the caitsthe and the wrythen, and what they had seen in the lower caverns. "Had it not been for Rix, I'd be dead by now. Or possessed by the foul creature— worse than death."

The cold night grew colder. The conspiracy was greater than she had thought, the danger more deadly. Was that why Rix had been watching Tobry earlier? Was Rix afraid the wrythen *had* possessed his friend? And had it? Was it looking out of Tobry's eyes whenever she turned her back? She did not think so—when the wrythen had taken over Tinyhead his eyes had been yellow and almost no trace of Tinyhead had remained. Unless the wrythen could conceal his eyes when he wanted to . . .

"I've been told my enemy can only be beaten by magery," said Tali, "but I can't find mine." She told him about her reluctant gift, which both her mother and Mimoy had said was different.

"It was certainly different when I killed Banj," she concluded, shivering at the memories. "But I had no more control than before."

"So the bursting sunstone roused your magery," said Tobry. "And woke Rannilt's hidden gift. Curious."

She looked up at his craggy face and realised, for the first time, that he liked her. She hesitated—it was hard for her to ask anyone for help, but she had to.

"Tobry, you know magery. Can you help me?"

"Me?" He laughed uneasily. "Don't be silly."

Heat rose to her face. What was the matter? Didn't he trust her with it? Or did he think of her as a child? Tali felt herself shrinking, but she had to convince him. There was no one else. "Why not?"

"It's not a good idea," he said evasively.

"Why not?"

"I'm . . . not my own man."

What was that supposed to mean? Or was it an excuse? "Tobry, he's after me. I just heard the *call* again. That's what woke me—"

"Even more reason," Tobry said.

She clutched at his wrist, not realising that she was shaking it. "Please, I'm desperate and you're all I've got."

He closed his eyes, turned away, turned back. "I can't, Tali. Please don't ask me again."

It was worse than a slap in the face. It felt like a repudiation of their friendship. She turned away, alone again.

"There are ways to uncover hidden or buried gifts," said Tobry. "Once we reach Caulderon I'll consult a friend who's far more skilled in magery than I am."

She swung around. The offer was worse than nothing. "You can't tell anyone about it!" she cried.

"All right, all right." He thought for a minute. "There was a device for this purpose, a very ancient thing . . . "

"A device?" she said grudgingly.

"It came from Thanneron with the Fleeters. What was it called? A pry-probe? Spectible?"

He shook the reins and the horse took off, sending a shuddery pulse of pain through her and robbing her of the strength to question him further.

She drifted . . .

"No," groaned Tobry. "Get out, out, *out!*"

Tali roused from tormented dreams with the *call* reverberating in her head like a pealing bell. She forced the shell to close around it and managed to choke it down to a whisper, though for the first time she could not close it off completely, and surely that meant . . .

Tobry moaned, a piteous sound.

She felt about in the dark. His left arm was thrashing up and down. She caught it and held him. "Tobry, what is it?"

"Urggh! Unrggh-rrggh, rggh!" He slumped onto her, squashing her down until her head hit the saddle horn.

She pushed herself upright. He was hotter than Rix had been when she'd laid her healing hands on him by the lake, and from such an awkward position she could not help Tobry.

If she dragged him to the ground, she would never get him back into the saddle. Tali heaved herself around until she was facing him, ignoring the spears of pain, and took his face between her hands. She was attempting to work the healing charm when her mind-shell was wrenched wide and the *call* went off like a shriek. No, like a beacon calling her enemy to her.

She tried to close the shell but something was forcing it wide open from the other side. Something far stronger than her was trying to snap it at the hinges so it could never be closed. She could barely hold it, and Tobry was growing ever hotter under her hands. If she could not summon her healing gift he would die, consumed from the inside. Yet if she did use it on him, she would not have the strength to hold the shell at all, and that would be very bad . . .

Mine, came a whisper, and she sensed shadows groping in a deeper darkness, familiar shadows, searching for her. *You're mine and you will bring her to* . . .

Tobry shuddered; panted; groaned, "No!"

It was as though two people were fighting over her. She felt resistance, then the voice continued, *I left my mark in you. You can't keep me out. Bring her!*

"I won't," she ground out, and lurched backwards in the saddle. "Get out of my head!"

Shock! Alarm, then the sounds retreated until they were a mean-ingless buzz—coming from Tobry's head!

The voice had not been speaking to her. It had been giving

orders to Tobry, orders about her. To bring her *where*? To the murder cellar?

The familiarity crystallised. Rix had been right to be worried—the wrythen *had* left something in Tobry when it attacked him in the caverns. Now it was trying to take control of him and make him do the job Tinyhead had failed at. The wrythen and her enemy *were* the same, and if he took command of Tobry, she was lost. Tobry must have been expecting it—that's why he had refused to help with her magery.

Tali could not see how to block a presence that was within Tobry, not herself. Wait! The wrythen was tracking her via the *call*, and only after he forced open the shell had he broken through to Tobry. The *call* had to be blocked before she tried to help Tobry—if she still had the strength to block it.

Tali squeezed her palms around her own head, one hand pressing against her forehead and the other on the back of her skull, as if by doing so she could prevent her enemy from doing to her what he had done to Tinyhead. She squeezed so hard that her thigh wound began to pulse. She had to ignore it; had to turn her enemy aside and block the *call* before it betrayed her.

Harder she squeezed, and harder, conjuring up the image of the protective shell and forcing it closed with all her driving will.

"Stop!" Tobry cried, swaying wildly and almost falling out of the saddle. "It's burning, burning. Tali, help!"

One flailing hand struck her on the cheek, hard enough to bring tears to her eyes. She lost concentration for a second, the shell was forced wide and she heard another voice . . .

The thing in the dark. Shadow and shape, shiftin', always shiftin'.

A huge, loping creature stopped, stood up on back legs until it would have towered over Rix, and turned in her direction, sniffing the air. Sickle-shaped pupils contracted to points; claws clotted with rancid fat and day-old blood extended; shadows fluttered around it, expanding and contracting. She caught a whiff, or imagined she did, of hot breath tainted with offal and carrion, then the maw opened wide, emitting not the roar she would have expected, but a repeated pinging sound, a false note like some corrupt mimicry of the note that was a distant reply to her call.

Pinnnng, pinnnng, pinnnng.

That's it, said the wrythen. *Fix on her. Steady, steady. Take her and you can drink the foul magian's blood. But do not harm her.*

Tobry's moan, deep in his throat, made her hair stand on end. His cheeks were glowing red in the dark, his eyes taking on the same gleam as Tinyhead's had before his head had been burnt through, now showing a trace of yellow.

Pinnnng, pinnnng, pinnnng.

The sounds rose and fell as though a beam was sweeping across her and back, and sick terror overwhelmed her. She wanted to fling herself off the horse and run, anywhere. Tali struggled to fight it. She could not run. She would be lucky to stand up. And without her, Tobry was going to die. Clamping her hands harder around her skull, she squeezed with all the strength remaining to her.

Pinnnng, pinnnng, pinnnng.

"Close, close!" she gasped, forcing physically and mentally at the same time.

With an audible snap, the shell slammed, and both the *call*, the pinging and the presence in Tobry's head cut off. So did the sense of that loping creature but she knew it was still out there, searching.

With a little sigh, Tobry toppled sideways out of the saddle. Tali almost followed him, for she was shaking so badly that she could not hang on. Twisting her hands through the stirrup straps, she half fell, half slid down, hit the ground and her bad leg crumpled under her.

Her head was ringing, her hands trembling so violently that she could not hold them against him. She crouched over Tobry and pressed her forehead to his.

"Heal, heal!"

Normally she could feel the healing force leaving her as she worked, but Tali was so drained that she felt nothing now. She lay beside him, her cold cheek touching his feverish one. From way out in the Seethings echoed an eerie shriek, so uncanny that she could not imagine any normal beast making it.

"Heal," she whispered. "Please heal, Tobry, or we're both dead."

CHAPTER 55

Tali was lying on hard ground, so drained that she could not move, while the horror hunting her drew ever closer. She thought she saw it fleetingly, a shadow darker than the night, shifting, always shifting from one form to another. Was it shadow, dream or hallucination? In her feverish state she could not tell the difference between reality and imagining, sleeping and waking, normality and nightmare.

Something leaned over her, half lifting and half dragging her. She flinched and tried to beat it off, but even the smallest movement speared jags of pain through her inflamed thigh.

"Try not to move," said a hoarse voice, Tobry's voice.

"You're alive," she whispered. She opened her eyes on a night black as a pit.

"Thanks to you."

"I thought he'd got you."

"He nearly did." The rasping croak sounded as though his throat had been burnt. "I don't know how you saved me, but—"

"It's not over. The shadow-creature is out there, hunting me. For the wrythen. It's big, Tobry. Bigger than Rix. And fast."

"Please, not a caitsthe," he said in a dead voice. "Was it cat-like?"

"Too dark to tell. Though it seemed hairy rather than furry. And foul—it really stank. And ... it ... the shadows seemed to transform it from one shape to another."

Tobry stiffened beside her, then slowly let out his breath.

"What's the matter?" said Tali. "What is it?"

"It sounds like some kind of shifter. And I'm mortally afraid of shifters. What if ... ?"

He did not speak for a few seconds, but his hands, on her shoulders, were trembling and she could hear his racing heart. She recognised the signs. He was close to panic, and he must not give way to it.

"Rannilt is all alone," she said. "We have to find her."

He gave a muffled sob.

"What is it?" she said softly.

"I've only known her a day, yet I love her like a daughter."

"She gets under the skin. Cling to it, Tobry. We're going to save her."

"Yes, we will." A little strength crept back into his voice.

"What are shifters?" Tali asked. "I remember you and Rix talking about them."

"Men that can change to beast-form. Or sometimes, beasts that can transform to man-shape."

"Isn't that the same thing?"

"Not at all. A beast doesn't gain human intelligence when it shifts, but it makes up for it in cunning, speed and savagery. A man loses some wit when he becomes a beast, yet he's still more clever than any wild creature. And more vicious. The beast-man kills because he must, but the man-beast kills because he enjoys it."

Tali pressed up against him. "You know a lot about them."

"A shifter helped to bring down my house—"

There came another howl, more shivery than the first.

"Could you make some light? The dark is suffocating me."

"I'm not sure that's a good idea," said Tobry.

"The thing I saw has other ways of finding us."

"I hope it's not another caitsthe," Tobry croaked. "More than anything in the world I hope it's not a caitsthe."

"What's a caitsthe?"

He told her.

"But you killed one in the mountains, didn't you?"

"Not me." He gave a mirthless laugh. "Rix fought it to a standstill while I lay on the floor in blissful unconsciousness. I've never heard of anyone else killing a caitsthe in single combat. Here."

The faint light from his elbrot revealed a scarlet face covered in blisters, and the whites of his crusted eyes were pink.

"Not a pretty sight?" he said wryly.

But at least the eyes were his again. Did that mean the wrythen had been driven out—or was it just hiding? She looked away. "You survived. That's what matters."

"For the moment. Did I thank you?"

"I don't need to be thanked."

"But I need to say it. Let's see if we can get you into the saddle. Can you stand up?"

"I'll try."

He took her under the arms and heaved, and such pain flared through her thigh that she cried out. It felt swollen to twice the size of the other.

"Sorry," said Tobry.

Getting her onto the horse proved to be the most painful few minutes she had ever experienced. Every movement was like having blunt needles forced into the wounds. When Tobry hauled himself up and took her in his arms, she closed her eyes and panted like a woman in childbirth, breathing to control the pain, concentrating on not screaming with every step the horse took.

Not even pain could erase the image of the shapeshifting carrion eater, hunting her for its master. *Pinnnng, pinnnng, pinnnng.*

"What if it finds Rannilt first?" Tali whispered. She would have no chance.

"Not even a caitsthe can catch a galloping horse."

"But Rannilt can't ride." And no horse could gallop through the Seethings in the dark. It would end up in pit or pool or bottomless quick-mud within a hundred yards.

She could not stop imagining Rannilt's terror as the beast stalked her, hiding and revealing itself again, catching her then letting her go. Playing with its food . . .

She bit down on a cry. Tobry put a hard hand on her thigh and began to whisper a healing spell. It was nothing like her own small gift of healing. This was real magery and she felt the pain fade, the hot tightness ease, the images in her head recede.

"Sleep," he said in her ear.

She was too on edge to sleep, but with his arm around her she felt safe enough to lapse into a daze. Tobry extinguished his mage-light, though from time to time he must have swung his elbrot through the air, for she could see moving trails through her closed eyelids.

They rode on, and on . . .

"Tali?" Tobry said quietly, squeezing her. "Don't make a sound."

Starlight showed that they were on the side of a small hill, moving through a patch of scrub. A wiry stem trailed across her shoulder, catching in the fabric of her ruined gown.

"What is it?" said Tali. "Are we out of the Seethings?"

"No, we're close to where we left Rannilt and the horses—" A sharp breath ruffled her hair.

"What's the matter?" An odd smell hung in the air—slightly sweet, organic, grassy.

"I don't know, but something's wrong."

"Maybe your horse took her home."

"I can smell fresh horse manure."

"Why don't I call her?" She took a deep breath.

"If it's here, we don't want to alert it."

As his arm tightened around her chest, she felt the tremors running through him. Tobry could have said that there was no hope of finding Rannilt, or proposed any number of reasons why going after her was futile, yet he had faced his fears and not mentioned the shifter again. Could any friend do more than he had done, asking nothing in return?

"If it's here, it knows we're coming. And Rannilt—"

"Don't say it," said Tobry. "That only makes it worse."

Could anything be worse than the fate Tali was imagining?

"Don't think about it, either," he added. "If this is a trap, she may be unharmed."

If it was a trap, Rannilt need not be live bait. Tali imagined the shifter creeping up on the terrified child, taunting her, batting her broken body about. Then waiting, covered in her blood, for the real prey.

She was tempted to snatch the reins and gallop away. She wanted to sweep Rannilt up in her arms and protect the child from all the horrors of the world. She burnt to hack the shifter to death, then destroy the wrythen the way she had killed Banj—

"When you saved me earlier," said Tobry in her ear, "how did you manage it?"

"I sensed my enemy, then blocked him out."

"See if you can sense him again."

"No!"

"Why not?"

"He'll hear the *call*."

"What do you mean?"

"I told you earlier," said Tali. "Before it attacked you."

"I don't remember—it feels as though I've lost an hour."

Because the wrythen is still possessing you, hiding in the background for the right moment? Tobry's arm was now confining her, binding her. She pulled away.

"Something the matter?" he said.

No, trust your feelings. If he is still possessed, you'll know it. Tobry wasn't himself when the wrythen attacked, and neither was Tinyhead. She had to trust Tobry.

"That's how the wrythen found me before. Via my *call*, and his reply. I think it's how he's directing the shifter after me."

"How *could* he track you that way?" mused Tobry. "What sort of magery can it be? Where does your *call* come from, anyway?"

"I don't know."

"What's making it?" Tobry mused. "To call across such a distance is no small matter. Only great magians can do it at all, and only with the aid of a powerfully enchanted device. I've never heard of anyone doing it mind to mind."

"Can you locate Rannilt with magery?"

"Mine doesn't want to work here."

"Why not?" she said hoarsely. "Does that mean *he's* here?"

"Could mean anything, or nothing. Some places the gift just doesn't work. It would be easier to sniff out the horses."

"I have a keen nose."

"You'd need to be well away from my horse. And upwind. But I don't think—"

"Help me down."

He did so reluctantly.

The pain in her thigh was still there, though muted, and the swelling had gone down. His healing had done more good than hers.

"Take this." Tobry was holding out a knife by the point. The hilt was wound with yellow, worn leather.

She took it, though she could not imagine it being any use against the shadow shifter. Tali moved upwind, into the dark, a herb-scented night breeze cold on her face. Her thigh felt peculiar, almost numb, though each time a spear of pain broke through it was worse than the one before. The healing was wearing off.

She caught the odour she now recognised as horse manure and began to follow it, moving slowly across the stony ground to avoid being heard, but lost it again. The night had too many other smells: leaves crushed underfoot, some pungent, others with a lemony sharpness; baked earth; her own sweat; fresh blood as the arrow wound broke open. Finally she picked up the smell of horse again and began to track it up the wind.

Tali stopped, took a deep sniff and gagged on the reek of carrion, blood and guts and ordure. The shifter could not be far away.

"Rannilt!" she whispered.

Light flashed behind her and Tobry's horse broke into a trot. "Stay where you are." He was holding the elbrot high, staring at the ground. "It's come this way."

A series of large, blurred footprints were steaming, the grass shrivelled around them and brown decay creeping out in all directions. What manner of beast was it?

In the light she saw a big, unmoving heap twenty feet ahead, a mound with long legs and guts spilled across the uneven ground. A dead horse, chestnut with a white mark on its forehead.

"Beetle," said Tobry heavily. "Stay back."

Tali wanted to be a thousand miles away. She knew what she was going to find next and could not bear to think about it, but she had to be sure. She had to keep searching, just in case. "Rannilt!"

There was no answer.

Tobry swung down from the saddle, drawing Rix's sword. The elbrot's light caused an answering shimmer along the curved blade.

"Is the sword—?" said Tali.

"It has an enchantment against magery."

They stood together. Chunks had been bitten out of Beetle's haunches, pieces of flesh the size of her head gone in single bites. Fear coiled up her backbone.

"Where's Leather?" said Tobry, looking around.

"What's Leather?"

"Rix's horse. A huge, ugly brute, much tougher than poor old Beetle."

Something gave a shrieking howl, a piercing note that rasped along every nerve fibre and echoed back from the rocky crest of the hill. It came from the same throat as those earlier cries.

Then a small golden light appeared between a group of rocks twenty yards ahead, a gentle, pulsing glow Tali recognised instantly, like a globe of sunshine held in cupped hands. Momentarily it lit up the small, skinny girl as though she were a princess, and Tali's eyes flooded.

"You're alive," she whispered.

"It's a trap!" shrilled Rannilt. "Run, Tali, run."

CHAPTER 56

What was worse? What Lady Ricinus was going to do to him, or the nightmares that were bound to return once he was back in his chambers with that voice in his head, ordering him to commit a terrible atrocity.

As Tobry had said, Rix's heritage was a honeyed trap. He would be better off abandoning it and galloping to the most distant outpost of Hightspall. He could still fight for his country there.

He was tempted to. Had it not been for his duty to his troubled house, he would have fled. Besides, wherever he went, Parby would come after him. The seneschal had been ordered to fetch Rix back and if he did not his own head would be on the line. Lady Ricinus did not permit failure.

"Where are the enemy?" he asked as they approached the city.

"Scuttled back to their rat holes." Parby spat on to the grass. "They won't find Caulderon such an easy target."

"You left before the attack, then?" asked Rix.

"Been searching for you for three days."

Rix's sole consolation was that the chancellor would be pleased with the intelligence he was bringing about the enemy's weapons and tactics, and what the wrythen was up to. Not as pleased as if Rix had been able to provide advance warning of the war, but the news might be enough to get him out of Lady Ricinus's clutches.

The road was full of refugees here, some pushing hand carts, some dragging their miserable possessions on skids, many staggering along with nothing save what they could carry on their bent backs. At every sound they whirled, staring, shaking. Rix saw terror in a thousand eyes.

The cavalcade passed two shattered towns and many razed villages. Here, in the rye fields to either side, burned crops were still smoking. The road turned a corner, passed through a copse of leafless trees and ahead, on the right, stood a rudely built stockade with guards patrolling outside the walls. Brown, greasy smoke rose from the far side, and they weren't burning wood.

"What's going on here?" He turned towards the stockade.

"Stay back!" said Parby.

Rix stood up in the stirrups to see over the wall, and quailed. The place was wreathed with stinking smoke, though not enough to hide the dozens of men, women and children imprisoned inside, some so covered in purple buboes that they could be seen from thirty yards away.

"They're be'poxed," said Parby. "We've seen the same, or worse, half a dozen times since the attack began."

Driven into pens to die, Rix thought bleakly as they rode on. The living burnt the dead, and doubtless some who weren't quite dead, on the pyre at the back—the last service the doomed ones could do for their country.

And all this in the first day of the war, from attackers no one had seen. The Cythonians had rained death and destruction on towns and villages, fish ponds and fields, using weapons no Hightspaller had ever encountered before. Then they retreated as silently as they had come.

Let Caulderon be unscathed, Rix prayed. But all he could think of was an enemy impossibly powerful, advancing on the unprepared city.

"Holy Gods!" cried Parby an hour later, as they came within sight of the gates of the city.

He reined in, and the troop stopped behind him, dismayed and not a little afraid. Rix, who had seen the blasted bridge near Gullihoe, was not surprised, though he was alarmed. Destroying an undefended bridge out in the country was one thing. Bringing down half of the massive and well-defended city gate was another entirely.

"How did they get close enough to do that?" said Rix.

The left side of the towering city gates, a thick-walled bulwark fifty feet across and sixty high, had been blown to bits. Rubble and charred timber lay everywhere, and bodies too, and the left-hand gate was propped up with poles, for its hinge pins had been blown out.

There were heavily armed guards everywhere, and more officers than in the New Year's military parade, most of them milling around in fearful confusion. Rix saw no evidence that anyone had taken charge and longed to do so. He'd make the bastards jump to attention.

"What news from the provinces, Lord Rixium?" said a voice on his left.

Rix did not recognise the speaker, who was dressed in a captain's uniform of viridian and mustard, with a red ribbon around his cockaded hat. The uniform did not appear to have been washed in a fortnight and there were food stains down his front.

"Bad," said Rix, curling his lip. "Gullihoe is half destroyed and abandoned, and the bridge over the river has fallen."

He rode through the gates. Inside, hundreds of shanty dwellers were carrying stone to shore up the wall under the direction of a team of harried masons.

"If the enemy can do such damage without even being seen, what will it be like when they attack in force?" said Parby, who had been an officer many years ago. "How can they be kept out?"

As Rix assessed the defences through the lens of war, his spirits plummeted. Caulderon had outgrown its walls hundreds of years ago and almost as much of the city now lay outside as within. Houses, inns and warehouses had been built right up to the ancient walls, offering the enemy ten thousand hiding places for an attack. From the higher buildings they could fire into the city and it would take an army many times the size of Caulderon's to defend it.

"The only way to protect the city is to clear every building for two hundred yards around the wall," he said.

"That would take weeks," said Parby. "And you'd have a thousand shopkeepers at your throat."

"They'll change their minds when the enemy starts shooting pox pins at them."

"Well, at least the defences of Palace Ricinus are in good condition."

"But our walls run for half a mile," said Rix. "We'd need thousands of men to defend the palace, and we've only got three hundred. What are we going to do, Parby?"

"Our damnedest!" Parby looked around at his troops, then lowered his voice. "We're glad you're back, Lord Rixium. Someone has to take charge, and the men will follow *you* anywhere."

It was the closest the starchy seneschal had ever come to criticising his lord and lady. "I'll do my best," said Rix.

Despite the attack, the mood inside the city walls was cheerful. Few people seemed to be taking the threat seriously.

"We crushed the scum once and we'll do it again," said a tiny, ancient woman, clay pipe clamped between her two remaining teeth. "Reckon I could take down three of 'em myself."

Rix shook his head in disgust and rode on, past the public scalderies and steam rooms, now closed forever because the geyser fields had recently gone dry, then the silent steam-driven mills and crushers of the manufactory quarter. On every corner, crowds of cold, hungry people had gathered, and they all stared at him.

It was growing dark and the lamplighters were out, their tasselled nose plugs inserted, lighting the stink-damp fuelled street lamps. Rix kept a safe distance away. Stink-damp gas, also tapped from underground, was a deadly poison that you could only smell when it was at its thinnest. It was also heavier than air, tended to collect in cellars, sumps and hollows, and was wont to explode without warning.

His gloom deepened as they rode up the long drive of Palace Ricinus, then around the corner past the baroque greenhouses full of tall, spiky-leaved castor oil plants, the family symbol. He glanced towards the rear of the palace and his own tower. The navvies were still in their trench, fruitlessly winding asbestos around the hot water tubule to keep the remaining heat in. The water had been cooling for years and was now only tepid.

Lady Ricinus was waiting at the monumental front doors, as he had known she would be. The chief guard would have signalled her the moment Rix passed through the gates.

Sweat soaked through his shirt, front and back. He would sooner have faced another dozen of the enemy—at least he knew how to combat them. He had no idea how to deal with Lady Ricinus, but as a dutiful son not yet of age he could not disobey her direct orders. Not when Hightspall was at war.

He had not expected his father to be there as well. It was Lady Ricinus's doing, of course, and to have enlisted Lord Ricinus in the cause of disciplining her errant son, her fury must have been monumental.

She would not display it in public, though. She stood outside the door, as rigidly upright as one of their drill sergeants, and presented her polished and powdered cheek for him to kiss.

"Welcome home, Rixium," she said through a mouthful of canines.

CHAPTER 57

Lord Ricinus slouched against a marble column, reeking of so many kinds of grog that he might have been swilling from the slops bucket in one of the lakefront taverns. He probably had been,

Rix thought ruefully. The last vestiges of Father's discernment had gone up against the wall long ago.

"Well done, Son," he said, shaking Rix's hand.

Rix was shocked to discover that his father's grip, once so crushing, was now soft, almost pulpy. A mirror to the inside?

"Father?" said Rix, not sure what he was referring to.

"For fighting through the encircling hordes. Killed a good few of them, I dare say?"

"A good few." Rix took a deep breath. He knew what his mother was going to say, but if he were quick he might bamboozle Lord Ricinus into pre-empting her. "Father, now we're at war I request leave from my duties to our house, to fight for my country."

Lord Ricinus understood, at least, and he wanted to say yes, but Lady Ricinus had got to him first.

"Your mother requires a word with you, and you'll obey her as you would me. Family unity is all in these troubled times, Son."

"Yes, Father," said Rix dismally, longing for a drink. Was he going to turn into his father? Were the seeds of his own destruction already sprouting in him?

"Come within, Rixium," said Lady Ricinus. "There are matters we must discuss." Her iron-hard lips thinned to blades. She looked down. "Where's the sword I gave you?"

"I—I lent it to Tobry."

"Get. It. Back," she said through her teeth. "Keep it by you, *always*."

It raised a question that increasingly bothered him. He looked to his father. "I can't read the inscription. Where did the sword come from, anyway?"

Lord Ricinus made a face. "From *her* side of the family."

"Mother's side?" Rix cried. Her family were of no account and it diminished the sword, somehow. "Where did *they* get it?"

Lady Ricinus looked outraged but did not reply. A servant held the door open and Rix followed Lady Ricinus down the hall to her suite of offices. She had lost weight lately; her limbs were becoming stringy and it did not suit her.

Rix's father was shambling into a side passage when she said, more sharply than she normally would have in public, "Lord Ricinus, if you please."

He made a stumbling about-face.

Inside his mother's offices, Rix waited for Lady Ricinus to seat herself at her tiny desk, and for Lord Ricinus to slump onto a settee close to the nearest decanter. He looked longingly at it and she waved an irritable hand. Rix perched on the edge of the other settee, which creaked under his weight. The immaculate chamber had a faint rotten egg smell from the stink-damp lamps, though only someone who had been out in the open would notice it. Rix smiled to himself.

His mother's nostrils flared as she looked at him and he tensed, involuntarily. She was not half his weight yet she dominated him in every respect.

"Did you set out to deliberately undermine all the work I have done for this house over the past three years, Rixium?" she said quietly. She seldom raised her voice; she felt it to be vulgar. Her gaze filleted him. "Or are you so stupid that you don't understand when I give you a simple instruction?"

"I've been having the nightmares again," he said, knowing how lame he sounded. "I had to get away for a bit."

"To risk your life doing things any paid soldier of this house could do better?"

"I didn't start out—"

"Don't lie. You went hunting jackal shifters."

"They're harmless. Not much worse than wild dogs, really—"

"They've taken dozens of our peasants and plenty of our guards—and *turned* three of them. Three good men who had to be put down." She fixed him with a frosty eye. "I inspected the portrait in your absence ..."

The damned portrait. Rix's hands were trembling. He clenched them around his knees, fantasising about snatching the decanter from his astonished father and swigging the lot.

"It's nearly done," he lied. "It won't take me long." The smile he put on felt like a death rictus.

"Seven days remain until the Honouring, and if the portrait is not done it will be a slap across Lord Ricinus's face. The powers will interpret it as disunity, and the survival of our house depends on absolute unity. You will not leave your quarters until the portrait is complete."

"But we're at war," he cried, leaping from the settee. "Surely you've heard what the enemy did to Gullihoe, and half a dozen other towns?"

"Craven surprise attacks. When they're face to face with our mighty armies they'll run like the rats they are."

"I don't think so. They've been preparing for this for hundreds of years. They've got new weapons that we don't know how to fight."

"What would you know about it?" she said coldly.

"I was in Gullihoe not long after they attacked. They destroyed the place without losing a single man."

"They're all cowards in Gullihoe," she sneered. "I've spoken to the chancellor and he assured me that we have the enemy's measure."

"I've got to see the chancellor; I have important news."

"It can wait."

"No, he'll be expecting me. He might have a command for me." Rix knew he sounded desperate, but it was his only way out.

Her small eyes glowed and he knew the hope was going to be dashed. Lady Ricinus had anticipated this escape, and blocked it.

"At your father's request," she said, and her smile was so snake-like that he expected her to lick her lips with a forked tongue, "the chancellor has given you a special exemption—"

This was too much. "I don't want an exemption," Rix bellowed, leaping to his feet. "I want to do my duty."

Two white spots appeared on her cheeks. "How dare you shout at me," she said, her voice even lower and more controlled. "Sit down, *boy*. You're not of age and you have no heir. Perform *that* duty and we will allow you to risk your life, but only in the defence of Palace Ricinus."

"But ..." Rix looked imploringly towards his father. "Lord Ricinus ... Father ... you know I have to defend my country ..."

Lord Ricinus buried his nose in his goblet. Rix wanted to smash it over his head. He steadied himself and made a last, desperate bid for freedom.

"Everyone will call me coward, Father. They'll say I'm hiding behind mother's skirts because I'm too gutless to fight."

Lord Ricinus looked up sharply at Lady Ricinus. "The boy has a point."

"No!" said Lady Ricinus.

"A coward and the son of a coward, that's what they'll say," Rix said bitterly.

Lady Ricinus rose deliberately to her feet, took six precise steps to Rix and struck him across the face. The blow rocked him, for all that he had been expecting it, but he controlled his face as rigidly as she did her own. She returned to her tiny desk.

"House Ricinus takes no notice of barking curs," she said thinly. "The servants will not allow you out of your rooms without a note written in my hand—and not one borne by you."

Damn. He had been planning on forging one—another of his less reputable skills.

"I will allow you one bottle of wine a day," she went on, "since you take after your father and can't produce anything worthwhile when sober." She studied her empty desk, her cruel mouth down-turned. "And one bed mate. I shall select one I deem suitable."

"Like hell!" he cried. "I've had enough of you interfering in my life."

"Do you think I relish it?"

"Yes!" he cried. "I know you do."

She studied him as if he were a recalcitrant child, her nostrils flaring. "Until you come of age, you will do as Lord Ricinus and I say. And then there's Lagger. He's always been a bad influence on you and I'm not sure you should associate—"

Rix sprang up again. "If Tobry goes, I will renounce my inheritance, walk out the door and never return, war or no war," he said, grinding the words out. "I mean it."

"Oh, very well," she said after a minute. "Now, where was I?"

She knew very well where she was. Lady Ricinus had a mind like a gimlet.

"Ah, yes," she went on. "Speaking of children—"

"No," he said mechanically, knowing he was beaten already. Her concession on Tobry made any other improbable. "I will not take a wife."

"In view of your risk-taking behaviour, the succession of House Ricinus must be provided for right away. Lord Ricinus and I are united in this. *Aren't we, my lord?"*

"United!" said Rix's father, his teeth rattling on glass as he swilled brandy from the decanter.

"Rixium, you will marry in ten days."

"No!"

"I will give you a choice of six suitable girls. You will have until the morning after the Honouring to choose one. I expect your wife to be pregnant by the end of three months. If she is not, I will come to your bedchamber each night to make sure you're doing it right. Do I make myself understood?"

No greater horror could be imagined. None could possibly be borne. Tobry would not have stood such treatment for an instant, but Rix had been brought up to be a dutiful son. It was his mother's right to choose a bride for him; he had always known that.

He bowed his head in defeat. "I will marry and produce an heir."

"Well," she said. "Get on with it."

"The choice?" he said dazedly.

"The portrait," she said between her teeth. "I will come each evening to inspect your progress and, if necessary, give you instruction in the art of portraiture."

You arrogant bitch! As far as Rix knew, his mother had never taken up a paintbrush in anger and, for all her carefully schooled conversation about the masters, he doubted that she knew as much about art as a common flea. The paintings in House Ricinus were chosen by an expert.

"That will not be necessary," he said, bowing. "And don't bother to send any bed mates to my tower. I've taken a vow of celibacy until the war is over."

"You won't last a week."

Rix bowed, insultingly low. "Mother, Father."

CHAPTER 58

It rose up behind the child, a vast, looming shape with the heavy shadows surrounding it wavering, shifting and drifting so that, despite the light streaming from Rannilt's fingers, it could never be seen clearly. Now it had the shape of a heavily muscled man with a frilled head, now it was more like a bear with clusters of whips instead of arms—or were they tentacles? Tali could not tell; it was transforming all the time, each morph more grim and ghastly than the one before.

It raised its head, tossed something into the air—a gobbet of horse haunch—caught it and swallowed with sucking noises and belches that glowed a sickly green and poisoned the air around it. And it seemed to smile, as if it delighted in death and ruin.

As the air thickened and congealed around it, Tali's long bones ached and she tasted foulness in the back of her throat. She closed her eyes for a second but its shifting *mental* forms were more terrible yet. It was reaching out, trying to get its psychic hooks into her and tear her down to its level.

"Why are you standin' there!" Rannilt screamed. "Run!"

But Tali saw instantly what the child could not, that Rannilt was a lure of no further use, a life to be savaged and trampled on the way to the real quarry. And not only because Rannilt was in the way. It was how the shifter had been created—as a weapon of terror, a destroyer.

Tobry choked and clutched at his blistered face with his free hand. His cheeks were the colour of an infected wound. He covered his eyes, as if he could not bear to look, and she thought he was going to break and run. But then, with a pitiful moan he shuffled forwards, Rix's sword upraised. Tobry knew he had met his nemesis but it was not in him to turn away.

If she were to rescue Rannilt, Tali had to be mobile. She could not have summoned healing magery in her own defence but the peril of an innocent child brought it forth. Clapping a hand to her thigh, she *twisted* the healing charm to numb her pain.

The relief was so instant that she lost her balance and nearly fell. Tali snatched the titane sword from Tobry's hand and ran, stiff-legged, for the golden glow. If the shifter was a creature of magery, the sword might help her to fight it. Her thigh felt peculiar and she was probably doing further damage but she put everything out of her mind save Rannilt.

The shifter took a swirling leap forward, the shadows writhing about it, arcing high and looming all around as if to cup the golden light in the petals of a savage flower. Another couple of leaps and it would be onto the child. Its right arm shifted to a cluster of metal-tipped flails, to barbed tentacles, to multiple arms terminating in hooked blades.

It was huge. One blow could shatter every fragile bone in Rannilt's body, and Tali's too if she went within range. But there was no other way.

She lurched forwards, swinging the surprisingly light sword while she sized the creature up for a killing blow. How, though? Since she did not understand what kind of creature it was inside, how could she tell where to strike? There was no time to reason it out; all she could do was hit hard and try to hurt it as much as she could.

It sprang again, shifter-shadows swirling about it like black flames, the heat of it blasting gusts of baked carrion at her. Tali gagged, choked down vomit and went at it, springing up to meet it as it leapt towards Rannilt to smash her out of the way.

As she closed in she saw a ragged mouth, eyes as black as the abandoned sinter pits of Cython and, above them, the deep indentation of a large hoof print, as if it had been kicked there. Such a blow would have killed any normal creature and might have dazed the shifter, perhaps weakening it. She took some comfort from that.

It struck at Rannilt from the left, a killing blow, but Tali was expecting it. She slashed safely above the child's head and across, and felt a surge of strength flow through her from the weapon. It made a buzzing sound, an arm or flail or tentacle went flying, and momentarily the shifter drew back, shrinking a little as if gathering its remaining members to it.

"Run to Tobry, Rannilt!" Tali roared, and sprang high.

Rannilt scurried between her legs. Tali hacked across and back, this time only severing shadows. A tentacular arm shot out past her, lengthening as it went.

"Look out!"

She flicked a glance over her shoulder. Tobry had ducked the blow but his horse fell to the ground, its skull crushed. The shifter's arm retracted for another blow. It could shatter him as easily.

But not her. It wanted her alive and that was her only advantage. Tali lunged and plunged the sword deep into the centre of the creature, twisting it where the heart and lungs of any normal beast would be.

Bone crunched, she felt tissue part beneath the point and almost-black blood gushed forth, but the creature did not flinch. The sword was stuck; she could not pull it free. Tali was backpedalling when an impossibly long arm curled around from the left, three bundles of flails snapped from the right and they all wrapped around her. The sword was ejected from the shifter like a bolt from a crossbow, whizzing past her ear. Its enchantments had done no good here.

The flail-arms tightened around her, binding her arms to her side. She had done just what it wanted her to do.

"Cel-lar," said the shifter. "Take to mur-der cel-lar."

It picked Tali up like an empty bag, tossed her over its shoulder and started down the hill, moving across the uneven ground as though supported on a raft of air. Its touch was hideous; she was sinking into it as though its skin was decayed, though there was hardness beneath, sometimes scaly, sometimes a claggy slime. She kicked feebly and dug deep, but could not summon any magery in her own defence.

Tobry was stumbling after them with Rix's sword but the shifter was moving faster than he could. Tali could not see Rannilt anywhere. Had she been caught by one of those flails as she had run for safety?

"Let her go, you stinking beast!" shrilled Rannilt from the dark, ahead. "Or else."

The shifter kept moving as if to roll directly over her, but as it reached the point from which she had spoken a ball of golden light flared so brilliantly that, for a second or two, it would have eclipsed the midday sun. A pure and perfect light that bathed Tali in a healing balm.

Though to the shifter it must have felt like venom, for it reared, shielding the region of its eyes and screeching like a sheet of metal being torn. Tali kicked but could not break free.

"*Put her down!*" shrieked Rannilt, dancing up and down.

The light grew until the fluttering shadows surrounding the shifter were blown away, revealing a lanky creature within, bone and sinew that was almost fleshless, though no less menacing.

The glow ascended as though Rannilt had raised the globe over her head, then shot towards the horseshoe indentation on the shifter's forehead, *whoomph-whoomph*, and struck. And stuck there.

The creature howled and flung up skeletal arms as the light brightened. It touched Tali like a bath of tingling bubbles, then she went tumbling down, down, to smack hard into the ground. Her healing charm snapped and the pain came shrieking back.

The shifter was swaying on its bony feet, evidently trying to transform, for parts of its body kept extending out to where the shadows had been, then freezing and retracting again as if, without filling in the shadows first, it was unable to change.

As Tali crawled away, her thigh so painful that she could only drag the leg, the shifter was whacking at the globe on its forehead, trying to knock it off. It kept flinching away from the light.

Rannilt tottered up, wobbly on her feet. Her skin was almost translucent. Taking Tali under the arms, she tried to drag her.

"Hurry, oh hurry! I'm losin' it. As soon as it goes out, the beast's gonna attack."

The golden glow did seem to be dwindling, the shadows returning and extending. There came a shrill whistle, an answering whinny, then Tobry was heaving Tali over his shoulder and running back to a gigantic horse, black as the inside of a skull and with rolling red eyes that went deep purple when the light from his elbrot passed across them.

"Leather!" said Tobry, stroking her muzzle. "Leather, old friend. If that's your hoof mark inch-deep in the beast's skull, you've done us some service."

He heaved Tali across the front of the saddle like a bag of carrots, clambered up and lifted Rannilt after him.

"Take this, child!" he said, handing her the elbrot and whirling Leather around. "Hold it up until we're on the Caulderon road."

Rannilt held it as high as she could reach, the light illuminating the slope of the hill and the Seethings beyond that. As Tali looked the other way, the golden glow went out and the surrounding shadows strengthened. The shifter whacked the globe off his forehead and began to transform.

"Go, Leather!" said Tobry, and the horse bolted down the slope.

When Tali looked back, the shifter was lost among the scrub.

"Thank you, thank you," sobbed Rannilt, throwing her thin arms around Tali and hugging her, accidentally whacking her sore ear with the elbrot. "I was so afraid. Horrid, smelly thing. But you saved me. I knew you'd come."

"You saved us all, Rannilt. You're the cleverest girl in the world—"

Tali had a sudden foreboding that Rannilt's gift should have been concealed from the enemy. Leather crashed down into a dip, sending a jolt of pain through her. She gasped and closed her eyes. Endure it. You've got to endure it.

Tears . . . pain without end . . . the pressure of small hands on her thigh, and a gentle golden light that warmed her over and drove the pain down deep until she could barely feel it. Until she slept.

"Facinore!" she cried, snapping awake.

"It's far away," whispered Tobry. "Go back to sleep."

The elbrot light was out and Leather was trotting along a smooth, hard surface. They must be on the road. Rannilt was asleep, her arms locked around Tali's middle.

"The shifter's called a facinore," said Tali.

"Where did you get that from?"

"It came to me in my sleep. The wrythen must have called it that. What is a facinore? Is it man? Beast? Phantom?"

"I've no idea," said Tobry, shivering a little. "But the word has an unpleasant ring to it."

"It won't give up. He won't let it."

"Nothing in Hightspall on two legs or four can catch Leather when she's racing. Besides, it'll never get through Caulderon's guarded gates. Go to sleep now."

She woke as Leather stopped. Tobry cursed and stood up in the stirrups, looking all around.

"Wassamatta?" said Tali, drowsily.

"Lights! Right across the Seethings from east to west, as far as the edge of Lake Fumerous."

"Do you think it's the enemy, looking for me?"

"More than likely. And by the look of those lights, they're heading directly for the city."

"To cut us off?"

"And form a cordon of war we'll find it impossible to creep through."

He thumped down in the saddle and flicked the reins. Leather began to trot, then canter, then moved to a rocking, rolling gallop.

Tali held Rannilt more tightly. "How far is it?"

"We just passed the five-mile post."

"Can we beat them to the gates?"

"The back roads are good in Suthly County, out to our left, and they'll make fast time there. But if anyone can outrun them, Leather can."

"Carrying the three of us?"

"I doubt that we three together weigh more than Rix. Go, Leather, old girl. Run like the very wind or we'll suffer the same fate as poor Beetle."

Their speed, at full gallop, was so terrifying that it almost detached Tali from the pain of each jarring stride. Almost. She dared not close her eyes. If Leather struck a deep pothole and broke a leg they would hit the ground hard enough to smash every bone.

Soon, far ahead she made out the glow of the city lanterns. Tali clung onto Rannilt, who was still sleeping, clenched her teeth, and prayed.

"How far to the gates now?" said Tali.

"Two miles."

"How long?"

"Less than four minutes."

"So fast," she marvelled.

"Rix has never lost a race on Leather."

"I can see lights to the left. Ahead of us."

"Yes."

"They seem to be cutting across to this road."

"They are."

"Will they catch us?"

"They'll certainly come within bowshot."

Skyrocket flares shot up from the left, one, two and then a third, hanging high in the air and burning with a brilliant yellow light that illuminated everything for half a mile around. Rannilt cried out in her sleep. Tali clutched her protectively, blinking against the brightness.

"Where are they, Tobry? I can't see them."

"Everywhere," Tobry said grimly. "They're everywhere. Thousands of the devils."

He had one hand over his eyes and was peering through his slitted fingers. Tali did the same, and started. The Cythonians had extinguished their lights and were running in a vast horde, the black cloaks swirling out around them making them difficult to pick out of the darkness.

Leather careered past the one-mile post. The Cythonians were curving around towards the road now, racing to cut them off. Ahead, Tali could see lanterns on the city gates, and guards moving restlessly there.

"The gates don't seem to be open."

"They never are, at night," said Tobry.

"Will the guards open them for us?"

"Depends how close the enemy is."

"You mean we could reach the gates and be trapped up against them?"

"More than likely."

Something shot past Leather's nose—a streak of silver accompanied by a hackle-raising screech. The great horse tossed her head and whinnied, but kept on.

"What the blazes was that?" said Tobry.

"I've heard talk of shriek-arrows," said Tali.

"If they're intended to frighten us, they're succeeding."

A shriek-arrow passed low overhead. Leather's eyes were rolling now. Tobry patted her and spoke soothing words. Another arrow shot by, trailing a fine wire that caught fire in the air and burned with the brilliance of the flares, though it was gone in an instant.

Leather let out a screaming whinny, leapt five feet high and seemed to double the speed of her precipitous dash. This time, Tobry had to reach forwards and place his elbrot on her neck, and even that did not fully calm her.

"What was that weapon?"

"I don't know," said Tali.

She did not see the next missile which, judging by its effect, had been hurled from a small catapult. It went off with a thudding explosion a little short of the road and spun in spirals, gushing white smoke that hung low to the ground and was carried towards them by the breeze.

"Half a mile," said Tobry. "One last effort, Leather old friend, for all our lives. Tali, wake Rannilt and be ready to run ... whatever happens."

Tali shook Rannilt awake, which took an effort. Despite their headlong pace, despite the howls and blasts and shrieks, she clung to sleep as if it were a lost friend.

"Wha—?" Rannilt said.

"We're nearly to Caulderon but they're after us again. Hold my hand."

More arrows were falling around them, ordinary ones this time, though only one came close. It thumped into the saddle horn in front of Tali and stuck there, quivering.

"I'm surprised they're not better shots," she said. "They shoot at targets all the time, in Cython."

"Not easy to hit a racing target when you're running flat out," said Tobry. "You can't train for that underground."

They were hurtling towards the gates, which remained closed. "Tobry?" Tali was afraid they were going to break their necks.

"It's all or nothing now." He stood up in the stirrups, waving furiously. "Recognise me, you bastards. Or at least, recognise Leather."

A hundred yards to go. The enemy was flooding in from either side. More burning-wire arrows threaded the sky, then from the corner of her eye Tali saw three Cythonians stop and raise their bows. They were only a hundred and fifty yards away and Leather made a huge target.

Forty yards. Thirty.

"Jump!" said Tobry.

As they fired Leather soared high, as though jumping a gate, and the arrows passed beneath her belly.

They were down to twenty yards when a small gate opened to the right side of the main gates. It was low and narrow, though. Would they fit?

"Heads down!"

Tali and Rannilt ducked, Leather lowered her long neck and they shot through the gate, tearing off the saddlebags and twisting the saddle so badly that Tali thought they were going to be flung to the ground. The gate banged shut behind them and dozens of arrows thudded into it.

Leather skidded to a halt on a broad avenue surfaced in yellow brickwork, blowing hard and covered in streaks of foam. Something went boom outside the gates, shaking them to their foundations, then all the pain Tali had been holding back for the past hours went off at once and she surrendered to it.

CHAPTER 59

Tali had no idea how much time had passed. It was still dark and someone was pounding on a door, every thump sending a throb through her head.

"Will you stop that," she said dully.

"Quiet," whispered Tobry. "We're here."

"Where—here?"

"The abbey."

She felt a spasm of panic. The past hours and perils had welded Rannilt and Tobry to her like brother and sister—or something stronger. The thought of being separated from them was unbearable.

"Don't want to be left with strangers," said Tali. "Take me with you."

"You need a healer and you've got to disappear. After our spectacular arrival, all Cauldron will be wondering who you are."

Tali slumped; she was beyond anything save enduring.

"I can look after her," said Rannilt. "Please, Lord Tobry."

"Tali needs the best healer there is," said Tobry. "I'll send her to you when she's better."

"I can heal her," Rannilt said desperately. "Please don't make me leave her."

"I'm sorry, Rannilt. If anyone speaks to you while I'm gone, pretend you're dumb."

"What's dumb?"

"It means you can't speak. And you're not a Pale, right?"

"Why not?" squeaked Rannilt.

"If the chancellor hears about you, he'll be after you too. You're only safe if no one knows who you are."

"Who am I?"

"You're a servant girl from Nitterlay, on the other side of the Crowbung Range—"

"Who's there?" said a woman's voice, old and quavery.

"Tobry Lagger. Let me in."

"Come back in the morning."

"I must see the abbess. I bear news of great value—and an injured girl who needs her special healing gift."

"Wait!"

"Hush," whispered Tobry to Rannilt. "Pretend you're asleep."

"You'll look after Tali, won't you?" Tears washed tracks down Rannilt's grubby face.

He gave her a quick hug. "Yes, and you too."

"Where are you taking her?" said Tali. Tobry had told her but she could not remember.

"To old Luzia. She was my nurse when I was little, and Rix's nurse after that. She'll look after her."

"She'd better," Tali said feebly.

The bolts were drawn back and the reinforced doors drawn open. Tobry took Tali in his arms.

"Who's that?" said the woman.

She was broad and stooped, her back so bent by a dowager's hump that she could barely raise her head above the horizontal, and her old face was covered with a crisscrossing network of wrinkles. Had she been on all-fours, she would have greatly resembled a tortoise.

"For Hildy's eyes only," said Tobry.

He followed the old woman down several halls and into a large, crowded room lit by a single lantern. Half a dozen tables were piled high with books, papers, maps, carved busts of the Five Heroes and other objects that could not be made out in the dim light.

"Lagger!" spat a woman from behind a large table on the far side of the room. "Your unlamented grandfather killed three of my novices."

"A terrible business," said Tobry. "But he's long in his grave."

"And you put him there." The abbess scowled at Tobry, making a finger sign over her head and heart. She had a soft, downy face and bright grey eyes, and was so plump that she was almost bursting from her skin. "What do you want?"

Tali stared at her in wonder. There were no fat people in Cython and she had never seen anyone like Hildy before. How could the abbey have so much food to waste? It was unimaginable.

"I claim refuge for an injured woman, in the name of the Five Heroes." He put Rix's bag of gold on the table.

She weighed it in her hand. "You don't believe in them."

" 'Course I do," Tobry said. "Seen the error of my ways."

The abbess's gaze turned to Tali, noted her unblemished skin and golden hair, the slave mark on her shoulder, and drew in a sharp breath.

"A *Pale*! Where did you find her?"

"She escaped from the Rat Hole yesterday. The first ever to do so, and she's not just any Pale. Rix and I—"

"Rixium of House Ricinus?" she hissed. "Never mention that house in my presence." She peered at Tali. "What's the matter with her? She's not diseased, is she?"

"There *is* no disease among the Pale," Tali said haughtily. "Not so much as a cold."

"She took a Cythonian arrow in the thigh," said Tobry.

"Bring her to the couch. Has the wound been attended?"

"We did what we could."

The abbess drew a sheet over the couch and rang a bell. A novice appeared, a stocky girl who appeared to have taken a vow of silence, her lips being pressed together so tightly that they made a straight line across her face. The abbess shooed Tobry away, stripped Tali's silk gown and sandals off and passed them to the novice. "Burn these and scrub your hands afterwards."

"That's my ancestor's gown," cried Tali. "We've kept it for a thousand years."

"And now it's ruined. Get rid of it. Bring hot water."

As the novice carried the once beautiful gown out, Tali felt as though her house was burning to the ground.

"What did this?" said Hildy, staring at the welt across Tali's belly.

"An enemy chuck-lash."

"What's that?"

"A chymical weapon, intended to cause great pain. It blasts and burns against the skin."

"What's it made of?"

"I don't know. There are many kinds. Some have shreds of metal inside. And then there are death-lashes—"

Hildy's eyes widened. "*Chymical* weapons?" She glanced at Tobry.

"Judging by the ruin they wrought on Gullihoe, they're masters of many forms of alchymie," said Tobry. He described what he had seen there.

"How does one fight such a foe?" said Hildy.

"I dare say we'll soon find out. Thousands of them pursued us to the city gates. Pursued Tali, anyway."

"Why would they bother with one escaped Pale?" said Hildy.

"To stop her mouth, of course."

The novice returned with buckets of steaming water, a towel and fresh garments.

Tali was stood in a dish, the novice holding her, and Hildy bathed her with a wet cloth. She appeared to be checking Tali for signs of disease.

Hildy examined the wounds with the light of a candle. "I see healer's work here."

"I have a minor gift," said Tobry hastily, as if he did not want Tali to reveal her own healings, or Rannilt's.

Hildy sniffed as she bent over Tali's thigh. "The wound has been broken open, more than once. Has the girl been mistreated?"

Tali studied Hildy from under her lashes. She had not realised that so much could be read from an injury. But then, Tobry had said that Hildy was a great healer.

"Enemies attacked," said Tobry. "We had to run."

Hildy laid a plump hand over the wound for a few seconds and the pain disappeared. She *was* a great healer. She pressed discs of a smelly unguent to the entry and exit wounds and bandaged them. The novice poured a measure of a gluggy white fluid into a cup.

"Drink," said Hildy, holding the cup to Tali's mouth.

"What is it?"

"It kills infection."

Tali drank. The novice handed her a grey blouse and baggy trews, and a pair of leather sandals. Tali dressed and lay down hastily; her head felt loose on her shoulders.

"Take her and go," said Hildy.

"What?" said Tobry, shocked.

"She's not welcome here. Get out, and never return."

Tobry's mouth opened and closed, then he picked Tali up and carried her outside.

"Where are you taking me?" she said dazedly as he put her in the saddle and mounted. Tali took Rannilt in her arms again. She was sleeping soundly and did not wake.

"I don't know," said Tobry. He raked his hair with his fingers, staring around distractedly. "I suppose it'll have to be Luzia."

He rode out and turned left into a narrow street. It was freezing here, a damp, miserable cold that her underground-adapted flesh had never experienced. And everything stank.

In Cython, every place had its distinctive smell, most being clean and natural. There was nothing pleasant about the smell of Caulderon. The alleys reeked of urine and human waste, rotting fur, burnt bones and other unpleasant things that she could not identify in the gloom and did not want to think about.

"It wasn't always like this," Tobry said quietly. "In my grandfather's day, even the poorest folk were well fed, well dressed, and healthy."

"What happened?"

"The land turned against us."

Shortly the sun rose, though by the time its light filtered through the brown smog of a hundred thousand fires there was no warmth in it. Now people appeared from every hole and hollow. It was like being back in Cython. No—in Cython every slave had a job and a purpose. And they had been clean.

The shanty dwellers were deeply engrained with grime, caked and crusted with it as though they had not bathed in their lives. Many were riddled with crater-like scars, others flush-faced as if freshly be'poxed, and they stank worse than the squatteries in Cython.

"How have the people fallen so low?" said Tali.

"We thought the good times would last forever. We put nothing by. Then the eruptions began, the weather turned, the crops and the hot springs failed, the ice began to spread and everything went bad."

"Except there," added Tobry as they rode along a red-brick thoroughfare. "Palace Ricinus."

It was gigantic and extraordinarily beautiful, a colossus of carved stone topped by an enormous dome and surrounded by dozens of clustered towers yearning towards eternity. Its windows were carved into the shapes of flowers and the snow-blanketed grounds ran for hundreds of yards down a gentle slope to a masonry wall, beyond which she saw the misty shores of Lake Fumerous.

Tali gaped. Palace Ricinus was magnificent enough for an emperor. How, when the poor of Caulderon lived in such filth and misery, could it be the home of just three people?

"Rix's chambers are next to that tower, there at the back," said Tobry, pointing. "Torgrist Manor is up there, if you'd like to see it." He jerked his head in the other direction. "What's left of it."

"Yes. I have to see it."

He glanced behind them and cursed. "Hang on!" He spurred Leather to a trot.

They hurtled around a corner, up a steep hill, then around another corner into an empty street with stone mansions to either side, all immaculate save one, which was a ruin.

"What's wrong?" said Tali, alarmed.

"We're being followed. Hildy's betrayed us."

"Who to?"

"I'd say the chancellor, and you don't want to fall into his hands." Tobry reined in. "Get off and over the wall, quick! Hide. I'll come back when I can."

"Is this –?"

"Torgrist Manor? Yes, go!"

Tali half fell to the ground, scrambled across the footpath and through a break in a high stone wall. Long grass and tall weeds on the other side ran up to a broken tower, a ruined manor most of whose roof had fallen in.

Rannilt woke with a cry. "What's happening? Come back."

"Sit up, child!" Tobry said urgently. "Try to look like Tali. Hold on tight!"

They galloped off. Tali had lost her hat somewhere in the night and the sky was rocking again. Hearing hoof beats approaching, she crawled along a rabbit track and into a spreading, thorny bush. There she hunched into a ball, fought the panic and tried to stop her crashing heart from giving her away.

CHAPTER 60

"You've no idea what it's been like here," said Rix when Tobry turned up at the guarded door of Rix's tower a day after his own arrival. "I'm confined to barracks. Lady Ricinus even wanted to bar you on the grounds of being a bad influence."

"I was a bad influence," said Tobry, who looked thinner than before and rather drawn.

"What's the matter? There's barely a laugh in you these days."

"It's different now. I've got responsibilities."

"Considering how often you encouraged me to neglect mine—"

"Leave it out. I'm not in the mood."

"You need a drink." Rix drew him into the vast salon and looked for a corkscrew. "Sorry about the miserable hospitality. I'm only allowed one bottle a day, guests or not."

"No thanks," Tobry said curtly.

Rix rocked back on his heels. "You've never refused a drink before. What's the matter?"

"I told you."

Rix poured two drinks anyway. "Can the man who doesn't believe in anything be lecturing me?"

"Remember all those weapons we don't know how to combat? The enemy has waited a thousand years to fight this battle and it's a holy war to them."

"I don't understand."

Tobry sat down. Rix put a goblet at his elbow and sat opposite, facing the heatstone. He did not like to look at it but it felt worse at his back.

"I've been in the Caulderon archives, reading ancient enemy documents," said Tobry. "They believe Hightspall is tainted because of the illegitimate way we came by our land."

"We won the war."

"They say we won through trickery, treachery, fraud, murder and foul, illegal magery. They call Hightspall the Tainted Realm and they don't just want victory—they want our annihilation." He picked up the goblet, put it down again, said, "What the hell?" and took a small sip. "How's the portrait going?"

"How's Tali?" said Rix at the same time. He had been fretting about her ever since they had separated.

"Sore, but—"

"Did you find Rannilt?"

"Yes, though it was a near thing. Several near things, for both of us."

"You'd better explain."

Tobry related what Tali had told him about her family's enemy, and the *call* that was being used to track her, then paused.

"This *call* ..." said Rix, struggling to comprehend something so far beyond his prosaic existence. "The way you say Tali's blocking it ... surely it's got to be coming from her ... from her own head."

Tobry stared at him. "Out of the mouths of babes and innocents."

"What do you mean?"

"I thought she was echoing the *call*, reflecting it back. But from the way she described it, Tali must be *originating* it."

"How can that work?" Rix's ignorance of magery was so profound that he did not know where to begin.

"I don't know, but I'm really worried now." Tobry began to pace in front of the heatstone. "How could it come from her? Is it a part of her hidden magery?" He sat down again, but rose at once. "And then there's *the one*."

"What one?"

"It's what Wil, the blind seer, called her. *The one*. That's why the matriarchs want her dead." Tobry told Rix all he knew about that.

"The *call*. *The one*. The wrythen. It's all a bit worrying, Tobe."

Tobry told him about the mental attack on himself, the boiling heat in his head, the voice urging him to bring Tali to Caulderon and how she had barely managed to save him.

"Is her enemy the same wrythen we fought in the caverns?"

"So it would appear."

"And he's killing the women of her family. Why?"

"I can't guess." Tobry rubbed his forehead, took another sip and told Rix about the rescue of Rannilt, the attack by the shadow-shifting facinore and their race for the gates of Caulderon.

"A facinore?" said Rix, gulping his wine and pouring another. "A new kind of shifter, part phantom and part flesh—or perhaps one alternating with the other? Are you seeing the connection I'm seeing?"

"To the caitsthe and the wrythen's caverns?"

"Yes."

"It's hunting Tali for the wrythen and it's almost impossible to kill. What are we to do, Rix? How can we protect her?"

"I don't know." Rix raised his goblet, had a sudden image of his father swilling brandy from the bottle and put it down again. "When I got home and they refused to let me fight, I didn't think things could get any worse. Now you're saying they're disastrously worse."

"And I'm not sure how long the city gates can hold."

"This doesn't seem like a simple war any more. It's starting to look like a conspiracy."

"But who's manipulating whom?"

Rix took a deep breath. "Tobe, I need your help."

"You want me to guard Tali and Rannilt. I was planning to do that anyway."

"Er, that too," said Rix, who had been focusing on a different crisis. "I've got to get the palace defences ready and the men trained to fight this new enemy."

"How do you propose to do that?"

"I've been training with Commander Horkoran since I was thirteen. He's a worrier, but he listens to me." Rix smiled mirthlessly. "He's got to, since Lord Ricinus takes no interest in anything beyond range of his drinking arm."

"What do you want me to do?"

"First we need to make a list of all the enemy's new weapons and tactics, then start thinking about how we can counter them."

"Our generals should be doing that," said Tobry.

"They aren't going to tell us though, are they? Maybe I can't fight in the army until I've got an heir, but no one's stopping me from defending my own people. If you can take Horkoran my written instructions . . . " Rix trailed off. "Pathetic, isn't it, but it's the best I can do."

"Your fanatical attachment to this house confounds me," said Tobry, "but no one can argue with your knowledge of military matters."

"Then you'll do it?"

"With all my heart."

Rix embraced him. "Thank you. We'll beat the devils yet."

"Of course we will," Tobry said unconvincingly.

"What did you do with Rannilt? Is she all right? Being trapped by a shifter, used as bait . . . I think I'd lose my mind."

"I know I would," said Tobry. "But she's a tough little creature. She seems in better shape than I am. I took her to Luzia."

Rix smiled. "That was kindly done. Rannilt will be good for her. It's a struggle for Luzia now, living all alone."

"I know. I often visit her . . . "

Rix took the hint, subtle though it was. "I've neglected her. I'll go and see her . . . as soon as the portrait is done."

"How's it going?"

Rix sighed. "Not well."

"Why not?"

"I hate it. What's wrong with me, Tobe? My father was a good man once, and he deserves my respect. Why can't I honour him with my art?"

They went up to his studio. Tobry stared at the huge portrait, walked back and forth, and studied it up close. Rix noticed that his coat hung lower on the left, as if he had something heavy in his pocket.

"No one could fault the artistry," said Tobry. "In fact, it's magnificent—"

"But?" said Rix. "Don't tell me you *like* it?"

"I don't. Not at all. Though . . . "

"For the Gods' sakes, say it."

"If you're painting to please yourself, you can do what you like. But when you're working to commission, doing a portrait for your father's Honouring . . . "

"What?" snapped Rix.

"Do you have to be so damned honest about him?"

"Mother says I've captured his essence."

"She would."

"What's that supposed to mean?"

"Sorry, but I have to be blunt." Tobry adjusted his coat, though it still hung lower on the left.

"I want you to be blunt."

"Do you? You can be a trifle blind where—never mind. Look, Lady Ricinus despises your father and you've captured it in his face—her contempt and his knowledge of it, the guilt at his drunkenness and bad behaviour, the wastage of the family fortunes. His face has it all."

"But?" said Rix, squirming as he realised Tobry was right.

"It's a magnificent portrait. It's going to be a masterpiece, but if it was my father I wouldn't hang it in my house. Assuming I had a father, or a house, you understand."

"Perhaps I have gone a bit far." Rix had loved his father once, and would never want to hurt him, though that was hardly possible. Lord Ricinus had the skin of a shifter pig. "It's too late to change it now. There's only six days until the Honouring."

"I'm not telling you to change it; just what *I* see in it."

"Anyway, I've begun another painting," said Rix.

"Really? Where do you find the time?"

"I haven't been sleeping well, and I've turned away Mother's bed mate. I'm not letting her have the pleasure."

"By depriving yourself of it. That'll *really* sting her."

Rix shrugged. It was rare to win a battle with Lady Ricinus but he was determined to beat her on this one.

Tobry pulled him close. "There's something else the matter, isn't there? Are you having the nightmares again?"

Rix cast an uncomfortable glance down the stairs. Though the great heatstone in the salon could not be seen from here, he could feel its brooding presence.

"I was dreading them all the way home, yet, oddly, I haven't had a one. I guess all that action drove them out of my mind. Or maybe the war did—something real to worry about. But—"

"What?"

"Come and look at this. I keep it in here so Mother won't find it."

"You can paint what you like."

"Until the portrait is done I can't even scratch my arse without permission."

Rix led Tobry into a storeroom full of blank canvases. From the back, facing the wall, he lifted out a smaller painting, only a yard across.

"I was planning to do a cruel satire on Mother," said Rix. "To balance my depiction of Father, I suppose. Anyway, I ended up with this instead. I don't know where it came from, but it scares me."

"As you said, sometimes your paintings can be divinations."

Rix turned the painting to face them. It was little more than a sketch rendered in quick, violent brushstrokes. A large, window-less chamber, crowded with junk and filled with a greenish mist. Dim lanterns to left and right, haloed rings around them, illuminating a black bench in the middle and, lying on it, the figure of a woman, just a few strokes of the brush.

"What's it supposed to mean?" said Tobry.

"No idea. The scene feels familiar, yet oddly remote."

"Perhaps it's a picture you saw as a kid. Remember those grim old paintings that used to be everywhere around the palace, full of bloody war and violent hunting scenes? What happened to them, anyway?"

"Mother got rid of them. She wanted art more in keeping with what the higher families had on their walls."

"Of course she would," said Tobry.

"I couldn't sleep after I painted this. I was afraid that if I dropped off I'd have another of those nightmares about blood, and an ice leviathan rolling over the palace, and the fall of our house."

"Hardly surprising, with the war going so badly." Tobry adjusted his coat again and took another look at the sketch. "I can practically smell the mould, the filth, the damp."

"When I close my eyes I *can* smell it."

"Paint the rest of it. That might get it out of your mind."

"I doubt it. I whited over it last night, but ten minutes later I was sketching the place again, exactly the same only more detailed. Where does it come from? What does it mean?"

"I haven't a clue, but ... "

"What?"

"The viewpoint is quite low. No higher than the bench."

"Why didn't I notice that?" said Rix. A shiver began, low down, then spread up his back to the top of his head. "It's as though it's being seen by a child ... "

CHAPTER 61

"Tobe," said Rix. "You've known me a long time."

They were in his studio again and he was trying not to look at the portrait, which was getting worse with each brushstroke. After Lady Ricinus's last inspection the water had frozen in the taps.

"All your wicked life," said Tobry. "I remember seeing you just after you'd been born. You weren't a big baby, oddly enough. And extremely ugly—a veritable horror." He chuckled. "We spent a lot of time at the palace when you were little ... before the scandalous fall of the House of Lagger."

Rix could not manage a smile. "Do you remember being here when I was ten? Something happened back then and I was sick for ages."

"I've never known you to be sick," said Tobry. "You're disgustingly healthy. Everyone in the palace is."

"I haven't been sick since, but I nearly died that time. A fever or something, and afterwards I'd lost a whole month of my life. You must remember it."

Tobry shook his head. "I wasn't allowed to visit then. We were disgraced; the House of Lagger was sliding towards the precipice and all doors were closed to us." He walked away and stared out the window.

"The nightmares started after I got well," said Rix.

"Fever can do that to you."

"But they've never stopped. They've got worse."

"Sorry. What with the bankruptcy, mother's disgrace, father's suicide, the manor being burnt to the ground with everyone but me inside, and our creditors taking the rest of the estate, I don't remember much about those years. Don't want to remember, if truth be told." He looked at Rix. "You're pale enough to be a Pale. You should have an early night."

"I can't. The damned portrait. I'll be up till three again."

"I'll get out of your way. I'm going to check on Tali."

"At the abbey?"

"Hildy wouldn't take her, and then I was followed. I shook them off, dropped her at Torgrist Manor and made a false trail—"

"Why didn't you tell me this before?" said Rix. "Who followed her?"

"I assume Hildy betrayed us to the chancellor."

"But Tali's wounded. You did go back? You made sure she's all right?" Suddenly Rix understood why Tobry was so flat.

He looked sick. "I tried to, but all the mansions in that street were watched, front and back. If I'd gone into Torgrist Manor the chancellor would have known within minutes that she was there. I'm really worried about her."

"Has she got food? Warm clothes? Fresh bandages?"

"No, nothing," Tobry said hoarsely.

Rix paced back and forth. "Damn it, Tobe, we've got to do something. At least, you have—they won't let me out." He handed Tobry a jingling bag. "Bribe the guards. Get her away where she can be looked after, then come back. I'm not sure I want to be alone with this, tonight."

He put the sketch back in the cupboard and closed the door.

When Rix could not bear to touch brush to the portrait again, it was four in the morning. Too exhausted to undress, he lay on the huge bed and blew out the lantern. Outside, big snowflakes were fluttering down in the moonlight.

The moment he closed his eyes, his father's face reappeared in his inner eye, as it always did after a long close-up session. Rix did not try to blank it out; that never worked. He concentrated on the brushstrokes until they blurred into a miasma—a green mist wreathing across a dirty, windowless chamber.

Though he never wanted to see that image again, he had been waiting for it, even longing for it in a strange kind of way. It was horrible, yet cathartic—or would be once he had seen it all.

He went back to the studio, took the sketch from the cupboard and focused on the figure lying on the black bench. He thought it was a woman but could discover no more about her. At the head of the bench, two blurred shapes might have been people, though no amount of analysis could extract more from them.

But why would it? Last night he had done the sketch in a creative frenzy, not thinking at all. Rix made some tentative dabs at the shadows, though as soon as the paint went on he knew it was wrong.

Loading his largest brush with white, he painted the scene out and fixed the blank canvas in mind. Now he could sleep. He rubbed his eyes, yawned, picked up the small brush again and, without thinking, swept it across the canvas. A dozen strokes recreated the windowless chamber, another two dozen the miasmic background and the bench with the indistinct figure on it, the shadows at the end, the lot.

But now there was a diminutive figure off to the right. Was she the one who had been viewing the scene before? He did not think so. She looked *too* little, though the viewpoint would depend on where she had been standing. Yet why would he see through the eyes of a child? It did not make sense.

"Still no faces?" said Tobry from behind him.

Rix jumped and his brush spattered grey paint across the right-hand lower corner. "There's nothing to identify any of them."

"That's definitely a child, though. A small girl. And I can tell you one thing about her, from the way she's standing."

"What's that?"

Tobry wore a different coat but it still hung low on the left. "She's scared. No, terrified—no, *horrified*."

"How can you tell?"

"I have a gift for it." Tobry adjusted his coat. "How's the portrait going?"

"Progress, though I still hate it."

Rix took a last look at the sketch then whited it out, wishing he could wipe his own imagination as easily. "What have you got in your pocket?"

"A packet of powdered lead."

"What on earth for?"

"I've a mortal fear of shifters, and especially caitsthes."

"A mortal fear?" Rix said curiously, then remembered the look in his friend's eyes when the caitsthe had been on his back—a terror that had nothing to do with dying, or being torn apart by the beast, but of something that to Tobry was far worse.

"If we meet another one, I'll be ready to burn its livers with powdered lead. Have I told you how the war is going?"

"Disastrously, you said, and I don't want to hear it again right now. How did you get on with Tali?"

"I didn't."

"What!"

"She wasn't anywhere in Torgrist Manor. I don't know where she's gone."

"How hard did you look?" cried Rix, chafing because Lady Ricinus's guards prevented him from going after Tali. "What if she's lying in a fever somewhere? Dying?"

Tobry was unnaturally pale. "I looked everywhere, believe me."

"Maybe the chancellor has her."

"I hope not. He's not a nice fellow."

"He's been good to me."

"Don't ever get on his bad side."

That night he slept badly, troubled by feverish dreams, though there were neither shapeshifters nor leviathans in them, nor that voice urging him to do something terrible. He had not heard it since they had left for the mountains. The dreams were about his sketch.

After waking at first light he went to the window, looking out on the snowy palace gardens but not seeing them. Who was the little girl, and why did she look horrified? Why was the sketch seen from the viewpoint of a child anyway? And why did it have such an air of menace?

The inspiration might have come from one of those violent, old-fashioned paintings that had come with the Palace when House Ricinus bought it, generations ago. Rix remembered being frightened of them as a child. They had also been masterpieces, the study of which, later on, had done much to develop his own genius.

Yet he did not think Tobry was right this time. More strongly than ever, Rix felt that he was sketching something he had seen before; though why did it seem so remote? Had it been something innocuous he'd seen before that terrible illness, leaving his memories distorted by the fever that had nearly killed him? He did not think so. Rix felt sick every time he worked on the sketch, as though he was glorifying a crime. Or wondering whether he'd been complicit in it.

Who could tell him? Certainly not Lady Ricinus, who had passed Rix into the care of Nurse Luzia and a succession of tutors when he had been a toddler—ah!

He opened the door and said to one of the guards, a sallow, crook-nosed fellow he had never seen before, "Would you inform Lady Ricinus that I wish to visit my old nurse, Luzia, down in Tumbrel shanty town?"

"Of course, Lord Rixium. Er, Lady Ricinus will want to know why."

"Surely I don't need a reason to visit Nurse Luzia?"

"I'm afraid so, Lord Rixium. Lady Ricinus was most adamant."

"Then tell her I wish to talk to Luzia about the good old days—*when I was happy.*"

The guard bowed and withdrew, shortly to return. "I'm sorry, Lord Rixium," he said, deeply embarrassed. "Lady Ricinus requires the portrait to be completed first."

"Bitch!" cried Rix.

The word escaped him before he realised that he was talking to a servant but, good servant that he was, the guard pretended he had not heard. No doubt he would tell Lady Ricinus, though. Keeping anything from her ladyship would earn the guards a place in the monthly flogging tithe. He went into Tobry's room.

"Tobry." Rix shook him awake.

"Yes?"

Rix lowered his voice. "Come up. I need you to do something for me."

Tobry pulled on a kilt and followed. "Why can't we talk down here?"

Rix did not answer until they were upstairs in the tower. He opened the window so the wind howled past and, even if someone had been standing two yards away, they would not have heard a quiet conversation.

"I'm not entirely sure that mother doesn't have some kind of spying device set up down there."

"What do you want me to do?"

"Find me a way out so I can talk to Luzia. I need to ask her about when I was ill."

"I'll see what I can come up with," said Tobry. "I'll need a bit for expenses."

Rix tossed him a coin bag.

"What are you doing today?" said Tobry, pocketing it.

"What the hell do you think? The cursed portrait—there are only five days left."

Tobry returned that night, after dark, whistling.

"What are you so happy about?" snapped Rix.

"Bad day?"

"I hate Father! I hate Mother even more, and I curse this stinking portrait to the Pits of Perdition."

Tobry inspected it. "It's going well, all things considered. Though the subject seems even darker than before. Grimmer. Bleaker."

"I can only paint what I paint." He put his mouth close to Tobry's ear. "Any luck?"

"Yes. Come upstairs."

Tobry had smuggled in a long length of woven strapping with hooks on either end. "We'll go out the far window and over the wall into Tumbrel Town. It'll be easier that way."

"And we won't be seen?"

"I've spread a few coins around. The shanty kids were glad to have them. Come on."

Outside the window it was overcast, freezing and black as a caitsthe's livers. Rix could not see a thing save for the enemy's blazing arrows arcing over the distant city wall.

"Don't they ever stop?"

"Only to come back with a new weapon," said Tobry. "It was fire ribbon this morning—horrible stuff that sticks to the skin and burns all the way down to the bone."

"Don't tell me any more. I want to enjoy the next hour."

"It'll be nice to see Rannilt again," said Tobry.

"It will," said Rix. He did not mention Tali, and neither did Tobry, though Rix knew he was still trying to find her.

As they went down, a strong wind kept banging Rix against the side of his tower, grating the skin off his knuckles, but it was worth it.

"This is just like old times," he said when they touched down at the bottom and crept across the grounds. "You and me, sneaking out after we'd been confined to our quarters."

"Save that there's a war on and we're losing."

"Cheerful sod, aren't you?"

"Sorry. I've got a bad feeling about tonight."

"Anything in particular?"

"Everything."

They climbed over an unguarded section of wall and down into an alley. Two small boys came scampering up. Tobry gave them a silver coin each.

"Wow!" Rix heard the smaller boy say. "Thanks, Lord Tobry."

"Guard our climbing irons and keep a sharp lookout for my enemies," Tobry said in a melodramatic whisper, "and there'll be another one each when we get back."

"What enemies?" said Rix. "You could stagger from one side of Tumbrel Town to the other in a drunken stupor and the meanest footpad wouldn't touch you."

"It makes the lads feel that they matter. They don't have much in their lives."

"Speaking of which, I wonder how Rannilt is getting on with Luzia?"

"Like a chick with a mother hen, last I saw," said Tobry. "Rannilt only stops talking to draw breath. It's done my cynical old heart a power of good to see her cared for; and see her looking after Luzia, too."

They made their way through the alleys to a slightly better part of Tumbrel Town, where Rix stopped at a small, single-roomed hut and rapped at the door. There was no answer.

"It's late," said Tobry. "Luzia's probably asleep."

"She never goes to bed before two," said Rix. "She's always up, a'doing."

"She's old now. Rannilt's probably tired her out."

Rix knocked again, and a third time. "I hope she's not ill."

"I told Rannilt what to do if Luzia took a turn, and left coin for a healer. Though with those healing hands of hers, Rannilt would hardly need one."

"It's a mighty healer that can heal old age," said Rix.

He lifted the latch, put his head through the door and shivers crept across his scalp again. "Something's not right, Tobe. What's that smell?" He knew, though. It was the smell that haunted his nightmares.

"Blood," said Tobry, pushing past and creating a fist of light in the dark room. "Don't come in."

Too late. Dear old Luzia, Luzia who had made Rix's childhood bearable, was dead in her red-drenched bed. Her throat had been savagely cut, only the vertebrae holding her head in place. And it had been done recently, for she was still warm.

Rix had seen plenty of violence in his time and would have said he was inured to it, but this was like one of his nightmares brought to life. His head was whirlpooling and if Tobry had not helped him to a three-legged stool he would have fallen down. Waves of hot and cold passed through his middle; he felt like throwing up. He looked away, praying that he had imagined it, looked back and gagged.

"Who?" he gasped. "Not the girl, surely?"

Tobry did not dignify that with an answer. He was walking around the little hut, touching the plank table, water jug, the ends of the bloody bed and the door latch, as if reading their stories through his fingertips.

"Where's Rannilt?" said Rix, clutching the sides of his stool, which seemed to be rocking like a dinghy in a heavy sea. "Have they killed her too?"

"Shut up, I'm trying to think."

Tobry waved his elbrot around the room. People-shaped shadows rose and fell, though if they had a story to tell Rix could not read it.

Abruptly, Tobry bent over Luzia, holding the elbrot to the hideous gash across her throat. "Incredible!" he hissed.

"What?" said Rix. The sickness was getting worse; it was all he could do to remain in the hut.

"The ends of the gash are *healed*," said Tobry.

Rix could not look. Not at the ruin of poor, kindly Luzia. "Ugh," he said, hand over his mouth.

"It's healed in for a good inch on either side. I wouldn't have thought that possible." He looked around at Rix. "Luzia didn't *heal*, did she?"

"No."

"Rannilt must have tried to save her. She must have a mighty gift."

"But not good enough to replace all that blood."

"Where's she run to?" said Tobry. "Wait here. I'll take a look out-side."

Rix lurched to the door. Nothing could keep him in this slaugh-terhouse by himself. Why Luzia? She'd never hurt anyone. Why, why?

Tobry found no sign of Rannilt.

"Poor child," he said. "After finding Luzia like that, and trying to save her, she must be out of her mind."

Rix did not reply. The nightmare was taking over and he had no idea how Tobry got him back over the wall and up into his tower. He vaguely remembered the reeking alley, and his friend taking care to pay the lookout boys the two silvers he had promised them. For a man who professed to believe in nothing, Tobry was metic-ulous in discharging his obligations.

After that, all was as much a blur as the fevered month when Rix had been ten. It was impossible that Tobry's wiry frame could have hauled Rix's bulk three levels up to the window of his tower. Utterly impossible, yet when Rix awoke in his bed at dawn the following morning, the scrape marks down his chest and arms could only be explained by his being dragged up over raw-cut stone.

He snapped upright and all he could see was blood. Blood and the gaping mouth and staring eyes of an old woman who had never had a bad word for anyone. A woman he had loved as he could never have loved his own mother.

"How could anyone do that to her?" Rix said, and wept until his dry eyelids rasped like grit rubbed on a plate. "In her whole life, Luzia never hurt a soul."

"We live in troubled times," said Tobry, holding Rix in his arms. "There's violence everywhere. People will rob an old lady for the contents of her pantry—"

Something rang false in his tone, and Rix thrust him away. "Never lie to me, Tobe. You don't believe that for a minute."

After a pause, Tobry said, "No, I don't."

"Why did she die?"

"To stop her talking to you about the time of your fever, I expect."

"Are you saying –?"

"I point no fingers. Anyone inside the palace might have murdered Luzia. Or anyone outside."

"How would they know I wanted to talk to her?"

"You know what the palace is like."

"I don't, actually."

"The servants gossip, and so do all the noble hangers-on."

Rix had no discrimination left. "People like you, you mean?"

There was a longer pause before Tobry replied, in tones carefully neutral, though not neutral enough to disguise his feelings from someone who knew him as well as Rix did. Rix had hurt him.

"If someone knows a piece of gossip or scandal," said Tobry, "everyone in the palace knows. Plus their families, *and* everyone who visits the palace or trades with it."

"Why did she have to die, Tobe? *Why Luzia?*" It came out as a howl.

"I don't know."

Rix staggered out of bed. "Get me a drink."

Tobry had brought a flask with him, circumventing Lady Ricinus's prohibition on more than one bottle a day, and this was a good one. Rix lurched up to his studio and emptied a quarter of it down his throat in one swallow.

"That's spirits," said Tobry, taking the flask, "and if you drink the lot it's liable to kill you."

"Father drinks three bottles of spirits a day," Rix snarled, making a grab for the flask.

Tobry held it out of reach. "Then he must have a liver the size of a whale. What are you doing?"

Rix had gone to his storeroom door. "I have no idea."

He dragged out the whited-out sketch, filled his brushes with scum-brown and miasma-green, and swiftly recaptured the essence of the dark chamber. Stroking another brush through luminous white pigment, he carved out the woman on the table. He did not know what he was painting; the strokes appeared on the canvas without conscious thought and, once they were there, he had no idea what they meant.

"What about her face?" said Tobry.

Rix blinked drunkenly at the sketch. The woman on the black bench—it was definitely a woman now, wearing only a rag around her hips—was small and slender, with pale skin and hair, though her face was a blank oval. The shadows at her head were hardly more defined than before, though he could tell that they signified a man and a woman.

He looked for the child away to the side, but she was not there. This time his unconscious mind had not conjured her at all.

"Rix?" said Tobry.

"Yes?"

"Do you really need to know what happened, all that time ago? If it killed Luzia—"

"Don't say it." Her death had struck Rix as few others could have. It was as though his real mother had been murdered. "Why did Luzia have to die, Tobe? Explain that to me."

"I can't."

"It's not fair."

"The world isn't fair," said Tobry. He paused, then said, "That's what Tali was trying to tell you."

CHAPTER 62

Tali huddled in the thorn bush as Tobry and Rannilt galloped away. Half a minute later she heard one of the riders follow. The other did not.

He must be watching, waiting for any movement that would give her away. It was freezing here, the bush was prickling her, the sky was rocking wildly and she needed to pee, but Tali did not move. She was an old hand at hiding, the best in Cython, and she had the patience of a slave.

She needed it. A small, wrinkled man with the hooded eyes of a hawk climbed onto the wall and paced along it, bobbing and ducking his head. He went up the overgrown carriage drive, around the back and reappeared from the other side. He went out and she heard the horse walking down the street.

The temptation to move was overwhelming, her need to pee desperate. Tali clenched down and waited, and ten minutes later she saw him again, head bobbing, hawk eyes scanning the grounds from an inconspicuous corner of the wall.

Only after another hour did she dare to wriggle out, turn the other way and gaze upon her ancestral home. Torgrist Manor was small and plain and very old. But it was hers. Her eyes misted.

Part of the left-hand wall had collapsed, the front door had rotted away and most of the roof was gone. And yet, as Tali looked down a broad hall floored in black flagstones caked with dust, she felt such a powerful sense of rightness that she could hardly breathe. This is my place, she thought. I'm home.

But the searchers would come back. She could not stay here. Besides, Rix was her best clue and she had to get into the palace. She

felt sure there had to be a tunnel from Torgrist Manor to Palace
Ricinus. Days ago, Tobry had said that the last Lady Torgrist had tried
to escape underground with her children *to the palace down the hill.*

Tali sat in each cobwebbed, roofless room until its smell was
embedded in her memory, then crawled back and forth, searching
for that distinctive subterranean odour.

Shortly, at the corner of a wall behind the stairs, she scented a
tunnel, then located the sensitive stone that opened into it. Time
had corroded the pins on which the stone rotated and she had to
clean out all the joins. She levered it open with the head of a bronze
shovel she found out the back, and she was in.

The sky stopped heaving. Going underground was like being
home and she felt an inexplicable yearning for the familiar, orderly
spaces of Cython. Safe at last, Tali curled up in a dry corner of the
tunnel and did not wake for a day and a half.

Hunger roused her. She had nothing to eat and her thigh
throbbed with every movement, though there were no signs of
infection. She limped down the tunnel, which descended steeply for
fifty yards before running on down a gentle decline.

After walking for twenty minutes or more, Tali caught a whiff
of a faint, unpleasant odour—mould and muck, rotting wood and
things long dead and decayed to nothing—and her hair stirred. The
mother and children had either been walled up to die, or had been
slaughtered in the tunnels, to keep the plague at bay. She fought the
fear down. The spirits of her own family could not hurt her.

Besides, the smell was chillingly familiar. She sniffed again and
her hackles rose: dry rot, mould, grime and the faint whiff of
vermin poisoned a long time ago. What did that remind her of?

She held her lantern up. Was it coming from the roof? No; the
seeps running down the passage walls were clear and odourless. She
shrugged and moved on.

Having lived all her life in Cython, where there were no signposts, Tali was used to making maps in her head. From the
direction and downward slope of the passage, and the number of
steps she had walked, she had to be under the grounds of Palace
Ricinus. Shortly she reached a dead end and smelled a fruity odour.
Wine?

Tali sat down to rest her leg. She had wasted too many oppor-
tunities with Rix. She should have confronted him and demanded
to know why he had been in the cellar at the time of the murder.
If she put it to him bluntly, his reaction was bound to give something away.

She found a concealed door, tugged and centuries of dirt broke
away, but as she put her head through, she heard the *call* again. She
stood in the doorway, trembling, and after a few seconds she heard
a *new* answer.

It was neither the distant, elegant note she had heard several
times now, which she associated with the wrythen, nor the false
mimicry of his depraved facinore. This answer was a discordant
three-note sequence, *di*-DA-*doh*, strong and clear as though it came
from somewhere close by, *di*-DA-*doh*, *di*-DA-*doh*, repeating over
and over like an unanswered question. And there was something
about it that put her nerves on edge—a ragged, self-pitying whimper. Definitely not the wrythen.

Someone else was looking for her, and who else could it be but
her mother's killers? *Di*-DA-*doh? Di*-DA-*doh?* Tali swayed and had
to grab hold of the door jamb. From the clarity of the notes they
had to be within Cauldoon.

Her initial impulse was to run back to the manor, but the comfort it offered was an illusion. Nowhere was safe. Everyone wanted
something from her, or wanted to do something to her, and no one
except Rix and Tobry would help her. And with the wrythen trying
to possess Tobry, could even he be trusted utterly?

Di-DA-*doh? Di*-DA-*doh?* A whining, boy-like voice spoke in
her head. *It wasn't my fault. The stupid bitch made me kill her.*

Tali froze. It wasn't the voice of the big man who had come after
her in the cellar. Was there another conspirator? The voice had a
yammering tone she had never heard before and would never forget.

Fury, bright and burning, drove away her panic. These people
had killed her mother; they had to pay. Momentarily, Tali indulged
herself with thoughts of black and bloody revenge, of killing them
the same way, but at the thought of doing such violence to another
her stomach heaved and her cheeks burnt.

She reminded herself that she was an agent of justice, and justice had to be sure, even-handed and unemotional. With an effort, she closed the shell and the *di*-DA-*doh* sequence was gone.

Once her knees had steadied, Tali slipped through the doorway and found herself in a real cellar, rectangular with a low, flat ceiling. Barrels of beer, wine and mead stood in wooden racks. Across the way, racks of dusty bottles extended for a hundred feet. Beyond that, steps led up. She sat on one of the middle steps, wondering how to proceed.

Since she knew nothing about the palace, making any kind of plan was impossible. First, get in, then worry about finding Rix. But what if she could not? What if he would not see her? No, they were friends now. He would help her, and hide her. And she really wanted to see Tobry again.

She was heading up the steps when a door above her clicked. She blew out her lantern and hid behind the racked bottles, only to realise that the cellar reeked of burnt fish oil and the smell was bound to be noticed.

A big man came staggering down, the light of his lantern dazzling her. What was the matter with him? Belching like a drain, he swayed to the racks of bottles, took the first that came to hand and turned away. He was so drunk that he could barely stand up.

The man turned back, his flabby belly wobbling, and she smelled sour drink on his breath. He began to sniff the air; he knew someone had been here. What if he searched the cellar? She took hold of a bottle. If he came close she would have to attack an innocent man, as she had already attacked poor, stupid Lifka. Tali's quest was leading her on paths her mother would have found hard to forgive.

He set down the lantern and, with a practised movement, uncorked the bottle, raised it to his mouth and drank from the crusted neck, draining half the contents with gurgles and gasps. After taking down another three bottles, he staggered up the steps, leaving the door open.

Taking off her sandals, she followed him in the semi-dark. He climbed three flights of steps, stopping several times to drink from the first bottle then, without warning, tossed it back over his head. The action was so unexpected that she watched it flying towards her before realising that it was going to hit her in the face.

She ducked and the bottle smashed further down the steps. The man kept going, drawing the cork of the second bottle, then followed a series of narrow corridors, evidently servants' passages. Finally he turned into a broader corridor with a red-and-blue patterned carpet, lit by lamps at intervals.

Tali peered around the corner. A large door at the far end of the passage passed through a curving wall that was unplastered and built from yellow stone. It looked as though it could be a tower, and Tobry had pointed out Rix's chambers, next to a corner tower. Two uniformed guards stood by the door, talking. Could they be guarding his rooms? How could she find out?

She ran back along the passages, planning to come out in front of the drunk. Her heart was racing. What she was about to do was incredibly risky, if he turned out to be more alert than she thought.

Tali put her head out, saw him ten yards away, and hissed, "Where's Rix?"

The drunk lurched around, looking in the direction of the guarded door. That did not mean it was Rix's, but it was worth the risk. Now she had to distract the guards, and the way was right in front of her. The drunk had turned and was shambling towards the door.

He stopped halfway along, where the next passage cut across the hall, set down his bottles and turned to the wall. What was he doing? The guards gave him disgusted looks and moved around the corner, out of sight.

Was he –? He was! The filthy brute was urinating on the wall and all over the beautiful carpet.

Tali's reservations vanished. Do it, now!

CHAPTER 63

The morning after Luzia's murder was endless. Rix had gone back to bed and had lain there all morning, wide awake with the covers swaddled around him, shivering. All he could see was the ragged slash across Luzia's throat and blood like the blood he kept seeing in his nightmares. Blood squeezed out of his people like juice from grapes. Blood on his hands and arms. Most horrible and inexplicable of all, blood being rubbed *into* a wound in his side.

At noon he hurled the covers away, stalked into the scalderium and, for the first time in his life, ran a bath for himself. After turning on all twelve taps he sat on the travertine floor, watching cold water flow down over a heatstone so thick and heavy that it must have cost the lives of dozens of Pale slaves to mine it. Until a few years ago heatstones had been unnecessary here, since endless hot water had flowed from the tubule network, but the underground source had gone cold.

It was another omen.

By the time the water poured from the grooves on the lower end of the heatstone it was steaming and in twenty minutes the tub was full. Rix sank beneath the water and scrubbed himself with a scouring cloth until the top layer of skin was gone and he throbbed all over. He still felt dirty, tainted, bloody.

He lay back, staring at the scintillating heatstone, which was already dry. By edict which, according to Tobry, Lady Ricinus had bribed to have passed, everyone wealthy enough to afford heatstones was required to use them for heating and hot water, a measure to cut down on Caulderon's deadly smogs. Those few houses permitted to share in the heatstone monopoly, including Rix's own, had made fortunes from it, and the trade disgusted him.

But since they were at war, all commerce with the enemy was banned. What would happen when the heatstones ran out? They only lasted a few years and the winters were getting ever colder. Rix shivered, though the water was still hot, then yanked the plug and went to his studio without taking breakfast. Food would have choked him.

The portrait accused him of neglect. He had redone the mountains in the background, turning them into a tortured landscape inspired by the volcanic ruin of the Seethings. He had also touched up the mighty wyverin. Now, instead of a savage predator rightfully slain, it was a noble beast, perhaps the last of its kind, cut down for the glory of killing.

But his father still eluded him. There was something about the man that wasn't right—

Tobry burst up the stairs, panting.

"Can't you knock?" Rix snarled.

"Sorry," said Tobry, unrepentantly. "I know how you hate being interrupted when you're *working*."

"I hadn't started." Rix tossed the brush down. "What's up?"

"Lady Ricinus is in an almighty flap. She's ordered a search of the entire palace."

"What for?"

"Good question."

"Could she know we sneaked out last night?" said Rix. "Maybe she thinks I smuggled something in."

"No, I think she's looking for—"

There came a thunderous rapping on the entrance door and Rix heard a snick. "I've had the locks changed a dozen times. I don't understand how she gets a key—"

"Who pays the locksmith?"

"Ah. I see."

"Where's your sketch?"

"In the storeroom. I always paint over it when I'm finished. Sit down and read a book. I'd better look busy." Rix picked up his brush. "I'm a grown man. I've fought a wrythen and cut down a caitsthe. I've killed more of the enemy than our First Army has, so why does she make me feel like a naughty schoolboy?"

Tobry settled himself on a couch with a ribald tome called *War and Wantonness*. Rix reached towards the portrait as if touching up his father's uniform.

Lady Ricinus's heels tapped up the steps. She inspected the painting and snapped, "You haven't done a thing since I checked last night."

"I've been working on it all morning," Rix said.

"Never lie to me, Rixium. All your brushes are clean."

"Can I help you?" he said, matching her coldness with his own. "It's impossible to work with constant interruptions."

"Artists!" She went to the top of the steps and called down. "Up here. Search the upper tower first. Lagger, don't move from the couch until we've finished."

"Your wish is my command, Lady Ricinus," said Tobry with an ironic bow.

She curled her razor-edged lip. "If it was, you'd be hunting walrus on the polar ice in a scorpion loincloth."

Four servants came up, two men and two women. "Begin up there and work down," said Lady Ricinus.

They went up the next flight and began opening doors and checking cupboards and storerooms.

She turned away. "Rixium, come with me. We have matters to discuss."

"Can't we do it here?" said Rix.

"In public? Certainly not."

"I'll need a note in your hand to get past your gorms on the door," he said sarcastically. Annoying her was never a good idea but Rix was beyond being sensible.

"Don't act a bigger fool than you already are."

He followed her out. Should he ask about Luzia's murder? No, she would spend the rest of the morning interrogating him as to how he knew about it.

Lady Ricinus was walking faster than usual and breathing noisily. To have rattled her, it had to be something serious, but Rix did not think it was the murder. To her, servants were cut-out humans, pressed into place to do a job. If one failed, ran away or was murdered, another would take the place. Not that Luzia had left any place to be filled. Once Rix married, *gulp!* his wife would pick her own nurse. Assuming she could stand up to his mother.

He contemplated the grim prospect. Did Lady Ricinus have the candidates lined up for his inspection? Unless, he thought hopefully, all the girls she's picked have refused me.

As if that would happen. Their families would decide and the money would clinch it. Nothing short of a reputation for disembowelling young women and brushing his teeth with their blood would get the selected girls out of a liaison with House Ricinus.

They passed a cringing orderly. In the distance, a slender, red-haired maidservant girl was sobbing. Lady Ricinus froze for a second, then strode on.

"What's the matter with Glynnie?" said Rix.

"I put her little brother in the month's flogging tithe."

"Why? Benn's a hard worker, always eager to please."

"The boy brought me *cold* tea. It won't happen again."

"You can't do that, Mother. It's not right."

She did not bother to reply. Rix stopped next to Glynnie, turned up her tear-stained face and said quietly, "It'll be all right. I'll fix it."

She gave him a tremulous smile and he continued.

"What's the matter, anyway?" said Rix. "What's going on?"

Without answering, Lady Ricinus stalked into her chambers, waited until Rix had passed through and slammed the door, which started another frisson of disquiet. He had never known her to slam a door before—quiet, viperish deadliness was her style.

"If you ever undermine my authority with the servants again," she hissed, "they will suffer."

"Take Benn off the flogging tithe," he said coldly, and forced himself to meet her eyes, to break her dominance, even if only for a minute.

After a pause, she said, "Very well. That's one favour wasted. Sit down."

His heart hammered as he went by. What was Lord Ricinus doing here? Mother only wheeled him in for emergencies, and this must be worst than most, for he was sober. Rix had not seen his father in that state since he was ten.

He gulped. His father was bad enough when drunk, but when stone sober he was an angry, bitter terror. Rix looked around for a flask but all were locked away. Lady Ricinus had planned for this meeting.

"Sit!" she said.

They sat. Rix stared at his father's grossly misshapen, purple-veined monstrosity of a nose. He could see the veins throbbing. Was this what he would look like when he was old? Was he halfway to becoming his father already?

"Where is she?" said Lady Ricinus.

Rix stared. "Where is who, Mother?"

"The Pale traitor you found near the Rat Hole."

So that's what this was about. He should have known that she would find out about Tali. Her network of informers was the best in the land.

"I didn't find a traitor near the Rat Hole," he said, matching her coldness and raising it a blizzard.

"Don't lie to your mother, boy," growled Lord Ricinus from the settee. "We know you met the scrag there."

Rix leapt up, shaking with fury, and for the first time in his life failed to show Lord Ricinus the respect due to him. He loomed over his father, dominating him with his own size and strength and knotted fists.

"The woman's name is vi Torgrist, Father, and hers is one of the oldest houses of all. Far older than yours."

His father tried to lurch to his feet. Rix was about to push him down again when his mother's voice cut through the room like a flaying knife.

"Sit down! Rixium, lay one finger on your father and I will have you flogged in the city square."

Since she made a fetish out of keeping the family's secrets, the threat indicated her dire state of mind. Rix went back to his seat, acid searing a track up his gullet.

"There is no House vi Torgrist," said Lady Ricinus. "It died out centuries ago."

Rix could have crowed. Her spies had failed her. It was the tiniest of victories, but any victory over his mother was rare and all the sweeter for that.

"*Lady* Tali can trace her name back to the Second Fleet. And she has her house seal. Tobry checked it, and as you know, there's nothing he doesn't know about the noble houses."

"It will do her no good," said Lady Ricinus. "Even if her claim could be proven after all these centuries, no Pale traitor can inherit."

Rix did not reply. The more he said, the more his mother would use against Tali.

Waves the colour of purple grape juice washed across Lord Ricinus's face. His slack mouth opened and closed; he clutched at his chest. "Drink! Need a drink."

Rix's mother tossed him a little key. "Get your lord father a drink. If I do it, I'm liable to jam it down his throat."

The expression stirred a troubling memory, but it submerged before Rix could ease it up into the daylight. He opened the locked case on the far side of the room, took down a bottle of brandy and gave it to his father. Lord Ricinus sank a third of it in one gasping swallow, wiped slobber across his cheek with his forearm, then lay back, "Aah, aah, aaaahhh!" His twisted mouth gaped.

Lady Ricinus looked as though she wanted to smash the bottle over his head, but swallowed her bile. She turned to Rix and said, through lips so pursed that a needle could not have been inserted between them, "Your impassioned defence of this woman disturbs me. Do you have feelings for her, Rixium?"

"Certainly not," he lied, meeting her eyes. Few people could deceive her but he'd had twenty years of practice. "She's not to my taste, insipid little thing that she is." He paused, wondering if he could make the planned half-truths convincing. "But I did help her escape the Cythonians."

"Why would you risk your life to help a Pale?"

"Tobry and I had just seen the ruins of Gullihoe. When Hightspall needs to counterattack, a Pale who knows the enemy's realm from the inside will be priceless."

"Indeed," she said, licking her lips, "and whoever can provide her will earn great favour with the chancellor. Favour we sorely need. In that, at least, you did well, Rixium. Tell me everything about her. Omit not the smallest detail."

Rix sketched out their rescue of Tali and the subsequent hunt, glossing over all the risks he had taken and the number of times he had narrowly escaped death. It would do no good to tell his mother that. He also omitted every detail she could use against Tali.

"Then why," she said when he had finished, "since you went to such trouble and took such stupid risks to rescue the chit, did you hide her from my seneschal?"

Rix was prepared for the question, though he did not imagine his answer would satisfy her. "After the enemy's cowardly attacks on Gullihoe and half a dozen other places, I feared for Tali's safety if I revealed her presence."

"Nonsense. Parby is a prudent man and would have recognised her value. Where is she now?"

"I don't know," Rix said truthfully. Tobry had found no sign of her, nor Rannilt, and he was terrified that the chancellor had captured them. He was a hard man who would do anything to protect his country—even torture secrets out of a girl and a child.

"Lagger does. Where did he take her?"

"To Abbess Hildy."

Lady Ricinus smiled. "But Hildy turned her away."

"Well, I haven't seen her."

So that's why she was so agitated. His mother thought he was having a scandalous affair with a Pale traitor. One that, if it got out, would ruin the Honouring and all she had been scheming for these past years.

"Liar! You sneaked out of your tower last night."

He nodded stiffly, afraid to speak. How did she know so much?

"Where have you hidden her?"

"I don't know where she is."

"I don't believe you."

"I went to see Luzia, if you must know, and I found her dead. *Murdered!*" It came out as a wail.

She rearranged her face into the appropriate expression. "I'm sorry. I know she meant a lot to you."

And she meant nothing to you.

"Rixium," she continued, softly now, almost wheedling, "if you have a liaison with this treacherous Pale, it could ruin your father's Honouring."

"The Pale have been slaves ever since Hightspall abandoned its hostage children a thousand years ago," said Rix. "Tali is the first to escape. She's strong and brave—*and* she saved my life. You should be thankful to her."

"I'll show her how thankful I am when I meet her."

Rix did not like the sound of that.

"What matters is not what she is," said Lady Ricinus, making a meaningless concession, "but what the Pale are universally believed to be—traitors. Nothing you or I can say will change that belief, and any relationship with her could ruin us."

She put on a smile worthy of a jackal queen. "But if we can make her over to the chancellor for use in the war, it will double our power and confound our enemies. We have powerful enemies, Rixium, and they will do anything to bring us down."

"I worry about them all the time," said Rix.

"Leave the worrying to Lord Ricinus and me. All I want from you is her hiding place. And the finished portrait."

"I have no idea where she is." Rix rose. "The portrait will be finished on time, if you'll allow me to go back to it."

"I am most disappointed in you, Rixium." Lady Ricinus waved him away.

"Mother will never give up," Rix said that evening. He was in his studio, dabbing at the portrait, which he hated more every time he looked at it. He wanted to hack out his father's image and burn it in the fireplace.

"I've never seen her so upset," said Tobry, who had come in without finding any signs of Rannilt or Tali. "This morning she seemed almost hysterical."

"You must have imagined it," said Rix. "Lady Ricinus is the epitome of control." But he had noticed it too. He laid the brush down. "I can't do any more. Let's have dinner, a bottle of wine, and then I'm having another go at the sketch. I've got to see the faces."

Tobry took a measured breath. "After what happened to Luzia, are you sure you want to know?"

"I have to know. It's killing me, Tobe." He changed the subject. "Is there any news about the war?"

"Nothing good."

Every enemy assault led to their victory, every counterattack by Hightspall's forces resulted in another crushing defeat. Rix had begged Lady Ricinus and pleaded with Lord Ricinus to be allowed to fight, but neither would relent.

One bottle turned into two, for Tobry had sneaked another in with him, and it was after midnight by the time they returned to the studio and Rix brought out the whited-out sketch. This time he did not have to look at the canvas—the scene was so familiar that he could have sketched it with his eyes closed.

"It's just the same," he said, slumping onto the settee once the creative fury had run out.

"There's a bit more," said Tobry. "Look at the little girl."

Rix stood up. "Her face is blank. I can't read anything into her."

"I can. Look at the way she's jamming her fist against her mouth, as though strangling a scream."

Worms squirmed in Rix's belly. "Where's all this coming from?"

Tobry shrugged. "No idea. I've never seen this chamber before."

"I don't recognise it either—" Rix broke off, head cocked. "What was that?"

"I didn't hear anything."

"Sounded like someone yelling in the west hall."

Remembering Luzia's fate, Rix grabbed his sword, ran down and opened the door. The passage was empty. "Where the hell are the door guards?"

CHAPTER 64

The carpet came up to Tali's ankles and her bare feet made no sound. Could this possibly work? The drunk was a large man and if he caught her she would be lucky to get free. But if she could push him over and smash the bottles, the distraction might give her a chance to check the door.

She was only a few steps away when he turned, raising the second bottle to drain it. He gulped and gasped, dropped it to the carpet and was levering out the cork of the third bottle when he saw her.

The drunk choked and swung the bottle as if to knock her out of the way. "No!" he slurred. "You're—"

She thrust him hard in the chest. The bottles fell together and broke, then he staggered backwards and his head made a soggy thud as it hit the corner of the wall. He collapsed into the servants' passage, blood pouring down his neck.

Tali stared at him, appalled. Had she killed him? The hall reeked of blood, urine and wine. She bent over him, not knowing what to do.

"Tam?" one of the door guards said loudly. "Sounds like the Lord's done it again."

Had they seen her? No, she was fully in the cross-passage, out of sight, but if she remained here they would find her in seconds. She ran down to the next corner and stopped to check.

The guards were bending over the drunk. "Is he dead?" asked the second guard.

"Wish the pig was," said the first. "If we're to survive the war, the sooner the young master takes charge the better."

"Shh! That kind of talk can get you flogged. Get a pad on that gash, quick."

Tali went cold inside. The drunk must be Rix's father, Lord Ricinus, and if he died, she would have killed him. But if he survived they would turn the palace upside-down looking for her.

She hobbled down and was hesitating outside the door when it was opened by Rix. "What the blazes are you doing here?" he hissed. "If you're seen—"

He caught her wrist, yanked her inside and locked the door.

Di-DA-*doh? Di*-DA-*doh?* It was coming closer. Tali clamped down on her shell but the pressure was trying to force it wide open.

Rix took her by the shoulders, holding her so tightly that it hurt. "Why have you come here? It's not safe."

She glared up at him. "Let—me—go."

"Sorry." Rix released her and stepped back, rubbing his hair until it stood up in tangles. "What am I supposed to do?"

"Do you want me to go?" she said stiffly.

Go where? Back to the manor, which was probably being searched at this moment? She looked around. She was in a broad hall. The tiles underfoot were polished white marble, large paintings were hung down either wall, and through an open door she glimpsed a bed the size of ten slaves' cells in Cython. The one imperfection was a faint, rotten-egg-gas smell from the hissing gas lanterns.

He hesitated a long time before saying, "Of course not. But . . . why are you here?"

Di-DA-*doh? Di*-DA-*doh?* Tali forced her shell closed. "I had nowhere else to go," she dissembled. "They're after me."

"Who's after you?" said Rix.

"My mother's killers."

His eyes were bloodshot and sunken, with dark circles around them. He looked as though he had not slept in days and her heart went out to him, but she had to harden it. She had to confront him about the murder, now. She might not get another chance.

"Rix?" she began.

He groaned and wrenched at his hair.

"Are you all right?" she said. "You look dreadful."

His laugh had an edge of hysteria. What could have happened since she last saw him?

"Mother has just searched the palace for you. She's also ordered that I marry."

"Marry?" she said, bemused.

"I have no heir and she won't allow me to fight until I produce one. Also, Father's portrait is a disaster, the war is a catastrophe— and dear, sweet Luzia, who never hurt anyone in her whole life, has been murdered."

"Your childhood nurse?" said Tali, her belly throbbing. Her voice rose. "The woman you sent Rannilt to?"

"Yes, and she's run away. Tobry can't find her. He's looked every-where."

Tali slumped back against the wall. Murdered? And Rannilt lost in a city at war, with no one to look after her. "Why was she murdered?"

"To stop her talking to me. I wanted to ask her about my childhood, a fever that nearly killed me—"

"When you were ten," said Tali.

"How did you know? I suppose Tobry told you."

He was shaking. Impulsively, she put her arms around him and he clung to her for a few seconds as though she was the only solid thing in the world. How could she confront him about the murder now? She would have to wait.

"Why did Rannilt run?" said Tali.

"She tried to heal Luzia but the wound was beyond any healer. Perhaps she ran in panic or terror. Poor child, the things she's witnessed. What are we going to do?"

"I don't know." She could not focus. "Rix, I keep hearing the *call*."

"Call? What call?" He picked up a water carafe and gulped at it, spilling water down his front, then put it down so abruptly that it shattered.

"The strange note in my head. My enemies are using it to track me."

Rix paced towards the front door but spun on one foot and came back, almost running, his limbs jerking. He looked as though he was cracking up.

"My family enemy is the wrythen you fought in the mountains," said Tali. "He ordered my mother's death. I told Tobry about all this—"

"Yes, yes!" cried Rix as though he had finally succeeded in dredging up the memories. "He told me, but what's the *call*?"

Tali explained. "I had it blocked. At least, I thought I did, but now I keep hearing it in my head, *di*-DA-*doh? Di*-DA-*doh?* Louder than ever, and closer. I'm sure it's them, Rix. My mother's killers are hunting me."

Her thigh throbbed. She pressed the flat of a hand onto it. Without direct skin contact she could not renew the healing charm but she imagined the pain had eased a little. "Why has the palace been searching for me?"

"Mother has some mad idea that I've got you hidden away."

Tali swallowed. He was head and shoulders above her and from this close she had to tilt her head at an uncomfortable angle to meet his eyes. "Why would she think that?"

"She thinks I fancy you."

She took a step backwards. "That's ridiculous ... "

"Isn't it?" said Rix. "How did you get in, anyway?"

She could not admit that she had knocked over his father and might have killed him. "Sniffed out an old tunnel. Having lived underground all my life, I'm good at that."

"But how did you get here unseen?"

"Er ... someone fell and hurt themselves ... down the hall. The guards went to help." The half-truth slipped out and it was too late to correct it.

Rix led her along the hall. Away to the right, a set of stairs ran up steeply into a tower. "How did you find me, anyway?"

"Um ... I've a very keen nose."

Laughter exploded above them. "Rix, you really must bathe more often."

Tobry was coming down the stairs, beaming, and Tali felt an unfamiliar surge of happiness and belonging. Tobry wouldn't panic; he would know what to do.

Rix scowled. "I spent an hour in the tub." He looked over her head. "Tobe, what the blazes are we going to do?"

"I don't know. The chancellor's turning Caulderon upside-down to find you, Tali. There's a reward on your head big enough to buy a castle."

Tali blanched. If any of the servants discovered she was here, they would turn her in.

"What's the matter?" said Rix. "You're trembling."

Tali had thought that she was hiding it. "It's just ... I was ... You'd have to ... "

"We defend our friends with our lives," said Rix stiffly, as if she had insulted his honour. He grimaced. "What if the palace is searched again?"

"Why would it be?" said Tobry.

"It's frightening how much Mother knows."

"Does she know we're friends with Tali?"

"Since Mother has no friends, she assumes I'm acting from an ulterior motive."

"What motive?" said Tali hoarsely.

"She believes I sneaked out the other night to bed you."

No one spoke for a minute. Tali felt flames creeping up her face.

"Is the war going badly?" she gabbled. There had been no news since their desperate flight through the city gates.

"It's going disastrously," said Tobry, turning to a map on the end wall. "The enemy have captured Suthly County and most of the land south of Caulderon between the Crowbung Range and the Vomits, and they're racing up the western side of the lake. Kleng must fall within days, Reffering after that, then Nyrdly County will follow. We still hold Lakeland and Fennery, but once they fall, the centre of Hightspall will be in their hands and they'll starve Caulderon out within weeks."

"What about all the counties over the mountains? When they march to our aid—"

"They're too far away. By the time they hear about the war, it'll be over."

"But Hightspall has stood for two thousand years." Never had Tali imagined it would crumble like this. "We must be beating them somewhere."

"We haven't had a single victory," said Tobry. "Their weapons are too strange and deadly, our generals too hidebound. Their tactics belong to the first war and they can't adapt them to this new enemy."

"The swine won't stand and fight," said Rix. "They melt away, fire on our armies, fields, towns and bridges from cover, then run and hide again. We can't get a grip on the bastards, and all the while they're killing us by the thousands."

He looked down at Tali. "But I've forgotten my manners. Come this way."

He led her into a vast and magnificent salon, bigger than the combined cells of a hundred slaves in Cython and with a painted ceiling soaring up to a point like a six-sided tent. A large fireplace in the right-hand wall was set with unlit wood and kindling, yet the room was pleasantly warm.

Pain spiked through her temples and she turned, knowing what she was going to see: the baleful coruscations of a heatstone the size of a cottage wall, set into a gilded metal frame. She could still see the marks of crowbar and chisel on the stone.

Genry had died mining heatstones for the idle rich, baked like poor Sidon. Rix's chambers were too big, just as he was. The ceiling must be forty feet high. How could all this be for one man?

"Sit down." He indicated a couch covered in a fabric so fine that it shone. "You must be starving."

Tali remained standing, the forgotten sandals dangling from her hand, mortified to realise that she was covered in the dirt and dust of the underground. She could smell it on herself and she couldn't possibly sit on that magnificent couch. No speck of dust had ever entered this room and every surface was waxed until it gleamed. What must Rix and Tobry think of her?

"Tali might like to freshen up," said Tobry. "I'll find something for her to wear."

Rix showed her into a room which he called the scalderium, and explained how the bathwater was heated.

"My father was killed in the heatstone mine," she said coolly.

Rix shrugged, turned on the cold taps and went out. Tobry returned with a fawn linen shirt and pantaloons, and a braided belt. When he had gone Tali stepped into the tub and yelped. The water was icy. She scrubbed clean and was getting out when she realised that she had not heard the *call* again. Had the killers lost her, or had they stopped searching because they now knew where she was?

Shortly, pink and glowing and dressed in clothes three sizes too big, she came out. Tobry was speaking.

"Better that Lady Ricinus thinks you're bedding Tali than she realises you're friends with a Pale."

"That she could never forgive," said Rix, who was calmer now. He looked up and smiled. "We'll have to get you out of here— Lady Ricinus wants you badly. If she can hand you to the chancellor, he'll be most grateful, and the house needs his gratitude right now. She'll search the palace again at the least hint of anything suspicious."

Like Lord Ricinus being knocked unconscious fifty yards from his son's door and gabbling about being attacked by a small blonde woman. Tali felt the trap tightening. Where could she go when the whole world was hunting her?

A furious rapping echoed down the corridor. Tali jumped and looked for a hiding place.

"That's Mother!" Rix cried.

"Go and see. It's probably nothing."

"Who but Lady Ricinus would make such a racket at this time of night?"

Rix headed for the door. Tobry ushered Tali around the corner and up the stairs.

"What are you going to do?" she said. If the only entrance was guarded, any search must find her in minutes.

"Tobe, Tobe?" Rix yelled from the door.

Tobry went halfway down the stairs. "What is it?"

"Father's fallen and knocked himself out. It could be bad." The door banged.

"There," said Tobry, leading the way up the stairs. "Nothing for you to worry about."

She limped after him, dread gnawing at her like a stomach full of alkoyl. Lord Ricinus would wake, describe Tali and accuse her of trying to kill him, and Lady Ricinus would be relentless. An attack on the lord of the house was an attack on the house itself and must be savagely punished.

It must also destroy the friendship that had developed between her and Rix, and perhaps Tobry too. They would know she had deceived them. They would believe she had attacked Rix's father while he was drunk and helpless, then had run away. Rix could not forgive that, any more than Tali could have forgiven an attack on a member of her own family. Why hadn't she told the truth?

Because the slaves' way was so ingrained in her that it was instinctive. Never admit anything, never notice anything and always be ready to lie yourself out of trouble.

"You're shaking," said Tobry. "Have you eaten?"

"Not—" Her voice went hoarse. "Not today."

"Sit down. I'll bring something up."

Tobry headed for the stairs, then turned back, as if he had forgotten something. Picking up a small canvas that was facing away from her, he put it into a storeroom full of other canvases and closed the door.

Now that she had no distractions, pulses of pain were spearing through Tali's abused thigh, following the line of the arrow wound, which had been repeatedly broken open in the past days. She forced herself to concentrate. When Rix discovered what she had done to his father, he would be furious. He had risked his life for her and she had betrayed his trust.

Would he give her up? No, he was too noble for that. He would put her out and tell her he never wanted to set eyes on her again. After all they had been through together Tali could not face that. She had to get away before he returned, and the only place she could go was back to the tunnels.

Could she glean any evidence about the murder first? How long did she have? Lord Ricinus had been very drunk when she'd encountered him in the cellar, and in the minutes after that he had swilled two more bottles. After he came to, he would probably sleep for hours.

Settling on a red leather settee, she pressed down on the hot arrow wound, working the healing charm as best she could, and re-examined the clues. There was no subtlety about Rix; his feelings showed on his face. If he knew anything about the killing, he would have given it away when she had told him about it. Therefore, he knew nothing. And yet, he had been there. She was not mistaken about that.

Tali desperately needed someone to share her doubts and fears with. What if she broached the subject with Tobry? She trusted him, but Tobry's loyalties had to be with his friend. If she told him that Rix had been a witness to the murder, Tobry would ask him about it.

"Here you are," said Tobry.

He set down a tray beside her. It held four wedges of something firm—one wedge white, the next two yellow and the last threaded with grey mould—plus sausages and slices of preserved meats, little onions with long yellow stalks, a green apple and a red one, and a couple of dishes whose contents quivered.

"What's that?" said Tali, pointing to the plain yellow wedge.

"Cheese. You don't have cheese in Cython?"

"There's no milk." She nibbled some cheese. It was pleasantly nutty.

"Wine?" He was holding out a brown bottle.

She could only see the drunken old man swilling it then peeing on the wall. "I'd rather have water."

He fetched some and sat on the other end of the settee. "I'm intrigued to know how you got into the palace."

"You mentioned tunnels, so I sniffed them out."

He was smiling. "That's quite a nose you have."

Was he mocking her? She did not know how to reply. "If this place is searched, what are you going to do with me?"

"Take you out the window and down into Tumbrel Town."

"If they know Rix sneaked out, won't they be watching the windows?"

"I expect so. We'll have to be quick."

"What if they've got men waiting below to catch us?" Panic flared. She was going to be caught and sold to the chancellor like a slave.

"I'll have men there too," said Tobry. "Trust me, I've played this game before. I'm going out to make the arrangements now. In the meantime, you've got to eat and sleep and give your thigh a chance to heal. Then, if we need to go in a hurry, at least I won't have to carry you."

"You once said you had a friend who was skilled in magery and might help me find—"

"And you said, 'Don't tell anyone about it'."

"I've got to have help. I can't do it by myself."

"Unfortunately she left Caulderon when the attacks began. If the enemy wins, those with magery will be taken first, and tortured longest."

"I've lost, then," she said bitterly. "And I'll be one of them."

"So will I," Tobry reminded her. He sighed. "Lie down, close your eyes and empty your mind."

"What are you going to do?"

"A little test."

"But you said . . . what if *he* sees into me, through you?"

"I'm not using *my* magery. Just the elbrot's. But only if you trust me."

"I trust *you*," said Tali. But she could also trust her enemy to use every advantage. And yet, without magery she was lost anyway. "I'll have to take the risk."

She closed her eyes and tried to think of nothing, but the memory of *di*-DA-*doh? Di*-DA-*doh?* kept intruding. Did the killers know she was in the palace? And what if her enemy still lurked within Tobry, just waiting for the right moment, this moment, to possess her? She would not be able to endure it the way Tobry had. A slave's mind was her last refuge when all else had been taken. If the wrythen invaded that sanctum she would go insane.

Tobry moved the elbrot back and forth over the top of her head, around the sides, and above her face. She could detect its glow through her closed eyelids.

"Your mind's so full it's bulging out your ears," said Tobry.

"Sorry," she said hoarsely. Don't think of the notes. Don't dwell on the *call. Di*-DA-*doh? Di*-DA-*doh?* What made the notes, anyway?

"Blank it all out." Tobry laid his callused hand across her forehead. "Turn yourself into a cork bobbing in a pond, just drifting, drifting."

She imagined that she was floating, empty, uncaring where wind and currents took her or what happened once she got there, at peace . . . But what if he *was* possessed, and her enemy was reading her gift at this moment, sneering at her weakness, preparing to enter her . . . ?

"Ugh!" cried Tobry, screwing up his face in pain. "For a minute there, I thought I was close, but it dropped away." His tanned skin was pale, his lips bloodless.

Because I blocked you, she thought guiltily. Despite all you've done for me, I didn't trust you. "Are you all right?"

"It was more painful than I'd expected."

"You knew it would hurt?"

"My magery often does."

CHAPTER 65

The inner peace faded and Tali was back on the red settee with her thigh throbbing and her belly so empty that it hurt. She ate as much bread, cheese and sausage as her small stomach could hold, fighting the urge to gobble like a starving slave and steal the rest for later.

"Why can't you reach my magery?" she said with her mouth full.

"It's not like any other magery I've come across."

"My great-great-great grandmother, Mimoy, said that too."

"Then she was a wise woman."

"She was a rude, cranky cow who never thought about anyone but herself." Tali was still annoyed at how she had been manipulated, and about Mimoy dying without telling her anything.

"How else could she have lived so long in Cython?"

Tali wasn't listening. "If my enemy can only be beaten by magery, and I can't reach mine—"

"I dare say the chief magian could help you, though . . . "

"He'd have to give me up to the chancellor, wouldn't he?"

"Unfortunately."

"What about that ancient device you mentioned the other day? A pry-probe, was it?"

He started, then put his hands on his cheeks, staring fixedly at the wall.

"What's the matter?" said Tali.

"I've just realised where Rannilt must be. In the chancellor's palace."

"Why would he want her?" But the answer was obvious.

"She also knows enough of Cython's secrets to be valuable, and he's got agents all through Tumbrel Town. They would have picked her up within minutes of her fleeing Luzia's murder."

"Where is the chancellor's palace?"

"Next door." Tobry pointed left, out the window.

She lurched to the pane. "Next door" clearly had a different definition to the fabulously wealthy—she could just make out the ice sheathed spires of another palace further along the slope of the hill. It was smaller than Palace Ricinus, a fierce, spiky building, black stone edged with red. She did not like the look of it.

"It's the most heavily guarded place in Caulderon," said Tobry. "Don't even think about going after Rannilt."

"I wasn't," she lied. Of course she was going after her. *Will you be my mother?* Little Rannilt had no one else, she must be desperate, and she had done her all for Tali. "He—he won't hurt her, will he?"

"The chancellor does nothing unnecessarily. Besides, he'll want her fit for questioning, for making maps of Cython and telling all she knows."

That made sense. Tali lay down. Heal, heal! But her small gift of healing seemed to have gone the way of her magery. "What's he like?"

"He's an ugly little runt ... and they say he has depraved tastes ... "

"But?"

"He's a cunning and brilliant man who thinks of everything."

"Everything except the possibility of war," said Tali sourly.

"Just weeks ago, he convinced Lord Ricinus to pay for the Third Army," Tobry pointed out.

She pressed her thigh. *Heal, heal*, Rannilt needs us. "What were you telling me? Oh yes, the pry-probe."

"I talked to some people about it," said Tobry. "It's called a spectible, and it's in the chancellor's collection, but I don't think it works any more."

"*Nothing* works," she muttered. "Every avenue is blocked."

It occurred to her that, since Tobry had known Rix all his life, he might know something about the time of the murder. But she would have to put it carefully.

"Did you know Rix well, when he was a kid?"

"Until he was five or six. I'm five years older but we spent a lot of time together. I suppose he was a substitute for Nimry, the little brother I lost ... "

"What happened to him?"

It took Tobry a long time to answer. He was rubbing his eyes. "He was such a bright little boy; sweet tempered, too. He was killed by a jackal shifter when he was four. Killed and eaten," he said savagely. "He—*it*—got into the nursery and killed all the little cousins ... I found them ... I was only nine ... "

"That must have been terrible," Tali said softly.

"It was the beginning of the end of my house."

"So you didn't see Rix much after he was six?"

He looked away, eyes unfocused, jaw knotted. "The *noble* House of Lagger was in its death throes at that time, and they were so drawn-out and horrible that I don't remember much else. Anyway, I wasn't allowed to visit House Ricinus then. I didn't see Rix again until he was twelve. He insisted that I be invited to his birthday week and we've been friends ever since."

She knew he was telling the truth, which meant he hadn't been around when Rix was ten. Another blockage. What else could she do?

"Why are you gritting your teeth like that?" said Tobry.

"My thigh is a little painful."

"I'm not surprised, after walking all that way underground. And no one saw you in the halls?"

"I'm good at hiding and looking ordinary—"

"You could never look ordinary," he said so passionately that her chest shivered. "Here, allow me."

He put a hand on her thigh, over the wound, and murmured a healing charm. "You were saying?"

Under his warm hand, something stirred in Tali, causing her to lose her train of thought. She yearned towards him, confused by the unfamiliar feelings. She wanted to know him better, and perhaps she wanted what her mother and father had found in each other, too, but she could not allow anything to distract her from her quest.

"And then, if I really need to hide, I press my fingers against my slave mark—that's what the Cythonians call it, but to me it's always signified the noble House of vi Torgrist—and it helps. Most of the time."

"I see it as noble, too."

The hidden hurt burst out of her. "But not Rix! He threw up when he saw it. I'll never forget that. Never!"

"He's a better man than you think. And I'm a worse one. You can't go wrong by putting your trust in him, but you can with me."

"I trust both of you." But you more . . .

He waved a hand, as if to say that he had lost interest. "Show me your thigh."

Tali pulled the pantaloons up as far as they would go, unwrapped the bandage and pressed the area. She winced.

"It's hot," said Tobry. "Let me feel your armpit." She raised her arm and he pressed his fingers in. "The wound is hot, but you're not." He studied her thigh as though he had not seen one before. "It's healing, though it would have healed a lot quicker if you'd kept off it."

"If I'd kept off it, you'd be possessed by the wrythen and I'd have been taken by the facinore."

He chuckled. "No need to get snarky. You must have a strong constitution."

"In Cython—"

"Only the strong survive," he said, sighing. "And those who *can* survive, those who flourish there, are strong beyond us normal folk."

Tobry decanted the wine from the black bottle, took a healthy swig and poured the red crust thrown by the wine into a saucer. He spooned half onto the entry wound, soaked the middle of a clean bandage in the rest and bound it up.

"And now," he said, "I've got to make arrangements and you need to sleep."

He lifted her legs onto the couch, tossed a blanket over her and bent to blow out the lantern.

"Leave it," she said. "I don't want to be in the dark just yet." Tali knew she would not sleep.

He turned the lantern down and went.

Rix did not come back. What if she had killed his father? Tali tried to tell herself that it was an accident but knew any court would see it differently. She had knocked down the Lord of the House, on whom everything rested, and the whole house would see her punished for it.

She limped to the window, stood in the darkness beside it where she could not be seen from below, and looked down. The wall of the tower fell away sheer and, even without an injured leg, she could not have climbed down without a rope. How was Tobry going to get her down that?

From this angle there was no evidence that Hightspall was fighting a desperate war that was likely to end in its destruction, or that Tali's enemies were closing in. The beautiful grounds were threaded with lights all the way down to the lake and the lawn was dusted with snow. It looked like a fairy kingdom, but Palace Ricinus was an enchanting trap. And Rannilt had to be rescued.

As she was returning to the couch, she noticed a large painting on an easel on the far side of the room, though only the back of the canvas could be seen from here. It must be the portrait Rix was doing for the Honouring.

She turned the lantern up, carried it around the other side and stopped, staring in wonder and alarm. He had a marvellous gift— the portrait was almost alive. The enormous winged creature draped across the bloody ground should have been dead, for a sword had been thrust through its heart, but the look in its eyes told otherwise. It was like some mythical beast playing dead, waiting to tear its attacker apart as he roared his vain triumph.

Her eyes drifted to the scalded landscape, which was not unlike the barren, boiling Seethings, and the rearing volcanic peaks in the background. They too were savage, tortured and uncontrollable. What had Rix said about Hightspall—*the very land is rising up against us*. The mountains looked as though they stood ready to blast Hightspall apart and bury the ruins in a hundred feet of red-hot ash.

And then to the man.

At first glance Lord Ricinus stood tall and proud, the heroic victor standing over the vanquished beast. But only until she looked at his face. Rix had not painted his father as a young man

who might have slain such a magnificent creature, but as the raddled sot he was now.

There was something terrible in Lord Ricinus's eyes—a shrinking away from the world, a refusal to *see*. The mouth was a ragged
twist, the cheeks mottled the colour of bruises, and the nose was a
monstrosity, a ruin, a bulging blob of red writhing with distended
purple veins. A nose covering up the failed man behind it.

She shuddered and looked away. The portrait was mesmerising,
yet horrible. And it was also an omen. A metaphor for the struggle now taking place between rising Cython and crumbling
Hightspall, and for the fall of houses and nations. Why would Rix
paint something so opposed to everything he believed in? Or had
he not yet realised what he had done?

Tali looked back, for there was something familiar about the *style*
of it—no, the savagery of the scene it depicted. Yet how could there
be? The only art she was familiar with was Cythonian, and it belied
their cruel nature. Their murals and wall dioramas were reflective
scenes of mountains, lakes, rivers and meadows, yearning back to
the distant time when their world had been at peace. Sometimes
animals were depicted—deer, rabbits, birds on branches—but
always alive and unharmed. Their art neither glorified the brutal-
ity of nature or the dominance of humankind.

So why was the violent realism of this portrait so familiar? She
could not think.

As she was returning to the couch, Tali remembered Tobry
taking a smaller canvas into the storeroom, as if he had not wanted
her to see it. Why not? Had Rix been painting her? She crept to the
top of the steps but saw no light below, heard no sound. She opened
the storeroom door.

It was full of canvases though, as far as she could tell, all were
blank. The storeroom smelled of oil paint and her nose led her to
a small canvas at the back, stretched tightly on a wooden frame. She
lifted it out, leaned it against the front of the stack and held up the
lantern.

Her heart began to gallop.

She was eight again, a terrified slave girl cowering in the skull-
shaped cellar with all those terrible paintings on the walls—that's

where she had seen them—and the stink of poisoned rats clotting in her nostrils. Tali looked closer, and choked.

There, on her back on the black bench, lay her beautiful mama. She had been sketched without a face, and the two people standing behind her head were also unidentifiable, but it was undoubtedly Iusia—*and those were her murderers*.

Tali shuttered the lantern and sat in the dark, rocking back and forth. Her legs had gone so weak that she could not have stood up again. Rix must know who the murderers were.

She shone a glimmer on the sketch again, shuddered and hastily closed the door, but could not stop the cascading memories: the tall man with the round pot of a belly hunting her with that enormous knife; the nail digging into her hip; the wee running down her legs from sheer terror.

Tali blew out the lantern and stood at the window, watching the snowflakes settle on the lovely grounds but not seeing a thing.

Was Rix protecting the killers? Had he lured her here? No, he had done everything possible to prevent her from coming to the palace . . .

And yet, could it be a coincidence that he and Tobry had found her so soon after she had escaped? Tobry, whom she would have trusted—*had trusted*—with her life, had hastily hidden the sketch. What did he know that he wasn't telling her?

CHAPTER 66

It was close to dawn when Rix staggered into his bedchamber, dropped his robe and fell onto the bed.

"How is he?" said Tobry from the armchair on the other side of the room.

Rix jumped. "Alive but delirious." His lip curled. "Though, judging by the litter of bottles, the delirium has nothing to do with his injuries. I've never seen Father this drunk before."

"What happened?"

"He raved about being attacked by a ghost, but—"

"I didn't think Lady Ricinus allowed anything so untidy in the palace."

Rix managed a wintry smile. "She doesn't. Besides, the bloody mark on the corner matches the gash across the back of his skull. There was wine everywhere, two broken bottles and an empty. He just fell over and whacked his head." He looked away, grimacing.

"And?" said Tobry.

"I shouldn't tell you this, but half the palace will know by breakfast time . . ."

"You don't have to tell me anything."

"Father had relieved himself on the wall, the disgusting old bastard! If I had any respect left for him, it's gone now."

"But you do respect him," said Tobry.

"I *owe* him respect as a dutiful son—he's my father! But as a man, he sickens me."

"And you feel guilty about that."

"I feel guilty because I feel *nothing*. For my own father!"

Tobry stood up. "He'll live, then? If he's not in danger, I need my sleep and so do you."

"I'll never sleep now. I'm going to work on the portrait."

"Are you sure that's a good idea, right now?"

"No, but it's like a wall across my mind."

"I'm not with you."

"I should be working out tactics to combat the enemy's new weapons . . . but how can I concentrate with the bloody portrait hanging over me like an executioner's axe?"

He climbed the stairs to the studio, donned a paint-spattered smock and directed his lanterns onto the portrait. And started.

Tali was lying on the couch, staring at him. His father had driven her out of mind and all he wanted was to get the stinking portrait finished without interruption.

"How is he?" said Tali.

"Drunk and delirious," he said curtly. "Nothing unusual."

"But he'll be all right?"

Why did she care? Or was she just being polite? "He'll sleep until he's sober—another ten hours at least—then wake as mean as a caitsthe with an axe through its ear."

She relaxed visibly. "I'm glad he'll be all right." He stared at her and she added, hastily, "I lost my father when I was six. I still miss him."

"Yes, well, I've got to work," he said pointedly. "You can have my bed."

"I can't take *your* bed."

There was a strange look in her eyes, a wary, trapped look, but Rix had to get on. He mixed paint on his palette and touched a fine brush to it.

"One of the downstairs couches, then. Anywhere but here."

"I don't like that painting," she said.

"I loathe it, but I've got to get it done."

She picked up her sandals and limped down the steps.

When Rix went down at midday, starving and exhausted, Tobry was on one of the couches chuckling over *War and Wantonness*, and Tali was curled up on the other, asleep. For the first time since Rix had known her, she looked at peace.

He studied her, wondering about her life. Her skin was so fine that he could see the veins underneath. There was hardly anything to her; she almost disappeared in Tobry's shirt and pantaloons, yet she was stronger than either of them. How had a slave race produced such a woman?

"How's it going?" Tobry said quietly.

"I don't want to talk about it." Rix collected a tray of food and a jug of water, and took them upstairs.

Tobry followed, inspected the portrait and studiedly took up his book.

Rix tried to paint on, but Tobry's presence blocked him. "*What?*"

"Did I say anything?"

"You don't have to. What's wrong with it?"

"I did suggest that you not work on it in this mood."

"If I don't it'll never be finished," Rix snapped. "And if last night is an example of the way Father carries on, it's no wonder House Ricinus is on the nose."

"On the nose," Tobry said meaningfully.

Go away, leave me alone.

"Does the portrait really matter that much?" Tobry added.

"I already told you. If the Honouring doesn't go perfectly, House Ricinus may fall."

"Take another look at it. Not even Lady Ricinus could accept that much truth."

"What are you talking about?"

"The nose. Why change it?"

Rix went to the window and leaned on the malachite sill, looking out. "It wasn't right."

"It was more right than it is now."

Rix had repainted his father's nose in a blind fury and had no idea how he had changed it. He always worked better when his mind was disengaged from what was in front of him.

"It looks like a drunkard's pizzle, and not even Lady Ricinus would allow you to portray your father that way. He'd be laughed out of the Honouring."

Pain stabbed through Rix's chest; he ran to the portrait and the nose was grotesque. It made him sick to look at it, even sicker to think he had painted his own father that way. What if Lady Ricinus came in?

He grabbed a brush, any brush, and painted the nose out.

"How did Father come to such a state?" he said, breathing heavily. "What turns a good man bad, Tobe? Is it one wrong step, or a lifetime of small errors until there's no going back?"

And how far had he, Rix, advanced down that path?

"I'm sure it's different for everyone," said Tobry. "In the great melodrama of the fall of the House of Lagger, for example—"

Rix stalked across to the storeroom, yanked open the door and the first thing he saw was his sketch, facing out.

"What's this doing here?"

Tobry strolled across. "You left it out, and I put it away after I brought Tali up . . . but I didn't leave it like that."

"How did you leave it?"

"At the back, facing the other way."

"You're sure?"

"Yes."

"So Tali saw it?"

"Does that matter?" said Tobry.

"I don't want the whole world to know about my nightmares."

"Calm down. Who's she going to tell?"

"That's not the point."

"What is the point?"

"Forget it. Leave me alone."

Tobry did not move. Rix made a couple of circuits around his studio, cursing his father, and himself for the way he was portraying him. Lord Ricinus was a deeply troubled man and he, Rix, should be supporting him, not flaying him in this portrait.

But Rix's art was the one thing in his life that was truly his—the one thing that was not given or withheld at Lady Ricinus's whim. He had discovered the gift within himself as a little boy, though only after his illness had it burst into magnificent flower. He had nurtured it against the wishes of Lord Ricinus, who considered fighting and drinking the only manly arts. Painting was an occupation for idle ladies and effeminates, not for his heir.

The people whose opinions mattered to Lady Ricinus viewed painting as a tradesman's occupation, unsuited to the son of a noble house. Not only had she refused to pay for his paints and brushes, or allow him to be tutored in his art, she had hidden him away in this tower at the rear corner of the palace from the age of twelve so no visitor could accidentally see his work. Only after the chancellor had heard about Rix's gift, came to see for himself and praised Rix, had she relented.

Nothing was too good for her brilliant son then, Rix thought sourly, and he resented everything she had bought him with.

"My art was always about truth. When one of my paintings reveals an inner truth, I feel as though I'm taking a stand, that my life really matters."

"Of course it matters. House Ricinus's army would follow you anywhere."

"That's not something I feel very often. Mostly I feel that Lady Ricinus has cut me out and pinned me to the wall."

Tobry rolled his eyes.

"The portrait doesn't matter a damn to me," said Rix, more calmly, "but this sketch does. There's a dreadful wrong here and no one else can find the truth in it."

He put the canvas on its easel and took up a handful of brushes. "What are we going to do with Tali?"

"I've made some arrangements. I can get her out, but it won't be easy to hide her from the chancellor."

Rix made some random marks on the canvas. "Haven't you got friends you could take her to?"

"Away over in Reffering. But it could fall at any time."

Rix shivered, for it was cold in the studio. He made a few more dabs, then stepped back, frowning at his palette.

Tobry inspected the sketch and swung around, fists clenched. "That's not funny!"

Rix dragged his gaze back. "What are you talking about?"

Tobry hissed at him, "You've painted Tali's face on the woman on the bench."

"Gods!" said Rix. "What's the matter with me today?" He clutched at Tobry's arm. "I've had a horrible thought."

"I think I know it already."

"Sometimes my paintings are divinations. What if she's going to be caught and killed, and I'm seeing it?"

He stared at the canvas, worms squirming under his skin. Why would he paint such a thing when Tali had risked her life to save his? The bond between them was indissoluble.

Tobry walked around the sketch a couple of times, reached out towards the woman's cheek, then drew back sharply and walked away.

Rix checked the sketch again. Why would he be seeing Tali's death? "Tobe? Answer me."

"I don't know what to say. Some of your paintings *have* divined the future."

"Most haven't."

"But this is a powerful imagining, the strongest I've ever

known from you. Even when you white the sketch out, the scene comes back the next time you pick up a brush—only more of it."

"I don't know what to do," said Rix. "I can't think."

"These two people at the end of the bench are the key. Paint them and, if we recognise them, we'll have the answer."

"I've tried a hundred times, but nothing comes."

"Keep trying. This is getting dangerous."

Rix had a sudden flash of poor Luzia and the red mouth opened across her old throat. "I know! Clear out and let me work."

There came a forceful rapping at the entrance door.

"That's Lady Ricinus," said Tobry. "White it out, quick! I'll bring Tali up."

"What are you going to do with her?"

"Take her out a window with the climbing straps."

"With an injured leg?"

"I hauled you back up the other night."

Tobry ran down the stairs. Rix painted over the sketch with broad strokes and put the canvas in the back of the cupboard. He was on his way down when he heard his mother's key in the door, and Tobry still had not brought Tali up. What was he supposed to do? How could he choose between Tali and his house?

He sprang the rest of the way and skidded across the floor at the bottom of the steps. Tobry was in Rix's bedchamber, looking under the bed.

"Where is she?" Rix hissed.

"I can't find her."

The door opened. "Rixium?" came Lady Ricinus's voice.

She was advancing down the hall, and next to her tottered an absurd, hunched little figure in shoulder-length wig, high heels, knee britches and stockings—the chancellor of Hightspall.

Absurd but deadly. His nose and chin formed a nutcracker and his eyes were like miniature black olives, so deeply sunken that nary a gleam escaped them. He was a small man with a big voice, and he was accompanied by a dozen female flunkies.

"Good day to you, Lord Rixium," said the chancellor, bowing. "Where is Thalalie vi Torgrist?"

CHAPTER 67

A bellow of fury shook Tali from a sleep blessedly free of pain and shifting shadows. She shot upright, her heart thundering.

Another roar. "Damn you to the Pits of Perdition!" It was Rix, up in his studio. What was the matter? Was he being attacked? She crept up the steps. He was across the studio, brush in hand, dabbing at his father's face and cursing the portrait with each stroke.

The shocking cellar sketch came flooding back, and all her previous doubts about him. She limped down to the scalderium and sat on the cold floor. Could he be a cold-hearted hypocrite, or did he genuinely not remember her mother's murder? How could he not remember? Was he covering up for the killers?

Another glimmer of memory came back. The boy had appeared some time after the killers had gone up that corkscrewing stair, and there was no evidence that they had known he was there. Could he have been in the cellar innocently? Had he witnessed the murder, or only arrived after Iusia was dead?

She had to confront Rix and demand to know what he had been doing there. It was risky, though. If he was covering up for someone and she forced him to choose, why would he choose her? But then, why sketch the murder cellar and leave it out where anyone could see it? It made no sense.

As she was sitting there, Tali caught a faint, musty-mouldy smell, which was odd since everything here was perfectly maintained. She walked around, sniffing. The smell reminded her of the tunnel through which she had entered the palace, though she could not tell where it came from.

Rix's studio was quiet now. She went up the stairs, taking them slowly, wondering how best to approach him. He was ten yards away and had his back to her, dabbing distractedly at the sketch and

talking to Tobry—the racket must have woken him. Damn. She
had hoped to find Rix alone.

"That's not funny," cried Tobry.

"What are you talking about?" said Rix.

Tali backed down the stairs until only her head was showing.

"You've painted Tali's face on the woman on the bench," said
Tobry.

"Gods! What's the matter with me today?" Rix clutched at
Tobry's arm. "I've had a horrible thought."

"I think I know it already," said Tobry in a low voice.

Tali raised her head, straining to hear.

"What if she's going to be caught and killed, and I'm seeing it?"

They gathered around the sketch, blocking her view. Tali
slumped onto the step, quivering. Could Rix be right? His paintings certainly had a power she had seen nowhere else. If he had
divined her death, her enemy was going to succeed.

She *the one*. What if Mad Wil had it wrong? What if Tali was the
one who made it possible for the wrythen to succeed, and for
Cython to regain the land it had lost two thousand years ago? How
could she matter that much? But if she did, and the fate of
Hightspall rested on what she did next, she had better think carefully.

She peeped again. Tobry paced around the sketch a couple of
times, reached out towards the woman's cheek then drew back
sharply and walked away. Or was Rix merely sketching her mother's
face from some lost childhood memory?

The killers at the end of the bench still had no faces and she
gathered that he was unable to paint them. It made one thing clear,
though—he wasn't covering up for anyone. He had lost all memory
of the murder and, if the sketch could not bring it back, what hope
did she have?

But if the sketch *was* a true divination, she might not have long
to live. She was withdrawing when a sudden resonance struck her
about that smell in the scalderium. It so precisely matched the
smell of the tunnel through which she had entered the palace that
there had to be a connection. *A connection!*

The original building on this site, she knew, had been a manor constructed at the time Caulderon was founded by the Five Heroes. Indeed, the manor had been built by the leader of the Heroes, Axil Grandys, and in subsequent centuries the palace had been constructed around and over it, enclosing it like a shell.

The Two Hundred and Fifty Year War had been raging then, and there could have been many secret passages and escape tunnels. Could there be another exit in Rix's scalderium, one long forgotten?

She walked around it, sniffing. The musty odour came from the far side of the enormous tub, where there was a narrow space between it and the wall. Tali wriggled into the space, which was as clean as the rest of Rix's chambers. Not a speck of dust had been missed by the meticulous maids.

She pressed high and low on the wall and the side of the tub, which was covered in large travertine tiles, and everywhere in between. The tunnel smell was stronger here; there had to be a space somewhere close by. She wiggled her fingertips into every tiny gap and under every ledge, and using everything that her mother had taught her about the workings of the secret hidey holes in Torgrist Manor.

A thunder of rapping on the entrance door made her jump and she cracked her forehead on the side of the tub.

"It's Lady Ricinus!" said Tobry from upstairs.

Should she run up and hope he could get her out the window and down the vertical wall of the tower in time? How could that succeed, in broad daylight? Lady Ricinus knew Rix had sneaked out the other night and she was bound to have people watching. The tunnel was Tali's only hope.

She scrunched into the narrow space behind the tub, probing for a hidden catch. Someone bounded down the stairs, opened the two bedchamber doors, then ran through the salon into the scalderium.

"Tali?" said Tobry

She was hidden behind the tub and did not answer. He cursed and ran out again.

Something had moved where Tali had cracked her head—one of the foot-square travertine tiles. She pressed her hands flat on it, pushed up and down and sideways, and it moved again. She dug her fingertips into a join concealed under the overhang of the tub, tugged and the tile rotated inwards, revealing a space. She wriggled into the humid dark, careful not to dislodge any dust from inside which might reveal her.

Her heart was thumping very fast. Dust stuck to her sweaty hands.

"The chancellor's here too," Rix hissed. "Where's Tali?"

"Don't know," said Tobry. "I've looked everywhere."

Footsteps advanced down the hall. Many footsteps.

Rix swore. Tali pushed gently on the tile, which slipped back into place, leaving her in Cythonian darkness.

"Where is she?" said a commanding voice, the chancellor. "Search the other chambers and the studio tower, all the way up to the roof. Put a watch on the doors and windows. Allow *no one* in or out until I give the word."

She caught a whiff of a cloying musk and cinnamon perfume. Booted feet clattered up the stairs. Tali could imagine what Rix must be thinking—since a determined search must find her, wouldn't it be better to reveal that she was in his rooms? If he did, she could not blame him.

Someone came into the scalderium, moving softly, rapping knuckles against the walls, the floor and then the sides of the tub. She put the flat of her hand against the swinging tile so it would not sound hollow and held it firm in case the catch was located.

"Nothing here, Chancellor," a woman said after many long minutes.

"Check the bedchambers."

"What have you done with her, Rixium?" said Lady Ricinus in a voice that sent shivers up Tali's spine. She had never heard anyone so cold.

Tali could not make out Rix's reply.

"I'll deal with this," said the chancellor. It sounded as though they were sitting in Rix's salon, next door. Tali pressed her ear to the tiny gap at the top of the tile. "I want Thalalie vi Torgrist, and I want her now."

"She hasn't been here," said Tobry.

They were protecting her, at great risk to themselves, and it brought tears to Tali's eyes. How could she have doubted them?

The silence lasted for a full minute. "Tobry Lagger," said the chancellor. "The last disreputable scion of a depraved and fallen house. But you can fall further, sir."

"I plan to," Tobry said lazily, and Tali was amazed at his self-possession. She was close to wetting herself. "I'm going to leave no depth unplumbed before I go."

"That might be sooner than you think."

"I've been expecting it since the terrible choice I had to make when I was thirteen. You can't frighten me."

"But I can threaten you, sir. A word from me and you'll be in the front lines."

"I have no fear of death. I stand ready to serve my country."

"Death isn't the only thing to fear in the front lines. *Life* there will soon curb your insolence. But I did not come here to bandy words with a penniless layabout. Get out, Lagger. And you too, Lady Ricinus—if you would be so kind," he ended mockingly.

"The heir to House Ricinus is not yet of age, Chancellor," said Lady Ricinus. "It is my right and duty to represent him."

"This is not a trial," barked the chancellor. "And in time of war, when the enemy is within the city walls, all rights are bestowed, and taken away, at my discretion."

"They're in Caulderon?" cried Lady Ricinus, shrilly. "Who allowed the savages in? The general in charge should hang."

"They swarmed up into Tumulus Town an hour ago, through rat holes we did not know were there. I dare say they're attacking other suburbs as well. I received the news on your very doorstep, Madam. Go! Close the door behind you, and look to the defences of the palace—if it's not too late. You should have listened to your son when he pleaded to defend it."

"How—how did you know that?"

"My spies tell me everything. Go!"

She went. No one spoke for some time, then the chancellor said, quietly, "Lord Rixium, great challenges lie ahead. I need the best men in the land at my side, and I've had my eye on you for some time. We greatly appreciated your news about the caverns at Precipitous Crag and the mysterious activities at the Rat Hole the other day, not to mention your insights into the enemy's new weaponry and tactics. Few men could have done what you did, nor rescued the Pale girl in the face of such odds, then gained her confidence."

Rix gave no audible answer and the chancellor continued.

"Your deeds do you honour, and House Ricinus too. They will not be soon forgotten, but ... " He paused, then went on. "This house stands in grave need of honour, after the depraved antics of your father which have caused so much offence."

"Father is not ... not a well man," said Rix hoarsely.

Tali imagined sweat running down his handsome face.

"I know more than I care to about Lord Ricinus," growled the chancellor. "Don't apologise for the scoundrel."

"I do not. But I do owe Father a duty of respect."

"Quite so. Your mother, however, is in full command of herself." The chancellor finished with a whip crack.

"I don't take your meaning, Lord Chancellor," said Rix.

"She has given mortal offence."

"I cannot see that, sir," Rix said weakly, "and I must defend her."

"That is your duty as a loyal son, but do so judiciously or you too may be tainted. I'm a realistic man—I allow for a degree of favours and douceurs. Many of the lesser hangers-on at court would be bankrupt were it not for their bribes, extortions and petty monopolies. But your mother, sir, assumes that everything is for sale—*and everyone*. She has gone too far and, should House Ricinus fall, it will be she who has brought it down."

"She can be a trifle abrasive, Lord Chancellor," said Rix, and Tali could hear the strain in his voice, the conflict. "Sometimes she strives too hard in her quest to serve our house, but—"

"Ricinus hangs by a thread, Lord Rixium. Were it not for your own valiant deeds, and your father's prodigious and sorely needed gift of the Third Army, I would have nudged your house off the precipice myself.

"But the gift has been made, gratitude is due and in war we need unity, not discord. Give me the girl and your house will survive. It may even rise to the absurd heights of Lady Ricinus's ambition. Who knows? In the past, equally villainous rogues have clawed their way to the top, loudly pronounced themselves noble, and even become noble, in time."

"Why do you want Tali?" said Rix.

"Her knowledge of the enemy, and Cython, could win the war for us."

"But you already have Rannilt," cried Rix.

"Who told you that?" snapped the chancellor.

"I too have my spies."

"No matter. Her knowledge of Cython was certainly useful, but full of gaps, and she sees things through a child's eyes. Besides, she's proven obdurate of late."

Tali smiled at that. How she missed the child.

The chancellor dropped his voice. Now she had to strain to hear what he was saying, but the power of his voice was all the greater.

"I want Tali, and I'm going to have her. Satisfy me on this and you will realise your dreams." He paused for a full minute. "But if you fail me, Lord Rixium, if Thalalie vi Torgrist is not delivered to me by the night of the Honouring, I swear that I will cast House Ricinus so low that a thousand years will pass before you can aspire to shovelling muck. From tonight, you have three days."

Rix did not reply. Tali would not have been able to. Such a threat to her own house would have stopped her heart.

"I find myself desperately conflicted, Chancellor," Rix said, his deep voice even lower than normal. "I love my House, and I have always done my duty to it, but I love honour too—my *personal* honour."

"Then look to the hierarchy, boy," growled the chancellor. "Your country comes first, *always*. Where your country is not under threat your House comes first, *always*. Next is family, *always*. Only then do you count friendship and lesser liaisons. You have until the Honouring."

Hard heels tapped across the floor. The entrance door clicked open, clicked closed. He was gone.

Tali felt sure that Rix would bow to the chancellor's threat. He must, as she would have done in the same position. Would she put an acquaintance, or even a dear friend, before the survival of her House and all the members of her family? How could she? How could anyone? Rix knew she was hiding here somewhere and, for the sake of his country, house and family, he would have to turn her in.

The door reopened. "Rixium?" said Lady Ricinus. Her voice had a quaver.

"The chancellor is displeased, Mother," said Rix.

Her voice firmed. "And so am I. I told you to find her—"

"It's you!" Rix said, choking on the words. "He's displeased with *you*, Mother."

"That's absurd. I'm the very model of propriety . . . "

"He's taken grave offence at all your bribing, conniving and manipulating."

"It's nothing that any other House has not been doing for generations. At least, any House with the least ambition—"

"If it's nothing, how come our treasury is so bankrupt that the palace army hasn't been paid?"

"How dare you question me!" she cried. "You are not—"

"Not of age," Rix snapped. "I soon will be, Mother, and if House Ricinus survives that long, I swear—"

"You don't get the keys to the treasury until you become Lord Ricinus."

"And that's unlikely to happen now, is it?"

"What are you talking about?" The uncertainty was creeping into her voice again.

"If Tali isn't produced by the Honouring, the chancellor is going to grind our House so low it will never rise again. And all because you tried to bribe him, Mother. The chancellor!"

When she finally spoke, her voice was low and savage.

"Then maybe it's time to ensure that he can't bring us down."

"Mother, that's treason!" cried Rix. "We're at war—the chancellor is a strong, capable leader, the only one we've got . . . "

"I spoke in haste," she hissed. "Erase my words from your memory. I never said them. Now get the damned portrait finished—and find that treacherous Pale."

Tali was trembling, shocked to her core. Taking her hand off the panel in case she made it rattle, she leaned back, thinking furiously. Rix had three days to save her, three days to betray her! And what if Lady Ricinus did carry out her threat?

If she did cast the chancellor down, Tali did not see how Hightspall could survive.

CHAPTER 68

At last, said the wrythen, *the host is where I want her. I have the alkoyl and everything is in place. Now to pull the pieces together.*

Why the Solaces? clamoured the ancestor kings and queens. *Why did you remake our people in a new image?*

He did not reply. Even if he had blundered there, he could not turn now. His next task was to complete the last leaf of *The Consolation of Vengeance* then, via the heatstone, wake the embedded command in Rixium. He was close to breaking point and the wrythen was confident that tonight he could tip Rixium over the edge. If necessary, he would take control of Tobry as well. It would be so much easier in the palace, where both men were bathed in the emanations from that enormous heatstone.

Yes, tonight Rixium would take Tali down and do the deed, and once the wrythen had the master nuclix he would use Tobry to dispose of the thieving magian, Deroe. Then the wrythen would kill Tobry from within, Rixium from without, and all five nuclixes would be his.

But he still had that niggling worry about the Herovians rising again. The wrythen had enlisted the intellects of all one hundred and seven ancestors in a collective mind-search for the *Immortal Text* but they had not found a trace of it. Surely it must have been destroyed.

CHAPTER 69

Rix dared not tell Tobry about his mother's threat. Not only was it high treason to threaten the chancellor at a time of war, it was high treason to know about the plot and not inform him.

My country first, always. So why was he keeping silent and praying that Lady Ricinus did not act on her threat? If Rix said nothing, and the threat was discovered, he would also be found guilty of high treason. But informing on his mother would destroy him.

He turned away from the malignly twinkling heatstone. "Tobe, what am I to do about Tali? The chancellor's left me no choice."

"I don't know," said Tobry heavily.

"If he makes a threat, he carries it out. I can't *pretend* to look for Tali. I can't let her escape, and I can't allow you to smuggle her away. Only one thing will satisfy him—that I deliver Tali to him by the night of the Honouring. If I don't, he's going to bring House Ricinus down."

"You have no choice. And neither do I."

Rix did Tobry the honour of not asking what his choice would be. It was better that he did not know. "How can I give her up? She saved our lives."

"I don't suppose he'll do her any real harm," said Tobry, over-casually. "And he does need to know about Cython."

Rix was never sure what Tobry was thinking, as when he had counselled Rix to leave Tali in the enemy's hands but had actually been provoking him to ride to her rescue.

"The chancellor is a vindictive swine. He'll torture it out of her. He'll break her."

"Tali wants to help her country, and a willing prisoner gives far more useful information than can be extracted by torture. She'll be well taken care of, so where's the harm in giving her up?"

"Dammit, I like her."

"So . . . so do I," said Tobry. "But no friendship between you and Tali can equal the bonds of House and family."

"If she were to agree to it there'd be no difficulty," said Rix.

"It would be a neat way out of your moral dilemma."

"Would *you* give her up—if you were me, I mean?"

Again that little pause. "The question isn't relevant. I've no House to protect, nor any family. Why are you so worried about this?"

"The chancellor is a man of his word, but I never said he was a man of honour. It's common knowledge that he despises the Pale."

Tobry sighed. "It's worse than that. I did some checking in the archives yesterday. After House vi Torgrist died out, his ancestors seized most of its estates on a dubious legal claim. They have them still."

"So he has good reason to want her out of the way. If I give her up, I could be collaborating in the doom I divined for her."

"I don't think so," said Tobry.

"Why not?"

"Murder in the dark isn't the chancellor's style. Anyway, since we don't have the faintest idea where Tali's got to, the question is academic."

"There's another thing," said Rix.

"From the grim expression you're wearing, I thought there must have been."

"I lay down a while ago and immediately had another of those ice leviathan nightmares."

"I'm not surprised. The polar ice spreads further north each day, and every day is colder than the one before."

"An early winter is a bitter winter. This nightmare was the strongest I've ever had, as if it had been building up all week, waiting for the right time to get to me." He paused, walked back and forth. "And the voice was back in my head."

"What voice?" said Tobry sharply. "You've never mentioned a *voice* before."

"Too ashamed," said Rix quietly. "And too afraid."

"That *noble* Tobry, fresh from presiding over the ruination of his own house, would judge you?"

Rix flushed. "It seems stupid now, but at the time . . . last week seems like half a lifetime ago."

"How long have you been hearing the voice?"

"Years and years, and it's getting stronger all the time."

"What does it say?"

"I can never remember the words. But . . . " The shame was burning him. And the terror that it might come true. Rix choked, then gasped out, "It's always got to do with *taking her down and cutting it out*."

"Taking who down?"

"Her. Just *her*. But it's obvious, isn't it?"

"It's beginning to look that way," Tobry said grimly. "Cutting what out?"

"I'm not sure it's ever been specified." Rix looked down at his big hands as if expecting to see blood there. "I feel sick."

He brought out the whited-out sketch and perched it on its easel.

"I can see every line and dab in my mind's eye," said Tobry. "I dare say you can, too."

They stared at the blank surface.

"I can't stop seeing it," said Rix. "No need to wonder who the faceless man is at the end of the bench, then."

Tobry attempted to speak but nothing came out.

"It's me," said Rix. "I've divined myself murdering Tali."

Tobry stirred, as though to deny it, but again failed to speak.

"Do you wonder that I think I'm going mad?" said Rix.

"You're not going mad."

"But you can't gainsay what I've divined, can you?"

"It's just a bloody sketch, Rix!" snapped Tobry. "We all think bad thoughts from time to time, but we don't carry them out."

"Then why do I feel so sick inside? Every nightmare tells me that I've committed some atrocity and I'm going to do it again."

"Have you committed any atrocities lately?"

"I don't know," Rix cried out. "But I've felt this way for years, and it's getting worse. It can't come out of nowhere, can it?"

Tobry shrugged and avoided his eye. "You wouldn't hurt Tali, or

any woman. You've always looked after the small and the unfortunate. It's preposterous."

"I think so too," said Rix. "There's just one problem."

"What's that?"

"In my nightmares, the voice always beats me."

"It must be the wrythen."

"And it always forces me to do what it wants."

"Then you'd better do the sketch again," said Tobry. "But this
time, don't let the divination control you—you've got to control
it."

"What if I can't?"

CHAPTER 70

The boy's memories hidden inside Rix were Tali's most
important line of evidence. She remembered the horror in his
eyes and the vomit splattered down his front. He might have followed the killers to the cellar in innocent curiosity. Then, when
they began their terrible work, he would have been afraid to move
in case they killed him too. No wonder he had blocked everything
out.

After groping her way around under the tub she discovered
rungs running down a round shaft. Should she go down, or back?
She needed to question Rix before it was too late, but the chancellor's searchers could still be here. Tali went down.

After descending twenty-four rungs she came to a side passage
that smelled of stale sweat, bad food and damp bedding. Thinking
that it probably led to servant's quarters, she continued past and
shortly encountered a cross tunnel. To the right, an air current carried a hint of cinnamon and musk that reminded her of the
chancellor. Not that way.

The other direction smelled of mouldering stone. No glimmer
of light penetrated these spaces but Tali's nose and fingers could

read stone in ways no one from the surface could understand, and this stone spoke of great age. She must be in the ancient, inner section of the palace, perhaps within one of its walls.

She climbed several steps, went along a horizontal passage and after some minutes caught a strong, ointment odour mixed with the reek of spilled wine and spirits—Lord Ricinus. She was feeling along the wall when her fingers encountered a small round plug standing proud of the surface. She wiggled it out and a thread-like beam shone onto her forehead—a peephole.

Going up on tiptoes, she peered into a large chamber decorated with arrays of spears, swords and shields, and other weapons. A coloured map of Hightspall covered one wall. Another held the stuffed heads of a great boar, several kinds of deer, one with curly horns, and other animals not covered in her Cythonian education. Clearly, a man's room.

The centre contained a canopied bed so huge it would have taken four housemaids to change the linen. Lord Ricinus lay in the middle, head bandaged. He was paler than before, save for his nose, which glowed as if he had a lighted candle up each nostril.

Did he not share a bed with his wife? On Genry's visits home, he and Tali's mother had clung together so desperately that a piece of paper could not have been slipped between them. But who would want to spend the night with such a disgusting creature as Lord Ricinus?

She continued and discovered other peepholes, and through the third saw Lady Ricinus. It had to be her; the thin-lipped, sharp-chinned, heavily powdered face matched the voice perfectly, and so did the talon-like red nails.

She was sitting at a small, curvy-legged desk, writing a series of notes. Each was inserted in an envelope along with some small coins that had the appearance of gold, and the envelope sealed with hot black wax.

Was she settling wages? More likely, judging by the conversation Tali had overheard earlier, Lady Ricinus was paying bribes. She stacked the letters and handed them to a uniformed orderly, who gave them to a messenger with instructions Tali did not hear.

Lady Ricinus locked a strongbox beside her desk and an orderly took it away. Now she stood up, grimaced as though she had to do something distasteful and left the room.

Was she going to see Lord Ricinus? Tali went back to his peephole. Shortly Lady Ricinus came across to the bed and drew up a chair.

"Ricinus?"

He did not move.

She shook him by the shoulder, her mouth tight. "Ricinus, I know you're awake."

He sat up. Apart from the bandage around his head, she saw no evidence that either last night's drunkenness, or the blow to the head, troubled him.

"Then get me a drink," said Lord Ricinus.

She took a small bottle from her bag and handed it to him. He sank the lot in one gulp and tossed the bottle over the end of the bed. "What do you want?"

"Lord . . . Ricinus . . . we're in trouble."

"We, or *you*?"

"The chancellor has demanded the Pale girl and we can't find her."

"So?"

"Ricinus, I . . . I need your help." She stretched out a bony hand, drew back, reached out again and took his. He did not look at her, but he did not pull away either.

"First time for everything," said Ricinus. "What have you done this time?"

"I—I—" She bit her lip, rubbed her free hand over her face. "I may have overreached myself."

Ricinus's mouth twisted into a gleeful grin. "Can my all-commanding lady be admitting a mistake?"

"I've only ever had the interests of this House at heart."

"The only interests you advance are your own."

"But to rise to the First Circle—"

"I never wanted to rise."

"And seldom did!" she snapped.

"If you want a favour, Lady Ricinus, you've an odd way of asking for it."

She pasted on a vulture's smile. "Ricinus, my lord, I went too far. I tried to bribe the chancellor, but it appears he's incorruptible and now—"

He snorted. "You went about it the wrong way, *my lady*. Your lack of breeding shows. You insulted him and he wants revenge."

"How—how do you know?"

"I talk to people while I'm drinking."

"My Lord, he says that, despite your magnificent gift of the Third Army, he's going to bring us down unless we hand over the Pale girl. And we can't find her."

"Who is she, anyway?"

Lady Ricinus did not speak at once. Tali gained the impression that she was concealing something from him. "Just a slave who got out of Cython."

"No ordinary Pale, then. What does she want?"

"To get her claws into Rixium, of course. The fool smiled at her, and now she's seen what he's worth she won't let go."

You bitch, thought Tali. Is there no lie you won't tell, no truth you won't twist to your vicious ends?

"Her knowledge of Cython will be worth a fortune," Lord Ricinus said thoughtfully.

"The chancellor won't pay. He wants to get her for nothing and take all the profit for himself."

"He always was a greedy swine."

Lady Ricinus swallowed, then laid a hand on his arm. "Ricinus . . . I've been a fool."

"What else have you done?"

"I—I made threats against his life."

"You what?"

"I was driven beyond forbearance. I snapped."

"Threats to his face?" growled Lord Ricinus. "I can't do anything about that, Lady. It's high treason just to know about it." He inspected her pallid face. Upwelling sweat was cracking her caked make-up from beneath. "No, if you had, you'd be swinging from the front gates by now with your belly opened and your entrails dangling out your mean little mouth."

"I made the threat to Rixium after the chancellor left, but he'll find out. Rixium can be indiscreet." She clutched at Lord Ricinus with both hands. "You must speak to him, Lord. Make sure he tells no one, especially not Lagger."

"You do realise that if Rix doesn't speak up, he's guilty of high treason as well?"

She reeled backwards. "No!"

"You haven't just put our house at risk, but its whole future. If this comes out, Rix dies a traitor's death as well."

"He won't speak. He won't betray his family."

"Won't he? What if he puts country above house? Or his survival above ours?" Lord Ricinus snapped his fingers. "Drink!"

She handed him another bottle. She already had it in her hand.

He drained half of it. "You stupid sow, this changes everything. No leader can tolerate being threatened in wartime. He'll hang us all and burn the palace to the ground. Even if we could give him the Pale, he'd erase House Ricinus to make sure."

"What if he were no longer chancellor?"

He stared up at the ceiling for a minute or two, then turned to her. "What are you on about?"

The backs of Tali's hands prickled. What was Lady Ricinus saying?

"I'm saying that we make good on my threat and take all the profit for ourselves."

He inspected her through the empty half of the bottle. "You've dealt us into a deadly game, Lady Ricinus." He considered. "On the one hand, ruin. On the other, should the chancellor be replaced by someone manageable, we make a majestic profit from selling the Pale girl to our generals."

"If we *rented* her knowledge of Cython to the generals for the duration of the war," said Lady Ricinus slyly, "we might treble our profit and retain the asset."

"Then redouble that profit in the coming peace—if we win the war." He scratched his chin. "But how to topple the chancellor in wartime? He's respected as much as he's feared. No one would support us."

"Toppling him is beyond us," Lady Ricinus said flatly. "But there's another way . . ."

He sat upright, staring at her. "You're not suggesting we have him assassinated? No, I won't have it."

It was cold in the passage but Tali was drenched in sweat and her knees were giving out. Monstrous woman, surely she could not be serious. But she was.

"Once he hears about my foolish threat," said Lady Ricinus, "he'll surround himself with guards and destroy us. It's us or him, Lord. There's no choice."

"You're a fool, Lady Ricinus," he said savagely. "Gods, how I regret the day I made you my wife."

To Tali's surprise, Lady Ricinus bent her head, deferring to him.

"You're right, I suppose," he went on. "Your folly has left us with no choice."

"Are we in agreement, Lord Ricinus?"

"I believe we are, Lady Ricinus. The chancellor has to die." He stared at her. "Are you in contact with our mutual friend?"

"I—I can be," said Lady Ricinus. "I'll make the arrangements."

"Do so, and we may yet survive."

"It will be costly," she said, biting her lip.

"Then you'd better find the Pale before the chancellor does. And before you make any deals, make sure of the price you're getting for her."

"I will, the instant I find her."

Once she had gone, Tali reinserted the plug and sat down in the darkness. Lady Ricinus must know that the palace had secret passages, and she had hundreds of servants at her disposal. They would soon find her, for wherever Tali went she left clear tracks in the thick dust. She shuddered at the thought of falling into Lady Ricinus's hands; she would be merciless.

What to do? She should tell Rix about his parents' high treason, immediately. It was his right to know, but that would both endanger him and put him in an impossible position. If he said nothing and the chancellor found out, Rix would be condemned just as much as Lord and Lady Ricinus. But if he betrayed them ... Tali did not see how a loyal son like Rix could survive it.

She could not tell him, though that meant that she had to act directly, and soon. Was saving the chancellor's life more urgent than her own quest? He was a calculating man who appeared to have ill intentions towards her, but could she stand by and allow him to be assassinated in the middle of a war? To lose Hightspall's leader at such a time would be devastating. She could not allow it.

Besides, the chancellor's spectible was her one hope of locating the buried magery she needed before she could go after the wrythen. Tali discounted that the spectible no longer worked. That could be a lie put out to deter thieves. She had to get it.

So: she must warn the chancellor about the threat on his life, urgently. She also needed to stay close to Rix, praying that his cellar sketch was not a divination of her own death but a record of her mother's that would reveal his lost memories of the murder. She had to protect herself from the wrythen's minions, who could locate her if her guard relaxed and she allowed the *call* out, and from the killers who were also hunting her.

And not least she had to rescue Rannilt. The poor child must be in agony.

The most urgent roads led to the chancellor, but how was she to get into the most closely guarded building in Hightspall? Remembering that whiff of cinnamon and musk she had caught earlier, Tali smiled. She would go via paths that any normal Hightspaller would find impossible. To a Pale brought up in the maze that was Cython, navigating the labyrinth of tunnels, caves, shafts and passages beneath this part of old Caulderon would be no harder than finding the way through the city streets.

She would go down to the tunnels and sniff her way in.

But first she had to talk to Rix and Tobry.

CHAPTER 71

"What about this nose?" Rix said exhaustedly when Tobry came up. He had redone the purple-veined bulb a dozen times but could not get it right.

"I don't care," snapped Tobry, who was ghostly pale. "Make it a bunch of grapes, a turnip, a crystal ball—anything as long as it doesn't look like a drunkard's todger."

Rix laid his brush down. "What's the matter with you today?"

"I'm so worried about Tali I can't think."

"I'm worried too, but I've got to get this done."

Tobry did not reply.

"You have to help me, Tobe. I can't do this by myself."

Tobry checked the nose, cursorily, and sat down. "It's beautiful. Perfect."

"I don't believe you," Rix fretted.

"Just finish the damn portrait. At this stage, it doesn't matter what his nose looks like as long as he's got one."

"There is such a thing as artistic integrity."

Tobry jumped up and took him by the shirt front. "Have you been out today?"

"I'm not allowed out."

"Would you like a report from the front?"

"No, but I'm sure you're going to give me one."

"You'd better sit down."

"I don't want to sit down."

Tobry picked him up by the shirt front and the belt of his kilt and threw him two yards onto the couch, which skidded backwards under his weight until it hit the wall.

"I've changed my mind," said Rix. "I'll sit. Spit it out, then."

"I'll start at the furthest distance and work in. Firstly, our forces have been attacked *and beaten* in Grume, Flekkitt, Ribrose and Tydderley. Oh, and the garrison at Plegm has been wiped out to the last man and the regimental donkey."

"That's bad," said Rix.

"Secondly, a thousand Cythonians have swarmed up from a rat hole at Tumulus Town—"

"Never heard of it."

"Yes, you have. The chancellor told you about the attack there."

"Oh," said Rix, rubbing his temples. "Right. Where is Tumulus Town?"

"It's a scabrous suburb on the south-east side of Caulderon. Thousands of tiny shanties, hundreds of alleys—"

"Why would they attack there?"

"It's a strategic hillside—the perfect base for an attack on the rest of the city. They already hold thirty streets, they've driven out everyone who could run and probably slaughtered those who could not, and it'll take us five times their number to gouge them out. And the enemy are gathering. At least thirty thousand of them."

Far more than all the armies in Caulderon. Rix was silent, shaken.

"Then," Tobry went on, "there's the outbreak of dead-lung in the villages near Plegm, and all around the Rat Hole." Rix sat upright, staring at him. "What, you hadn't heard about that?"

"I told you . . ." said Rix.

"You can imagine who's being blamed for it," said Tobry. "The treacherous Pale. If Tali is seen outside, she's likely to be killed on sight."

Rix put his head in his own hands. "Is that all?"

"I've hardly started. Packs of jackal shifters have attacked dozens of villages that we know of, and doubtless many more where no one survived to tell about it. They go for the children first. It's horrible, Rix. Unbearable to see what they do to them—" Tobry's voice cracked.

Rix shivered. Nimry, Tobry's little brother, had been killed by a jackal shifter and Tobry had never got over it.

"A few have even been seen in Caulderon," Tobry went on, blank-faced, "though the Gods know how they got here."

"I suppose the mushroom eaters sent them up through their secret tunnels."

"And there was an attack on the gates of Palace Ricinus, just hours after the chancellor left."

Rix leapt up. "The enemy, here? Why wasn't I told?"

Tobry lowered his voice. "It wasn't the enemy. The people from Tumbrel Town next door were rioting. They're calling for a revolution and an end to the rotten system run by the greedy noble houses."

"Revolution?" whispered Rix. "When we're at war? What's Hightspall coming to?"

"A question that might have been better asked before things came to this state," said Tobry. "Their leaders were taken and are being tortured; a hundred of the rabble were executed and the rest driven off. The disgraceful business is being hushed up, though that's hardly the end of it. They seem to think that the nobility are using them as a wall between themselves and the enemy. Which they are. And ... "

"What?"

"It seems as though most of the trouble is focused on Palace Ricinus."

Rix's gaze fell on the portrait and his father's eyes were on him. He kicked the easel, sending it skidding around until the accusing eyes faced away.

"I should be out there, fighting. Why am I stuck here with this monstrosity?"

"Because it's necessary to the survival of the family," said Tobry. "And you don't have an heir."

"Tell Mother to pick a wife for me," Rix said recklessly. "I'll marry her now and be out defending the walls in the morning."

"Even for a scion of one of the noble houses, that seems an unsound basis for matrimony."

"What the hell would you know about it?"

"You're right," said Tobry. "What would I know about anything?" He walked to the top of the stairs then came back. "If you're done with the portrait for now, why don't you have another go at the sketch?"

"I'm afraid to. I can't face any more bad news."

"If you are divining Tali's future, we need to know now."

"What if I make it worse?"

"Get on with it, damn you."

Rix sketched the windowless chamber on the whited-out canvas, clenching his jaw as he tried to reproduce what had always previously been blind inspiration; clenching so hard that his teeth began to ache. It took but thirty brushstrokes to recreate the last one, exactly as before. It was always easy to get back to the previous sketch, but every stroke after that was agony.

He stared at the two standing figures at the end of the bench as if he could force their faces and identities onto the canvas, but nothing came.

"They're mocking me, Tobe. They know I know, but they won't let me remember. Do you think if I got drunk –?"

"With the enemy on all sides and rebellion at the palace gates, that would be a mortally bad idea."

Rix slumped down, the brush smearing paint across his kilt.

Tobry walked back and forth in front of the sketch. "I'd swear that's Tali on the bench, and she looks dead. But what have those faceless figures to do with it? Did they kill her, or are they trying to save her?"

Without realising he was doing it, he looked at Rix, consideringly.

It was as if Tobry had punched him in the mouth. *My oldest friend, who knows me better than anyone and has always supported me, thinks I'm going to murder the only woman I've ever been friends with.*

Rix buried his head in his hands. And what if he was? What if, as the nightmares whispered, he'd already done something as bad, or worse? He had never wanted a drink more. He wanted to get blind drunk—no, he wanted to *be* blind drunk, instantly, and never sober up. He wanted . . .

I will not become my father. I will not!

Tobry was walking back and forth in front of the sketch. Then he stopped. "What's that in the woman's hand?"

"Where?" Rix said without raising his head.

"There. Hanging down. Looks like a pair of tongs."

Rix went to see, and of its own volition his hand rose to the canvas, the brush making a series of small strokes there. With another brush he touched at the hair of the girl on the black bench, then another couple of dabs at the tongs, before the inspiration went as mysteriously as it had come.

"It's definitely tongs," he said, "and the woman is holding something in them. Something small, round, red."

"Not red," said Tobry, and his eyes were staring again, as if he was looking into his own nightmare. "It's black as a caitsthe's livers. It's just got red on it—"

He walked away, very fast, raking hooked fingers down his cheeks, then ran back and peered at the woman's blonde head. "There's red in her hair, too. Blood."

"Her hair's almost the same shade of blonde as Tali's," said Rix. "It's got to be her."

Pain spiked his chest. Was she going to die because his sketch had forecast her death? Why had he done the sketch anyway? Had the voice in his nightmares ordered him to paint it because sometimes Rix's paintings came true? Was it fixing him onto an immoveable path that led to him killing Tali?

"But why the tongs?" said Tobry. "And—what's that in them?"

"The red on that black marble is her blood," said Rix. "Are they trying to put it into her head?"

Tobry blanched and whispered, "No!"

"Tobe?" cried Rix.

Tobry swallowed, let out a parched croak, then gasped, "Have you heard of ebony pearls?"

Rix studied the black, red-flecked object in the tongs. "No."

"I think that's one."

"What are they?"

"No one knows much about them, but there are nasty rumours . . . "

"For the Gods' sakes, spit it out."

"They're the most powerfully enchanted objects ever discovered and they have a dreadful origin. They're incredibly dangerous—any non-adept who touches one with bare skin is liable to die most unpleasantly. And they're so priceless, I doubt that the chief magian has ever seen one."

Rix walked around the easel, trying not to look at what he had painted. Finally he said, "Who has?"

"I don't know."

"Then why," said Rix, feeling sick, "are they putting one inside Tali's head?"

CHAPTER 72

"They're not putting it in," Tali said quietly.

Rix spun around. She had climbed the steps and was swaying on her feet. Her pale features were stark, her gold-blonde hair hanging lank as straw.

"I've just remembered—"

She crumpled and was about to tumble backwards down the steps when Rix leapt three yards and caught her. He carried her to the couch, holding her tightly as if it was the only way to save her.

Tobry poured a splash of brandy into a goblet, sat her up and pressed it to her lips.

Tali grimaced, swallowed and looked up. "The woman on the bench isn't me. It's ... it's my mother, ten years ago."

"How do you know?" said Rix, waves of relief sweeping over him. It wasn't a divination at all.

"That's the cellar where she was killed. Mama made me hide, but then they caught her and—they did it."

"You were there?" said Rix. "You saw your poor mother murdered?"

"I told you that already." Tali gave him a peculiar look and took a deep breath, only to shake her head and close her mouth without speaking.

"If you know more—" began Rix.

"Those are my mother's killers, at the end of the bench," she said in a tight, controlled voice. "I was eight. I must have blocked most of it out."

"How could anyone block that out?" said Rix. "I'd remember it to my dying day."

She gave him another strange look. Her arms hung rigidly by her sides and her small fists were knotted. Rix frowned. What was the matter with everyone today?

"The woman told the man to kill me," said Tali, "and he came after me with a knife, but I was too good at hiding."

"What kind of monster would order a child killed?" said Rix, slumping onto the other end of the settee. It was horrible, but nothing to do with him. The relief was dizzying.

"When I saw the new sketch, I remembered the woman ... gouging at Mama's head. She pulled out something round and black with the tongs and ... " Tali frowned, trying to remember. "She put it in something." Tali shuddered. "Then she licked the blood off the tongs, the evil bitch. I remember *that*!"

"It's an ebony pearl," said Rix, haltingly. He felt battered, assaulted. "Your mother was killed for it."

"So that's what the wrythen wants." Tali rubbed the top of her head as if to feel a lump through the skull. "Four of my ancestors have died with their heads opened. Four pearls have been taken already, and I'm to provide the fifth."

"The master pearl," said Tobry.

"What did you say?" cried Tali.

"From what I've read about them, each pearl is different from the one before. And stronger. And the fifth pearl is the master. It can be used to unite the others, and command them—assuming one is strong enough to withstand it."

"The master pearl," said Tali with dawning hope. "He wants *my* pearl."

"Kirikay!" Rix said softly.

"Where did that come from?" said Tobry.

"I heard it when you were unconscious in the cave," said Rix. "As the caitsthe died, it reached out towards the wrythen, saying, 'Kirikay, Kirikay'."

Tali started. "Not Kirikay, *Khirrik-ai*. It's the Cythonians' familiar name for their last and most beloved king—King Lyf."

"The oath-breaker who started the war," snapped Rix.

"Or a trusting man terribly betrayed by the Five Heroes," said Tobry, "depending on who you listen to."

"Why was he their last king?" said Rix. "You'd think that, with a war to fight—"

"He disappeared and was never found. Without a body, Lyf could not be given the rituals that allowed their sacred king-magery to separate from the king's soul before it passed on, down through the Abysm. And without receiving that king-magery, no new king or queen could ever be crowned. That must be why the Cythonians are ruled by matriarchs."

"Khirrik-ai doesn't have to mean Lyf, though," said Rix. "The name could mean any number of people."

Tobry shook his head. "Every king and ruling queen had a different name. They never re-used them, and neither were they bestowed on commoners. It must be Lyf."

"So your wrythen, and my enemy, is Lyf's ghost," said Tali.

"A wrythen is far more than a ghost," said Tobry. "It has a strong hold on life."

"He's partly solid, too," said Rix. "I felt it when I put my blade through the bastard."

"To burn through Tinyhead's skull from a distance, and nearly possess me," said Tobry, "Lyf's no empty spirit. He's got real power."

"Where would he get it after two thousand years?" said Rix.

"He could be a psychic vampire, stealing the life force of anyone venturing inside his caverns."

"It explains why he's attacking my family," mused Tali. "Lyf must have discovered that certain women of my line were forming ebony pearls, and he wants them for their power. And now he needs the master pearl, my pearl, to unite and control them."

"But your mother wasn't killed by a wrythen," said Rix, staring at the sketch. "This pearl was taken by real people, so who are they?"

"I don't know. They were masked."

"Lyf's after me too, because I used the titane sword on him in the caverns. *Traitor's blade*," he called it. "*Liar's blade. Oathbreaker's blade*—"He broke off, staring.

"Why does Lyf hate the sword?" said Tali.

"I don't know that either," said Rix. "But I'll bet it's got something to do with the inscription."

"We'd better find out who owned it when Lyf was alive." Tobry's eyes narrowed. "What were you going to say about the Oathbreaker's Blade?"

"Lyf knew me," Rix said slowly. "He said, *I have not seen you since you were a boy.* And later he said, *You belong to me.* He told me to put the sword down, and I started to obey. I had to fight hard to stop myself."

"I wish you'd told me this before," said Tobry. "Lyf must be the presence in your nightmares."

"But why choose me, out of all the people in Hightspall?" said Rix. "No one has less magery than I do."

Tobry shrugged. "It beggars belief that all this isn't connected. And it explains why you keep imagining the murder scene. He's putting it into your head."

"Not all of it," said Tali, who was tense as wire.

"How do you mean?" said Rix, frowning.

"You were there," she said, almost inaudibly.

"What?" Rix was not sure he had heard her correctly.

"You were there!" she shouted, her voice cracking. "In the cellar. As a boy. Just after Mama was killed."

"No," cried Rix, a cry of pain because he recognised the truth in her voice. "No, it's not possible."

"I saw you."

"Saw what?" The horror swelled like one of his nightmares. *"What did I do?"*

"You were wearing a plum-coloured velvet coat with gold buttons. An emerald kilt. Black shoes with shiny buckles. You'd thrown up all down your front. *And you had blood on your hands.*"

Tobry was staring at her, mouth agape. Then he turned to Rix and said stiffly, "Is this true?"

Rix felt like a prisoner accused of a terrible crime and afraid that, in some madness, he might have done it. "I've never seen the cellar before."

"But you lost a month of your life when you had the fever," said Tobry. "Ten years ago—at the time when Tali's mother was murdered. The nightmares began after that, and the voice telling you that you'd done something dreadful. Lyf's voice!"

"Rix had nothing to do with Mama's death," said Tali.

"Then what are you accusing him of?" said Tobry furiously.

"I'm not accusing you of anything, Rix," she said, taking his trembling fist in both hands.

He put his other hand over hers, clinging to her as if she was the only person who could save him. "What are you saying?"

Tali was staring into his eyes, her hands giving his little shakes as she strained to remember. "I think something went wrong for Lyf when my mother was killed . . . "

She seemed to be looking to the sketch for inspiration.

"Yes," she went on, "Lyf's face was carved into the end wall of the cellar . . . and yellow moved in his eyes . . . and . . . and there was a hand, a foggy hand reaching out towards the woman who'd taken Mama's pearl . . . but there came a flash from behind a pile of barrels—even as a child I knew it was magery—and the hand recoiled . . . and the woman licked Mama's blood off the tongs."

She went so pale that Rix was sure she was going to faint. He tried to digest what she had said, but could not get past the horror of the scene he could not remember yet could imagine perfectly.

Tobry let his breath out in a gust. "So the killers stole the pearl Lyf was after."

Suddenly Tali understood what the triple call, *di-DA-doh*, really meant. "The pearls call out to one another, and three of them always call together, *di-DA-doh*. And the call is always close—in Caulderon."

"Therefore the killers must have stolen three pearls," said Tobry, "and Lyf only has one. That's why he's so enraged, so desperate to get yours. With the master pearl, he may be able to command the stolen ones."

"There's more," said Tali to Rix. "When you came out from behind those barrels, there on the left, I saw a faint pink aura around you—"

"I don't have any magery," said Rix, trying to deny what she was saying.

"I knew it even then," said Tali, "but the aura was definitely there."

"What if the killers put a blocking charm on you?" Tobry said to Rix.

"Why would they?" said Rix, pulling free and burying his face in his hands. He wanted to scream.

"It could have been designed to go off when Lyf appeared, to stop him getting the pearl. The charm would have been painful—perhaps that's why you've always been afraid of magery."

"I repeat, *why?*" Rix's voice was muffled by his hands. "Why was I there at all? Such a spell could have been put on any object in the cellar. Why put it on me?"

"I haven't the faintest idea," said Tobry.

"Lyf blames you for him losing the last pearl," said Tali. "That must be why he's sending you nightmares."

Rix felt as though he was trapped under a weighted shroud, screaming with claustrophobia. Why had be been there? Why put a spell on him? *Why, why, why?* The shroud kept tightening around him, suffocating him, and he could not heave it off.

"Rix?" Tali said softly.

He did not reply. Could not.

"Rix?"

"Yes?"

She pulled his hands away. "I've got to know what you saw that day. Did you see the killers' faces?"

"This is all I know." Rix swiped at the sketch. "And I've had to fight for days to get it."

There was a long silence.

"What if it represents both the past and the future?" said Tobry. "Such symmetry might appeal to a wrythen two thousand years old. What if the sketch depicts both Iusia's murder, *and* Tali's?"

No, Rix thought. I don't believe it. I can't accept it. I won't do it. *No, no, no!*

"So that's what the nightmares are all about," said Tobry. "After Lyf was robbed of your mother's pearl, he chose you, Rix, *because* you have no magery. That's what it's all about—he means you to kill Tali and take her ebony pearl for him."

The black shroud tightened until Rix could hardly breathe. "What am I supposed to do?" he said, gasping for air. He felt the way Tali must have done in the water: overcome by panic, helpless, drowning. But there was no one to come to his rescue.

"Do the sketch again, and finish it. But this time, *you* have to control the divination."

"What if I can't?"

"Tali, I think—" Tobry looked around sharply. "Where's Tali?"

Rix knew he should go after her. She must be just as traumatised as he was, and the best way to deal with it was to talk everything through with her, but he was drained to the last drop.

"She can take care of herself," he said in a faded croak.

"Not in the state she's in. She's bound to do something reckless."

Rix raised a boneless hand and let it fall.

"Come with me," said Tobry. "We've got to find her."

"Tobe, I've got nothing left. And I've got the stinking portrait to finish."

Rix flopped onto the settee and lay there, staring up at the timbered ceiling.

Tobry gave him a look of deep disgust and went out.

Rix closed his eyes, but could not rid himself of the scene in the cellar, and the mental image of himself at the end of the bench, eyes wide with horror as he cut the pearl out of Tali's head.

CHAPTER 73

Every shape in the chancellor's palace was curved and bulbous, like intestines herniating through muscle walls, and the only colour was the red of curdled blood. It made Tali's stomach churn and her thigh throb. Even the air felt clotted; it tugged at her as she moved, as if she were trapped in a gigantic, pumped-up liver.

The colour sharpened her wrathful mood. How dare Lyf abuse her family so? How dare he bring them to such brutal ends, simply to steal their pearls? And how dare he manipulate Rix so cruelly?

Lyf must have been sending Rix the nightmares for ten years, whispering the lies that had made the boy think he had committed some hideous crime. Lyf had to pay, and she was the only person who could do it. But not without magery, and for that she needed the spectible. It was the one thing that could protect her now.

It wasn't the only reason she'd fled Palace Ricinus, though. What if Lyf succeeded with Rix? She had to get away from him, just in case.

Getting into the chancellor's palace had been the easy part—for an underground dweller, at least—but where to look? The shapes of the rooms and halls confused the eye and dulled the wits. It was hard to tell whether she was seeing a place for the first time, or the tenth.

She edged along a sinuous hall decorated with unnerving sculptures and paintings. Some were just gaunt shapes, pared almost to nothing, others so bulbous that they appeared to extend into other dimensions, and all were warped or twisted. What kind of a man filled his palace with such oddities?

Ignore them. Concentrate. Lady Ricinus's hired killer might already be stalking the chancellor, and the Cythonians could attack at any time. She had to find the spectible, uncover her magery, rescue Rannilt and leave a warning about the threat on the chancellor's life. Then, go after Lyf.

Ahead, two servants turned into the corridor, chatting as they walked. Tali pushed back against the sinuous wall, which was as warm as living flesh, and rubbed her slave mark. *Don't see me. Turn away.* They did not turn aside, and it was impossible that they would not see her pale outline against the red wall. *Look past me. I'm not here.*

One woman was a tall, slender redhead, the other small and curvaceous, dark of skin and hair and eye, and both were remarkably pretty. Every servant in the chancellor's palace was young, attractive and female. What kind of a man was he? Tobry had mentioned unnatural appetites, and if the chancellor caught her here . . .

"Has he come after you yet?" said the small servant.

"Not so much as a sidelong glance," replied the redhead, with a regret-steeped sigh. She stopped at a cross-corridor only a few yards ahead.

"Me either," said the small woman. "Mother will be furious. I'm the last hope of our family and it cost a fortune in bribes to get me a place here. If it's all been wasted, I don't know how I'm going to tell her."

"How could he not like you?" said the redhead. "Your face and figure are perfect; you're clever, but not too clever ... "

"Do you think he inclines the other way?"

"If he does, why surround himself with women? There's not a single man in his palace."

Heaving another sigh, the redhead turned down the other corridor. The small, dark woman came on.

Don't see me.

She passed Tali only a yard away and, though she must have been visible from the corner of an eye, the woman kept going and disappeared around the next corner. I've still got it, Tali thought. I can still hide in plain view, better than anyone.

Shortly, she caught a faint scent of the grubby child she had held in her arms for hours as they escaped to Caulderon. Rannilt! Her scent was coming from a door to the left.

Tali poked her finger into the oval catch, flicked upwards and it opened, revealing a large, bi-lobed chamber like two fused circles. The right-hand lobe was half filled by a curved table of dark red wood polished to a mirror shine. A series of scalloped shelves, partly in shadow, curved around the walls behind the table.

In the centre of the other lobe, scattering dirt onto pink granite flag-stones, stood a battered set of wooden punishment stocks such as Tali had seen several times in the ride through Caulderon. Dirty hands and feet protruding through them belonged to Rannilt, who was fast asleep and apparently unharmed, though so pale, so wan. And no wonder, after finding Luzia bloodily murdered.

Tali rubbed her eyes, momentarily overcome. "Rannilt," she whispered, gently shaking her. "Wake up."

Rannilt slept on. Was she drugged or bespelled? Her breathing was strong and, when Tali pushed her eyelids back, her pupils weren't dilated. Tali was looking for a way to unlock the stocks when an amused voice spoke behind her.

"I confess myself disappointed, Lady vi Torgrist."

She whirled. A small man sat in the shadows in the far corner, high-heeled boots up on the table. His crimson pantaloons were patterned with sequins, the lurid yellow velvet coat had ruby buttons and the cravat was purple. But the chancellor's commanding voice did not fit—that hollow chest should have supported no more than a breathless whine. Tali reminded herself that he was a brilliant and powerful man, and cunning too. And he would have guards everywhere.

"Why?" she said warily.

"I never thought you'd walk into such an obvious trap. I don't know that I can use you after all."

"Good! Then I'm taking Rannilt with me," said Tali, though she had no idea if she was ever getting out of here. Surreptitiously, she felt along the top of the stocks, found the catch, and pulled. "I trust you're done with her?"

"I could be persuaded to give her up as an exchange."

"For me."

"Why do you think I lured you here?"

"You have an over-healthy ego, sir," she said in her best Lady vi Torgrist voice.

He chuckled. "I'm chancellor," he said, as though that were answer enough. "The best hope of my people in this dire war."

"And I love my country and want to help," she said passionately. "But I don't know anything about the enemy's alchymical weapons."

"I didn't ask you about their weapons," he said softly. "Approach the table."

She did so, trying not to creep, until she was brought up by its curved edge. The chancellor frightened her more than Lady Ricinus. Everyone said how ruthless he was, and he controlled a nation. What did he want? She felt that he was looking inside her, reading her strengths, weaknesses, capabilities and potential, and judging how he could use her. She squirmed.

"It's said you claim that the Pale are slaves, not traitors," he said lazily.

"It's said you're a clever man!" she snapped.

He quirked a pencilled eyebrow.

"Only a fool would believe that absurd lie about us. And you're not a fool, Lord."

"What lie?"

"That a group of noble child hostages would go over to the enemy."

"Hostages, if held long enough, often end up taking the side of their captors."

He said it as a fact known to all, not trying to convince her. Tali felt the ground shifting beneath her feet.

"Not us! All our tales say the same thing, and so do the enemy's. They often gloat about it."

"What tales?"

"That one hundred and forty-four children, from the noblest families in Hightspall, were given up to the enemy as hostages a thousand years ago—and never ransomed!"

"All traitors seek to justify their betrayal."

"Hightspall abandoned its children to a thousand years of slavery. Why?" she said furiously, leaning so hard into the table edge that it was bruising her.

"If it did, it's not in any history I've read."

"They would have covered it up!" she cried. "Then justified *their* betrayal, the mealy-mouthed hypocrites."

Her passion seemed to amuse him. "If they did, how can it be proved after so long?"

"There must be letters, reports, all manner of documents in the city archives. You'll find them if you bother to look."

"I don't have time. I've a war to prosecute, one we're losing badly."

That shook her. Things must be really bad if he was prepared to admit it. She considered the man. Pleas for justice would never move him, but self-interest might. "There are eighty-five thousand Pale, Chancellor."

"So many?" he said, and bright reflections drifted across his eyes.

"And right in the middle of Cython," said Tali, improvising desperately. "If managed well, they might turn the war from the inside."

"Weaponless women and beaten men?" It was almost a sneer, but not quite. Was he giving her the chance to argue her case?

"If you offered them something to fight for, if you gave your word as chancellor that the Pale would be welcomed home and the truth told about their slavery—"

"And their ancestors' property torn from its current owners and bestowed on them?" he said harshly. "Is that why you're really here?"

"Is that why they were never ransomed? So the families would die out and their estates be given to others?"

"I'm losing interest," said the chancellor.

Tali had to make a big concession, or lose. "The Pale must have *some* recompense, Lord. But there can be no justice in taking all from the present to restore to the past."

"Set the lead, then."

"I want House vi Torgrist's plague manor. Nothing else."

"Satisfy me and you will have it. And for the other Pale?"

"A tithe of what they once owned."

He leaned back, the deep little eyes peering into hers. "A tithe divided among so many would hardly amount to a cottage each. How can that satisfy?"

"To a lifelong slave, a cottage is a palace."

"Ah!" he said, smiling. "Just so."

"You agree?" said Tali, amazed. "You give your word?"

"Would you accept it?"

"I'm told you're a man of your word, Lord."

"If only that were all they say about me. Very well, you have my word. And in return, you will do something for me."

"Submit to interrogation about Cython?"

"You'll do that anyway, out of love for your country." He inspected her again, weighing her. "I wonder . . . if there were to be an uprising in Cython—"

Tali had a sudden vision of Mia's beheading and tunnels running with the Pale's blood. What had she done? "But . . . but they're weak, unarmed and cowed. They'd be slaughtered."

The absurd little man sprang up, his nutcracker jaw working, and for the first time she saw the fervour in him.

"I have no time! The enemy are at the gates and my people are being slaughtered right now. Pregnant women! Children! The frail elderly! Cython's chymical weapons and incurable poxes and vile shifters are killing them indiscriminately." His tone moderated; he met her eye. "If the Pale wish to be accepted back as equal citizens, they have to fight. And yes, many will die."

"They can't fight Cython by themselves."

He sat, calm again. "Did I say they would be alone? The uprising must come at the moment we counterattack."

"When will that be?"

"When we understand the enemy's weapons and have developed tactics to defeat them. Months, perhaps years."

"Can Caulderon last that long?"

"Not unless I can pull off some brilliant counterstroke." Again she felt that he was weighing her for a perilous task. "I fear we'll have to abandon Central Hightspall and, in time to come, lead an army back here from over the mountains—if the ice doesn't crush us first. Enough of tomorrow. Why are you really here?"

"I came for Rannilt."

"Or did you come for this?" said the chancellor.

He reached back over his head, plucked something off the lowest of the shelves and sat it on the table. It was an oval frame made from engraved silvery metal, enclosing a sheet of translucent, lustrous black mica. Two knobs spaced across the top of the frame were so worn that the knurling was almost gone.

"This spectible," he said, leaning back with a self-satisfied smile that revealed small, perfect yellow teeth. "That's what you really want."

"How—" Tali's chest was so tight that it was hard to breathe. "How did you know?"

"Lagger may have thought his inquiries were discreet, but if anyone asks about one of the seven devices brought here from Thanneron I *will* hear about it."

"The spectible was brought here?" said Tali. "It's that old?"

"It came on the Second Fleet and it was an old device then. You want it to find your buried magery, I'm told."

There was no point denying it. "Find it, and free it," said Tali. "Can it do that?"

"It may be able to *find* it, since its purpose was to spy on magians from afar—"

Tali leaned across the table, studying the ancient device. "How?"

"By amplifying the subtle emanations that even the smallest magery creates."

"But if I'm not using my magery, surely it won't be producing any emanations?"

"I wouldn't know," said the chancellor. "I don't have that gift. Besides, the spectible can't liberate your magery. All it does is *see* its emanations. You'll have to find another way to free it, assuming you can get the spectible to see at all. My chief magian says it's long dead."

Yet you've taken the trouble to show it to me, she thought, though you've no time to waste on anything save the war. You must think it can be made to work, and you want me to do something no one else can do. If she could get the spectible to work, and wake the master pearl somehow, then let her enemies tremble.

"I don't know another way to free my magery."

"How did it appear the first time?"

"It was after I smashed a sunstone at the Rat Hole." She started.

"What?" said the chancellor.

"There are no sunstones here, but heatstones are stronger. So if I broke a small one—"

"Ingenious."

"Can I try the spectible?"

"You can earn it."

"How?"

He was watching her, his eyes giving nothing away. "Make me an offer."

What did he want? A liaison? The thought was revolting. "It's said you have unnatural appetites ... "

He laughed. "I spread that story myself."

"Why?"

"The weak-minded need something to gossip about. And I like to be underestimated."

"But is it true?"

"You've nothing to fear. In truth, I have no carnal appetites."

"Liar!" she cried. "Your palace is full of beautiful young women. I haven't seen a single man here."

"There are none, save me. Beautiful things are my particular joy, beautiful women most of all. Perhaps I should add you to my collection."

She jumped, cracking her knee on the leg of the table.

He chuckled. "I ask nothing of them save a servant's normal duties. It disappoints a surprising number of fortune seekers. How will you earn the spectible?"

Tali did not like telling tales. It felt underhand and dirty, but what choice did she have? "You said you know everything that goes on in Caulderon."

"Little escapes me."

She took a heavy breath. "Then you'd know about the threat on your life."

His small eyes narrowed. "Threats from fanatics and lunatics are one of the hazards of leadership. I'm well protected."

"Are you protected from a treasonous threat from a powerful family?"

That made him sit up and his nostrils pinch in. "If you know of such a threat, and seek to make capital out of it, you're close to treason yourself."

"I don't like you, Lord," she snapped, "but I will never stand by and allow my sovereign to be assassinated."

The chancellor laughed. "I'm beginning to like *you*, Thalalie vi Torgrist." He pushed the spectible forwards a few inches. "If what you say is true, you shall have it. Who seeks to bring me down?"

"Lady Ricinus."

The smile vanished. "House Ricinus's loyalty is not in question. It has just made Hightspall a mighty gift, one that could save Caulderon."

Tali forced herself to stare into his eyes, hoping he would read the truth there.

"Ricinus is so rich and powerful that even I have to tread carefully," he went on. "Do you realise what they'll do to you, should they hear this allegation? Lady Ricinus will tear out your beating heart and choke you with it."

CHAPTER 74

Lady Ricinus would do it, too. No wickedness was beyond her. Tali's stomach knotted, though not only from fear. If Rix discovered that she had informed on his parents it would destroy her friendship with him and Tobry. Well, she had started out alone; she would finish it alone.

"I've so many enemies," she said, trying to pretend indifference, "I don't see that one more matters."

"This one does." The chancellor steepled his fingers, which were as soft and smooth as a noble lady's, though somewhat twisted, and stared at her over the tips. "Your evidence had better be good."

She related how she had been hiding under Rix's tub while the chancellor had given that ultimatum, and what Lady Ricinus had said afterwards.

"The viper!" he hissed. "I've always detested her. And Rixium heard this threat?"

"I—I can't say." She had not expected the question and knew her stumbling reply had betrayed him.

"Of course you can. You're trying to protect him and it won't work." He met her eyes. "If he doesn't inform me of this threat, he's also guilty of treason and must suffer a traitor's death."

"But you know, now," cried Tali.

"Rixium doesn't know I know."

"Why does he have to pay? He's always defended you."

"In war, a leader has to know who he can rely on, and whom will betray him wilfully—or by omission. In war, one's country must always come before one's family. Let him stew on that conflict." His laughter was like a set of false teeth chattering on a draining board.

"He's a good man!"

"And I'm a swine who'll enjoy seeing him squirm," said the

chancellor. "But a tough swine, just what our country needs. What else do you allege Lady Ricinus said?"

Tali related the conversation she had overheard with Lord and Lady Ricinus through the peephole, and as she spoke, the chancellor's thin face set in ever grimmer lines. He questioned her about every detail, then leaned back and studied his fingers.

"The question is, do I believe you?"

Tali felt the blood drain from her face. She had not considered that, either.

"A despicable Pale," he went on, "a habitual liar desperate to save herself, might make up false accusations against one of our noblest families. Accusations so incredible that no one could believe them.

"Should I call Lady Ricinus over and give her the opportunity to defend her house?" he said after a menacing pause. "She's savage in protecting her own. She would tear your face off with her nails."

Tali remembered how red her nails had been, and how sharp.

He looked her up and down. "You're terrified, yet you neither defend yourself nor attack House Ricinus. Why not? You must have heard dirt on the lady of that house—everyone else has."

"I've told you what I overheard," said Tali, fighting to keep her voice steady. "I don't smear my enemies' names."

"I put my boot heel through their teeth," the chancellor said matter-of-factly, "and grind them into the muck until they drown in it."

Again she felt the weight of his regard, as if he were peeling away skin and bone to look inside her head and heart. Nothing could elude him. What was he going to do to her?

"Extraordinary!" He withdrew his boots from the table with a small thump. "I read much falsehood in you—hardly surprising in one who has lived as a slave—yet not an iota in this matter."

"You believe me?"

"Never trusted House Ricinus. The lord's a pig, the lady an adder. There's nothing so foul that she would not do to raise the family higher." His eyes met hers. "And you're not going back to warn them."

Gulp! "Why would I?"

"Because you're friends with Rixium and Tobry, and if they don't tell me about the treason, they'll swing for it."

"But Tobry doesn't know anything about it," she cried, caught off-guard.

"I've never liked the man," said the chancellor chillingly, as though that were reason enough for Tobry to die. "Can't trust a fellow who believes in nothing."

"What are you going to do to Lord and Lady Ricinus?" said Tali, with a kind of fascinated horror.

Again, that malicious smile. This was not a man she would want to make her enemy.

"I'll see their necks settled into the noose, first." The chancellor studied Tali's slender neck in a contemplative way, then called for a large sheet of blank paper, a pencil and a wedge of brown rubber. "Draw me a map of Cython. Mark every tunnel and chamber, and its purpose and use, and everything you know of Cython's defences. Then tell me all about the Cythonians."

"I only know the main level of Cython. I've never been lower down."

"All I ask is what you know. Rannilt has also helped me, and some of the captured enemy will reveal a scrap or two before they die. It should be enough."

"Enough for what?"

He rang the bell and the tall redhead Tali had seen earlier appeared. "Note down everything she says, Verla."

Though Tali could envisage any route she had ever taken through Cython, the underground city proved surprisingly difficult to map. After some hours, and many sheets of paper, she was still ending up with rooms and workshops where she knew they could not be.

"I'm sorry," she said, when her latest sketch showed the eastern edge of the heatstone mine intersecting the straight line of the main floatillery. "The mine should be half a mile this way."

"Note it on the map. My cartographers will sort it after we've tortured enough of the enemy. Describe the kinds of wall carvings in every area—their art may prove more reliable than signposts."

"What are you going to do with all this?" she said at the end, after Verla had gone as silently as she came, without saying a word the whole time.

"That's my business." He met her eyes. "You have done me mighty service today, and I pay my debts." He sent the spectible spinning across the table towards her. "It's yours."

She caught it before it hit her in the belly and felt it with her fingers. The metal was cold; the mica felt warm to the touch.

"How is it used?"

"One puts it across one's eyes and forehead, then turns the knobs until the emanations of magery come into focus."

Tali had no idea what it was supposed to show, but she saw nothing save the lustre of the dark mica and the chancellor's blurred features through it. She slowly turned the knobs. Nothing, nothing, nothing. "You said it's dead."

"So my chief magian says. But Hightspall's magery has dwindled over the centuries and perhaps he lacks the strength to work it." Again it felt as though he was peering into her head. "It's said you have a unique gift."

"Who told you that?" she said sharply.

"One of my rangers caught an eyeless fellow called Wil, a Cythonian seer. Unlike the other prisoners, he was eager to talk. Especially about you."

"Mad Wil," said Tali. "You can't take any notice—"

"Oh, yes I can," he said softly, the gleam back in his eyes. "A mad seer might see more clearly than all one's spies and advisers together. Wil said you're *the one*, and I believe him, because I've also read something rare and wild in you."

Whatever he really wanted of her, she did not like it. She kept turning the knobs until they would go no further, but saw nothing. "What does *the one* mean?"

"The one who changes the future, and not to Cython's advantage. The matriarchs are afraid of Wil's foreseeing, which they call *shillilar*."

She squirmed. Her life was being moved by forces beyond her understanding.

"Years ago they had dozens of little girls killed, to make sure *the one* was dead," said Tali, shivering. "But Wil lied—he told the matriarchs I had black hair and olive skin." She raised her head, looked him in the eye. "What do you want of me?"

"If *I* fail," said the chancellor, "Hightspall will be swept away. And the war's going so disastrously you can't possibly make things worse. Yet if you are *the one* . . . " Tali held her breath, but he shook his head. "I must think on it. Wil says he's been *all the way down*. What does that mean?"

The sudden change of tack was disconcerting. "To the lowest level of Cython?"

"If you don't know, don't guess. What about the Hellish Conduit?"

"I overheard the master chymister mention it once. He said *I'll have to send down the Hellish Conduit for more.*"

"More what?"

"Alkoyl." Tali told him about the young woman whose leg had been eaten away.

"Fascinating," said the chancellor, "though not immediately useful. What's the Engine?"

"Cythonians believe that everything in nature comes from the working of a great machine, at the heart of the world, called the Engine."

"How do you mean?"

"If the Engine gets a wobble, the ground shakes. If it overheats, the Vomits erupt . . . "

"And?" he said when she did not go on.

"They also believe the Engine is fuelled by an unstable cauldron deep in the Earth. And sometimes it blows up. That's all I know."

"It's said that Lake Fumerous fills the chasm where a fourth Vomit blew itself to pieces." He made a dismissing gesture. "How goes the spectible?"

She looked down. "I've turned both knobs as far as they go. Did the chief magian say why it stopped working?"

"He said the *source* it drew from could no longer be reached."

"If a new source could be found, might it work again?" An ebony pearl, perhaps? Careful, don't even think about them here or he'll have the secret out of you—and perhaps the pearl, too.

"Possibly. Hold the first knob steady and turn the other all the way. Then rotate the first knob one notch and the second all the way back, and so on."

She began to do so. Nothing for the first notch, nothing for the second, nothing for the third. Then, as she moved her head from side to side, a pinkish rainbow flashed across the black mica.

"Ah!" said the chancellor.

"You saw it?"

"No, but you did."

"What was it?"

"The emanation of magery from this speaking egg." He picked an oval yellow object, egg-sized, from the shelf behind him. "Abbess Hildy has another. It's how she told me about you, soon after you arrived."

"So the spectible does work."

"It does for you."

But could she use it to locate her own magery? Tali set it down on the table. "What are you going to do with me now?"

"In return for my concession to the Pale you must do me a service—assuming you're a woman of your word?"

Tali swallowed. "I said it, and my word holds." She fought to hold her voice steady. "What must I do?"

"A trifling task." He examined his buffed and manicured nails, drawing out the tension.

"How trifling?" she rasped.

"Before we counterattack, you will return to Cython and rouse the Pale to rebellion."

"No!" She snatched at the table edge for support. "I'm no leader. And the enemy will kill me on sight."

"If you're truly *the one*, you'll find a way."

"And if I'm not, I die an agonising death."

"Thousands of my people have already died such deaths in the war," said the chancellor, "and more fall every minute. Until the enemy is stopped they will continue to die."

"Unless they wipe us out first," said Tali.

His head shot up, the impassive face cracked. She had shocked him. "You think that is their intention? Not just to take back the land, but to erase us from Hightspall forever?"

Tali considered everything she knew about the enemy. "Yes, I believe it is."

He did not speak for a very long time, and when he did, though he fought to control his voice, it had the faintest tremor. "Worse than I had thought; far worse. What can I do?" He thought for a moment. "I have no choice but to go on—and neither do you."

"I'm not up to it, Lord Chancellor."

"Do you imagine you're the only one tormented by self-doubt?"

Had she not seen his anguish a few minutes ago, she would have said he had no demons. Perhaps he was more practised at hiding them. She shook her head.

"A while ago you argued passionately for the Pale. You must know what the enemy will do to all eighty-five thousand of them when they no longer need slaves."

She thought about the people she cared for—Nurse Bet, Waitie, Little Nan—and the people she owed, like Lifka and the first eunuch at the loading station. How could she let them be cut down?

"Well?"

"I know," she whispered. "I've long feared it."

"Can any other Pale save them? Or anyone from outside Cython?"

"No. They have only me." And she had sworn that oath on Mia's blood, to make up for all the injustices done to the Pale. To free them from bondage. Even her enemy, Radl.

"Then your duty is clear."

"Yes," she said despairingly. She could not do it, but neither could she refuse. "It is."

CHAPTER 75

"Your word on it," he said, coming around the table. His back was hunched; he wasn't much taller than her. He extended his hand. "And my word to you."

She shook his hand, which was surprisingly firm, though a trifle claw-like.

"It is done," said the chancellor. "Sit down. Take refreshment while I think. Be at ease—what you fear may never happen." He grimaced. "We may be driven over the mountains to the furthest reaches of Hightspall and crushed by the ice. We may never regain the strength to counterattack."

"I hope you're not planning to say that publicly."

"Nor even to my allies, privately. Morale would never recover."

It suggested that he thought more of her than his allies, which confounded her.

Food and drink was brought in—smoked meats, yellow and green pickles, a mound of dried fruits, a blood-red cordial. Everything was delicious yet she ate absently, watching him across the table. He studied the maps, then read through Verla's notes, marking several passages with an orange crayon. His face became ever more drawn, his cheeks turned a bloodless grey.

"Lord Chancellor?" she said tentatively. "You seem shaken by what I said."

"That the enemy's intent is genocide? It changes everything. Only in the past few days has Caulderon begun to take Cython seriously. Even now, people sneer and call them rock rats. But they were a formidable enemy before, one it took us two hundred and fifty years to defeat, and they're stronger now. While we're weak and unready, and the magery that saved us last time dwindles daily—"

If he knew about the three ebony pearls stolen from Lyf, she thought guiltily, and could gain them, it might change the course of the war. But she dared not mention them. "What are you going to do?"

"Take desperate measures." He went into the hall and spoke to his servants in urgent tones for some minutes, then returned. "I understand you have a quest—to avenge yourself on a family enemy."

"I will have justice for my murdered mother," said Tali.

"Justice." He chewed over the word as though he had not heard it before. "Extraordinary! And this enemy dwells in the caverns at the base of Precipitous Crag. Is he the wrythen Rixium fought there?"

How did he know that? "So I believe."

"A wrythen in the pay of the enemy." The chancellor was watching her from the corners of his eyes. "A powerful, uncanny creature breeding shifters for Cython to use in the war."

This was getting dangerous. If the chancellor learned that she was host to the master pearl, she was lost. *They're the most powerfully enchanted objects ever discovered*, Tobry had said. *They're so priceless, I doubt that the chief magian has ever seen one.*

Magery was the one weapon the Cythonians could not use, and in the chief magian's hands the master pearl could turn the war Hightspall's way. The chancellor would have to take it. What was one life—her life—compared to the fate of a nation?

"That's what Rix and Tobry said," said Tali.

"Interesting. Perhaps this wrythen is Cython's way around the prohibition against magery." He tap-tapped two fingers on the table. "Were the wrythen to be eliminated, it would strike a mighty blow against the enemy." He looked up suddenly, weighing her. "I wonder . . . "

"If Rix and Tobry couldn't harm it, it would take an army—"

The small servant appeared at the door with a package the size of a wrapped book. The chancellor put it on the table beside him. "I can't drive a squad of soldiers through the enemy's lines to attack this wrythen, but . . . "

"What?" she said uncomfortably. Was he planning to send Rix and Tobry there, in revenge for House Ricinus's threat against him?

"I can get *the one* there."

"No!" cried Tali. Was he insane? No, it was a calculated gamble by an utterly ruthless man, and if she failed he would shrug his shoulders and try something else.

"I thought you burnt for justice," he said mildly.

"I can't fight . . . the wrythen without magery." She had almost said Lyf, and naming him would raise too many dangerous questions. "Powerful magery."

"I think you will find it. I think this is *the one's* first great task. I'm going to send you there."

"What if the wrythen kills me?"

"What if Lady Ricinus assassinates me in spite of all my precautions?" said the chancellor. "What if the Cythonians tunnel under my palace and collapse it into a gigantic pit? Any of us may fail through error, or the unexpected, or the sheer perversity of life. You're a gamble, but my instinct, which is seldom wrong, tells me you're worth it. And here is the key."

He slid the wrapped package to her.

She untied the cords, unwrapped the linen and discovered a book-sized heatstone inside. Tali felt no relief, only a numb horror. What if it didn't work? What if her magery came and went again? In any case, that storm of white needles, so devastating against human flesh, might have no effect on a wrythen.

"Take it with you," said the chancellor. "Smash it when you need magery."

"The wrythen nearly killed Rix and Tobry. How can you imagine I can do better?"

"I can read people better than anyone in Hightspall."

"What do you read in me?"

"That you're a risky investment, but a worthy one."

"I'm not ready," said Tali. "Magery takes years to master. I'll only make things worse."

"Neither am I ready, but as chancellor I have to act now. The enemy could break into Caulderon tonight or tomorrow. What if they intend to kill every man, every woman, every child and babe-in-arms in this great city? Think about the horror of all those individual deaths, then tell me that you'll do your duty to the country you profess to love."

This nightmare was all the more terrifying because it was what she had wanted. Now she realised how unprepared she was, how naïve she had been to think of attacking Lyf. What if she failed and he gained the master pearl?

She had to do something. She checked around her. If she could leap on the chancellor, and bind and gag him, could she get back to the tunnels with Rannilt and the spectible before the alarm was raised?

The instant she moved, he snapped his fingers and two guards appeared at the door. They were much bigger than Tali and their blades were in their hands.

"Chancellor?" said the first of them, an oval-faced brunette almost as tall as Rix.

"Take the child away."

Chills spiralled through Tali as the brunette unfastened the stocks and picked Rannilt up. She woke, beamed and threw her arms out towards Tali.

"Knew you'd come," said Rannilt. "I told the old man so."

"Take her away," said the chancellor. "I hold her hostage for your conduct, Tali."

It was like history repeating itself. "Will you enslave *her* descendants for a thousand years?" cried Tali.

"Why would I harm a child?"

"I don't want to go," cried Rannilt, struggling furiously. "Tali, help, *help!*"

Tali trembled with a mad urge to hurl herself at the guard, but the smaller guard blocked the way with her blade.

Tali swallowed. "Rannilt, I'll come back for you, I promise."

"Don't leave me," Rannilt wailed, and reached out to her with both hands. "Here—use your gift."

Golden bubbles formed at her fingertips, expanding and bursting into fragments that pattered gently on Tali's face and hands. A sharp pain cleaved through the top of her skull and she felt a tight pressure there, as though a balloon was swelling inside her head, pressing so hard on her skull bones that they creaked.

She had felt that pressure before, in the sunstone shaft. Coloured lights swirled madly; the pain intensified; more balloons formed in her chest; her eyes misted and her vision swam. Then something rose up in her, something powerful, dark and uncontrollable, and she thrust her right arm towards the chancellor's meagre chest. Her fingertips ached for release.

Considering his peril, he was eerily calm. "Don't mistake an ally for an enemy," he said quietly.

The balloon popped, the mist vanished, and her rising gift sank out of sight and out of reach. Tali sagged backwards against the wall, almost as drained as if she had used magery. She felt a profound disappointment, a deep and troubling loss. The gift longed to be used and, horrific though it was, she longed to use it.

"Ahh!" He was smiling. "But you truly *are* worth the gamble."

Tali stared at him. He seemed pleased, even vindicated. Had he manipulated the situation so she would reveal her gift? Truly, he was a dangerous man.

"Remove the child," said the chancellor.

Rannilt was still screaming a hundred yards down the corridors. Her helpless, hopeless cries stabbed through Tali's heart. Rannilt had given everything she had for Tali, over and over, and Tali could do nothing for her.

"Well?" he said.

She was beaten. "How are you going to get me through the enemy lines to Precipitous Crag?"

"There are secret ways."

This could not work. Even if breaking the heatstone did liberate her gift, it must take years to master. And without mastery, how could she take on a wrythen who had survived two thousand years after death? How could she attack a magian so powerful that he could create shifters, possess other magians and burn through Tinyhead's brain from many miles away?

Without mastery of her gift, there was no hope. Lyf would take the master pearl he so coveted, and when he cut it out, she would die, just as Rix's sketch predicted.

She was *the one*, all right. The one who opened Lyf's path to vengeance.

PART THREE

HUNT

CHAPTER 76

Plague stalked the streets of Caulderon, poxes of Lyf's own creation to which his people were immune, and for which there was no cure. Neither could Hightspall's frantic magians and alchymists find any defence to Cython's chymical weaponry. The enemy's morale was crumbling and Lyf's vast armies were in place. Caulderon would soon fall.

All was well.

When Lyf last haunted Rix's nightmares, the compulsion had been close to taking him. On the next visit, it would, and Lyf would have neutralised his most pressing worry, the Oathbreaker's Blade. Then Rix would bring the host to the cellar and cut the master nuclix from her.

But before he did, Lyf had to make sure of his most cunning enemy. Deroe had strengthened his wards further. A triple layer now surrounded the magian in his cliff-top manor and he believed he was safe. He believed he had beaten Lyf and was closing in on the host who bore the master pearl. The pearl that would allow Deroe to drive Lyf out for good, then exact a terrible vengeance on him.

Let Deroe think that until the very moment when Lyf slid between the wards and, striking like a cobra, tore his throat out.

Yes, all was very well.

CHAPTER 77

"Wake up!" shrieked a high, desperate voice. "Chancellor's got her—"

Little fists pounded Rix's shoulder, then a pair of cold hands dragged him rudely off the settee. It was a long way to the floor and he hit with a thump that rattled his teeth.

Tobry chuckled. "Well done, Rannilt. Serves the sod right for napping at this time of night."

"How did you get here?" said Rix, focusing blearily on the child.

"Escaped." She was half sobbing, half choking. "Get up, we got to save Tali."

"What's the chancellor got to do with her?"

"Tali sneaked into his palace," she panted, her bird-like chest heaving. "Hurry!"

"Why would she do such a thing?" The sleep-fog lifted. Tali had disappeared after the revelation about ebony pearls and Tobry had gone after her. Rix, who had barely been to bed in days, had lain on the settee for a minute and must have slept for many hours. "You didn't find her, then?"

"Lost her in the tunnels," Tobry said coolly.

Elbowing Rix aside, he crouched before the girl and took her dirty hand. Belatedly, Rix remembered all that Rannilt had gone through, including Luzia's murder and an interrogation by the chancellor. It was a wonder she wasn't under the bed, screaming.

"She sneaked in to rescue you, didn't she?" said Tobry.

Rannilt sniffled and wiped her nose on her arm, not successfully. Tobry handed her a piece of white linen. She smeared dirt and mucus across her face with it.

She nodded. "But the chancellor caught her and sent her off."

"How do you know?" said Tobry. "Rix, go and get a cloth. Rannilt wants to wash her face. And a drink of water."

Rix did so and she scrubbed her face and hands with it. Her eyes were huge, the sockets purple as bruises. She gulped the water, spilling it everywhere.

"Better?" said Tobry.

She nodded.

"How do you know he sent her away?"

"Was pretendin' to be asleep. Heard them talkin'. He said he was sendin' her on a quest."

"What quest?"

"To find the wrythen. At Precip—Precipitous Crag."

Tobry let out an inarticulate cry.

"Why in the name of the Gods would he send Tali to her enemy?" said Rix.

"Stupid Wil told him Tali was *the one*," said Rannilt. "Chancellor thinks she can beat the wrythen and save Caulderon."

"Clearly he doesn't know about the—"

At a slashing motion from Tobry, Rix broke off. If word got out about the master pearl, Tali would be hunted ruthlessly for it. And if Lyf got it, he would win.

"The chancellor's taking an almighty risk," said Tobry.

"Said Tali was worth the gamble." Rannilt hugged herself with her thin arms. "I'm really scared, Tobry. We've got to save her."

"We don't know how he got her out of the city," said Rix.

"I can find out."

"How?"

"Tried to wake Tali's gift with my golden mage-light, but it . . . um, spliced us. And when—"

"How do you mean, *spliced us*?" said Tobry in an odd voice.

"It leaves threads floatin' in the air behind her. I can see where they took her."

"Are you saying you can track Tali?" said Rix.

"As long as we're quick. Threads are fadin'."

"When did they take her?"

"Hours ago."

Rix looked at Tobry.

"Last time, your excuse was you had the portrait to finish," said Tobry pointedly.

Anything to avoid that. "You've swayed me. Let's go."

"Sure you're not using Tali to escape your *responsibilities*?" Tobry sniffed.

"If she's killed," said Rix, "if the wrythen takes—" Tobry was shaking his head. "Get Rannilt some winter gear."

Tobry ran out. Rix hurled all the necessities into a pack, gathered bow and arrows, made sure his sword was sharp and filled a couple of storm lanterns. The urgency was a welcome distraction from the unanswerable questions. Why had he been in the cellar? Why the blood on his hands? How could he warn the chancellor without betraying his own mother?

Rannilt watched him in silence. He wasn't sure she trusted him, and he knew damn well she did not like him.

"Haven't you got anything to do?" said Rix.

She did not answer, and he was pleased when Tobry returned a few minutes later with fur-lined gear and boots in the child's size. While she dressed, Rix studied the hole under the great tub, which Tobry must have enlarged when he had gone after her.

"I don't see how I'm going to get down there."

Tobry put his elbrot to the side of the hole and screwed up his face. A high-pitched whine shook the mortar behind the tiles to dust and they fell off. Tobry put his foot on one of the stone blocks and shoved. It slid into the shaft and fell, hitting far below with a muffled thud. He sent half a dozen more blocks the same way, leaving a hole a pony could have passed through.

Rannilt went first. Like Tali, she was accustomed to making her way through tunnels in near darkness. Rix shuttered his lantern to a glimmer and followed.

The tunnel was close, humid and dripping, and he did not like it. "No wonder the rock rats are desperate to take Hightspall back," he said quietly. "Imagine spending all your life in a place like this."

"Cython ain't like this," said Rannilt. "It's dry and warm, and it don't smell. And the walls are carved into beautiful places."

"What kind of places?"

"The way Hightspall is *supposed* to be," she said rebelliously. She sniff-led, went to wipe her nose on her arm, then used Tobry's rag instead.

"I would have liked to have seen it in the olden days," said Tobry. "The First Fleeters said Cythe was a paradise."

They followed the passage for miles, up and down, through a narrow pinch like a dyke eroded out of black rock, then through a broad passage of cream limestone crisscrossed with veins of a pink mineral that twinkled as the light caught it. Finally, along a dipping tunnel where they splashed through ankle-deep water, stirring up silt, and up again.

"Shh!" Rannilt stopped, staring up the dark passage. The rock was greatly fissured and water dripped from every crack.

Rix shuttered the lantern.

"What is it?" said Tobry.

Rannilt sniffed the air. "Horses."

"What would horses be doing down here?" said Rix, who could not smell anything save dust and damp.

"For the chancellor's private use," Tobry said drily. "To escape when the city falls."

"To run away like a coward!" Rannilt said in a fierce whisper.

"When Caulderon does fall, it'll take more courage to fly and fight again than it would to lie down and die."

CHAPTER 78

"Rannilt, can you tell how many guards there are?"

She sniffed the air. "At least one, in with the horses."

"Wait here."

"Don't hurt him."

Rix slipped into the stables, a cross-shaped space excavated out of yellow limestone. The left-hand end of the cross was stacked with dark cubes of silage which gave off a rich, malty odour. The floor of the central area was worn in an exercise circle. A rock salt lick was set in a metal frame near the far wall, while the right-hand end contained a series of stone-walled stalls, reeking of manure and urine, each with a horse inside.

Further down, he made out a trundling squeal, a stable boy barrowing manure away. Rix waited in shadow until he returned, a stocky, brown-haired lad of twelve, then rose like a golem into the lantern light and took him by the arm.

"Don't make a sound."

The boy jumped, groped for a knife on his belt, then stopped, smiling tentatively. Two of his front teeth were missing. "Lord Rixium?"

"You know me?" Rix was constantly surprised at the number of people who recognised his face.

"Everyone's talkin' 'bout how you beat the enemy out in the Seethin's," said the lad, breathily. His eyes were shining. "You're the hero of Caulderon."

Rix raised an eyebrow. "Well, we've come for the horses." He studied the stalls. "And we'll need a change of mounts, so four of your best."

"I haven't been told about this," said the boy.

"It came up rather suddenly."

"They're the chancellor's horses."

"And he's sent me, so go and rouse them out."

The boy was starting to sweat, but he stood his ground. "Sorry, Lord, I can't let them go without a docket."

There wasn't time for debate. Rix drew his sword, its curved blade glittering in the lantern light. "This is my authorisation, lad."

The boy took a deep breath, as if to yell for help. Rix twitched the sword. The shining light vanished from the boy's eyes. His face flushed and he looked bitterly disillusioned.

"You're no hero," he said crushingly, jerking free and scrambling away. "You're runnin' like a stinkin' coward, and I'll die before I let you have them."

Rix started after the lad, the sword dangling uselessly. He could never use it on a child. The boy bolted, roaring, "Thieves! Traitors! Help!"

"Sorry, kid," said Tobry. A low, fizzing sound, a narrow streak of emerald light, and the boy crumpled.

"I didn't know you could do that with magery," said Rix.

Tobry tied the lad up. "It only works on the unformed minds of children and innocents," he said with more than a hint of bitterness.

Rix, shaken by the boy's accusation, did not reply. Was he doing the right thing or making an inevitable disaster worse? But how could Tali take on Lyf? It was impossible.

Shortly they emerged through a cobwebby illusion concealing an exit screened by boulders and scrub, partway down a warty hill. It was not long until dawn and the moon was an eerie red through gauzy clouds and heavy smoke.

"Where are we?" said Rix, leading the largest horse, a rangy, red-eyed grey, up the hill.

The Vomits were smoking balefully to his left, and every so often the ground gave a faint quiver. Ahead, a couple of miles away, the orange glow of Caulderon's burning shanty towns was clearly visible. Thousands of yellow flares illuminated the dark mass of Cython's armies ringing the walls.

Tobry cursed under his breath. "How many are there?"

"We've got eighteen thousand troops in Caulderon, counting the injured. The enemy must be three times that number by now."

"And nothing we can do save go on," said Tobry. "We're a little south of Nollyrigg. If we strike towards the Brown Vomit, we should reach the Caulderon Road in half an hour. Though I'm not keen on risking the road—"

"Or Rannilt," said Rix.

"You're not leavin' me behind again," said Rannilt.

"No, we can't do without you," said Tobry.

He shook Rix's hand, then Rannilt's tiny paw, gravely.

"The enemy seem to be massing for an all-out attack," said Rix, wondering if there would be anything left to come back to. "The boy was right. People will say I've run like a coward."

"People say all manner of things," said Tobry.

"Tali is hours ahead. She could be captured by now." Or dead.

"She saved you," said Rannilt. "Now you've got to save her."

"I should be defending my family and my house, not riding into a certain trap."

"Tali comes first."

Rix could not bear to argue. The conflict was already unendurable.

As they reached the road and headed south, all three Vomits were smoking. He spurred his horse and they raced towards the mountains in the blood-red moonlight. The world was eerily quiet. The towns they passed were dark, every window shuttered, the people cowering inside. Or horribly dead of plague or pox.

Several hours passed. Dawn broke under a heavy, yellow-brown overcast sky, not much brighter than twilight. Closer to the Vomits, the ground shook constantly and they had to slow because cracks had opened across the road, some wide enough to trap a horse's leg.

"Do you think all three Vomits are going to erupt?" said Rix, reining in.

"I hope not," Tobry said direly. "According to Cythonian legend, that presages—"

"Let me guess," said Rix. "Apocalypse? Armageddon?"

"What's Armageddon?" piped Rannilt.

"The end of the world, child. Ruin in fire, then ice."

Tobry, who was holding her as if she were his own precious child, seemed to be in physical pain. Not a trace remained of the reckless hedonist Rix had known all his life.

As they approached the mountain climb, ruddy glows lit the sky. Sudden hot winds rushed down the Vomits, which now lay ahead to the right, and billowed across the Seethings to the road, only to be driven back by icy gales from the mountains on their left. One minute Rix was sweltering in his heavy gear, the next, freezing despite it. Tobry's sweaty face had a demonic aspect in the baleful light. It certainly looked like the end of the world.

The wire-handled sword rattled. As Rix steadied it, he saw the opalised figure again, contorted in agony. He had only ever seen it on the way to the caverns—the caverns the sword had led him to last time. What was it up to? He had never discovered where the sword came from and that now felt like a fatal error.

"I've got a bad feeling, Tobe," Rix said quietly. The foreboding was so thick that he could have painted it.

"What's that?"

Rannilt turned to stare at Rix, but even with her all-seeing eyes on him he could not hold back.

"That we'll be too late to save Tali; that Lyf will win and bring Hightspall to ruin. That we won't all come back alive."

"*I* haven't given up," said Rannilt coldly. "Tali will beat the nasty old wrythen-king, I know it."

"It might be an idea to get a move on," said Tobry.

"I'm not going quietly!" Rix drew the enchanted sword that he had once feared, and now was his mainstay against the foe at journey's end. Raising it high, he roared, "Ride, ride, or the whole world is dead!"

Hours later they stopped at the lookout where they had rested briefly on the way to Precipitous Crag, over a week ago. Smoke and fumes hid both the Vomits and Caulderon now, though the sky was clear to the south and the red moon rode high, reflecting off a white ocean for as far as they could see.

"The sea-ice clamps around the coast of Hightspall like a fist," said Tobry. "The end can't be far away."

The nightmare almost choked Rix. "How can it be the end? Why are we being punished? What have we done wrong?"

No one had an answer.

They navigated the narrow valley in the brooding darkness under the blood-bark trees, the hooves making little sound in deep snow, then left the horses next to the boulder-studded strip of open land where the caitsthe had attacked.

Tobry wiped icy sweat from his forehead. His terror of shifters could not be contained. *And perhaps he's still blaming himself for letting me down last time,* Rix thought, *which was absurd. Tobry never gave less than his all.*

As they were crawling through the vine thicket, Rannilt let out a little, hoarse cry. "I can smell blood."

They scrambled out into the open, next to the looming bulk of the Crag. It was frigid here. Tobry's lips moved in what looked suspiciously like a prayer, surely the first that had ever crossed his disbelieving lips.

Let it not be Tali's.

CHAPTER 79

The horses wore goggles, and so did Tali's guards, lighting their way with black-light lanterns that reeked of magery. They did not speak all the way, and neither would they answer Tali's questions, but she could smell the fear on them. They wanted to go to Precipitous Crag no more than she did.

What if Cython was planning genocide? There might be nothing to come back to—no Tobry, no Rix, no Rannilt, nor the chancellor himself who, despite his failings, was the main hope of Hightspall.

But if she did love her country, if she could give Hightspall a chance, she had to try. How could she take Lyf on, though? Tali did not know where to begin.

She reminded herself of her other victories against impossible odds, but her disquiet only strengthened. Rix and Tobry were powerful and experienced, yet they had nearly died here. How could she survive when she had no idea how to combat her enemy? The heatstone gave her no confidence—she might break it and nothing happen.

When they dismounted below the cave entrance in the early hours after midnight, mounting terror turned her bowels liquid. Even had her magery been in full flower she would not have been ready to take on Lyf.

"What am I supposed to do?" she whispered.

There was no way of knowing what defences he had inside, or what forces he commanded here at the centre of his power, though she knew he had shifters penned below. Even had she been armed she could not have fought such creatures.

"Why ask us?" said the taller guard, a muscular blonde with shoulders like a blacksmith. She handed Tali a small pack containing food, drink and the heatstone. "You're *the one*."

"You'll still be here when I come out?" asked Tali.

"We have our orders," said the other guard, who was compact and had a cap of black, dancing curls. "Go!"

She shot a crossways glance at the tall guard and Tali saw fear in their eyes, skilled fighters though they were. They crawled through the vine thicket and disappeared. She was on her own.

Hunching down out of the keening wind, she tried to plan. The chancellor might be desperate but he wasn't reckless; he would not have sent her here unless her chance of succeeding outweighed the risk of losing her. Tali took comfort from that thought—until she remembered that he did not know about the master pearl. He would never have risked it.

It was perishing here, yet the cave was worse: it was breathing out air frigid enough to shatter iron, a bone-aching cold that sucked the resolve from her. How could she hope to beat a wrythen who had surmounted death for two thousand years and was driven by such implacable purpose? A wrythen who possessed an ebony pearl and knew how to use it?

The master pearl had to be cut out of living tissue. If he knew she was here, he would try to take it. Or would he? If he could extract the pearl himself, why had he directed Tinyhead to carry her to the murder cellar in Caulderon? Why involve others and take such a risk of being robbed of the pearls—as, indeed, he had lost three of them? Perhaps he could not take them himself.

She edged down the passage at the rear of the cave. She had no lantern but there was enough light for an underground dweller like herself to see by. Ahead, the centre of the passage was heaped with broken stone where Lyf had brought the roof down and knocked Tobry out. The caitsthe's corpse was gone but she could smell its blood.

She shoved her arms deep into her fur-lined pockets and was veering left where the rubble was lowest when she felt a shivery pain in her shins and heard an outraged whisper, *Oathbreaker's blade!*

Tali shot around, staring into the gloom. Rix had hurt the wrythen here and driven it off. Were the words and the pain just an echo of Lyf's trauma, or did he know she was coming? Was he already sharpening the knife?

She went on, so cold that a deadly lethargy, almost impossible to fight, was creeping over her. Every surface was glazed with pearly layers of ice, so slippery that it was a struggle to walk. She did not recall Tobry mentioning ice; the change must have come since he was here. But why? Could Lyf be behind the ice packs encircling Hightspall? No, that was absurd; no man could wield such power—could he?

At the maze of passageways she put the spectible over her eyes and saw, by the faint twinkle of magery, which path to take. She lurched on and reached the junction Tobry had mentioned. One way led down to shifter pens but her hackles rose at the thought of going near them. The other plunged to an uncanny cavern where the wrythen dwelt. But which was which?

The air was so cold it carried no scent. Because it felt right, she took the glassy-walled path, which became a steep set of steps leading down beyond sight. In the semi-darkness, where the stone beneath her could barely be distinguished, she had to concentrate on every step.

After taking three steps she knew it was too easy. Where were the shifters, the alarms and traps? Lyf had been outraged at Rix and Tobry's trespass, so why didn't he show himself?

Tobry had said the stairs ended in mid-air, but this one ran down into a space she struggled to understand even when it resolved into a tall chamber that resembled an upside-down flask bent around and through itself. It felt unnatural, though Tali could not see it clearly enough to know why. She measured each step, careful to make no sound. Lyf could be anywhere, watching from the shadows, hiding within the wall, preparing to strike.

Her heart was beating erratically—racing one minute, deathly slow the next, and sometimes missing beats altogether. Her blood seemed to be thickening in her veins, her heart fighting to pump at all. She swung her arms, clenched and unclenched her fists, though it did not help.

Statues ringed the circular top of the chamber, at least a hundred of them, all dressed like the images of kings and queens she had seen in Cython. Their eyes followed her, and she sensed both rage and curiosity, though none moved, none spoke.

She reached the bottom of a twilight world, turned left and gazed about her in wonder. It was like being inside one of the glass retorts she had seen chymisters carrying in Cython—was that symbolic?—though this one was upside-down with the bulb high above her and the broad neck curving down, flattening at the base where she stood and sweeping up again to pass, *impossibly*, through its own wall halfway up.

Away to her left towered a platina-distilling apparatus a good twenty feet high. Three chairs shaped like beans were grouped around a low table with an egg-curve sculpted out of it. A library in the distance held more books than she had seen in her life, magnificent volumes inlaid with silver, gilt and slivers of precious stone. She ran light-footed to the bookcases and reached for the nearest book but her fingers passed through it with only the faintest resistance. A wrythen might have read it but she could not.

Another book lay open on a lectern, an illuminated volume of verse, perhaps an epic, though she could not read the words. She blew on the edge and the page turned to reveal another lovely illumination, then another, so perfect that the book must have taken half a lifetime to complete. But then, the wrythen had lived for a hundred and fifty lifetimes; time must hold a very different meaning for him. As she studied the pages, waves of sorrow washed over her, as though the books were the last record of masterpieces that no longer existed.

But not what she was here for. She tried to imagine the coming confrontation. How could she defend herself when she did not know how Lyf would attack? If only she could use her pearl. She longed for it, hated it, feared it.

Tali looked through the spectible and reeled at the radiance flooding from it. There was magery everywhere: in the books, the chairs and table, the walls and floor, the row of standing statues high above—and the wrythen fluttering in the gloom ten yards away!

She jumped, gasped and sprang backwards, but it continued to hang a foot above the floor, rippling like an empty suit in a breeze. After her clattering heart steadied, she studied it through the spectible. The aura haloed around it was static, while every other enchanted object had a moving aura.

Seen directly, the wrythen was translucent and its eyes had a fixed and empty stare. Lyf wasn't here! What could its empty form tell her about him?

She saw a man apparently only a few years older than herself, neither tall nor short, with the silvery ghosts of kingly tattoos on his face and throat. He wore a short, flaring cape over a loose blouse and silky pantaloons bunched at mid-calf, below which protruded several inches of shattered bone.

Had Tobry mentioned that the wrythen's feet had been hacked off? She had a vague memory of it. Why hadn't Lyf, who clearly had created everything here, restored them? Did he stay this way as a reminder of what had been done to him? Well, his absence was her opportunity, though a fraught one. It might only take him seconds to return.

Where would he keep the pearl? It would be hidden so no casual intruder could stumble upon it. Tali scanned the cavern through her spectible, trying to filter out the auras that streamed out from books and tables, the walls of the cavern, the kingly statues high above, and even the junction where the cavern looped up like the neck of an alchymist's retort before passing back through its wall . . .

She froze, staring at the junction, through which she had fleetingly glimpsed a single, striking aura. Tali moved her head left, right, left again. Ah, there it was, a circle of quiescent blackness unlike anything she had seen before. Could it be his ebony pearl?

The only person who can teach you how to master your gift is your enemy, Mimoy had said. Could Tali do so by reading how he'd used his pearl?

The junction was high up, the wall of the cavern smooth. She tore off her pack, gloves, boots and socks, and scrambled onto the wall. It had a clinging feel, like soft rubber. She went up it in a rush, and fell. And up again. And fell.

The third time, by digging her nails into the springy surface, she reached the junction where the neck passed through its own wall in that way that baffled the eye. Clinging on with toes and one hand, knees trembling with the strain, she peered through the spectible, searching for the pearl.

The junction was so narrow that a hair could not have passed through it. Nonetheless, it was where she'd seen the pearl. Tali put the spectible away, pressed both hands against the wall and rested her head on the junction. What to do?

With a dazzling flash and a splitting-skull pain, she was drawn towards the junction. *And hurtled through it*—but not out the other side.

She was inside a white, cylindrical shaft extending up and down beyond sight. It was softly lit though she could not tell where the light came from. Below her the whiteness, perhaps the whole shaft, appeared to be rotating slowly.

She was floating above an enormous drop! Tali's head spun, she made a grab for the side but found nothing to grip and began to fall, though not nearly as fast as she would have done in the real world. Where was she falling to? She could see only white.

Magery, she thought, if ever I needed you, stop me!

She stopped, hanging in mid-air, but had magery done it, or the shaft itself? She had been floating at the beginning, after all. Tali looked for the ebony pearl, a sphere of perfect black, but saw only white. The spectible showed neither, rather a catastrophe of colours so brilliant that she could not think for them. After clicking the left-hand knob, the brightness reduced a thousandfold and she saw magery streaming out of the walls, but no little circle of blackness.

Yet she had seen it from outside; it had to be here. She scanned the white walls, covering every inch, clicked to reduce the brightness another thousandfold and suddenly it stood out against the pale—a tiny knot of intense colours emerging from a crevice above her. She reached up towards it and slowly rose in the shaft.

It wasn't a crevice, rather a concealed opening in the wall, invisible to the eye but revealed by the spectible. The perfect hiding place—no thief could steal what he did not know was there.

And there it was, resting on a flat disc of grass-green metal—a little globe of black. The ebony pearl. Lyf's pearl. Could it be the first of the five, cut from her great-great-grandmother's head a hundred years ago? There was no way of knowing. She extended her fingers towards it and heard a small, mewling peep, its *call*. Tali's mental shell burst open and, before she could close it, her own pearl answered.

Lyf's pearl called again, a higher note, a question. What question, though, and what had her own pearl replied? Tali shivered; it was as if the pearls had their own agenda. As her pearl responded to the second call, pain speared through her skull and rainbows of light cascaded through her inner eye, colours she did not know existed.

Lyf's pearl kept calling and she sensed a desperate urge for completion with the other pearls. What would happen if it found what it was looking for?

She reached out to the pearl. It retreated. She reached further. It retreated further.

"Don't run away," she said quietly. "I have one too. You were hosted in one of my ancestors, and all the pearls are linked to me, so why would I harm you?"

The pearl stopped, quivering a little.

Without thinking, Tali said, "Come!"

And, with another peeping call, it came.

CHAPTER 80

"Die, magian, die!"

But Deroe struck back, sending a mind-numbing spell whispering towards Lyf. Lyf twisted, allowing it to sigh past, then caught his enemy with a nerve-fire enchantment that made him gasp and twitch with a million pain pricks.

Deroe fired a thesaurus of emotions, trying to overwhelm Lyf with aggression and alienation, shame and bewilderment and rage, melancholy, spite and a hundred other conflicting feelings all at once. The assault would have driven any ordinary man mad, but over the aeons Lyf had mastered his own mind. He used the cool aggression to reinforce his own, allowed the other emotions to glance off him like hailstones from a helm and struck back.

Deroe screamed like the stunted boy he was inside, threw up a barrier and huddled behind it, whimpering, "Don't hurt me, don't hurt me."

But despite the whining, he was far from beaten.

Inside the magian's head, the battle had been going on for half a day, veering from imminent victory to looming defeat and back again. Deroe, an old man emotionally frozen in adolescence at the time Lyf had first possessed him, could never be Lyf's match in wit or magery. However, Deroe had a real human body to draw upon and it gave him far more strength than Lyf could take from the wry-then form he had left behind in his distant caverns. The longer the struggle went on the weaker Lyf became, and the greater the likelihood that Deroe would cast him out permanently.

If Deroe ever realised how physically weak Lyf was, if Deroe knew for a moment that Lyf could be beaten, he would attack mercilessly. Deroe had to die.

But he had the three stolen nuclixes close to hand to bolster his power at need, while Lyf's, the weakest of the five, could not be used at all from so far away. Unable to match Deroe's strength, and afraid to use magery that might be turned against him, all Lyf had left was cunning, and patience.

And knowledge of a weakness Deroe was not aware of. A vessel in his brain had a flaw and, if it could be induced to rupture, the magian's death would come within minutes. Not so fast that his death would trap Lyf too—for that was the greatest peril of fighting a man while possessing him—but too quick for Deroe to save himself with magery.

Lyf had been subtly attacking the flaw for hours, picking at it with what little force he could muster while the mental struggle went on. It was like trying to cut a pipe with a feather, yet in time a feather can wear away rock and he was close now. Just a hundred more strokes. Just fifty. Just thirty—

The *call* shrieked through his mind, but this time it was *his* nuclix, calling frantically—an intruder had entered his caverns. And *The Consolation of Vengeance* lay open on its table, unprotected. What if the intruder stole it? Or worse, catastrophically so because the last leaf was blank—what if the intruder wrote another ending and transmitted it to the Chamber of the Solaces?

Lyf burned *quessence* like a spendthrift, desperate to see, to *know*. The intruder was the host, Tali, and somehow she had gained entrance to the white shaft of the Abysm, his nucleatory. How had she got in?

Again this admirable enemy confounded him by going where no living human should have been able to go. It had not occurred to Lyf that one person could easily penetrate the sacred Abysm— someone who also had a nuclix. She was close to the *source*; her master nuclix might already be charging itself from it and if she took his nuclix, the plans of two thousand years would collapse.

He had to fly at once.

But Lyf could not simply disengage from Deroe. That would leave him exposed and vulnerable for an eternal minute, time enough for the magian to strike. Lyf had to ease out of Deroe's mind so subtly that he did not realise what was happening.

Deroe, correctly interpreting Lyf's inactivity as weakness, struck a ferocious blow. Lyf deflected the worst of it, yet it hurt him, and in reflex he hit back with the nerve-fire enchantment. It failed, as he should have known it would—Deroe was too subtle a foe to be caught by the same spell twice.

He's crumbling, ha, ha! Deroe hooted like a schoolboy and attacked with seven spells at once, spending power promiscuously to overwhelm his enemy.

Suddenly, even as Lyf sensed Tali reaching out for his nuclix, he was fighting for his life. Every instinct screamed at him to withdraw and run, but he had to maintain his defences and go slowly, slowly. Deroe must not realise what was going on.

Lyf sneaked through a low blow and the magian howled, but did not retreat behind his barriers this time. The advantage was his, and if he kept up the assault it was only a matter of minutes.

Then Lyf saw Tali's fingers close over his nuclix and it went to her with a little sigh. Catastrophe was only a breath away. He thought furiously. Even if she stole his pearl, she did not know how to use it. And it was a long way out of the cavern; an even longer way back to Caulderon. The worst could not happen. But what if it did?

The facinore should be close to the caverns by now. So profane a creature could not enter the Abysm, but the moment Tali emerged with the pearl she must be taken. Lyf directed his failing strength into a command to the facinore. A command he prayed it would obey.

Find the host. Hold her.
Do not feed!

CHAPTER 81

The blood moon broke free of racing clouds, illuminating a body—no, two bodies—sprawled ten yards away up the long rubble slope leading to the cave mouth. The broken rock was stained all around, as though the blood had burst forth when the victims were torn open.

Rannilt was gasping, in, in, in with never an out-breath to balance. Tobry went so still in the saddle he might have frozen to it.

Too late, Rix thought bleakly, and it was his stupid fault. Why, after the revelation about the ebony pearls, hadn't he gone after Tali at once? She had been in such a state that she was bound to do something reckless, like racing off to rescue Rannilt from the chancellor. And the chancellor was utterly single-minded. To protect Hightspall he would use anyone, even Tali. He would cast her into any danger to give himself a tiny advantage, then discard her wreckage afterwards.

Rannilt let out a despairing cry and tried to throw herself from the saddle. Tobry clamped his arm around her. She jammed an elbow into his belly, squirmed under his arm and dropped to the ground.

Rix leapt after her to shield her from the dreadful sight, but she was too quick for him. She scrabbled up the slope on hands and knees, rubble clattering behind her, then froze, staring. The first body was a tall, broad-shouldered woman, the second a smaller one with dark, curly hair, and both had been opened at the belly as if their attacker had feasted on their living organs, then left them. Nothing else had been touched.

"Facinore did this!" whispered Rannilt, shedding tears that froze as they fell and shattered to jewel-like shards of ice with the lustre of gold.

"I've seen her before," said Tobry, bending over the dark-haired woman as the moonlight waxed and waned. "She was one of the chancellor's most trusted guards, and almost in your class with a blade, Rix." He gave a convulsive shudder.

Rix gripped him by the shoulder. Tobry had vowed to never come back here. "How far behind are we?"

Tobry checked the bodies. "There's a trace of warmth left. Doubt if they've been dead an hour."

"An hour's a long time when you're up against a facinore. Can you still see the threads, Rannilt?"

Her dark eyes showed white all around. She nodded but did not speak. Tobry took her hand and they went up the rubble slope and in. Despite the cold, which became fiercer with every step, the stone basin was unfrozen. Rannilt turned towards it, as if to drink, but before Rix could warn her she threw up her hands and backed away.

"What is it, child?" said Tobry. "What can you see?"

"Mad patterns." They passed by. Something squelched underfoot. "What's that horrible smell?"

"Shifter dung," said Rix, scraping it off his boot on a projecting rock. The back of the cave, and the cavern beyond it, reeked of their manure. Were the shifters from the pens below roaming free? "I've got an unpleasant feeling we're being watched."

Tobry's jaw was clenched tightly enough to crack his teeth. Why was he so afraid of shifters? Was it the fear of becoming one, like Tobry's grandfather who had brought House Lagger to ruin? Rix had never asked about the details and Tobry had not volunteered them.

Some friend I am, Rix thought bleakly. He's always supported me, and what have I ever done for him? How can I do this to him again?

The fear was contagious. Rannilt was clinging to Tobry's hand now, looking anxiously up at him. Rix swallowed. Lyf had nearly beaten them here last time and, down in his lair, close to his ebony pearl, he must be far more powerful. He had tried to possess Tobry and take control of him more than once. What if he succeeded?

Why are all my choices so bad, Rix wondered. I can only save the chancellor, and perhaps Hightspall, by betraying my mother and my house. And if Lyf possesses Tobry . . . ?

He shook the unease off and concentrated on now. They were at the maze and he did not know the way through. Nor did he want Tobry to use magery here.

"Come up here beside me, Rannilt," said Rix. "Show me the way with your threads."

She crept forwards, looking up at him. He extended his left hand. Rannilt bit her lip; he did not think she trusted him over-much. But when she put her small hand in his huge one he felt a surge of protectiveness and understood how Tobry felt about her. Why had they brought her here? They'd known where Tali was headed.

"This way. Come on." She tugged at his hand, her courage showing them both up. No, what she had was far greater than mere courage. Rannilt was terrified, yet she never faltered.

They went down, following the drifting threads only she could see. Why were the shifters free? Were they guarding the place for Lyf? Or had they been sent to the war? Rix prayed they had—there was no hope of surviving a pack attack in here.

Rannilt was breathing hoarsely, the air whistling through her parted lips, and her hand kept clenching against his. What was she sensing? Where was the facinore? The back of his neck prickled. He still felt sure they were being watched; stalked.

They went down the glassy steps that had previously ended in mid-air but now continued into the flaskoid chamber Rix had distantly glimpsed last time. Its top was ringed with kingly and queenly statues, save that their translucent heads turned and their eyes moved as Rix, Tobry and Rannilt approached.

"Ghosts!" whispered Rannilt, her nails digging into Rix's hand.

"The greatest kings and queens of ancient Cythe," Tobry said quietly. "But not real ghosts. Lyf must have created them."

"As a first line of defence?" said Rix.

Tobry waved his elbrot. Rannilt let out a little gasp.

"Don't use magery here!" Rix hissed.

"I don't *think* they can harm us," said Tobry. "Besides, Lyf must know we're here by now."

"Is that supposed to comfort me?"

"Shh!" said Rannilt.

As they passed on down, several of the kings raised translucent hands, cursing them in reedy voices and ordering them back. Rannilt let out a moan. Rix's stomach clenched painfully, as if around a broken brick.

"Where's the wrythen?" said Rix. "Where's Lyf?"

"If he's not here," said Tobry, "it's more than we could have hoped for. Keep moving."

"I don't like it. Why isn't he here?"

"Get going."

At the bottom, Rix went right and, a third of the way around the curving wall, encountered a bookcase with four shelves formed from the same shiny substance. The top shelf held five books, the second, nine. Even to Rix's prosaic eyes there was something strange, beautiful and deadly about them, but he had not come here to look at books.

Tobry stopped and studied the titles of the age-worn volumes on the top shelf, whose covers were written in the Hightspall script. *"The Songs of Survival,"* he said, frowning. "Have you heard of them, Rix?"

"I don't even read Hightspall's great books," snapped Rix. "Come on!"

Tobry turned to the second shelf. *"The Lore of Prosperity.* And the titles are, *On Delven, On Metallix, On Smything, On Catalyz* ... Do they sound like instruction manuals to you?"

As he reached out to touch *On Catalyz,* Rix's sword rattled in its scabbard. He dropped a hand to steady it but the sword shot upwards, slamming into his palm, and auras flared around all fourteen books.

Tobry whipped his hand back and the auras faded, but the aura around another book did not—a book made from grey sheet iron, with cast-iron covers, lying open on a pitted stone table. An engraver's scriber lay beside the book and a corroded platina flask on its side on the table, as though cast there when empty. Most unnerving, the deeply etched letters on the open pages were the colour of burning blood.

"The *Solaces*," Rannilt whispered.

"What are the Solaces?" Rix approached the iron book, warily.

"Wil said they're precious books that tell the matriarchs of Cython what to do."

"But what are they doing *here?*" Rix bent over the open book.

"Don't touch *anything*," said Tobry, staring at the book through his elbrot, then shaking his head. "Rannilt, can you tell—"

She was staring the other way, up at the point where the flaskoid passed back through itself. Her teeth chattered.

Rix could see nothing save a slight blur there. "What is it?"

"Tali!" Rannilt screeched, tearing her hand free and running forwards. "Look out! It's waiting for you."

CHAPTER 82

I cy waves crept down Tali's back as the black pearl drifted off the disc and crept towards her outstretched hand. Was Lyf's pearl responding to her own?

Take it and run! You don't have to fight Lyf now. Steal the pearl and you damage him, and strengthen yourself to fight him on your own ground. And it'll help the war too, and please the chancellor.

She was about to close her fingers around it when the gift rose inside her, though it had done that before only to retreat again. How could she bring it to the surface? It was a question Tali had asked a thousand times without ever finding an answer, but she sensed the answer was not far away.

You can only defeat your enemy with magery, but the only person who can teach you how to use your magery is your enemy.

Her head throbbed as though something hard—the master

pearl?—was grinding against the inside of her skull, and the bands of colour were dazzling. She was close to a source of phenomenal power, but where was it? Within the pearl, or were pearls merely the key that unlocked a greater power?

And if unlocked, how could she use it? The white torrent that had shorn Banj's head off had been uncontrollable, and she had been so ill afterwards that without Rannilt she would have been killed. But Banj had been just a man. To fight such a master as Lyf she too must have mastery, yet magery rarely came easily and mastery never quickly.

A first-day apprentice could not hope to defeat her master. Take the damned pearl and go, before he comes back.

The pearl quivered and, without knowing how, Tali understood that she was trespassing in a forbidden place. Not Lyf's place, but something far older. Something private, sacred, never to be entered by her kind.

The pearl *called* like a lost, frantic child, and instinctively she tried to calm it, stroke it, but as her fingers grazed the black surface, patterns began to radiate inwards from all around the shaft and she did not need the spectible to see them.

Complicated bands of swirling colour, twisting and writhing, spinning out and frilling and coiling back on themselves, and every little bump and node and coil had its own coiled pattern that mimicked the greater structure, down to the smallest size that she could see. Could the pattern be the key to power? The temptation to look deeper, to win the prize, was irresistible.

She looked down, wondering where the Abysm led to. Tali stroked the pearl and sensed a throbbing power far below, beyond anything any mortal could wield. If she could take a tiny fraction of it, could she command her magery?

Ssst, sssst!

Now grey flecks and threads were revealed, whizzing down the shaft all around her, and she caught snatches of sonorous, solemn speech. The words made no sense, yet vague rumours rose unbidden—half-remembered conversations between Cythonians, overheard ages ago, about their most secret and sacred place. A place where none of them would think of venturing, the very conduit between creation and destruction, life and death . . .

Could this shaft be part of the Abysm down which Cythonian souls were said to pass after death? It must be, and her presence here was a dreadful sacrilege. Tali's cheeks were scalding—not even in war would she willingly trespass on her enemy's sacred places, but she did not know how to get out. There was no sign of the crack through which she had entered.

Way down, as far as she could see, something reflected brightly, the colours changing constantly as it moved. It was a tiny figure of a man, apparently carved from black opal. No, not tiny, it was life-sized, with furious, glaring eyes that could almost have been alive. It was drawn down, only to bob up again, over and over, as if something prevented it from going deeper. Was it a relic or offering cast into the Abysm to accompany a soul as it passed *beyond*?

It had nothing to do with her. Focus! Why had Lyf hidden the pearl here? For its protection, or did he haunt the Abysm because he had not been given the proper rituals after death? Because his spirit had never passed on, Tali knew that the sacred king-magery had been lost upon his death, and without it no new king could be crowned. Was that why he was so desperate to get the five pearls? To gain a new source of magery?

The pearl was still now. The rush of threads past her slowed, the snatches of speech faded, then Tali's hair stirred in a warm up-current that carried with it a familiar oily-sweet odour with an underlying bitterness. Alkoyl—the deadly chymical fluid that had eaten that young woman's leg off in the back tunnels of Cython, the stuff Wil had used to set the sulphur ground in the Seethings ablaze. Why was she smelling it here?

"I'll have to send down the Hellish Conduit for more," the master chymister had said, "if I can get anyone to go."

He had shuddered as he spoke. Was the Abysm linked to the conduit, and if so, what lay at the other end of it that contained such awful power?

Tali dismissed the distracting questions she could not resolve. Take the pearl and run. She was reaching out for it, and it was trembling as if it yearned for her touch, when she heard that strident, angry, *false* call . . .

The facinore must have scented her and it was moving her way.

Was the shadow shifter in the Abysm, or outside? Terror numbed her for a minute; Tali fought it down. Outside, she thought. Lyf would not allow that foul creature into such a holy place.

If she went out, it would attack. But she could not stay here either, because Lyf could return at any time. To take on the facinore, however, she had to have magery and lots of it.

She edged towards the pearl, trying not to alarm it. It occurred to Tali that, when she had used her gift as a child, she had also seen tangles of colour in her head. Each time, in a fury, she had snatched at one of those tangles and hurled it at her foe, not realising she was using a clumsy kind of magery.

The spectible revealed spirals of colour spinning out of Lyf's pearl in a complex pattern where the smallest part contained the whole. Prudence told her to fly with Lyf's pearl, but when would she have a better chance to decipher her own pearl than here in the Abysm, where the patterns of magery were so bright and clear? I'll give it one minute, she thought, and if I learn nothing about my pearl, I'll go.

She concentrated on the tangles writhing through her inner eye, trying to reconcile them with the endless spirals coming from Lyf's pearl. The colours in her head were whirling and twisting ran-domly—or were they?

What if she was only seeing a tiny part of the pattern, because she was looking at it from *inside*? It would be like trying to deci-pher the structure of the universe by peering at the night sky through a pinhole.

She fixed the spiral from Lyf's pearl in her memory, tried to imagine a similar spiral coming from her own pearl and, for a moment, Tali glimpsed the whole glorious pattern radiating from her pearl, and *understood* it. Before it could disappear she reached out with her mind's eye, took hold of a tiny piece of the pattern and drew it into herself. And as she did, her magery rose inside her all the way to the surface, not in a chaotic, uncontrollable surge, but steadily, like a well that could be drawn upon at need.

Tears stung her eyes. At last!

But a long time had passed. Quick! Grab the pearl. Go!

The instant she snatched at it, Tali knew it was the wrong thing to do, but the realisation came too late. The pearl shot backwards out of reach, shrieking the *call*. And far away, Lyf answered in a strangled cry of fear and fury.

She sensed him attempting to separate from the unpleasant mind he was possessing—a magian and killer who had *three* pearls, stolen from Lyf. And Tali's mental shell was wide open; she could not close it without also closing off her magery. Even if Lyf was in Caulderon, where she had previously sensed the triple call, *di*-DA-*doh? Di*-DA-*doh*, his consciousness could cross the distance quickly.

Trapped! Why had she delayed? Outside, in the flaskoid chamber, the facinore howled and clawed at the crack.

"*Come*!" Tali made the word a command.

The pearl spun away towards its hiding place. She dived after it, but it vanished, then the crack opened and she was ejected into the main chamber.

She raised her hands to blast the facinore but her magery sank out of sight like the water level in an over-pumped well—as if only in the power-saturated Abysm was it possible. A repulsive stench blasted up her nostrils then something scabbed and slimy clamped around her ankle.

The facinore had her.

CHAPTER 83

Rix saw a golden nimbus form around Rannilt only to be slammed back into her. She yelped, clenched her pointed jaw and the nimbus reformed, brighter. Again it was driven back into her. Rannilt let out a strained groan, pressed her hands together like a diver and thrust them upwards at the blur.

The facinore was clinging to the wall like a chameleon to a branch. It reached up, yanked and Tali appeared there, upside-down, suspended by the ankle from its right hand.

"Rix?" Tali wailed, "why did you bring Rannilt *here*?"

Rix was asking himself the same question. The facinore had felt Rannilt's great gift before, and it would not be long before Lyf knew she was here.

Its arms shifted to wings, to crab claws and back to arms; the shadows writhed and fluttered all around it. It drew Tali towards it, hissed a visible breath in her face and a silver aura appeared like a halo above her head. The facinore snatched at it, tore part of it away and swallowed it. The rest of the aura faded.

Rix's skin crept. Was it trying to feed on her psyche, attacking her mentally as well as physically? He raised the sword, wondering if he could hurl it true and impale the beast. No, the risk was too great.

Rannilt shrieked in fury and thrust her folded hands up again. The facinore reared backwards, Tali tore free, tumbled and landed hard on her feet with the beast close behind.

She darted towards the shelves, looking around desperately. The facinore's legs shifted to frog's legs; it leapt over her head and blocked her, spreading its arms wide. Bare feet skidding on the black floor, she shot back towards Rix. It sprang over her head again.

Its back was to Rix, only three steps away. He lunged, aiming to pierce its heart from behind, but it shifted and the sword tip skidded off thick, ridged armour, then it leapt over Tali again, out of reach. Rix cursed and went after it.

"Tali, you can kill the beast," cried Rannilt. "I know you can."

Tali was trembling, her eyes darting. What was she looking for? A moan burst from her but she strangled it. She made hand-over-hand motions as if raising a bucket from a well, then extended her right hand towards the creature. A jagged grey clot shot forth, though it only shattered against the facinore's chest like mushy ice.

"Your gift's there!" yelled Rannilt. "I can see it."

Rannilt flung a golden globe at the facinore, which ducked and shot out a chitinous fist, striking her a glancing blow to the left temple and sending her tumbling. She took a shuddering breath and rolled over, holding her head with both hands and trying not to cry.

"Rannilt, stay down!" Tali blasted again and again but her feeble gift could only produce harmless, rotten ice.

"Out of the way," said Rix.

Tobry yanked him back by the shoulder. "The facinore was created by magery, and only magery can finish it."

His arm was trembling, his voice thick. Fear of the shifter was choking him and Rix knew he couldn't do it. If Tobry took on the facinore he would die.

"I can deal with it, Tobe," said Rix.

"I let you down last time," Tobry said bitterly. "I'm not doing it again."

Rix knocked him aside and extended the titane blade, gauging his foe. It did not retreat. It was leaning towards Tali, a humanoid core with those eerily shifting limbs and the fluttering shadows surrounding it that made it nine feet tall. It reeked of blood and sweat and the carrion it had been feeding on.

It was a creature of the magery he had always feared, and powerful magery at that, stronger than anything he had come across outside these caverns. But Rannilt had hurt it out in the Seethings and surely he could do as much here. Rix lunged and struck at its back.

It whirled, the left fist clubbed and shot out like a Cythonian war rocket. Rix tried to parry it but the air clung to his blade like tar and he barely got it up in time to protect his face from a blow that would have pulped it. The facinore's fist struck the flat of the blade, driving it against his forehead so hard that Rix saw coloured lights. He staggered, momentarily dazed, went to one knee then recovered as the other fist came looping around, shifting and opening like lobster pincers.

Instinct jerked the edge of his blade into its path. The pincers split down the limb and the left half shot past his head. The right half struck him a skidding blow on the cheek that knocked him sideways and almost tore his ear off. Defence was going to be fatal. His only option was to attack.

The severed pincers withdrew, *shifted* to the serrated blade of a sawfish and the muscles behind it swelled as it prepared for a killing blow. Rix settled into the warrior's mindset where his sword became an extension of his arm and he simply reacted. The sawfish blade swung. Rix did too, hacking it off, and when it clattered to the floor it sizzled into a black, glutinous stain.

The facinore shifted its other arm to a narwhal's tusk and tried to spear him through the groin. He leapt onto the six-foot tusk, swung low and clove it off at the shoulder. The facinore shrieked and stumbled, and its enveloping shadow shrank, retreating into flesh. The shifter seemed smaller than before, though it was still bigger than he was. He was only one lucky blow away from death, but luck was an unreliable ally.

His own warrior's heart was not; attack was the only defence worth pursuing. He lunged, weaving between the blows, and struck at its chest, turning the sword tip in a circle as if to cut out its heart. Fire seared up the blade, the facinore reared and the sword withdrew. He'd hurt it.

A rhino's foot struck his kneecap, numbing the whole leg. He staggered sideways and the blow that would have smashed his pelvis glanced off his hip and spun him around. He went with it, whirling and putting the momentum into his swing, and was aiming for its neck when an icy needle blast pierced his shoulder.

Before Rix could check behind him the facinore attacked with a pile-driving flurry of blows, driving him backwards, and suddenly he was fighting for his life. A dozen chisel-shaped protrusions shot at him. He severed three, then another two, and ducked the rest. The facinore shrank and withdrew a step.

Ha! Rix thought.

Before he could strike a fatal blow, another rain of cold needles spiked into the back of his shoulder. He was under attack with *magery*. The ice set alight his nerve fibres, spread to his heart and it began to race and burn as it had done when he had been attacked by Mijl the pothecky, by the lake. When he had nearly died . . .

There was no one behind him save Tobry. Rix turned, free hand pressed to his heart, the other hand fighting the titane blade which had begun to shudder as though thirsting to drink the blood of his dearest friend.

A friend with someone else glaring out of his eyes.

Lyf had returned, and in the chaos he had slipped into Tobry's unprotected mind like a key into a lock.

CHAPTER 84

"What's the matter with Tobry?" Rannilt whispered, probing the huge bruise where the facinore had struck her.

Tali swayed, struggling to take in all that had happened. Her magery had been pathetic; she had done more with it as a little girl. And Rix, who had driven the facinore back in that furious attack, was gaping at Tobry, his free hand clutched to his heart and the titane sword shuddering so violently that he could barely hold it.

The mixture of horror and revulsion in Tobry's eyes chilled her, but worse was the familiar yellow growing in their centres. Tobry's right hand pointed the elbrot at Rix as if to blast him apart. Tobry's left arm kept jerking upwards, his hooked fingers clawing at his own eyes as if to tear them out, but it was forced down again. He was fighting Lyf with everything he had, but that was not enough.

"Lyf's possessed him," said Tali.

"What do that mean?" said Rannilt.

Tongues of fire sizzled from the elbrot, crimson and jagged. Rix deflected most of them with the sword and they shot upwards, striking a red-haired king in Lyf's ancestor gallery and dissolving him in an instant. A single flame caught on Rix's left ear and flared, singeing hair. He yelped and smashed it out but it flared again, and again until Rannilt directed a wobbling little globe at it. It splattered on the side of Rix's head, drenching him and extinguishing the flare.

"Thanks!" he said without looking around.

"Tali?" said Rannilt.

"Lyf has got into Tobry's mind and is making him attack Rix."

"But . . . that's horrible."

Rix's eyes were locked on the yellow eyes as if he could drive Lyf out by sheer force of will. The facinore stood to one side, statue-still now. Awaiting Lyf's command? Or an opportunity to break free of him?

"Possession is an enemy you can never escape," said Tali. "He can take you over at any time, make you do terrible things, and you know that even your friends are afraid to trust you."

"I'll always trust Tobry, same as I trust you," Rannilt said fiercely. "No one's stoppin' me."

Tali hugged the child, overcome by her loyalty and her simple faith. Tobry and Rix had risked their lives to return to this terrible place, to help her. Rannilt had done the same, and what greater gift could anyone give?

"Can't we drive Lyf out?" said Rannilt.

"I don't know how."

"Get her out of sight," Rix said from the corner of his mouth. "Don't let her use her gift."

Tali jerked Rannilt behind her. "Stay there. Don't move. Don't try and help."

"But no one else can stop the beast," said Rannilt.

"Rix can. Just do what I say."

Tobry's elbrot fired a spray of tiny emerald shot. Again Rix's sword deflected the attack, seemingly of its own accord, the little balls pattering against the walls and eating fuming holes where they touched. If one touched Rix, presumably it would eat into him, too.

A shudder wracked him. Once more the sword leapt in his hand and he dragged it back only inches before it spitted Tobry's throat. Lyf threw Tobry backwards, away from the blade, but Tobry drove himself forwards again. Tali pressed her hands to her cheeks. What if Rix could not stop it next time?

Tobry moaned, his right arm jerked up and he tore open his shirt, baring his chest to the blade. He made a series of incoherent grunts, trying to force out the words Lyf was holding back. Foam oozed from his mouth.

He gasped, "Do it, Rix!"

Rannilt took a breath that seemed to go in forever. "You'n me, we've got to save 'em, Tali."

But Lyf was far more powerful than they would ever be. For two thousand years he had been strengthening his plans and tightening his control. Tali's spirit faltered; her feeble and troublesome gift could never stop him. "How can we, child?"

"They helped us so we can't let them go. I've still got some golden magery left."

At the earnest look on Rannilt's face, Tali bit her tongue. The war, if Rannilt survived it, would force her to grow up all too soon. Let her cling to the absolutes of childhood as long as she could. And who knew, maybe she was right. She hugged the skinny, determined waif.

"Keep it ready, but don't use it unless it's an emergency. I'll think of something. We'll save them, somehow."

How? The heatstone! Where was her pack? She had dropped it before climbing the wall.

Rix's sword leapt in his hand so powerfully that his boots slipped on the floor. This time the tip drew blood on Tobry's scarred chest before Rix heaved it back.

"Why is the sword trying to kill Tobry?" said Rannilt. "Has Lyf taken it over too?"

"I don't think so," said Tali. "That would be like attacking himself. I think ... the sword hates Lyf, and Rix said Lyf was afraid of it. *Oathbreaker's blade*, he called it."

When had Lyf encountered it before? As a wrythen, or as a living man two thousand years ago?

The foam oozing from Tobry's mouth went pink. He was gasping and grunting as he tried to fight the possession, but the yellow eyes within his eyes were relentless and his arm was slowly rising, the elbrot in his left hand glimmering as if Lyf were charging it up for a killing blow. And the facinore stood guard to stop Rix getting away.

Tobry spat out bloody foam. "Cut me down, Rix, or all's lost."

"I—can't." Rix jammed the point of his sword against the floor to hold it back. It screeched across the polished stone and whipped up at Tobry again, shrilling as it cut through the air. Rix grounded it at the last second.

"Once he's fully—possessed me—never be free. Sooner—be dead."

"Rix, don't!" gasped Rannilt.

The sword lunged, dragging Rix with it, and he barely managed to turn it aside from Tobry's heart. If Rix had to kill his friend, how could he live? And if Tobry killed Rix, even while possessed, it would destroy him.

For the moment, no one was looking at Tali. She backed away, motioning to Rannilt to stay out of sight. Lyf wanted Tali's pearl and it was almost within his grasp, for whatever Rix did, it would fail. If he killed Tobry, Lyf would reoccupy his wrythen form and attack again, or order the facinore to kill Rix, and Rix would surely give up. She could see the horror in his eyes at the thought that he might cut Tobry down.

Ah, there was her pack, at the base of the wall. She felt inside it for the wrapped heatstone and began to peel the wrappings away. Her fingers were shaking so badly she could barely hold the cloth. She pulled and the stone slipped through her fingers. It was uncannily warm and the feel of it on her skin made her squirm. Her heart was beating wildly as she drew it out.

The heatstone was an inch and a half thick. How to break it? The walls of the flaskoid looked like rock glass but the surface was rubbery and would not serve. And the bookcases were of the same material. She raised it above her head, mentally prepared herself for the pain and the surge of power when it broke, and hurled it at the floor.

It bounced and flew towards Tobry, but Lyf thrust Tobry's elbrot into its path and the heatstone slammed into it, bursting in an implosion of light and sound that wrenched a scream from Tobry and speared pain through Tali from skull to groin. She was reaching out desperately for the power when the facinore snatched part of it and grew two sizes. Lyf swirled the elbrot in a spiral, gathered the remainder into himself and forced Tobry to bow, ironic thanks.

The mud in Tobry's eyes disappeared—they were Lyf-yellow now. Frustration rose inside Tali like a scream. She had hurt Tobry, strengthened Lyf and gained nothing.

She searched her inner eye for the patterns she had seen so clearly in the Abysm, patterns that were both the source of power and the key to magery. They were faded here, and so blurred it was a struggle to bring them into focus. As she tried to draw on a small loop, Lyf's eyes flicked towards her and her head gave a painful throb. Her protective shell snapped shut and the colours vanished.

He smiled with Tobry's mouth, a sneering twist of the lips that mocked her pitiful attempt to use the pearl he regarded as his. She stepped backwards, involuntarily, and smelled alkoyl again. Why was she smelling it here?

The sword dragged Rix a step towards Tobry. Rix's eyes were starting out of his head and a trickle of blood ran from his left nostril, luminously red in the uncanny light. Tali could hear his teeth grinding.

"If you care for me at all," said Tobry, "do it!"

Rix did not move.

The facinore's eyes revolved as it digested the stolen power. It doubled over, choking up wisps of brown shadow, then exploded across the chamber, smashing down the bookcases and colliding with the platina still, sending it crashing to the floor. Droplets of green sprayed from its lower end and fumes belched up. It was an alkoyl still.

Alkoyl held a different kind of power and it had saved Tali once before. She surreptitiously checked around her through the spectible. On a stone table, thirty feet away in the gloom, a book lay open with a silvery aura of magery wisping up from its pages. An *iron book*.

In the Seethings, Wil had mentioned a series of secret books called the Solaces. *Touched the iron book, I did. Saw you in the future.* But not this book, surely, since Wil had never been out of Cython before. What was the connection between Wil and that iron book, and this one, and alkoyl?

The eyes in Tobry's eyes were fixed on the titane sword. No one was watching Tali. She edged towards the table. The book had cast-iron covers and its thick pages, numbering no more than thirty, were sheets of beaten iron, deeply engraved with Cythonian glyphs she could not read. The book lay open at the third-last page, the writing ending halfway down it, and the last two pages were blank.

The smell of alkoyl was strong here. Her head was spinning. Then, standing over the book, she saw that the bottom of each etched letter was thickly crimson, as if half filled with boiling blood. She turned the pages forwards and discovered that she could read the title on the cover—*The Consolation of Vengeance*. Vengeance she understood in her bones, but why consolation?

"Paralyse—him!" Lyf forced the words through Tobry's unwilling lips.

Tobry's eyes appeared for a second over Lyf's and he cried, "Rix, he's eating me alive. Cut me down."

Rix's jaw knotted like a bag of walnuts. He raised the sword, took a slow step forwards, then another. The elbrot spat more emerald shot at him but the blade diverted it, almost contemptuously. The yellow eyes retreated to the back of Tobry's eyes. Tobry's free hand rose, making a hand signal to the facinore.

It came hurtling back, out of control. Its muscles bunched and it formed new appendages on its arm stumps. The stumps lengthened, extending towards the back of Rix's head, crossed and joined. Rix did not notice; his eyes were fixed on Tobry as he took another slow step, like a marcher at a funeral. He was close enough to strike. The facinore's two hands formed a set of nutcrackers, yawned wide enough to crack a skull-sized nut, then slowly began to close around Rix's head.

Tali threw out her arms, knowing she could do nothing to save him and momentarily forgetting her most important duty. Rix, that wonderful, generous, heroic man, could not die this way.

Rannilt ran out into the open, screaming, "Rix, behind you!"

Tali dived, trying to stop her, but Rannilt hurled a ball of light at the facinore.

"Ah, *quessence*," said Lyf, and smiled, and reached out to draw the golden globe to him.

And in that second, Tali realised that every good thing she and Rannilt and Rix and Tobry had done in the war was about to be undone.

CHAPTER 85

"Take it back!" Tali shrieked as Rannilt's little globe shot across the chamber.

Lyf was smiling, reaching out for it with Tobry's glowing elbrot. Rannilt evaded Tali's clutching fingers, raced across the chamber and tried to draw the globe back, but it shot up beyond her reach.

The facinore's skull-crackers snapped at Rix's head. Tali choked, but the paralysis broke and Rix ducked and whirled, striking up at it and re-severing both arms in the one blow. Its legs shrank, it stumbled, the fluttering shadows withdrew to a dark band surrounding it, then began to flare and fade. With a screechy whine, the facinore dwindled until it was smaller than Rix, and then it backed away.

Tobry lurched forwards, stiff-legged, stretching up on tiptoes for the drifting globe. Rix swung the sword at his friend's neck. Rannilt wailed and covered her eyes. Tali choked.

But Rix twisted and lifted the blade at the last instant, slamming the flat of it into the side of Tobry's head and he crumpled, unconscious. His eyes emptied and Lyf's yellow eyes reappeared in the wrythen's empty form, which filled like a balloon, soared up to catch the golden globe and thrust it into its chest. Its middle— Lyf's middle—darkened until Tali could no longer see through it, as if it were changing from wrythen to a real being.

Lyf was floating ten feet high, out of reach of the sword he so feared. White bone gleamed in his shin stumps and he was staring at Rannilt as if he had never met anyone like her before. Then he smiled and met her eyes and pointed a finger. Rannilt was panting now, shaking her head, covering her eyes and trying to get away, but he whispered, *Come forth*, and more golden light burst from her. Taking hold of a thread of it, he reeled it in and rolled it into a ball around his arm.

Rannilt collapsed with a little sigh. Lyf thickened further and, while the golden draw continued, extended his left hand towards the armless facinore. It let out a squeal of fear as it was pulled towards him. Lyf clenched a fist around the upper part of its shadow and drew it into his chest. Rannilt heaved like a caterpillar on a leaf. The facinore screamed, a shrill, ugly sound as, bit by bit, its shadow halo was stripped away and also incorporated into Lyf.

Without it the facinore was a gaunt, shuddering monster, a scrawny thing all bone and sinew and stringy lengths of desiccated muscle. Lyf gestured and a second globe was wrenched from Rannilt's mouth. She moaned, faint and feeble now, and Tali felt a pang of fear. Lyf was taking so much from the little girl, how could she survive?

Lyf swallowed the globe and momentarily his chest glowed golden-red, as if real blood was beginning to flow in him. He was getting stronger every second. Tali willed her gift to come. If it did not, she could not save Rannilt or any of them.

Rix took a slow step towards Lyf, who held up a hand. Rix ground to a halt as though the air had set hard to hold him back. Lyf gestured towards the facinore's legs, twirling his fingers. The facinore screamed as a layer of muscle was stripped off its legs in sprays of black blood, then drifted towards Lyf. He continued to twirl his fingers and the muscle strips wrapped around his wrythen legs like lengths of ribbon, slowly building them into reality, all the way down to his stumps.

Tali covered her eyes, peeped through her fingers and covered her eyes again, shuddering at how quickly his power had grown. His chest pulsed red, gold, red—he was using Rannilt's life force and gift to cannibalise the facinore's body into his own, and if he was this strong with only part of a body, she dared not imagine what he could do when it was completed.

Lyf drew the elbrot from Tobry's hand, pointed it at Rix's head and spoke, mind to all their minds.

Ten years I have worked my compulsion on you. Now you are mine and you must atone.

"No, Rix!" Tali screamed. "He's a stinking liar and a murderer. Don't listen to anything he says."

Rix might not have heard her, for he choked and the tip of his sword struck the floor, scattering chips of smoking stone. He jerked his head from side to side as if his neck joints were fused together.

"Done nothing wrong," he slurred.

Remember the blood?

Rix dropped the sword, *clang*, stared at his hands then rubbed them furiously on his coat as though they were smirched with blood. Tali remembered the blood on the boy's hands, in that cellar of long ago, and her scalp crawled. Such was Lyf's power that even she wondered what Rix had done.

She fought it and spoke the words she no longer quite believed. "He's a liar, Rix. You've done nothing wrong."

Obeying me is the only way you can gain peace.

"Get out of my head!" cried Rix.

It belongs to me. You will cut it out of her and bring it to me.

The top of Tali's head throbbed. Rix was cracking, falling under Lyf's power, and any minute now he would break.

Rix's cheeks shivered as if worms were crawling under the skin. "Go away, leave me alone." He groaned and bent for the sword.

You are mine. I own you.

Rix's fingers closed over the hilt of the sword.

Cut it from her.

He hefted the sword.

Not with that! Lyf tossed down a tool with a circular cutting edge. *Cut it out now!*

An image flashed through Tali's head—the murder cellar, the way Rix had sketched it. She heard a tooth crack in his tightly clenched jaw, then he took a slow, grinding step towards her and the look in his eyes was not Rix at all. Lyf had taken command of him. Was this the end?

Tobry was unconscious, Rannilt dying and Rix was out of control. Tali had to do something and, if her magery would not work, all she had left was her own strength. Lyf might not be expecting physical attack from a small woman he had always underestimated.

With an effort, she heaved the iron book off the table and swung it out to one side, for it was incredibly heavy. Rix stopped as if he had been frozen to the floor.

Put that down! Lyf shot towards her, arms outstretched.

She swung the heavy book, slowly at first, then gathering momentum that would make it difficult to stop, and as Lyf dived she smashed him in the face.

The blow passed right through his translucent wrythen head, driving his more solid upper body backwards. Blood-red ink—or red-tinged alkoyl—was driven out of the etched letters in the book to form seething globules inside his skull.

Lyf screamed.

The pearl in the Abysm shrieked and so did Tali's own, agonisingly, then, faintly, the three distant, stolen pearls. She let out a sigh, and knew that the master of the three pearls had realised where she was. Then the half-wrythen with the legs made from a facinore fell to the floor like an empty cloak.

Where was Lyf? Had he possessed Tobry again? No, Tobry still lay unconscious. Tali's head was shrieking, but she scanned the chamber through the spectible and caught a flash from the corner of an eye as Lyf's disembodied consciousness hurtled through the crack into the white shaft of the Abysm. The crack vanished.

Her fingers stung from the iron book. She dropped it on the table and Tobry shot upright as if propelled by a spring. Pale and dazed and swaying, he looked down at his right hand in bewilderment. It was swollen and purple; huge, fluid-filled blisters covered his palm and fingers, burns from the bursting heatstone. Then he must have remembered, for the colour rose to his face and she saw the sick horror in his eyes. He raked at his skull as if it carried some vile infestation, then doubled over, retching.

Rix shook his head as though waking from a nightmare. With a roar that echoed through the flaskoid chamber, he snatched the titane sword, jamming it through the facinore's mouth and out the back of its head. It flopped and fell, twitching beside the empty wrythen, but did not die. Lyf must be keeping it alive until he could strip the rest of its flesh from it.

Tali fell to her knees beside Rannilt, who lay as still as before, and pressed her hands to the girl's chest. "Heal, heal!" she whispered, but her hands did not warm, nor did Rannilt react.

"Come on," said Rix, lifting the child, "before Lyf comes back. Bring the book."

Tali wrapped it in a piece hacked from the hem of her coat and pulled on her discarded boots. Tobry recovered his charred elbrot. Then they went up, looking over their shoulders all the way. They passed out through the cave mouth and down the bloodstained rubble where the bodies of the two women were nothing but bones, and under the vine thicket to the horses. Several jackal shifters lay broken there, kicked to death. There were eyes all around in the darkness.

Tobry would not meet Tali's eye. Rix hacked at every branch they passed as if the whole world was his enemy. Rannilt lay in Tali's arms, breathing steadily now, a little colour had returned to her pale cheeks, but nothing could wake her.

A defeat or a victory? Tali had not beaten the wrythen, as the chancellor had hoped. Rather, the intrusion had strengthened Lyf. Nonetheless, she had gained some understanding of her magery and almost taken his ebony pearl, and he had been shaken to be attacked in his hitherto inviolable realm. The facinore, the most potent of his shifter creations, was finished, and they had his iron book. It was a victory of sorts—or would be when Rannilt woke.

If Rannilt woke.

CHAPTER 86

The ride home, under the twilight of that choking brown over-cast sky, was silent and endless. What was *The Consolation of Vengeance* for? And what did it say? Though cold to the touch, it radiated heat. Tali could feel it through the leather of the saddle-bag.

And why, since it was Lyf's book, had it hurt him so badly when she had struck him with it? Had taking it been a master stroke, or a fatal folly? She could not tell. Not even Tobry, who knew five lan-guages, could read the glyphs inside.

He was slumped in the saddle, eyes dead, and she did not know how to aid him. Tobry was a man whose word was unbreakable, a man who would do anything to help those he held dear, yet Lyf had forced him to attack his friend. It was eating him alive.

Something ailed Rix, too, something that bit even deeper than the wrythen taking command of him and ordering him to *cut it from her*. He alternated between furious rages and intervals of slack-jawed apathy.

"Tobe," said Rix, riding stirrup to stirrup with him, "do you think –?"

"It's finished, Rix. I'm utterly and irretrievably dishonoured." *"How do you think I feel?"*

Something snapped and Rix spurred away, hacking down an innocent needlebush as he passed, then several branches off a blood-bark tree.

"Damn you!" he roared, racing back to them and brandishing his sword towards Precipitous Crag. "You will not command me!"

The echoes chased themselves back and forth between the bluffs to either side, mocking him.

"Ride away, Tali, and ride fast," he said, biting the words off and flinging them to the wind. "When next Lyf comes, I'm not sure I'll be able to resist his compulsion."

Tali forced herself to swallow her fear. She could no longer fight alone, and without Rix and Tobry she was lost. She reached across and put a hand on his arm.

"I believe in you, just as I believe in Tobry. When Lyf comes, you will resist him."

"He's stronger each time!" said Rix, wild-eyed.

She tightened her grip. "So is Tobry, and so are you. You're much stronger than when I first met you, and a better man, and I trust you, no matter what. And if Rannilt was—" she had almost said *alive*—"was *awake*, she would say the same. We have to hold together. We're all that stands between Lyf and victory now."

Rix stared at her as if she had gone mad. He swallowed and rubbed his eyes, but not before she saw tears form there. He nodded stiffly, as if afraid to speak. "You have no idea what that means to me."

Tobry turned those empty eyes on her. "Have you ever been violated?"

"No," she said quietly.

"It's as though he's emptied all his fury into me, a festering rage at what was done to his people. He owns me now, Tali. How can I fight him?"

"He's not as strong as you think. We can still beat him." They were empty words. Tali had none that could comfort him.

A mile or two further on, Rix said suddenly, "I envisaged that opal sculpture again, Tobe."

"When?" Tobry said dully.

"As we left the caverns."

"I saw one too," said Tali, and told them about the contorted figure she had seen bobbing up and down, deep in the Abysm. "But it looked too perfect to be a sculpture."

Rix drew a sharp breath. "What else could it be?"

"It looked like a man turned to opal . . . yet . . . "

"What?"

"I'm sure the eyes were alive."

No one could guess what it meant. Hours later, they were riding up a high hill when Rix cried, "They're gone!"

"Who's gone?" said Tali.

"The enemy. From Caulderon."

Smoke still belched from the burning shanty towns outside the walls and brown trails issued from a dozen places within the city, but the grey shadow of the Cythonian armies was no longer there.

"The city's fallen," said Rix bleakly. "We're too late."

Tobry checked with Rix's telescope. "The gates are still standing, and they're manned by our troops." His voice rose. "And . . . I can see dozens of prisoners, chained to the walls and the gates . . . "

"Can we have beaten them?" said Tali.

"You must have hurt Lyf more than we thought," said Tobry. For the first time that day, she saw a hint of hope in his bruised eyes.

"We'd better make plans," said Rix. "If we ride in together, the palace's spies will hear about it in minutes. I'll go alone. Tobry, come later with Tali and Rannilt. Bring them underground to my chambers."

"The chancellor will surely guess I'm there," said Tali. "And Rannilt."

"There's nowhere else to go," Rix said distractedly. "I've got—" He swallowed. "Got a duty to pay."

He galloped off, leaving Tali and Tobry staring after him.

The streets were a drunken carnival clogged with people, and every stride of the way they clutched at Rix's stirrups, crying out their glad tidings.

"We showed them. The gutless rock rats are running for their lives."

Rix shook them off and rode on, grim of face. He could only think of one thing now—his mother's treason and his duty to report it. Acid burnt up his throat. How could he make the threat known to the chancellor without implicating her?

He used his horse to force passage through the throngs, heading for the chancellor's palace, and was admitted at once. The chancellor was at a red-jasper-framed window, looking down on the celebrations.

"Caulderon is doomed," he said without turning around, "yet for the sake of morale the poor must have their street parties. And the rich their Honouring, tomorrow."

Rix remembered, guiltily, the portrait that had to be completed tonight.

The chancellor took an upholstered chair by the fire and gestured to the other. "Clearly, the encounter at the Crag was not a complete success."

"No," said Rix. "But Tali hurt him." He told the story briefly, omitting any details that could harm her.

The chancellor listened without comment, then said, "Why have you come here?"

Rix stared into the flames, but found no assistance there. When he looked up, the chancellor was studying him, impassively. Rix looked down again. "I've overheard a plot. To get rid of you."

"Don't mumble, boy!" The chancellor leaned forwards, his face unreadable. "When did you hear this?"

Rix had never found it easy to lie, except to his mother. "Two days ago."

"Before you stole my horses and galloped to Precipitous Crag."

He shivered. Minds were open books to the chancellor. What did he know? Was this a test?

"Yes."

"How long before?"

The noose was tightening. If he lied and said days or weeks, it would make him an accessory. "Less than a day."

"I know you're a brave man, and I'm told you're an honourable one," said the chancellor. "Since you're only telling me about the treason now, the plotter must be friend or family."

Rix could not speak; he could hardly breathe.

"And the name?" said the chancellor.

"I—can't say," Rix said in a strangled voice.

"Allow me to assist you. My spies watch your windows and one of your door guards is my man. On the day before you left, you did not go out of your tower, and no one entered save myself, Lady Ricinus, Tobry Lagger, Tali vi Torgrist, and servants. You would not keep silent for a servant, and I know it wasn't Tali." He leaned back and his hard little eyes met Rix's. "I hope it was Lagger. I've always despised the man."

Out in the city, every steam whistle went off at once. Rix sprang up. "What's that? Are we attacked?" The whistles died as though they had run out of steam.

"Sit down," said the chancellor.

As Rix sat, a drop of sweat ran down his nose. The chancellor would order Tobry's execution without a qualm. But if Rix denied it was Tobry, it was the same as betraying his mother.

"If you don't deny it," said the chancellor, "your silence affirms his guilt and he dies a traitor's death." He reached for the bell pull to his left.

A black-haired servant girl came in, carrying something heavy on a large silver tray covered by a silk cloth. She set it down on a low table between Rix and the chancellor. The chancellor nodded, she lifted the cloth and withdrew.

Rix jumped, sending his chair backwards. A small white dog,

contorted by the agony of its death, lay on the tray. Blood had leaked from its mouth and bowel. The chancellor leaned forwards, stroking the small head, then looked up.

"Ricin," he said. "The deadliest poison in Hightspall, the most agonising death, and there is no antidote."

"How did it happen?"

"I thought myself well protected. I had employed every protection at my disposal, yet still the assassin got through. The poison was meant for me."

"It wasn't Tobry," Rix gasped.

"But he knows about the plot? You're his best friend. You tell him everything."

"He knows nothing. I dared not tell him."

The chancellor leaned forwards again, eyes impaling Rix. He felt like a worm with a hook through its guts.

"If Lagger is innocent, only one person can be guilty."

Rix kept silent, clinging to the pathetic illusion that not naming his mother lessened the betrayal.

"That poison is both a trademark and a challenge," said the chancellor.

"I—I don't understand."

"Ricin comes from the castor oil plant, also called *Ricinus*, which is on your house crest. Poison is a woman's weapon, isn't it? And she'll try again."

Rix stared at the dead dog, afraid to speak.

"Name the name," said the chancellor inexorably.

"I—can't betray my own!"

"If you don't, you're betraying your country at a time of war. That won't just bring you down, it will topple your house."

"My house?" Rix whispered.

"Your country comes before your house—*always*."

"If you know who made the threat, why do I have to say it."

"Traitors must be named. *Name her!*"

"I'm sure she didn't mean it," said Rix. "She retracted it at once."

"Then where's the difficulty?"

"Naming her is her death sentence."

"Such a cunning, ruthless and well-connected woman is far more use to me alive than dead—especially if her life, *and her house*, relies on my favour."

Waves of relief coursed over Rix. The chancellor was right. Lady Ricinus could help him in all kinds of ways. He met the chancellor's eyes.

"Name the plotter," said the chancellor.

The hook twisted in Rix's guts. He tried to speak, but could not; tried again.

"It was Mother," he gasped, staring at the black tiles. "Lady Ricinus made the threat."

CHAPTER 87

Sickness churned in Rix's belly. He had broken the greatest taboo of the noble houses. He had betrayed his mother and was utterly dishonoured.

The chancellor bared his teeth. He had all he needed to bring Lady Ricinus down. "So House Ricinus falls, brought down from within."

It was like a blow to the groin, as agonising as it was unexpected.

"But ... but ... " Rix felt like a stupid schoolboy, crushed by a master and a rule he could not understand. "You gave me no choice—you said, 'My country first, *always.*'"

"That was a test, and you failed it."

"A *test?*"

"You're brave, strong and a born leader. Had your other qualities matched those, you would have been a great asset to me in the fight-back. But you're a bitter disappointment, Rixium. You failed in the most vital quality of all—loyalty."

"Loyalty," Rix said numbly.

"I lied to test you. A chancellor must put his country first. However the first duty of the heir to a noble house is always to protect his house."

"I *was* protecting it!" Rix cried.

"By condemning your own mother? If you could not even show *her* loyalty, how could *I* expect it? How could I ever trust you?"

The chancellor pulled the bell and said to the two guards who came at once, "Escort him from my palace."

Rix stumbled across the snow-covered grounds towards a side gate to Palace Ricinus, his head reeling. He was lower than the street scum down at the docks, where life was bought and sold for a length of copper wire or a worn pair of shoes. And what if the chancellor tried Lady Ricinus for high treason, and called Rix as the chief witness against her? Shame burned him like mage-fire.

Beyond the wall, a rocket soared high, exploding in multi-coloured pyrotechnics, but the cheering only made things worse. Morale had to be maintained and, despite his mother's treason and her sickening hypocrisy, there was no hope of the Honouring being cancelled. For the nobility, the well connected and the disgustingly rich, it would be the high point in their celebrations.

He sneaked into Palace Ricinus via a side door and headed for his mother's rooms. First, he must abase himself for disappearing for a day and a half, leaving the portrait uncompleted. Then, warn her that the chancellor knew about her plot, though how was he to do that without revealing that he had betrayed her?

Rix was tempted to say that the chancellor had told him about the treason, but lying to his mother would only compound his shame. And the worst of it was, Lady Ricinus did not make idle threats. Rix knew she had meant the poison for the chancellor.

He stopped halfway, unable to face her. Knowing himself to be a craven coward, he slunk away to his tower and sank into a scald-ing tub, shivering uncontrollably. For a man so dishonoured there were only two ways out—to take his own life in atonement, or renounce all worldly things and ride into the wilderness, never to return.

But he could not do either. He had a duty to defend his city, look after his people and protect his house. If it could be protected from the chancellor who, he felt sure, was determined to destroy it. And Rix had given him the means to do so.

He took no food. His stomach would have thrown it up. He

drove himself up to his studio and spent the afternoon and evening working at a furious pace. Completing the portrait could never make up for what he had done, but he would not compound the betrayal by breaking his word and ruining the Honouring.

"That's it," said Tobry, who had come in silently. "Don't do another stroke."

"It's the most hateful thing I've ever done."

"It's repellent, yet perfect. You've captured every aspect of Lord Ricinus, the bad and the good. Even Lady Ricinus will be pleased."

The thought gave Rix no pleasure, even if such a miracle did happen. "In my entire life, Mother has never been pleased with me."

He stepped back, studied the overall effect, then examined the portrait from one side, then the other. "It's not bad," he said grudgingly. "Better than I could have hoped ten days ago." He began to clean the brushes he could never use again. "Where have you been?"

"Getting Tali and Rannilt into the city, unseen."

"Where are they?"

"Down in the tunnels."

"Is Rannilt—?"

"She hasn't woken. I'll bring them up late tonight, once it's safe, and put them to bed under my bed." Tobry rubbed his bruised eyes. "I'm going to have a lie down."

"Now? I thought we'd have a drink."

"To celebrate completing the portrait?"

"If you like."

"I'm too exhausted."

"Then sit with me for a minute; I need to talk about something."

Tobry lay on the settee and closed his eyes. Rix fetched a bottle and took a swig of a red wine so strong that he could feel the enamel being etched off his front teeth. "I'm in trouble, Tobe."

"Thought you might be. What have you done now?"

"I've betrayed my mother," Rix blurted.

Tobry stared at him.

Between gulps, Rix told him the bitter tale.

Tobry got up, poured himself a goblet and topped up Rix's.

"I make no excuses," said Rix. "There are none. I'm dishonoured and I can't go on."

Tobry did not speak.

"Say it!" Rix cried.

"Considering the ruin of House Lagger, and my part in it, I'm in no position to judge anyone." Tobry sipped, grimaced, then took both goblets and the bottle and threw them out the window. "Wait here. Don't do anything stupid."

He went down the steps. The fishhooks were back in Rix's belly; he felt as though he was torn open inside. Seeking any distraction, he took a huge, primed canvas from the storeroom, set it up and redrew the murder cellar in a series of quick strokes. Painting normally soothed him, but this sickening divination only made things worse. Tobry reappeared with an ancient, dusty bottle and two goblets.

"What's that?" said Rix.

"The only bottle that survived the fall of our house. I've been keeping it for a suitable occasion."

"Like the end of the world," Rix said grimly.

"How better to celebrate it than with the finest port in existence, one hundred and twenty-seven years old." Tobry cleaned the bottle, eased out the blackened wooden stopper and sniffed it. A spark lit in his eyes. He poured Rix a generous measure.

They clinked goblets and sipped. "To friendship, and the world's end," said Tobry.

Rix echoed him. The magnificent port glided down his throat like buttered gold leaf, but he could take no pleasure from it.

"Betraying your mother, even for her high treason, is dire," said Tobry. "I can't deny that, even done in defence of your country and your house. But you have to go on."

"I don't think I can, old friend. I've poisoned my soul and there's no antidote."

"No man is irredeemable. You can still make up for it. Indeed, you must."

"How?" Rix said dully.

"Finish the cellar painting. Then, when the war resumes, defend your city and your people with your life." Tobry leaned forwards and clasped Rix's forearm. "The enemy are bound to come back, and when they do, they'll be planning to finish the job."

"I'm sure they will."

"Maybe, maybe not. Tali is *the one*, remember? She's bloodied Lyf's nose several times, without magery. And twice you've driven him off through sheer strength—"

"And the enchanted blade."

"He has his weapons, we have ours. This is the moment you were made for, Rix. Don't fail us now, or it really will be the end of our world."

"Even if I'm killed defending my house and my people, it can't wipe away the taint."

"Death wipes all," said Tobry, leaning back with his nose in his goblet and sighing in pure pleasure.

Once that had irritated Rix, but he was beyond such trivial vexations now. "In a hundred years, they'll still be talking about how I betrayed—"

Tobry sprang up. "Will you stop talking crap? In a hundred years, *if Hightspall still exists*, history will portray you as a troubled man who gave his life defending his people. What more can anyone ask?"

Rix stared at the cellar sketch. "Changing the subject, if Tali recognised me when we first met, why didn't she say so?"

"She thought you were covering up for the killers."

"No wonder she was so afraid of me." Rix whited out the sketch and put the canvas back.

"Are you still required to hand her over to the chancellor, to save your house?"

"He didn't mention it, but once Tali's here, he'll know. He's got spies everywhere."

"Well," said Tobry, "I'm going down to get her and Rannilt. I expect I'll be a while."

Rix barely noticed his going. Lady Ricinus had committed high treason in defence of her house. Rix had betrayed her to the chancellor for the same reason. Which was worse? He knew the answer. A son owed a duty to his mother and, while her crime was monstrous, his was unforgiveable.

CHAPTER 88

Shortly after Tobry left, Lady Ricinus appeared. "They told me you'd come slinking back. Is it done?"

"It's done," Rix muttered. Shame burned him. He could not look her in the face.

"It had better be perfect."

He led her upstairs and she inspected the completed portrait, her small eyes darting.

"It will do. Box it up. I'll send for it in the morning." She went out without a word of thanks.

Good riddance! He never wanted to see it again. After he had crated up the portrait, Rix slumped on the couch, feeling oddly empty and not knowing what to do with himself.

The month-clock on the wall said ten-thirty p.m. Twenty-four hours until Lord Ricinus's Honouring, which was to take place immediately after the Honouring Ball. Would Lord and Lady Ricinus lead the dancers onto the floor of the Great Hall? That would be a sight to see—his father and mother holding each other close, pretending that they had not despised each other for twenty years.

Distractedly, Rix re-sketched the cellar scene on the big canvas, then sat back with a goblet of wine, deliberately not looking at his work. Even the urgency to see the faces of the killers paled before the looming catastrophe if Lady Ricinus succeeded in her plot against the chancellor. Or if the chancellor had lied, and he planned to bring her down . . .

His head was spinning. He had drunk a bottle and a half on an empty stomach. Too damn bad. Rix filled another goblet, blinked at the canvas, then went to his palette to mix colours. As he was doing so, something began to nag at him about the sketch, something he had promised Tobry he would do, but it would not come to mind.

When he began to paint, Rix did not have to think about it, for he had all the colours in his inner eye: the dingy grey-greens of the streaked and oozing cellar walls; the slimy, brown-stained flag-stones; the pearly lustre of the black bench; the stacks of crumbling crates, their grey timbers dotted with yellow mould and threaded with white dry rot; the piled barrels on the other side. The blonde of the young woman's hair contrasting with the reflective gold of the tongs. The eerily beautiful ebony pearl highlighting the shiny beads of blood clinging to it.

Blood. A gloved hand was rubbing it into his wounds again, murmuring softly all the while. Rix shook off the nightmare, took another goblet and began to work. His eyesight was blurring now but that did not matter—his subconscious was guiding his hand.

Later, when he had to squint to stop seeing double, Rix was astonished to discover the canvas covered in paint. It was long after midnight; he had been working furiously for hours. He reached for the bottle but it was empty. He kicked it across the floor and it rang against the other two.

Had he really drunk three bottles? He could not remember fin-ishing the second, much less opening a third. Rix looked around for another but there were no more up here.

At the top of the steep steps he had just enough wit to realise that his only way down was by falling. He staggered back to the painting, pressing on his eyes to fuse the two wavering images into one. There was something he had to see, though he could not remember what. A vital, urgent revelation—

Something dragged him out of unconsciousness. As Rix tried to sit up, his head spun sickeningly. It was still dark outside, and he was so drunk he could barely stand up.

His sword was propped against the wall. Using it as a walking stick, going with exaggerated care so he did not stab himself in the foot, he wavered to the painting and blinked at it. His head was slowly revolving though the blurred vision had gone.

The painting was complete, yet utterly different to the meticu-lous realism of his father's portrait. The murder scene was an anguished work, done with furious strokes that made little sense up close. He backed away and the scene glided into focus, imagined as perfectly as memory.

There was the little girl, fist up to her mouth as she stifled a scream. Her blue eyes were huge, her hair not quite as golden as now, but there was no doubt who she was. He remembered her furious cry as he had scrambled up the stairs, "I'm going to get you."

There was the young woman on the slab, freshly killed. It could almost have been Tali as an adult, save that the blonde hair was too pale.

And there were the killers.

"No!" Rix gasped. "No, no, *no!*"

The wine came up in a paroxysmic heave that splattered the floor for yards around. His brain was shrieking, his head splitting, and the one thing he could do, that he had to do, was get out of there.

He lurched up the stairs to the next level of his tower, unlocking the door with shaking hands. He had to be alone; he could not bear the thought of meeting anyone. Up he went, and up, past the little observatory he had not used in years, eight flights in all to the topmost, open floor. Around him, nine slim columns supported the zinc roof that rose in a barley-twist spiral for another fifty feet. The shoulder-high outside wall was covered in yellow tiles, now glazed with ice.

Rix lay down on a snow-covered bench and bawled like a baby for the family now lost forever. When his tear ducts were as dry as the saline flats of the Southern Seethings, he crawled across to the nearest wall. He had to end this tainted house that, clearly, had been bloodstained for generations.

But would his death end it? The chancellor cared only for the survival of Hightspall and might even reward Lady Ricinus if that ensured her cooperation. Rix staggered down again. He had to make sure; had to put House Ricinus beyond recovery.

Shortly, he returned to the roof. The cellar picture swam in his mind, but the two faces, though much changed now from ten years ago, remained perfectly clear. They did not have a sorcerous bone between them, so why had they killed Tali's mother for the ebony pearl? Surely not just for the money?

The faces of Lord and Lady Ricinus.

His own mother and father.

And why had he, Rix, been there?

He would never know. There was only one way to make up for the evil of such a family, and the dishonour of betraying them. He was going to end it now.

He climbed onto the tower wall, swung a leg over it, slipped on the ice-glazed tiles, and fell.

CHAPTER 89

The iron book burned red-hot in Tali's dreams, as if its maker had cast it back into the chymical furnace to forge its pages anew. She jerked awake in the makeshift bed concealed under Tobry's big bed. It had been after three in the morning when Tobry had brought them to Rix's chambers, which were unguarded now the portrait had been completed.

Rannilt whimpered in her sleep. "Leave me alone. Didn't do it, *didn't do it.*"

Tali put an arm across her shoulder. The girl clung to her briefly, then sighed and rolled over. Her steady breathing resumed. She seemed a little better now.

After Rix left them on the road, it had taken ages for Tobry to sneak them into the city unseen, and he'd had to hide Tali and Rannilt in a damp tunnel on the other side of the city all day. The hidden entrance into Rix's scalderium had been blocked and Tobry had to wait until the early hours to bring Tali and Rannilt into the palace. Tali had collapsed into sleep the moment she lay down.

Now, though still exhausted, she was wide awake. She had hurt Lyf with the iron book but he would attack again, and he knew her weaknesses now. He knew she had little control over her magery, knew where she had gone and probably where she was now. He would try again for the pearl, and it would not be long.

Her mother's killers would not have given up, either. Had Rix completed the cellar painting and discovered who they were? He was not here to ask, and neither was the sketch.

With every passing minute the killers must be drawing closer, eliminating possibilities and following clues to track her down. Lady Ricinus would be doing the same. She would be desperate now, with the Honouring and the deadline of the chancellor's ultimatum only hours away ...

Rap-rap. It was the front door.

Tobry raced in. "Stay under the bed, that's Lady Ricinus."

Tali crouched there, fingering her knife. If discovered, she would be caught and sold back to the chancellor. She could think no further than that.

"Where is Rixium?" came Lady Ricinus's chilly voice as her heels clicked along the hall. "It's five-thirty. He should be dressing for the Honouring."

Tali started. She must have slept all day.

"I don't know, Lady Ricinus," said Tobry politely. "He wasn't here when I returned in the early hours."

Lady Ricinus gave a disapproving sniff.

Tobry must have felt a mischievous urge for he said, "Perhaps he's run off to a monastery."

"He will be there," said Lady Ricinus in a voice so cold it made Tali's teeth ache.

Lady Ricinus's breathing was quick and shallow; a musky perfume wafted off her. Her heels tap-tapped through the salon and scalderium, then up to the studio and down again. Rix's door was flung open, then Tobry's. Tali clenched the knife, though she could hardly use it on Rix's mother, could she? Oh yes.

"When my son returns, tell him I require audience with him immediately."

"I will so inform him," said Tobry virtuously.

Lady Ricinus swept out. Tobry bolted the door. Tali crept from beneath the bed and followed him into Rix's bedchamber, where he began rifling through an enormous wardrobe. "What time is the Honouring?"

"The ball is at eight o'clock and the Honouring will be straight afterwards. I'm sure he'll be back any minute."

"Are you going to the ball?"

"Of course," said Tobry, picking out a crimson velvet tailcoat and holding it up against himself. "As Rix's closest friend, I'm required to be there."

There had been no dancing in Cython, save in the privacy of one's cell. "I suppose it will be a very grand affair," she said, sighing.

"The grandest of the year. House Ricinus isn't well liked, but it's so exceedingly rich that none of the nobility, nor indeed Hightspall's vulgarly wealthy commoners, would think of missing it."

"It doesn't seem right, with all the war and ruin outside."

"It's a sign of defiance, and therefore good for morale."

"I don't understand."

"The enemy may break our walls and burn our shanty towns, they may have taken the outlying provinces and be marching on Caulderon again, but they will never crush our spirit. That's what the Honouring says, to our own people as much as to the enemy, and it's why even *I* want it to go ahead. Where the blazes is Rix?"

"I'm sure he'll be there."

"I'm worried now. He ... wasn't in a good state when I saw him yesterday evening."

"You didn't tell me that."

"It's ... a private matter. Dreadful." Tobry looked away. "He was so distraught ... "

"You're afraid he's done something terrible. Is it—" There was no one around but she lowered her voice. "Is it about the treason?"

"How did you know about that?"

Tali told him everything.

"And you informed the chancellor of this?"

"Before I went to the Crag."

"The bastard! He set a trap and Rix fell right into it." Tobry told her about the poisoned dog, and what the chancellor had said to Rix.

"The worst poison of all," said Tali. What did that remind her of? The clues were starting to fall into place, and everyone would be at the Honouring. She had to go.

She glanced at Tobry from under her eyelashes. "I'd love to see it," she said wistfully. "The beautiful ladies in the gowns, the handsome noblemen in their uniforms ... "

"Not to mention the unhandsome fallen nobility." Tobry pointed out. "But the guests will also be there for a baser reason."

"What's that?"

"To be witness when House Ricinus rises even higher or, should rumour prove well founded, to delight in its destruction."

Tali limped into the scalderium, absently studying herself in the full-length mirror. She took a deep breath, fluffed up her hair and walked back to Tobry, who was inside Rix's wardrobe now, frowning at a collection of kilts.

"Tobry?" she said, fighting an urge to chew her fingernails. No, she was Lady Tali, heir to the ancient, noble House of vi Torgrist. She would act like a lady at all times.

"Mmn?" he said absently.

"Are you taking anyone to the ball?"

"Certainly not. Why be tied to one dreary woman when you can have the choice of dozens?"

He had not intended to insult her. He had no idea what she was thinking, yet she felt insulted. However, Tali could not be cowed that easily.

"Do you think *I* am dreary, sir?" she said, practising the coldness she had heard in Lady Ricinus's voice.

He turned sharply. "Of course not. You're the loveliest—" Tobry studied her, head to one side. "What are you saying?"

She twisted her fingers behind her back. It was up to the man to ask, wasn't it, and the lady to be asked. What if he said no? What if he laughed? What if he was so thunderstruck that he could not reply?

"Will you take me to the ball, sir?" There. She had done it.

He did not speak for a minute. He just gazed at her in a way that made her blood rise and her ears burn.

"It's a terrible risk," he said.

"Worse than hiding here? Wherever I go in Hightspall, I'm hunted, but who would expect me to be at the grandest ball in all the land?"

"Your enemies will consider all possibilities."

"If I am to be caught, to fail in my quest and die, just once I would like to go to a ball."

She looked at him so wistfully that he sprang forwards and gave her a hug, before stepping away, bowing and looking more than a little surprised at himself.

"I will take you to the ball, my beautiful Lady vi Torgrist." He pursed his lips, then smiled. "You shall be a distant cousin of mine, Lady Felysse Tybell, from the remote, cold and rainy county of Murge. That will explain your pale complexion and unfamiliar accent, while make-up applied by my own skilled hands, and a mask, will further conceal you."

At the right-hand end of the wardrobe, among a series of gowns, were several in her size. She picked out a pale blue, gauzy one that reminded her of Eulala's gown and held it up before her. It was almost weightless and she knew she would feel free in it. In a loin-cloth she had always felt free, slave though she had been. "Can I wear this?"

"Only if you wish to attract every eye in the ballroom and pro-voke the most delicious scandal."

"What's wrong with it? Does it plunge too low at the front?"

"Not at all," said Tobry, inspecting the area. "Bosoms are in this year, by which I mean, half out. It is not the custom, however, for the rest of a lady's anatomy to be visible through the fabric, no matter how charming her figure may be." He rotated her as if to confirm her charms for himself. "I'll go out and find something suitable, but not sleeveless. Your slave mark must be concealed. Hmn."

"I don't want you to go to any trouble ... " Yes, she did.

"My Lady Felysse, I shall go to as much trouble as I please," said Tobry with a gallant bow. "And a mask, of course. What would you prefer? Fox, cat, eagle, owl?"

"What about a mouse mask?" said Tali, thinking of her poor little Poon, taken by that dreadful cat in the moment of its free-dom. Mice were clever at hiding and not being noticed. They also had sharp teeth.

"A mouse it is." He went out.

Two-and-a-half hours later Tali was standing by Tobry, clutch-ing his arm, among the gaudy throng outside the ballroom door. The sapphire gown he had found for her was pretty and suited her complexion, but it was heavy and confining and she was already beginning to perspire. The elastic of her mouse mask was cutting into her ears.

"Lady Felysse?" said Tobry in a low, amused voice.

It took a moment before she realised that he was talking to her. "Yes, my lord?"

"You're crushing my poor wrist bones to splinters."

She unclenched her hand. "Sorry. Is there any sign of Rix?"

"No, and I'm really worried. It's not like him. It'll be a mortal insult if he fails to appear for his father's Honouring and the portrait's unveiling." He put her hand on his arm in the correct position.

The huge double doors were opened and the couples began to enter the ballroom, their names being announced as they did. Tali could hardly breathe. Her figure required no corset, but the gown was so tight under the bust that it was an effort to breathe.

"You're clenching again," muttered Tobry. "Relax."

"I'm scared. What if Lady Ricinus recognises me when we're introduced?"

"She's never seen you before. Besides, she's not going to take a second look at any girl on *my* arm."

"Why not?" she said, bristling for him.

"I have no land, no family, no money and no prospects. The House of Lagger was utterly disgraced before it fell, and I'm only here because Rix insisted on it."

His words did not alleviate her anxiety. "What if she talks to me?"

"Blush prettily and look confused. An air of charming vacantness goes a long way in such situations."

"How would you know?"

The line moved forwards. Lord and Lady Ricinus were just ahead. Tali realised she was clenching Tobry's arm again and consciously relaxed. She allowed her jaw to go slack, her red-tinted lower lip to droop like Lifka's. Now, that was a look she could emulate.

"*Charming* vacantness, not doltish stupidity, Lady Felysse," murmured Tobry.

She corrected, and just in time. They were being announced.

"Lord Tobry Lagger of House—er, Lord Tobry," said the announcer, "and his second cousin, Lady Felysse Tybell of Murge."

Lord Ricinus, who was immaculately dressed but swaying like a sailboat in a heavy sea, took Tali's hand. His hand was oozing sweat and had a revolting, pulpy feel. She released it and turned to Lady Ricinus.

Lady Ricinus extended two gloved fingers and said in a bored voice, without looking at her, "Charmed."

Tali bowed and they passed on.

"That wasn't so bad, was it?" said Tobry. "Now, some of the gavottes are particularly tricky and you don't want to attract attention to yourself. I should have asked this before, but—which are your best dances?"

Tali fell from a great height. "I've never danced in my life."

CHAPTER 90

Rix groaned, opened gummy eyes and saw nothing. Had he gone blind? Was he dead? His head felt as though an axe was embedded in it, his mouth was dry as a vulture's armpit and the fur on his tongue had fur on it.

He rolled over and cried out. There was a lump on the back of his head the size of a half melon. He groped around him, felt a stone wall and pulled himself up on it, and saw the familiar outline of the palace roof beyond. What was he doing at the top of his tower? He hadn't been up here in months. An icy wind whistled in between the low perimeter wall and the spiralling roof. It was a wonder he hadn't frozen to death.

His mouth tasted of wine gone sour and stale vomit. He must have been royally drunk last night, though he could not remember anything after Lady Ricinus had left. Rix smelled painter's oil on his hands and a glimmer of memory came back.

He'd been painting the murder scene in the cellar; painting and drinking.

So drunk he could barely focus on the canvas.

The staring, haunted girl.

The young woman's head torn open.

The bloody ebony pearl . . .

Rix groaned. His head was bursting with the effort to remember. Then another glimmer: two faces, finally emerging from his frozen memories, the killers on the canvas.

Lord and Lady Ricinus.

"Why, why?" he cried, but the howling wind drowned him out.

Rix was pounding his fists against a column when he remembered one final fragment. Utterly dishonoured and with no way out, he had staggered up here to throw himself off his tower. Evidently he had fallen and knocked himself out. He couldn't even kill himself successfully.

It must have been many hours ago, otherwise his mouth would not be so dry. But why was it still dark? Had he lain unconscious all day? No wonder his tongue was like a leather strap hung over a fence. He was lucky to be alive.

Lucky to be the son of vicious killers?

Lucky to have betrayed his own mother for high treason? He remembered that.

Judging by the stars, it was around ten o'clock. The Honouring Ball would be nearly over. He had promised to be there, and he was not. He had broken his word, shamed his father and humiliated his mother. And, oddly, their crimes could not excuse his own behaviour. If a man's word was not sacred, what kind of a man was he?

He must attend the Honouring. He would perform that last duty for his parents. And then? What came first, duty to them or obedience to the law? Was he supposed to turn them in for murder? That would, unquestionably, destroy House Ricinus. Did his duty to House and family outweigh the victim's need for justice?

He did not know, but one thing was very clear. If he turned them in it would destroy him too, because he would know in the chambers of his heart that he had betrayed those whom he had vowed to honour.

Rix stumbled down to his studio. The cellar painting was gone. Tobry must have put it away and Rix thanked the Gods for that. He could not bear to look at it.

He smiled grimly as he put on the ceremonial garments Lady Ricinus's maid had laid out for him, adjusted the angle of the lapis cravat and his scarlet, plumed hat, and wiped a speck of dust from his gleaming boots. After buckling on the titane sword, he checked himself in the scalderium mirror. He would perform this final service, put on this final show, as best the heir of House Ricinus could.

Not even Lady Ricinus could fault his presentation this time. Even if she had brought the chancellor down, Rix would see his unworthy father honoured, then walk away. Let House Ricinus rise, or all come crashing down behind him. He would never look back. He would go to the front lines and die there, defending his country and trying to assuage his blighted honour the only way he knew.

The halls were empty—every servant in the palace would be called to witness the Honouring. Outside, people were still partying in the streets. Fireworks climbed the sky near the city gates, though the celebrations rang falsely in his mind. If they thought the enemy had gone, they were as deluded as the priestesses who gathered on the sacred mountain and commanded the ice to withdraw from Hightspall, the magians who tried to melt ten thousand cubic miles of icecap with their pathetic spells.

And always, always in the back of his mind, was the unanswerable question—why had the ten-year-old Rix been there when Tali's mother had been murdered?

He thrust open the doors of the Great Hall so hard that they slammed back against the wall to either side. He was not going to sneak into this hypocritical ceremony. The ball was over and the dance floor crowded with people, all looking up at the stage where the dignitaries were taking their places for Lord Ricinus's Honouring.

Rix's heart missed three or four beats before restarting with a lurch. The chancellor sat centre stage, smiling. Had Lady Ricinus's plot failed, or were her assassins waiting for the end? Or would the executioners be the chancellor's? Rix faltered.

The high constable took his place on the chancellor's right, the lady justiciar to his left. The chief magian was there too, and Abbess

Hildy. All the mighty of Hightspall were in attendance. Had they come to witness the rise of House Ricinus, or to gloat in its fall?

He reached the edge of the stage unnoticed. Rix's head was throbbing and he felt a dire urge to scream at his parents, *Why did you murder Tali's mother?*

The preliminaries must be going well; even Lady Ricinus was smiling. How could that be? The chancellor had threatened House Ricinus with ruin if she did not hand Tali over. Did Lady Ricinus's smile mean that she had taken Tali and was ready to deliver her? Or, after events at the Crag, did the chancellor no longer care?

Abbess Hildy, a plump, soft-faced woman of indeterminate age, lumbered to her feet. "Lord Chancellor, Lady Justiciar, High Constable, Chief Magian, Dignitaries, ladies and lords, welcome to this Honouring."

She paused to catch her breath.

"Much has been written about the House of Ricinus, and much has been said. That they were thieves and brigands who made their gold in dirty trades."

Someone in the audience tittered, and Lady Ricinus looked uneasy. Was this a set-up to lull House Ricinus into false hope, then bring it crashing down? The chancellor's ironic smile suggested he had such a plan in mind.

Hildy continued, in a sneering tone. "That they were upstarts who bribed their way to the top. Scoundrels unworthy to sit among the noble houses of Hightspall, or to occupy this, the most magnificent palace in Caulderon, which was first built by the greatest of the Five Herovians, Axil Grandys himself, not long before his mysterious disappearance.

"I too looked down on the upstarts. I knew that, generous though they were to all manner of causes, House Ricinus was beneath contempt. And I told the chancellor so, that he might find a way to topple this unworthy house."

The whole room was buzzing now. Lady Ricinus's red fingernails were gouging varnish from the arms of her chair. Was this the chancellor's revenge—the Honouring to be a public humiliation? From the gleeful faces of the nobility, they hoped so.

Hildy paused, looked around the gathering and, after a dramatic pause, said, "But I was wrong."

Heads turned. People whispered among themselves. The chancellor rose halfway from his chair, his famous composure lost for a few seconds, before settling back, tight-lipped. What was going on? Had Lady Ricinus won after all? Rix prayed that she had not. Any such victory would be a travesty. And yet, for the sake of his house . . .

Hildy opened a flat leather case, withdrew a ragged, dirty piece of parchment, and held it up.

"For two thousand years it has been held that our founding hero, Axil Grandys, died without issue, despite that he was renowned as a vigorous and lusty man."

She paused for a full minute, until the whispers died away.

"This document proves otherwise. This parchment shows that Axil Grandys fathered a daughter, Mythilda, and acknowledged her before his disappearance. And Mythilda's line, it has been proven to my satisfaction, runs unbroken all the way to the present time. To the father of Lord Ricinus, and therefore to his son, Rixium Ricinus."

"Bastards sprung from bastards, back to the beginning of time," sneered a red-faced nobleman on Rix's left.

Rix was not inclined to disagree.

"House Ricinus," said Abbess Hildy, taking a sheaf of documents from the case, "has always been seen as the lowliest, its lord and lady as greedy upstarts. But no more. Should these papers pass the final test, Ricinus will take its place among those houses who can trace their line all the way back to the founding fathers."

She bowed to Lord and Lady Ricinus.

"I present the documents for authentication," said Abbess Hildy, handing the stunned chancellor the parchment and the other papers.

And Rix knew, from the smile on his mother's face, that the critical document was a forgery. It would be a masterful one, doubtless written on two thousand-year-old parchment in ink equally ancient. And the monumental bribes she had been paying for the past three years, that had almost emptied their treasury, had been to smooth its passage to authentication and her house's rise to the top.

The chancellor rubbed the parchment between his fingers, held it up to the glow from a brazier behind them, then raised it to his horn-like nose.

"It *looks* authentic," he said reluctantly, sourly, and handed it to the chief magian. "Though I can scarcely believe it is."

The chief magian probed the parchment with the heel of his staff, and then with the tip, and passed an object like an ivory-rimmed spectible over it.

"This parchment is ancient," said the chief magian, a tubby, balding little fellow with tiny feet and hands, after some minutes of increasingly frustrated magery. "So ancient that it was not made in this land. It came, no doubt about it, on the First Fleet from our lost homeland of Thanneron, now crushed beneath the ice that draws ever closer to our own fair isle."

"Damn the parchment!" snarled the chancellor. "It's the writing that matters. When was it written?"

The chief magian studied the parchment again. A tap of his staff made the writing glow leaf green, then flesh pink and finally indigo.

Rix held his breath. Part of him yearned for it to be authentic, and for the legitimacy that would bring his house. Another part prayed that Lady Ricinus would not get away with so monstrous a lie.

"This ink flowed from the nib two thousand years ago," said the chief magian.

"My Lady Ricinus," said the chancellor with a vulture's smile. "We cannot fault the critical document, therefore House Ricinus's *claim* can not be challenged. Welcome to the First Circle, House Ricinus."

He extended his hand, though from the look on his face the chancellor would sooner have cut it off than shake hers, or Lord Ricinus's.

Rix had to admire his mother's cunning. She had neutralised the chancellor's threat to bring down their house unless they delivered him Tali, for not even he had the power to topple a house of the First Circle for so minor a reason. But why hadn't he acted on the treason? Because Lady Ricinus was far more use to him alive than dead? Or was this just the first move in a deadly game between them?

"Lady Ricinus," the chancellor continued, "before we began the Honouring, you mentioned two matters of moment. What is the other?"

For a second, Lady Ricinus's poise failed her, and her triumphant smile revealed her lack of breeding. Then the sickening false humility was back.

"My beloved Lord, Ricinus, is unwell." She extended a hand to him. Lord Ricinus lurched across the stage and flopped his pulpy hand into her bony one.

"He was savagely struck down by the escaped Pale slave just days ago," said Lady Ricinus, "and our healer fears my lord's remaining days are few. Lord Ricinus regrets that he is unable to discharge his duties, either as a husband," several nobles tittered, "or as the head of House Ricinus. Therefore he begs to be released as lord, that he may spend—"

"It is customary for the lord of a noble house to be released from his duties only by death," said the chancellor.

"An earlier release is not unheard of," said Lady Ricinus. "I can cite the precedents."

"I'm sure your notaries have documented every instance." The chancellor turned to Rix's father. "Lord Ricinus, do you solemnly declare that you are no longer fit to discharge your duties as lord of your house?"

"I declare it," said Rix's father. "Where's my drink?"

The nobles muttered in outrage. Lady Ricinus ground her heel into Lord Ricinus's instep.

"In these extraordinary circumstances," scowled the chancellor, "I will approve the abdication of the present Lord Ricinus." Then he smiled vengefully. "And installation of the new lord, Lord Rixium Ricinus."

Rix nearly fell against the stage. Lady Ricinus staggered and clutched at her lord. Her mouth opened and closed, then she slipped a new mask over the old. Clearly, she had expected that the stewardship of House Ricinus would be given to her for her lifetime. It was a reasonable expectation, since a third of the noble houses were led by women, but her vulgar birth was a fatal flaw.

"Thank you, Chancellor," she said with a cracked smile. "I will do my duty as steward until—"

The chancellor looked down at Rix, who knew he had forgotten nor forgiven nothing. What game was he playing now?

"Rixium will be installed as lord immediately," said the chancellor.

"But he is not yet of age."

"He defeated a caitsthe with his bare hands, did he not?"

Several mature ladies, who must have heard the story, tittered. A trio of young eligibles eyed Rix boldly and inflated their assets.

"He also took the war to the enemy," said the chancellor, "and rescued a Pale who has given us priceless intelligence about Cython."

Lady Ricinus knew when she was defeated. "Rixium, Lord of Ricinus, come up." She extended her hand towards her son.

"Not yet he isn't," growled the chancellor. "First, we finish the Honouring."

Rix took his place between his mother and father, barely able to keep his throbbing head upright, and afraid he was going to throw up again. This was monstrous, a travesty.

"May I see your sword, Lord Rixium?" said the chancellor politely, as though nothing had ever happened between them.

Rix handed it to him. The chancellor studied it for a moment, then passed it to the chief magian, who ran his little fingers along the worn inscription, causing multi-coloured auras to flicker around it. Momentarily the words stood out, black against the bluish metal—*Heroes must fight to preserve the race*. The chief magian started, then mimed several words.

The chancellor nodded and took the sword. "Search the archives," he said softly. "Find a test."

The chief magian resumed his seat. The chancellor's mouth hardened. He looked Rix up and down, then handed the sword back.

What was that all about? Rix's restless gaze passed across the audience and he noticed Tobry at the back of the hall. And there, clutching his arm, as Pale as if she'd had the word painted on her forehead, was Tali. She was gazing up into Tobry's eyes, quivering with suppressed emotion, and his eyes were locked on hers. What was she doing here?

Rix started, then realised that his mother had fixed on the small girl in the blue gown and the mouse mask.

"*Lord* Rixium," she said softly. "You have no idea how sweet my revenge is going to be."

CHAPTER 91

C *an this unexpected boon outweigh the disastrous loss?*

Lyf had been floating in the Abysm for a day, evaluating hundreds of possibilities, each a branch of the unknowable future. *I have a body!* he exulted. *I'm free!* Or at least, the framework of a body, ugly, misshapen and clumsy though it was. With flesh stripped from the facinore and the power stolen from the gifted child he would soon complete his body, and no longer would he be bound to the place of his death.

Lyf had discovered how to create a body for himself seven hundred years ago, and ever since he had fought and schemed and struggled to glean the power for it. And had failed every time.

Then those foolhardy intruders had brought the Pale child to his caverns, bearing within her a gift neither she nor they understood, one he had not realised he could feed on until the moment she had hurled that golden globe. Truly, fate was unknowable. He had always discounted luck and serendipity, but he should have made allowance for them—chance had given him in a moment what centuries of planning could not. He would not make that mistake again.

But could this prize outweigh the loss of *The Consolation of Vengeance?*

The balance was poised. If his enemies learned to read the iron book it would reveal almost the entirety of his plan. But could they read it? He had written it in an ancient script that had never been common, and the enemy had burnt most of Cythe's books at the end of the war. Lyf doubted that any books survived in this script, save in his own library, yet if there were, Hightspall's scholars might decipher the iron book in time. That would be a dreadful setback, though he could recover from it. Thankfully he had not yet written the ending.

But the theft raised another possibility, one that was terrifying. That they might understand the magery of the book, obtain a measure of alkoyl and write their own ending, one he had no way of knowing about or dealing with.

That possibility could not be allowed. His armies must encircle Cauldeton so tightly that a flea could not escape. At the same time, he must set his traps from within.

First, allow Deroe to discover that the host of the master pearl was on her way to the cellar, and to believe that with her pearl he could break the possession for good. Deroe would follow her, carrying the three stolen pearls that never left his side.

Next, using Rix's heatstone, tighten the compulsion on him and bring him to the cellar to kill the magian and cut the pearl from Tali's head. Lyf's new body, even when complete, would not have the dexterity to remove it safely. Then Lyf would take the pearl, kill his remaining enemies and rise in triumph as his armies broke into Cauldeton.

Last, recover the iron book and write the true ending. Then the real war could begin.

CHAPTER 92

Lord Ricinus swayed on his feet while the chancellor praised his staggering gift of the Third Army, studiously avoiding mention of his personal attributes or character. The Honouring medal was fixed to Lord Ricinus's chest, the official artist completed his sketches and the chancellor beckoned Rix forward.

"Would you unveil your portrait, Lord Rixium?"

Lady Ricinus was glowing now. This night was the culmination of two decades' dreams and schemes and, despite several scares and stumbles, it was going well.

The crated portrait rested on a wooden frame behind them, high enough for the audience to see it over the heads of the dignitaries. Lady Ricinus drew Rix's ancient blade and handed it to him, hilt first.

As he rose, pain speared through his skull and he stumbled, for his head felt worse than when he had roused on the tower roof. The audience must have thought he was tipsy but everyone smiled indulgently—he was soon to be the lord of a house of the First Circle, after all, and many of them had daughters.

With the titane blade Rix cut the sealing wax and the bonding cords, and lifted the front of the box away. Behind it, the portrait was concealed by grey silk.

"With a flourish," said Lady Ricinus.

Rix forced himself to bow to his father, his mother and the chancellor. He took hold of one end of the silk and turned to the assembled nobility.

"Father," he began, choking on his own hypocrisy. "Father, with this portrait I reveal the true man behind the mask. With all—with all my art I honour you . . . "

With a single heave, he tore the silk away to expose the portrait he never wanted to see again.

The nobles stared, open-mouthed.

Lady Ricinus throttled a gasp.

Lord Ricinus's red eyes bulged. Bubbles popped from his nostrils and he let out the squeal of a pig being slaughtered.

The chancellor smiled.

Rix spun around, focused on the image and it was as though he had been smashed in the face with it. His knees buckled. It wasn't the portrait; the crate held his frenzied depiction of the murder in the cellar. How had it ended up here?

His blood froze—had he, in a drunken rage after he'd seen the killers' faces, swapped this painting for his father's portrait? Did he secretly long to destroy the family and the house without which he was nothing? But why do it this way? Why not accuse them openly? Was he such a coward? Rix could not believe that, even blind drunk, he could have committed such a betrayal. Nonetheless, shame scalded him.

A clamour broke out at the front, a hundred people talking at once. Those at the back, too far away to see clearly, were whispering and crying to their neighbours, desperate to hear the scandal. From the corner of one eye Rix saw Tobry urging Tali towards the door, but she stood firm. She had waited ten years to see the killers' faces.

"What is this?" said the chancellor in a low voice, beckoning the justiciar and the high constable behind his back.

"The stupid boy has crated up the wrong painting." Lady Ricinus, as always, was the first to recover her poise. "It's one of his nightmares; he's always painting them. I'll have the portrait brought down immediately." She gestured to her attendants. "Take this to the furnaces." Then, to the chancellor, "I told you he's not fit to be lord—"

"Be silent!" said the chancellor, silkily. "Rixium Ricinus, did you paint this abomination?"

Rix's throat was so dry he could barely croak. "Yes, Chancellor."

"When?"

"Last night, after I finished the portrait of Father."

"Then why is this picture here in its place?"

"I can't say," Rix gasped. The room was boiling, his head whirling, the air almost too thick to breathe. "I—I was drunk. After I saw what I'd painted, I went to the top of my tower—to jump!—but I fell and knocked myself out. It appears I lay there unconscious all day."

"Why have you portrayed your mother and father, whom any *dutiful* son would honour, as vile murderers?"

The truth was screaming at Rix but he could not utter it. "I don't remember."

"Really?" The chancellor's voice went low and deadly. He gestured to the right side of the painting. "And what is this black object in your mother's golden tongs?"

"Don't know," Rix lied. "It . . . just came to me."

The chancellor's eyes glowed. He had his teeth in Lady Ricinus's throat and, whatever explanations she put up, he would never let go.

"Chief Magian," said the chancellor, "would you come here?"

The dumpy little man hurried across, examined the object in question, then straightened up, his mouth curling in disgust. "I believe it is an ebony pearl, Lord Chancellor."

"For the benefit of Lord Rixium and our noble audience, what is an ebony pearl?"

"A nuclix. A sorcerous talisman of prodigious power. A forbidden object, my lord."

"Forbidden?" said the chancellor.

"Indeed. I have never seen one. It is rumoured that there are only four in existence, that only five *can* exist."

"And these would have a high value?"

"Beyond price," said the chief magian.

"How far beyond price?"

"A single ebony pearl would be worth as much as this palace and everything in it."

A stir ran through the audience.

"*This palace*, which House Ricinus bought for cash a hundred years ago," said the chancellor. "Tell us more."

"With two such pearls, even a minor magian's powers would exceed my own. With four, all the magians of Hightspall together. If one man should also get the fifth, the master pearl—"

"If you've never seen one, how do you know about them?"

"From a parchment written by an obscure magian half a century ago."

"And they're only known from this source?

"Yes."

"Where do they come from?"

"It's said they're cultured within the heads of Pale girls and grown there over many years, before harvesting after the girl comes of age."

Rix's mouth went dry. This was a deadly moment. If the chancellor saw a connection between *the one* and the master pearl, he would not scruple to cut it out of Tali.

The chancellor's disgust was unfeigned. "Cultured? In the heads of *living* girls?"

"Just so."

"To *harvest* a pearl, would it be necessary to kill the girl?"

"Ebony pearls must be extracted while the host is alive, then stored in her warm, uncongealed blood for several days. After her head has been cut open and the pearl gouged out, and enough blood taken, how could she survive?"

"And this is what Lady Ricinus is doing in the portrait? Extracting such a pearl and killing the young woman who was the host?"

"There can be no doubt," said the chief magian.

"Justiciar, High Constable," called the chancellor, "would you come forward and inspect the evidence? You too, Abbess, if you please."

They approached.

"It's just a stupid painting," cried Lady Ricinus. "The fantasy of a sick boy. He's addled, everyone knows that. He has been ever since—"

"Ever since he was ten!" cried a high voice from the crowd. "When he witnessed this murder—the murder of my mother—and it nearly drove him insane."

"Mouse Lady?" said the chancellor, smiling grimly. "State your name."

Sweat was pouring down Rix's face. If the chancellor didn't know about her pearl yet, he soon would. Tali, run for your life.

But Tali wasn't going anywhere. She wrenched off her mask and climbed onto the stage. She was the smallest person there, and her left knee was trembling beneath her gown, but she was not going to be robbed of this moment.

"My name is Tali vi Torgrist," she said with quiet dignity. "I am the last survivor of the ancient, noble House vi Torgrist, and that woman is my mother, Iusia. I was there. I witnessed the murder. That's me when I was eight." She pointed to the little girl.

Her bosom heaved. "I name Lord and Lady Ricinus the killers, and I demand justice in my mother's name, and in—"

Rix put on a frenzied fit of coughing that almost made him throw up, and she broke off. He was terrified that she was going to list her other murdered ancestors. If she did, the chancellor, and many others, would jump to the obvious conclusion—that she also hosted a pearl.

Tali stood alone, surrounded by enemies, and Rix's heart went out to her.

"You are the escaped Pale," said the chancellor.

"You know I am. We talked in your palace just days ago—about honour and betrayal, among other matters."

Lady Ricinus's head shot around. She stared at her husband, her lips moving.

"Shut your face, woman," growled Lord Ricinus.

"Can you prove your identity, girl?" said the justiciar.

"The mark of my noble house is on me." Tali drew up her sleeve.

Those people close enough to see the slave mark gasped and drew away, scowling and muttering.

"The symbol was burnt into my shoulder as a child with this, the family seal of House vi Torgrist." Tali held it up on its chain.

The justiciar, a tall, cadaverous woman with eyebrows like mouse skins, inspected the seal and nodded. "I recognise it."

"I can also recite the names of every one of my ancestors—"

"Not now," the justiciar said hastily. "Please continue, Lady vi Torgrist."

At the acknowledgement, Tali's back straightened and her feet almost left the floor. She wiped her eyes and went on.

"We Pale are accused of betraying our country," Tali said in a ringing voice. "And willingly serving the enemy. That is a vicious lie!"

"How dare you?" cried a jowly, bejewelled woman from the crowd. "Chancellor, this cannot be tolerated."

He waved her to silence, savagely.

"My people were given up to the enemy as children," Tali said, her blue eyes burning into the jowled woman until she had to hang her head. "One hundred and forty-four of the noblest children in the land, given as hostages, and meant to be ransomed, but Hightspall never came. Why did Hightspall abandon its own children to the enemy?"

"Important questions," said the justiciar, "but this is not the forum for them. Lord Ricinus, Lady Ricinus, you have been accused of a terrible crime. How do you plead?"

"Not guilty," said Lady Ricinus. "And my lord pleads the same way."

Rix looked around. Where was his father? At the back of the stage, where evidently he had secreted several flasks earlier. His head was tilted back and he was draining the dregs of a flask of brandy.

"Lord Ricinus?" said the justiciar. "How do you plead?"

Lord Ricinus turned to face him, drawing the bung from a second flask. "Pissed!" he roared. "I plead pissed as a lord," and laughed like a hyena.

"My son is insane," said Lady Ricinus with quiet venom. "He gets it from his father. And the evidence of a child witness is worthless. Children can be made to say anything, made to—"

"Made to *do* anything?" said the justiciar.

"The girl is a lying slut," cried Lady Ricinus.

"Curb your viper's tongue," said the justiciar, then turned to the gathering. "Can we rely on the evidence of a child who was only eight at the time, or on a picture painted by a man who admits he was blind drunk when he painted it?"

She turned to Tali. "Did you see the faces of the killers?"

"Not clearly," said Tali. "They were masked."

"Masked?" said the justiciar. "Then you have no evidence—"

"The woman stood on my mother as though she was rubbish! I heard her ribs break," Tali cried. "And Rix was there. I saw him."

"You saw *Lord Rixium* there? At the murder scene?"

"He came out from behind the barrels after the killers went up the stairs. Rix was shaking and his clothes were covered in vomit. He went over to Mama—to my mother. He stared at the blood on his hands, then vomited all over his shoes. They had shiny buckles. He made a horrible moaning sound, like an animal in pain, and raced up the stairs."

"Lord Rixium?" said the justiciar. "What do you remember of this?"

"Nothing," said Rix.

"And yet you painted it?"

"Yes."

"This is a conspiracy," said Lady Ricinus. "She told him what to paint. They're trying to cast me down and take my place."

"You confined Rix to his tower with guards on the door," said Tobry from the edge of the stage. "You searched his rooms three times, yet found no trace of her."

"Where is the cellar where the alleged murder took place?" said the high constable.

"I don't know," said Rix. "I've no memory of ever having seen it."

"This story is a vicious fabrication," cried Lady Ricinus.

"I know where the cellar should be," said Tali.

"Where, Lady Tali?" said the high constable, a pink-faced globe of a man no taller than her.

"Below this palace. I smelled it the day I first entered Palace Ricinus, underground."

"You *smelled* it?"

"I didn't realise it at the time, though it made my hair stand up. Until I die, I'll never forget the smell of the murder cellar."

"You say your mother was killed in this cellar, but how did she get there when no Pale can leave Cython?"

"We were led there, underground, by a Cythonian traitor I called Tinyhead. Mama thought he was helping her to escape."

"An enemy traitor who, presumably, was paid by traitors to Hightspall," said the chancellor, eyeing Lord and Lady Ricinus malevolently.

There was a great stir at this. The palace's master mapmaker was called and he listened to Tali's description, marked the area on his maps, then shook his head. "I have mapped all the palace passages and know of no such cellar."

"That's good enough for me," said the justiciar. "And therefore, without any corroborative evidence, I must dismiss—"

"It's said that Axil Grandys frequented a deep chamber below his manor," said Hildy thoughtfully. "And carried out arcane experiments there. Indeed, that he was working in that chamber when he disappeared."

The justiciar called for the palace historian.

"There was such a chamber," she said, "though it is believed to have been a Cythonian temple, originally."

"What?" cried the chancellor. "Why wasn't it destroyed?"

"Axil Grandys was the First Hero and the founder of Caulderon, and he ordered it kept. Previously, the Palace of the Kings of Cythe lay on this very spot, but Axil Grandys demolished it after their city was taken and built his own manor in the same place. No one knows why he kept the king's temple."

"High Constable," said the justiciar, "take these maps and a dozen men with sledgehammers, and find this cellar. Chief Magian, go with them."

They went out. Tobry came up to Rix, who slumped into a chair with his head in his hands. "Please tell me you didn't switch the painting for the portrait."

Even Rix's best friend doubted him. For the first time in his life he was utterly alone.

"Who else could have done it?" he said, wanting to throw up. "But if I did, I have no memory of it."

CHAPTER 93

After forty agonising minutes, the floor shook and a series of crashes rumbled up. Not long afterwards the high constable's party returned and he conferred with the chancellor and the justiciar.

"Speak," said the chancellor, who was warming his hands over the brazier.

"We found a cellar six levels down," said the high constable. "It is exactly as Rixium has painted it."

"Are you saying—?" said the chancellor.

"The black bench and the floor have old bloodstains. One stone box holds the bones of four women, each with a hole in the top of her skull. Several rib bones of the skeleton on top are broken."

Everyone turned to stare at Lady Ricinus.

"It proves nothing," she said, her face a mask but her eyes darting. "The bones could have been there a thousand years."

"The chief magian's dating spell says otherwise," said the high constable. "There's little doubt these are the bones of Lady Tali's mother and several other women killed the same way. But there's more. Worse."

"Worse?" said the chancellor, frowning.

"We also located a tunnel whose entrance was hidden by a prodigious charm of concealment," said the chief magian, rubbing his tiny hands together. "I nearly had an apoplexy breaking it."

"There are tunnels everywhere around here," said the chancellor.

"I divined where this tunnel goes."

"Oh?" the chancellor said sharply.

"It runs south-east for two miles, then south-west for another six. All the way to Cython."

"To *Cython?*" bellowed the chancellor. "Are you sure?"

"Quite sure."

"A *fresh* tunnel?"

"No. Quite old. Perhaps a hundred years."

"A secret tunnel to Cython, built a hundred years ago," said the chancellor relentlessly. "An illegal tunnel for trafficking in ebony pearls with the enemy. An unguarded tunnel through which the enemy could attack at any time."

"We know nothing about it," said Lady Ricinus, and now she had a look of trapped ferret about her. "It was hidden, he said."

"It's your palace, *bought a hundred years ago*. Who did you sell the pearls to, Lady Ricinus? Who could afford their staggering price?"

"I have no idea what you're talking about."

"Lady Ricinus," said the chancellor, lowering his voice, "these pearls could change the course of the war. Tell me who has them and you'll be surprised how forgiving I can be."

Her face worked through a range of emotions. Rix could see she was tempted, but it was not in her to admit her guilt. She would fight and deny all the way to the end.

"What pearls?" said Lady Ricinus.

"Have it your own way," said the chancellor, with a malicious smile. "House Ricinus became wealthy very suddenly, did it not, a hundred years ago? Wealthy enough to buy Palace Ricinus for cash. It will be interesting to see your ledgers for that time."

"Unfortunately they were lost in a fire."

"How convenient."

"You can't prove anything against us."

"Perhaps not on the *current* evidence."

"Then I'll have a public apology," said Lady Ricinus, giving him that viper's smile again. "And reparation for the ruin of the good name of House Ricinus."

"You'll get nothing, you upstart bitch," hissed the chancellor. "There's still the tunnel."

"You can't prove we know anything about it," sneered Lady Ricinus.

He cocked an eyebrow at the justiciar. "Would you be so kind as to describe the legal situation to Lady Ricinus?"

"Having an illegal tunnel to Cython is a capital crime at any time," said the justiciar. "But having an unguarded tunnel in wartime is treason."

"You are not unfamiliar with treason, are you, Lady Ricinus?" the chancellor said softly. "Even *high treason*. Would you like me to enlarge on that?"

Rix realised that the Honouring was always going to end this way. The chancellor was a vengeful man. He had allowed Ricinus to be raised to the First Circle solely for the joy of crushing it.

"I don't know what you're talking about," Lady Ricinus blustered.

The chancellor snapped his fingers. From behind the curtains at the rear of the stage, his pretty, black-haired servant girl came forward with slow and stately steps, bearing the covered tray. She sat it at the front of the stage where everyone could see and removed the cloth to reveal the chancellor's sad, poisoned dog.

"My faithful hound was killed by *ricin*," said the chancellor.

"It must have taken a rat bait," said Lady Ricinus.

"Ricin comes from the castor oil plant that is the symbol of your house, and the poison was meant for me."

"Poison—the worst," Tali said to herself. "That's what Mimoy was

trying to tell me. And Tinyhead hinted at it as well, *Lay-lay-lay*. Lady."

"The weed grows wild all over the city," said Lady Ricinus. "Anyone could have done it."

"Two witnesses say you threatened me."

"They're liars!"

"Reliable witnesses."

"Name them!"

The chancellor smiled but said nothing.

Lady Ricinus seemed to take heart from his silence. "You can't prove I had anything to do with this, either."

"I don't have to," said the chancellor. "Justiciar?"

The justiciar continued. "Lady Ricinus, Lord Ricinus and yourself are in charge of these premises. In law you are deemed to own the illegal tunnel to Cython, whether it can be proven you knew about it or not."

"Not me." Lady Ricinus would never concede, not even when her world was collapsing around her. "My husband is the lord."

"I need another drink," said Lord Ricinus.

"I'll pour it down your throat until you choke," she snarled.

Rix jumped, then the layered sweat froze down his back. He had heard her say that before, but where? Tali was staring; she remembered it too.

"You've pulled Lord Ricinus's strings for fifteen years and more," said the chancellor inexorably.

"Rixium is Lord Ricinus now," said Lady Ricinus. "Let sanction fall on him."

The pain was as bad as if she had cut open his own head. What kind of a woman would try to save herself by shifting blame onto her son? Rix felt something building up inside him, like a mudslide of memories banking behind a wall. The wall quivered as more and more memories built up behind it, then it cracked and crumbled and burst into pieces and he was back in the cellar as a small boy.

"You did it to me!" he howled. "*Deliberately*."

"What are you talking about, mad boy?" sneered Lady Ricinus, shaken but unyielding.

"I was dressed in my best clothes—you said you were taking me to a party."

"He's lying," cried Lady Ricinus. "Everything he says is a lie."

"You don't know what he's going to say," said the chancellor. "Or do you?"

"You led me down to the cellar and told me to hide behind the barrels," said Rix. "To watch and learn the family business that was going to make us the richest house in Hightspall."

"Lies, all lies," said Lady Ricinus.

"You had blood on your hands," Tali said suddenly. "I saw it—"

"Rixium must have cut the woman's head open," said Lady Ricinus. "He was evil from birth."

"Stop the bitch's mouth," said the chancellor, and she was gagged.

"I've often wondered why Rix had blood on his hands *before* he touched my mother," said Tali. "Lady Ricinus must have put it there so he would think he'd been involved."

"You told me to make no sound," Rix said to his mother. "*Hide until the business is done, and if you're a good little boy you'll get a reward.*" He felt the vomit swirling in his gut. Every eye was on him, every mouth gaping.

"Then you hacked that beautiful young woman's head open." He choked. "I couldn't move. I heard a child cry . . . and then . . . then you said to Father . . . I still can't believe you said it—*Find the brat and finish it.*"

"At first I thought you meant *me*," Rix whispered. "But Father didn't cut the little girl's throat because he couldn't find her. She didn't come out until you left me behind with the body."

"Lies, lies and more lies," mumbled Lady Ricinus through her gag.

"And after I came up, out of my wits with horror, you gave me a potion. Why?"

"To make you forget until you came of age," said Lord Ricinus, lurching across the stage with tears flooding from his sunken eyes.

"I was delirious for weeks," said Rix, "and when I recovered, my memories were gone. But the horror never goes away."

"How could any mother do such a thing to her son?" said Tali. "How could any father allow it?"

Lady Ricinus was coldly blank; she would never admit anything. Then the brazier flared as high as the ceiling. Lord Ricinus was holding his second bottle of brandy upside-down over it, the golden fluid feeding the flames. He dropped the empty bottle and looked sideways at Rix.

"Every word my son says is true. The previous Lady Ricinus, my mother, did the same to me when I was a boy."

Lady Ricinus tore free, wrenched off the gag and threw herself at him, clawing at his face. "He lies!" she screeched. "He did it, not me—"

The guards dragged her off, bound and gagged her, thoroughly this time.

Her nails had scored bloody marks the length of Lord Ricinus's ravaged face, but he stood up straight for the first time in years.

"I was eleven when my parents made me complicit in the killing of a different Pale. They gave me a potion of forgetting until I came of age, then blackmailed me into taking over the family business when my father died. But when it came time to take the next pearl, Tali's mother's pearl, I couldn't do it. Unfortunately, my mother had chosen the *perfect wife* for me. Lady Ricinus threatened to destroy me and I was too weak to resist. She led and, like a craven dog, I followed. Do you wonder that I drink? It's the only way I can forget."

Lord Ricinus looked up at the justiciar. "My lady and I are guilty of every crime you accuse us of. And more. She murdered poor old Luzia, and I plotted with her to kill the chancellor."

On this confession, the brutal years fell from him; for a moment, Lord Ricinus looked noble.

"I know," said the chancellor. "Your son informed on her."

Lord Ricinus stiffened. Lady Ricinus squealed and tried to chew through her gag. The nobles muttered to one another, then studied Rix as though he was muck to be scraped off a boot.

"Who bought the pearls?" said the chancellor.

"I never met the fellow," said Lord Ricinus, "but his name is Deroe—a minor magian. He must be ancient by now."

"Deroe?" said the chancellor to his chief magian.

"There was such a magian, Lord, though not of any account. I thought he'd died half a century ago."

"What does he want with these pearls?"

"I can't imagine."

"Find him," the chancellor said to the high constable, "and get the pearls. They could turn the war our way." He rubbed his hands together. "This has been a good night." He eyed the Ricinuses, mother, father and son with the same contempt, then called the justiciar and the high constable into a huddle.

Tali was making urgent signs to Rix. "What is it?" he said under his breath, putting his body between her and the others so they could not hear.

"Remember when I first came here, and someone was hunting me with a triple call, *Di*-DA-*doh? Di*-DA-*doh?*" she murmured.

He nodded. "It must have been Deroe."

"And he hasn't given up."

The chancellor's little group broke up and the justiciar went to the front of the stage.

"Lord and Lady Ricinus have been proven guilty of treason in a time of war. Lord Ricinus has confessed to other dishonourable crimes committed at his wife's behest. They will be hanged from the front gates of Palace Ricinus at dawn—"

Lady Ricinus chewed through her gag and spat it out. "House Ricinus is First Circle. I demand a proper trial where my lawyers can examine—"

The chancellor's smile oozed such malice that she broke off, trembling.

He picked up the two thousand-year-old parchment, tore it in half and tossed it onto the brazier. As the sheaf of documents followed it and burst into flame, Lady Ricinus let out a ragged screech.

"How can your house be First Circle when there's no evidence?" he said softly. "No evidence of *any* nobility whatsoever. You will die common traitors' deaths and your corpses will hang from the palace gates until they rot to pieces."

Lady Ricinus's nightmare had come true. Not the public execution, but the public humiliation, and the undoing of her life's scheming at the moment it had come to fruition. The chancellor's eyes were ablaze. How he revelled in his vengeance.

"What about my son?" she said.

"He is under age. And by switching that painting with the portrait—"

"I didn't switch it!" cried Rix, but no one believed him, least of all his own mother. She would go to her death believing that her son had betrayed her. And he had, though not this way.

"By switching the portraits," the chancellor repeated, "he brought this filthy matter to light. Rixium survives—*assuming he can live with himself*. All assets in Lord and Lady Ricinus's possession are forfeited. And it does not end there.

"House Ricinus has grown fat on this evil trade for generations. Under law, the whole house stands condemned. Take the heads of all its departments," he said to the high constable. "They will hang beside their lord and lady, since they must have known evil was at work here, yet stood idly by."

Rix sprang up. "That's not justice. How could the chief ostler know of such matters, or the head gardener?"

"Justice lies in the majesty of the law, and the law says all the heads must die with their lord and lady. Let it be done. Seal the palace doors. The remainder of the household will attend the hangings and everyone in this hall will bear witness.

"The new Lord Ricinus may keep this palace, and such moneys that are his own by right, *if* they are untainted. The staff will be dispersed and may never return. This Honouring is ended."

Lord and Lady Ricinus were stripped of their clothes and jewellery, and thrown to the floor. Ropes were bound around their ankles and they were dragged away.

The guests followed, falling over themselves to escape from so tainted a household, but the doors had already been locked.

Tali and Tobry came up but Rix waved them away. "Leave me!"

He had been brought up to do his duty, to speak the truth and act with honour. To believe in his country, his house and his family.

But where did duty lie when his sovereign had condemned his

family and destroyed his house? What price honour when, for generations, his house had acted so dishonourably? What value truth when his parents' whole existence, and the truths he had been brought up to believe in, were based on lies?

Everything Rix had believed in was tainted beyond redemption. He had loved House Ricinus and honoured his parents. Now he had destroyed them, and many others, guilty and innocent alike.

And for what?

CHAPTER 94

D*i-DA-doh, di-DA-doh.*

Tali had been hearing the triple call for hours and she now knew where it came from. Deroe was hunting her for the master pearl. He had ordered her mother killed for her pearl, and he had to pay, though Tali wasn't sure she would get the chance.

The chancellor's eyes had been on her at the end of the Honouring. For Hightspall, magery meant the difference between victory and defeat, and once he realised that she carried the master pearl, she would die for it.

Outside the palace gates, thousands of shanty dwellers had gathered to see the fall of House Ricinus, though few seemed to be enjoying the spectacle. How could the wealthiest house in Hightspall, one that had endured for generations, be toppled so quickly? And if Ricinus could fall, what hope was there for their miserable selves, with the enemy bound to return and no one to come to their aid?

It was not yet sunrise but Tali's day felt week-long. Was Deroe watching her now? How would she recognise him? With the magery of three pearls, he could disguise himself as anyone.

Inside the gates, the guests from the Honouring watched silently, the men in their crumpled dress suits, the ladies bleary-eyed and bedraggled. They weren't rejoicing either: the fall of a noble house that had, albeit briefly, inhabited the First Circle, reminded them of the fragility of their own positions.

Where was justice when the innocent were taken with the guilty? That kindly old man, the Master of the Palace, hung silent and still, as did the nine heads of his departments, four from the left side of the gate beside him, five from the right. They, at least, had been hanged with their clothes and their dignity. Lord and Lady Ricinus, naked, scratched and bruised after being dragged all the way from the palace, shuddered in the bitter cold. Tali's toes were freezing in her ballroom slippers.

"Hang Ricinus and his wife together," said the chancellor as the sun rose.

They were forced onto the scaffold below the great arch of the gate. Without her clothes, make-up, corsets and back brace, Lady Ricinus looked smaller and older, and walked with a stoop. It was impossible to see, in this pathetic baggage, how she had intimidated so many for so long. Tali avoided looking at Lord Ricinus's drink-ruined body.

She could not bear to witness Rix's agony, either. He was standing so still that he might have been turned to basalt, his fingers clawed over his heart as if tearing out his own falsity. Who would want to watch such a sight? But his parents were the last of House Ricinus, that had fallen and would never rise again, and he was required to see them on their final journey.

The barbed ropes were placed over their heads. No words were spoken for their souls; no priest or abbess was permitted to attend them. They were to die unshriven, cursed by the Five Heroes and forsaken by their Gods.

The chancellor gave the signal. Rix's mother and father fell together. Lady Ricinus's chicken neck snapped like the frail rib bones she had once stood on so contemptuously and she died at once. Lord Ricinus hung there, slowly choking, and though his death took five dreadful minutes, no mercy stroke was permitted.

A thousand klaxons howled, all over the city. Tali turned away as the ritual disembowellings were carried out. And we call the Cythonians barbaric. This was not justice; it was vengeance.

*

"Who would have thought the execution of noble traitors could be so good for morale?" Tobry said bleakly that afternoon. "I knew Lord and Lady Ricinus were hated, but . . . " He trailed off.

"I'm amazed there's any fireworks left in Caulderon," said Tali.

It was still an hour until dark, but the rockets and the fiery wheels showed up clearly under the gloom created by a heavy brown overcast sky.

"Or any grog. If the enemy were to attack now, they could walk in."

They were watching the celebrations from the tower inside the palace gates, wondering what, if anything, was left for them after such a disastrous night and day. The surrounding streets were clogged with drunken men and women, and even children, moving in colourful surges this way and that.

"It's not the enemy we have to worry about tonight," said Tobry.

Down the road, several dozen thugs were attacking the gates of a mansion with a ram. On the third strike the hinges tore out and they swarmed through, followed by hundreds of drunken shanty dwellers. The guards were torn to pieces, the rioters flooded into the mansion and shortly the leaders reappeared, dragging a plump man and a small grey-haired woman with them. The woman was struggling furiously, the man curiously listless.

"Thissel and Teala of House Neger," said Tobry, shaking his head. "I knew them well, once."

"What have they done?" said Tali.

"Treated their servants too well. They're good people—and that's a fatal weakness now."

"They're not going to kill them . . . "

"It's happening all over Caulderon. So *glorious* Hightspall rots and falls—from within."

She looked where he was pointing. Smoke rose from half a dozen of the great houses and another was fully ablaze.

"Why are they destroying those beautiful houses?" said Tali, aching for her own, ruined manor.

"What they can't take with them, let no one have."

"But what does it gain anyone?"

"Vengeance is power, the only kind the shanty dwellers have ever had, and how they glory in it."

A huge man raised an axe. The heads came off, the bodies were strung from the broken gates, upside-down, and pelted with muck. The mob split, one part heading to the next manor, a smaller wedge heading up the hill towards Palace Ricinus. Only then did Tali realise the inevitable and remember that Rannilt was all alone.

She ran for the palace, pain spearing through her thigh with every step. Tobry matched her stride, but as they reached the front steps the horde came streaming towards them.

"Lock the doors! Hurry." Tali took hold of the left-hand door and heaved.

"Leave it!" Rix stalked out, thrusting the doors wide, and the look in his eyes was so haunted that shivers crawled across Tali's back. If ever a man wanted to die, he did.

"There's a hundred of them . . . " began Tobry.

"A *hundred*?" said Rix. "A thousand, ten thousand, it makes no difference."

He stood at the top of the six broad steps outside the palace doors, hand on his sword hilt, waiting.

Tali hesitated, then moved out to his right. Tobry took position on the left.

The horde reached the foot of the steps, led by a huge, raw-boned fellow, taller than Rix and broader across the shoulders. His threadbare shirt and trews had diagonal sprays of blood from the earlier killings. He carried an axe with a six-foot handle and a bloody blade a foot across.

"It's the lording who betrayed his own parents," sneered the axeman. "Run, little lord—let's see how far you get before I spill your guts."

Rix put his hand on the wire hilt of his sword but did not draw.

The axeman hefted the gigantic axe. "I'm going to chop your arms and legs off and split you for kindling."

As he lumbered up the steps, Rix took several steps backwards. The axeman grinned and called the rest of the mob with a sweep of his arm. At least twenty followed, carrying axes, mattocks, knives and a sword or two. Another hundred waited below.

Tali's belly throbbed. A rasping sound beside her was Tobry drawing his blade, though what could it avail him against so many? They were going to die here. And Rannilt inside, without waking.

The axeman's weapon was back over his shoulder, ready to swing, yet Rix had not drawn his sword. Surely he wasn't so far gone as to let the brute cut him down?

"Rix?" Tobry said in a strangled gasp.

The axeman swung. Tali let out an involuntary scream. Rix moved like a flash of silver, then the axe came clattering across the flagstones towards her and she had to leap out of the way.

The axeman was clutching his belly but could not hold his entrails in; he had been slashed across and back. They squelched out of him, splatting on the top step and oozing down while he stood there, his wet mouth slack. Rix's sword was back in its sheath and she had not seen that, either.

Rix spun the axeman by the shoulder, put a foot in the middle of his back and sent him flying into the group halfway up the steps, knocking several of them over. He landed face down, making sickening gurgling sounds while his red fingernails raked at the treads and blood poured out of him to stain the white stone. The other thugs stared at the steaming entrails.

"Reckon I can disembowel twenty of you before you kill me," said Rix. "Who wants to be next?"

They longed to see him die. Tali could read it in their eyes. They wanted to tear Rix to pieces and feed him to the dogs, then pillage Palace Ricinus of its treasures, defile it in every way and smash it to pieces the way life had smashed them. And if they attacked at once, not even Rix could stop them.

The axeman thrashed and screamed, his cries strangled for want of air, and muck dripped from his middle. His entrails slid down the next step and came to rest beside his cheek.

The thugs eyed each other and gave a collective shudder.

"No?" said Rix, after another minute. "Then take your meat and go."

Two of them took the dying axeman's legs and began to drag him away, his head thumping on the ground. The blood on the steps was already icing over.

"All of him," said Rix with frosty menace.

A man wearing a leather butcher's apron took it off, scowling, scraped the entrails into it and slung the dripping mess over his shoulder.

"What sort of a man betrays his own parents?" he said savagely. "Cut your own guts out and make Hightspall a better place."

Rix choked, and even after they were out of sight he stood there, staring sightlessly across the grounds.

"Come on, old friend." Tobry took him by the arm.

Back in Rix's chambers, Tali checked on Rannilt, who lay in Tobry's big bed, breathing shallowly. Though she was twice wrapped in blankets and had his thick quilt over her, her hands were cold.

"Nothing can warm her," Tali said to Tobry. "I think her end must be near."

"All our ends are near," Rix said harshly. "At least she goes peacefully."

"Rix!" Tobry said sharply.

Rix's eyes, which had looked ever to the horizon since Lord and Lady Ricinus were condemned, focused on Tali.

"Forgive me," he said. "No truer friend have any of us ever had, and Rannilt is an innocent child. Tobe, see what's happening outside."

Tobry went out. Rix picked Rannilt up in her covers and carried her to the salon.

"Bring the blankets," he said over his shoulder. "I'll make a bed for her in front of the heatstone. If anything can warm her in this dreadful winter, it can. We'll sleep here tonight—if we're allowed sleep. Should she rouse, she'll know she's among friends."

He laid her on the couch close by the heatstone. It did seem a little warmer there.

Tali heard a faint rustle, like someone creeping down steps.

Rix drew his blade, wrenched the door open and was about to strike into the darkness when a boy cried, "Lord Rixium!"

Rix hauled a stocky, red-haired lad, no older than Rannilt, down into the light. "What are you doing here?"

"Nowhere else to go, Lord."

"You're Benn," said Rix.

"Yes, Lord." Benn bowed and called up the stairs. "It's all right, Glynnie, it's the lord. He'll look after us."

A slender girl crept down, her emerald eyes as round as plums. Her hair was redder than the boy's and her nose and forearms were freckled. At most she was sixteen, Tali thought, and she was shaking.

"The High Chancellor forbade any servant to return to the palace, Glynnie," said Rix sternly.

"S-sorry, Lord," she said.

"Then why are you here?"

"After the hangin's, and all the killin's, we wus too scared to go out the gates. We been hidin' up in the passages. We didn't take anythin' though. Not even a crust of the pigs' bread."

The boy's stomach rumbled. Glynnie tried to shush him. "Besides," she added softly, "you saved Benn from a floggin'. We owe you—"

"You owe me nothing, and you're welcome to whatever you can find in the pantries," Rix said wearily. "But you'll have to go."

"Please, Lord." Glynnie reached out to him with both hands. "We'll slave for you night and day."

"I don't want anyone to slave for me."

"But the shanty people hate us." She clutched at his arm. "They won't have us, Lord. Benn will have to steal to survive, and when he's caught they'll cut his hands off. And . . . you know what will happen to me."

Rix flushed. "Yes," he said, "I know. Damn the chancellor. You can stay."

"Thank you, Lord, thank you." She bowed three times, mechanically straightened the blankets and tidied the table. "Don't stand there idle, Benn. Get to work."

"You don't have to wait on us," said Rix,

"How else will we earn our crusts?" said Glynnie, scanning the room. "But you haven't anything to eat."

"Can you cook?"

"I can do *everything*," said Glynnie. "Benn, we've work to do." She ran out, dragging the boy after her.

Shortly they came back with hot fish soup. Tali spooned half a cup into Rannilt, though there was no change in her condition afterwards.

Rix sent Benn to keep watch then sat on the couch. Tali lay beside Rannilt, holding her cold hands. When Tobry returned, ice in his eyebrows and on the stubble of his beard, they were sitting in the malign twilight of the heatstone.

"Are we to live the night?" said Rix.

"The chancellor has hanged three hundred of the rioters, flogged another thousand and locked up the alehouses. There'll be no more trouble tonight."

"And tomorrow?" said Rix.

The floor shook so violently that the table jumped a foot across the salon and the empty bowls fell and smashed. Tobry threw open the door to the tower stairs. Brilliant red light flooded in.

"Fire!" Tali gathered Rannilt in her arms.

"Benn!" wailed Glynnie, racing the other way.

Tobry ran up the steps, then called down. "It's not the palace. It's far off."

Rix followed him to the studio. The light grew until it was bright as sunlight, though not in written history had such a baleful crimson sun illuminated this land.

"Chymical fire!" Tali clutched Rannilt to her chest and struggled up the steps. But how could anyone create such a vast and terrible conflagration, so quickly? "It's as though the whole world is burning."

Another shudder shook her off the step. Rix steadied her and helped her up. At the top, the glare streaming through the tower windows made her flinch.

"It's the Vomits," said Tobry. "In full eruption."

"Is it always like this?" Tali set Rannilt on the settee and peered through slitted fingers at the distant fountains of fire and the red lava clots spinning through the sky.

"It's never like this," said Rix. "All three Vomits are erupting at once."

"And that last happened after the First Fleet landed," said Tobry. "It's held to be a sign of the fall of nations."

"Ours, or theirs?" said Tali.

CHAPTER 95

The butcher was right, Rix thought in the blackest part of that night. *The taint on my house is so foul that only annihilation can cleanse the ground it stands on.*

It was eating at him like a cancer. All the world despised him for being Ricinus, for betraying his own parents, and most of all for not dying with them. Why had the chancellor allowed him to live? To punish him even more?

The cherry wood month-clock said two in the morning. Despite the constant shaking and quaking, everyone else was asleep. Rix longed for that oblivion but sleep was a lifetime away. He rose quietly, pulled a cloak around him and went up to his frigid studio. The mess he'd made in his drunkenness had been cleaned away but all else lay as it had when he'd completed the cellar painting that had ruined his life.

Snow was falling thickly now, concealing the lights in the chancellor's palace next door and even the eruptions, though their glare turned the night into ruddy twilight and the fat snowflakes to crystals the colour of engorged leeches.

Where was the cellar painting now? Probably taken by the chancellor. In its own way it was as much a masterpiece as the portrait, and he was a connoisseur of twisted arts. Rix lay on the settee, cloak wrapped around himself, and closed his eyes.

Ice creaked and cracked around him. A moving mountain was pulverising everything in its path as it ground towards the palace walls . . .

Tomorrow you will take her down. You will cut it out and bring it to me.

He woke so violently that he hurled himself off the settee. The voice was Lyf's, and as Rix hit the floor he remembered his earlier promise to Tobry, and how he had failed to keep it. In the final cellar painting Rix had meant to take control of the divination about Tali, but he had been so drunk that he had allowed the divination to control him. Had his folly doomed her too?

He stood up, pressing his palms against the nearest window and peering out into the volcanic glare. Could Lyf drive him to commit an even worse betrayal—the murder of a friend?

No! The evil must be scourged from the flesh, the cancer burnt away. Lord and Lady Ricinus's quick deaths could never make up for a hundred years of House Ricinus's infamy, but the debt had to be paid and Rix was the only Ricinus left.

As he reached that resolution, calm settled over him. When the enemy reappeared he would ride out to battle against them and give his life away. It could never be full atonement, but it would end the threat to Tali and thwart her enemy, and deliver him to the peace he so craved.

It was enough. He slept at last.

Day dawned, almost as black as the night. The floor was shaking constantly now and a crack had appeared over the lintel of the entrance door.

"The eruptions seem to be building to a climax," said Tobry.

As Rix joined him at the window, sparks jumped from his fingers. The sky was black as mud and gritty volcanic ash rained down. The malachite windowsills were inches deep in it; it covered the palace grounds like dark snow.

"Can that be ice riming the shore of the lake?" said Rix.

"I'd say so."

The lake was warmed by the same subterranean fires as had created the Seethings and Rix had never seen ice on it before, though it had cooled in recent years. He thrust open a window. It was achingly cold outside and the air tasted of burnt rock.

A yellow glow appeared under the trees down to the left, then drifted across the grounds, several yards up—a fiery sphere no bigger than a pumpkin. The air crackled; the globe jagged towards a majestic tree Rix had often climbed as a child, *zipppp,* and the trunk exploded like a firework. The ash rain fell, heavier than before.

"What manner of vile weapon is that?" said Rix, grieving for his childhood tree even though he had renounced all worldly things.

"Nature's own," said Tobry. "Ball lightning."

Tali limped up, little and barefoot and rubbing her eyes, to stare out the window. "The land wants rid of us."

"And we're running," said Tobry, "as fast as we can, on everything that will float."

The circular harbour away to the right was jammed with hundreds of boats, all making for the entrance. The shoreline was a similar scene: fishing boats, yachts, merchant's barges, canoes, even hastily built rafts were loaded with goods and heaved into the sullen waters.

"How many do you think will reach the other side, and safety?" said Rix softly. He might be doomed but he still cared about his people.

"Not many," said Tobry. "Though the risk is less than staying here. I'm ducking out for a minute. We have to know what's going on." He went down.

Tali moved closer to Rix, shivering. He put an arm around her shoulders and they stood together, watching the uncanny storms out over the lake, storms that began from dark clouds only hundreds of feet up and discharged red lightning in all directions. Storms that were drifting towards the city.

Rix raised a hand to the iron window frame and static discharged, stinging his fingertips. Outside, the air was crackling continuously now and more ball lightning rolled across the grounds, two globes sometimes meeting in fiery incandescence. Over the city, dozens of lightning bolts were visible at any time, striking trees and manors and sparking fires, and then hitting a raft on the lake, returning it to logs and flinging a dozen passengers into the rime-flecked water.

"Those poor people," said Tali. "Is there anything—?"

"It's the most merciful end they could come to," said Rix. "Come down into the warm."

He was turning away when the floor jerked half a yard to the left, then back again, tossing them both off their feet and turning the easels over. Brushes and paint pots went flying. The windows rattled; glass burst out of several panes, scything across the room. Outside, masonry thundered to the ground.

"What was that?" said Tali.

"One of the palace towers falling," said Rix. "Only eighty-seven to go."

"Pardon?" said Tali.

As he got up, the dark sky lit up more brightly than day. The ash clouds cleared and he saw across to the Brown Vomit as it went into full, terrifying eruption.

"What's happened to the mountain?" said Tali, holding onto the windowsill as the floor jerked again.

An enormous chunk of the right side of the volcano, up near the crater, had vanished. A series of dark flecks partially eclipsed the red lava fountains, flecks that must be rocks hundreds of yards across, blown miles into the air. And when they fell—

"Run!" Tali yelled.

Rix caught her by the arm, steadying her. "There's nowhere to run to. If one of those rocks hits the palace we die without ever knowing it."

"What if they fall into the lake?"

He did not answer. The floor shook three times as chunks of rock thundered to the ground out in the Seethings. Another tower toppled then, half a mile away, a mansion collapsed into boiling dust.

And then he saw it, a gigantic piece of the mountain wheeling across the sky out over the lake, rising, seeming to hover for a second, then plunging down. Momentarily the lake vanished in an explosion of boiling water, and when it cleared . . .

"What's happened to the water?" said Tali, winding her arms around Rix.

The lake had receded, exposing its muddy bed out for a hundred yards and grounding eleven boats plus a raft built from the side of a timber cottage. All along the shore, people shouted and pointed at the marvels exposed in the mud. Children ran to gather stranded fish and eels.

"No!" whispered Tali, going up on tiptoes to see more clearly. She put her head out the window and shrieked, "Grab the children. Get out of the way!"

"They can't hear you," said Rix, who had been slower than Tali to realise what was going to happen. "They're dead anyway. They just don't know it."

And then it came, a swell that rose until it must have been a hundred feet high, racing towards the shore faster than a galloping horse. Now the people screamed; now they ran, abandoning their boats and rafts and even their children, labouring through the mud in desperate attempts to get to the safety of the shore.

But the swell became a monster wave towering above them, breaking and thundering and crashing down onto boats and rafts and people, then picking them up and driving them towards the lake wall to smash them, and it, to bits.

Rix clung to Tali without realising he was doing so. As the wave struck the shore, in the lower grounds of the palace a column of pressurised water spurted two hundred feet in the air from some long forgotten tunnel, carrying ancient stonework, snow and turf with it.

The earth heaved, then disappeared under a boiling brown flood of muddy water, broken bodies, smashed boats and the rubble of the wall itself. It surged up the slope, drowning the navvies working in the tubule trench, smashing the castor oil greenhouses to bits and racing towards the palace doors.

"Should we go higher?" said Tali, eyeing the stairs up to the higher levels.

"The flood's spending itself. It's nearly done."

It tore through the downhill wing of the palace, rose higher and curled around to wash the blood off the front steps and cover them in mud. The water stilled. Objects bobbed to the surface, then it slowly ebbed, leaving a strandline of ruin curving across the grounds—trees and timber, stone and drowned animals and bodies all tangled together.

As the water retreated, carving ten-foot gullies through the lawn, the ground heaved and a scattering of sinkholes appeared across the lower grounds, exposing ancient ruins Rix had not known were there.

After the first flood withdrew, and the succeeding, smaller waves had passed, the shanty towns had vanished along with the lake wall. The city defences had been breached for three miles along the shore and could not be repaired, for the stones lay under the water.

"Nature does the enemy's work for them," said Tobry, coming up.

"Hightspall is tainted," said Rix. "The reek has to be cleansed from it. And the biggest stink of all is right here. As soon as the enemy reappear, I'm riding out to face them—alone."

"Rix?" said Tobry.

"I took the wealth and the privilege, and all the good things that came from it. Now there's a price to pay and I'm the only one left to pay it."

"Better you pay it by staying here with us."

"I betrayed my own parents, Tobe. No matter what they'd done, I can't escape that dishonour. I can't live with myself any longer."

CHAPTER 96

Tali did not try to dissuade Rix. In his current mood, nothing could change him. Besides, it hardly seemed to matter now.

Nature's omens were clear—the sea-ice was thickening and closing in on the coast, the cataclysmic eruptions and the roaring waters were conspiring to bring Hightspall down. The enemy would soon return and there was no lake wall to keep them out. The end could not be far away now, for any of them.

Least of all for Rannilt, who was fading by the hour. Tali sat by the sleeping child's side, watching the hours drag by on Rix's month-clock and holding the thin fingers that not even the great heatstone could warm. No medicine in the palace had roused Rannilt; neither Tobry's magery nor the small power of Tali's healing hands could help her. Whatever was draining the life from her, they could not touch it.

"I'm sorry, Rannilt," Tali whispered as she chafed the child's cold hands. "You gave everything for me and I can't do the same for you. I tried, and I failed. Failed at everything."

Her quest for justice had come to naught. The storm of magery that had killed Overseer Banj had been a life for a life, but in his own way Banj had been a good man obeying his laws and doing his duty. She had done no justice to him.

Lord and Lady Ricinus had deserved to die, no doubt about it, though how could their executions be justice when such grave injustice had been done to every servant in the palace?

Had she achieved anything at all? Her escape had not caused the war, but it had brought it forward. Had she remained in Cython, and Rix and Tobry had returned to Caulderon to warn that war was brewing, Hightspall would have had ten days' warning and might have driven the enemy back.

But her greatest blunder was with Lyf. By failing to protect Rannilt, Tali had allowed Lyf a source of power he'd had no chance of finding as a wrythen, not to mention the physical body he could not have obtained by himself.

Her head throbbed. A knot beneath the top of her skull went cold, then hot. Rannilt's pallid face blurred and shifted, then a wave of nausea flooded through Tali and she had to run to the scalderium to throw up in the basin.

She was washing her face in icy water when her mental shell burst open and her pearl sent out a frantic call, as if trying to call the other pearls to it. She forced the shell closed and slumped onto the side of the tub, fantasising about hacking the pearl out herself. It was an alien thing inside her and she dreaded what it was going to do—or make her do—next.

She looked up and Tobry was frowning at her. "You look like—"

"Just tormenting myself with my failings." Tali put on a feeble smile.

"I know all about that," said Tobry. "Have you talked to Rix lately? I'm really worried about him."

"He won't listen to anything I say."

Tali returned to Rannilt and to her agonising. The chief magian had said that the master pearl could command the others, but how?

What else did she know about pearls? Hers had woken when the sunstone smashed in the shaft, liberating her magery briefly and uncontrollably. Her pearl was also affected whenever she was near a heatstone—it was one of the first things she'd noticed after she reached Rix's chambers. The pearl seemed more agitated here.

Rannilt jerked in her sleep. As Tali stroked her chilly brow, she sensed Lyf working, but what was he doing? Wrapping strands of wrythen muscle around something, she thought, though not his legs or any limb this time. This object was hardly bigger than her fist, and almost complete. He sighed, pointed a finger, and the object went *thump-thump*, *thump-thump*, *thump-thump*. He had made himself a heart!

Tali could not have said why it filled her with such dread. He might be days away from having a working body, even weeks, but she did not think so. She could sense his exultation. And a physical body would free him from being bound to his caverns. With a body, he could roam wherever he wished.

He would go to the cellar that had once been the most sacred part of the kings' palace, the place where the other pearls had been cut from their hosts. Perhaps, with a body of his own, Lyf could take it for himself.

"Tobry, tell me about Lyf."

"You know him better than I do."

"Tell me what you know."

"He was younger than Rix when he disappeared, only nineteen. Lyf was quiet, their history books say, reserved or shy. Nonetheless, a hospitable man who welcomed the First Fleeters when they came. Some of the enemy historians said he was too trusting, but Cythe had seen neither war nor invasions in thousands of years."

"Was he clever?"

"He had a keen mind. Had his brother the king not been gored to death on a hunt, Lyf would have been a scholar and a poet. He loved art and books and beautiful things, and it's said his mastery of calligraphy was almost magical."

Almost magical, or *actually* magical? That would put an entirely different complexion on the Solaces. Tali heaved open the cover of the iron book. "In his caverns, I saw how he wrote it."

"How?" Tobry said curiously.

"With a hollow-pointed scriber filled with diluted alkoyl." It would not have been easy to write with such a tool, yet every glyph was perfect in its elegance and grace. "It's a beautiful book, for all it's called *The Consolation of Vengeance*. Why did he make it this way, I wonder?"

"For permanence, I suppose," said Tobry. "Paper burns, and worms eat it. It rarely lasts."

"And iron rusts," said Tali. "Why not bronze, if he wanted it to last?"

Tobry shrugged.

"What are his weaknesses? I see none, now he's making himself a body."

"Who knows?" said Tobry. "Self-doubt, perhaps?"

"He's afraid of Rix's sword," said Tali.

Rix came down, shivering from his tower-top vigil. "Hand me my titane sword, there's a good fellow," he said to Tobry.

"What for?" said Tobry, unmoving.

"The enemy are back."

CHAPTER 97

"The wind changed at four o'clock as if Lyf had ordered it personally," said Rix, buckling on the sword.

"Maybe he did." Tobry handed Rix his chest plate.

He frowned at it, as if thinking that a man bent on self-sacrifice had no need of armour, then put it on.

Tali watched them, aching inside. Why was Tobry arming Rix for a one-way trip to the enemy lines? Had he decided that, where Rix's honour was concerned, he had no right to interfere? She wanted to scream at them and demand answers, but who was she to interfere between friends who had known each other all their lives?

No! Rix's strength was their only hope now. Without him they could not survive and Tali had to stop him from sacrificing himself. She had to do whatever it took and she was beginning to think of a way. An ignoble way she was bound to regret, but she would worry about that later—if there was a later.

"A wicked sou'wester blew the ash away," said Rix, "and when I could see beyond the walls again, the armies of Cython were there—all of them this time."

"What do you mean, *all of them*?" said Tali, rising.

Rix tucked his telescope under his arm and led them up eight flights to the top of his tower, one of the highest points in Caulderon. Tali hadn't been there before and looked around curiously. Above them, the leaf-patterned, zinc-clad roof spire soared in a twisted spiral for another fifty feet. On this level the sides were open, save for nine slender columns supporting the roof and a tiled surrounding wall, shoulder-high to Rix, though too high for her to see over.

Rix looked out. "Seventy-nine," he said with a grim smile.

"What?" said Tali.

"He's counting the palace towers," said Tobry. "Until this morning there were eighty-eight of them."

"At this rate, the palace won't long outlast its lord and lady," said Rix. "And that's only fitting after what they got up to here."

An icy wind licked the back of Tali's neck. Already Rix seemed to have gone on so far that he could not see back to the real world.

A feeble, blood-red sun was skidding below the horizon, and glad to go by the look of the sky, which was mottled the red and black of rust blisters on iron plate. The air already smelled like the dead.

Tobry dragged over a bench. Tali stood on it and pointed the telescope towards the city gates, though she did not need it to see the Cythonian armies—they stretched to the horizon. And once they attacked, every soldier would be looking for her.

"For every man, every squad, every army they had before," said Rix, "they now have two. There must be a hundred thousand of the bastards."

"What are they doing?"

"Waiting," said Rix.

"What for?"

"Lyf's word, I suppose."

"They're taunting us," said Tobry. "Telling us they can do what they want, when they want, and nothing we can do can make a jot of difference."

Tali looked across Lake Fumerous. Its northern cliffs were steep and ragged, like a hole smashed through a stone window—the chasm made when the fourth Vomit had blown itself to bits. She turned back to the Brown Vomit and her stomach twisted into a knot. If it blew up, neither Hightspall nor Cython would have anything to fight over.

"What's north beyond the lake?"

"The sunken lands of Fennery," said Rix. "Ten miles of treacherous swamp and mire, and Lakeland after that. We have an estate on the largest lake—" He tightened his jaw. "We *had* one, bought with blood, no doubt." Goose pimples rose on his arms as though something had scuttled over his grave. "Come down. I can't put it off any longer."

Tobry was unnaturally pale beneath his tan. "Wait a moment." He took the telescope and pointed it down towards the streets around the palace.

"Can we possibly beat them?" Tali asked Rix. "Or is Caulderon doomed?"

"It takes a lot of soldiers to capture a city," said Rix, pacing jerkily around the low wall. "Far more than to defend one. Had the wave not washed all the lower walls away we might have held them out for a month, even two. But nothing can stop them now."

"Hightspall has magery, and the Cythonians aren't allowed to use it. Surely magery can make a difference?"

"Our magery has been dwindling ever since the First Fleets grounded here," Tobry reminded her. "And it was never so powerful that it could destroy such an army."

"What if the chancellor gets the three pearls from Deroe?"

"I don't think Deroe will be easy to find."

He'll come after the master pearl, Tali thought. She had to be ready.

"No one is celebrating now," said Tobry, who was still studying the streets. "The eruption has everyone on edge—the people believe it was *sent* against us."

"And the tidal wave?"

"That too. They knew it presaged the end, even before the latest rumour."

"What rumour?" Tali said curiously.

"That the entire First Circle fled in the night," Rix grated. "Caulderon is finished, Tobe."

"We can still fight," said Tali.

"The common folk have given up," said Tobry. "You can see it in their eyes. They're not even looting any more."

"Their *best* hope is to be carried into slavery." Rix's eyes met Tali's, briefly.

"*I'm* not giving up," said Tali. Her head gave another painful throb and she felt fingers prising at the mental shell she'd built to prevent the *call* from getting out. She clamped down hard.

"Will you do one last thing for me, Tobe?" said Rix, turning to the door.

"What?" said Tobry.

"Take Tali and the child, and get out now."

As Rix headed down, Tali grabbed the back of his coat. "I didn't escape from Cython to run away."

Rix stared at her vacantly. His mind seemed to be fixed on the last fatal ride that, if it did not pay for all, would at least end all. "If you stay, you and Rannilt will die the deaths they reserve for escaping Pale. Do you want that for her?"

He jerked free and headed down the steep stairs.

"We can't let him go like this," said Tali as Tobry came down beside her.

"Can you stop him?"

"No, but you can." She prayed that Tobry would. Otherwise she would have to use her own plan, and that would shatter him.

"Tali, Rix was brought up as the heir to a great and noble house," said Tobry, "one that had raised itself by its own prodigious efforts. He may not have liked his parents, but he honoured what they were and all they had done. Honour and duty and truth were everything to him, and now his world is revealed to be a lie. His family's rise was bought with the blood of innocents, the parents he honoured were corrupt, and everything that was good about his life has been befouled."

"But he's a good man. Surely people must see—"

"To the chancellor, it wasn't Lady Ricinus who plotted to have him killed, it was *House* Ricinus. House Ricinus committed high treason and House Ricinus had to pay. But that's not what ails Rix most."

"What does?" said Tali.

"Betraying his own parents."

"He was trying to save his house."

"Does that lessen the betrayal?"

"They were evil, murderous monsters."

"Even so, in Rix's eyes his dishonour can never be redeemed, and there's only one way out."

"Would you take it?" Tali hissed, "if you'd been put in such a position?"

Tobry's eyes turned opaque. "Before my house fell, I *was* put in such a position," he said harshly. "But I lacked the courage to do the honourable thing afterwards. Do you wonder that the chancellor loathes me almost as much as I despise myself?"

His eyes forbade questioning. He pushed past and went down. Tali stood there, aching for these brave and decent men, neither of whom she could help. But Rix had to live and only Tobry could save him. To convince Tobry to do so, she had to tell him this terrible lie.

Would he believe her, though? If the positions were reversed, Rix would not believe her for a second—but Tobry had been in Rix's shadow most of his life, standing beside Rix while he got everything. Yes, she thought Tobry would believe her lie.

"Tobry?" It came out as a strangled cry.

He stopped ten steps below, staring up at her. "Yes."

"Stop him. For me."

He frowned. "For *you*? Why?"

Tali's heart was racketing around her chest. She felt the colour rising up her throat at the dreadful lie she was about to tell. "Because," she gasped, "because I love him."

He went so still that his feet might have frozen to the step. "You—love—*Rix*?"

She forced herself to meet Tobry's bruised eyes, but they were even more unreadable than before. She needed him to act on the lie; she also wanted him to call her on it.

"I think I have ever since ... since Rix carried me down the cataract ... I—I can't do without him." She reached down towards Tobry, pleadingly. "Please. Save him from himself. For me."

Tobry took a shuddering breath, lifted one foot and then the other. "You do know the fairy tale about the girl who called her lover back from death?"

She went down, step by slow step. "Rix isn't dead."

"Isn't he?" he said stiffly. "I can't refuse you. But he won't thank either of us."

But Rix would live! In a rush of relief, she threw her arms around Tobry and he recoiled, holding her away with upraised palms.

"What's the matter?" She would never understand men.

"You've just pledged yourself to Rix."

"But ... that doesn't mean you and I can't be friends ... "

"I won't dishonour myself further, Tali."

His eyes cleared and, for an instant, she saw the despair and loss he was desperately trying to conceal. Then he turned and ran down.

What have I done? Tali thought. And between these two good men, how can I possibly undo it?

When she entered Rix's salon, he was wearing a sword on each hip and had his boots on. "Well, old friend," he said to Tobry, "it's been good knowing you. Don't come after me, will you?"

"Not if you don't want me to."

"Try to remember me the way I was ... before all this." Rix extended his hand.

"I'm the last person entitled to judge anyone."

As Tobry put out his hand, Tali held her breath. Was he going to do it, or not? And if he was, how?

His other hand was in his pocket and she saw the outline of his elbrot there. As they clasped hands there came a small emerald flash and crackle. Rix was hurled backwards, his head thudded against the heatstone and he fell, dazed. Tobry disarmed him, clamped a set of manacles around his ankle and locked them through the frame of the heatstone.

Rix groaned, tried to get up and discovered that he was shackled. His eyes opened wide. "You utter bastard, Tobe."

"Yes," said Tobry. "I am."

CHAPTER 98

Though she bedded down in front of the heatstone, Tali ached from the cold that night. But even had she been warm, even had the shearing pains in her head not been worse than ever, she would not have been able to sleep.

Rix, sitting as unyielding as a set square by the left-hand end of the heatstone, never took his eyes off her. Had she done the right thing? She could not tell. He knew she had put Tobry up to it and his silence was an accusation—three times I risked my life for you, and when I most needed your understanding you turned on me.

It wasn't the only thing between them. Rix had not betrayed his mother, because Tali had already informed the chancellor of Lady Ricinus's treason. But she could not find the words to make this confession. Or perhaps she lacked Rix's courage.

Tobry lay on his back with his eyes closed, so rigidly that she knew he was awake. He had avoided her eye since the incident on the stairs. How long had he loved her? Thinking back, Tali suspected it was from the moment he first set eyes on her at the oasis.

And what about herself? She cared for him as a friend, yet until her quest was fulfilled and justice done she could not allow any man to be more than a friend. Even so, that magical night at the ball, when she had spent two hours in his arms, still made her glow inside.

She shook off the memories. Glynnie and Benn were curled up together on one of the couches, bathed in the light from the heatstone, sleeping soundly. Their faith in their lord was absolute.

Rannilt's pulse was barely there now. She was slipping away and there was nothing anyone could do. Fretfully, Tali whipped the iron pages of *The Consolation of Vengeance* back and forth. What else was the book apart from a call to action? A philosophical work, or a manual for revenge?

From Wil, she knew it was the latest of a set of books called the Solaces. Lyf had made them and, via some incomprehensible magery, transmitted perfect copies to the Matriarchs in Cython, page by page, over hundreds of years. The Solaces told the matriarchs what to do, Wil had said, but what did this book say, and how could she find out? Might the book be translated with magery? Why did it smell faintly of alkoyl? What was alkoyl, anyway?

Why were there never any answers? She flipped the iron page, a ragged edge tore her finger and a speck of blood fell on the bottom of the book. As she was wiping it off the etched glyphs seemed to blur into words, though when she rubbed her weary eyes and looked again she saw only glyphs, as unreadable as ever.

The book was densely clotted with magery—she could tell without resorting to the spectible. What was the magery for? She turned the last, blank leaf. Who was supposed to write the ending? Lyf, or the Matriarchs?

Tali fantasised about writing it herself, turning his plan back on him and his vengeance into her just retribution. Why not? She was *the one*, after all. But before she could write it, she must discover how to read it. And then she would need alkoyl to etch her words into the iron.

Beside her, Rannilt jerked, stiffened and cried out. Tali dismissed the fantasy and sat up, the covers falling around her and the book hitting her knee with a painful thump.

The child's eyes opened wide and she said in a little, awed voice, "He's coming!"

Her eyes closed, then her mouth opened and a tiny bubble of golden light was pulled out of her, trailing threads like a bandage torn from a healing wound. The bubble spiralled upwards and vanished, but another followed it, then another.

Tali was stroking Rannilt's brow when the ragged, three-note sequence went off in her head, *di-DA-doh*, though this time the *calls* were close and seemed to come from three different directions. Had Deroe separated the pearls so he could triangulate the location of the master pearl?

"What's the matter?" Tobry, beyond the far end of the heatstone, and not illuminated by it, was only an outline in the dim salon.

"Lyf's on his way," said Tali. "Deroe too. Whoever gets the master pearl first can control the others and take all. What do we do?"

"We wait."

Trapped in the palace in a besieged city, she had no way to escape either hunter. But was there a way to use them against each other? She glanced across at Rix, who was still sitting upright, eyes closed. As much by the lack of tension in his face as by the rise and fall of his chest, she knew he slept at last.

"What if I were to lure Deroe into the cellar?" she whispered to Tobry.

He did not look at her. "Lyf's been trying to trap Deroe for years, and *he's* never succeeded." The implication was that she had no hope.

"But until now, Lyf's had no body and hardly any power. And he's been bound to the caverns. The only place he could go from there is to the cellar. Besides, I've thought of a plan Lyf could never use."

"Go on," he said dubiously.

"Deroe must be a very old man, yet when I heard his thoughts the other day, he sounded like a whining boy—as though his emotions were frozen at the moment Lyf possessed him. And I think he's desperately lonely. No one likes him, no one cares for him, yet that's what he yearns for. If I listen to his troubles and pretend to care, I might discover how *he* uses the pearls and command his three with my own. Then, when Lyf comes, I might be able to take control of his as well—"

"That's a lot of *mights*," said Tobry.

"I can't think of any other way to save Rannilt. Or Caulderon."

Rix let out a muffled gasp. His eyes were flicking back and forth beneath their lids as if he was having another nightmare. Since his house had already fallen it must be the other nightmare—the one he had painted, the future he had divined, where Lyf told him to go down and cut it out of her, *and Rix obeyed*.

Tali pulled her blankets up around her throat and chafed her aching hands. How could Lyf, who had not been able to leave his caverns, get to Rix from so far away? There was no spell or magery on him, nor any enchanted object nearby through which Lyf could have worked the compulsion. She had checked him with the spectible and Rix was—as Tobry had often joked—as lacking in magery as a log of wood. She had also checked his chambers and found no trance of an enchantment.

So how was Lyf sending the nightmares to him?

CHAPTER 99

All was ready. Now was the hour. Secure in his newly fashioned body, Lyf drifted to the top of the flaskoid to seek the advice of his ancestor gallery. And, if he could admit it, to gain their admission that he had been right after all.

For several minutes the shades of the kings and queens of old surveyed him in silence.

"The facinore was both a treacherous and an ill-made beast," observed Queen Hilga, a white-haired spectre with enormous popping eyes and a penchant for pronouncing doom. "That body is liable to betray you when you can least afford it."

"Ah, delicious irony," said Errek, First-King. Though faded to a wisp, his voice remained strong and, with the perspective of ten thousand years, all human follies amused him.

"I don't follow," said Lyf coldly.

"An aesthete king forced to cloak himself in so awkwardly fashioned—no, frankly—so hideous a guise." Errek chuckled.

Lyf scowled. He'd recreated the ancestors to support him, not mock him. "In wartime, perfection is a luxury. This body, while neither handsome, strong nor complete, frees me from a wrythen's bondage. Are you not pleased that we'll have our land back at last? And our vengeance?"

"The tale has not yet played out," said Hilga. "We were a gentle, cultured people once. Now you've robbed our people of their past, disconnected them from the land and your so-called Solaces have turned them into a warped reflection of the enemy."

"It will be a tragic irony indeed if you've made it impossible for our people to live in harmony with the land," observed Errek. "Or for their kings to heal it."

"What else could I do?" said Lyf. "They had been reduced to filthy, raddled *degradoes*; they would have been forever tainted by that past. Our only hope was to begin again: three unblemished matriarchs recreating our people from the youngest and least scarred of the children."

"You should have let our people go."

"I couldn't bear the pain!" Lyf cried.

"Well," said Errek, "it can't be undone now. But Lyf, before you go, enlighten us about those dreadful, er, feet."

Lyf looked down at his twisted, nodular, bare-boned extremities and might have flushed, had facinore flesh been capable of it.

"The traitor's blade that clove off my feet bore an enchantment that, even after two thousand years, I cannot break. It took my strongest healing powers to fashion any kind of bone there, but no magery can clothe it in flesh."

"Not even the black flesh the facinore offered up to you?" said Bloody Herrie.

"Not even that. But I will have everything back, before the end."

"That will depend on the end," said Errek. "And now?"

"I've restored the link to my most faithful servant," said Lyf, "and healed him as best I can. He's about to convey my battle orders to the matriarchs."

"You can't do battle until you hold the pearls in hand," said Hilga, her eyes protruding out of their sockets. "Should an enemy gain them, or worse, one of our own kind—"

"Do I not know it?" snapped Lyf, vexed that his own creations, meant to support him, were more critical than ever. "I've ordered a horde of shifters into the tunnels. At the critical moment, my faithful servant will lead them the secret way to the cellar under Palace Ricinus."

"How will you ensure the critical moment?" said Bloody Herrie. "You have not yet succeeded in commanding the boy-lordling."

Lyf had been waiting for the question. "I soon will!" His glee burst forth, unrestrained for the first time since his death.

"You'd better explain," said Bloody Herrie.

"The magian, Tobry, has chained Rixium to the heatstone in his salon—the very heatstone I've used to send nightmares to him these past ten years."

"But it carries no enchantment," said Bloody Herrie. "We don't see—?"

"Heatstone doesn't need enchantment," said Lyf. "It's mine, of its very nature."

That gained even Errek, First-King's attention. "How?"

"Because I died unshriven, my king-magery could not be passed on to the king-to-be, and thus our people have had no king to this day."

"We know this," snapped Bloody Herrie.

"Neither could my king-magery take the way of the Abysm, to dissolution," said Lyf. "But it had to go somewhere. It drifted through solid rock for hundreds of years until it came to rest beneath the Seethings—and turned a hundred yards of stone to heatstone."

"Ahh!" sighed Errek.

"The king-magery is no more, but my connection to it remains, through the heatstone deposit and every stone cut from it. Now, bathed in its emanations and with no way to escape them, Rixium slips ever closer to the compulsion I've spent half his life reinforcing. The moment he sleeps it will take him over, and no power of the enemy's, not even the Oathbreaker's Blade, can break the compulsion until it carries him all the way to the bloody completion."

CHAPTER 100

An hour after midnight the golden threads drawn from Rannilt snapped.

She sighed and shivered, but did not wake. Tali prayed that this was a good sign, and that Lyf had failed in whatever he was doing, but logic whispered that he had succeeded so well he no longer needed to rob a child.

Suddenly Tali's shell burst open and the *call* was like five alarms going off together in Tali's head—Lyf's pearl was calling, and so were the other three, *di-DA-doh*, *di-DA-doh*, and her own pearl was answering. And then she felt a jarring rasp, as though a bone reamer were being sharpened.

Tali shot up in the blankets, her heart thundering, then scrambled across and shook Tobry's shoulder. "He's found me."

He woke at once, if, indeed, he had been sleeping. "Who?"

"Deroe, with the three pearls, and Lyf knows it too. I've got to go down. Tobry . . . will you help me?" She wasn't sure he would.

"I want Rannilt saved as much as you do," he said deliberately. "And our enemies thwarted."

But not a word about her. It hurt, but she had created the mess and she must live with it. She dressed quickly and stood looking down at the child. "I'm afraid to leave her here in case she . . . slips away."

"Bring her. The pearls are her only chance—if you get them."

And if I don't, Tali thought, and I probably won't, better we die together than alone. She hefted Rannilt, who seemed to weigh nothing now. Tobry stood waiting, sword at his side. Rix's eyes were still racing under their lids, and Glynnie and Benn were asleep, her arm protectively around him.

"Why is the cellar at the heart of it?" Tali said quietly.

"It was once the private temple of Cythe's kings. And it's the only place Lyf could travel to as a wrythen."

"But why did Axil Grandys preserve it when he'd done his best to erase Cythe from the map? What did he hope to find in the cellar?"

Tobry had no answer.

"What do you know about Deroe?" said Tali.

"Nothing. I haven't found anyone who's met him."

Tobry led the way down, following the path the high constable and chief magian had broken with sledgehammers on the night of the Honouring. Tali followed, her thumbs pricking and her throat so dry that each breath rasped. The passage was as dark as a tomb, yet before they were within thirty yards of the cellar she knew it lay ahead. The hackle-raising smell gave it away: dry rot, mould, caked grime and the faint stench of long dead, poisoned rats.

Memories overwhelmed her. She was a little girl again, hand in hand with Iusia in her bid for freedom and trusting her mother's judgement utterly. If only she had whispered her worries about Tinyhead ...

Tobry slid the stone door open and went in, raising his lantern. Tali's skin crawled—the cellar might have been closed the day she'd fled from it and only now reopened. All was as she remembered it—the broken crates she'd hidden between, the ferocious stone raptors, the black bench where they had laid her mother. She could not look at it or she would never stop remembering.

"This is an evil place," she said, frozen in the doorway. "I can feel it. Something terrible happened here before the murders. Long before."

"But not wholly evil," said Tobry, softening at her stricken look. "In olden times, the kings of Cythe worked their healing magery on the land from here."

"How could anyone have the power to change the land?"

"King-magery was rooted in the land." He walked around the cellar, elbrot out, touching things with it. "And Cythonian magery wasn't spread out across thousands of magians, as ours is. King-magery was concentrated in one person, trained from birth to use it wisely and only for healing."

"But to heal this great land ... " It was beyond imagining.

"Hightspall's bounty comes at the cost of violent eruptions, devastating floods and landslides, and disasters of many other kinds. It's a land much in need of healing and this is where the kings of Cythe did it. And because they did, pockets of good still linger here."

"Enough to heal Rannilt?"

"I don't know." Tobry stopped by a stone box the size of a large coffin, with a cracked lid. He slid it aside, looked in and said gently, "Here is best, for you and for her."

She knew what lay inside; the chief constable had mentioned it after the Honouring. Tali paced across, as if in a funeral procession, and looked down at the bones of her mother and her three older ancestors who had been hosts to the ebony pearls. She had not known her ancestors—they had all died young—but her eyes burnt that her beautiful mother had been reduced to this sad little pile of bones.

"You're right," she said. "I do feel something good here."

He slid the lid over the bones. Tali laid Rannilt on the dusty surface, wrapped in her covers, and she sighed and breathed more steadily. Perhaps some protection did linger in the gracile bones of the four Pale women killed here.

Thump-thump.

"What was that?" Tali whirled, staring into a misty green gloom that Tobry's lantern could not dispel.

"Sounded like someone jumping down a step."

Di-DA-doh, di-DA-doh!

"Oh, poor Rix, leave him alone ... " said Rannilt in a croaky little voice. Her eyes were screwed tightly shut, as if she did not want to see.

"What's she talking about?" said Tobry.

"Lyf must be waking the compulsion on Rix." The *call*-clamour grew, *di-DA-doh, di-DA-doh*, along with the spiking headache, and now the three calls were coming from the one place. "And Deroe's coming. He knows I'm here. Hide! I'll try to gain his confidence, then you come in behind him and take the pearls."

Thump-thump.

Tobry went out into the very pitch of darkness. Tali turned down the lantern and waited. The greenish mist hung in curtains, the foul air was thick in her nostrils and her terror was rising. She was in the murder cellar and if this went wrong she would suffer the fate that all her life she had dreaded. The fate that Rix's sketch had divined for her. That Rix himself would do to her, if the compulsion on him could not be broken. But how could it be broken when no one knew how Lyf had put it on him?

Thump-thump. The *call*-clamour faded.

An old man materialised two feet above the floor, right in front of her, and grabbed her wrist before she could dart away. He landed unsteadily, *thump-thump*, made a thread-like mesh of light with his fingers and she saw a darting head on a wrinkled, tortoise neck. The grey eyes were rimmed with black; a spreading cloudiness partly obscured the pupils. Cracked, flaking skin ran up his arms into the cavernous sleeves.

His grip was an old man's grip, feeble and shaky and no match for hers, save that a sweaty numbness had spread out along her arm from his touch. She fought the terror—where were the pearls? Tobry could not attack until he knew Deroe had them. The magian's hands were empty and his grey robes had no pockets she could see, though they could be on the inside.

He scratched the crusted skin on his left wrist and grey flakes, brown with old blood, stuck under his long nails. Raising his hand, Deroe stared at the flakes and the blood. His mouth hung open and he was breathing noisily, as though it was a struggle to draw in enough air. His breath wasn't so much foul as dead, and it fogged her mind.

"What do you want?" Tali croaked.

She had to stick to the plan—get him to hold Lyf back, then deal with Deroe. Only with his pearls would she have a chance of fighting Lyf.

He scratched at his wrist again, breaking the papery skin. Muddy, grey-brown blood ebbed out.

"Lyf's coming," said Tali, eyeing the stone head on the end wall. She had seen Lyf's eyes there as a girl. "And he has a body now, a better one than yours."

"But I have his pearls," Deroe crowed. The high pitch, like a boy whose voice had not yet broken, jarred with the decrepit old man's body.

"Wards!" he said. A series of fist-sized globes appeared, studding the edges of the oval ceiling. They were pretty things, patterned in grey and white swirls like polished agate, and each had a moving glow as though a perpetual flame flickered inside.

"He won't get through now," Deroe piped. "Barrier!"

A grey, transparent sheet blocked the doorway. Tobry hit it with his shoulder from the other side but bounced off.

Tali's numbness faded a little. "You paid House Ricinus to cut out the ebony pearls. You had my mother killed, and my grandmothers back for three generations. Why?"

"Wasn't my fault," he whined, staring at the top of her head as if figuring out where to cut. "I didn't grow the ebony pearls in them."

"You ordered their deaths."

"They should have stayed away. They made me kill them."

"You contemptible little worm!" She struck him in the face.

He fell to his knees and it surged out of him like the draining of a blocked privy. "You can't know what it's like, being possessed. What did I do to him? I was just a lad, exploring in the ruins, collecting things no one wanted. I didn't mean any harm. Then he slithered *into my head* and squatted there like a toad, sneering at my terror and pouring his venom into me. He has such hate for us . . . such hate . . . "

His fingernails tore the skin of his wrist again, three long, ebbing cuts. It would have been the time to strike, had she known where the pearls were.

"He forced me to take the first pearl for him," said Deroe. "She was such a pretty little thing, your great-great-grandmother, and he made me gouge the pearl out of her head. Ah, the pain! I feel it to this day. I had no choice; I could not resist him. *Not then.*"

His whining self-justification sickened her. How could his suffering compare to the victims'? But she forced herself to say, "That must have been agony for you."

"It was," he wailed, as if this was his first confession. "It was. And none my fault. He made me do it."

"Tell me about my great-grandmother," said Tali. "How did it go with her?"

"Lyf thought he still controlled me," said Deroe with a wink and a leer, as though she ought to admire his murderous cunning, "but the touch of the first pearl had woken a gift I never knew existed. A tiny gift, no match for his, yet with it I drew magery from him whenever he possessed me. And when he did not, which was most of the time, I made my plans to outwit him and take the second pearl for myself."

"With the aid of House Ricinus."

"They were greedy for gold, and with the magery I'd learned from Lyf I could find cartloads of gold. The old Lady of Ricinus extracted the pearl for me, held it in the host's life's blood until Lyf was so weak that the possession broke and he was drawn back to his caverns, then I gave her gold for it."

You stinking mongrel, how dare you boast about killing my ancestors? If Tali's magery had come then, she would have splattered the walls with him. He didn't seem like a man at all; rather, a selfish, immature but incredibly powerful boy trapped in an old man's decaying body. She could not predict what he would do next.

"Clever," she said, nearly choking on her words. "But Lyf must have been furious."

"He was bound to his caverns, he could not come after it."

"But when he repossessed you—"

"I'd already put the pearl out of reach. You have no idea of the agony I endured, but he could neither find the pearl nor force me to give it up."

"And the same for the third and fourth pearls, when they were mature?"

"Lyf dared not send his own people after the pearls, and could not take them himself, yet he could not possess anyone but me. He had no choice but to use me. Each time he tried harder to outwit me; each time I beat him, ha, ha. I have three, and he only has one."

His voice had a sing-song quality now. From the look in his eyes, he expected her to applaud his cleverness. "Once I have the master pearl I'll be able to command his pearl, too. And then," he said viciously, "I'll stamp him to pieces like a toad in the garden."

Tali fought the urge to smash his yellow teeth in. "Aren't you afraid I'll use the master pearl to control your three? I too have a gift, magian."

His face lit and Tali realised, uncomfortably, that he had been hoping she would ask.

"I worked that out as a boy," he chortled, "after he made me take the first pearl. Your thrice-grandmother had the gift stronger than you, and she tried to fight me, the stupid bitch! But the pearls aren't meant to be used within the host and she fell into a swoon, bleeding from the eyes and ears." He shuddered. "The emotional connections are too dangerous; the host can never control it."

No wonder Tali's every attempt to take control of her gift had failed, and would always fail. It could not be done.

"How is the pearl made safe, then?" she said dully.

He came closer. "It must be cut from the *living* host, severing all connection with her, then healed for three days in her healing blood."

As Lady Ricinus had done, putting the pearl inside that green-metal glove filled with Iusia's blood. "And killing the host," Tali said.

Closer. "The trauma is great, but it's separation from the pearl that kills."

If I can't rely on the master pearl, Tali thought, I'll have to outwit him of his three. And then, deliver him to my own justice, since there's none to be had in Caulderon.

Oh, how he would pay.

Reaching out with his free hand, he stroked the top of her head, though not in any sensuous way. Deroe cared nothing for the human flesh, only what had been cultured within.

Tali's scalp crept and her mother's cries echoed within her skull, then the splintery gouging sound she had not recognised as a little girl. She tried to dart away but toppled forwards. His magery had fixed the soles of her boots to the floor, and now Tali knew fear as she had never known it before. If she could not break his magery, his tools would soon bore through her skull.

Deroe sniggered, turned to the black bench and reached up with his hands. The mesh of light threads that had been clinging to his fingers hung in the air there, illuminating the bench with a ragged cone of light. The greenish mist drifted back and forth through it, highlighting the edges of the cone. The poisoned-rat smell thickened in Tali's nostrils.

He wiped the bench with a rag. The black, slightly domed bench top had the gleam of the ebony pearl in Rix's finished painting—a pearl at the centre of the skull-shaped cellar like the pearl in her mother's head, and now her own.

He walked into the darkness. Objects clicked and rattled as though he was feeling in a cluttered cupboard. Tali heaved and lunged but could not tear free. Deroe came back carrying a small, upside-down parasol on a stand, though the silver ribs lacked any fabric covering.

"What's that for?" she said.

He did not reply.

In his other hand he had a circular disc made of white wood, as thick through as her closed fist and the diameter of her open hand. Five round depressions had been cut into the top, four at the corners of a square and the fifth at the centre.

He took three black pearls from a case lined with yellow velvet and put them in the depressions at three corners of the square. Tali struggled to draw breath. Each pearl had been cultured in one of her ancestors. Which was her mother's? They looked identical. The top right depression, and the slightly larger hollow in the middle, remained empty.

After fixing the parasol upright on a small table near the head of the bench, Deroe closed and opened its metal arms, set the pearls beneath, rotated the disc by ninety degrees, then nodded.

Now me. And Tali still could not move her feet.

He took a small hammer and narrow chisel from a bag. Was that to crack her skull? Now a thin-bladed saw, a steel gouger and two reamers, which he handled as gingerly as a first-day apprentice in a slaughterhouse. As though he was afraid to use them . . .

A savage urge for vengeance boiled inside her. If she got the chance she would jam them through his wattled throat. But how could she beat him? What were his weaknesses?

In a land where it was rare to live beyond sixty, he had to be double that, at least. Either he had lengthened his life by uncanny means, or the pearls had. But the greater the magery, the greater the cost, and it had cost Deroe dearly. Was that why he seemed as decayed inside as he was decrepit outside? And with those clouded eyes, his sight must be poor. If she moved swiftly once he freed her feet, she might beat him.

He turned and shuffled towards her. Tali tried to look like a terrified slave. It wasn't hard; the urge to scream was overwhelming. Her stomach muscles were so tight that it was difficult to breathe. Outside, Tobry was hacking at the grey barrier and attacking it with flashes of emerald magery, but he made no impression on it.

As Deroe reached out, she avoided his eyes in case her own gave her away. His crusted hand touched her biceps and her feet came free. She swung, fast as a striking adder, burying her fist in his belly below the diaphragm and driving it up.

Tali was strong for her size and there was so much power behind her small fist that she felt his papery skin tear. The blow forced air from his lungs and he doubled over, gasping. His spell broke and the light threads went out, leaving the cellar in darkness save for the faintest glimmer from her lantern, which she had left on the other side of the stacked crates.

Tali dived for the pearls.

But Deroe called them up, high above her head, to him.

CHAPTER 101

Rix woke with the voice ringing in his head. Lyf's voice.

It is time. Go down.

"Damn you!" he said aloud. "You'll never force me." But even in his own ears, he sounded unconvincing.

Lyf seemed amused. *You divined this night, this scene, this death. You had the chance to seize command of the divination when you painted the scene in the cellar, but you did not. Now it is set and can't be changed.*

"I won't do it!" Rix roared, though he could see no way of escape. Why hadn't he ridden out to give his life away yesterday? Why had he told his treacherous friends his plan?

In the shadows, a girl cried out in fear. It took some time for him to recognise Glynnie cowering behind the couch, sheltering her little brother with her arms. But before he could speak ...

Ten years I've worked my compulsion on you, preparing you for this night.

I'll fight you.

Yes, you will do everything in your power to break the compulsion. And you will fail. You will go down. You will cut the master nuclix from Tali, submerge it in her blood and keep it safe for me.

"I won't!" But the willpower was draining from him as Lyf wrapped the compulsion ever tighter. Only Tobry's shackle was keeping Rix here now. His shin was chafed to the bone from straining against it.

Call for your sword. I will have my due.

"Damn you, no!" But against his will, Rix turned to a wild-eyed Glynnie, who clearly thought he had gone insane, and said, "Fetch my sword, girl."

Clutching Benn tighter, she shook her head.

Good, Rix thought, but the compulsion stabbed him and his treacherous mouth said, "Who took you in, at risk of his own life, when the chancellor cast you out?"

"You did, Lord," she whispered.

"Am I your master?"

"Yes, Lord."

"Then obey me or be thrown into the street."

Trembling all over, she took the wire-handled sword from the shelf where Tobry had left it and carried it to Rix, holding it out by the tip as if she expected to be cut down with it. At any other time, that would have hurt.

He raised it high, then drove it down with all his strength onto the chain fixing his ankle to the heatstone. The enchanted blade cut through the chain in a shower of sparks.

Get the implements.

What was the point in fighting when he was bound to be defeated? He stalked out, the chain dragging, and down the halls to Lady Ricinus's rooms. The door was locked; he kicked it open and hacked her tiny desk in two.

A hand reamer tumbled out, along with a woven, green-metal glove and a pair of golden tongs. With these implements she had murdered Tali's mother and grandmother, and taken their pearls. She had planned to kill Tali the same way and she had shown no remorse.

Don't touch them. Turn around, walk to the front doors and ride out to face the enemy. Your death means Lyf's defeat.

But though he fought with all the strength he possessed, Rix took up the fatal tools. He could not stop himself. The compulsion was strengthening with everything it forced him to do and he could not overcome it.

He stalked the empty halls, following the path Lyf mapped in his head, and across to the secret stairs that, worked by a lever, plunged five flights before corkscrewing down through the roof of the cellar to the black bench.

At the top of the stairs Rix stopped, fighting to summon a shred of defiance.

Go down. The voice was softer now. Lyf knew Rix was beaten.

The assumption was just enough to summon a wisp of resistance. Before the compulsion could deny him, Rix pulled the stair lever, pressed the enchanted blade against himself and threw himself head-first down the stairs. Even if the blade did not open him from belly to throat, he would surely break his neck before he struck bottom.

He hoped so. After a life etched in failure, death was all he had left.

But the blade twisted in his hands, turned away from him and, though on the endless plunge he struck every step with head or shoulder or knee or hip, Rix tumbled through the mist of the cellar and landed beside the bench, winded and battered and bruised all over, but otherwise unharmed.

Do it.

Rix had no resistance left. He picked up the bone reamer, the green-metal blood glove and the golden tongs, and looked around for Tali.

CHAPTER 102

A s Deroe took hold of the pearls, the eyes in the stone head on the wall went yellow. The trapdoor in the ceiling burst open, then the screw-shaped stairs that Tali remembered from ten years ago spiralled down between her and Deroe, grounding beside the black bench.

Deroe let out a squeal of terror, rolled his hand across the three pearls and the agate wards around the walls flared. Tali sprang at him, knowing she had only seconds to get the pearls, but he scrabbled past the stone raptors with them, slipping and skidding in his panic to get away.

A sword came clattering down the stairs, striking sparks with every impact—Rix's sword. Tali's heart stopped for several beats. This must be the time.

The sword was followed by several jangling objects she could not make out in the dim light, then a series of thumps and grunts, and Rix came tumbling through the air to slam into the floor.

The impact would have broken her bones but he sat up and picked up the objects, one by one. Tali recognised the bone reamer, the green-metal glove and the golden tongs. Rusty barbs scraped down the knobs of her spine.

She backed away, trying to make no sound, but Rix's horror-filled eyes picked her out of the darkness and he took a slow step towards her. He was fully conscious of what Lyf was forcing him to do and it was eating him alive. Away to the left, Tobry was hacking desperately at the transparent barrier.

"Rix, stop!" Tobry screamed, until his voice went hoarse.

Rix could not meet his eyes, nor Tali's. She had never seen a man with a greater longing for death.

"You should have let Rixium ride out to war." Deroe, sheltering behind one of the raptors, let out another incongruous giggle.

"Rix?" said Tali, fighting her own urge to scream. She had to stay calm. There had to be a way to get through to him. "You've got to fight the compulsion."

"Been fighting it for ten years." Rix's voice was as dead as his eyes. "Lost!"

He turned towards her. One of Deroe's pearls *called* to hers and Tali's gift rose in a flush of anger, though not her own. The anger came from outside her, as if Deroe was manipulating her gift for his own ends, and it was one step too far.

"Kill him," said Deroe. "You've killed before; I can read the blood lust in you."

Her hand rose, involuntarily. She fought it down—she would not be dictated to like a slave—and her gift sank with it. Deroe cursed, pointed the parasol frame at the face on the end wall, caressed the pearls and an ultrasonic screech turned the stone nose to powder. Lyf's yellow eyes disappeared behind a puff of dust.

Cut down Deroe first, said a voice in her head that she knew to be Lyf's voice, though he was not talking to her.

Rix stopped in mid-stride. His eyes crossed, then he swivelled and headed after the magian. Deroe scuttled away and took shelter behind a low granite pedestal. A square trophy case stood on top, its sides made of crystal so grimy that Tali could not see what it contained.

Deroe's mouth twisted into a lopsided grin and he began to rub the dirt off the trophy case.

Stop!

Rix stopped, his arms dangling like a run-down clockwork toy. Deroe cleaned the last of the crystal faces, stepped aside, and within the trophy case Tali saw a pair of skeletal feet, severed at the ankles as if by the blow of a sword.

"Axil Grandys's most prized trophy," said Deroe, looking up at the crazed stone face, "and your greatest weakness. Ha-ha-ha!"

One stone eye cracked out and a shadow-clad finger protruded through the hole. A whisper of sound swelled to a howl, then a cloudy rock-glass barrier rose between the trophy case and Deroe, locking him into the right-hand end of the cellar.

Take the master pearl and bring it to me.

Rix rotated, the soles of his boots grinding on the gritty floor. Tali could see the sick failure in his eyes, that his life had been pre-ordained ever since he had been taken to the cellar by his mother ten years ago and ensnared by Lyf. How could she stop him?

"Rix," she said desperately, "how did he get to you?"

Rix shook his head. He did not know.

Tobry broke off his futile attack on the barrier, for the question had set his mind racing. Rix only had nightmares in the palace, and then only in his own chambers. But Tobry had checked them for magery many times and had found no trace of an enchantment save in Rix's sword. Unquestionably, the compulsion did not come through the sword.

That left only one possibility—the heatstone.

Tobry turned and ran. To his knowledge, no inanimate object

was enchanted in its natural state—only through deliberate human intervention did magery come about. The heatstone in the salon contained no enchantment, so how had Lyf, who could only travel to the cellar, used it to get at Rix?

Tobry raced up the dusty stairs. There was an ache in his side and his healing wounds burnt as though they were tearing open, but he dared not rest. Tali could not hold Rix off long. Either he would kill her for the pearl, or she would find her gift and kill him. The one possibility was as dreadful as the other.

He reached the ground level and hurtled along the halls to Rix's chambers, bursting the door open with his shoulder and skidding the length of the hall into the salon, where the heatstone twinkled as balefully as ever. If he broke it, surely it must snap the link that allowed Lyf to control Rix through the compulsion.

Glynnie started up from the couch with a cry of fear.

"Get out!" he bellowed. "Take the boy with you. *Now!*"

She took one look at his face and ran, dragging Benn behind her.

The heatstone was a good four inches thick; it would take a sledgehammer wielded by a blacksmith to break it. Tobry ran around the room twice, cursing. There was nothing here that could even knock a chip out of it. Perhaps it was just as well. When Tali's little heatstone had smashed on his elbrot in the caverns, it had burnt him badly. If he succeeded in breaking this one, there would be nothing left of him, and it would be a hideous way to die.

But if the heatstone remained, Rix would kill Tali and Lyf would get the master pearl. Tobry could not allow that. For the sake of his friends, and the woman he loved who did not love him, he had to make the sacrifice.

He was looking around wildly when *The Consolation of Vengeance* caught his eye, lying on the blankets where Tali had dropped it. The iron book was potent with magery, and without further thought he picked it up and slammed it against the centre of the heatstone.

The impact jarred all the way up to the back of his neck. The heatstone was unmarked, though small red flecks of spent alkoyl, driven out of the deeply etched words, had splattered across the middle, outlining the title in reverse.

Tobry was swinging the book again when the heatstone cracked beneath each red fleck. The cracks spread and merged and fire licked along them, then the centre of the heatstone swelled, showering him with blistering chips of stone.

He dived behind the couch, knowing it could not save him, as the centre of the heatstone was drawn inwards. It pulled in the rest, crumbling the enormous stone to dust which collapsed to a bright red mote, then vanished with a roar like an erupting volcano.

At the moment of the implosion, every captured Cythonian in the chancellor's cells next door to Palace Ricinus fell unconscious, save one.

Wil the Sump rubbed his aching forehead, stared around him with the blind eye sockets that saw so much further than any ordinary man, then giggled, "She *the one*. This *the ending*."

Using a smear of alkoyl from his hidden stock, he burnt through the door of his cell and scuttled along the red, contorted passages of the palace.

"Clever Wil," he said, for no one he encountered noticed him. "Stupid chancellor."

Outside, Wil scurried across the grounds to the unguarded side gate to Palace Ricinus, and through it, drawn inexorably to a cellar he had never seen. The ending was close now, but who would win the contest—the Scribe or *the one*? Which story would prevail? He had to be there, had to see it first. Wil was so tense he struggled to draw breath.

Back in his palace, the chancellor listened to the reports of Wil's progress, smiled, and called for the captain of his personal guard.

CHAPTER 103

I t had been bad enough killing an enemy, Banj. How much worse would it be to cut down a friend? Could Tali kill Rix, even to save herself?

He stopped six feet away, within lunging distance, and still she did not know what to do. The magery Deroe had raised in her was bubbling beneath the surface, and if there was no choice she would use it on Rix to save her life, but she was afraid to bring it all the way too soon in case she lost control. She could not attack Deroe with it. He had cleverly blocked that way.

Rix was gasping and grunting as he strove to overcome Lyf's compulsion but she knew it was futile. Now Lyf had a body, he was far stronger than before and Rix could never break free of his own accord.

He took another step, reaching out for her. Tali backpedalled, blinking away tears as she prepared to defend herself the only way she could. Her fingertips tingled. The fury that had killed Banj was only a breath away, a thread, a sigh . . .

The floor shuddered, then a golden light burst from Rannilt, driving the misty shadows off and revealing the simple beauty of Lyf's ancient temple for the first time. She cried out in wonder and sat up.

Pain sheared through Tali's skull, worse than the time the sunstone had smashed in the shaft. Her gift rose uncontrollably, as it had that time, and her fingertips began to sting. The sensations were unmistakable—someone had broken Rix's gigantic heatstone and the cataclysm must have burnt him to charcoal. Who could have done it? Who would have known it was the only way?

Only one man.

"Tobry!" she screamed, but then the white blizzard was forced out through her spread fingers and she could not stop it. Her eyes flooded until she could not see. *"Rix?"* Had she killed him?

Not Rix as well! Was she to lose everyone she cared about? Tali swung aside and rock shattered with a roar, chattering off the ceiling and walls, falling all around. She blinked the tears away. She was pointing towards the left-hand stone raptor and her white torrent was tearing the stone apart.

"Rix, where are you?" she gasped as the well emptied, and the flood faded. Her gift—if gift it was, and not a curse—was gone again.

Her burning fingertips were covered in hundreds of tiny red specks. The room was full of dust and smoke. She could not see anyone.

"Garrimoolish! Flisseroomph blorrgggg! Gebblinengle-googaah!"

Rix came reeling through the clouds, shaking his head between his hands and raving like a madman. What had she done? Had she burnt his brain? She could see no sign of injury—it must be the effect of the shattered heatstone.

He stopped, swaying on his feet and utterly bewildered. The dust began to settle. His mouth gaped; his eyes flicked back and forth as though he was watching a fast-moving scene. He frowned, nodded and extended his right hand as though mixing paint on a palette. Then, with sweeping movements of an invisible brush, Rix painted a moving picture in the air for all to see.

It was another scene set in this cellar, though the filth and clutter was gone. The walls were carved with gentle Cythian dioramas, the floor marked with the swirls of a kingly tattoo. As Rix imagined the scene, he painted it so vividly that Tali could have been there.

But this was not a divination—it was a revelation.

A slender young man stood at the door, wearing the scarlet king's robes of old Cythe. He held out his arms, welcoming five Hightspallers into the most sacred place he knew, the private temple where he worked king-magery to heal his land. The temple was bright with light, and uncluttered. A simple stone altar stood at the far end. The young man, Lyf, indicated a low table and the visitors sat around it, talking merrily while he treated them as honoured guests, bringing them food and drink, and serving them with his own hands.

The biggest of the Hightspallers, a florid, yellow-haired giant, produced a parchment document, evidently a charter or contract, and handed it to Lyf. The jollity faded; he read it, frowning, then shook his head.

The giant scowled and brandished a slender book at Lyf, pointing to the words on a particular page. Lyf scanned the text, thrust the book away as though he had read an obscenity and stood up, furiously indicating the door.

One of the women—thin-faced, with a prow of a nose and hair cropped close like a soldier—drew a swirling object like an elbrot and pointed it at Lyf. He stared at it as if he did not know what it was.

The elbrot lit a muddy green, like the misty light in an endless swamp,

*like the light that pervaded the murder cellar. Lyf convulsed, recovered,
then ran for his staff which stood by the door. The elbrot flashed and he
was brought down, trembling all over and his legs thrashing. The yellow-
haired man dragged him to the table and, while the other four held him
down, put a quill in his hand. The elbrot flashed a third time and,
though Lyf fought the enchantment with all his strength, his hand
inscribed his kingly signature on the charter.*

*The five shook hands, grinning and congratulating one another as if
they had just won a kingdom. The king collapsed, shuddering violently.
The yellow-haired man drew a curved sword—the same sword that now
hung by Rix's side—and said something to the others, laughing.*

*They cried "No!" as one, but he strode to the fallen king and, with a
mighty blow, hacked his feet off, then stood them on the king's own altar
as a bloody trophy. The five dragged Lyf out, his stumps trailing blood,
like a living corpse to be disposed of.*

The final image hung in the air for a minute, slowly fading. Rix
stared at it as if he had no idea what he had done or how he had
done it, then his shoulders slumped. It was over.

"That can't have been the Five Heroes," said Tali, dismayed.
"That brute of a man wasn't Axil Grandys. It's a mistake; a lie . . . "

But she knew it to be truth as only Rix could portray it. She had
also recognised the dark-haired woman as Sporrealie, the Hero she
had always revered.

Tali could not take it in. The revelation was too shocking, the
betrayal too monstrous, the implications too far-reaching. The
Hightspall she loved was based on a lie, the realm irredeemably
tainted at the moment of its founding.

No one spoke. Rannilt lay quietly again, her golden light gone.
Rix was swaying, his eyes staring. Behind his protective wards,
Deroe let out a brief, incongruous snigger. He, alone among them,
had not been affected by the imploding heatstone.

The stone face cracked and crumbled. Now Lyf's face could be
seen behind it, cold and implacable. Only Deroe's wards held him
out, but for how long?

"Two days before that scene," said Lyf, speaking aloud this time,
"I saved the yellow-haired man's life, and that is how he repaid me.
It was just the first betrayal by your *glorious* Five Herovians, who

used their foul *Immortal Text* to justify stealing our land. Then they walled me up, bleeding from my stumps, in a forgotten catacomb. Left me to die unshriven in unholy darkness, screaming and clawing at the walls."

"Why?" Tali whispered.

"To prevent my king-magery being passed on. Axil Grandys planned to destroy our kingship and take the magery for himself."

"Is that why he tore down the rest of your city, yet preserved this cellar?"

"It wasn't a filthy, rat infested hole then," Lyf said bitterly. "The king's healing temple was the very crux of Cythe. But until Grandys's living petrifaction at my wrythen hands—oh, yes, I made him pay! I turned him to opal and hurled him into the Abysm, to spend eternity in helpless agony—he haunted this place, carrying out his profane experiments that have befouled it forever, vainly trying to find the lost secret of king-magery."

Rix shivered, closed his eyes, then opened them again. So the opalised man was Axil Grandys. Rix's sword had once been Grandys's sword and he was Lyf's enemy. But had the sword led Rix to the caverns to attack Lyf, or to recover Grandys's opalised body?

"Now you understand," said Lyf, "why the land you plundered so ruthlessly rises up to cast you out. You don't know how to heal it and would not if you could. Your presence is a blight, a corruption of all good things." He gestured to Rix. "The compulsion still binds you. Cut out the pearl."

Rix studied Tali for a moment as though he had never seen her before, then turned back to Lyf. "I am unbound. You have no hold on me, nor ever will again."

"Do it," grated Lyf, "or I shall visit such torment on you—"

Rix spread his arms, making an offering of his own body. "No pain you inflict on me can atone for my house's crimes or my own betrayals."

He turned his back on his enemy as if to say, *Do your worst*.

The face withdrew, then the cracks in the stone lit yellow as Lyf attacked the wall. Deroe's agate wards began to rattle and shake, flaring and dying and flaring again. Little chips of stone spalled from them and fell all around. How much longer could they hold Lyf out?

"Tali, I can never repay you," said Rix, misty-eyed. "How did you free me?"

"It wasn't me. Tobry must have broken your heat—" Tali choked on the thought.

"What's the matter?"

"When my sunstone imploded in the shaft, it burned the Cythonians to char. Tobry—" She choked. "How could he survive such a blast?"

Rix rocked backwards, staring into infinity. "Despite what everyone thought, even me, he was always the greater man. If he's given his life for us, we must honour him by the manner of our own living—and dying."

Tali took his hand. It was warm and strong. Her own fingers ached from the cold. "What now?"

"I can't fight magians." He drew his sword. "Use your gift on Deroe."

"It spent itself when the heatstone burst."

"Can't you get it back?"

"I've never been able to command it. Deroe said ebony pearls are too unstable to be controlled by the host. They have to be cut out first."

"Then we'll find another way," said Rix.

Staggering footsteps sounded in the passage outside, then Tobry called, "Tali, Rix?" He sounded at the extreme of exhaustion.

"Tobry?" Tali cried. He was alive and that was all that mattered.

He lurched to the transparent barrier, supported by Glynnie, and clung to the door frame, his burnt hands smearing red on the stone.

She gasped. His hair had been burnt away and his chest was a mass of weeping blisters.

"Tobe, what have you done?" said Rix, running through the barrier to him. "Here, let me help you through."

"I'm all right," said Tobry. "The book protected my face and throat, at least. I've had worse injuries."

"Not much worse," said Rix.

IAN IRVINE

He backed through the barrier and took hold of Tobry but it would not allow him to pass into the cellar. Deroe's spell still held him out. Tali tried to push through; it would not allow her, either. She reached out to Tobry and managed to lay her healing hands on his chest but the burns were beyond her small gift.

Sconts! said Lyf, mind to minds. *Kill the man called Tobry and feed him to the shifters.*

"Who the blazes is Sconts?" said Rix.

"Tinyhead," said Tali.

And then she heard them: a horde of small, dog-like creatures, their claws scratching the flagstones as they raced down a nearby passage. Jackal shifters. And Tobry was mortally afraid of shifters.

He forced himself upright, thrust Glynnie and her little brother behind him, and took his elbrot in his left hand and sword in his right. Rix looked from Tali to Tobry, not knowing what to do.

"Lyf is my battle," said Tali. "Stand by Tobry."

"It should have been me," said Rix.

CHAPTER 104

"I'm glad you're here," said Tobry.

"Me too." Since it was the end, Rix would take a savage joy in fighting and dying beside his friend.

"Where do you think the shifters are?"

"Not far away."

Rix went down the passage for fifty paces, holding up Tobry's lantern. The girl and the boy followed him, holding hands. Rocks rattled in the distance and he heard a frenzy of barking and growling.

"They're coming," whispered Glynnie.

Benn cried out, stumbled and fell. Glynnie picked him up, pushed him behind her and drew a small knife. A useless weapon against jackal shifters, Rix knew. If they got that close, they would have her, and the boy too.

"Run back and see if you can get into the cellar," said Rix.

"Lord?" said Glynnie, terrified but reluctant to leave him.

"That's an order."

Glynnie and Benn ran. Rix backed after them, watching the tunnel. He would see the eyes first, the lantern light reflected there. Water had puddled on the floor here, seeping from crystal-encrusted fissures in the roof. As he splashed through, the first of the jackal shifters came creeping along the wall of the passage, eyeing him sidelong to minimise the reflections. They were more cunning than normal jackals.

"We can't get through, Lord," called Glynnie. Her voice had a squeak. "It's all right, Benn," she whispered, hugging the wild-eyed boy. "Lord Rixium and Lord Tobry will look after us."

She didn't believe it and neither did Rix. This was a battle no two men could win. Tobry joined him, trembling. His mortal fear was of being bitten by a shifter and suffering the fate of his grand-father—whatever that had been.

The shifters went back on their haunches, pink tongues lolling. There were eleven of them and, if they all attacked at once, some would break through. They were cowardly creatures, like real jack-als, yet quite as relentless. They would try to avoid the men with the sharp swords and get through to the easy meat, the girl and the boy.

Rix sprang and lunged, and his enormous reach was six inches more than the leading hound had expected. He skewered it through the chest, shook it off the blade and, with the toe of his boot, heaved it at the others. They did not retreat.

"One down."

Three sprang at once, before he had his sword back in position. Rix batted the first away with the side of the blade, breaking bones. The second went for his calf. He kicked it in the snout but it snapped and fastened onto the toe of his boot. If those powerful jaws tore through, if its teeth drew blood . . . He swung the sword, cut-ting it in two, though he had to lever the teeth out with the point of the blade.

Tobry had dispatched his beast and kicked it forwards. The other seven sat on their haunches, saliva dripping. Something was caught between the crooked teeth of the beast on the left—the last joint of a slender finger, complete with red-painted nail. A lady's finger. The beasts had fed recently but their hunger had not been slaked.

Then, through the doorway came a long, shivery scream.

"Deroe must be going for Tali's pearl," cried Tobry.

"See if you can get through. I'll hold them off."

Tobry lurched off and attacked the barrier again. Rix dared not look back—if he turned away, even for a moment, the jackals would tear him down. Besides, he could imagine the cellar scene all too well. He *had* imagined it—he'd painted it, and now it was coming true just as he'd dreaded it would. He had divined her fate with the cellar scene that he could not stop painting but had failed to control.

The floor shook and there came a low rumble, like distant thunder, though it could not be thunder down here. He pressed forwards, using his blade like a surgeon, and coldly killed another two. The other jackals let out a synchronised howl and backed away. Rix wiped his brow.

"No luck," said Tobry, appearing beside him.

"But we've taught them a lesson," said Rix.

"No, when they retreat, it's bad."

A huge, cat-like shape was approaching, its slitted eyes green-gold in the reflected lantern light. A familiar shape: leonine, red and black, paws the size of dinner plates. The jackals slunk aside, their coarse fur rasping against the walls.

The caitsthe stopped twenty feet off and crouched, swishing its red tail. I can't do this again, Rix thought. The first time I beat one was sheer dumb luck, and killing it in the caverns was more of the same—it could as easily have finished me. It beggars belief that I can do it a third time.

"Rix," said Tobry, staggering and nearly falling, "one of us has to sacrifice himself, and it'd better be me."

"Like hell. We'll get through this."

"Will you listen?" Tobry croaked. "Even if we beat the caitsthe, those jackals are only the advance guard. There'll be a whole pack up the passage. And did you hear that rumble?"

"Just a tower falling," said Rix.

"No, it's the enemy, clearing rubble out of the secret tunnel to Cython, and they'll soon be here in force. Go! If you can cut through into the cellar and kick Deroe in the guts, you might get everyone away up the corkscrew stairs before Lyf breaks through."

"Be damned. We'll cut the caitsthe down, seal the cellar door and both go."

"Look out!" cried Benn.

Rix had not seen it spring. It was soaring towards him, twenty feet in a single leap, and he only just got his sword up in time to stab at its heart. Its claws batted the blade aside and it tumbled the other way. Tobry, swinging wildly, trimmed fur off its left shoulder and Rix pinked it in the chest, though not deeply enough to do real damage.

Again it slashed at the flat of the blade, nearly tearing it out of his hand and throwing him off-balance. It swiped at his unprotected throat but Tobry's savage thrust tore through its gullet and out the side of its neck. The caitsthe shot backwards, blood spurting from both wounds, then began to shift to the more powerful and deadly human-form.

"Now!" Rix and Tobry yelled together.

Rix's blade went through its neck, aimed for the spine, and severed it. Not even that could kill a caitsthe, but until it finished shifting and the damage was repaired it would be paralysed from the neck down.

He threw it onto its back, exposing the belly. With one slash, Tobry unseamed it from the up-arching breastbone to the furry groin.

"Hold its head back, Rix. It can still bite."

Rix thrust his sword in between its teeth. Tobry put a boot into its belly, heaved its steaming intestines out of the way and made a series of hacks, then thrust. When he raised his sword, it was skewered through the caitsthe's twin livers.

"Oh, well done," said Rix, though he caught his breath at Tobry's recklessness. If a spot of caitsthe blood fell onto his raw chest, he could end up one of them.

Tobry seemed to have drawn strength from the victory, for he was steady on his feet now. He flung the livers down ten yards away and fumbled a paper packet from a pouch on his belt. Tearing open the packet, he sprinkled grey powdered lead over the black livers, which began to squirm.

"Oil, quick!"

Rix snatched the lantern from Benn and poured half of the oil onto the livers. Tobry lit it and backed away hastily as it caught fire and white fumes belched up.

"Cover your noses," he said hoarsely. "Lead fumes are deadly." He rinsed his bloody sword under one of the springs issuing from the wall. "What are you waiting for? Use your enchanted blade and cut the blasted door open."

Rix hacked across and back. This time, Deroe's spell twanged apart.

"Benn, Glynnie, go through." He looked back. "Tobe?"

Tobry had a rag over his nose and was alternately looking from the fuming livers to the caitsthe writhing on the stone. It had been caught halfway between beast and man but would never complete the transformation now.

"I've got to make sure the livers are destroyed. If they aren't, it might restore itself."

"It won't come back from that," said Rix. The livers were a charred mess covered in shiny, molten lead. "Come on."

An air current drifted the poisonous fumes towards the jackals. They retreated, coughing and howling. This is our chance, thought Rix. If we can seal the door against them . . .

Tobry staggered and had to prop himself up on his sword. "Go! I'll be along in a minute—"

A furious baying and howling began further up the passage, then a pack of jackals came rolling around the corner—ten, twenty, fifty, a hundred of them. They hurtled up and stopped just beyond the low-hanging fumes.

Rix's knees trembled. It was over. As jackal-men they would soon open the door and pull everyone down.

"This is where it ends, Rix," said Tobry, panting. "Go through to Tali."

"You can't fight that many jackals."

"Not as a man. But as a caitsthe I might."

Rix goggled. "That . . . that's always been your greatest fear."

"It still is. But if I don't, we're all going to die, aren't we?"

"Yes, but . . . "

"A while back, you felt so dishonoured that you were going to ride out to die."

"And you chained me up," Rix said mildly. The fury was long gone.

"That was wrong, but I don't regret it—we needed you. Listen, Rix. I too was put to a terrible choice, many years ago, and I've got to atone for what I did."

"I can stop you," said Rix.

"I know you can, but what would be the point? If I can hold the jackals back for five minutes, it'll give you and Tali a good chance. Besides, even being a caitsthe is a kind of life . . . "

Rix shuddered. He wanted to say, "Let me do it," but couldn't. He would sooner die than turn shifter. "You're a better man than I am, Tobe. But then, you always were."

A small piece of liver lay near Tobry's right boot, perhaps left for such an emergency. Before Rix could stop him, Tobry bent, put it in his mouth and swallowed.

Rix wanted to scream and punch the stone with his fists, but that would have been a poor way to honour his friend's sacrifice. He saluted Tobry, then sprang through the door and slammed it behind him.

The shrieks as Tobry transformed for the first agonising time were like a red-hot poker thrust through Rix's belly.

CHAPTER 105

Deroe slapped his flaking hand across the three pearls, jeering like a malicious schoolboy, "Ha, ha, got you!"

His wards flared brilliant orange, then Lyf was driven backwards out of sight and the crystal wall burst. A sharp fragment speared into Tali's forehead, sticking there, and when she pulled it free, blood flooded into her eyes.

"Come," said Deroe, touching her cheek, and again she was paralysed.

He dragged her to the black bench, panting. Tali fought the paralysis with all her strength and again it eased a little. Outside, there was more baying of jackal shifters, more furious howling and a series of thumps that shook the door. How long before they killed Tobry and Rix, and broke through? Not long. Deroe was going to win and everyone else was going to die.

The numbness faded. Tali swung the fragment of crystal at his right eye but he whacked her elbow with the chisel and she dropped the shard. He renewed the paralysis, heaved her onto the black bench then bent double, wheezing.

Die! she prayed.

He spat on the floor and turned away.

As she lay there, Tali saw Rix's cellar painting truly for the first time. It *had* been a divination. He *had* seen her future. The murdered woman was both her mother and herself, and she was cast back to the day when Iusia had lain here. The vision was so real that, momentarily, she *was* her mother. She screamed.

The magian shuddered and blocked his ears. Taking up a crystal of pale green tourmaline, he passed it back and forth over the top of her head, his lips pursed and brow furrowed. It did not light up as—another memory surfaced—the stubby blue crystal had when Lady Ricinus had pointed it at her mother's head.

"Where is it?" Deroe hissed. "Tell me. I must know where to cut."

Tali strained to wriggle a finger, a toe, but all she could move were her lips and tongue. "I wouldn't have thought you'd care, you murdering swine."

"The least nick will ruin the pearl; it has to be plucked from a live host. Death, even if only a heartbeat ago, and the pearl's vitality is lost."

Tali spat in his eye and braced herself for a return blow. If she was going to die, she would not die meekly like her mother.

Deroe wiped his face, ran flaky fingers over her scalp then stood back, gnawing on a cracked nail. "What if I saw the top of the skull all around?" he muttered, "then prise it off in one piece."

He shuddered. "That horrible paste of blood and bone and hair. Yecch! The grinding of the saw as it chews through bone! But I must have the master pearl. The others only keep the wrythen at bay. They can't hold it out when it comes possessing; they can't destroy it. It must be done, despite the blood and the slimy, oozing brains."

This was her living body he was talking about, and her pain, her suffering, her life meant nothing to him. Tali wanted to punch his cracked teeth through his tonsils. What could she do? Her *inner* magery would not return quickly—she'd drained her personal well with the blizzard. But what about an *external* power? She visualised the whirling, multi-coloured patterns she had seen in the Abysm and drew on one small part to try and break the paralysis. Nothing happened.

Something was watching her. Someone. She rolled her eyes backwards. Lyf's yellow eyes were back in the cracked stone face and he was studying her, consideringly.

A small, quivering loop of brightness appeared, not in her inner eye, but in the air in front of her. Had he sent it so she could attack his enemy?

You can only defeat your enemy with magery, but the only person who can teach you how to use your magery is your enemy. Could she learn magery from him?

Or was it a trap? Probably, but how could she be worse off by trying it? She took hold of the loop, drew strength from it and her right index finger moved.

"It's the only way to be free of him, so it must be done."

Deroe was talking to himself again. It sounded odd, though she supposed he had spent so much of his life in hiding that it was natural to him. He walked around the bench, eyeing her from all sides.

"Make a cut all the way around the top of her skull, yes. Peel back the skin; expose the living bone and saw it like an eggshell. But she must be still as death. One twitch and all is ruined. That's the way, and you can do it. Yes, you can. You must."

He sounded as though he was trying to talk himself into something unpleasant. Tali got another finger to move, then a third, but it would take more than that to save herself. She worked on releasing her right hand, freeing the arm.

The magian rubbed his face furiously, as if scrubbing away blood, and flakes of skin drifted in the mage-light, lifting and circling in rising air. They reminded her of the flocking vultures she had seen out in the Seethings.

He began to set out his instruments. So, he was afraid of blood. The thought of cutting her head open was practically making him sick. But he had done it to her great-great-grandmother and he would do it again.

He picked up a lumpy herbal bolus, something to knock her out, she assumed. His other hand held the fatal knife. Do it now!

As he bent to press the bolus into her mouth, Tali snatched the knife and drove the point deep into her wrist, through the vein. Blood spurted and she directed it over his face in red, splatting gouts.

Deroe shrieked in disgust and backed away, dropping the bolus. Tali rolled off the bench, forced her numb legs to hold her upright and lurched after him, spraying blood into his eyes, his nose, his mouth. His eyes rolled up and he staggered away, whimpering.

Tearing strips off her gown, she made a pad with one strip and a bandage with the other and tied the pad over her bleeding wrist, using one hand and her teeth. But Deroe was coming again. Tali hurled the bone saws, grinders, gougers and reamers at him, one after another. They all missed save the heavy, tapered reamer, which struck him between the eyes and embedded there, quivering.

Deroe reached up to tear it out, saw his brown blood dribbling from its handle and, with a thin, terrified cry, fell to his knees. She ran after him, knocked him onto his back and tried to twist the reamer in. A pointed knee crashed into her hip, knocking her aside.

Before she could attack again he sat up, wrenched the reamer from his forehead and thrust it at her belly, though the feeble blow did no damage. She kicked it out of his hand. More blood ebbed sluggishly from the wound, forming coiled brown ribbons down each side of his nose.

He was struggling to rise when a yellow streak shot across the room and through the dribbling hole between his eyes. Lyf's faci-nore body might not be able to pass Deroe's wards, but Lyf's consciousness had slipped between them and repossessed his enemy.

Deroe's legs kicked and his arms thrashed; grey saliva dribbled from his gaping mouth, then brown foam. Was he having a fit? No, he was shamming. He made it to his knees and slashed at her with the bone saw. Tali wove aside, kicked out the way Nurse Bet had taught her and struck him under the jaw, almost breaking her toes. His head snapped back and he was driven onto the beak of the stone raptor. He convulsed, slid off and she felt the last of his power over her fade.

She ran back for the knife to finish him. Justice be damned; Tali burnt for revenge. But as she loomed above the magian, ice-blue vapour began to ooze from around his eyeballs, a miasma that began to pull together into a face as solid as history itself and as stern as justice denied. A face that would give no quarter even after two thousand years.

"Kill him," gurgled Deroe, slimy bubbles extruding from his mouth to burst on his lip and chin. "If not for me, then for Hightspall. Kill Lyf now and the war is over."

"How?" said Tali, a dawning hope warring with her instinctive fear that Deroe was lying.

"I set a mind-trap for him in case he tried to possess me again, and it's forcing him out before he's ready. He can't do anything about it, but I'm dying. I can't close the trap, but you can. Catch him with the soul grippers, then destroy him with the pearls."

The soul grippers must be the parasol skeleton Deroe had flexed earlier. "There's only three pearls," said Tali.

"Use the master pearl before he recovers. *Now!*"

"You said it couldn't be used inside the host."

"I lied."

And perhaps he was lying now. Deroe was a liar and a murderer many times over. How many lives had he destroyed over the past hundred years? How many families had he torn apart? Whatever he wanted, she should do the opposite.

"He's your real enemy," he sobbed. "I've never been more than his puppet. *Kill him while you can!*"

Tali did not believe him, and wasn't sure he was dying, either, but the miasma dribbling from his raw eye sockets was thinning now. Lyf's face was almost complete. What was there to lose by doing as Deroe asked? Everything, or nothing?

Tali snatched the parasol from the bench, and the disc with the pearls. She limped back to Deroe, pointing the parasol at Lyf's face. "Like this?"

"*Close!*" said Deroe in a magian's command.

The skeletal arms of the parasol closed on the misty face, which writhed and shifted and tried to stream away, but could not escape. Tali touched each of the pearls with the fingers of her right hand, these enchanted, marvellous spheres that had been cultured inside her closest female ancestors, and she felt a connection there that no one else could have used.

"*Kill!*" whispered Deroe, reaching for the pearls.

Tali pulled them away. She was not giving him a chance.

"*DIE!*" said Lyf.

There came a wet, tearing sound from inside Deroe's head. His eyes went the muddy brown of his blood, then blood began to ooze from his eyes, his nose, his mouth and ears. He fell back and the breath whispered out of him. He was dead.

Tali looked down at the body. Another of the killers was dead; another stage passed on the long road of her quest, but all she could see was the pathetic man-boy trapped within that crumbling shell.

Deroe's wards failed. The misty face dissolved into air and Lyf streaked back through the wall into his facinore body. Then, a thousand times more powerful, he tore the wall apart.

"For my weeping country," he said softly, and soared out, racing for the pearls.

Tali had only seconds to command them. She put her hand across the three and drew deep within her. Each of her murdered ancestors had hosted one of the pearls, each had lived their short lives with a pearl growing inside her, connected physically and emotionally, as she was linked to her ancestors and to her pearl. Surely, even if she could not use the pearl inside her, there had to be a familial connection she could employ to command the other three.

But before she could try, a small, skinny man came stumbling down the corkscrew stairs, crying, "She *the one*. Look out, Lord, she *the one*!"

Wil the Sump hit the floor so hard that she heard a rib crack, and a needle-tipped alkoyl vial slipped from his pouch and rolled across the floor towards her. She hastily moved her foot aside. Wil bounced to his feet in oblivious ecstasy.

Lyf froze in mid-air, then hovered fifteen feet away. "What do you mean, *the one*?"

Tali was astounded. She had always assumed Lyf knew about *the one*. Was there any way she could use this before he thought it through?

"Wil had *shillilar* about *the one* rewriting the book," said Wil. "Changing the ending. Matriarchs tried to kill her to stop *shillilar* coming true."

Lyf looked from Tali to Wil, then back to Tali, weighing the implications.

Tali was pressing her hand against the pearls, trying to read the imprint of how Deroe had used them, when Rix leapt through the door, sword in hand, and slid it closed. He was spattered with blood, and very pale.

"What's happened to Tobry? He's not—?" She could not say it.

"A hundred jackal shifters came; no way to stop them. One of us had to make a stand or they would have broken through and killed us all. Tobry sent me to get you away. To give Hightspall a chance."

While Tobry died alone, facing his worst nightmare? This could not be borne. Tali spun towards Lyf and her lips were forming the word, *Die!* when he extended a hand. Silver cords unreeled from it into Rannilt's chest, into Rix's and out through the doorway towards Tobry.

Rix tried to pull the cord free but it snapped tight. He gasped and doubled over, clutching at his heart.

"With the pearls you may, *perhaps*, find the power to end me," said Lyf to Tali. "But if you try, with my last breath I will tear out their hearts. Who will you sacrifice, to end me? The dying child who has given her all for you? The friend outside who endures his nightmare in a vain attempt to protect you? Or the tainted hero forced to choose between betraying his family and helping you?

"Or for the sake of vengeance, will you sacrifice all three?"

CHAPTER 106

On her mother's body, on Mia's blood, Tali had sworn unbreakable oaths, and now her fingers were quivering on the pearls. By killing Lyf—*if* she could—she might end the war, or at least delay it until Hightspall could defend itself, and thousands of people who would otherwise die would live. Was that *the one's* true purpose?

And why not do it? Rix longed for death, Rannilt was slipping away and, outside, the shifters would soon take Tobry, if they had not already. A painless end was the greatest kindness she could do her friends.

But if she broke her oaths, saved her friends and let Lyf go, a host of innocent people would pay with their lives. She could see them in her mind's eye, folk she had encountered on the way into Caulderon last time: a crippled girl hobbling on broken crutches, that wailing baby whose limbs were like sticks, the white-haired ancient staggering under the weight of his ailing wife. All were begging her to save them, all dreading she would condemn them.

The chancellor would sacrifice his allies and not be troubled by it afterwards, and perhaps he would be right to do so, for Lyf would never give in. If she let him live, his armies would crack Caulderon open and he would revenge himself on the whole city. What point saving her friends if they were going to die anyway?

Tali's fingers clenched. She was about to use the pearls when Lyf looked up and smiled, and she choked. He wanted to see the failure in her eyes. He wanted revenge on her most of all.

Damn him! The reckless fury she had suppressed ever since Mia's death boiled up and Tali saw another way—a terrible way. He'd always protected the master pearl and, if she could destroy it, it might ruin the other pearls as well. It might even finish him—if she had the courage to do it.

Did she? Tali so wanted to live, but if this was the only way to bring Lyf down she had to make the sacrifice, as Tobry had done outside. Yet her sacrifice would be a dreadful way to die.

If she thought about that, she would never be able to do it. Tali doubled over, as if in pain, then grabbed the alkoyl tube Wil had dropped, jerked the cap off and pressed the tip of its needle against the top of her head.

Bracing herself, she prepared to ram the needle through her skull into the shuddering pearl. The alkoyl would destroy it, then eat through her head the way it had burnt through that poor woman's leg in Cython. A moan rose in her throat; she could still hear those wrenching screams.

Pain flared around the tip of the needle. It was going to be agony, but it had to be done. As Tali thrust, Lyf extended his arm towards her and the tube was wrenched from her fingers and sent bouncing across the floor. Her pearl shrieked the *call* so loudly that Tali's head spun and she fell to her hands and knees.

"I salute your courage," said Lyf. "But you should not have hesitated."

"She not *the one*," sneered Wil, turning his back on Tali and bowing to Lyf. "Lord Scribe, you *the one*."

Lyf set Deroe's implements up at the end of the black bench. The top of Tali's head was throbbing as if the reamer was already grinding through her skull and her bones felt as soft as marrow. She tried to get up but her legs would not support her weight. She had lost.

Lyf was making his preparations when Rix moved so fast that, once again, she lost sight of him. One second he was slumped against the wall, the next his sword had cut through the three heartstrings and the blade was outstretched towards Lyf.

"Don't try it," Rix said coldly. "Once cut with this blade, they can't be remade."

He lunged, the titane sword slid between Lyf's arms and its tip cut him across the chest. Lyf bit down on a gasp as the red ribbons streamed down his front.

"Having a body means you can die," said Rix.

Lyf made an involuntary gesture towards him, but froze it halfway. Tali saw fear in his eyes, quickly hidden.

"Ah, but when I take your head with the Oathbreaker's blade," said Lyf, "it breaks the enchantment forever."

"My head is already promised," said Rix, with the smile of a man walking gladly to his end, "but not to you."

Lyf pointed the reamer and Tali saw a curse quivering on his lips, but another blow tore it from his hand. Rix took a step forwards and Lyf backed away, hobbling on his remade feet. Rix was forcing him past the stair towards the piles of barrels. Soon Lyf would have to fight. Could this be the end? Tali could not believe that he could be beaten this easily.

"This the wrong ending," said Wil in a nasal whine, and rubbed the brown nodules in his eye sockets until they bled. "Lord Scribe has to finish the story."

As Rix passed the corkscrew stair, a huge figure leapt off it. Tinyhead had crept down, unseen, and all his weight landed on Rix's shoulders, driving him to the floor and knocking the sword from his hand.

Tinyhead drove his knees into Rix's back, pressing him down and punching him repeatedly in the head until Rix went still. Tinyhead sprang for the sword and came up with it in his fist.

Tali pulled herself up with the aid of a crate. Rix staggered to his feet, swayed and had to support himself on the stair. Tinyhead struck at him, missing by inches. If he killed Rix with his own sword it would surely break its enchantment and its power over Lyf, because Rix was the last of his line.

"This too *easy*," wailed Wil. "Scribe's great story can't end easy."

Tinyhead glanced at the quivering little figure, shaking his head contemptuously. He took another step, then another. Rix lurched backwards, trying to protect himself with his bare hands.

Tinyhead was about to cut him down when Wil sprang. He landed on Tinyhead's back, locked spindly legs around his waist and those unnaturally large hands closed around Tinyhead's throat. Tinyhead dropped the sword and tried to prise the fingers away but

Wil's grip was too strong. He seemed bent on crushing Tinyhead's windpipe.

Tinyhead threw himself backwards, trying to dislodge the little man. Wil swung around Tinyhead's waist, landed on top of him and, as Tinyhead kicked and flailed, slammed his head against the floor. Tinyhead's eyes glazed. He slumped, dazed from the impact and, as Tali watched in horror, Wil calmly strangled him.

Wil rose, breathing heavily through his bloody nose cavity. "Contest is even now." He put one foot under the sword and flicked it away from Rix.

Tali remembered Lyf's weakness and saw her opportunity in the same instant. Could he, who had never gone through the proper death rituals, still be linked to his bones? The bones he had protected so carefully?

Lyf must have come to the same realisation, for suddenly he was diving for the sword.

"Yes, yes!" cried Wil, dancing a jig. "This how it supposed to end, Scribe against *the one*. Kill her, Lord. Kill her now."

Tali beat Lyf to the sword and swung it around so fast that it whistled through the air. Lyf flinched and swayed aside.

"I *am the one*," she cried, and let fly, but not at him.

Tali hurled it at the trophy case, which shattered. The titane sword speared through, struck the skeletal feet which it had severed from Lyf two thousand years ago, and a conflagration of magery flared so bright and fierce that it burnt the bones to ash.

Lyf shrieked. His nodular extremities, constructed at such cost from the dark bones of the facinore, were charring away, belching smoke that began to fill the room like black fog. His severed shins spurt boiling blood, then he vanished.

Wil stumbled away, sobbing, "Scribe beaten, *the one* prevails. Solaces wrong! Scribe's stories *just made up*!"

He stopped, sniffed the air, then his face lit as though there were little lamps in his eye cavities and he scuttled up the stairs out of sight.

"We did it," said Tali, clinging to Rix. She could barely stand up.

"Lyf's not dead," said Rix.

"But we hurt him badly. We drove him off."

She knelt beside Rannilt, whose breathing was stronger now. Tears stung Tali's eyes. "I think she's getting better."

Rix was staring at the stone door. All was silent outside.

"Tobe?" said Rix, retrieving his sword. The tip was melted. He forced the door open. "Tobe?"

A shiver made its way up Tali's back. He must be dead, and it hurt more than Mia's death. More than anyone's. She wanted to scream out her pain and loss.

In the passage, hacked jackal shifters were piled in heaps five bodies high; there must have been a hundred of them. Blood slimed the floor for thirty feet, save for an oval space where a charred mess was surrounded by a silvery, metallic halo of condensed lead.

Tali cried out. No man could have survived such carnage. But he must have. Tobry could not be dead. She would not accept it.

His sword lay near the door, covered in blood and bits of brown and red fur.

"Where is he?" said Tali, heaving the small corpses aside with her bare hands. She had to see him. "Rix, where's Tobry?"

His kilt lay on the floor, torn to shreds. His boots looked as though his feet had burst out of them. Pain spiked her belly, unbearable pain. "Tobry!" she wailed.

Rix steadied her. "He was dying. He took this way for you. If he hadn't, you could never have beaten Lyf."

"What are you talking about?" she said frantically. "What way? *What has he done?*"

"It's for the best," said Rix. "No *human* man ever fought against such impossible odds and won."

"No!" cried Tali. "No, no, no!"

One of the heaps moved. The jackal corpses were pushed aside and a creature the like of which she had never seen before lurched to its feet. It was almost as tall as Rix, though more like a cat standing on its hind legs than a man. Its short fur dripped with gore, splattered brains oozed down its front and several canine teeth were stuck there.

The creature was bleeding from a dozen wounds, and she was

backing away when she saw something familiar in its grey eyes. A gentleness that did not fit the beast before her.

"Tobry?" she whispered.

With wild shrieks and savage cries, the cat-creature began to shrink and change from cat to man. The fur withdrew into the skin, the muck fell away and Tobry stood there, naked but for the belt of his kilt.

His burns were gone, healed in the transformation. So were the many scars and bruises he'd had before, apart from the injuries he'd taken as a caitsthe. Tobry was wounded in all the same places as the cat had been, though the bleeding had stopped and the smaller gashes were starting to scab over. It wasn't quite the old Tobry, though. His ears were slightly pointed, his cheeks were furred and the silvery grey of his eyes now had a hint of green and gold.

"Tobry!" She threw herself at him and wrapped her arms around him, joy and horror intermingled. Lyf gone, Tobry alive—it was too much to take in.

He fell, carrying her down with him. He was too weak to stand up.

She lifted his head. "What's happened to you?"

"The damn fool ate part of a caitsthe's liver," Rix said harshly, helping Tobry into the cellar and closing the stone door, "and now he's become a shifter-cat, as if he'd been bitten by the beast. And therefore, he's condemned."

Tali swallowed. "Tobry? Tell me it's not true."

He looked into her eyes and, momentarily, he was the same wonderful man who had taken her to the ball and whirled her about like all the other couples, though she had not danced a step in her life.

"It's true," he said in a voice from which all laughter was gone, all hope.

"Why? Why?"

"Had I not, Rix and the children and I would be dead, and the jackal men would be holding you down for Lyf to gouge out the pearl."

She crushed him to her, ignoring the gore smeared across his chest. "You're such a fool. Such a brave, stupid fool."

"Don't say it." He tried to push her away but she clung tighter.

"Let me go. I'm a monster and I have to be put down."

Tali jerked free. "Rix, tell him that's nonsense."

"It's the law," said Tobry, "and rightly so, as I know better than anyone." He looked around. "What happened here?"

"Deroe's dead," said Tali, "and Lyf's gone. We hurt him badly."

"Not badly enough!" said Rix.

"What do you mean?"

"The three pearls are gone. Lyf must have taken them with him."

CHAPTER 107

"We've got to have a fire, Rix, or Rannilt will die." A freezing wind spat ice crystals in Tali's face. They had gathered at the top of Rix's cracked tower to see the end. Since Lyf had four pearls now and she could not use the master pearl within her, the end would not be long in coming.

Rannilt lay still, cocooned in blankets. Tali had on all the clothes she possessed, and one of Rix's cloaks, yet she was shuddering convulsively. It was six-thirty in the morning and just starting to get light. In the distance, all three Vomits were erupting again, an unequivocal portent of the fall of a nation.

"Caulderon is finished," Rix said harshly.

He looked down at the child and his face softened. He limped down the stairs, shortly to reappear lugging his easels.

Rix smashed them to kindling and lit a fire in a corner of the wall. Tali winced with every symbolic splinter he fed to the flames.

"Burning your bridges?" said Tobry, who was slumped on a bench in an exhaustion so total that she wondered if he would ever move again.

Tali laid Rannilt on a bench beside the fire. The child was no better after all, but no worse, either. The wind howled in between the columns, whirling smoke in their faces. This defeat is due to my failures, she thought. I didn't protect Rannilt and I couldn't help Rix when he most needed it. Then I lied to Tobry and he lost hope. But my biggest failure was with Lyf. I should not have hesitated.

In the background, another failure nagged at her. Something that might have made the difference if only she could have thought of it, but she could not dredge the memory up.

Glynnie and Benn carried up a forequarter of deer from the palace stores. Glynnie cut it up and they threaded chunks of red meat on skewers and set them over the fire. Juices dripped and sizzled on the coals. Tali stared at the feast, her mouth flooding. The only meat slaves were given in Cython was poulter, and that was only once a year.

"What's going to happen now?" she said.

Rix stared over the wall, his jaw clenched. "I should have jumped the other night."

"What's that?" quavered Benn, who was standing on a bench looking towards the gates of Caulderon.

A lean, footless outline had appeared above the gates, a mid-air manifestation hundreds of feet high.

My people, it boomed, *I am Lyf, your last, lost king. Two thousand years ago the enemy's Five Heroes betrayed and murdered me, but even in death I could not leave my people unprotected. As a wrythen I have watched over you all this time, guiding your matriarchs via the secret books called the Solaces.*

Tali started. "I forgot the iron book. We can't let him get it back."

"Forget it," said Rix. "It's over."

Lyf's shattered shinbones were still smoking. *See how they treat your king, as foully as they have brutalised our beautiful Cythe. Yet the very land rebels. The earth rains fire down on them, the waters rise to tear down their filthy shanty towns. Even the eternal ice draws in all around to crush them into oblivion.*

Cythe is close to ruin and will need much healing. We must take it back before it's too late. The invaders deserve no mercy and will be given none. Take Caulderon, now!

The top of Tali's head, where she had touched the needle point to it, throbbed. She rubbed it and her finger came back bloody.

Memories stirred, of blood and alkoyl, and those fleeting words on the iron book.

"I know how to stop him. Rix, come on!"

She ran for the roof door, yelling over her shoulder. "Look after Rannilt. We won't be long."

"What are we doing?" said Rix as he caught her on the stairs.

She hurtled down. "I saw it, but I didn't take it in."

"Saw *what*?"

"The iron book was written with alkoyl that he distilled drop by drop from the Abysm. Remember that tube of alkoyl Wil dropped in the cellar? We can write our own ending."

"How? We can't read the damned book."

The flood of hope was choking her; Tali could barely speak. "Blood," she gasped.

"You're making even less sense than usual."

She stopped on the fourth landing to catch her breath. "Last night a drop of my blood fell on the book and for an instant I saw words there, but I was too exhausted to take anything in. Blood must decode the book and, if we write our own ending, it'll stop Lyf."

"Even if that were true," said Rix dubiously, "he's got four pearls. Why does he still need the book?"

They ran on. "Because his magery is bound up with everything he's written in the Solaces. Everything he's done in the past thousand years has been directed towards *his* ending, but he never got the chance to write it. If we write our own ending, it's got to be a powerful blow to him. It could change everything."

"But it's just a book."

"If your paintings can *divine* the future, why can't a book written with powerful magery *change* it?"

"I'll take your word for it."

They reached the dimly lit chaos of Rix's salon. "Run down and grab the alkoyl tube," said Tali. "I'll look for the book—"

"It's found," said Rix.

A white-faced Wil was crouched on the far side of the salon, hugging the iron book to his hollow chest. "Wil's book now," he whimpered. "Wil's got to be the Scribe."

He turned his raw eye sockets on her, jumped, then squeezed through a ragged crack in the wall, squirted alkoyl around its edges and was gone.

"After him!" Tali yelled.

Rix held her back. "Nothing can get through there now." He put a brawny arm around her waist and turned her back to the steps. "We tried."

"Not hard enough," she said bitterly. Why hadn't she listened to the inner voice last night, when it had whispered about the book?

He was still holding her, lifting her so her feet skipped over each step. "What more could anyone have done?"

"I don't know," she wailed. "Everything I've tried has gone wrong. I'm useless."

Rix smiled, the first she had seen from him in days. "You broke out of Cython where no other Pale ever had."

Tali sniffed.

"And you saved Rannilt's life. You can't dismiss that so easily."

"All I gave her was one lousy week."

"Rannilt would say it was the best week of her life."

"I suppose so," she said grudgingly. "But my quest has failed. I'm—"

"The killers are all dead," said Rix.

"But I don't feel any better." She turned to look up at him. "What's the matter with me? I thought the pain would go away once they'd been punished, but it's as bad as ever."

"You're asking *me* for advice," Rix said wryly.

"Yes."

"The pain has nothing to do with the killers, only with the crime you and I witnessed. The pain is inside you, and only you can deal with it."

"Lyf's not dead!" said Tali. "That's why it still hurts."

"And you're determined to ignore the truth," said Rix, restraining himself with an effort. "You found his weakness, you hurt him badly, and he's lost the iron book. You've done more than you could have hoped for. Isn't it enough?"

Tali had to think about that. "It's more than I ever expected, but nothing will be enough until Lyf pays for his crimes. And he never will, now."

"He'll pay," said Rix. "But not today."

As they reached the top, the sun tipped the horizon and a cascade of bombast blasts rippled along the south-eastern wall of the city, half a mile from the main gates where the First Army waited in its ranks. When the dust and smoke blew away, a section of wall a quarter of a mile long was gone and the enemy soldiers were scrambling over the rubble. Another great force was attacking from the unwalled lake shore.

"They're encircling the First Army on three sides," said Rix directly, reporting on the scene through his telescope. "They've pinned our soldiers between the gates and the buildings along the avenue. They're blocking all the side streets . . . "

"But our soldiers are better than theirs," said Benn. Even standing on the bench, he only came up to Rix's shoulders. "We'll beat 'em, Lord, won't we?" His voice went shrill and he fought to hold back tears.

Rix put an arm across the boy's shoulders. "I wish I could say so. Hop down, lad. You don't need to watch."

But Benn, though white-faced and trembling, shook his head. "Got to see what they do to us, Lord. Got to know."

The enemy began to cut the First Army down, rank by rank, for the soldiers had no defence against Cythonian ferocity, their unusual tactics or their strange, chymical weaponry. From other breaches in the wall, more enemy streamed in to trap the Second and Third Armies.

"If House Ricinus hadn't paid for the Third Army," said Rix, "would those men be dying now?"

"Yes, they would," said Tobry, whose eyes never left Rannilt's blanched face.

"Caulderon will fall within the hour," said Rix.

"Is there no hope?" Tali was still praying for a miracle.

"None," said Tobry. "And little for you, if Rix still retains his suicidal urge. If anyone can get you across the mountains to plan the counter-attack, he can."

"We're going to fight," said Rix. "And win Caulderon back. Gather your gear. We'll take the chancellor's secret way."

Before they could move, a squad of burly troops burst through the tower door, wearing the livery of the chancellor's personal guard, and the chancellor followed. The tubby, balding chief magian was there too.

The chancellor inspected Rix, the servants, Tali, then Tobry's cat-like ears, and smiled. "I told you to leave this place and never return," he said to Glynnie and Benn.

Rix stepped forwards, carrying his sword, with light-footed menace. "I ordered them home," he lied. "I protect my servants with my own life, sir. Every one of them."

The chancellor shrugged. "It doesn't matter now." He turned towards Tali, his eyes glittering.

"I did what you asked of me," she said defensively.

His voice was ice smashing on an anvil. "You neglected to mention the most vital secret—that the wrythen was Lyf."

She had not dared, knowing that he would ask dangerous questions.

"Had I known Lyf was our enemy," the chancellor grated, "had I known *he* had been plotting against us for two thousand years, had I known *he* wrote the Solaces to guide his people every step of their way back to power, I would never have sent you to the Crag."

"I hurt him," Tali said feebly. "It made him pull back his army."

"For a day and a half!" He was like a cobra waiting to strike, and Tali knew she had made a deadly enemy. "You also strengthened him immeasurably and drove him out, bent on vengeance."

She could not deny it. "Lyf's only attacking the armies. He's not killing indiscriminately."

"Yet!" The word was a whiplash. "But once my people have been enslaved and forced to tear Caulderon down, he will." The chancellor pulled her aside, saying in a low voice, "I know you're holding out on me—"

"I don't know what you're talking about," Tali blustered. She had not mentioned her murdered ancestors at the Honouring, but too many people knew the truth. He would soon guess that she bore the master pearl.

"Take your hands off her," Rix snapped.

"You consider the girl who attacked your helpless, drunken father and knocked him out a friend?" said the chancellor.

Rix froze with his hands outstretched. "Tali? Tell me this isn't true."

"He—he swung the bottle at me," said Tali, feeling sick. "I only pushed him. I didn't mean to hurt him."

"I know what Father was like," he said coldly. "Why didn't you tell me he was hurt?"

Her denials and half-truths had been instinctive, a slave's way of keeping out of trouble. How bitterly she regretted them now. "It—I—the guards were looking after him—I was afraid—"

"Never make excuses to me!" Rix stalked off.

The chancellor turned to Tobry, wrinkling his nose. "As for the shifter-cat, the law requires that it be put to death."

"No!" cried Tali.

"I was aware of the penalty before I ate the beast's liver," said Tobry, with a trace of his old insolence.

The chancellor gestured to an attendant carrying a flask and a sealed box. "You have the powdered lead?"

"Yes, my lord," said the attendant.

"Stand ready to burn the livers the moment they're taken."

Tali stepped in front of Tobry and spread her arms. "There has to be a way to save him."

"There isn't, as he knows better than any," said the chancellor.

"What's he talking about?" said Tali, twisting to look up at Tobry's furred cheeks.

"His grandfather was bitten by a jackal shifter and House Lagger tried to save him," said Rix. "Though I've never known why that was such a mistake."

"You can't bring anyone back," said Tobry. "Once you're *fully* a shifter, you remain one until you die. They should have put Grandfather down, but he was greatly loved and the best magians in the land were called in to break the shape-shifting curse."

"But they didn't succeed?" said Tali.

"It looked as though they had but, inside, the shifter madness was taking him, and he stalked the halls by night, hunting his own family. He got into the nursery, killed my little brother and all the young cousins, and *turned* several others, though it was years before we realised the culprit was Grandfather."

"Oh, Tobry, I'm sorry."

"Father had no choice but to hunt down his own father-in-law. It tore our house apart."

"But there's more, isn't there?" said Tali, seeing the pain in his cat eyes now and remembering things he'd said previously.

Tobry stared back through time and space. "I was thirteen," he whispered. "Just a kid. When Father called for help I didn't understand what was going on. Grandfather still had the shifter's strength and he was going to tear Father's throat out. What could I do? I saved Father; *I* killed my grandfather."

"You could have done nothing else," said Rix.

"Mother went out of her mind and Father was destroyed by the guilt—not for trying to do what had to be done, but for failing and calling on a boy to do a man's job. Afterwards, Mother burnt Lagger Mansion down with the rest of the family inside it, all save me."

Tobry looked into Tali's eyes. "So I'm certainly not going to inflict—"

"I don't have time for this," said the chancellor to his guards. "Cut the beast's livers out."

CHAPTER 108

Tali remembered a detail of her mother's murder that was not on Rix's painting. "What if there's another way?"

"Magians have been looking for a solution ever since shifters were first created a hundred years ago," said the chancellor.

"It's not a spell," said Tali.

"Really?" His eyes picked at her, peeling the layers away, trying to prise open her head again. "Many people have been bitten by shifters since the war began—valuable people we can't afford to put down. Tell me more."

Could he know about her pearl? Was he just toying with her? Tobry was sweating—he was worried about it, too. A stench of burnt meat drifted her way, from the skewers forgotten on the fire, and Tali lost her train of thought. "What?"

"'What if there's another way?' you said," said the chancellor.

"Oh! Yes! After she killed my mother, Lady Ricinus collected a tin of her blood."

"She took *blood*? Why?"

Tali was working it out as she went along. "In Cython the Pale are half starved and worked like dogs, but hardly anyone ever gets ill."

"You asked me what a cold was," said Rix, momentarily forgetting that he was angry with her.

"And in Hightspall, whole houses have died out from plague and pox, yet no one in Palace Ricinus has caught any disease in years. People in the palace are really healthy."

"I nearly died of fever when I was ten," Rix pointed out.

"But you haven't been sick since," said Tali. "And you keep having nightmares about someone rubbing blood *into your wounds*."

"I never understood why I kept having such an odd dream—" Rix stared at her. "Are you saying Lady Ricinus kept your mother's blood to use on me?"

"To give you our immunity to disease," said Tali. "Perhaps she put some in the palace water, too, to protect the household."

"Get to the point," growled the chancellor.

"What if Pale blood can protect against shapeshifting?"

"I wouldn't call shifting a disease."

"But what if it is?" Tali persisted. "What if Lyf *created* the first shifters that way?"

"Such creations would be an utter debasement of his king-magery," said the chancellor thoughtfully. "And the oath each Cythian king swore to use magery only for healing."

"Perhaps he felt the end justified the means," she said pointedly.

"Let's see it, then."

The gleam in his eye was alarming. But if she failed, Tobry would be butchered. Tali reopened her wrist vein, put her thumb over it and reached out to the largest gash on Tobry's chest.

He backed away. "If *my* blood gets into that cut it'll condemn you. Bleed into a cup."

The attendant held out a drinking mug. Tali allowed her blood to spurt into it until the bottom was covered a fingernail deep, then pressed her thumb to the wrist puncture and murmured her healing charm. The flow stopped. Tobry held his hand out for the mug.

She felt a spasm of fear. What if she was wrong? How could her blood heal, anyway? She rubbed her slave mark, for luck, then tipped blood into her cupped hand. The deepest gash across Tobry's chest had not scabbed over. It was a jagged, zigzagging wound, still raw.

The chancellor leaned forwards, his lips parted. He wanted her to succeed—but why? Tali's throat had gone dry. What if she failed? What would happen if she succeeded? She fought the fear down, steadied her shaking hand and pushed her blood into the wound. Hoping to reinforce it, she murmured her strongest healing charm. Tobry must not die. She could not bear it.

"More?" she whispered.

All the little hairs on Tobry's cheeks were standing up. "Yes, more."

As Tali rubbed the blood inside the ragged edges of the gash, Tobry's fingers hooked and the tendons of his neck stood out.

"Is it—?"

"I've felt worse," he said, forcing a smile. "But not much worse."

Then, as she watched, her blood was drawn into his flesh until all trace of it was gone.

"Wash your hands, very carefully," said Tobry.

The attendant brought water in a bucket and she scrubbed her hands, then Tali looked up and started. "But you're bleeding! The wound's bleeding." Tobry's teeth were bared; he seemed in more pain than before. "I've made it worse."

"Bleeding and pain are good," gasped Tobry. "It might mean there's not enough caitsthe in me to heal the wound."

"An impressive demonstration," said the chancellor smoothly. "Though the shifter side may restore itself the way a damaged liver can regrow. Lagger may always require the healing blood, and so may all those *valuable* people who will be bitten before this war ends."

Tali stared at the chancellor, trying to work out what he meant. Each breath rasped in her throat. Had she made the most dreadful mistake of her life?

"I can only take a handful of people into exile," he went on, "and if we're to counterattack and win Caulderon back, I can't lose any one of them."

He paced across the room, then back, studying Tali all the while. "Saving those bitten will require much Pale blood, and there's only one place we can get it." He looked down at Rannilt. "Two places, if the child survives."

Tali reeled and the scar on her shoulder burnt. It had once been her slave mark, then the symbol of her nobility. And now enslavement again, by her own people? A far worse kind of slavery—to be milked of her blood like a beast of the stables? No, it could not be borne.

The chancellor gestured to the captain of his personal guard, who had moved in close without anyone noticing. "Bind the two Pale and bring them."

Rix let out a great roar and sprang for his sword, but two guards brought him down from behind and pinned him to the floor. Tali darted for Rannilt, unable to leave her yet knowing that any attempt to rescue her was not only hopeless, it would doom them both.

The captain seized her around the chest. Tobry staggered towards her, trying to shift, but before he could do so another pair of guards disarmed him.

"Chief Magian," said the chancellor, his eyes glittering like chunks of anthracite, "would you put Rixium's blade to the test you found in the archives?"

"What test?" said Rix.

His captors allowed him to rise but held his arms behind him. Rix wasn't struggling, though Tali felt sure he was planning to break free, and two ordinary men could hardly hold him. Could he save them? The chancellor had fifteen men here, and surely not even Rix could beat those odds.

The black writing Tali had seen from a distance at the Honouring appeared on the sword. *Heroes must fight to preserve the race.* The chief magian passed a copper-coloured elbrot above and below the blade and a green aura shimmered around it, which slowly turned blue, and then finally a deep purple.

"It's Maloch!" said the chief magian, and the small amount of grey hair on his head stood up.

Rix tensed. "What the blazes is Maloch?"

"The dire sword that Herovian swine Axil Grandys brought here." The chancellor's smile twisted, his eyes burned. "A foul blade, enchanted to protect none but himself and his direct descendants."

"But I'm not his descendant. Mother had those documents forged . . . " Rix faltered. "What are you saying?"

"Oh, yes," said the chancellor softly. "*Her* documents were fakes, but Maloch was well forged. It doesn't lie."

"I don't understand."

"Your father wasn't descended from Axil Grandys," the chancellor said with gleeful malice. "The sword came to you down your *mother's* line."

Rix's mouth opened and closed. Tali felt sick. If revenge was meat and drink to the chancellor, this was a royal banquet.

"The sword protected you," said the chancellor. "Therefore, you were already of the First Circle. You're descended directly from Grandys—via your mother."

"You utter bastard," spat Tobry. "You guessed that at the Honouring, yet you allowed Lady Ricinus to go on so you could publicly humiliate her."

The chancellor did not bother to look his way. "Two days before the Honouring, Tali informed me that Lady and Lord Ricinus were plotting my assassination."

Rix's head shot around and she saw the shock in his eyes, the accusation, the feeling of betrayal. *I thought we were friends. You should have told* me.

"How could I tell you?" she said softly. "It would have put you in an impossible position."

"I was already in an impossible position. It was my right to know."

"If I told you, it would have endangered you too."

"Am I a child, that I need to be protected?" Rix said, low and deadly.

She could not reply. He was lost to her now.

"The treason had nothing to do with Rix," Tobry said hastily. "Besides, he told you ..." He trailed off.

"The lord and lady stand for the house. Therefore *House Ricinus* plotted high treason and it had to pay." The chancellor turned to his captain. "Take Tali and the child away. Feed them well; we could be milking their blood for a long time. Leave the others."

"Rix is one of our greatest fighters, and an inspiring leader," murmured the captain.

"And I wanted him by my side," said the chancellor, "but I could never trust a man who would betray his own mother, and I won't have a Herovian at any price."

"I never knew I was," Rix said. "But since you've taken away everything else I had, and now name me Herovian, *a Herovian I will be*."

In her head, Tali heard an irresistible ice sheet grinding against an immoveable glacier. What was Rix going to do—*or become?*

"Your kind will be at the top of the enemy's death list," said the chancellor, unperturbed. "I'll leave you to them."

Two guards began to drag Tali towards the door. "What about Tobry?" she cried, struggling uselessly against the lashings. "What's he going to do without my blood?"

The chancellor's smile was terrifying. "He won't need it. Heave him over the side."

Two burly guardsmen swept Tobry up and began to drag him towards the wall. His eyes met Tali's and she saw the same despairing look there as when she had told him she loved Rix.

"*Shift!*" she screamed, kicking her guards and trying to reach him. "As a caitsthe, you can beat them."

But Tobry did not shift. Had her healing blood doomed him? Or did he just want it to end?

"Rix! Do something!"

Rix seemed to be in shock, for he simply stood there. Then in a blinding movement he wrenched free, flattened his captors with single blows and leapt towards Tobry. Another pair of guards, swords out, blocked him. Rix went into a crouch, swaying from side to side.

"Tobry, why?" he said quietly.

"I'm making way," said Tobry. "You're the better man."

Rix let out a great groan. "You bloody fool! Tali lied to save me from myself. It's you she wants."

"Me?" Tobry's head inched around towards Tali.

"Yes," she whispered, realising what she should have known ages ago. "Ever since you took me to the ball."

Tobry's eyes blazed and he tried to tear free.

"Get him over, quick," rapped the chancellor.

Three guards took hold of Tobry, dragged him to the wall and tried to heave him into the air. He punched one in the throat, jammed an elbow into the eye of another, then convulsed and Tali saw his nails lengthen, his back arch. He was trying to shift, but it was going too slowly. Tali's breath thickened in her throat. Could he do it? Not with so many guards swarming after him.

Rix kicked one of his opponents in the knee, the other in the belly, snatched a falling sword out of the air and attacked. His first blow, with the side of the blade, hurled one of Tobry's captors ten feet, into the wall. A bone-breaking left hook to the jaw took down the next man. Rix was thrusting at the third when the captain kicked his feet from under him, stretching him prone on the flagstones.

"Take his right hand," said the chancellor. "With Maloch."

Rix must have been dazed, for he did not move. This could not be happening. Tali brought her knee up into one guard's groin and he doubled over. The other man, knowing she had to be protected at all cost, hesitated. She chopped him across the larynx with the side of her hand, evaded a third guard and ran at the captain.

But before she could reach him, the captain raised Maloch and, with a savage blow, severed Rix's right hand at the wrist. His hand shot into the air, struck her on the knee then flopped onto her foot like a bloody spider. Tali jumped, instinctively flicked it aside, shuddered and had to look away.

Rix let out a roar and staggered to his feet, his wrist pouring blood. The captain struck him on the back of the head with the sword hilt and he collapsed.

Tali ran for Tobry, but before she could reach him, and before Tobry could shift, the guards raised him high and hurled him head-first from the top of the tower.

Rannilt woke, screaming and spraying golden light in all directions, and it took three soldiers to hold her while another wound layers of cloth across her mouth. Only on the fifth winding could they block out the dreadful sound.

Tali stared at the wall where Tobry had gone over. Could he survive such a fall—more than a hundred feet? Surely it would even kill a shifter, and Tobry had not fully shifted, had he? She did not see how he could have completed it in time. Her healing blood had doomed him.

She stumbled to the nearest wall and drove the top of her head into the stone, trying to smash the cursed pearl that had robbed her of every good thing in her life and brought her nothing but despair. But the pain, terrible though it was, could not mask the agony that would never end.

A guard stopped her. Others held her while her bloody head was bandaged and her wrists bound. Tali did not struggle. It felt as though her heart had been cut out. She stared at the wall until the soldiers led her away, then went with them, indifferent to her fate, weeping until her burning tear ducts ran dry.

She was alone again. Every friend she made, every bond she formed, ended in a disaster of her own making. She had failed them all when they most needed her. Iusia had been right, back at the beginning—but for the wrong reason.

You'll never be hurt if you *trust no one.*

CHAPTER 109

Lyf stood on crutches at the top of Rix's tower, brooding. Had he done the right thing by his people? The urge for vengeance had carried them to their first victory but, even if the rest of Hightspall fell as quickly, could they ever regain the gentle, harmonious society they'd had before the First Fleet came? Or had he fatally corrupted them, alienated them forever from their own land?

Now was not the time for self-doubt. He addressed the officers and soldiers gathered outside the front entrance of Palace Ricinus.

"You have done well. The city is ours. Identify all the Herovians, separate them out and march them to the special place. Then, take the rest of the Hightspallers into slavery. Gather their provisions and carry them to the warehouses on the lakefront. Collect all the enemy's weapons. Lock them in the four designated armouries and make sure they are well guarded."

"My king, these things are already being done," called the squat, muscle-bound General Hillish, "and will be done as you order. And then?"

"Sift the rubble of Lord Rixium's salon and find the iron book."

"At once, my king." Hillish gave the orders. "And then?"

"Scour the city for a vicious little tome called the *Immortal Text*. If it is found, or any copies of it, bring every page to me for destruction."

"It will be done." Hillish looked at Lyf, expectantly. "And finally?"

"Do unto Hightspall as Hightspall did unto us," said Lyf.

"My king?"

"Visit an equal ruin on Caulderon as its Five Heroes did to our city of Lucidand, which stood here until the invaders came. See where Lucidand's foundations have been exposed by the great tidal wave?"

Lyf gestured towards the ravines carved through the lower grounds, and the stonework visible there. "Burn Caulderon's libraries and raze its temples. Leave not one stone laid by Hightspall standing on another."

"Even this palace?" said the general. "My king, it's a creation of unsurpassed beauty. Perhaps there's more to the enemy than we know. I would not have thought them capable of it."

"Especially this palace," snapped Lyf. "It was once home to the brute Axil Grandys, who murdered me and plotted Cythe's ruin.

When Caulderon is grit and ashes we will rebuild Lucidand according to the ways of old Cythe. Begin with Palace Ricinus. Leave nothing save this tower, which will stand in its cracked ruin as a monument to our victory, and a warning to the enemy that all their works are doomed to fall."

Their bombasts had toppled twenty-two of the palace towers when a young female soldier came panting up to Lyf, hauling an enormous rectangle wrapped in cloth. She dragged it across, avoiding a puddle of congealed blood.

"My king," she said, bowing to the ground and blushing, "I found this out the back. General Rochlis told me to bring it to you for assessment."

When she took off the covering, Lyf caught his breath. The painting was mesmerising—a defeated wyverin pretending to be dead while a dissipated warrior posed before it. It was magnificent, yet terrible—the noble creature secretly waiting for the moment to strike at the strutting, deluded warrior whose life's failures were etched deep into his face. Clearly, the painting was a metaphor for the two races and their forever war, and a warning—to both sides.

"It's a masterpiece." He knew at a glance who had painted the portrait, and what it had cost him. "The finest work of theirs I've ever seen."

"Even the common soldiers think so," the girl said, shivering. Every child in Cython knew how to paint and carve; every Cythonian could tell the difference between good art and bad.

Lyf closed his eyes, reliving the pain of long ago as Cythe's treasures had been smashed and torched by the barbarian enemy, and remembering his own despair at the loss of everything he cared about. Was Rix's painting evidence that even the despised Herovians had changed? It portrayed a cultured and creative side Lyf neither wanted to see nor admit to.

Yet had he not grown over the centuries? Could he not rise above the urge to slake his grief in vengeance? He wanted to. A truly great king would have, knowing that was the way to end the war.

He tried, but the bitterness of two thousand years could not be overcome. Far better that the enemy be seen as brutes without any redeeming features. It would make it easier to deliver them to the final resolution when the time came. That was the other way to end the war.

He opened his eyes. The painting was magnificent but, as Errek, First-King had once pointed out, *Posterity is rife with oblivion*.

"Burn it."

CHAPTER 110

In a passage far below Rix's demolished salon, Wil the Sump hugged the iron book to his hollow chest and howled at the stones. No one loved books the way he did, and he had believed the iron book to be perfect, but it wasn't. His life had been robbed of meaning.

"Scribe got it wrong," he sobbed. "Scribe's story untrue. Ruined the iron book."

But Wil could not believe in *the one*, either, because the *shilillar* about her had also gone off track. How could he find the true story, the right ending?

It had to be right, for Wil now knew about the creeping ice. If it was not stopped, it would wipe Cythe clean, as it had already erased life on the island of Suden.

There was only one thing to do. He must erase every glyph from the iron book, recast the pages and rewrite it himself. If he used enough of the magical alkoyl, the pure weepings that could only be found deep down, surely he could make the story go right. He had to. No one else could be trusted to do it.

Wil crept down and down, cradling the book in his right arm as if it were his own child. With his free hand he sniffed his alkoyl tube until blood dripped from his ruined nose and his liver bulged like a grapefruit, but he felt no pain.

"Down the Hellish Conduit, yes, yes. All way down to the Engine. Engine must be beating too slowly. Yes, Engine cold, that why ice coming. How can Wil fix?"

He thought for a minute, an hour, perhaps a day. Time no longer had any meaning to him. Wil took a deep sniff, mad images danced in his head and he lurched on.

"Heat! Heat melt ice. Engine fuelled by great cauldron, down at heart of world. Wil must open stopcocks, flood Engine with cauldron fire. Make Engine race and melt ice away."

He stopped for a moment, troubled by an elusive thought that the cauldron might be unstable, even dangerous. But Wil did not like to think about such things, so he took a huge sniff and the worry went away.

"This the true story, the right ending. Wil going to write it."

He made what he thought to be an elegant sweeping motion with his alkoyl tube, practising the calligraphy he must master before he could write the book anew. This time the iron book was going to be perfect.

"Wil really special now. Wil the Scribe, and *the one*."

The End of Book One

The story continues in book two of
The Tainted Realm Trilogy
Rebellion

ACKNOWLEDGEMENTS

I would like to thank my publisher, Bernadette Foley, my editors in the US, DongWon Song; the UK, Bella Pagan; and in Australia, Abigail Nathan; plus everyone else at Orbit Books who had worked so hard and so long on this series. I would also like to thank my agent, Selwa Anthony, for her support, encouragement and assistance over the past fifteen years and many, many books.

extras

meet the author

Mike Benveniste

IAN IRVINE, a marine scientist who has developed some of Australia's national guidelines for protection of the marine environment, has also written twenty-seven novels. These include the internationally bestselling Three Worlds fantasy sequence (The View from the Mirror, The Well of Echoes and Song of the Tears), which has sold over a million copies, a trilogy of thrillers set in a world undergoing catastrophic climate change, Human Rites, and twelve books for younger readers, the latest being the humorous fantasy quartet Grim and Grimmer. Ian is currently working on the second book of The Tainted Realm, *Rebellion*.

Email Ian: ianirvine@ozemail.com.au
Ian's website: www.ian-irvine.com
Ian's Facebook page:
http://www.facebook.com/ianirvine.author

interview

***Why did you write* Vengeance?**

I've long been fascinated by the fragility of political power, and in particular how the means of seizing or maintaining power can undermine the legitimacy of a nation. It happens all the time in history, and we've seen it recently in Australia, where I live. The current government is constantly undermined by the way the prime minister's predecessor was overthrown in a backroom plot. In the US, Nixon's presidency was fatally damaged, then destroyed, by the Watergate affair.

Musing on such events gave me the germ of the idea behind The Tainted Realm. The once great nation of Hightspall has been so stricken by earthquakes, eruptions and plagues that it's in danger of collapse. Its people are burdened by a growing sense of national guilt about the nation's brutal origins, and they feel that the stolen land is rising up to cast them out.

Then, at the worst possible time, they're about to face a resurgent enemy they have no idea how to fight. This idea has all the elements I'm looking for in a story.

Who/what would you consider to be your influences?

My influences... tricky.

I read a huge amount of SF when I was growing up and at uni, though I wouldn't say my writing was influenced by any of those writers—apart from fostering a love of grand adventures set in exotic lands.

I didn't discover fantasy until my early twenties and switched almost instantly from SF to fantasy. I particularly loved *The Lord of the Rings* at that age, and I dare say my love of epic fantasy has been influenced by it and other massive tomes (such as Mervyn Peake's Gormenghast trilogy, which I read on a two-month Greyhound bus odyssey around North America in the early seventies). Though later, when I formed the ambition of writing fantasy, I deliberately avoided rereading Tolkien and my other favourite authors so I wouldn't be influenced by them.

When I began writing, in the late eighties, most popular fantasy seemed heavily influenced by Tolkien—all those struggles of good versus evil, frequently where the villain was evil for the sake of it, set in imaginary lands that often resembled Western Europe in the Middle Ages. I read dozens of such books, and enjoyed them, too, but I didn't want to write fantasy like that. A story can develop from any of hundreds of possible themes; why restrict it to just good and evil?

Also, I wanted to take my readers to places they had never been before, to plausible worlds and environments they could never see on our world, and show them sights that no one had ever seen—like the Dry Sea (an environment that hasn't existed on Earth for five million years) in The View from the Mirror.

But you haven't answered the question.

Sorry, got carried away there. I also loved Fritz Leiber's Fafhrd and the Gray Mouser books, and everything by Jack Vance, and the exotic stories of Clark Ashton Smith, though not for a microsecond did I think of imitating their work or attempting to write in a similar style. Rather, if I notice another writer's influence in my own work, I rewrite to get rid of it.

So, my influences. Essentially I write the kinds of books I would have loved to read when I was younger—great, action-packed adventures roaming over vast and unusual canvases.

But I've also been influenced by my own working life. I'm a marine scientist, an expert in contaminated sediments, and for the past thirty years I've investigated pollution problems in Australia and around the world. My scientific background gives me a different way of looking at things and I often realise that I'm using scientific imagery to describe the things that happen in my books.

Perhaps that's why I called my first epic fantasy quartet— The View from the Mirror—a Darwinian fantasy. It's not about the battle of good versus evil but rather a struggle for existence between four different kinds of humans, all of them great, none of them evil, and each with a burning desire for survival.

Do you have a favorite character? If so, why?

I do, though it changes all the time.

Often it's Karan, the heroine from The View from the Mirror quartet, because she's strong and brave, sharp-tongued yet gentle and kind. She's my sentimental favourite because she was the first character I ever fully created and I spent twelve years trying to understand her while writing and rewriting that series, over and over.

Sometimes it's the scrutator and sorcerer Xervish Flydd, a scrawny, scarred, ugly yet charming little man who dominates large parts of The Well of Echoes quartet, and parts of the Song of the Tears trilogy that follows. Flydd emerged on the page fully formed; I didn't know he was coming and didn't have to work at him at all. Perhaps he's unconsciously based on the author!

A few months ago I would have said my favourite character was Useless Ike, the protagonist of my humorous children's series Grim and Grimmer, because Ike posed a particular challenge. I'd never written a series before about a character who was useless at everything, bottom of the class, got everything wrong and was so clumsy that he was constantly falling over his own feet. It's not easy to convincingly turn such a character into a genuine hero. And yet, by the last book of the quartet, Ike is a genuine hero, and I'll always love him for the way he did it.

But at the moment my favourite has to be Tali, from *Vengeance*, because she starts out a pitiful slave, her ancestors have been enslaved for the past thousand years, and at the beginning of *Vengeance* she's lost everything, yet she never gives up.

How much of you is in your characters?

The good ones or the evil, lol?

A well-travelled writer will, in a lifetime, meet thousands of interesting, unusual and often quirky people from different cultures. And writers often have long-time partners and lifelong friends, yet ultimately the only person any writer can truly know, from the inside, is himself or herself.

Every character I write about is based in some way on my own life, thoughts, feelings, emotions and experiences. For example, when I'm writing about Tali being very afraid, I'm thinking about times in my life when I've been uneasy, frightened or even terrified. Then I stretch or twist or invert my own remembered feelings until I have something that fits her character in her present situation. It's much the same process for every character I write about, and every situa-tion—the writer's challenge is to make the character's feel-ings real, yet different each time.

Are any of your characters based on real people?

None of the people I know are interesting enough to be in one of my stories, he chuckles.

Characters in popular fiction need to be larger than life; they should be the kind of people who say things we wish we had the courage to say, and take the kinds of risks in life we would never dream of taking. Sure, I know people who are larger than life in one small aspect of their lives, but at the end of the day they have to take the kids to school, then go to work and pay the mortgage.

What do you do when you aren't writing?

Think about what I'm going to write next.

I used to bushwalk and scuba dive and do other similarly adventurous things. I also used to travel a lot for work. But, having been on about two thousand plane flights over the past few decades, I don't have the same travel urge as I used to. These days I mainly read, walk, sit and think, plan new stories and, when it's not raining, which is hardly ever where I live, I work in the out-of-control jungle that's laughably called our garden. We live in the country on a few acres so there's always work to do, and it's nice to escape the com-puter screen and do some useful physical labour.

Have you always been a writer?

The funny thing is, I never wanted to be a writer when I was a kid.

I hated writing at school, and was in fact a rather lazy boy.

I spent most of my time up the back of the class, daydreaming. But around the age of fourteen I decided I wanted to be a scientist, and at uni I studied chemistry and geology before eventually doing research in marine pollution. I became an expert in this field three decades ago, and set up my own little consulting company in 1986 to do this kind of work. And I still do it, when I have the time from writing.

How does a marine scientist end up writing fantasy novels?

I was doing interesting scientific work in great places, but it wasn't enough.

About twenty-four years ago I decided I wanted to write a fantasy novel. I'd been reading fantasy for a long time by then, and ten years previously I'd designed my own fantasy world with maps the size of doors, dozens of ecosystems, nations and cultures, and ten thousand years of history. I began writing *A Shadow on the Glass*, the first book of what was to become the eleven-book Three Worlds series. At first it was incredibly hard and frustrating work but, within a month of beginning to write, I knew it was what I wanted to do for the rest of my life.

What's next?

I'm presently doing the final edits of *Rebellion*, book two of The Tainted Realm, and at the same time I'm working on detailed planning of *Justice*, the final book in the trilogy.

And after that—

When are you going to write another Three Worlds series?

Ah, my most frequently asked question.

At the end of each big fantasy series I always write something completely different. I do this for a number of reasons, one being to freshen and rejuvenate my writing. The problem with writing such vast sagas (the Three Worlds sequence runs to 2.3 million words thus far) is that I've used up an enormous number of different characters, settings and plot elements, and the more I write, the more I'm prone to repeat myself. Not that this is necessarily a problem—quite a few writers have made a career out of writing the same book over and over again. But I don't want to do that.

Another reason is that, like most other writers, I crave variety: I don't want to write the same kinds of books all the time. And a third reason: by the end of the last Three Worlds novel, *The Destiny of the Dead*, I was creatively exhausted and desperately needed a rest from that place.

That's all very well, but what about the Three Worlds? What about the story you've been promising to write for more than a decade, the follow-on from The View from the Mirror to be called The Fate of the Children?

It's next, I promise. Honest!

I'll be finished with The Tainted Realm around the end of 2012, and I'm planning to start the new story straight after that. At this stage I don't know whether it'll be a single book, a pair, a trilogy, or longer. That will depend on what comes up when I reread The View from the Mirror, which I haven't opened since the series was finished back in 1999. I'm looking forward to seeing how it reads after so long, and hoping I've forgotten enough of the story that I can see it with a fresh eye.

You can write to Ian at: ianirvine@ozemail.com.au
Or talk via his Facebook author page:
  http://www.facebook.com/ianirvine.author
Ian's enormous website is here: http://www.ian-irvine.com/

introducing

**If you enjoyed
VENGEANCE,
look out for**

SEVEN PRINCES

by John R. Fultz

It is an Age of Legends.

*Under the watchful eye of the Giants, the kingdoms of Men rose
to power. Now, the Giant-King has slain the last of the Serpents
and ushered in an era of untold peace and prosperity.
Where a fire-blackened desert once stood, golden cities
flourish in verdant fields.*

It is an Age of Heroes.

*But the realms of Man face a new threat—an ancient sorcerer
slaughters the rightful King of Yaskatha before the unbelieving
eyes of his son, young Prince D'zan. With the Giant-King
lost to a mysterious doom, it seems that no one has the
power to stop the coming storm.*

663

It is an Age of War.

The fugitive Prince seeks allies across the realms of Men and Giants to liberate his father's stolen kingdom. Six foreign Princes are tied to his fate. Only one thing is certain: War is coming.

SEVEN PRINCES.

Some will seek glory.

Some will seek vengeance.

All will be legends.

SUNSET IN YASKATHA

The stranger came to Yaskatha at sunset.

The city had taken on the color of blood, a mound of rubies stacked beside the blue-green mirror of the sea. Shadows glided through streets and gardens. In the royal orchards weary harvesters carried bushels of lemons and pomegranates. Along the wharves a flock of trading vessels folded their sails for the night. Mariners prowled the taverns in search of red wine and the red lips of women.

In the airy palace of King Trimesqua the Feast of Ascension began with a legion of musicians, a flourish of dancers, and a quartet of fire-eaters. Before the throne sat a long table piled high with delicacies. Prince D'zan sat at the head of the board, looking far more regal than his sixteen years would suggest. Behind him, as always, stood Olthacus the Stone. The solemn warrior wore a massive blade on his back. It had served him well in three wars, but he seldom drew the sword from its jeweled sheath. A glance of the Stone's gray eyes sent fear fluttering into the hearts of brave warriors. To D'zan, laughing at the antics of a fool who juggled flaming brands, his fearsome bodyguard was little more than a stiff-lipped uncle. Yet no man could have been safer at court than the young Prince. Not even the King himself.

In the midst of the revels, as the sun poured the last of its lifeblood into the sea, a stranger appeared before the throne of Trimesqua. No one saw him enter the palace gates or move between the ranks of armored guards. He flowed like a shadow across the motley crowd and stood before the King. When first he spoke, the music overpowered his words so that only the King could hear him.

Trimesqua set down his golden goblet, raised a hand heavy with rings, and commanded silence. All eyes fell upon the stranger. He was a tall man, gaunt, and as pale as the jungle dwellers of Khyrei. His hair fell long and gray down his back, and his robes were black as pitch. An arc of rubies hung across his chest like drops of frozen blood, mimicking the cold moon with a red smile. The nails of his fingers were long and sharp, making claws of his hands. Shadows rimmed his eyes.

"Who is this mad vagabond?" Trimesqua asked a nearby courtier.

"I am Elhathym," said the stranger. His voice was deep and cold. "I knew this city when it was called by another name . . . but I have lingered a great while in distant lands. Tonight is my homecoming."

"Say again, Elhathym, what you said to me when first you caught my eye," said the King. "If you dare."

Elhathym nodded. "I said that your reign has come to an end, Trimesqua." He glanced about the crowded hall. "Step down from your marble seat. This city belongs to me."

A flood of gasps and muttered curses filled the hall. Prince D'zan stood up from his feasting chair and stared at the stranger. His guardian, the Stone, did not move or even blink an eye. A moment of silence fell across the assemblage.

The exquisite tension was broken by the King's laughter, which spread like bubbling water throughout the courtesans, nobles, entertainers, and servants. The stranger stood mute and grinning as the laughter surrounded him. Guards along the walls drew their curved blades and moved closer to the throne, but the King raised his glittering hand again, halting them.

"Surely you are one of the fools sent to amuse me?" said the King, regaining his composure. He quaffed red wine and chuckled again. "A rare jest!"

"I assure you," said Elhathym, "I am no fool, and this is no jest. This land is mine by ancient right. I could bring your city to its knees with sorcery and shed the blood of all these beautiful soldiers, but I am not a cruel man. Therefore I give you this chance to surrender the throne without any deaths on your conscience but your own. I will make your execution quick. You will feel no pain. Deny me... and all will suffer."

Now the King did not laugh. Nor did anyone in the hall. A deathly silence hung between the pillars with the smoke of feasting, broken only by the crackling of torch flames. D'zan drew the long dagger that he always wore and moved toward his father, but his silent bodyguard placed a hand on his shoulder. Despite the nervous twitching in his stomach, the Prince stilled himself.

The King stood up and tossed his wine cup down the steps of the dais, turning white marble to crimson. Guards rushed forward, but a third time Trimesqua raised his hand, and they halted. "My father, and his father, and all their fathers before them ruled Yaskatha from this high seat," said Trimesqua.

"Neither men, wizards, demons, or tidal waves shook them from this throne. Here is what I think of your threat, Elhathym the Sorcerer."

In the blink of an eye Trimesqua, who was seasoned in the same wars as Olthacus the Stone, drew his silver sword and swept it down upon the stranger's head. Elhathym's skull split with a meaty crack that rang the length of the hall. He fell backward in a shower of gore, staining the fine carpet at the King's feet.

"Remove this trash!" commanded the King. He tossed his soiled blade to lie upon the chest of the dead man. Guards rushed forward and dragged the body away; one of them would clean and anoint the sword before returning it to him. Servants exchanged the ruined carpet for fresh one, and the Festival of Ascension resumed. Music and wine flowed through the heart of the palace like blood through a living man's body, and the corpse of Elhathym was thrown into a deep furnace. Later, his charred bones were tossed into the midnight sea.

That night Prince D'zan fell asleep after exhausting his passion with a comely courtesan. Instead of the sweet oblivion born of drink and exertion, his rest was plagued by nightmares. He found himself wandering through the ancestral burial vaults deep below the palace, where lay the bones of his grandfather, his great-grandfather, and all the generations of his family going back a thousand years. He was cold and without garments as he wandered those lightless, musty catacombs, and the eye sockets of decaying skulls glared at him from the shadows.

Somewhere among the vaults he knew his mother lay, for she had died when he was an infant, and he did not remember her face. Still, she must be here in this realm of chill darkness and creeping grave mold. Royal families throughout the centuries filled the numberless rows of niches, and sometimes favored servants and war heroes earned the honor of burial in the royal crypts. In terror, D'zan wandered this mansion of the dead, calling the name of his father into the dark. Only echoes answered him.

He called, too, the name of Olthacus, his bodyguard. Not even the Stone came to help him navigate those dark depths, and he could not find his way out. He found only chamber after chamber of mummified ancestors, the population of the city's long history, and the crumbling, engraved sarcophagi in which they lay. Here was a city of death that slept beneath the living city, and at last he gave up looking for the exit and lay down in the dust near a pile of bones. It seemed to him then that he heard a faint laughter ringing through the tombs.

He woke to a sweltering bedchamber, lying next to the senseless girl who shared his bed. He could not sleep again so he walked along the open balcony of his room and let the ocean breezes dry his sweat. The girl joined him on the balcony and soon lured him back to bed.

The following day was like any other in Yaskatha's thriving capital. D'zan arose early and walked the palace garden with his fair-haired cousin Lysinda. He spoke to her of his nightmares and she comforted him like a mother with gentle kisses on his forehead and cheek.

"I've dreamed of my mother before," D'zan told his cousin. "But never of the place where she lies."

"There is nothing to fear," said Lysinda, taking one of his hands in her own. "Dreams are only passing fancies. They cannot hurt us."

"Do you truly believe that?" he asked.

"Of course," she said.

"But...this dream seemed so real. It was...a warning of some kind. I know it."

"Don't be silly," said Lysinda, ruffling his hair. "Look about you: the sun is shining, the sea is laughing, the blooms of the garden rejoice. The stranger is dead and forgotten."

"I'm afraid," he whispered. She cradled his head in her lap awhile. She did not have to tell him that Princes of the royal house were not supposed to speak of fear or weakness. He knew that well enough.

D'zan forsook his studies for the day, and the two cousins went riding along the pounding surf. They rode twin mares the color of honeyed milk, and Olthacus the Stone rode some distance behind on his black charger, a single shadow for them both.

When sunset fell on Yaskatha once again, the King sat on his throne listening to reports of trading galleons from Mumbaza, Murala, Shar Dni, and the kingdoms of distant continents. D'zan reclined nearby on a lesser throne; his father was grooming him in the ways of statecraft. Behind D'zan stood the vigilant Stone, his eyes hidden beneath the hood of a heavy cloak. Olthacus scanned the throne room for potential threats among the comings and goings of the court.

Despite his keen sense for danger, not even the Stone saw the stranger's second arrival. As before, the dark-robed Elhathym simply appeared before the King's throne without any warning. His hoarse voice interrupted and overpowered the voice of the King's viceroy, who read a cargo list from an unfurled scroll.

"Trimesqua," interrupted the sorcerer, his sallow face looking even more skull-like than yesterday. "You have spurned my offer of mercy. As you can see, my death is beyond your power to grant. I give you one more chance to abdicate your throne. Since you refused my first offer, now it falls upon your people to suffer if you refuse a second time. Everyone inside this palace will die if you deny me again. Blood will flow through your streets and orchards. The shadows of your own past will tear you from your throne. What say you?"

Olthacus the Stone drew forth his great two-handed blade, and D'zan rose from his own chair to unsheathe his ceremonial scimitar. He felt again the terror of his dream...For a moment he was lost in the lightless crypts. Then he was staring at the broad back of the Stone, and guards rushed forward to encircle Elhathym in a thicket of bronze spear points and shining blades.

King Trimesqua did not rise from his throne this time, but his wrath was great.

"Charlatan! Chicanery will gain you nothing! Your fatal mistake was in returning to the scene of your previous treason. Now your death will be slow and agonizing. You will scream and beg forgiveness on the rack! Take him!" Spittle flew from the King's lips to fleck his dark beard.

The palace guards swept over the sorcerer, a vast wave of silver and gold drowning a single black pebble. Olthacus the Stone did not move, but kept his place shielding D'zan in case the sorcerer unleashed some dreadful magic in his direction. But Elhathym did nothing as soldiers loaded his limbs with heavy chains and dragged him from the throne room. He did not even scream as they dragged him down below the living levels of the palace and into the sulfurous glow of the torture chamber. Here, among the half-dead relics of political prisoners, murderers, rapists, and traitors, he endured the worst of torments the torturers could envision. For hours the hooded ones plied their trade, but not once did Elhathym scream. Instead, he *laughed*. As if all the processes of his own bodily pain and dismemberment offered some private delight.

In the throne room far above, the condemned man's laughter drifted like a fetid smoke. D'zan, sitting at the arm of his father, shivered in his cushioned chair. He recognized that hollow sound from his dream of the tombs, and a nameless terror swelled in his heart. He could not speak to his father of his true feelings. He must be as brave and valiant as his sire, as grim and unfazed as the Stone. So he hid his quietly growing horror, and stuffed his ears with pieces of silk to drown out the faint laughter of the tortured man.

That night D'zan dreamed himself into the tombs again. He wandered, naked and alone as before, looking for the sarcophagus of his mother. In the living world he had visited her grave a thousand times, and such a familiar landmark might give him some hope of egress from the nightmare maze. But he could not find his dead mother, only legions of those who had died before his birth, a necropolis of winding corridors leading nowhere. At last, he saw a pale light and ran toward it. It seemed to draw away from him in the ever-lengthening distance that only occurs in the midst of dreams. Finally, he came close enough to realize the glow came from a single face, gleaming in worm-pale moonlight. It was the face of the sorcerer Elhathym, and it smiled at him in the darkness, floating wraith-like before him, bodiless. The face laughed, and the flesh sloughed away like that of a leper, leaving only a cackling skull that hovered in the endless dark.

D'zan woke screaming, and seconds later the Stone came into his bedchamber.

"It's all right, Olthacus...I'm fine." D'zan waved his guardian away, but the big man would not leave the room. He stood in the corner while servants dressed D'zan. The Prince called for a cup of morning wine, but could eat no breakfast. He spent the day in the library, poring over ancient texts from Khyrei detailing legends of sorcerers and necromancers who had haunted the Old World. In one of these tomes, after hours of meandering through moldy pages, he discovered mention of a wizard bearing the same name as the one who'd come to plague his nightmares. "The Tyrant Elhathym," said the *Book of Disgraced Savants*, "ruled a southern kingdom before the Age of Serpents." Nothing more than that brief passage.

Such texts were widely discredited by Yaskathan sages, because there were no civilizations that existed before Giants out of the northlands drove the race of fire-breathing reptiles from the earth. According to D'zan's history tutors, the Giants then claimed the north for themselves, forcing the Four Tribes of humans to flee southward to ultimately form the five kingdoms: Yaskatha, Khyrei, Uurz, Mumbaza, and Shar Dni. How could there be a southern empire before any of this happened? Unless history was wrong…a lie invented to cover up horrible truths. And why would this present-day sorcerer take the name of a tyrant from an age of mystery?

It did not matter, he told himself. The sorcerer was finally dead now, tortured to death last night by order of King Trimesqua.

Or was he?

As the sun slipped once more into the sea, D'zan closed the musty volume and walked with urgency into the lowest level of the palace proper. Behind him, a second shadow, came the imposing figure of the Stone. The Prince hated the reek of the torture chamber, a blend of feces, sweat, blood, and fear. Even more he despised the terrible sounds that resounded among the boiling furnaces and intricate devices of torment. He usually avoided this part of the palace. But the sorcerer's laughing had finally stopped, and he had to be sure that Elhathym was dead.

The smells of scorched flesh and decay drowned all others as D'zan entered the chamber. There was no sign of the sorcerer. Only the bodies of the three hooded torturers lying across the floor, blood pooling about their split bodies, their limbs askew in impossible angles. All the racks, cages, and shackles were empty, even those that had encased rotting corpses to terrify victims.

The sound of screaming came from somewhere above. D'zan raced back up the steps and ran toward the throne room, the Stone pounding at his heels. Courtesans, servants, and soldiers fled the great hall, mouths agape, eyes wide with terror. A cacophony of shrieking filled the arched corridors, and the odor of ancient decay was everywhere. The stench from D'zan's dreams... the acrid reek of the tomb.

D'zan raced into the throne room to see his father the King surrounded by a trio of grasping mummies. The smell of long-rotten flesh filled the chamber like a fog, and two of the mummies grasped the King by his arms, holding him immobile while the third decomposing corpse raked its claws across his flesh, spilling royal blood across the dais. D'zan heard his father scream, and his legs were frozen; he could not move forward or backward, but only stood staring at the tableau of impossible slaughter.

On the King's throne sat black-robed Elhathym, a grim smile on his lips, his skull nearly visible through the tight, pallid flesh of his face. He bore no marks of torture on his person; not even his black robes were disturbed, and his necklace of blood-drop rubies hung gracefully upon his emaciated chest.

A legion of the dead swarmed the hall. Already several guards lay bleeding on the flagstones, their throats ripped out by fleshless fingers and the teeth of withered skulls. Swords and spears clove into dry breastbones with little effect. The mummies of previous dynasties were now ravening ghouls, splashing gouts of blood across fine tapestries as they tore the palace guards to bits. D'zan recognized the tattered raiment of the ghouls, and saw on the head of more than one a royal diadem or crown out of Yaskathan history. These were the inhabitants of the royal necropolis crawled up from the underworld beneath the palace.

The shadows of your own past will tear you from your throne.

More lurching corpses poured into the hall; the screams of women and children rang from the walls in every wing of the palace. A grinning mummy rounded the corner and reached for D'zan's throat, but the Stone's blade took off its moldy head. Olthacus' booted foot crushed the corpse against the floor; as he tamped its ribcage into dust, its fleshless arms kept grasping at his legs, tearing through his leathern leggings and drawing blood. D'zan backed away, inspired by the Stone's bravery to draw his own weapon; a reeking cadaver grabbed him from behind, pressing its rotted skull against his ear. Its jaws snapped like those of a turtle, and he dropped his sword clattering to the floor as horror suffocated him.

The Stone tore the mummy from D'zan's back and pulverized it with blade and boot. His big hand slapped D'zan across the face, ending his paralysis. "Come, Prince!" growled the Stone. "I know a secret way."

"No!" shouted D'zan. "We can't abandon my father!"

"Your father is *dead*, boy!" said the Stone, pointing his blade at the cluster of ghouls who tore at a mess of scattered flesh upon the royal dais. Above the horrid feast sat Elhathym, the bloodstained crown on his head now, smiling at the devouring of Trimesqua. Still the ranks of blood-hungry dead things continued filling the chamber, the last of the guards falling before their voiceless assault.

The Stone grabbed D'zan's arm and they ran through milling clouds of grave dust. They never stopped running, all through the winding corridors of the servants' wing, the Stone's great blade demolishing one desiccated corpse after another. Everywhere the dead feasted upon the living. None in the palace were spared the bottomless hunger of the corpses; royal and servant alike died under the raking of bony claws. So Elhathym had promised, and he had delivered on his ultimate threat.

D'zan wondered if his mother's corpse was among the hungry dead. *Would I recognize her? Would she tear out my throat with the same hands that gave me life?* Stifling a bottomless scream, he drove such thoughts from his mind, closing his eyes and mumbling a prayer to the Sky God.

The Stone brushed aside a wall hanging and opened a hidden passage, leading the Prince along the dark and narrow way. D'zan, fearful of dark places now that his nightmares had come to life, closed his eyes while Olthacus dragged him along that winding route, up and down seldom-used stairwells, through crawl spaces, and finally out into the night air. Once again the screams of the dying filled D'zan's ears. He dared to open his eyes and found that the Stone had brought him to an outer palace garden. They ran for the orchards beyond. Behind them flames danced among the towers and courtyards. The dead were heedlessly knocking over braziers and torches, spreading flame and death throughout the royal domain.

Where can we go to escape this damnation? His unconquerable father was dead and there was no safe place left in the world. The Stone grabbed his arm and pulled him onward.

Once in the deep shadows of the orchards, they seemed free of the undead plague a while, steeped in the tangy aroma of hanging citrus. But when they crossed the outer wall into the seaside quarter, they saw again the terror and panic that had claimed Trimesqua's house. Here, too, corpses walked the streets and tore at living flesh. It seemed every graveyard and mausoleum in the capital had vomited forth its dead at the command of Elhathym. Citizens fled for the hills or locked themselves inside their houses. The Stone smashed another mummy to powder as he drew D'zan on toward the wharves, where towers of flames writhed and flickered. All across the city, walls of orange-white fire leaped toward the sky. *They must be fighting the dead with fire*, D'zan thought. *But they will burn their own city to ash...*

Many ships in the harbor had already launched, heading out to sea to escape the apocalypse of Elhathym's making. Citizens jostled and fought one another for passage on one late-embarking galleon which flew the Feathered Serpent of Mumbaza among its white sails. The Stone hacked his way through the crowd, leaving a bloody trail in his wake, dragging D'zan by his elbow. The panicked Yaskathans gave way before the big warrior. Without a word the Stone gained passage from the ship's captain at the point of his dripping blade.

The deck of the galleon was crowded, and the sailors had to beat back the mob with oars and clubs before they could cast off. D'zan collapsed on the deck, near the prow. The pitiful cries of women, children, and men—all doomed—filled his ears even when he clasped his hands over them. When he dared to look out over the railing, the capital was a flaming, screaming mass of chaos separated from him now by an expanse of dark water. The horned moon hung pale and implacable above the dying city. Towers gleamed brighter than rubies in the glow of the roaring fires.

Those who had escaped by securing passage on the galleon were weeping, or cursing, or both. A few had brought entire families with them. D'zan stood in the prow watching his inheritance burn, thinking of his father's bloody crown sitting upon the sorcerer's head. Hot tears burned his cheeks. Behind him, as always, stood the Stone, silent and still as the moon.

In the blood-spattered throne room, Elhathym drank wine from Trimesqua's goblet as his army of undead Yaskathans preyed on their descendants. He smiled at the irony of using the past to remold the present in such a way. Among the entrails and filth littering the hall, a great white panther glided toward him. The beast licked at Trimesqua's blood, and the snapping ghouls ignored it as they wandered off to find fresh victims.

The white panther came close to Elhathym's knees and rubbed its silky fur against him. His thin hand caressed its head between the ears, and it growled.

"You see, my dear?" the sorcerer told the panther. "I told you my birthright would be easily reclaimed."

"So you did," said the panther. "But what of *my* desires?" Now the cat was a pale-skinned lady sitting at his feet, her voluptuous body draped in strings of chromatic jewels. A thick mane of hair, gleaming white as silk, fell across her shoulders. Her eyes were as dark as his own.

Elhathym, the new King of Yaskatha, smiled at his lover.

"Patience," he whispered. And he kissed her ruby lips, which tasted of royal blood.